THE OPENING

THE OPENING

James Christie

112
"There was the door to which I found no key
There was the veil through which I might not see
And voices talked of us and Him; but none
Unlocked the door or raised the veil for me."

114
"Not earth, nor air, nor water gave the clue
To teach the soul to know the false and true;
But Heaven's revealing fire would blaze, methought,
And end the night that covers me - and you."

115
"Therefore with faith to awful Heaven I cried,
Asking: "What lamp has Destiny to guide
Her little children stumbling in the dark?"
"Only a sightless instinct," Heaven replied.

Khayyam - The Rubaiyat

Humdrumming Ltd.
75 Withermoor Road
Bournemouth, Dorset
BH9 2QN

This Paperback Edition 2005

First published in Great Britain by Humdrumming 2005

The Opening Text © 2005 by James Christie

Cover design © 2005 by Lee Thompson

James Christie asserts the moral right to be
established as the creator of this work.

All rights reserved. No part of this book may be used or reproduced in any manner whatsoever without written permission from the authors, except in the case of brief quotations embodied in critical articles or reviews.

All characters in this publication are fictitious and any resemblance to any real persons, living or dead, is purely coincidental.

This book is sold subject to the condition that it shall not, by way of trade or otherwise, be lent, re-sold, hired out or otherwise circulated without the publishers prior consent, in any fom of binding or cover other than that in which it is published and without a similar condition including this contition being imposed on the subsequent purchaser.

Published 2005 by Humdrumming
www.humdrumming.co.uk

ISBN 1-905532-03-2
ISBN 978-1-905532-03-2

Printed by Antony Rowe Ltd in the United Kingdom

*This book is dedicated to the real magicians and healers who wait,
on guard, all over the world. It is also deidicated to my wife Joanna,
and to special friends in Jimena de la Frontera, especially Karl and Carmen,
and of course, Señor Calvo – wherever he may be!*

"Those who disbelieve in Magick are those who have never felt its power."
- *Dione Fortune, 1921*

"Given the fact that two thirds of Man's brain is dormant it never ceases to amaze me how little he uses the one third which is active. If Man pushed just a little harder what miracles there might be!"
- *Albert Einstein, 1932*

"The magic of a beautiful sunset is not to be confused with that other kind of magick wherein the adept raises the human vibration to change the parameters of natural law. Men of science say this cannot be done. Those of use who have done it tend to ignore the men of science."
- *Eliphas Levi, 1896*

"Believing in the power of magic/k is one thing. Practising the craft and seeing it work is something entirely different."
- *Alaister Crowley, 1939*

"Wise old men say that magic does not work and this reassures those of you who fear the shadows. And yet long after you have taken your women to your bed it is those same wise old men who conjure up the spirits of dead ancestors that they may ever increase their knowledge and their power."
- *Ali Al Hadin, 847*

"Magic changes things."
- *The Rev. John Light, California, USA, 2005*

1.

Mage

It had been a long and tiring drive from Santander and it was with a sense of relief and achievement that Mage navigated the Land Rover around the last curve in the tightly winding road and allowed the vehicle to coast to a stop by the side of the street... A small square really, with a couple of bars and three ancient Mercedes taxis, all of which had seen better days. Slapped against a wall which had once been white, was a peeling bull fight poster, and the door of an estanco was flaky with dark green paint.

Mage closed his eyes and rested his head against the steering wheel, allowing the exhaustion to settle within him. Once, when clean, the Land Rover had been pale blue, but now it was tan and brown and dirty grey with streaks of mud and dried red clay acquired during the last two hours of his journey along the rain swept N340 from Malaga.

It still rained now. A persistent drizzle that did little to wash away the grime, but added to a sense of loneliness and desolation. His arrival in the village of Castillo was hardly a welcoming experience.

The stilled engine ticked with the rapidly cooling temperature and opening his eyes to reach for a cigarette, Mage wriggled his toes in his cold and wet boots. Yes, he was certainly tired, but also he was quietly satisfied. Against innumerable odds, not least of which had been the appalling condition of the roads for the last three hundred kilometres, he was here on schedule - the daylight hours of April 14th. Later, whether he saw it or not, a new moon would rise above the horizon of the world, and seen or unseen, its energies would be appealed to and tapped.

'You must arrive at the correct time,' the old priest had said. *'If the evil is as you believe it to be, you must be there at least one full lunar month before it, and the potency of a new moon cannot be ignored...'*

He lit the cigarette, then pulling his hat down more securely, low across the forehead, he pushed open the Land Rover door and stepped down on to the wet pavement. He stood still and silent for a few seconds, aware of the symbolic importance of the moment.

He allowed his eyes to roam and his senses to reach out and touch. It was cold on this late Spanish afternoon and the air was redolent with the smell of wood smoke. Details that he savoured along with an awareness of the tall trees behind him and the jumbled terraces of white houses that arched upwards towards the imposing edifice of the ruined castle that dominated not only the village but the whole of the Castillato valley.

His eyes lingered on the castle. *Would it be there?* he wondered. *The Battleground? Would there even be a battle?*

Made opaque and misty by the rain cloud, the castle rose up out of the bedrock. To the South, a single Christian keep with serrated walls and broken battlements, bnattlements that stretched Northwards towards a Moorish citadel with arches and the remnants of a minaret... A clash of architectural design that spoke volumes about the clash of religious and historical ownership.

Red roofs of village houses, many of them covered with green moss and yellow lichen, reached towards the castle as if in supplication... Or for protection? Or in fear? Clearly, whoever held the castle controlled the village and the valley.

From the castle his eyes moved on to the more distant mountains, the Sierra Morenos, to the North and the East and West. Barely perceptible through the curtain of moisture, they were nonetheless there. Dark jagged sentinels in the mist. The village of Castillo de la Frontera hung to a hillside at the head of a valley that stretched upwards from the flatlands of Marchenillas and El Campo de Gibraltar, guarding the single lane highway that disappeared into the mountain passes towards Ronda, some sixty kilometres further North. The village seemed to press against the mountains, but the mountains appeared to push back harder.

Mage gave the Ronda road a passing glance, but he knew there was no escape or retreat along that avenue. *This is where it ends,* he thought. And then, *did it begin here, too?*

Looking at the two bars, he allowed intuition to make the decision and crossed the street towards the larger of the two establishments. The three taxis eyed him forlornly as he passed them by and pushed open the faded blue door of the saloon. A rough sign, pale green printing on a dirty white background, told him this was "Jacinto's".

There was a stainless steel bar counter, cruelly lit by two hard neon strip lights. Behind the bar were shelves of bottles with unfamiliar labels. Brown tables, cheap chairs, dust on the floor and a motley selection of crushed and empty cigarette packets. Ducados, Celtas, and the occasional red and white of a crumbled contraband Winston smuggled across the border from Gibraltar for a few pennies and enormous profits for the marketeers. An immobile fan hung beneath a fly stained ceiling, and in one corner there was a fireplace without a fire.

If anything, it was colder inside the bar than out in the street and the place was devoid of warmth or cheer. Three men propped the furthest corner of the bar, silently drinking Anis; the taxi drivers waiting for the call that never came? And in the rear of the bar, tucked against a grimy window, a younger man, little more than a boy really, sat with a mongrel dog at his feet and strummed desultory minor chords on a badly out of tune guitar.

Mage ordered coffee from a weasily thin bar tender. He desperately wanted a brandy to go with it, but alcohol was forbidden. All false stimulants dulled and distorted the natural senses, and God alone knew that the caffeine and the tobacco were bad enough; something had had to go, and the alcohol was the obvious choice. It would be those same senses that might just keep him alive in the weeks ahead and he could not afford to do anything that might blunt the finely sharpened edges of his awareness.

He sighed inwardly and lit another cigarette as a substitute. The tobacco was almost as bad as the booze, but – and he grinned sheepishly to himself – once a smoker, always a smoker. Besides, he would stop quickly enough if – no, not if but *when* it became necessary. He drank the coffee, ordered another and smoked quietly – feeling the boy's eyes boring into the back of his neck.

***

Angel Guadiaro, sometimes called Rubio for his uncharacteristic fair hair, had watched the Land Rover with the English license plates pull up outside the tabacalera, and he had watched the extranjero get out of the cab and sniff the wind before he'd crossed the street and had entered the bar.

I will call him El Moreno, Angel thought, for here is a brown man. Brown leather jacket, brown trousers and boots – good boots – and even a brown shirt. True, his hat is black, but he has a brown moustache and a brown beard, and beneath the brim of his hat, I think his hair is also brown... And his eyes, when he looked at me but did not see me, yes I'm certain that they too were brown. And so, Señor El Moreno, The Brown Man is a good name for you.

But what are doing here, El Moreno? You do not look like the typical extranjero or llaneto from Gibraltar who seeks a new life in my pueblo. Are you going somewhere then? And if so, where? The road to Castillo leads only to Castillo.... Ah, but perhaps you have a friend here, or friends, and with the increasing number of extranjeros who come here every year, this may well be possible. And yet, Señor, there is something unusual about you, something strange... You stand at the bar drinking coffee, but you are tense and poised, just like a cat before it pounces on some poor unsuspecting bird...

Angel unconsciously fingered the vicious cold sore at the side of his mouth – well, he told himself it was a cold sore, but in his heart of hearts he knew it was a bad case of the clap. Every time he'd urinated for the past three days it had been like pissing cut glass. One half of him cursed the filthy whore in Campamento who'd given it to him and the other half of him cursed himself for going with her in the first place. If this was all you got for one hundred euros, he'd learn to go without. Three minute's physical pleasure and sexual release wasn't worth a dollop of clap, was it?

Still, what was a fellow to do? Seventeen years old and living in a village full of old married women and tight assed virgins, who might, and only might, mind you, give you a hand job and let you lick their tits while they did it – but only then if you promised to marry them first. Certainly there were a few foreign girls, English mostly, who fucked easily and readily, but you had to have a motor bike or a car and plenty of money to buy unlimited drinks in the bars or down at Castillo's apology for a discotheque before you caught that particular piece of pussy.

And even then, his friends, Curo, Lorenzo and Xavier, had all taken English virgins the previous Summer and all of them had ended up taking penicillin throughout the Autumn and most of the Winter. At least The Ra Ra Club was more honest and you knew the risks you were taking.

Angel turned his attention back to the foreigner at the bar. I'll bet you don't get the clap when you fuck virgins, he thought with frustration and irrational anger. And with your good, good boots and your fine black hat and your Land Rover (even though she is old), I bet you've fucked plenty of virgins!

And then to Angel's horror, the stranger turned and looked straight at him across the room.

Oh Jesus, Angel thought with certain intuitive knowledge, he heard me thinking about him. He heard me thinking!

Mage finished his coffee, then with a slight smile, walked across the bar and sat at the table next to the boy. The mongrel looked up once from the floor, yawned, then closed its eyes again – showing a far greater deal of sang froid than its owner. Angel's eyes darted everywhere, at first refusing to meet Mage's steady gaze and his discomfort was a palpable thing. Then Mage reached out through the confusion and gently touched the young Spaniard's mind. Angel's agitation diminished and Mage's smile broadened.

'Is it possible you can help me?' he asked quietly. 'I am a stranger here and wish to stay in this village for some time. I need to rent a house for three, possibly six months. It does not need to be large, but it must be clean and with hot water and electricity. I have money and will pay in advance for the right place.'

Angel was surprised and impressed. The extranjero spoke perfect Spanish and albeit with the hard Castillano accent of Madrid, the timbre of his voice was pleasingly soft and deep. Was he after all an extranjero? Was he not possibly from Catalunia or Navarre? Or even Galicia? Not that it mattered, for suddenly Angel's world seemed a little brighter with the possibility of easy financial pickings at a time when he desperately had to have money for the penicillin injections and tablets that would be needed to combat the herpes or (please God no!) the syphilis that threatened to ruin the most important aspect of his youthful existence.

There was his Grandmother's house in Calle Granadillos. It was large and dry and furnished with a good bed and a modern kitchen. Although the hill was steep, the views were good and all extranjeros liked good views, didn't they?

His Grandmother had spoken to him only the week before. 'I'll not sell the house,' she'd said, 'so don't bother to look for a buyer.' She would, however, consider renting the house, so he should see if he could find her a tenant. If he looked, she thought he might find someone somewhere... She wanted two hundred euros every week and anything he made on top of that was his own business.

Angel did a rapid calculation. If he could charge the extranjero four hundred euros, and took three months in advance, then (thank Jesus Mary and all the Saints) he would be immediately richer by almost five thousand euros! A sigh of relief ebbed through his body and a beatific smile lit his face. He hardly noticed as the cold sore cracked and began to suppurate.

'Yes sir, I do know of a house, not three hundred metres from where we sit. It is strong and has all of the things you will need.' Angel paused and considered. 'The house has been empty for several months and, although it is dry and has no leaks, it has been a very wet winter and so it may be a little damp. You will need to light fires, but there are two full bombonas of gas and many good dry logs that have been kept inside away from the rain. If you wish to see this house, I will take you there now. It belongs to my Grandmother who has charged it to my care and thus I even have the key in my pocket! If you like the house, sir, perhaps we can do a deal this very afternoon?'

'Yes, Angel, I'm sure that we can...'

Go there and on your journey pray very hard, Father Paul had said. *When you arrive, perhaps God will provide you with an angel...*

Mage stood up. 'Let's go and look at this house, shall we?'

Mage strode over to the Land Rover and pulled a large soft carpet bag from the front seat. It looked, and was, both full and heavy. Angel reached out eagerly to take the bag, swinging his guitar round on the strap so that it hung across his back, but Mage shook his head.

'No thanks, Angel. I'll carry the bag. You just show me the way to the house...'

So, with dog trotting at his feet, the young Castillato led Mage through a maze of winding back streets, ever climbing upwards across wet cobble stones and flanked by white walls and black wrought iron window bars. It was both quaint and picturesque and, although Mage's thoughts were elsewhere, the atmosphere of Andalucia did not go entirely unnoticed.

They walked up an increasingly steep hill and then on a corner where the street gave way to wide serrated steps, Angel stopped and fumbled in his pocket for the keys.

'This is the house, sir. Perhaps not impressive from the outside, but as is the case with many village houses, the beauty is within.'

Mage allowed another small smile to play across his face, although it contained little humour. The house was built of white stone and apart from the scrollwork on the black window bars, it seemed little different from all the rest. It stood at the end of a terrace of similar structures, falling away down the cobbled hill at a gradient of about twenty degrees; it was of two stories with a red tile roof and a dark, almost black, wooden door. Above the door, painted upon the white stone, was the number fourteen.

One and four – five – the number of the pentagram, the number of magicians and magic and in the discipline of numerology, his own significator name number.

Angel conducted Mage through the building, but it was no more than a formality. The currents that had moved him half way across Europe and that had brought him to Castillo and the boy called Angel in Jacinto's bar, were exactly the same currents that had brought him to this particular house.

On the ground floor, there was a tidy kitchen and dining room and also a bathroom. A narrow staircase escalated in a half spiral up to the first floor where there was a large salon filled with solid furniture and featuring a large open fireplace. A door led through to a bedroom with an ancient double bed with tarnished brass end rails. French windows opened onto a small balcony, giving an uninterrupted view of the castle keep and the battlements.

The grand tour had begun in the kitchen, and it also ended there.

'All right.' Mage nodded thoughtfully and sat down at the kitchen table. 'How much? In advance, remember, and in cash.'

Angel squirmed. This was the difficult part. Should he ask for the four hundred euros a week and risk scaring the extranjero away? Could he ask for more than four hundred euros and get it? How familiar was the extranjero with the Spanish property market? Pulling himself to his full height of five feet and four inches, he took a deep breath.

'I think that four hundred euros each week is a very good price to pay for this very fine house.'

Mage laughed. 'I agree it is a very fine house, but I think that three hundred euros each week is a much better price.' And then, carefully... 'Will your Grandmother not be happy with two thousand and four hundred euros, and can you not be happy with twelve hundred?'

Mage brought out a bulging wallet and began to count out high denomination bills. 'Remember, there will be the same again three months from now. I dare say I'll know exactly how long I intend to stay within the next few weeks.'

Angel sat down and looked at the money in befuddled confusion. What was this? The extranjero knew that his Grandmother's price was two hundred euros and that the extra was to be for him. How was this possible? How did the extranjero know? Was his Grandmother testing him? Had she employed an actor from the theatre in Algerciras to see how honest her grandson was? Was the extranjero a mind reader? Or worse – a witch? And yes, there was another thing, wasn't there? Back in the bar and again by the Land Rover, the extranjero had called him by name! He had not spoken to Jacinto other than to order his coffee, so Jacinto could not have told him, and yet this extranjero had known his name!

Angel studied the money on the table. Mage had divided it into two piles: twenty four one hundred euro notes to the left and twelve one hundred euro notes to the right. He now produced a scrap of paper from a small notebook and scribbled a few lines of writing before pushing it, along with the pen and the money, over towards Angel's side of the table. Angel read it quickly, not really surprised to find that it was in excellent Spanish. It was a receipt for thirty six hundred euros and in a few brief words, a rental contract for the house. Almost automatically and without thinking, Angel picked up the pen and signed his name.

'This is satisfactory?' Mage asked.

'Yes sir.' Angel's finger picked at the cold sore. 'This is satisfactory.'

Mage watched. Almost with a sense of guilt, Angel picked up the two piles of money and stuffed them into an inside pocket.

'If there is any other way in which I can be of service, you only have to ask, sir...'

'Can you drive?'

'Of course, sir.'

Mage tossed him a bunch of keys. 'If you'd bring my truck up to the door I'd be obliged.'

Aware that by Spanish standards no small honour had been bestowed upon him, Angel de Guadiaro picked up the keys and, with his dog at his heels, went to fetch the Land Rover. Walking down the slippery cobbles he had to press a handkerchief to the sore on his mouth; the scab had flaked away and it was now bleeding quite profusely.

Antonia de Guadiaro had been alive for almost seventy nine years and, although she was old now and partially crippled with arthritis, her mind was still sharp and her eyes were still clear.

She counted out the pile of one hundred euro notes that her Grandson had brought her and looked at Angel shrewdly, though not without affection. He seemed sick and feverish and she wished he would eat more and take better care of his health. At least, she consoled herself, he was not taking drugs like some of the other young ones in the pueblo. This latter fact she was not certain of, of course, but she felt that she would know if it were the case.

By perfidious twists of fate, she was his sole relative, and he hers. Angel's father, who had been her only son, had died with his wife three years before: a bizarre accident in one of the late Summer storms. Lightening had struck their car on the road from Ubrique and the car had gone over the cliff and down into the ravine five metres below. Pepe and Marie had been killed outright, while their son, Angel, asleep in the back, had clambered out of the wreckage unscathed.

Unscathed, but not untouched by the tragedy.

Angel had been a boisterously happy, almost hyperactive child, but since the double death of his parents, he'd become quiet and withdrawn... Not moody or sulky, but it was as if a spark of life had departed from him in pursuit of his mother and father. In many ways this was only to be expected, but still she worried, hoping that time would heal. After all, three years was not a very long time to get over something like that, especially if one was young and impressionable.

Angel had come to live with her... Her and Jacobo... And then eleven months later without any kind of warning, the man who had been her husband for sixty one years, had dropped down dead with a massive heart attack. One moment he'd been lifting a glass of wine and then he'd been falling... Dr Sanchez had told her that he'd been dead before he even hit the floor!

...And this was something that had certainly not left *her* untouched or unscathed! True, Jacobo had been over eighty, but he was a fit and hail man who'd never had a day's serious illness in his life. Good God, he'd still done a full day's work in the fields well into his seventies!

Antonia still grieved and would always grieve. The marriage, although there'd only ever been the one child, had been a good one. Never a day had passed without Jacobo expressing his love and appreciation and although he'd been a stranger to her on the night he'd taken her to the marriage bed, her love for him had blossomed and grown more fierce and prideful with every tender year they had been together.

For twelve months, she and Angel had carried on living in the house in Calle Granadillos, but the hill was steep and her legs were old, and neither she nor her Grandson had been able to find any peace there. In the space of one week, with little discussion but tacit agreement, they had moved into Pepe and Marie's house down by the Paseo. Angel seemed to be happier, living again in the home of his childhood, and life was certainly easier for her without the hill. Without the memories.

Many times since she'd almost been persuaded to sell the house in Granadillos, but she'd always drawn back. Angel could sell it if he wanted to after she was gone, but as long as she was alive there was something which prevented her from letting go of the place which had been her marital home for more than half a century.

The idea of renting the house had never really occurred to her until recently – only ten or twelve days ago, in fact. There had been one restless night filled with periods of wakefulness and fitful, dream filled sleep. Jacobo and Pepe and Marie had been with her, though she could not remember what they had said. There had been visions and memories of her own youth and childhood and the impression of having been with her own parents had been very strong. But there had been tension and darkness in her dreams as well; it seemed that shadowy faceless forms hovered above her bed and battled for her soul. There was no resolution to this conflict and she awoke in the morning with only two clear thoughts. One was that her own death, while not imminent, was not that far away. The other was that she would rent the house in Calle Granadillos; that it would be needed and that in fulfilling the need she would be doing no evil.

Thus, it seemed oddly coincidental that less than a fortnight later a tenant had been found – or more accurately if Angel had told it correctly, a tenant had found them. She had listened to Angel's report, unsurprised and with a sense of deja vu. She wondered about the stranger, this Englishman who wrote and spoke such perfect Spanish and who had good cash money in his pockets. This was April, not July or August; few tourists found their way to Castillo at the best of times and this early in the year it was almost unheard of.

She counted through the money again then looked up at Angel. 'How much did you make?' she asked without preamble.

Angel, who was in no mood for long discussions, told her the truth. 'Twelve hundred euros for me on top of the twenty four hundred for you. If you think this is too much, I'll give it to you and then you can pay me what you consider fair.'

Good boy, she thought. Good boy! 'Keep it,' she sniffed, betraying no emotion. 'You've done well and I'm pleased with you.'

'Thank you, Grandmother.'

'Now, who is this extranjero?'

'I'm not quite sure what you mean. I told you, he walked into Jacinto's with money in his pockets, looking for a house.'

'What does he do?'

'Grandmother, how should I know what he does!' Angel could not keep the note of exasperation from his voice.

'Well, what do you think he does? Will he write? Does he paint? Will he work with the llanetos in Gibraltar?'

Angel shook his head slowly. 'No, not Gibraltar. As for the rest, I don't know. An artist perhaps, but I'm only guessing.'

'Well, what does he look like?' Antonia asked. It was her turn to sound exasperated.

'Brown.' Angel grinned. 'He wore brown clothes and had brown hair. A brown beard and moustache and brown boots. He was brown!'

'And is El Moreno tall, short, thin, fat; does he wear glasses? Has he got a limp? How old is he?'

'No,' Angel sighed. 'He does not wear glasses and he does not have a limp. I think maybe he is about forty, maybe forty five, and although he is of medium build, I would neither call him fat or thin.'

'Well is there nothing about him that you thought unusual?' Antonia persisted, drumming her long fingers on the table.

Oh yes indeed Grandmother, indeed there are quite a few things about this extranjero which I think are unusual, but we're not going to talk about them tonight, not until I've had a chance to think about them on my own for a while.

'Nothing I can think of,' he lied. 'Perhaps I'd better bring him down here to meet you, then you can judge for yourself.'

'You have arranged to meet him again?'

'No – but it would be an acceptable formality to issue such an invitation.'

'Do it.' Antonia said promptly. 'I would very much like to meet this extranjero, this Mr Colin Mage. See him tomorrow morning and bring him in the afternoon after the siesta.'

'Yes Grandmother,' Angel got up to go and kissed her lightly on the top of her iron grey hair. And then he asked, 'Why are you so interested? We have the money and it is a good rental. Why are you so filled with curiosity about this man?'

Antonia could not tell him and she doubted whether she would have done even if she'd been able to articulate her confused feelings and thoughts. Dreams of dead ancestors and shadowy night phantoms were for the very old, not for the very young. She could not begin to explain the disquieting sensation of expectancy that tingled subliminally beneath the threshold of her consciousness, nor the constriction of inexplicable excitement that her Grandson's news had stirred within her blood.

'Calle Granadillos was my home for fifty years and if there is to be a stranger living in it, even if it is for only three or six months, then I want to see the man. I want to know him.

'Now, enough talk. Leave me to my thoughts. Go and spend some of that money you've come by, but not all of it at once, mind me, not all of it at once.'

He sat silently in the darkened room - no longer wearing brown but dressed in a black jalaba made from light Moroccan cotton. He'd slept and bathed and then, standing by the open window, had waited and watched for the moon. It had finally teased into existence; the slimmest wafer thin silver crescent, lifting above the mountains. Then and only then had he sat down – in the middle of the floor, head bowed and legs crossed in a half lotus.

The Hurting was upon him now, upon him and within him, causing nauseous emptiness in his stomach and making his cheeks burn with heightened blood pressure. It coursed through his body like a virus, causing his temples to pound with pain and making limbs and joints ache as he fought to control the flood of bitter memory. The control came, albeit slowly.

By eleven o'clock he was almost in a comatose trance, swaying gently from side to side and keening softly. By eleven fifteen the silence had come upon him and he was calm and still... The Hurt having become a concentrated ball of controlled energy at the top of his solar plexus.

At eleven forty five, his eyes, governed by an internal body clock, snapped open. He then concentrated on his breathing and waited. At one minute to midnight he lit the five long black tallow candles that he had previously placed at strategic points around the room and as the town hall clock began to chime twelve o'clock, Mage began to recite words in a language that was neither English nor Spanish. Gradually, almost in slow motion, he outstretched his arms and lifted his face upwards until he was looking directly into the faint amorphorous cloud of shimmering silver blue light that seemed to hover somewhere between the top of his head and the ceiling.

'Ateh Malkuth,' Mage began to chant. *'Ateh Ateh Malkuth, veh geburah veh gebulah, ley aolahim omm.'*

At more or less the same time Antonia de Guadiaro woke from a light sleep, and for one brief second would have sworn that Jacobo was sitting on the bed next to her, stroking her hair. The after image of the dream, if that was what it had been, was slow to depart, and suddenly Antonia was crying, which was something she had not done for many long years. She cried for her husband and for her son and her daughter-in-law; she cried for Angel and she cried for herself – long, gentle sobs that gently led her back into the sleep state.

Half a kilometre away, in a mindless fight down at The Supernova discotheque (a converted barn behind Cuenca's bar), Miguel Torres drew a knife. The fight had been going on for the better part of ten minutes already and was rapidly reaching a bruised but amicable solution. Miguel Torres, with bloody nose but pride intact, was as surprised as anyone else as he plunged the switch blade into the soft and unsuspecting belly of Paco Camino.

Beyond the castle, on the hillside of The Hozgarganta ravine, a half wild dog suddenly turned and savaged one of its pack mates, sinking its bared fangs into the other animal's jugular vein.

In a remote farm house, fifteen kilometres to the West, an expectant mother, seven months into her pregnancy, experienced an excruciatingly painful contraction, and with that certitude given to expectant mothers the world over, she knew that something was very, very wrong.

In the private apartment of the Hotel Miraflores, not two hundred metres from where Mage chanted his mantra, the hotel's owner, Henry Holloway, was more than a little surprised when his wife, Valerie, suddenly rolled over in their bed and began to stroke his testicles. Valerie had been 'off' sex for more months than he cared to remember and her present actions – within seconds she was down on him, his penis fully pressed into her mouth – came without any indication or warning. When Henry climaxed, and after five months of enforced celibacy it didn't take very long, the eruption was volcanic and violent, made more so by Valerie's refusal to let go. 'Jesus Christ!' Henry bellowed... And then she was on her back, legs stretching towards the ceiling as she pulled him into her. He was still amazingly rigid and it wasn't long before Valertie started to shout at the top of her voice.

In a small house in the Northern barrio of the village, a man flew into a rage and began to beat his wife. The fact that she was already dead and had been laying in her coffin for the previous five or six hours, seemed to make no difference at all whatsoever.

As the town hall clock chimed twelve, the clock on Hector Sanchez's mantle piece chimed thirteen. He looked up from his armchair, uncertain whether or not he'd heard what he thought he'd heard. Doctor Sanchez was both very tired and deeply depressed, so he put the thirteenth chime down to imagination. In a bedroom in another part of the Sanchez household, the Doctor's twenty two year old daughter stirred in her sleep, a smile on her pretty face. She dreamed that the operation in Madrid had been successful and that she would not, after all, go blind before the end of the year.

In a field close to the railway tracks, two brothers, high on marajuana, suddenly thought it would be a wonderful idea to tie their Doberman dog to the railway sleepers... The train from Algerciras would be along in less than fifteen minutes… And in another field close by, a cow gave birth to a premature calf that only had three legs. Almost as if to compensate, the beast, which thankfully would die within minutes of breathing, had two heads.

Sitting alone with his thoughts in a quiet back street bar, Angel Guadiaro began to feel sick and dizzy. The handkerchief that he'd held to his mouth almost constantly during the latter part of the evening was now all but covered in blood and the degree of pain had increased beyond belief. As the midnight clock chimed its twelfth note, the bile and vomit rose from his gut and then he was up and racing for the lavatory. He didn't make it.

There were two churches in Castillo and two priests. Father Francisco, priest for the church of Santa Maria in the Southern barrio, masturbated for only the second time in his young life and wept while he did it. Father Ignatious, older by forty years and pastor for Santa Clara's in the Northern barrio, paused in his nocturnal meditations. Then smiling a somewhat unholy smile, he reached for the telephone and placed a call to the United Kingdom.

'Yes?' said the hard, almost nasal voice in England.

Ignatious felt warmed and aroused by the voice and in common with Henry Holloway and Father Francisco, he found that he was sexually erect.

'It is Ignatious in Castillo,' he spoke with a sibilant sycophantic tone. 'He is here.'

'Impossible,' said the voice from England.

'No Lord,' Ignatious said quickly. 'He is here. I have just this moment felt his presence.'

There were a few long seconds of silence and then, 'You say you have felt him, but you have not actually seen him?'

'Would I know him if I did, Lord?'

'Nobody has reported his presence to you?'

'No, I have but felt him.'

'Very well. I still think this is very doubtful, but seek confirmation and telephone me again in twenty four hours.'

'Yes Lord,' breathed Ignatious, finally allowing his hand to drift downwards to between his legs. 'It shall be done.'

...And in another part of England, another man looked up from the glow of candles and smiled quietly to himself. 'Ah,' he murmoured, 'he made it on time.' He then took a single strand of hair from a parchment envelope and held it over a candle until it burned and frizzled into nothing.

2.

Castillo

The village of Castillo de la Frontera stretched along the Eastern face of a hog back ridge, the ridge itself being part of an unkind hill that half heartedly elevated into a small mountain crag. Upon the crag and overlooking the pueblo, stood the castle, its dark brown and grey stonework counterpointing the predominantly white walls and red and green roofs that huddled beneath it.

Following the contours of the ridge, Castillo was a long thin place, its houses and shops and bars clustered around a single main street that ran on a perfect North-South axis. There were dozens of cobbled side streets and a multitude of small courtyards and back alleys and, as a focal point of attention, in the southern barrio, there was an attractive main square – officially called Plaza de Constitution, it was more familiarly referred to as El Paseo. The square was paved with terracotta red stone and was protected from traffic by a low wall and a row of mature orange trees on three sides.

While not a remarkably pretty village, it did have character and a quaint mediaeval charm that solicited an unusual degree of pride and devotion in equal degrees from those who knew it as their only home and those foreigners, the extranjeros, who came to call it home.

By Andalucian standards, it was a large pueblo. A sign at the side of the road announced a population of four thousand eight hundred and forty, but this was probably a conservative figure, not allowing for those who lived in the outlying Campo, and certainly not for the insidious influx of foreigners that had been going on quietly for the last fifteen or sixteen years. These were the foreigners, mostly English but with a scattering of Americans and a handful of Scandinavians, who still sought that elusive place in the sun, but who were disillusioned and disappointed by the busy and increasingly expensive urbanizations on The Costa de Sol. To them, perhaps more so that the indigenous Spanish population, Castillo represented the Spanish ideal – the "real" Spain, whatever that was.

True, Castillo had no sandy white beaches to offer, but there were the mountains and the fields, the forests and streams. Gibraltar was less than an hour away, Jerez and Seville two and three hours respectively and if one actually wanted the Costa del Sol (although God alone knew why anyone would), then both Estapona and Marbella were within easy reach.

In the Summer months, due in part to the evangelical efforts of Henry and Valerie Holloway, the village (and in particular, the Hotel Miraflores) played host to the occasional groups of bird watchers and walkers, but the true tourist was a rarity. Castillo was too far off the beaten track. There was little to attract the sun seekers of the Club Med set and even less to attract the loud mouthed lager lout who over the past decade had caused such havoc from Malgret to Malaga.

Of those foreigners who had bought homes in the village, a good few were professional people with careers either in Gibraltar or the blossoming white elephant of property speculation that was Sotogrande. Others fell into two main categories. There were those who had retired, usually on a fixed income, and the remainder were the artists, the writers, the dreamers and the visionaries, who saw in the Campo de Castillo the font of their own personal holy grails.

Though these extranjeros were few, perhaps less than a hundred all told, they were not easily absorbed into the ambience and the atmosphere of the village. There were too many eccentrics and archetypes, too many egos and strong wills. There was also a dichotomy between those who went native, trying to become more Spanish than the Spaniards (much to the latter's tolerant amusement) and the other, smaller cabal of those who still maintained an infuriating aura of old colonial attitudes and values, which frequently caused the lips of younger Castillatos to curl in contempt.

'But Dahlings,' one maiden lady had been heard to say – a lady who'd spent more years than most in Castillo and really ought to have known better – 'Dahlings, what possible point is there in learning to speak Spanish? After all, the natives here...' it came out "heah" – ' – the natives here don't speak Spanish either. It's this ridiculously stupid Andalucian lingo! And besides, dahlings, one must always remember that one is English!'

On his first day in Castillo, Colin Mage knew none of this, but in the following days and weeks he was to learn much. He stood now on that bright, cool morning of April 15th, balancing upon the ramparts of the crumbling castle and with a feeling of exhilaration, surveyed the scene below and all around. With the cobalt blue skies and a low, almost Wintry sun, it was a spectacular scene to behold.

To the South, the Castillato valley descended between undulating hills to the distant pale blue smudge that was Gibraltar, more than thirty kilometres away. This was the Campo, filled with rich red soil, ideal for both the vine of grape and grove of orange.

To the North, the mountains were immediate – soaring foot hills covered with Cork Oak and Pine, lifting to granite buttresses and jagged peaks. To the East, higher more majestic mountains thrust upwards towards the sky, but these were much further away and the rolling hills rose more gradually before they gave way to the monolithic ramparts of The Sierra Morenos.

To the West, a deep gorge cut through to high and rocky land and at the bottom of a steep ravine, a river, swollen now with the last of the Winter rains and melting snows, tumbled angrily with a mute roar towards the distant sea. This was the Rio Hozgarganta, and Mage allowed his eyes to follow the winding white ribbon of water Westwards towards its unseen source. The Hozgarganta wound its way on an erratic course, full of steep twists and bends until it disappeared behind a huge bluff of granite two kilometres upstream. His eyes narrowed. He felt uneasy about this river.

The Hozgarganta – or in English, The Giant's Throat.

What lay beyond that which he could not see? And why should it be important? He closed his eyes and imagined *whirlpools and caves and the waters of the river rushing out of a tight and narrow cut, forced to the surface by millions of tons of subterranean pressure...* He opened his eyes and thought about caves. *There would have to be caves.*

With an angry shake of his head he turned his attention towards the village below him. It was certainly attractive with its white walls and richly coloured roof tops and although long and thin in its geometry, the two church spires at opposite ends of the pueblo with the crest of the hill roughly half way in between, created an odd but pleasing symmetry that rested easily on the eye.

Mage sat on the end of the parapet and, with some difficulty, lit a cigarette with an old brass zippo. He drew the smoke deeply into his lungs and as the cool wind ruffled his thick tawny hair, he again closed his eyes, this time in quiet satisfaction. In his life he'd had more than his fair share of failures, but he'd also accomplished some major achievements: perhaps the most significant of which, certainly in recent times anyway, was getting to this place, this hill village of Castillo, at this time. The timing had been critical and it had been a close run thing.

Quite independently of each other, both Father Paul and The Merlin had emphasised the importance of the timing and Michael Fry, The Merlin, had been coldly adamant.

'Go there Mage, believe that it's true and stop it if you can.'

'Can you believe that it *is* true?' Mage had asked.

The Merlin had looked down at his beautiful hands. 'I don't honestly know, but can we, can any of us, afford to take the chance that it's not?'

'But what do I have to do?' Mage had asked in desperation.

'Be there,' The Merlin had answered promptly. 'If you are wrong it can be no more than another wasted journey. If you are right, then you, and we also, will know it soon enough.'

'Can you do nothing to help?' Mage had almost pleaded.

'We shall pray for you,' said the Chief Druid of All Britain. 'And we shall do what we can to monitor your progress and we shall also do what we can to offer some measure of protection... But from all that you have told me it would seem that you are the one chosen to face this challenge and conflict and if you can't stop it, then nobody can. But Colin...' The Merlin's voice had softened as he'd used Mage's Christian name for the first time in what had been a long and hitherto always formal association, 'be careful. Pay attention to the tides and the moon; the highest tides in known history will rise in the Western Hemisphere on April 14th. This should be a full moon, but it's not. A new moon falls on that date. A high tide on a new moon is a scientific impossibility but never the less, this is what is going to happen and if you can be there by then and announce your presence, the power you will gain will be phenomenal. You may have to wait some time for your adversaries to arrive, but every day that you are there before them is a day of doubly gained strength for you and your cause.'

Mage had been silent for a moment, then had broached the subject he'd sought to avoid. 'My Lord Merlin, the personal aspects of this matter... Do they detract from the validity of what I believe?'

'Who can say?' The Merlin had replied. 'Who among us can really trace the interlinking strands of human destiny? In your case, your personal grief may be the one single factor that binds you to this business, or your grief may be no more than the result of destiny's devious path. Either way, the emotional aspects of your past are dead – and if they are not, you must kill them quickly. At this time you need intellect, knowledge and spirit.Nothing more. Emotions are weakening influences that you can well do without...

'Now, to another matter. If we are to help you, we shall need sacrifice and psychometric link. You agree?'

'Yes.'

'Good. Then bow your head.'

Mage had lowered his head and had felt a thrill of energy as The Druid had lightly touched his temples with his well manicured finger tips. Both men had remained silent for several long seconds and then The Druid had taken a razor sharp knife from his desk draw and had severed a good sized lock of Mage's hair. Placing the hair in an envelope he had then produced a small silver chalice.

'We shall need blood,' he had said quietly.

Without comment, Mage had unfastened his shirt sleeve and had extended his right arm across the table, his wrist above the chalice. With the deftness of a surgeon The Druid had drawn the knife across the wrist, cutting deeply, then holding Mage's hand lightly as the chalice steadily filled two thirds of the way up with the Magician's life force.

'You will heal quickly,' The Druid had said, pressing a dressing against the cut. 'Now, one other thing...' He'd removed the chalice from the table and replaced it with a small square of black silk. 'Your wedding ring.'

Mage had paused.

'Colin, she is dead to you, and yet this ring can still be used against you. If we have it then perhaps we can use it to peep into the enemy camp and, if nothing else, our possession of it will protect you from your own weakness.'

Reluctantly, Mage had removed the ring and had placed it in the centre of the silk. Immediately The Druid had removed it from the table, depositing it with the hair and the blood in the unseen drawer.

'When will you leave?'
'Within the week.'
'Good. You take with you the blessing of The Merlin.'

Incredibly this conversation had taken place only nine days previously and yet to Mage it seemed like half a lifetime ago. He tossed the butt end of the Marlboro in to the wind and glanced at his wrist; there was a fine white scar, two inches long, and although by rights he should have had stitches, as The Merlin had prophesied, it had healed quickly – too quickly to be totally natural! Wrapped around the same wrist there was a small green cord of braided silk. This had been Michael Fry's parting gift and it brought Mage more comfort than he was able to express.

He was cold now, but chose not to move from his perch. He lit yet another cigarette and thoughtfully tried to work out a detailed plan of campaign – then grinned at himself when he realised that this was impossible.

They would come – but he did not know when. It could be days although he did think that he might have at least a few weeks' grace, may be even months. *But they would come and they already had friends here in this place* – that much he already knew. But who were the friends? What did they know? Were they willing collaborators or were they just being fooled and manipulated? How important were they to the overall situation?

Perhaps if he were to form any kind of strategy, finding the answers to these questions should be his first task... And with his talents, both old and newly found, that might not be altogether too difficult. All he need do was to watch, listen and maybe if the circumstances warranted it, reach out and touch.

And there were two other questions he would have to consider. Namely, why here in the first place, and where abouts exactly? After all, Castillo and its outlying Campo covered many acres and The Opening need not be large.

Mage coldly remembered the first time he'd heard of "The Opening" and suppressed a grim shiver that had nothing to do with body temperature. But here again, this gave voice to another question. What precisely was The Opening? Was it an actual portal, a gateway, a conduit... Or was it a ritual act?

As for the previous two questions, there were at least a few clues he could follow, Maggie's report on the ley lines being the most obvious starting point.

According the Maggie – Maggie who had slipped into Castillo for two days in the middle of March – Maggie who was a founder member of Mage's very close inner circle of friends – Maggie who had learned most of all she knew from Colin Mage – Maggie who was a dowser, earning thousands of quiet dollars every year from petroleum and mining companies who sought her unusual and never disappointing abilities – Maggie who had dowsed this Andalucian village street by street...

Well, according to Maggie – 'Colin there are no fewer than four ley lines meeting and intersecting in your funny little town, and that's really way out and wild because that gives you a perfect inner diamond, eight secondary legs, ten external angles and four perfect inners! I got a map for you from a weird little hotel... Hang on, ah yes, here we are! It's called The Hotel Miraflores and it's a cross between Fawlty Towers and something out of a Hammer Horror film... Anyway, I got this map, and as best I can, I've plotted the ley lines for you...'

Mage pulled out a creased sheet of A4 paper and studied Maggie's map. The ley lines, or lines of natural Earth energy, cut across the page like a flattened diamond; north east to south west, and north west to the south east. The northern intersection was at the end of the main street, cutting through the simplistic map at a point half way between a restaurant called La Bodega and Santa Clara's church, which Maggie had also marked as being a convent. The eastern intersection was in a street called Calle Llanette, the last street on that side of the village before open fields sloped downwards to the distant Ronda road. The southern crossing of lines was fair and square on top of the Hotel Miraflores, while the western intersection was more or less where he sat now...

At the castle.

Wouldn't it, Mage mused, be so wonderfully convenient, so logical if The Opening should be in the centre of the diamond created by these intersecting lines! But it couldn't be that easy, could it? One thing was certain, he had to start somewhere and it would do no harm to look.

Mage began to slide off his rock and then paused. 'No...' he spoke aloud to the listening wind. 'Let's put it into words. Let's be clear. I'm going to look for The Opening, I'm going to look at this village and I'm going to look at its people. I'm going to look along these ley lines. I'm not just going to sit here and wait for Dolorean to show up – I'm going to work and I'm going to be ready!' He was self consciously aware of the melodrama and a part of him winced at the sound of his own voice. However, melodramatic or not he felt better for saying the words out loud.

Then Mage pulled himself to his feet in one smoothly fluid and catlike movement. He stood on the battlements, legs astride, hands bunched into fists. The wind blow steadily into his face and in his heart he shouted at the wind, giving voice to his anger and also to his fear.

'Come on, come on, because I'm going to be ready for you...' The wind fanned anger into hatred and defiance... 'You *bastards!*"

Angel sat in a quiet corner of The Miraflores bar. It was late morning and there were few customers. Apart from himself, there were the two Americans – he admired the blond girl's bottom clad in skin tight blue denim jeans – and felt regret that she was with either her lover or her husband. Whoever he was, he was blond too, and massively big. He wore good clothes and managed to carry his gold – the watch, the chunky identity bracelet and the large signet ring – without appearing either ostentatious or flashy. He reeked money, and although his face seemed old (anyone over the age of twenty five was old to Angel) there was a craggy clean shaven handsomeness: no wonder the girl found him attractive despite the fact that she herself was much younger.

When they'd arrived in the village a couple of weeks previously, Angel had first thought that they might be father and daughter, but there were few secrets in a village like Castillo and fewer still at the Hotel Miraflores. Juanita, who worked in the kitchen mostly, but who sometimes also cleaned the bedrooms, told him things. For one thing, the Americans spent a lot of time in their room and it was a room with only one large double bed... And in fact, according to Juanita, the Americans were seldom out of it! She would be called to take up coffee and tostados at eleven in the morning and they were in it then... And sometimes when she'd gone to try and change the sheets in the middle of the afternoon, they were *still* in it. The noises she'd sometimes heard when she'd been passing the door made it very clear that they were not just lying on the big camadoble holding hands!

Even as Angel watched, the American's hand casually stroked the girl's thigh and the girl giggled mid-sentence in her conversation and pushed herself closer to her man.

Beyond the Americans, in the corner by the telephone at the end of the bar counter, Diego Matan perched morosely on his stool, his leathery face a grim picture of dissatisfaction as he sipped at the alcohol free beer that he was condemned to drink... And in the other corner, leaning with his back to the wall next to the log fire, was Jaime Gomez, chief of Castillo's diminutive police force.

Gomez was a short plump man with slicked back hair and piggy eyes that sat like hard almonds in a puffy face. His skin was sallow and baby smooth, falling to flabbiness with a pronounced double chin. A pair of rubbery lips completed the picture of a very ugly man, almost beyond caricature. There was a slyness about the policeman that nobody in the village really liked and least of all Angel, who'd lived in apprehension and loathing of Jaime Gomez for almost two years.

It had been the first anniversary of his parents' death and Angel had ridden up to the cemetery on his moped (long since defunct and sold at a great loss). This was in contravention of the village bylaws, but it had been a very hot day and everyone else (that is to say everyone else who had a bike) flagrantly ignored the stupid laws anyway. The cemetery, on the brow of the hill to the north of the castle wall, was a good place to buy marijuana or to feel a girl, away from prying village eyes...

...So Angel had ridden up there, had stood speechless and dry eyed for fifteen minutes in front of his parents' dual grave – and Gomez, the policeman, had been waiting for him when he came out.

There had been an on the spot fine... Gomez was making an example, he said, and so it was severe, taking every duro from Angel's youthful pocket. And yet this was nothing compared to the cold tongue-lashing he'd received, delivered in a flat toneless voice that had systematically flayed him of every ounce of pride. Gomez had finished by sneering at him, accusing him of desecrating the last resting place of the dead with his noisy little motor bike... And Angel's inner hurt was shocking and profound.

For the sake of the saints, did not Gomez know that his parents were interred in there? Didn't he know that there was nothing Angel would ever do to desecrate their memory? Gomez *must* have known! On that day, in Angel's heart, hate was born and he glowered across the bar now, albeit surreptitiously, wondering what the police chief was doing here. Granted, he was out of uniform, but even so, this was not one of his usual hangouts.

Angel reached to pick the cold sore, then disciplined himself not to. The unsightly mess seemed to be getting a bit better – he knew it was still there, but it no longer hurt and itched quite so much. In fact, after the previous night's mini eruption, it was more like an ordinary cold sore that you got when you had a bad cold and not a case of the clap...

...And even that was questionable. Last night he'd still been pissing razor blades, but this morning, blessed relief and bless the virgin, there *was* blessed relief. He'd urinated three times since breakfast and there hadn't been a problem. Could you go into sudden remission with something like VD? Could it suddenly vanish? Had he really had it in the first place?

Of course he'd fucking well had it! Doctor Sanchez (and half a dozen friends who also knew the symptoms well enough) would not make a mistake like that, something so glaringly obvious! Besides, some instinct or intuition, call it what you would, had told him the prostitute was dirty even as he'd been taking her. Even so, he'd go round and see Sanchez again that evening after he'd taken Señor Mage to see his Grandmother – that is if he was able to find El Moreno to offer the invitation. He'd not been at the house and Angel had scoured the village fruitlessly. So, he'd come to the Miraflores to wait, certain that El Moreno would arrive here eventually. All the tourists and extranjeros found their way to the Miraflores sooner or later, like water finding its own level.

While Angel was right in his surmise that Mage would find his way to the Miraflores, it did take some time.

Mage sauntered down the steep cobbled path from the castle and wound his way into the labyrinth of narrow streets that formed the Western barrio of the village. Off the mountain and sheltered by the buildings, it was pleasantly warmer. He paused to unfasten his jacket, smiling slightly at a street sign painted in bold black on the brilliant white of the wall.

"Caminette de la Luna" the sign said, which he translated as "the passage of the moon". True, the street was little more than a passageway, an alley really... A couple of donkeys might have negotiated it, but certainly not a car. The name enchanted him, but he would have cause to remember it later with greater curiosity and more than a few misgivings.

Strolling the length of the alley, he came to a T junction, both streets sloping downwards. He chose the left hand path which brought him into a tiny picturesque square, little more than a cobbled court yard with an old well in the middle. Plaza de Toro, the sign said, which brought another small smile to his lips. No much of a bull ring, he thought. They'd have to be very small bulls! And apart from a couple of wrought iron balconies festooned with hanging baskets of colourful flowers, there was no space for spectators. Hardly enough room to swing a cat, let alone march a quadrille of torreros!

He back tracked to the T junction, then followed the right hand path, a street called Calle Sol, which turned another corner and headed down one of the steepest hills he'd thus far found in the village. As it descended, it broadened and while losing nothing of its Spanishness, acquired something of a more cosmopolitan atmosphere. At the bottom of the hill and on the corner of the street he would have to take to find his way back up to Calle Granadillos, was the Hotel Miraflores.

The tempting thought of a gin and tonic crossed his mind – and he pushed the thought aside. Tea, he told himself firmly and entered the hotel through a pair of thick oak doors studded with coach bolts and a large antique hasp and lock.

The moment he crossed the threshold, the atmosphere reached out and enveloped him. Despite his earlier mood at the castle, it came suddenly and he was caught off guard. He stopped and let the atmosphere touch him... Old wood, wood smoke, age... Polish and wax and an undercurrent of something elusive that was almost like a pulse of sexual excitement, enigmatic and mysterious. But even beneath this, there was something else... Something darker and more deeply malevolent.

Mage breathed deeply and took stock of his surroundings. Two glass doors in front of him led into a vine covered restaurant, closed now until the summer. Chairs stacked upside down on the tops of empty tables. On his right there were two rest rooms with mannequin figures nailed to the doors denoting Señoras and Caballeros. To his left a plain white wall with two framed photographs, one of Queen Elizabeth and Prince Philip, the other, hedging the bet of divided loyalties, of King Juan Carlos and Queen Sofia. Ahead of him, escalating upwards and to his left, there was a narrow open staircase... Leading to where? The Bar? The hotel reception? The rooms?

From the top of the stairs came the sounds of muted conversation, a woman's laugh, the gentle clink of glasses and the epicentre of the atmosphere... And quietly, Mage put an identity to the elusive ingredient. It was subtle and hiding beneath the clutter of everything else, difficult to pin point, but there just the same.

Threat.

Mage closed his eyes and concentrated on his breathing in the process of building up some physic defences. He murmured a mantra in time with the inhalations and built the visualisation of being covered head to foot in pale blue fire. He conjured the mental image of the pentagram, the five pointed interlocking star contained within a perfect circle, and imagined it held above his head, beneath his feet... *Around me flame the pentagrams*, he whispered quietly to himself. Then he expelled the air from his lungs and climbed the stairs...

...And entered the bar.

It was a character filled room with a large open fire, low beams, several glass cases containing scale model trains. On the walls there were old railway posters, faded timetables, advertisements from magazines not published for more than thirty years: a book case, an arm chair, a ship's bell, various antique agricultural implements either propped strategically or hung from the beams on thick hemp rope. The bar itself, monolithic in heavy oak, dwarfed the half dozen high stools and a few hard back wooden chairs scattered around three small round tables.

Mage immediately saw Angel sitting in the nearest corner and nodded in acknowledgement of Angel's half raised hand and shy smile. Instead of joining him at the table, Mage went and stood at the bar, inviting Angel to a drink from that vantage point and giving him the opportunity to scan the hotel's other customers.

Where was the threat?

A fair hared couple on his left. Nothing there. They hadn't noted his arrival and even though he now stood almost next to them, they were so totally engrossed in each other they failed to register his presence. *Nothing there.*

Old man in cloth cap sitting a little way off to his right – a diffused fugue of alcoholic oblivion covering unfocused feelings of failure and bitterness; nebulous and introspective. *Nothing there.*

Fat man standing by the fire. A policeman? Some sort of official? Full of anger and suppressed resentments, a kaleidoscope of confusion and violence beneath which there was the acid bitterness of cold contempt. Mage pushed gently forwards with his mind and almost recoiled when he came in contact with the seething mass of sexual repression and perversion that dwelt within the little fat man's libido, making him as ugly on the inside as he appeared to be on the surface.

But was he a threat?

Mage was not sure – he was no longer sure that there was the kind of threat he had initially perceived. The little fat man by the fire was so charged with negative energy that it was quite conceivable that this was what Mage had brushed against in the hotel lobby. Nonetheless, he boosted mental energy into his defensive screens and making eye contact with the little fat man across the room, nodded politely. The policeman – Mage was sure he was a policeman – met his gaze briefly before his eyes fell away and there was an imperceptible nod in return.

He was studying me and now he knows that I know it, thought Mage... Then, still keeping his screens in place, he turned to order drinks from a slim, young barman. Mage pushed into him and discovered thoughts that centred around motor cycles, marijuana and vaginas. Mage smiled to himself. There was certainly no threat there, leastwise, not to him anyway.

To Angel, watching from his table, Colin Mage had simply walked into the Miraflores bar, had seen him, smiled and had offered him a drink. Now, as Mage brought the drinks to the table, Angel was aware of some tension in the man but that was all. The mental examinations that Mage had made had taken no more than a few casual seconds, unnoticed by all present... Or so Mage hoped.

And yet, as he sat with Angel, his back to the rest of the room, his hackles rose with the sure knowledge that someone was trying to reach into his psyche.

Who?

Mage employed an old and well tried technique. He separated his mind, and while one half of him conversed with Angel and accepted the boy's invitation to visit his Grandmother that afternoon, the other part of his mind played with the incoming psychic probe. It was not very strong and was not co-ordinated enough to be described as a psychic attack, but try as he might, Mage could not follow it back to its source. So, after bouncing it around the pentagram images that he still held tightly around him, suddenly and without warning he sent the probing thoughts back across the ether from whence they came, along with a powerful blast of his own mental energy.

The probe terminated immediately and from behind him came the sound of breaking glass followed by a low moan and a heavy thud. As Angel's mouth hung open mid-sentence, Mage casually turned in his seat.

The alcoholic old man's head rested face down on the bar amid shards of his broken beer glass. Beer trickled from the edge of the bar on to the top of his dirty grey trousers, without reaction. The old man was oblivious. He was out cold.

The blond couple looked on with quizzical bemusement. The policeman wore an evil, almost self satisfied grin and an English voice shouted from behind the counter...

'Oh fucking hell! Valerie? Valerie! Get up here will you. Diego's pissed again!'

It was early evening. The first stars shone, most of them dimmed by the brightness of the planet Venus which hung low over the horizon of the mountains. With the setting of the sun, the temperature had dropped like a stone and although a roaring log fire blazed half way up the chimney, there was little heat in it and Mage, stretched out on a sofa, still wore his jacket. Hands clasped behind his head, he stared up at the ceiling and let his mind wander over the events of the day, trying to assimilate them into some form of order.

He had still not resolved the business at the hotel. Had the old man, Diego, been responsible for sending out that psychic probe? If so, he had been very skilled in hiding his ability when Mage had first studied him. If not Diego, then had it been the policeman? In which case, the little fat man must have had deep training in the craft to have been able to hide the power from Mage's own probe and even more so to have deflected the energy that Mage had unleashed. Had the policeman channelled Mage's energy into the old man, using him as a repository and causing him to pass out, or had the old Spaniard flaked out at an acutely coincidental moment, caught in the backlash, perhaps?

Colin, there's no such thing as coincidence – his Grandmother had told him that once while he was still very young and he words had followed him down along the years, amassing corroborative evidence with every new thing he had learned.

Who else had there been? Angel, the blond couple, the bar boy and the proprietor of the hotel, lurking somewhere in the background. There had been absolutely nothing in any of them, so that meant it had to be either Diego or the policeman, although both seemed unlikely candidates.

Diego had been carried from the bar, unconscious, and shortly afterwards the policeman had departed under his own steam, still wearing a smug self satisfied smile...

Why? Why that smile?

Mage grimaced and lit a cigarette. He didn't know why, but he did know he'd been caught unawares with his guard down and that it mustn't happen again. This village of Castillo de la Frontera may have been quaint and charming, but it was also enemy territory and he'd better not forget it.

And carrying on from that, it would be wise, he thought, to make a few friends and allies in the enemy camp and he felt that he had done this that afternoon with

Angel and his Grandmother. If he was right, and Mage knew that he was right, this village would be a battle ground before the end of the year. In which case, he thought grimly, he might well be in need of a few friends. He was also well aware that they might need him even more.

He swung his legs off the sofa and three another log on the fire, causing long shadows to leap across the room as the embers of the old fire ignited and flamed the dry tinder.

White walls, ponderous black furniture, austere and yet emanating a certain warmth – the room was not unlike its mistress of fifty years. Indeed, although not physically present, Antonia de Guadiaro was very much a part of this room. Her personality was stamped indelibly on every room in the house, but especially so up here in the main salon. Having met her that afternoon and learned something of her history, Mage could easily understand how.

Antonia had received him in her parlour and Mage was drawn to her immediately. For one thing, she very much reminded him of his own Grandmother, not only in her physiognomy, but also in her stature and bearing – and for another, she emanated a powerful aura of basic – *goodness?* – yes, goodness. There was really no other word to describe it. Also, when Mage reached out and touched, he found great strength of will and brightness of spirit, built on layered degrees of pain and suffering.

As Angel performed the introductions, he took her hand and was immediately aware of the arthritis; it was in her legs and hands, but mostly in her right hip. He sensed bereavement and loss and felt the strength of her pride and her dignity. There was something else, too... A worry, a niggle, a fear... something deep down inside her that had not yet surfaced from the subliminal to the conscious.

She had served mint tea and they had discussed the rental contract. Was the house to his satisfaction? It was. Did he consider the financial arrangements fair? He did. Did he require a more formal agreement with a notorised contract? No, that was not necessary. Would he like someone to come and clean for him? No, that was very kind, but also unnecessary. Well, he was paying good money for the house so he should consider it his home for three months or six months, or however long he needed it.

She had dismissed Angel from their presence at that point and had then gone on to talk about him at some length. He was a good boy, honest and reliable. If he, Señor Mage, needed a correador or a guide or if there was any problem with the house, then he had only to speak with Angel. In fact, if Señor Mage could find some occasional work for her Grandson, she would be willing to consider a substantial reduction in the rent.

Mage thanked her, then listened politely as Antonia told him something of her own life centred around the years spent in the house in Calle Granadillos. She neither gossiped nor rambled and Mage was aware that she was telling him in an obtuse Spanish way that house he was renting from her was a most precious part of her life and that she was entrusting it to his care.

Following an impulse, Mage had reached over and had laid his hand across the old woman's wrist. He charged the healing power of his spirit into her ancient body, thinking of the pains in her joints and the pain of her memories.

'Your house is safe with me, Señora,' he'd spoken gently '... and should you care to visit, then we will both remember the importance of its history.'

He'd felt the power go out of him and then had withdrawn his hand. Antonia had smiled an uncertain smile and Mage had smiled back reassuringly, covering this woman who so reminded him of Elsie Maud, with the blue fire of his own etheric body... Holding her, loving her and giving what hope and protection he could.

It's easier to give than it is to take, so give what you can whenever you can... Elsie Maud's words crossed the gulf of time and Mage smiled again with the memory.

'And now, Señor Mage,' Antonia's words, cautious and hesitant, had brought him back to the reality of the moment. 'Tell me what brings you to our village of Castillo? It is not the time for tourists and even if it was, I do not think you are much of a tourist anyway.'

Mage laughed – and had his cover story well prepared. 'No Señora, I am not a tourist. I've been working very hard for the last two years and I've done a great deal of travelling. Now I want a long quiet summer in which I can do a lot of resting and some reading and possibly even some writing.'

'Ah you are a writer!' Antonia had exclaimed. 'I wondered if this might be the case. Tell me, what kind of books do you write? Adventure stories, perhaps, or romances?'

'Neither, I'm afraid. Textbooks.'

Antonia had seemed momentarily disappointed, but then she'd brightened. 'And what is the subject of your textbooks?'

'Psychology, mostly. Very dry. Very boring.'

'And you have done much travelling, yes? You have visited many interesting countries?'

Oh, they were interesting all right. Even after three months, he could still taste the sand of the desert...

'Many interesting countries' Mage had confirmed without elaboration.

Too many interesting countries; Israel, France, The United States, Ireland... all in the space of a few weeks, the fear and the tension ever present, sometimes salving The Hurt, sometimes enhancing it...

'Ah,' Antonia had sighed. 'I have never travelled, although it was frequently my wish to do so. In all of my years, do you know I have never been further than Ronda and Algerciras.' She'd chuckled. 'In fact, the last time I left the village would have been in 1972 when Pepe and Marie got married over in San Pablo.' She'd chuckled again. 'A great journey that. All of fourteen kilometres there and back!'

'Are you not happy here?'

'Oh happy enough. Here I was born and here I shall die. I just wish, sometimes, that the times in between had been a bit more exciting.'

Mage had nodded in understanding and silently hoped that Antonia's wish for more excitement was one wish that would not be granted.

The shadows grew longer as the fire dwindled and as Colin Mage fell into fitful and dream filled sleep –

...as Doctor Hector Sanchez puzzled over the microscope in his small laboratory wondering how the herpes 'A' virus could mutate into the herpes 'B' virus over night –

...as Police Chief Jaime Gomez stared flush faced at a pornographic film that was illegal even in its country of origin –

...as Antonia de Guadiaro snuggled down to what would be the best night's sleep she'd had in months...

Father Ignatious de Santa Clara made his telephone call to England.

'Yes' said the same nasal English voice.

'It is me, Ignatious,' said Ignatious, feeling less excitement and more trepidation than he'd felt the night before.

'Yes?' said the voice again, making Ignatious think of icicles and breaking glass.

'It is definitely him. The one you have warned us about. He has been observed during this day and we have reached out and examined him – and I – we – are certain that it is he.'

'I see.' The voice paused thoughtfully, giving nothing away. And then: 'Was he aware of your examination?'

'Only once.'

'And the result?'

'Our brother is sick with a scrambled mind, but he should recover well enough within a few days.'

'And the other occasions?'

'No, I do not think he felt us. If he did, he gave no indication.'

'And the incident with our ailing brother – was that occasion at the beginning of your examinations, during the course of it, or towards the end?'

'Towards the end. We feel it was the physical proximity of our brother to The One that caused the problem. Our other examinations were carried out from a greater distance. It was only because we wanted to be quite certain that we placed our brother as closely as we did.'

'I see,' said the nasal voice, again lapsing into thoughtfulness.

Ignatious could not bare the silence. 'When will you be coming Lord? We long for your presence and we are impatient for The Day. The One who is here now, he cannot change things, can he?'

'No,' the voice laughed mirthlessly. 'He can change nothing. He is a nuisance with very limited power, so you need not be afraid, my friend...' Ignatious sighed, partially with relief, though mostly through being referred to as "friend". 'However,' the voice continued in a more calculating tone, 'it will still be some weeks before we can arrive. The time of The Opening is not yet at hand and there is still much to be done elsewhere in preparation. The Magician is a minor distraction, but nonetheless, one that we could well do without. I want nothing to disturb The Placing of The Key...'

'What would you have us do, Lord?' Ignatious asked, his excitement rising now, though still leaving him ill-prepared for his Master's answer.

'Kill him,' said the voice.

3.

Ritual

Mage dreamed. Dreamed of the time when he was still married. The good time, the happy time, before things became bad and strange. He dreamed of Alexandra's laughter, the joy of her company, the warmth and tenderness of her kisses. In his dream, Alexandra leaned across his naked body and kissed him with lingering passion.

But in reality things had changed. Alexandra had changed and in his dream, now becoming nightmare, Alexandra changed again. Even as he held her, her hair became lank and the gentleness in her eyes became cold, old and evil. Her skin paled and when she smiled it was a smile of corruption and triumph. Her teeth darkened, apart from two milk white canines that lengthened, becoming vampyric fangs and, as she lowered her mouth to his throat, he could smell the stench of filth and rotting decay. There was a throaty bloody laugh and then the waves of pain washed over him as she tore into his jugular vein. Throughout the transformation and his mounting fear, he'd been unable to move... And now, even more powerless, he screamed out loud as he began to die. Even the scream was denied him. It emerged as a strangled whimper... But in his mind, he was screaming, screaming, screaming...

His last vision before death lifted him from the haze of red mutilation, was of Alexandra clawing at his chest with razor edged finger nails, then plunging her hands into the wound that she had opened and clutching greedily for his heart. In the way of dreams, he knew that it was important that she took it still beating from his body...

He moaned and came close to consciousness, but sleep took him again, leading him into the second part of the dream.

He was dead.

His discarnate spirit rose into pale blue ether while below him striations of red light flickered like lightning amid a seething cauldron of midnight blue black clouds. He elevated on and upwards, this in itself a fulfilment of a multitude of precognitive dreams; out of body and out of control.

The pale blue ether eddied, carrying him gently in an unspecified direction. There were no landmarks, no terms of reference, but he felt that he was moving towards something or somewhere and indeed after a while – it could have been minutes or hours – it seemed that his momentum increased. As he gained velocity the blue etheric mists began to swirl and form in a cylindrical vortex; the blue darkened and the vortex became a tunnel, causing him to feel stabs of fear and suspense. At the end of the tunnel there was something he did not wish to experience, but he was powerless to arrest his flight.

Again in the way of dreams, the ether solidified becoming dark grey stone, illuminated by a blue glow that emanated from the walls. He was carnate now, walking rather than flying, but he had no control over his feet. The blue light eddied and changed in hue to a pale sickly green... This green light frightened him and he wanted to close his eyes and pretend that it was not there – and yet he found this was something he could not do. He could not close his eyes!

In the distance there appeared a black speck, a black speck that grew in size with every unwilling footstep, until it took on the shape of a doorway. The closer he moved towards it, so much greater were the feelings of fear and dread that grew within him. The doorway took on shape; it was round, made of wood and studded with dark metal. There was a hinge to the left and a handle to the right... A handle that began to turn of its own accord, even as he watched.

Now standing, before this circular door at the end of the tunnel, he was petrified – feet cemented to the ground, he was incapable of movement – and he very much wanted to move, as fast and as far away as he could from the slowly opening door.

The door opened, swinging silently back on itself, then disappeared into a void of stygian blackness that was the other side of the threshold. This black void filled him with horror: it was total nothingness, enigmatic and anathema to his every sense of rightness and reason. It filled him with awful panic and he wanted to turn and run from the terror of this phenomena. He knew that if he entered the void, not only would his life be lost, so also would his soul!

He willed himself to step backwards, but instead he moved even closer and then as he was propelled forwards and began to fall into the midnight black vacuum, turning over and over, all light disappearing until he was nothing in nothing, his terror finally found voice with a long wailing cry of abject misery and dispair.

Mage sat bolt upright in the bed, beads of sweat covering his brow, the aftershock of the dream causing confusion and disorientation. Closing his eyes, he fell back on the pillow and after a few moments tried opening them again more cautiously.

Sunshine danced into the bedroom causing motes of light to float across the white walls and ceiling. It was summerspring warm. A gentle breeze sighed against the cortina and from the street came the sound of children laughing counterpointed by the jingling of goat bells and the friendly bleats of baby lambs.

He breathed deeply, then forced himself to sit up. His head cleared and he centred himself in the real world away from the terror of his nightmare. Even so, he still felt far from well: the flu virus still lingered and his head hung heavy with cold. His bones ached with fatigue and as insult to injury, his bowel suddenly went into spasm and he forced himself from the bedroom into the bathroom with barely seconds to spare.

He felt marginally better after showering and dressing and made himself face a breakfast of dry toast and weak tea without milk. Things improved even more as he went and sat on the balcony and lit his first cigarette – but the improvements were only relative.

This was bloody ridiculous, Mage swore. He'd been in Castillo for a week and for the past four days had been immobile and incapacitated by whatever it was that he'd caught; it had hit him out of the blue during the morning of his third day and for seventy two hours he'd been delirious with a raging temperature and the most violent bouts of nausea and diarrhoea. Nothing from his homeopathic dispensary had helped and even allopathic drugs like kaolin and morphine and paracetamol had had little or no effect.

And yet in many ways he was not too surprised by his own weakness. The previous months had robbed him of many reserves and the tension involved in getting himself to Castillo on time had been intense. Now he was here and much of the immediate pressure was off. The body organism that had kept him together through more than thirty thousand miles of frantic travel schedules, that had sustained him through too many months of irregular and unhealthy meals, that had kept him going when there were far too many nights without sleep – had now finally gone on strike. One could not live indefinitely beneath the burden of pressure such as Mage had experienced without cracks emerging sooner or later.

His chest wheezed and he dispensed with the half smoked cigarette. A cleansing ritual, he told himself firmly, and then a good regular diet with plenty of fresh fruit and vegetables. There was work to do in this village that he couldn't do if he was flat on his back with the gripe. But what about that dream?

Mage's eyes clouded and he replayed the dream through his conscious mind... and nor was this the first time he had done so, for the nightmare had been a regular if not constant companion these last six months. Although occasionally there were subtle variations, the dream always followed the same pattern – Alexandra's kiss of love turning into the deadly kiss of The Beast, the tearing out of his heart leading to death and the terror of the tunnel and the opening of the curiously circular door.

Sometimes, especially in the early days of the dream, Mage had awakened long before the door had opened to reveal the horror of the nothingness that was The Void... But he'd dreamed the dream on four consecutive nights now and, on each occasion, not only had the door opened to reveal the abyss, he'd actually been forced across the threshold and had fallen (or was he pushed?) into it! This had to be significant of something, hadn't it?

Mage smiled thinly. Even if the significance was elusive, he didn't have to be Freud to interpret the cause of the dream, or to find the parallels and allegories.

In reality, Alexandra's metamorphosis from loving wife into some alien being that weakened, terrified and finally almost destroyed him, was no less horrific than the visions thrown up by his subconscious. As for the journey along the tunnel, he saw this as being forced into the unknown against his free will. The opening of the circular door worried him the most. It was clearly allegorical to that other Opening that had dominated his thoughts and actions since he'd first learned of its existence. His falling into the darkness of The Void was a clear precognitive warning of what would happen, not only to him but to many, many others, if he were to fail in making sure The Opening never took place.

He shivered at the awesome responsibility that had been placed, unsolicited, upon his shoulders and gave silent grateful thanks for Michael Fry and the handful of people like him who had listened, educated and on occasion had provided individual pieces of the jigsaw that made some dreadful sense of the chaos that had turned Mage's life upside down in less than a year – The Chaos that stretched human credulity to the limit and even beyond the limit. The Chaos which, if not checked and neutralised, would become The Armageddon of legend and historic prophesy. The Door had to remain closed, The Opening denied. Armageddon contained.

How he, Colin Mage, had become involved in this cataclysmic confrontation, defied all explanation. Obviously Alexandra was the catalyst, but even that in its own right demanded explanation. Why Alexandra? Why him?

Mage was under no illusion of false modesty. He was a very fine psychic craftsman, with sound and solid training and more than twenty years of practical experience. His gifts were remarkable, not least of which were his powers of healing and telepathy. He'd earned a very good living for more than half his lifetime as a precognitive seer and his four published books on the practice and psychology of magic had been modest best sellers among the very small fraternity who specifically sought that literature. He was a careful man, almost to the point of conservatism; he had a reputation for thoroughness and was highly regarded by his peers. In short, he was very good at what he did, but there were others, and he could have named a good half dozen, who did it better.

Surely this task should have fallen to one of them? To one of The Masters? Hershal of The Negev? Light in California? Kiku in Calcutta, or even Paul of Ireland? Or what of Michael Fry, The Druid Merlin of All Britain? Any one of these people were far better qualified to fight the forthcoming batter than he was and arguably each of them had more to lose if they failed – and yet undeniably he, Mage, was the one chosen.

The Chosen One.

Yes, it sounded melodramatic, but that's what it came down to, didn't it? Just because of Alexandra? Why?

His eyes drifted upwards towards the castle – the western linchpin of the intersecting ley lines – and he pondered on the dark enigmatic slabs of stone. There was more to the old ruined fortress than met the eye – of that he was certain – and the site warranted a much more critical investigation. What was also interesting was the fact that the southern intersection of ley lines (if Maggie was right) cut directly through the Hotel Miraflores – so wasn't that situation with the old man and the mind probe just a little too coincidental?

Colin, there's no such thing as coincidence!

He'd fully intended to explore the other ley lines and establish the exact whereabouts of the northern and eastern intersections, but then the flu virus had struck with its vicious onslaught and he'd been laid low... But four days was quite enough; was all that he would allow himself.

He pushed up from the chair and went back into the house. He paused when he caught sight of himself in a long wall mirror, not at all pleased with what he saw. The plump well fed look of a year ago had gone; now, in its place, there was a stocky hardness. All the surplus fat had been burned from his body and what had once been a pot belly was now well toned muscle. Never a tall man, he now at least appeared to be taller and yet at the same time, even more solidly built. It seemed that something other than excess flesh had been taken from him (which indeed it had) and had been replaced with something new and different that, as yet, he neither fully recognised nor was totally aware of.

There were streaks and speckles of grey that lightened his brown hair and beard and his face had acquired a gauntness which might have been attractive were it not for the pallor still noticeably visible beneath the residue of his sun tan. What once had been laughter lines were now lines of fatigue and although he still retained the ability to smile, it seemed that all genuine humour, once such an integral part of his personality, had been stripped from his soul. His eyes, eyes that had once danced with laughter and compassion, were alternately cold and bleak, or brimming with such profound sadness that they almost seemed to be on the brink of tears.

'What a bloody mess,' he muttered laconically to himself – then turned his back on the mirror and carried on through the house.

Not knowing where he was going, but aware of the fact that he needed fresh air and space as part of the healing process, he drove the Land Rover out of the village, heading south. After half a kilometre, and before hitting the main Ronda road, he impulsively turned off the sweeping S bend avenue flanked by tall Eucalyptus trees and headed along a gravelled side track and followed this as it swung back around the base of Castillo's hill, marching with the eastern bank of the River Hozgarganta.

With the steep southern face of the castle and the crag ahead of him, the village half obscured, the gravel track did a sudden left hook and he crossed the river courtesy of a narrow iron bridge that brought him to the other side of the surging mountain torrent. Here the track forked, one route deteriorating rapidly as it curved to the right and followed the western bank of the river, while the other became tarmac and wound it's way up the hillside into the mountains. One car, a battered green Renault Four, had already come to grief on the riverside road, bonnet up and buried up to its hubs in loose gravel. Mage took the hint and headed for the hills.

The road was tortuous with sharp hairpin bends every fifty or sixty metres; it was pockmarked with deep pot-hols and Mage had to drive slowly and carefully to avoid overtaxing the suspension.

Stunted cork oaks pressed from both sides of the road, growing in eratic profusion amid huge boulders and slabs of stone the size of small houses. Occasionally there were breaks in the tree line and Mage was gifted with tantalising views of the valley below.

The road climbed steadily for almost twelve kilometres, never widening to more than a single track, before it levelled out and wound its way along the spine of a long ridge. He was above the tree line now and the views were breathtakingly spectacular. Then the road curved around a last bend and abruptly petered out into the soil and scrub, with a couple of dirt tracks going off at opposite tangents. He hit the breaks in surprise and managed a perfect stall.

He was on a small plateau; one of the dirt tracks carried on more or less where the road should have been, winding down over the brow of the ridge towards a distant stream and small farm house, maybe three or four kilometres further on. A wisp of grey smoke drifted skywards and there were sheep and goats grazing in a nearby pasture. The other track led off to his left towards an ugly concrete building, obviously derelict and disused. Mage was reasonably sure that this had once been some sort of telegraph relay station, perhaps the original reason for the road's existence in the first place but, like the road, it was falling to rack and ruin and he guessed that it hadn't been used in years.

To his right he had an uninterrupted view of valleys and mountain peaks. He could just discern the white smudge that was the village of Castillo and a thumb nail skyline of the castle and the keep. Beyond were the Sierra Morenos and beyond them the blue haze of the higher and better known Sierra Rondas. He climbed out of the Land Rover, marvelling at the vista and inhaling the invigorating fresh mountain air deep into his lungs. Already he felt better than at any other time during the last four days and, as the weak spring sunshine caressed his face, he knew that it had been a good idea to get out of the village for a while.

Pulling the carpet bag from the front seat, he walked a few dozen metres down the hillside until he came to an arena of fresh green grass, partially surrounded by small boulders and wiry pine bushes. He looked approvingly at the rich earth beneath his feet, then squatted down and opened the bag.

First he removed a long bladed knife. It was wickedly pointed and razor sharp on both cutting edges. The hasp and handle were made of plain unpolished wood, into which had been carefully carved runic sigils and hieroglyphics. The blade of the knife was tempered from the finest English steel, milled at a time when the British steel industry had been at its height: the handle was much older and had once been a part of a Runemaster's staff. Steel and wood had been brought together by Mage's Grandmother in 1921 and it had been Mage's since 1978 – the year his Grandmother had died.

Laying the knife by his side, he then produced a silver flask; oval in shape and without a standing base. It was plain and unornate, but nonetheless, exquisitely made and it had cost Mage a lot of money – in that time when there had been money for such luxuries as solid silver flasks! Incredibly, the contents of the flask, purchased much more recently had cost almost three times as much as the flask itself... This, however, was not a luxury, but an absolute necessity for the work in hand. Mage was in no doubt that the contents of the flask would be put to good use on more than one occasion in the time that lay ahead.

Laying the flask next to the knife, he took a third and final item from the bag. This was a longish piece of yew wood, twenty one inches in length, and with a diameter of two inches. It, like the knife handle, was intricately carved and was bound at both ends by a wide thong of black leather. From one end, set deeply into the bowl of the wood was a long shard of clear quartz crystal, naturally shaped to an arrow point. It caught the sun's rays in its prism and flashed alternatively silver white and cold ice blue.

Mage closed the bag and sat thoughtfully, facing the East. It's a good place, he thought. Good earth...

Mage stood and took off his hat, jacket and shirt. The mountain air was cold, but he suppressed the natural urge to shiver and let the air come into contact with his body. Then he stooped and, picking up the knife, held it horizontally to the sky, the blade tip pointing towards the Sierra Morenos. Then squatting again, in one long fluid movement, he drew a circle in the earth all around him, using the blade to scar the soil and cutting deep. This done, he then used the blade to etch in the points and intersecting lines of the pentagram.

Coming to his feet, again he raised the blade of the knife to the east. Slowly, and with great deliberation, he drew the sign of the pentagram in the air before him, imagining the knife cutting lines of golden fire into the atmosphere. As he did this, he spoke low firm words in a language practically older than time itself. It was a polyglot patois of ancient Hebrew, Aramaic and Sumerian. The words were strange and alien to the untutored ear; consonants clashed with diphthongs and monothongs causing the rhythm of speech to ululate in odd and unexpected ways. And yet there was a powerful beauty to the overall sound, creating an impression of majesty and grandeur that was not out of tune with the wildness and isolation of his location.

From the east, Mage turned to the south and repeated the ritual words and the drawing of the imaginary fire lines... Repeating them twice more to the west and the north. Resting the knife on the ground by his feet, he picked up the silver flask and splayed his legs out very wide. He undid the flask and raised his face to the sky.

After standing this way for a number of minutes, regulating his breathing and tuning in to his surroundings and the magnetic pulse of the Earth, he tipped the flask into the palm of his right hand and deposited one drop of the oily liquid on his forehead, directly above the bridge of his nose.

'To be cleansed,' he said softly.

He placed another minuscule droplet upon his throat, two inches below the Adam's apple.

'To be cleansed,' he said again.

Now he carefully shook another few droplets into his hand and massaged the oil into his stomach, directly beneath the sternum.

'To be cleansed...' he spoke a third time then, capping the flask, pushed it deeply and securely into the back pocket of his jeans. Around him now was a rich aromatic scent as the contents of the flask came into contact with the fresh air. Mage smiled, almost reverently, with the thought of what had gone into the preparation of the lotion.

There were a number of ingredients.

First, a distillation of the oil of the apricot kernel taken from the Hunza Valley in the northern Himalayas, then a mixture of ambergris and verdigris oils, held together by frankincense and myrrh. Into this concoction had gone two tiny vials of human blood – Mage's own and that of an unknown female virgin. Then there were the waters from the four holy rivers... The Jordan, The Nile, The Ganges and The Euphrates, mixed at matrix with Holy Water from the shrines at Lourdes and Bethlehem. The market price of this potent lotion was over one hundred pounds sterling per millilitre, and Mage's flask contained thirty millilitres!

Perhaps the most potent ingredient of all was the blessing given to the lotion by The Merlin of Britain – this, and the fact that the High Druid had prepared the concoction himself before the High Altar of England. Mage was fully aware of the potency of this action and it warmed him spiritually to know that Michael Fry had taken him seriously enough to go to such lengths.

Now Mage closed his eyes and very slowly raised his arms until they were level with his shoulders, turning the palm of his right hand up to face the sky and the palm of his left hand downwards to face the Earth. Then he waited...

It began as a trickle, but he immediately relaxed as he felt the Earth energy start to move through him, causing his right palm to tingle with the sudden drop in temperature, and his left, Earthbound palm glow and gently throb with warmth. Mage's breathing became very long and soon the trickle became a steadily flowing surge, wave upon mounting wave, buffeting gently and causing his face to break into a smile of pure tactile joy.

The air above his head became opaque and began to crackle with static electricity – a breeze pulled at his legs and ruffled his beard and a pale blue light began to emanate from his body... A light that writhed and eddied, strengthened, weakened, then strengthened again and solidified, covering him from head to foot. The light pulsed in counterpoint to his heart beat, a heart beat that accelerated now as the electricity striated the blue with shards of silver white lightning, streaking from the crackling star of pure energy that hovered in brilliant whiteness just above and beyond his imaginary vision.

Minutes passed and Mage moaned gently in the face of the growing wind. Then without warning, the star seemed to detonate, blossoming and exploding, bathing his head and shoulders with an incandescent radiance. Mage opened his mind to it, drawing it down through his skull into those key body terminals known as the chakras. His right hand was ice, his left hand fire as the energy... Gods, there was so much of it in this place... coursed through him, cauterising and sweeping away the dark areas of illness and infirmity within.

'Be cleansed. Be clean and well!' A voice, Mage's own voice, roared and echoed around the mountains. 'Be out of me and gone, infirm darkness!' He yelled against the rising cosmic wind that now howled around him, making him flex muscles as he leaned into the gale to maintain his stance and position. In huge lungfulls he sucked this same wind into the soul of his being, feeling it leap through his blood and organs with all the keenness of a surgeon's scalpel.

'Out Demons and be gone from me!' His voice was a scream A scream that died to a whimper as the wind tore into him with fresh ferocity, curling and curving around the pentagrams in the soil like a controlled tornado; his hair stood on end and he began to float above the ground losing all contact with reality.

He fought for control, reached out for it, drawing the blue and white fire into himself, suppressing the wind, holding it captive in his heaving chest. He came to Earth, aware that he was now on the most dangerous of ground, also frantically aware of the formidable degree of negative energy he had released... That same energy that would destroy him were it not diffused or discharged.

Colin Mage the Magician was also very human and, lowering his arms, aching dreadfully from having been held outstretched for so long, he dipped his hands into the dimension of the negativity and hurled it with venom through the wind.

'Against the darkness!' He bellowed. 'Against The Opening!'
There was a millisecond of questioning, and then a crack in the air that sounded like tearing fabric. And then the air was still and silent. Mage's arms fell to his sides and his head fell forwards, bowed towards the ground. His breathing eased down from a point near hyperventilation to a regular pattern and his heart beat slowed from its rapid-fire hammering to a normal rhythm. He stood like this for several minutes before pulling on his shirt and jacket and, packing the knife and the wand into the carpet bag, headed back towards the Land Rover. He realised that he had not used the wand, but even so, the crystal prism was clouded and opaque, no longer alive with the dancing light motes of the sunshine. He clambered up behind the steering wheel and lit a Marlboro, still thinking about the crystal in the wand. Someone, somewhere, was certainly soon going to know that Colin Mage was alive and well and living in the mountains of Southern Spain.

Alive and waiting.

To the casual observer, had there been one, Mage's actions on that April morning may have appeared a little odd, even virging on the eccentric. Beyond that, they would have elicited little comment. The casual observer would have watched him scratching in the air and earth with a knife and then they'd have seen him apply some droplets of lotion to his body from a strangely shaped flask. If they'd not been bored to distraction, they'd have seen him standing in the same position, legs and arms stretched wide apart, for more than thirty minutes before he'd relaxed and walked back to his waiting truck. They'd have heard him mutter words in an unintelligible language and they would have heard him shouting in what roughly might be described as biblical tones...

They would not, however, have felt any variation in either wind force or temperature. They would not have seen stars of crackling blue and white light. They would not have seen the steady build up of dark mist that swathed his legs and stretched and eddied over the rim of the mountain down into the valley below.

They might have assumed he was involved in some form of deep meditation or that possibly he was preparing for some kind of martial arts demonstration; had they been told he was practising some religious or pagan rite, this they might have accepted, albeit with a raised eyebrow. If they'd been told the truth – that this was a modern day magician about his business of a ritual of cleansing, then most, if not all, would have either scoffed and walked away or laughed with sympathy and derision. Nonetheless, truth is truth, and although there were no casual observers, there were others who felt something of Mage's power on that sunny April day.

In England, the woman who, until quite recently, had been Mage's wife, sat astride her new partner's pale white body. She was about to lower her grossly misshapen frame onto his erect penis, when despite the drugs that had been given to her, she inexplicably went dry, losing both her juices and her desire. She felt giddy and opened her mouth to say something to the man who lay beneath her – but then the crushing hammer blows of migraine started pounding in her head and she half collapsed over Jack Dolorean's chest. Dolorean, caught off guard in more ways than one, felt something cold and snake-like uncoil in his belly: his discomfort was significantly enhanced as Alexandra's knee caught him squarely in the testicles.

Also in England, The Druid, Michael Fry, paused mid-sentence in an important telephone conversation as he felt a sudden hollowness in his solar plexus. His computer-like mind assessed his psychic emotions and came up with data almost immediately.

'Mage,' he thought out loud. 'He's cleansing. That means it's already begun.'

'I beg your pardon, Lord Merlin?' queried the voice at the other end of the telephone.

'I'm sorry.' Fry was immediately apologetic. 'I'm afraid my mind slipped for a moment. Now, what were you saying?'

In the Negev desert, an old man called Herschal looked up from his camp fire and thought it might be a good idea if he moved further north towards Beer Sheba. He hated villages and detested towns, but there were telephones in Beer Sheba and he thought the time might be coming close to when he needed one.

On the tiny island of Cael off the West coast of Ireland, Father Paul O'Connor lowered himself to his knees in the long grass of the abbey gardens: there was an empty lightness in his chest but a dull ache gripped his left arm. Knowing clearly what was happening (God knew he'd been warned often enough), he managed to bring the palms of his hands together and recite the first two lines of The Lord's Prayer before the pain in his arm leapt upwards and exploded in his heart. He slowly toppled forwards, cheek coming to rest against the velvet green of the overgrown lawn. The Lord's Prayer abandoned, he nonetheless smiled as The Nazarene's hands reached down from the tree tops to lift him from the garden. 'Thank you, Lord Christ,' he whispered through the wetness of his tears and then, almost as an afterthought: ' – And God help Colin!' Thus, only two days before his eighty third birthday, Paul O'Connor finally died.

In the small village of Gangit, thirty kilometres South of Calcutta, a thin scrawny woman dressed in a deep saffron coloured robe looked up from the fire into which she had been gazing and stared instead at the statue of the Goddess Kali that stood to the left of the fire. Two rubies formed the Goddess's eyes and they twinkled now with life and animation. *It is the reflection from the fire*, Kiku told herself rationally. *And yet I have been waiting for something, some sign all week. How many times have I thought of the Englishman? Is this it? Is this the start of it?* She shuddered and, impulsively, overturned a large pale of brackish water into the embers of the fire causing a huge billowing mass of smoke and steam to rise towards the ceiling of the mud hut with a long drawn out hiss. Unconcerned about the consequences, she then three a thick skin rug across the fireplace and turned again her gaze back to the statue of the Goddess. Now, in the gloom without light or reflection, the twin ruby eyes gleamed even more malevolently. *So be it,* Kiku thought with sadness and resignation. The ritual she had hoped to avoid would have to take place after all and the boy would have to be offered as the ultimate sacrifice. A great, great pity. Rajad was not only a lovely child in his own right, he was also her favourite Grandson. Still, what was the life of one good child in the face of the possible alternatives? The Englishman, who had sent her that strange and powerful letter that she still read at least twice a day but had never bothered replying to....what was there to say? How could she possibly answer his questions? Well, he had been right – far more right than he'd known. If The Demons of Shiva were released, it would mean the end of everything!

In an even more distant country, many time zones away, The Reverend John Light, one time hell's angel, one time Satanist, now evangelical crusader for The True God, thundered threateningly at the thousands of faces in his captive audience. He was aware of the tens of thousands, maybe even hundreds of thousands more that would be watching spellbound (he hoped) on their television sets as he preached live (oh yes, baby, this was live all right!) from The Hollywood Bowl amphitheatre.

'... And I'm telling you The Light is coming... GOD's light is coming and you better be ready for it, 'cos the Good Ole' Lord's gonna be mighty angry if you aint! Yep, the Big Boss is gonna be mega peeved...'

He nearly said pissed off but the TV people had done a good job of putting the fear of God into *him*, warning him of what would happen to the transmission if he slipped into bad language patterns. They liked the idea of a six and a half foot tall, three hundred pound Negro wearing a white suit and doing his 'thing', but they didn't like the idea of offending more orthodox Christians and the thought of offending the advertisers and sponsors was complete anathema.

'...Yes, The Good Lord's gonna be angry and in His mage He's gonna sort out all the good from the bad. Now, if you're in with the Good Guys, you get to go up...' he jabbed an ebony black finger amply decorated with gold and diamond rings into the air, '... and you'll enjoy all of the joys of heaven. But if you're in with the Bad Guys,' he jabbed a finger down towards the boards of the stage, ' – why, you're gonna go down into the deepest black, and baby I mean BLACK bowels of Lucifer's living perpetual Hell! So, how're you gonna avoid that? How you gonna avoid God's mage...'

Mage? What was this Mage crap? He'd' meant to say rage and yet twice now he'd said Mage? So what or who was Mage? Oh yeah, fuck, that weird English wiz and all that shit with the opening crap. Fucking limey shit! Fuck off outa my head, Mage. Fuck you and fuck your opening shit. Just fuck off and stop fucking up my sermon. Hope the fucking opening opens up right under your ass and gobbles you up, prick first...

'God's RAGE!' Jonty Golightly more latterly called the Rev. John Light roared into the battery of microphones that had suddenly started howling with a major feedback problem. Fuck the fucking TV people! Didn't they know fucking anything? 'I'll tell you Motherfuckers how you're gonna avoid God's rage. You're gonna do it by being good and seeing The Light.'

Much much closer to where Colin Mage had ritually cleansed himself in the mountains above the Castillato Valley, others felt the force of his power much more acutely.

In the village, an old man called Diego Matan who'd been ill for five days since having some sort of fainting fit in the bar of the Hotel Miraflores... had a stroke. Truth to tell, it was not a major one, but in his confused and befuddled state, it was quite enough to kill him.

At precisely the same time, his son, Lorenzo Bautista Matan, began to have a heavy nose bleed. He lost more than a litre and a half of blood in less than ten minutes. Hitherto, he'd never had a nose bleed in his life.

At precisely the same time, Father Ignatious de Santa Clara began to bleed – from the rectum. He also began to be physically sick and by the time he reached the nearest lavatory, he was covered in his own ordure, blood and vomit.

At precisely the same time, Father Francisco de Santa Maria also began to bleed. From the palms of his hands.

Somewhere between the two churches a very strange little girl of about nine years old, suddenly thought it would be a wonderful idea to play with a dead bird – and later, when she became hungry, she would eat it. Raw.

At precisely the same time, a man who'd already beaten his dead wife in her coffin less than a week before, hung himself in the small room that served as a kitchen. He could find no rope, so used a strand of barbed wire.

At precisely the same time, a boy called Miguel Torres killed himself in his Algerciras prison cell. He did this by trying to eat his own tongue. He was successful, and choked to death.

At precisely the same time, an expatriate English lady who'd lived in the village for fifteen of her sixty one years, began to menstruate for the first time since 1973...

And at precisely the same time, a house shifted on its foundations in Calle Llanette, causing pots to crash to the kitchen floor. The TV, which had been tuned to GBC, continued to work, but now broadcast a programme from Morocco. Annette Salt, another expatriate who'd been in the village for only twenty months, dashed out of her home to find that her next door neighbour, a Spaniard called Paco Carlos, was smashing the windscreen of her brand new car with a seven pound sledge hammer.

At precisely the same time, four children playing on the northern outskirts of the village, heard the unmistakable sounds of gunshots coming from the direction of the war memorial. Typically without caution, the ten year olds raced up the hill and were both disappointed and mystified to find that the war memorial was deserted.

At precisely the same time, and without warning, the plate glass window of the Bar Vargas shattered and dissolved into a thousand flying pieces. Only one person was injured... the owner, one Xavier Mendoza. Two pieces of glass struck him. One in each eye.

At precisely the same time, Valerie Holloway decided that come hell or high water she was going to have the baby that Henry had always denied her – and if Henry didn't want to be the father then she'd just have to find someone else. Elsewhere in the Hotel Miraflores, a young American girl called Christina Carol finally succumbed to the gentle persistence of her mentor and lover and allowed him to bugger her.

At precisely the same time, Angel de Guadiaro looked into an unused bedroom of his home and heard his mother laughing.

And at precisely the same time, in the Commissaria of Police, Chief Jaime Gomez looked up from the report he was writing and saw the Virgin Mary

4.

Sanchez

Mage gunned the Land Rover into life but only drove a couple of miles down the mountain before he stopped again, pulling over into a small cork oak forest. He got out of the truck, and walked around the trees, some of them shaved of their bark up the the frist forks of their branches. He spent a few minutes marvelling at the sense of peace and stillness, felt the vibrancy of the earth beneath his feet, felt the crackling of nature's energy around his head.

Sitting on the soft ground he pulled out a packet of cigarettes, lit one and inhaled deeply, and let his mind replay the process of the ritual he had just peformed. He felt that it had been effective. If he used his own physical state as the barometer, it had worked well. All traces of his fever had gone and he felt brightly alive and alert.

Not for the first time in his career he found himself contemplating the psychology of magic. Was it the case of an individual mind working over matter, the brain tricking the mind into believing what *most* people would regard as being as being impossible – or was there a separate reservoir of power that could be tapped into by a trained intelligence, and once tapped into, could that power not be moulded and shaped to change the natural law of narture and the sequence of events nominally govered by the dictat of cause and effect?

For more than twenty years he had swithered between the two theories but over the past twenty months he had come down firmly in favour of the second option. This was where the evidence pointed anyway, and over the past twenty months he'd had more evidence that he'd had in all the previous twenty years put together. Nor was it second hand evidence gleaned from dusty old books and third parties. He measured the results on what he himself had been capable of – and whast he had *become* capable of.

His first real introduction to the craft had come on his fourteenth birthday. His gypsy grandmother had taken him to one side and said – 'Gorra special present for you, our Col!'

They had bewen in the vack parlour of her old Yorkshire stone cottage. The room was sparse and Spartan but a big bay window gave spectacular views over the sky hugging panorama of the North Yorkshire Moors.

'What is it, Nan?' the fey young fourteen year old asked with quickening interest.

'Coom an' sit at table an' I'll show thee.' The wrinkled old lady had said with a sly smile. 'Yer fourteen now Col, an it's about time yer learned a few things about benefits of bein'me only grandson!

'Now I want yer to cup yer hands.' Elsie Maud had said and when Mage had brought his hands together the old lady had cupped her own hands beneath them, her palms lightly touching the back of hius hands – the slightest and lightest of contacts, so subtle that it might not have been there at all.

'Now then, I wants yer to look into yer palms and think of a colour – don't tell us what colour yer thinkin'of – jusat empty your mind of everything else an' think of yer colour…'

Mage had found himself thinking of blue. At first it had been difficult to rid himself of intruding every day thoughts, but after a few moments it seemed as though he was dipping into a blue reverie; images of guitars and footballs and fast cars slipped away to be replaced by a shining effervescence that filled his senses and brought his a reassuring sensation of inner peace and safety.

'Right now…' He was aware of his grandmother's voice speaking to him but as though from some great distance and not just the other side of the kitchen table. 'Next thing for yer to do is to imagine a fire burning in yer 'ands – a cool fire wi' flames the same colour as the colour yer bein thinking of – can yer try that, Col? Go on lad, try it an' see what yer can do!'

To his surprise he found it quite easy to visualise bright blue flames coruscating from his upturned hands. There'd been a tingling tickling sensation, but certainly no feeling of heat or warmth…

'Ah that's good,' Elsie Maud murmoured approvingly. 'Now, let's get to the heart of it. Col, think of someone special that you really like, y'know, someone you'd really like to be with, someone who mebe you might want to want to be with you. Just think o'that one person as 'ard as yer can. Don't think of owt else…'

It had not been difficult for him to visualise one person – the one person who had occupied a lot of his fourteen year old thoughts and had done so for the past four months or so ever since she had become part of his geography class the previous term. Her name was Rosalyn Harrup – short silky fair hair cut in a page boy bob, creamy clear skin with full pink lips and baby blue eyes. The first curves of provocative breasts and ther longer curves of graceful hips and tight taut buttocks. Rosalyn of the mellifluous voice and the mischievous smile, Rosalyn who inspired romantic daydreams and caused dangerous nocturnal emissions.

…And now, wonder of wonders, here she was, smiling at him from his upturned palms, pivoting, talking laughing, happy to be there, not afraid of making eye contact – at one point unfastening the top b utton of her virgin white school blouse – *just for him! Just for him!* – and with the unspoken promise of secret kisses yet to come... And he was there with her and she was there with him; he coult smell her perfume and the scent of soap and although he had never kissed her he could feel the touch of her lips on his mouth and he could feel the contours of her lithe and nubile boby beneath his tentatively searching hands. Now lost from all sense of time and place, he felt her naked flesh upon his hands, felt himself become sexually rigid in the relity of the waking dream – and yet at the same time part of his mind was constantly aware that this was no dream – it was actually happening, albeit in a private cavern of his most secret imagination.

He'd felt a cold prickling sensation in his hands and then just as suddenly as it had appeared the vision of Rosalyn's beautiful face had been lost, leaving him only with a retinal memory of the miracle he had just been party to. He'd looked at his grandmother with a mixture of wonderment and awe.

'Nan.' He had said with all the respect befitting the old woman's talents, 'that's one hell of a birthday present!'

'Oh that's not yer present,' the old lady had retorted scornfully. 'Yer present, if yer wannit, is that I'm gonna teach yer 'ow to do it fer theesen.'

He smiled quietly to himself in the warm shadows of the forest. It had been thirty years ago, and now thirty years on, if he was to be totally honest, he would have to admit that he still did not know exactly how the power of magic actually worked. But at least he had the satisfaction of knowing that the power was there in place and that it *did* work when called upon

Pushing himself to his feet, he climbed back into the Land Rover and carried on down the mountain.

Doctor Hector Sanchez was a big man, standing well over six feet tall and topping the scales at two hundred and fifty pounds. At fifty three years old, his thick black hair and bushy moustache were only just beginning to fleck with grey and, although much of his stomach paunch came from a mild excess of good food and Rioja wine, there was hard muscle beneath the fat and he carried his weight with panache.

He was a sensitive man with soft tawny eyes, more often filled with good humour than with anger. The pain he had sustained in his own life shone out of those eyes as compassion rather than as bitterness or defeat. He had an easy laugh and essentially an optimist, he laughed far more often than he frowned. Slow to anger and mild of temper, he radiated an aura of confident calm that patients and friends alike found attractive and reassuring in equal proportions.

As a doctor, he was the best that Castillo had – which, as he frequently reminded himself, was not difficult because he was the only doctor Castillo had! Even so, behind the jovial modesty there was an excellent medical mind and not only was Hector Sanchez a first class GP, he also held degrees in pharmaceutical analysis and gynaecology.

Unlike many of his colleagues in the medical profession, he had a refreshingly open mind – and sometimes some had said too open – and over his years of practise he had looked at many different aspects of healing. Homeopathy and hypnotism had fascinated him, along with aromatherapy and reflexology. He'd delved deeply into such concepts as psychosomaticism and very early in his career had come to the conclusion that factors such as stress and basic human unhappiness accounted for much of the modern world's ill health and disease. An open man, he had aired his views on innumerable occasions, sometimes with confidence and enthusiasm, sometimes with a cautious curiosity that searched for confirmation of his ideas and answers to his thought provoking questions.

This had done little to endear him to his various superiors at the succession of hospitals that had littered his pathway in the early days and nor had he been popular with the vast majority of his peers, who accepted homeopathy and herbalism with reservation and caution, but openly derided him for the rest.

Now, and thank God, especially in Spain, there was more acceptance of new ideas and alternative medicine, but thirty years before he'd been preaching heresy and had rocked the boat too many times for comfort in the process.

Hector could have been more than a competent surgeon and indeed surgery had been both his intention and ambition when he'd first entered medical school back in 1955. But he soon realised that specialisation closed the door on so many other interesting aspects of his profession and there was a radical curiosity fermenting away in the front of his brain, growing ever stronger with every year that passed.

Nor had he been impressed by the conservatism and "by the book" attitude that prevailed in Spain at that time and after an unhappy internship at one of the larger hospitals in Madrid, he'd wandered... Barcelona, Paris, London, New York, then The Philippines. It had been in Manilla, he'd met and married an extraordinary girl, half American and half Philippino, called Mariana Ortega. They were married within two months of meeting at a hospital party and three years later while working in a panic stricken central African republic for The World Health Organisation, their daughter Anna Maria Sanchez had been born.

Three days after that, a passing band of guerrillas –
terrorists, freedom fighters, call them what you would – had stopped briefly at the bush hospital in respite from a new and very effective offensive by the government forces. They'd drained the gasoline from the two old ambulances and had sacked the dispensary. After which, and quite casually, almost as a matter of course, they'd sub-machine gunned every patient and member of staff present... Four doctors, three doctors' wives, thirteen nurses and forty one patients, fifteen of which were children under the age of ten. The body count at the end of the day was fifty one dead, eleven wounded and one unharmed.

Hector had been hit by two bullets. One had passed through his left arm, missing the bone by millimetres, while the other had creased his temple, leaving him unconscious and concussed for days. Which, in the circumstances, was probably just as well.
His wife, Maria, had been shot at point blank range and died in her hospital bed, falling in her death throes across the small form of her newly born daughter and thus, more by accident or quirk of fate than by design, had saved her baby's life. No other child survived the massacre and Hector was the only doctor to pull

through. Two nurses were lucky and recovered from their wounds, but several of the patients were destined to spend much longer recuperative periods in various hospitals across the belt of Central Africa than they'd originally anticipated or had been led to believe would be necessary.

Grieving in a profoundly silent way for his dead wife, but rejoicing with the life of his child, Hector moved first to South Africa and then to England. Half a year in London was followed by another half year in Rome and then Tel Aviv. Tel Aviv was but a small stepping stone to the peace and tranquillity of the Ein Geddi kibbutz beneath the mountain of Masada on the shores of The Dead Sea. Anna Maria was now almost three years old and in the first three years of her life had lived in four different countries, looked after by her doting father and an ever changing stream of professional nannies. At Ein Geddi, this pattern of life changed.

Hector was quietly content, having found a degree of inner peace after five years of loneliness and mourning and Anna Maria blossomed in the kreshlike company of children her own age. Ein Geddi became their home and remained so for a further four years.

More violence in the form of constant terrorist activity by the Hamas and the PLO shattered Hector's ideal and with sadness but relief at the final acceptance of the inevitable, he took himself and his daughter back to Spain. Anna Maria Sanchez was a Spaniard, and she set foot on her native soil of Spain for the very first time on her eighth birthday.

Hector had no family and had long since lost contact with the friends of his youth. No strong ties pulled him to either Madrid or Barcelona, and anyway, he sought the slowness and simplicity of the countryside, not the noise and the grime of a city. He was a man who had travelled half the world and yet there were still vast areas of his own country totally unknown to him.

Acting on instinct and following his intuition, he bought an elderly Volkswagon Microbus and, filling it with six suitcases, five cardboard boxes, one eight year old girl and a ten week puppy that Anna called Golda after her heroine of the moment, he set off from Madrid and toured the land of his birth.

It took them twelve long beautiful months to find Castillo de la Frontera... Months of swimming in the sea on the Costa Brava, buying inexpensive antiques at Burgos, eating fresh fish off the quay at Santander, getting belly ache through eating too many apples at Manzana. They jousted at Windmills in La Mancha, ate tortillas in Toledo, gawked at the Alhambra in Granada, admired the bulls in Cordoba and listened to the music of the Moors in Malaga.

By the time they reached Malaga, father and daughter and dog (suddenly a much bigger dog than daughter had assured father it would be) were seat sore and weary. They'd travelled more than ten thousand kilometres criss-crossing the Iberian peninsular and Hector knew it was time to make a few decisions. Apart from anything else, there was Anna's education to think of. She might have been very advanced for her age and she might have been fluent in three languages, but that didn't make up for the continuity of school discipline, nor for the company of other children.

Thoroughly spoiled by her freedom and her father's undivided attention, Anna precociously assured Hector that she really didn't need the company of other children and that she could easily catch up on any schooling she might miss. But Hector Sanchez knew when he was being conned! Also, he'd happened across a small advert placed in a medical journal by the Junta de Andalucia. There was a village between Ronda and La Linea that desperately needed a doctor; the fact that there was a tithed house and surgery in with the deal, coupled with his dwindling financial reserves, caused Hector not to hesitate. He made a phone call and three days later was motoring westwards along the N340 with a very disgruntled little girl and an incontinent dog.

That had been thirteen years ago. In those thirteen years, Hector had become an integral and essential part of the village, practising allopathic medicine when the case warranted it, but not afraid to use herbs, homeopathy and Bach flower remedies when and where he knew they would work. The VW had long since disintegrated making way for a new Renault Four. Golda, long in the tooth and slothfully lazy after having produced five enormous litters of multicoloured pups, mooched around the village streets when and where her limited energy took her. And Anna Maria had grown in to a beautiful - a tragically beautiful - young woman.

Hector's calm and good humour were stretched to breaking point that afternoon. He humped and heaved at the Renault Four until the cords of muscle in his neck and shoulders bulged; his shirt clung to his back and perspiration found its way from his forehead into his eyes making them sting... The Renault stubbornly refused to move and indeed the more he pushed, the more deeply embedded in the gravel it became.

He paused to mop his brow and reflected upon his own stupidity. He'd known the river road was still soft from the Winter rains and he'd known that the Renault's clutch was slipping – but he'd still insisted upon taking Anna out for an afternoon drive. Anna, quietly compliant, had gone along with the idea although he knew she'd rather have stayed at home listening to her music. But that was half the trouble! She spent far too much time these days mooching around the house. Nothing excited her any more. Nothing stimulated. She had become withdrawn, retreating into herself, quietly waiting for the inevitable. It was in a desperate bid to break this mood, present since the result of the eye tests in Madrid, that Hector had suggested the morning drive down by the riverside.

Well, they'd got as far as Torre Grande before the road became impassable – Hector had managed a delicate eight point turn – and it had been during their return journey that disaster had struck. Fifty metres from the road junction and the bridge, the clutch had slipped badly. Toeing and heeling to compensate, he'd used too much power and that had been enough to put the small green car into the softer gravel by the side of the road. It had stalled and stopped and, with the clutch all but burned through, it certainly wasn't going to get out under its own steam.

He'd sent Anna back to the house, uphill most of the way but only a kilometre distant. She'd offered to push, but she didn't have the strength these days.

'No,' Hector had told her. 'You go. If I'm not back by four o'clock phone Pepe at the garage and tell him to come with his truck and the long rope.'

'All right, Papa.'

Hector had watched her walk across the iron bridge, her tall willowy figure moving slowly, the gentle breeze ruffling her short raven wing hair. Once the hair had been long, almost down to her buttocks, but in a moment of fury and as a gesture of defiance, she'd recently had it all chopped off, cut into a boyish style, razored at the back, gently quiffed at the front. Hector had not remonstrated with her. He knew exactly why she'd done it.

In a highly uncharacteristic burst of rage and frustration, he violently kicked at the wheel of the broken car, cursing profusely and forcing the anger to hold his other more vulnerable emotions in check.

He directed his anger against the marooned Renault, alternately pushing and heaving for all he was worth. The little green car would rock forwards six inches, then fall back eight inches. God damn it, it wasn't fair! How much suffering did one man have to take in a single lifetime? God damn it, God damn it to hell! Why Anna? Of all people, why did it have to be Anna?

'Do you need some help?' asked a quiet voice from behind him.

Once the cable was firmly secured to the Renault's front chassis section, the Fairey winch mounted on the Land Rover hauled the small car out of the gravel and onto the road with the greatest of ease. Hector beamed happily and stuck out his hand.

'Sanchez,' he grinned.

'Hello,' said Mage. 'I'm Colin Mage.'

'English?' queried Hector.

'English,' Mage confirmed.

'Your Spanish is excellent,' Hector laughed. 'In fact it is better than some of the Spanish spoken by Spaniards in these parts. Where did you learn?'

'Here and there.' Mage smiled, 'Though mostly in the bars along the Costa del Sol.'

Hector shook his head with mock severity. 'No, no, I do not believe this. Your grammar is too perfect and I do believe I detest the accent of Madrid and no one learns Madridliano on the costas.'

'Ah well Señor Sanchez, although at a guess I'd say you hadn't been there in quite a while. Your consonants have softened and there's lots of Andaluz in your vowels.'

'My God you are right!' Hector was impressed and his notoriously inquisitive mind fretted with curiosity. 'But seriously, I must ask again, where did you learn?'

'First, at school. We had a choice between French, German or Spanish and Spanish seemed to be the easier option. *Then* came the bars of the Costas and a few years after than I did do a proper language course for eighteen months while I was studying in Madrid. After that, put it down to a lot of usage. It is a beautiful language!'

'You studied in Madrid! Unbelievable! So did I, so many years ago. Tell me, what and where did you study?'

Mage leaned against the bonnet of the Land Rover and lit a cigarette to hide the discomfort of lying. He didn't like lying and, ergo, he was not good at it. Thus he resorted to the half lie, based on fact but bending the hard core of the whole truth.

'I studied psychology mostly – and of course Spanish, at the International Language School...'

This seemed to satisfy Hector, for which Mage was grateful. He had no desire to elaborate the lie. He *had* been in Madrid for eighteen months and he *had* studied psychology and he *had* studied Spanish – but only in his spare time when his other studies had permitted.

Hector declined Mage's offer of a cigarette and instead pulled out a large and bent stemmed briar pipe. Filling it from an equally old leather pouch he looked sadly at the Renault and then hopefully at Mage. He was wondering how to ask his question when Mage resolved the matter for him.

'Well Doctor Sanchez...'

'Please call me Hector!'

'Fine – and I'm Colin – come on. Let's get you towed in to the nearest garage and see if we can get that clutch repaired.'

It had been a fraught afternoon and Hector had had many painful things on his mind. It did not occur to him until much much later that he had not mentioned the Renault's clutch problem to the Englishman, and nor had he told him that he was a doctor. But by then, in comparison with other things that had happened, it did not seem very important.

Mage towed the Renault to the small garage on the far side of the village and after depositing it with the mechanic, Hector insisted on buying drinks in the dusty little bar across the street. Mage accepted the invitation: the afternoon had become unseasonably muggy and the blue skies of the morning had veiled over with flat white cloud. An ice cold beer, even if it was of the non alcoholic variety, slid down very well indeed.

One drink led to two and two to three and Mage was thoroughly enjoying the other man's company. With a pang of guilt, Mage realised that he was deliberately courting Hector Sanchez's friendship, perhaps to learn something of importance, perhaps just to find an ally for later on, but this did not detract from the pleasure of talking and listening to Castillo's slightly larger than life doctor. Hector may have lived in Castillo for a while but he was no Castillato. His years of travelling had broadened his horizons, giving him an unselfconscious sophistication. With the innocence of his simple enthusiasms, it created a most attractive and engaging personality. Mage did not doubt that this genial giant would be well loved by his patients.

From Hector's point of view, talking with the Englishman was delightfully refreshing. Sharing stories about Madrid and Paris and London with someone who had actually been there and knew those places as well as he did himself was an invitation to wander backwards along the pathways of memory and nostalgia and Hector found himself speaking with more enthusiasm and animation than he had done for quite a few years.

Hector wasn't aware of it, but throughout Mage wove his own experiences around the theme of being a psychologist, encouraging the older man to do most of the talking. When Mage cautiously divulged the fact that he'd recently been in Israel, Hector spoke at great length about his own time at Ein Geddi... before finally asking if Mage happened to know the place.

Mage grinned. 'I spent Christmas there.'

'Where? Ein Geddi?'

'Ein Geddi.'

'But my dear man,' Hector was almost beside himself. 'This is incredible! Such a small small world! What on earth were you up to in Ein Geddi, of all places?'

Why Doctor Sanchez, I was nearly dying. Dying of sunstroke, fear and exhaustion. Getting caught in a tear gas attack in a Jerusalem riot the previous month didn't help much and, oh yes, I was preparing a major ritualistic ceremony to be carried out at the top of Mount Masada. You see, I'd just spent three weeks in the middle of the Negev desert with a man called Herschal who'd been telling me all about the end of the world and I was seriously considering jumping off the top of the mountain to see whether or not I could fly. Frankly, I was as mad as a hatter and was waiting for a sign from God.

'I was looking at Masada,' Mage said, 'trying to build a psychological profile of what happened there. Ein Geddi was the nearest place to stay.'

'A psychological profile?' Hector looked puzzled. 'I'm not sure I quite understand.'

'You know what Masada is famous for?'

'Yes, of course, it is where the Jewish rebels, the Zealots, made their last stand against Rome after the big rebellion of whenever it was. I know they held out for a long time, but then in the end, rather than be taken prisoner, they committed mass suicide.'

Mage nodded. 'Yes, but what really made two thousand Zealots commit mass suicide and was it actually suicide or something else? From what we know, first the men killed the women and children, then the fighters either fell on their swords or jumped over the edge of the cliff in ascending order of seniority. Certainly the Roman army had them boxed in and they were well on the way to finalising an assault that might – or might not – have been successful, but the Zealots had held the third and seventh legions at bay for nearly three years; there was ample food being smuggled in to supplement what they were able to grow up there and if they'd wanted to, they could have held out almost indefinitely... So what suddenly made them throw in the towel in such a ritualistic way?'

'Ritualistic?'

'Look,' Mage elaborated. 'If you were a Zealot freedom fighter stuck on top of a mountain top with your wife and family and you decided for whatever reason that it wasn't worth carrying on the fight, wouldn't you at least examine the possibilities of escape? After all, if food was being smuggled in, surely people could be smuggled out! If this wasn't feasible, wouldn't you at least consider the option of a dignified surrender, especially if you'd been offered fairly generous terms?'

'Were the Zealots offered generous terms?' Hector asked, thoroughly fascinated by what he was hearing.

Mage shrugged. 'By Rome's standards, yes they were. They would have been treated as bona fide prisoners of war. Life might not have been pleasant breaking rocks in some Syrian quarry, but it would have been life. True, Rome would probably have broken its word and executed the leaders, but even so, the majority would have lived, especially the women and children. Rome may have been barbarically cruel, but the Romans themselves were not barbarians...

'But anyway, say, after all your deliberations you came to the conclusion that suicide was the only way out. How would you do it? Logically, would you not lay with your wife and maybe your children, taking the poison cup together, falling asleep in peace and dying as a family? Or, if you had a flair for the melodramatic or were so impassioned by your Zealotry that you wanted to make a grand gesture, would you not all gather together in front of Jahweh's altar and take the poison together as a group – or fall on your sword, or slit your veins, or jump over the edge. It wouldn't matter what specific means you used as long as it was a simultaneous group action.

'Either of these options would fit into an acceptable psychological profile, but from what we know, and we do know quite a lot, it simply didn't happen like that. It took one whole night for the Zealots to die in isolated pockets and in a variety of ways. Mothers poisoned their children, fathers put their wives to the sword and then the men committed suicide by rank. In modern terms, the privates went first, then the NCOs, then the officers... Each standing over the other to make sure the deed was done, either by blade or by poison or by flying over the edge of the cliff.

'The psychology was all wrong, Hector, and I wanted to see what I could make of the place where it all happened.'

'And tell me, my friend, what conclusions did you arrive at?'

'I didn't.' Mage smiled. ' – But that's what I was doing at Ein Geddi this last Christmas.'

Their conversation was interrupted as the blue overalled mechanic from the garage poked his head around the door of the bar, grinning broadly.

'Hey Hector, Anna's on the phone. She says to take my truck and a tow rope down to the river road because you're stuck in the gravel. I say, oh no you're not, you've been drinking in Bar Estacion for the last hour and a half with the Englishman who towed him in with a blue Land Rover. She says she wants to talk to you and will I come and get you – I say I will, so I'm here telling you and she's waiting on the other end of the telephone line and if you want my opinion you'd better have a good excuse, because she sounds pretty pissed off!'

'Okay, okay, tell her I'm coming. I'll be there in a second!' Hector stood up, sighing resignedly. 'My daughter treats me like a little boy sometimes. I swear she's worse than a harridan wife when she gets upset...' Then a mischievous look broke across his face. 'I think, however, she will forgive me when she learns that I've been talking with someone who is recently come from Ein Geddi! I'd better go and talk to her Colin – please excuse me – and if nothing else it will give me the chance to tell her that we shall be having a guest for dinner. You shall dine with us this evening and I shall hear no refusal or excuse. Here, before I go I will draw you a little map and we shall expect you at eight.'

Hector left the bar, leaving Mage amused and bemused by the reactions and attitudes of Castillo's doctor – and thinking of doctors made him pleasantly aware of the fact that he felt remarkably well. Since the cleansing ritual of earlier in the day, the residual feverishness had gone along with the knotted stomach and heavy head. He found himself looking forward to spending an evening in Hector's company and wondering what his daughter, Anna, might be like.

Anna Maria Sanchez was not happy: specifically she was not happy with her father, who *did* on far too many occasions behave like an errant school boy. Although her anger soon began to fade (she cold never stay angry with him for long and, after all, he was all she had in the world), the exasperation and mood of peak still remained.

'Well, who *is* he?' she asked.

'I have already told you,' Hector replied, equally exasperated. 'He is the Englishman, Colin Mage, who has rented Antonia Guadiaro's old house for six months while he writes a book about psychology. He has done much travelling and has just returned from Ein Geddi. I'm sorry Anna, but I thought you would like to meet him.'

'Oh Papa, you know I don't like meeting people when I'm – when I'm like this!'

Hector rested his hands tenderly on his daughter's shoulders and lightly kissed the top of her head. 'Listen Precious, despite all of our tragedies, the world keeps turning and life goes on. You can't turn your face from the world and live like a nun just because you might be going blind.'

'Papa, there is no *might* involved here. I *am* going to be blind. We both know it, so please don't try to humour me or be patronising. I'm working as hard as I can to accept what God has ordained for me – it's just a little difficult sometimes. I cannot bear other peoples' sympathy. It's too much like pity. Their curiosity I find both morbid and intrusive and just about everyone I know is either sickeningly sympathetic or blatantly curious. Do not scold me then, if I choose too much of my own company. It's easier this way.'

Hector hugged her to him and, stroking her hair, tried to swallow the lump in his throat that threatened to choke him. 'I'm sorry, my little one,' he whispered gruffly. 'I do know how difficult these days must be for you. But Anna, have faith. Believe in God and let us both pray for a miracle. Something may happen to change things. The scientists make new and wonderful discoveries every day.'

'I do believe in God, Papa, and I do pray to Him. But I can't afford to believe in miracles, so I just pray to Him for strength and understanding.' She pushed herself away from Hector's chest and managed a small smile. 'Come along Papa, don't look so tragic. As you say, something might happen and even if it doesn't, it's not the end of the world.

'Now,' she deliberately changed the subject. 'What shall we give this Englishman for his supper?'

'I shall prepare gaspacho,' said Hector, taking his cue. 'Then we will have fish, merluza, I think, with a light green salad. Then we will finish with cheese and fruit.'

'It does not sound very spectacular.'

'It will have to suffice,' said Hector simply. 'It's all we have. Besides, I do not think my English friend will mind, especially if we put an extra bottle of wine on the table.'

'What is he like?' asked Anna.

'I like him!' exclaimed Hector.

'That,' said his daughter, 'is quite meaningless. You like everybody.'

'No I most certainly do not!' Hector was indignant. 'There are dozens of people that I don't like.'

'Name them!' Anna challenged. 'I'll bet you can't name six!'

'Well there's Jaime Gomez...'

'That's one and he doesn't count.'

'Why not?'

'Nobody likes him.'

'Well I don't see why that should count against me!'

'Name some others,' Anna insisted.

'Well I don't like Pablo Ramirez, the mayor...'

'Didn't stop you voting for him,' Anna observed.

'There was nobody else to vote for!' Hector countered defensively.

Anna let that pass but she wasn't going to let her father off the hook lightly. 'Very well. You have named two. Now, name some more!'

'Well, er... Well, I don't like those young boys who ride those silly little motor bikes and smoke marijuana and I don't like that old witch Imaculada Morro from Calle Loba. I don't particularly like Father Ignatious of Santa Clara (may God forgive me for saying so!) and, er...' Hector fumbled. 'I didn't like that extranjero, that Englishman who was her last year – you know, the one who bought the big house in Calle Sombra and cheated old Pepe Ortega of all that money. And,' Hector finished defiantly, 'if you put all those people together that's a lot more than just six!'

'All right.' Anna was smiling now. 'But you still haven't told me what this new Englishman, this Señor Mage, is like...'

'He's quiet and intelligent and he speaks excellent Spanish; he seems very sincere and I'm sure you will like him.'

'I hope you're not up to your old matchmaking tricks,' Anna said sharply, suddenly suspicious.

'No of course not. The thought never crossed my mind for a minute. In any case, much as I think it is about time you found yourself a new boyfriend, I suspect that Colin is far too old for you anyway. He's nearer my age than yours. Now, young Pedro from San Pablo, he's always liked you and...'

'Papa! Leave it alone! Please!' Anna's voice held warning and Hector fell diplomatically silent.

Yes, Anna thought, there was Pedro of San Pablo and although I could never have married him, he was fun to be with and I did like him. He liked me too until he learned that I was loosing my sight. Then, despite all his brave talk about wanting me in his life for ever, he scuttled back to San Pablo and I haven't seen or heard from him all winter!

A grim scowl tugged at the corners of Anna's pretty mouth. 'Let's get back to your Englishman. What time is he coming?'

'About eight.'

'That's early.'

'He's English.'

5.

Anna

Mage meditated for half an hour, then showered and changed into some suitable clothes for the evening. The barometric pressure had continued to fall during the afternoon and now it was breathlessly close. There was no doubt in his mind that there was going to be a storm and he wished that it would break soon. The heaviness of the atmosphere made his head ache dully.

He considered building a fire, but then dismissed the idea and went and sat at the kitchen table and lit the calor gas heater instead. He turned on the lights and studied the rough drawn map Hector had given him in the bar.

There were two routes he could take from Calle Granadillos to Calle Santana. According to the doctor, one could walk up the wide steps to Calle Alta and at the end of Alta turn right down Caminette de la Luna, walk a little way down Consuelo then turn left into Caminette de Serpientes, which would lead him down onto the main street. If he...

Caminette de Serpientes? Mage's eyes flew back across the sheet of paper. *Was that right?*

With the flexibility of the Spanish language and the Andalucian patois in particular, Caminette de Serpientes could be translated a number of different ways. Snake Alley; The Pathway Of The Snakes, or even The Passage Of The Serpents... Mage pursed his lips thoughtfully and checked Hector's spelling – a rapid scrawl, but there did not appear to be a mistake. Therefore, was Mage's translation suspect?

He read on.

Once he was in the main street, he would walk up the hill as far as the post office and then turn right into Calle Santana. The other route also involved walking to the top of Calle Alta, but instead of turning into Caminette de la Luna, he could carry on down a long hill which would join the main road just beyond the post office. It would then be a simple matter of approaching Santana from the opposite direction. As flew the crow, this was obviously the longer way around, but Hector had assured him it was the easier walk with fewer hills.

Thinking speculatively about Caminette de Serpientes, Mage decided on the longer route. He had a pocket of time to fill and a pre-supper stroll would do no harm. Resolving to ask Hector what his interpretation of Caminette de Serpientes might be, he slung his jacket over his shoulder and stepped out into the street.

Night had fallen and the cobbles glistened in the lamplight from an earlier shower of rain that had done nothing to ease the oppressiveness. There was a stillness, most unusual for a Spanish hill village. It was almost as though the residents of Castillo knew that a storm was on it way and had already battened down their hatches in preparation. Even as he walked past the turn off for Caminette de la Luna, a distant rumble of thunder echoed across the mountains from the West.

Cresting a small hill at the very end of Alta, he realised that he was now in the most westerly street in the village; above the roof tops to his left he could see the darker outline and shadow of the castle's battlements as they marched south to north from the circular keep to the more angular Moorish citadel. Even as he looked they were thrown into black silhouette by a distant stab of forked lightening.

A cat slunk across the paving in front of him and in a side alley two small dogs scavenged among piled litter. A shadow, Mage's own, flickered and danced along the wall – but it was enough to make him catch his breath.

He was not the kind of man to get the jitters, but by the time he arrived at the end of this long and brooding street all his hackles were risen and his psychic self defence mechanisms were on full alert. He was not sorry to reach the intersection with the main road, and gratefully turned right towards the post office which was no more than a hundred paces distant. He cast a backwards glance at the name of the street he'd just walked along, and for a second his blood froze.

Calle Loba.

Street Of The She Wolf!

Something quietly clicked and fell into place within his magician's mind. So now, he thought coldly, we not only have a Serpent's Passage, we also have a She Wolf Street. We have a Pathway To The Moon, and we have a Calle Sol, which is Sun Street. And remember that small courtyard I found the first day I went exploring, it wasn't Plaza del Toros, was it? No, it was singular. Plaza del Toro. The Place Of The Bull. Not quite the same thing at all!

Mage experienced a thrill of excitement. It was based on the sure knowledge that Castillo was much more than it appeared to be and it was also based on that most fundamental of all human emotions. Fear.

***

Calle Santana was a pleasant street and although the barometric pressure still indicated an imminent storm the atmosphere that Mage had encountered in Calle Loba was noticeable by its absence. Here the houses seemed more orderly, still old, but free of the flickering shadows that had been his dancing companions by the castle wall. There were a few trees, small Sevillana Orange protected by wrought iron rejas, and welcoming amber light fell onto the pavement from a dozen different doors and windows.

The Sanchez house, number fifty, was not difficult to find. The paint work seemed a little brighter, and rather than the usual ironwork around the windows, there were wooden shutters. Above the door, made from the inevitable heavy wood with studded coach bolts, there was a small square lamp that bathed the doorway in an ambient yellow glow.

Mage pulled on the long old fashioned bell rod and waited. Seconds later the door swung open and an effusive hector welcomed him into his home.

'Perfectly timed, Colin! You have beaten the storm by a whisker!'

As if specifically stage managed to confirm Hector's words, there was a loud clap of thunder and even as Mage crossed the threshold into a neatly kept hallway with white walls and black furniture, the skies opened and rain began to fall in a heavy torrent, raindrops bouncing two feet into the air as they crashed into the street.

Hector slammed the door shut and led Mage into the dining room. A table was laid for three, silver cutlery on pale green linen. One wall was totally covered with book cases and shelves, and opposite a heavy red velvet curtain hung across a large window that faced out into the street. Opposite the entrance doorway was an open fireplace piled high with logs and burning merrily. There was a mantelpiece that supported two candelabra with cheerfully flickering candles, their gentle light adding to the warmth and welcome of the room. To the left of the fireplace was an over stuffed easy chair and, to the right, a small two seater sofa. In one corner of the room, close to a door which presumably led off to the kitchen, there was a small office desk overflowing with files and papers. An antiquated telephone served adequately as an effective paperweight. Well to the right of the fireplace and near to the window curtain, there was a drinks cabinet and standing in front of it was Anna.

'This is Anna,' Hector said with simple pride.

Mage stepped forwards and took her outstretched hand. As their palms made contact, there was an immediate and unexpected tingling in his finger tips.

'Good evening, Anna,' said Mage, studying her intently. He noted the high cheekbones and the generous mouth... Naturally dark pink lips over even white teeth and there was a squareness to her jaw that hinted at stubbornness and determination. It was not a beautiful face in the sense of cheesecake glamour, but it was strikingly attractive, full of interest and vivacity. He worried that he couldn't quite see her eyes properly. She was wearing large glasses with smoked lenses which created an incongruous effect and yet at the same time generated an air of mystery.

What's the matter with her eyes? There's something very wrong here...

She was wearing a straight black skirt into which was tucked a crisp white blouse. Long legs, Mage guessed, and good breasts: he could faintly see the outline of her bra beneath the sharp white cotton and he experienced a small stab of sexual arousal. She was a tall girl, easily Mage's own height and very statuesque. Unlike many of her compatriots, her complexion was flawless.

'Good evening Mr Mage and welcome to our home.' When she spoke it was in a well modulated contralto voice, and in English.

'It was kind of your father to make the invitation – and, please, I'd be much happier if you called me Colin.'

'As you wish – Colin. May I offer you a drink?'

'Thank you. Anything non alcoholic will be fine.'

'A fruit juice then? Or a glass of Casera?'

'Casera? Fruit juice? Hector's voice boomed across the room. 'Colin, my friend, I have a find selection of good Rioja wine and...'

'Sorry Hector, but I don't drink,' Mage said as gently as he could and looking Hector in the eye. *Let him think what he wants. Even if he thinks that I'm an alcoholic on the wagon. It's easier than trying to explain the real reasons.*

'Papa, if Colin does not wish to drink, then you must not make him.' Anna handed Mage a long glass of lemonade and Mage caught the half smile that played around the corners of her mouth. *Damn. I bet you think I'm on the wagon too. What's the matter with your eyes, Anna Sanchez? What's the matter with your eyes.*

Mage's own eyes inexplicably began to water and he turned from Anna, tuning in to what Hector was saying about the relative virtues of Rioja versus Valdepenas, listening with a feigned interest as Hector elaborated on the story of how, a few years previously, a small quantity of Rioja had been smuggled into France and had been covertly entered into the Appellation Controllée's annual contest. The Rioja had walked away with the grand prix masquerading as a little known Beaujolais.

Hector guffawed with triumphant laughter. 'It simply goes to prove that there is more snobbery than a good nose when it comes to deciding what is a good vintage! Anyway, come! We will eat! I am famished! Our food will be simple fare, but fortunately, there is no shortage of quantity. We shall sit at the table and I shall serve while you tell Anna all about Ein Geddi.'

Mage realised that he was hungry and although he may have denied himself the pleasure of sampling Hector's wine, he spared himself not at all when it came to the food. The gaspacho was light, piquently flavoured with garden herbs and the fish melted in his mouth. He broke the rough bread with gusto and thoroughly enjoyed the limited selection of strong Spanish cheeses. There were apples, crisp and green, and small oranges with thin skins that had, Hector assured him, been picked fresh from the tree that very evening.

Mage spoke of Israel and Ein Geddi, and of the work that had taken him to other places of interest in the world, and Hector filled the room with laughter as he regaled Mage with anecdotes from his own vast range of experience. Anna listened with polite interest, smiling on cue, but offering little to the flow of conversation.

Mage was enjoying his evening, but he was far from totally relaxed. He was aware of an atmosphere of expectancy and suppressed excitement and, although this might have had something to do with the storm that had begun to rage outside, rattling the windows with each fresh crash of thunder and providing a background noise of water pelting down and cascading in the street he somehow doubted that it was the storm alone that was responsible for his feelings. It had as much to do with the girl, Hector's daughter, who sat, almost primly, opposite holding herself in like a coiled spring. She was a lithe young woman, but her movements lacked flow and spontaneity. Her every action seemed excessively self disciplined and controlled.

On more than one occasion Mage reached across the table with a gentle psychic probe, but met with such turbulent resistance that he retreated quickly. To get inside the girl's head would need some patience and concentration, neither of which seemed appropriate or possible at that precise point in time. Hector was a demanding host and, either through shyness or psychic awareness, the girl was very much on her guard.

But Hector Sanchez was not alone in having an overly inquisitiveness nature and Mage employed an old and often used occult technique to try and resolve something of the mystery. He was here in this village at this time to learn and to prepare and to make what friends he could. He could not bring himself to believe that his chance meeting with Hector earlier that afternoon had been entirely accidental in the great cosmic scheme of things, and he freely admitted that he was not the kind of person who made new friends easily. And yet with Hector there had been an immediate rapport and also with Anna there was thrumming buzz of suppressed energy that attracted him and teased his curiosity. She emanated a baffling aura.

Elaborating on the technique he'd used in the Hotel Miraflores, Mage divided him mind and, while one part of him listened and made all the right responses as Hector related the tale of a man who owned a pet pig, taking it for walks each day, complete with collar and lead, the other part of him went mind wandering around the room, viewing Anna's troubled aura from different and more objective viewpoints. Most people, he know, had some ability to do this, but he'd practised and honed the technique over more than twenty years and had refined it to such an extent that it required very little effort to effect. There were, however, no absolute parameters to this gift and every time he used it the results were always a little different and sometimes wildly unexpected.

He took a position next to Anna, perching in an imaginary way upon her left shoulder and looking at himself sitting opposite, smiling attentively at Hector's story. Slowly, and oh so very tentatively, he tuned into her thought patterns, aware that he was invading the sanctity of her privacy, but not moralising on the right or the wrong of it. That, he thought grimly, would come later.

At first there was clutter and confusion, but then – *My God, she's frightened of me... She senses something and she can feel the power, although she can't identify it for what it is. She's frightened to death about something else as well... Something about her eyes. Very well, then. Let me look behind the eyes... Let me look behind your eyes, Anna Sanchez, and see as you see...*

Immediately Mage's vision blurred. He became a dim shape of vague outline and then from his own chair it was Anna, then Hector, who became dim shadows. Then the rest of the room kaleidoscoped and degenerated into a muddy pool as hard objects hazed and defocused. The fire became an indistinguishable oval shape of moving red and orange; the candle flames became six discarnate orbs of floating light. And there was pain, a barely tolerable pounding ache of pain that emanated from somewhere deep inside her skull and held her temples in a cruel vise.

Oh lord, her eyesight's going! She's nearly blind! No wonder she's scared! She uses what little vision she's got, then fakes and bluffs the rest, relying on memory to know where things are. She can see enough to walk down a street without bumping into walls, but she can't distinguish clearly between pavement and road. She can't read or write anymore without her nose almost pressed against the page and... It's getting worse all the time... And does Hector know how bad it really is? Does he know about the pain... And God, all of the other stuff! The fear of never knowing love, the fear of rejection... God, you're still a virgin and you've resigned yourself to staying that way. Who will want a blind girl for a wife and how can you face life without love, without children and what will it be like when the total darkness finally comes? Will you be able to live with that? You don't even want to find out, do you? You're thinking more and more each day that

'Colin?'

it would be better, simpler and easier, if you swallowed a bottle of tablets or gave yourself a careful little injection; you're a doctor's girl and you know how to do it, you know what to take... No, of course you haven't told Hector how you're feeling, it's bad enough for him as it is. If you die, he'll be badly hurt, but better that than being tied to a helpless blind daughter for the rest of his life. But what's caused this? The optical nerves are going, but why? How? It isn't

'Colin, are you...'

diabetes and it certainly isn't psychosomatic and I want to help you Anna Sanchez, but what makes an otherwise healthy girl start going blind? Yes I can feel the glaucoma, but what's causing the glaucoma? Is it a brain tumour, is it a...

'Colin!' His name was being spoken urgently. 'Are you all right?'

Hector glanced at his daughter in some alarm, then looked back at their dinner guest. One minute, Mage had been chuckling gleefully, then he'd suddenly gone deathly pale, eyes glazed, and obviously no longer listening. His head had half slumped forwards, supported by a hand that, to Hector's experienced eye, definitely seemed to be trembling.

Mage focused on the table cloth; a used spoon, a half filled coffee cup, three crumbs of bread. He fought to clear his head, then looked up first at Anna, then at her father.

'I'm sorry. Just a momentary dizzy spell. A legacy from the 'flu. Forgive me, Hector, what were you saying?'

'Are you sure you're all right?'

'Yes absolutely. Now what happened to the pig when it met the Alsatian?'

'Ah,' Hector beamed, reassured that Mage had been listening after all and that all was well. 'The Alsatian's owner goes up to old Arturo and says...'

Mage listened, fully attentive, satisfied now that at least some of the mystery had been solved and successfully hiding the distress that his new found knowledge caused.

Later, Hector served coffee and they moved from the table to the fire. Mage was content to sit on the small sofa in front of the crackling logs, listening to Hector talk and covering Anna with the incandescent pale blue mantle of his own aura.

People are like plants in a garden. Elsie Maud had once told him. *Sometimes a plant gets sick and starts to shrivel and die and there's no reasoning why it should, but it just does. Imagine yer the gardener. What do yer do? Yer water the plant and tend it and care fer it a lot more than t'others. People is like plants, so when yer comes across one that's poorly, shower 'em with yer spirit. Cover 'em with feelin's of love an' protection. It always 'elps. Not everyone can do it, but you, you've gorrit in yer Col, so don't ever be afraid to use it and give it away whenever yer comes close to a sick soul in need. It'll cost yer nowt an' it'll 'elp keep yer straight wi' God.*

Over the years, his young years and her last years, his Grandmother had taught him how to contact the fountainhead of healing spirit within himself. Even fewer were those who could reach inside themselves, touch the spirit and channel it to where it was needed. She taught him that there were different elements of spirit; earth energy, air energy, fire energy, water energy and, most potent of all, soulspirit energy...

Elsie Maud had died when she was ninety three years old – when Mage was still only in his mid twenties. During the last eight years of her life, she'd taught and trained her grandson well, leaving him a potent and powerful legacy of arcane skills and knowledge. He'd been her only living relation and tradition and need dictated that she should not die without first passing on her knowledge to someone. Apart from the fact that Colin was the obvious choice, there really wasn't anyone else but him.

She'd tried when Mage was still in his early teens, but it had been too soon and his interests had been elsewhere; music, theatre, sports and although he'd always been a shy and sensitive boy, girls... But she'd always known he had the gift within him and she found she had a more responsive student when Mage reached his eighteenth year and found himself suffering from the first of several broken hearts. *Nan, how can I get her back? Don't you know a spell or something?* Now he came to her, granted for all the wrong reasons, but did that matter if the end justified the means?

Once he'd accepted the unacceptable, she'd had little difficulty in turning him in on himself where he began to find the true source of temporal and mystical power, then it was simply a matter of guiding and directing, presenting him with the route map and allowing him to choose his own pathways.

Elsie Maud had been dead for fifteen years, but he still missed her. She'd been a great healer, and he remembered her now as he tried to touch Anna Sanchez with his own healing thoughts.

Anna perceived a subtle difference in her father's new friend during the second part of the evening, but could not for the life of her put her finger on what it was. Maybe it was just that she was feeling a little better herself: the crippling headache that was now such a permanent part of her life, had begun to ease off as they'd finished dinner. As they moved to the fire and drank a second pot of coffee, she found herself talking a little more openly to the man called Colin. She spoke in English, he answered in Spanish, and she began to enjoy the novelty of such unusual conversation. Now that she was much closer to him, she could study him as he sat listening to her father and, really, he wasn't bad looking for an older man and she found that she quite liked sitting next to him on the small sofa. He smelled spicy and clean. His voice was low but strong and, in some odd way, with him next to her and her father sitting closely opposite, she felt secure and safe.

The telephone call that was to bring Hector's soiree to a premature close came through at five minutes past eleven. The machine jangled on the desk behind him and, excusing himself, Hector leaned over and picked up the receiver. Immediately he frowned.

'Yes Jaime, of course I know him... Yes, well, she's due in another four weeks but... Yes, of course that could happen, but this is her third child and there were no problems with the other two... Yes. Look, is he there with you now?... Good, put him on and let me talk to him. Hello Manolo... Manolo, slow down and just tell me quietly... All right, all right, now what time did you leave?' Hector glanced at his watch with a muttered 'Damn!' and then 'All right Manolo, I do understand. Now listen carefully, because this is important. When you left, was she bleeding much?... Right, *listen* to me Manolo, was she conscious?... Yes, yes of course I'm coming... Hang on Manolo...'

Hector turned from the telephone, devoid now of all bonhomie, and a serious frown creasing across his expressive face. 'Colin, my friend, I need a favour. I've got an emergency situation. It sounds like a premature breach birth and I've got to get out into the campo immediately. I need your Land Rover.'

'You've got it,' Mage said promptly, standing and moving quickly towards the door. 'I'll be here within ten minutes.'

'No, go straight to the police station on the main street. It'll be quicker. We've got to pick up Manolo. He's walked all the way in from Torre Negro. It's taken him more than six hours and, by now, if it isn't already too late, every moment counts... Manolo...' Hector turned back to the phone. 'Stay where you are with Jaime, and I'll be there in a few minutes... Yes I know the conditions are terrible, but we have a friend who will bring a Land Rover with four wheel drive!'

Anna followed Mage into the hallway, feeling – no, she could not describe her feelings. One minute she'd been sitting with father and friend, snug and secure, and now suddenly the trinity was broken. Both men were dashing out into the hostile night. A rude and unsettling end to a pleasant evening – leaving her worried and strangely unsettled.

Mage was pulling on his jacket and opening the front door at the same time.

'Here, take this. You will need it.' She tried to pull an umbrella from the rack stand and push it into his hand, but the light in the hallway was dim and it was a fumbled gesture. The brolly fell to the floor and Mage, with both arms momentarily trapped in his sleeves, one foot holding the door, was in no position to retrieve it. Anna stooped to rescue it, but Mage saw that she did it more by touch than by sight and, oh *shit*, he was suddenly sprouting an erection as Anna crouched at his feet, her head bowed and not four inches from his crotch!

'Let me help.' He bent and helped her up, one hand under her elbow, and taking the umbrella from her with the other. She rose, standing almost in the crook of his arm. He could smell the sweet red wine on her breath and the subtlety of a modest perfume. He could even detect the starched linen crispness of her blouse.

In that millisecond, and for the first time in more than a year, he felt the hunger of physical desire – and he crushed it coldly and ruthlessly. To feel compassion for an attractive young woman was one thing, but there was absolutely no room in his life for the other.

One millisecond became two milliseconds, and with her own dormant psychic ability, Anna felt something pass between herself and the Englishman. Or maybe it was the other way round. Maybe something passed from the Englishman into her. Either way, he was holding her eyes with his own, and this close, even Anna could discern something most peculiar in their expression.

'Colin, why are you looking at me like that?'

Then her father's friend, and perhaps hers too, did something very strange. A small thing, but one that would occupy her mind for a long time afterwards.

'Anna,' he said, in a tone of voice that was different from the way he had spoken to her over the course of the evening, speaking so softly that it was almost a whisper and she had to strain to hear. 'Anna, you are very beautiful, and I promise you...' he touched her forehead as lightly as a feather with the first and second fingers of his right hand... 'I promise you, everything is going to be all right.' And then before she could protest or react, he leaned forwards and kissed her gently on the lips - and then he was gone! Out of the door and into the pouring rain.

Three minutes later, wrapped in an old gabardine mackintosh and carrying his large brown leather bag, Hector also left. 'I'll be back when I'm back. Don't wait up, and Anna, leave the dishes.'

'All right Papa - ' But as the front door slammed, she doubted that he'd even heard her.

Slowly, thoughtfully, she put another log on the fire, then poured herself a full glass of wine. She sat in front of the flames, knees almost drawn up to her chin, and gazed into the secret canyons and cityscapes within the glowing embers.

He had kissed her, and not in the Spanish way either, but full on the mouth. She could still feel the soft – sensuous? – tickle of his beard and moustache, and he had called her beautiful. No, not just beautiful, but very beautiful. No man other than her father, and even then only when she was still a little girl, had ever called her that. She knew that she was attractive, pretty even, but never beautiful... And yet there was absolutely no doubt in her mind that Colin had meant it.

But what had he meant when he'd said that everything was going to be all right? He *could* have been referring to the situation out in the campo with Manolo's wife, but in which case, why had he said it *like that?*

Like What?

She didn't know, but if he hadn't been referring to Manolo's wife, then what *had* he been referring to?

She reached up and touched her forehead where his fingers had brushed against her skin. Odd, but it was as though his fingers still rested there. And *why* had he touched her there and what did it mean? It was almost as though he had been conferring a blessing which, of course, was impossible. Only priests could do that, and the nuns, and Colin wasn't a priest, was he? No, of course he wasn't, and – she smiled at her own humour – he certainly wasn't a nun!

A thought began to take shape in her mind. He couldn't have been referring to her blindness, could he? No, that was preposterous! He didn't know, couldn't have known. Hector would never have told him and she'd covered herself all through the evening apart from that wretched business with the umbrella – and that on its own could never have given the game away. And so, no, he could not have been talking about her eyes...

And yet, as she sat there for more than an hour, thinking about the incident in the hallway, the thought that the Englishman *had* been talking about her blindness when he'd said "I promise you, everything is going to be all right" was a persistent thought that would not go away.

6.

Storm

Mage toed and heeled the pedals of the Land Rover and hurled the heavy machine around the impossibly tight corners of Castillo's forbidding one way system. When he intersected with the main street he put his foot down and accelerated up the steep hill towards the town hall and the police station. The rain hammered in a cacophonic din against the roof and the single speed wipers were hard pressed to cope with the deluge of water that exploded against the glass pains of the split windscreen. The Land Rover was in excellent condition for its age, but it was old and lacked the sophistication of later models. The de-mister hissed pathetically and drops of water leaked in from a variety of places – a window panel here, a strained rivet there...

And yet Mage was filled with a wild elation. It was hard for him to describe, but something was happening. He was *doing* something instead of just thinking, wondering and planning. It brought a gleam and glint of excitement to his eyes.

Eyes!

The eyes of Anna Sanchez danced before him and his excitement intensified. Why had he kissed her? This was not in character with his normal behaviour. Usually he was reserved and correct with women, at least until he knew them well. Intimacy, both mental and sexual, had never been immediate. Even when he'd first met Alexandra it had taken him three weeks to seduce her and, even then, it had been she who had finally taken him to *her* bed. This was not to say that he was naive or without experience, it was just that he preferred things to develop slowly and with a degree of control. In his teens and early twenties there had been too many disastrous light hearted relationships – they'd been disastrous for him, anyway – and too many flash in the pan romances that had burned themselves out with predictable inevitability, though never without causing some pain. The cumulative effect of half a dozen burned fingers had been enough to teach him what manner of man he was and what he could, and could not hope to get away with.

Even so, following wild impulse or some more deeply motivated instinct, he had kissed Anna Sanchez, and hoped he wouldn't live to regret it. Furthermore, he'd made her a promise – and he alone knew what he'd been referring to – a promise that he had no idea how he was going to keep.

A clip from an old video danced across his mind. A scene where the heroine screamed in extremis: "Flash, hurry! You've only got four minutes to save the world!"

A quirky grin crossed his face, then filled with the electricity of the night and the madness of the storm, he laughed out loud at his own black humour. *I might not be able to save the world, but Anna Sanchez, I'll break my balls trying to save your eyes!*

He came to a careening halt outside the brightly lit entrance of the ayuntamiento – the town hall, of which the police commissariat was but a part. Immediately figures crowded round the vehicle, among them Jaime Gomez with flattened hair and black serge uniform. As he swung open the passenger door, Hector hauled himself up onto the bench seat next to Mage, followed by a small man with rain slicked hair and sodden wet clothes. Mage only had the briefest of glimpses in the opaque light, but it was enough to see the ashen panic in the little man's eyes.

'Colin, there is no need for you to...'

'I'm driving! You navigate and direct!' Mage had already let out the clutch and the Land Rover was moving rapidly up the hill.

'Very well. I won't argue. Take the road to the Hozgarganta where you met me this morning...'

My God was it only that morning?

'... then take the mountain road up to the telegraph relay station. You were there, yes?'

'Yes.' Mage had a flash vision of the relay station and also of the single isolated farm house further down the other side of the mountain. He was suddenly certain that this was to be their ultimate destination.

'When the road ends there is a cart track that cuts across country down to Manolo's place. It's about another five kilometres on and the track will be bad: the rain has been heavy. Colin, again my thanks! I would never have got through in the Renault, even if she had been on the road.'

'Did Manolo walk all that way?' Mage asked, almost shouting above the engine noise which had risen dramatically now that they were driving along a short straight and he was able to pick up some real speed.

'Yes. As I say, it took him more than six hours.'

'What exactly is the problem with his wife?'

'She's gone into premature labour with her fourth child. She's a full month early. From the sound of it there are some nasty complications. If Manolo is right, she haemorrhaging badly and she's in great pain. I'll not be sure till I get there, but it does sound as if the baby is breached, and if that's the case I'm probably going to have to do a caesarean.'

'Don't you need a hospital for that sort of thing?'

'Colin, this is Campo Spain! The nearest hospitals are in La Linea or Algerciras! Campo women have been breach birthing since the beginning of history without the benefit of hospitals. True, it's a messy business and the mortality rate is high, but that's the way it is in this part of the world. We may have joined the EC and given up many of our old ways, but that's Cosmopolitan Spain, the Spain of the cities and the costas. This is The Campo, and Colin, although the rest of the nation may be racing to catch up with Europe, it's still like a third world country out here in the backlands. Normally, with a little luck, we'd probably be all right with what I've got here,' he patted the brown leather case that he hugged to his chest as it balanced and bounced on his knee, 'But on this particular occasion I must confess to being a little worried, which is why we're speaking English, by the way. I examined Dolores only last week and she seemed well enough then. Her other three children popped out as easily as peas from a pod. I'm hoping that our friend here is exaggerating somewhat. It's an Andalucian tendency after all. If he isn't, then I must tell you, I'm not looking forward to what is ahead. It will be a bloody night's work.'

The Land Rover hurtled across the iron bridge, at one point hitting a pothole and bouncing boneshakingly into the air. Mage was driving at no more than twenty five miles an hour but in the high seated vehicle with the visibility so dangerously restricted by the onslaught of the storm, it seemed much faster. Once on the hairpin mountain road he dropped the speed to under twenty in deference to the gradient but even this seemed too fast as Mage flung the car into the tight curves of the looping bends, using the four wheel drive to its maximum advantage.

'Colin, watch out for fallen trees and rocks. Even in a few hours, a storm like this can cause havoc.'

As if to confirm Hector's words a solid wall of water crashed across the bonnet and roof, and for a long second visibility was down to zero. Mage realised that they'd forded a small stream and the water falling down on them was only that which their passage had first thrown upwards. The Land Rover missed a beat and the ignition light flickered red until he built up the revs. There had been no stream crossing the road that morning and, duly sobered, Mage dropped into a lower gear, allowing their speed to decrease even more. It made for marginally easier handling, causing fewer bumps and enabling Mage to take a lighter grip on the madly bucking wheel, but the little Spaniard, sitting hunched and cramped in the corner, began to fret.

'Señor, can we go no faster? The children are alone, and Dolores, she...'

'Patience Manolo,' Hector soothed. 'It is a bad road and the English does well. It is better to get there a little late than not to get there at all. A few minutes will not make that much difference.'

I hope, thought Hector, full well knowing that in situations such as this more seconds could make the difference between a patient's life and death... And another thought came unbidden, one that had been lurking malignantly at the back of his mind ever since Jaime Gomez had phoned from the police commissariat. *What if this one is like the others?* His eyes hardened. *Well, if it is* – he thought of the extra hypodermic syringe he'd put into his bag before leaving Calle Santana, *if it is, then this time I know what I must do.*

A light flared. It was Colin, expertly lighting a cigarette with one hand, the Marlboro gripped firmly between his teeth. Good god, Hector thought, I really do believe that he's enjoying this! Yes, well I hope he continues to do so, and if he's going to come inside when we get to Manolo's I hope he has a strong stomach! This was not a night to be "enjoyed" but an emergency with a definite death risk, and yet – Hector's momentary resentment sparked and died as quickly as it had been born – and yet, when he'd needed the favour the Englishman had not hesitated and was this not the same man who had stopped that morning without being hailed down and asked, never forget, and had pulled Hector's car out of the gravel? The same man who, again without being asked, had towed Hector into the garage, saving him not one but two bills from the avaricious little mechanic.

Hector watched him now: the cigarette jutting defiant from his lips, the black hat pulled down firmly, brim low across his forehead. His hands were a blur of movement on the steering wheel and the gear lever as he guided the lumbering vehicle around the steep hairpins. Hector would have been willing to drive himself if he'd had to, but was nonetheless glad that it was Mage who sat behind the wheel on this bloody awful night.

The branch of a tree cracked against the side of the cab. The Land Rover swerved, hit a deep rut, then bounced out again. Hector's head banged against the roof and he grabbed at the dashboard to steady himself.

'Sorry,' Mage grinned.

He is a strange one, Hector thought, and he *is* enjoying himself. Even stranger was the way that Anna had warmed to him. Despite her aversion to strangers, she'd been more animated and alive in Mage's company than Hector had ever seen her since the discovery of the glaucomas the previous year. Well that made Colin Mage all right in Hector's book. Anything, or anyone, who could bring Anna out of herself was once, twice and three times welcome.

'We're at the end of the road,' Mage shouted, hitting the brakes. 'The relay station's up there on the left. Which way from here?'

'Keep going straight on. Can you see the track?'

'Just about.' Mage leaned forward and peered through the almost opaque glass. He could barely discern the path they had to take. It was mostly pooled with water and visibility was less than ten feet. 'How well do you, or does he, know the road? I mean, can you talk me through it?'

Unthinkingly Mage had automatically spoken in Spanish. Manolo, even more agitated than before, responded immediately.

'A straight slope downwards for about thirty metres, then a sharp right curve followed by a longer left bend, with a much steeper down hill slope...'

'Got it,' Mage said, and pushing the gear selector into low ratio, eased the Land Rover forwards... The machine lurched sickeningly as the wheels went into soft mud and Mage concentrated on keeping the wheels moving. To stop now would be disastrous.

If Hector had asked, Mage would have owned up to the fact that this was the first time he'd tested the four wheel drive in really adverse conditions... That he was relatively new to the concept of off road driving! The Land Rover had been bought only a few weeks previously, half on intuitive impulse, half out of common sense, specifically with this trip to Spain in mind. Mage's low slung classic sports car would never have coped with Spain's rough roads, and the right deal had presented itself at the right time.

He'd been in the TVR, driving back into York after his second meeting with Michael Fry. As he'd turned the last corner into his street, an elegant tree lined avenue in one of the city's nicer districts, the garage on the corner had been moving the Land Rover out onto the forecourt. Mage had backed up and parked, attracted by the 'Rover's clean condition and solid chunky lines.

Rick Jackson, the proprietor, had sidled over. He and Mage had known each other for years and Mage also knew the Rick had long coveted the crimson Tuscan, now cooling at the curb.

'What's this Colin? Thinking of getting into FWD are we?'

'What's FWD?'

'Four Wheel Drive. The biggest selling new old idea since diesel.'

'This runs on diesel?'

'Nah. This is the petrol version. Fuel economy ain't so hot. You're only gonna get eighteen or twenty to the gallon and only then if you're driving her gently, but it's a lot quieter than a diesel, and a lot faster, a damn sight cheaper to put right if owt goes wrong. Not that it will,' he added hastily. 'This un's a good 'un. Fifteen years old, but only a genuine forty thou' on the clock and with a full service history to prove it. She's taxed and tested and comes with a no quibble six month guarantee.'

'How much?'

'To you Col, 'cos you're an old mate, a straight two and a half grand!'

Mage had walked around the Land Rover. The RAF blue paint work was without chip or flaw and the interior was nicely valeted in a plasticky utilitarian way.

'Really nice condition,' Rick had pressurised. 'Built of aluminium so they don't rust like ordinary motors. You can go through floods an' 'urricaines in sommat like this...'

Mage had paused by the driver's door, one hand resting on the handle. A sudden precognitive image flashed across his mind of a stormy night, the Land Rover bucking, a sense of tension and excitement...

'All right Rick, you've talked yourself into it. Go and fetch your cheque book.'

'Me cheque book?'

Mage had nodded. 'If I've just bought your Land Rover for two and a half thousand pounds, you owe me about a thousand pounds because you've just bought my TVR.'

They'd haggled, but Mage had still walked away with the blue Land Rover and a cheque for nine hundred pounds. Now, less than six weeks later, the flash of clairvoyance was being proven accurate and the Land Rover was being put to the test and proving its worth with every yard travelled.

'A big rock and a sharp bend that goes left and very quick down at the same time!'

'Got it,' Mage yelled again, nearly hitting the rock and side sliding down the steep incline. The rain did not abate and jagged forks of lightening continued to dart and stab across the heavens. The cab of the Land Rover was damp and chill. His feet were wet and there was a prevalent smell of rubber and hot oil, but Hector was right! Despite the fear of risk, maybe even because of it, Mage was enjoying this Valkyrian ride through the night. He felt totally alive and charged with energy and he briefly wondered if Rick Jackson had kept the TVR or had sold it on.

They careened around one last treacherous bend and emerged into a waterlogged grove of eucalyptus trees. Over to the left was a low slung adobe bungalow with cracked walls and a broken porch. A dull orange glow shone dimly through filthy uncurtained windows.

'We are here,' Manolo shouted and immediately jumped out of the truck and half ran, half stumbled towards the house. Mage swung open the driver's door but felt Hector's restraining hand on his arm.

'Colin, there is no need for you to come inside. Wait for me here.'

'No, I'll come. Maybe I can help.'

'My friend, you have no medical skill – and it will not be very pleasant in there.'

'Hector, we're wasting time. Let's go.'

Mage jumped from the cab and sank to his ankles in freezing cold rainwater. Hurrying round the Land Rover he followed Hector into the house and walked straight into an earlier century.

The room was lit by candles and oil lanterns. An open fire flicked dolefully in one corner beneath a substantial black cauldron. The walls were adobe white and grey plaster and in most places the plaster was peeling. There was sawdust strewn across the floor and bundles of hay stacked haphazardly against the far wall. Three hens and a small dog clucked and yelped and had free run of the room. The furniture was obviously home made and rough hewn. Sitting at a table were two grubby and wide eyed girls, no more than four or five years old; a third child, little more than a babe, lay equally wide eyed in a cot, nervously pulling at something that had once been a doll.

To the left of the fire and in that part of the room that had the most light, there was an ancient iron bed, and writhing on the bed was the swollen and blood covered body of Manolo's wife, Dolores. Along with darkly oozing pools of crimson, she lay in her own ordure and frantically clutched at the head bars of the bed frame with whitened knuckles. The stench of filth and excreta was gagging and the sounds of her hoarse shrieks and moans was nothing less than pitiful.

Mage stood transfixed, but Hector moved forwards muttering 'Holy Mother of God' beneath his breath.

And then, 'Manolo, get the children out of here. Put them in the barn or in Colin's Land Rover and then come back and help me find some hot water.'

'There is hot water in the pot Señor. I filled it before I left and Sophia should have been topping it up.' Manolo crossed in front of Mage, moving towards the children. He glanced at the cauldron as he passed. 'Yes, there is much hot water. More than thirty litres.' Then he gathered up his children.

'Colin,' Hector snapped. 'Don't just stand there. Drag that cauldron over to the bed and let's get her cleaned up a bit. I can't see what I'm doing amid all this carnage.'

Mage broke out of his momentary fugue and, not without some effort, hauled the heavy black cauldron from the hearth, half carrying, half dragging it across the littered floor towards the end of the bed. Hector immediately scooped it up in handfuls and splashed it vigorously over Dolores' body, then, towelling her off with a less than clean piece of sheet, he began his examination, deftly and gently moving his hands across the grossly distended belly.

To Mage's eyes, the woman's skin seemed to crawl and ripple, as though there was something trapped inside her stomach that was determined to get out and escape any way it could. He suppressed a shiver and contained his feelings.

Snapping on a pair of rubber gloves and ignoring the woman's cries, Hector leaned forwards and began a cursory internal. Dolores' screams became more shrill and after only a very few moments Hector pulled back. Discarding the bloody gloves, he reached over to his bag and took out syringe. 'This is impossible! Let's see if we can get her on her side. I'm going to have to give her an epidural...'

But the woman, never less than eighteen stones since the birth of her first child and now deliriously crippled with pain, was not to be moved. Even with Manolo's help, the combination of dead-weight, angle of bed and the risk of inflicting unknown damage, defeated them. In the end, Hector exchanged syringes and injected into her wrist.

'It will quieten her down a bit, but not as much as I'd like. At least I'll be able to do the internal properly...'

Her screams diminished, although not by much. Hector produced new gloves and eased his way in. Mage watched, both fascinated and sickened as first Hector's fingers, and then his whole hand disappeared within the swollen and still bleeding vagina. After what seemed to be an eternity of tension, Hector finally groaned and withdrew his hand. Consigning the gloves to the fire, he tiredly took off his overcoat, paused for a moment, then turned and took Manolo's arm, looking him firmly in the eyes.

'I hate to do this to you my friend, but if it comes to it and I think it might, then who am I to save? The mother or the child?'

Manolo blanched. 'Doctor that is no decision to give me! How in the names of Jesus and Mary am I to make this choice?'

'I'm sorry Manolo, but choose you must – and there is precious little time for deliberation.'

Tears streamed down the little Spaniard's swarthy cheeks. 'Doctor Hector, give me at least one minute, one half minute with this...' He turned away, sobbing silently, head bowed.

'Is is really that bad?' Mage asked quietly in English.

'It's worse,' Hector looked at him strickenly. 'I cannot guarantee to save either life. If I do nothing, certainly both will die. If I can cut, then maybe and only maybe I can save one or the other. The child is breached but part of it is already jammed in the birth canal. I have to do a caesarean section and I have to do it as swiftly as I can to save the child. I can work just a little more slowly if I am to save the mother but that still means cutting the baby free and, either way, without a proper anaesthetic the shock to her system is going to be enormous and...'

Manolo touched Hector's shoulder, stifling his emotion and fighting for control. 'Señor Doctor,' he spoke formally, pulling himself up to his full height and full of gypsy pride. 'I know that you will do all that you can. I know that you will do your best. But if this choice must be made... Señor, I have three fine children but only one wife. Please, you must work for Dolores.'

'Very well. Now, go to your children. There is nothing you can do here. Give you little ones what comfort you can and do a little praying for us all, eh Manolo!'

Manolo nodded then quietly left.

'Damn,' Hector swore sadly and yet dispassionately. 'I wish I could save them both... But at least, thank God, he's given me the easier task.'

Again he showered her body with warm water, then drying his hands, pulled on a third pair of surgical gloves and produced a variety of syringes and scalpels. 'There'll be no cosmetic bikini line on this one,' he said gruffly.

' Hector – ' an odd tone in Mage's voice made the doctor look up. 'Would it help if she was deeply asleep and could feel no pain?'

'That would be the miracle of modern medicine, the wonder of a nice clean hospital delivery room with all the latest drugs. Regrettably we have no such facilities here.'

'But would it help?' Mage insisted. 'If she was deeply asleep and could feel no pain, would that help you save both mother and child?'

'In those circumstances I could virtually guarantee it, but...'

Mage was moving to the head of the bed. 'Then give me two minutes, Hector. Just two minutes. I'll tell you when you can start cutting.'

'But what are you going...'

Mage turned and just for a fleeting second, to Hector's eyes he no longer looked like the Englishman with whom he'd spent the better part of that day. For the space of one heart beat, he looked somehow taller and there was something of a different colour in his eyes.

'Trust me, Tio Palyasso, and I'll give you your anaesthetic.'

Something warm and unearthly exploded gently in Hector's solar plexus. *Tio Palyasso!* How had Mage known that name. None had called him Tio Palyasso for twenty three years and even then it was a unique name that Mariana had thought up for him when she'd wanted to tease. *How did the English have this name?* Not even Anna Maria knew of it, so how could Mage know?

Hector opened his mouth to speak, but Mage had turned his back on him and was now sitting on the edge of the bed near the sweaty and vomit stained pillow.

'I'll tell you when to cut...' It was Mage's voice and yet it *wasn't!* 'Be ready, and once you start, keep me informed as to how you're progressing.'

***

'Yeva vishua, yeva yeahod, sooshi kosh quandosii...' Mage chanted the mantra over and over again, never varying the pitch or phonetic emphasis. Leaning over the woman he massaged her temples with the first and second fingers of each hand. His thumbs held her eyelids open and holding his face close to hers, forced her to focus on his eyes. At first her pupils darted all over the place, not seeing him – but then as her screams diminished to moans and whimpers, eye contact was made. For a second there was blind panic as she tried to close her eyes and couldn't, then her eyes defocused completely and rolled backwards into her head. The whimpering fell away into a silence that seamed deafening. Outside the rain crashed against the leaves of the forest and the tin roof of the nearby barn counterpointed by the buffeting wind and distant thunder. The fire crackled in a desultory way, there was a steady drip of water leaking from the roof, splashing with regular monotony against the stained metal of the sink. Dolores' breathing became deep and regular.

Mage ceased the softly chanted mantra and removed his thumbs from the eyelids which immediately closed shut. Maintaining the gentle pressure against her temples with his finger tips, he called quietly over his shoulder.

'All right Hector. You can start.'

'I do not believe this!'

'Start cutting Hector, but take your time. There's no rush now. I can hold her like this for as long as you want. She will feel nothing.'

With one part of his mind in a daze – he would not have believed this possible had he not seen it for himself – Hector picked up the tools of his trade and went to work. He cut deeply into the abdomen from just below the navel right down to the pubis. Dolores made no sound and nor did she flinch as Hector's scalpel cut into her. She simply carried on breathing regularly as if in a deep and dreamless sleep.

Hector freed the embryo from the womb and birth canal and lifted it from the body. He looked at it only once, feeling a coldness clutch at his heart and bowels. Bile and vomit rose in his throat. Laying the body on the floor and ignoring its tiny bleats of life, he swiftly took a hypodermic needle from the secondary pocket of his bag and, kneeling on the dark tiles, injected the contents of the syringe directly into the baby's chest. It died immediately and he covered it with one of the discarded sheets. He then went back to work on Dolores, stitching, suturing and steadily closing the gaping caesarean wound.

'How are you doing?' asked Mage, not turning from the head of the bed.

Hector was silent for a second. 'I'm closing her up now. How long can you keep her like this?'

'How long do you want her to sleep for?'

'Twenty four hours?' Hector laughed coldly. 'Can you do that?'

'Yes, if necessary, but I'll have to let her sleep naturally, so if you're serious about twenty four hours it means I'll have to sit here for twenty four hours, taking her down again every time she starts to regain consciousness.'

'All right. Just hold her until I'm finished here then I'll give her a couple of jabs, one for the body shock and one to keep her knocked out for half a day. At least, I can do that now...'

'Hector - the baby?'

'Stillborn.' There was ice in the doctor's voice and beads of perspiration on his brow.

In the light of the rain swept dawn, dark grey clouds scudded across a washed out sky. Instinctively, Mage pulled the Land Rover off the road and the two men sat silently surveying the village, drenched and dim in the dawnlight, half a mile away.

Mage brought out a crumpled pack of cigarettes, took one then passed the packet to Hector. The doctor unthinkingly helped himself then tossed the packet onto the dashboard and reached for his matches. They were wet and would not light. Mage passed over the brass zippo.

Hector inhaled the smoke deeply, then turned to look at his companion. There was a calmness in the Englishman that simply had not been there before... But there was also challenge. Mage met his eyes and in the end it was Hector who finally looked away.

'What did you do back there, Colin?'

'What do you think I did, Hector?'

'I don't know.' The doctor, tired beyond belief and battling with conscience and the Hippocratic oath, looked up from the cigarette. 'Some kind of hypnotism? Let me tell you, my friend, that I know something about hypnotism and I have even practised it on occasion, but never in all my life have I seen anything like what you did to Dolores... And,' he hesitated, 'how did you know about Tio Palyasso? Answer me that, my new English friend, for if you can't, then our friendship can travel no further than this night.'

'It was mostly hypnotism,' Mage conceded carefully, 'but please don't worry about it and please don't ask too many questions because it's impossible to give you all of the answers. I have certain – talents and it's difficult to explain how they work, even to myself. I have a psychic gift. It enables me to see things and know things about people that I have no right to know. It doesn't control me, but then, nor can I always control it. Sometimes the gift isn't a gift at all, but a curse, and I have to work very hard on occasion to ignore what my senses are telling me. That isn't always possible and I find that I've done something or said something before I've had time to think about it. So it was with Tio Palyasso... I know that it means Uncle Clown, but I don't exactly know what it means to you. Things were getting very tense back there and I knew that I had to get your attention... I knew that I had to make you trust me and Tio Palyasso just popped out of its own accord. I'm sorry if I worried you, but at lease we can be thankful that my gift was put to some good use.'

Hector sighed and closed his eyes. 'I've heard about people like you, but you're the first one I've actually met.' He smiled mirthlessly. 'I would welcome the opportunity of talking to you some more on the subject, but while you are in this part of Spain it may be to your advantage to keep your gifts to yourself. The people here are superstitious. They would soon start calling you El Bruho...'

'I'm not a witch, Hector.'

'No of course you're not but that's what people would call you anyway. And I am thankful for your help tonight, for without it I'd have lost both child and mother...'

In his mind's eye, Hector remembered walking into the forest, bundle under one arm, spade resting in the crook of the other. He'd sweated, digging deep in the soft wet soil for more than half an hour, before depositing the bundle at the bottom of the grave, then filling in the hole, covering the loose surface earth with large stones and small rocks. Afterwards, he'd had to tell Manolo what he'd done, a defiant Manolo who'd insisted that the baby be given a proper burial in the village until Hector had whispered furiously in his ear.

'Manolo, the priests would never bury it. The baby was wrong, very wrong. That's what nearly killed Dolores! Do you understand, Manolo? The baby was wrong!'

Comprehension of what Hector was saying came slowly to the campero's face, but when it finally did arrive, he'd nodded silently, gripping the doctor's hand in mute gratitude. How much better to say that the baby had been stillborn and had been buried with prayers and dignity on his own land than to risk the pointing fingers and wagging tongues of the village. There had been too many tales of wrong babies over the last few seasons. Far better he be thought of as a miserly peon than the carrier of bad seed.

'What was wrong with the baby?' Mage's words cut through Hector's reverie like razor blades.

'What makes you ask such a question?' The doctor asked indignantly. 'I told you. It was stillborn.'

'If you say so then I shall believe you,' Mage spoke softly, 'but as I said, I have certain talents and I felt there was more to it than that. If we are to be friends, Hector Sanchez, let us remember that truth is a two way thing. If the baby was only stillborn, why haven't we brought it with us to be buried in Castillo? I know enough of Spanish customs to understand this would be the normal thing for us to do.' And then, as Hector felt the younger man's eyes boring into him... 'There *was* something wrong with it, wasn't there?'

The doctor looked out of the window, absently wiping at the condensation with a grubby sleeve. Two hundred metres away, the Rio Hozgarganta churned beneath the iron bridge; its waters, brackish brown, were filled with debris – branches of trees, the corpse of a goat. He shivered in the damp of his clothes and fumbled for his pipe. This was a futile gesture for the old briar was jammed with wet tobacco and would need a thorough decoking before it would smoke again properly. Nonetheless, the took some comfort from holding the familiar oval shape in the palm of his hand.

'The child was deformed.' He spoke in a low voice, slowly and pedantically. 'Badly so...' He blinked his eyes and saw again the monster that he'd taken from Dolores' distended body. The head was twice as big as it should have been and the arms and feet had been stunted and claw like. The scales on the thing's body had been the most repulsive element. The scales and the eyes, eyes which had been green slits of malevolence that had watched with dispassionate intelligence even as Hector had injected the massive killing dose of pentothal. What would have been the outcome of allowing the thing to live? And there was no doubt in Hector's mind that the thing would have lived and thrived unless Dolores had quietly smothered it or until Manolo had hit it with an axe in the solitude of the forest.

There would have been the speculations, investigations and accusations, just as there had been before, and look at what that had let to! In one case divorce, in another murder and in a third case suicide and madness. Simple ordinary lives turned upside down and thrown into an abyss of pain and confusion, and born of what? Certainly not superstition for there was nothing of fantasy or imagination in the physical reality of the dozen or so deformed creatures that he had seen in the past months. So *what* then?

Something in the water? No, he'd checked and double checked. Something in the food chain? No, because he'd checked and double checked that as well. Something in the air? A spore or gene or virus, possibly drifting over from the big American base at Rota or from the nuclear stockpile in Gibraltar? In the best traditions of investigative medicine, Hector had been most thorough in his checking, analysing both the water supply and the food chain and also the quality of the air. He'd found nothing.

Then he'd made very discreet phone calls and learned that nowhere else was affected. Only Castillo and the Castillato Valley was producing this pattern of premature births, some stillborn, all badly misshapen and mutated. And those few that had lived had only lived for a few hours until some fatal domestic accident befell them, leaving the inevitable aftershock of guilt and accusation.

Few knew the true figures, although most were aware of one or two occurrences. As the area's only doctor, Hector knew exactly how many times it had happened and the numbers frightened him.

'How many times?' Mage asked, and Hector's eyes narrowed. What was this? Was the Englishman reading his mind even as his thoughts were forming?

'Thirteen times in eighteen months. Three times this year alone since January.'

Colin Mage sat and thought furiously about what Hector had told him. The implications were very relevant to Mage's purpose for being in Castillo and although he couldn't tie in all the data, he was certain there was a link somewhere.

'What about the birth rate in general?' he finally asked.

Hector shrugged. 'It's above normal, about twelve or fifteen percent, but the harvests have been good for the last two years and the people have been happier and more relaxed, and with more money in their pockets. That could easily account for it...' Hector trailed into silence, the great ball of grief moving up from his solar plexus to his throat, threatening to choke him. His load was a heavy one and he'd carried it too long alone. Tentatively, he reached out for Mage's arm... When he spoke again, it was barely more than a whisper. His was a soul in search of absolution.

'Listen Colin, I gave Dolores' baby an injection. I put it to sleep. For the sake of the family. For the sake of this village and its people. I have played God and will answer to the angels for it with a broken oath. I tell you this because my heart is aching for what happened back there and for what seems to be happening in our Valley.' And then, 'I needed to tell someone. I have been tempted to do this thing many times and always before I have drawn back. But last night... Last night was too much and I had to do something.'

Mage rested his hand lightly on the doctor's shoulder. 'You don't have to explain it. I do understand.'

'Do you? How can you?'

'I understand very clearly...' Mage paused, thinking and making a decision. 'Hector, I never really knew my parents and I was more or less brought up by my grandmother. She was an incredible woman, as tough as old boot leather. We were very close and it was always an intense and unusual relationship. She was mother, father, teacher and friend, all rolled into one.

'She never had a day's serious illness in her life and she never lost her wits or determination to live life on anything but her own terms. I can remember her painting and decorating the house one year...' Mage chuckled quietly. 'She was up and down ladders like a yo yo, slapping on paint and papering walls and she was in her late eighties even then!

'Anyway, sooner or later it had to happen and one day she felt poorly. The next day she was in hospital with pulmonary pneumonia. She came home a couple of weeks later, but the spark had gone out of her. She was well over ninety and she'd started to die.

'After a few weeks it got so that she didn't bother getting out of bed any more and most days she was asleep more often than she was awake. But it was a painful process and she loathed it. She'd lost the energy to live, but not the will.

'There wasn't anybody else. Only me. Towards the end I had to do everything for her – you know, from spoon feeding to changing the bedclothes, the dirty linen – everything. She couldn't even use the lavatory without me being there to hold her in place. Then she became incontinent and it didn't really matter any more, although it made my work load ten times heavier and it was a grave offence against her dignity. She was in permanent pain and discomfort, but nothing hurt her more than her loss of independence and the even greater loss of her pride. She simply couldn't cope with the helplessness...

'The social people wanted to put her into a home, but the thought terrified her and I can't say that it appealed to me much either. We both knew that once in, she'd never be coming out again and we both fought bitterly against that truth.

'Towards the end it got so bad that she begged me to end it for her. I knew that I *couldn't* and when I mentioned it, very carefully I might add, to our attending doctor, he made it perfectly clear that he *wouldn't*...

'Anyway, this particular night, she was moaning and whimpering. She'd been bed bound for fourteen weeks and the bed sores were all over her frail old body by then. I was exhausted and couldn't sleep – God, I hadn't slept properly for weeks – and in the end, when she eventually fell quiet for a while, I finally found the courage to do what she'd been asking me to do for ages.

'I took a pillow from my bed and walked down the hall to her room. I tell you, Hector, I felt awful. I was crying and hurting, but I knew I couldn't let her go on suffering. In the end I went in and I was just about to cover her face with the pillow when something, I'm not sure what, made me wait a second. And then a shaft of moonlight came in through the window and rested on her face.

'She was calm and serene, looking like the old lady she'd been at seventy. She seemed to be sleeping, but...'

'She'd already gone?' Hector asked quietly.

'Yes, she'd already gone... But if she hadn't, I know I would have done it. I'd not have let her go on with any more of the awful suffering she was going through. Looking back now, I just wish I'd found the courage to do it many weeks earlier. But the point of all this is to let you know that I do know how you feel and you'll have no criticism from me...' And then as a deliberate afterthought... 'And no breach of confidence either!'

'Thank you, Colin. Thank you.'

'Tell me about Anna. What's the matter with her eyes?'

Hector looked up, momentarily startled by the sudden shift in conversation. Then, the tiredness and overloading emotions taking over, he visibly relaxed. After all, this was the Englishman who could defy the laws of medicine, the Englishman who had known that he was a doctor even before he had been informed of the fact. This was the Englishman who knew what you were thinking even as you thought it. The Englishman who could read minds. Why then, should he be surprised if he knew about Anna?'

'Anna has a brain tumour,' Hector said bleakly. 'She is going blind. She will be without sight before the end of the year... and unless some miracle happens to arrest the tumour's growth, she'll probably be dead by the end of next year. She knows about the blindness, but she doesn't know the rest. Now you know. God knows why I've told you, but I have done and I charge you not to breathe this information to another living soul...'

Hector rubbed at the misty windscreen with the back of his hand and peered out into the growing light. 'I have lived in the village for fourteen years and it has been a good place to live. But now something is changing. Something is going wrong... The people are changing and the changes are too sudden to be natural. We have rich harvests, but badly deformed babies... And it isn't just the children either. Some of the things that are falling from the bellies of our sheep and cattle come straight from the bowels of hell! People are becoming frightened and aggressive; we have murders and suicides and cases of insanity... Things which would have been unheard of in a place like this a couple of years ago. The whole atmosphere, the ambience... Seems to have fallen down the face of the cliff.'

He turned and looked enigmatically at Mage. 'I'll tell you something now which is funny, but I don't think it will make you laugh much. I am a man of medicine, if you like, a man of science. I am not given to flights of fancy or the wild imaginings of a village washer woman, and yet I look out of your Land Rover's window upon the village that has been my home for all these years, and do you know what I feel? I'll tell you what I feel! I feel frightened. Something very strange and wrong has come to dwell among us in Castillo de la Frontera. Now, my very clever Englishman, tell me you think I'm mad, eh?'

'No Hector,' Mage stubbed out his cigarette and turned on the ignition. 'I don't think you're mad. I think you're right. There is something wrong in Castillo...' He shot Hector a look that Hector would not easily forget. '... And that, Doctor Sanchez, is why I'm here.'

7.

Other People

Michael Fry sat at his desk. It was an expensive oak affair inlaid with dark green leather. A single table lamp stood at one corner next to a modern push button telephone. The telephone and lamp were the only concessions to the twentieth century, the rest of the room reminiscent of a bygone age. Thick tapestry curtains hung across leaded windows and, where the walls were not covered with book cases, there was a deep green velvet wall paper, matched by heavy shag pile carpet, also in dark green. A single oak panelled door faced the desk and a small but exquisitely elegant chandelier hung unlit from the frescoed ceiling.

Fry leaned back in his chair, causing the fine silk of his expensive suit to rustle imperceptibly. He closed his eyes, face pulling into a slight frown as he concentrated on the problem that had caused him to leave his company in search of the privacy and silent sanctuary that this room alone was able to give.

He was a slight man with well groomed ash blond hair and aquiline features. His eyes were grey and sat either side of a longish, slightly hooked nose. His mouth was thin and could easily have been described as cruel; he seldom smiled and was not renowned for having a great sense of humour. He was thirty four years old and, unless one studied him carefully, one might have said that he was at least ten years younger.

There were many things that had caused this man to become The Merlin – The Chief Druid of Britain – but boyish good looks was not one of them. Mostly, he conceded, it was the incredibly long bloodline of his family. This would have counted for much even if he had not been named heir apparent by the Old Merlin who had died some six years earlier. Named Heir Apparent not because the Old Merlin had been his great uncle but because he was the obvious (and some said only) choice on merit alone.

Fry had many talents. He was a capable seer and had a powerful clairvoyant gift. He'd been born a Druid and was expertly versed in the movements' lore and law. And yet it was none of these things that had guaranteed him the accession to The Merlin's Throne. Druidism was, at a conservative estimate, four and a half thousand years old and yet Michael Fry was very much a man of the twenty first century. His clinically modern mind, tuned to various levels of expert knowledge in subjects as diverse as the stock market and parliamentary politics, gave him a phenomenal degree of organisational ability. This ability was needed at a time when The Faith was fundamentally disorganised and splintered. To survive, Druidism had to expand in a credible and acceptable way...

Fry had many contacts, both in politics and in the media. His international links were also seen as being a favourable aspect. He spoke five languages with total fluency and eight others passably well. His argument that there were too many splinter groups that had to be unified and that the movement had to do something to shake off the public's perception of what The Faith was all about, was an argument that fell on fertile ground and eager ears. His belief that Druidism should become an international faith, rallying behind a single banner, was enthusiastically applauded. His determination to see the religion demystified and made more accessible to the man in the street was met with a more cautious response until Fry explained that it was only be travelling this pathway could Druidism hope to take its rightful place alongside Christianity and Islam and exert its influence (only ever for the good!) over the masses. This latter philosophy had acolyte and adversary alike eating out of his hand and in the Salisbury Gathering of the new millennium he was almost unanimously elevated from the Council of Thirteen to The Merlin's High Throne.

That had been six years ago and for six years Fry had fought tooth and nail, sometimes working twenty hour days, to make his visions real. It was slow work and, although his successes had been spectacular, he frequently despaired. There was so much apathy and so much opposition. He didn't know which was worse! And now, just as things were beginning to come together and fall into place – Holy Oaks! England, Ireland, Scotland and Wales united after thousands of years of independence and dissension – there was this business in Spain. This thing with Colin Mage.

It would be so easy, so convenient, to dismiss the magician's story as so much nonsense – but there were many reasons why he could not do that. First of all, there was Mage himself. Fry had known him for a number of years, not well, but well enough to have an accurate impression of Mage's strengths and weaknesses as an active occultist. The four books that he'd written were both thoroughly researched and sensibly presented and Fry had heard him lecture on more than one occasion and had been impressed, not only by the degree of Mage's knowledge, but also in his ability to communicate it.

As a matter of course, he had interviewed three people who had sat with Mage in readings. One had been a deliberate plant at a time when it was thought that the magician from York would make a good Druid himself. If Fry remembered correctly the girl had been rumbled within five minutes, although she'd been a trained priestess and ought to have been able to disguise her identity and purpose rather better than that! Both the priestess and the two others who had subsequently joined the movement, had been inspired by Mage's accuracy and also by the detail that he had gone into.

Thus, Mage could not be dismissed lightly as some seaside fortune teller with delusions of grandeur. He did not sensationalise and nor did he resort to theatrical gimmicks. In his own way he was as dedicated to his craft as Fry was to his own and, therefore, if he'd sought audience with The Merlin in search of guidance and to issue a warning, then both Mage and the warning had to be taken seriously... Especially if there were other things which seemed to corroborate Mage's story which, of course, there were. Too many isolated incidents that made little sense at the time began to make sense once they were tied in with Mage's theory.

And yet it was impossible to believe. Mage could not be right. Not entirely. There had to be some flaw, some missing link, for if not the scenario that presented itself was too awful to contemplate. Not the end of the world, certainly not in the sense of nuclear holocaust, but it would be the beginning of the end of all that was good in the world, the dousing of the spiritual flame that he, as Chief Druid, along with many many others, had striven so hard to kindle and nurture.

Fry had spoken with Mage five times in four months, the last time only two and a half weeks previously. It had seemed expedient to help the magician, to listen and to push him, where he could, in the right direction. At their last meeting The Druid had taken blood and hair and a wedding ring and, ever since, Mage had been too frequently in his thoughts, both waking and sleeping.

The wedding ring. Michael Fry wondered about Mage's ex-wife. The fact that she was involved complicated matters. She was the flaw, wasn't she? Destroying the objectivity of Mage's beliefs and taking the magician's fears into the realms of psychosis. And yet, The Druid argued with himself, without the wife's involvement Mage would not be involved either and, therefore, what better catalyst could there be?

Fry switched his thoughts to another curious area. For once, perhaps the first time in years, his organisational skills and powers of leadership were working remarkable well. He and his Inner Councils were on top of everything; there were no panics or pressing emergencies that demanded his time and attention and his diary was relatively free...

Question: was he worrying about Mage purely because he had little else to worry about at this time – or had he, subconsciously and with the power of the Gods, deliberately created a situation wherein he was free to worry about Mage and to do something about it?

He wasn't certain, but he suspected the latter. Mage had been too frequently in his thoughts and dreams. He admitted that he did not want to believe what Mage had put before him, but it was about time that a few things were put to the test. That was certainly a responsibility he could no longer afford to ignore.

He opened his eyes, eased himself out of the chair and walked over to the window, pulling back the curtains and gazing out at sweeping vista of parkland shadowed in the starlight by the thnick copses of old oak trees which represented the outer fringe of Shewrwood forest. Beyond trees and some eight or nine miles distant was the amber sodium glow of Nottingham, reflecting against the low blanket of cloud.

Nottingham. Not the most obvious location for the High Druidic Altar of All Britain, but it was a long standing tradition that wherever The Merlin was, so also was his throne and temple. In the past the altar had been in many other unlikely places, but Fry was more than happy with this prime location in central Nottinghamshire. He was, after all, a man of that county and, furthermore, as his duties took him travelling all over the country, Nottingham was conveniently equidistant to everywhere of importance. Two hours from London, four from Edinburgh. Four hours from Caernarfon, three from Salisbury. Seven hours from Truro and Tintagel, seven also from Inverness and Aberdeen. Five hours from West Anglesey, four hours from Glastonbury. Certainly the traditional Druidic altars remained in those places, but as long as Michael Fry remained The Merlin, the High Altar would remain beneath the grounds of The Oaks.

Early resistance from the die-hards had diminished once the convenience of The Oaks had been experienced – and not only the convenience but also the comfort. The substantial mansion house that had been in the Fry family for generations offered all the facilities of a modern five star hotel and The Temple itself, three metres beneath a private grove of thirteen sacred oak trees, offered not only warmth and space, but also total privacy. Access was from the tunnel deep in the mansion's extensive wine cellar and although it may have fallen short of the splendour of Stonehenge, it was at least accessible, which was more than could be said for Stonehenge these days and it offered its own intimate magic and mystery without the problems of prying eyes or inclement weather. Druid gatherings had taken place at, or rather, beneath The Oaks for more than three hundred years and, although it was still a new temple in the eyes of some, it nonetheless had a degree of tradition.

Fry closed the curtains and coming to a decision, crossed the room and left through the heavy door. The sound of laughter and clinking glasses lilted up from the floor below and he was mindful of the fact that he had been absent from the soiree for five minutes too long. No matter. The time had been well spent and there were people that he would put to good use. The party, small and private, was a birthday celebration in honour of one of his most senior bards and although he had no intention of curtailing this gathering, he would use the opportunity to set certain things in motion.

He descended the ornately carved staircase and lifted a glass of good champagne from a convenient try. Casting a glance at the thirty or so people who chatted and laughed in the reception hall before, he detected the person he sought and, with polite nods and smiles, eased his way through the throng until he came to the large and statuesque woman with iron grey hair. She was in conversation with two younger females, but turned her attention towards him immediately.

'Margaret, a word?'

Nodding politely at her companions, she allowed Fry to take her by the arm and steer her towards a quiet corner of the room.

'How is the party going?' he asked.

'Very well,' she answered with a merry twinkle in her pale blue eyes. 'I don't think you were missed.'

'You missed me,' he said pointedly. 'And I wasn't gone for very long, was I?'

'I am your Mother, Michael, and there are times when I am so closely in tune with your thoughts that I can sense your presence even when you're out of the country, never mind out of the room. And incidentally, you were gone for fourteen minutes. Now, what's the matter – and please don't say nothing because I know you've been pre-occupied all evening... On and off, for a number of days, in fact.'

'I think we might have a problem,' he said shortly.

'I see.' She hesitated. 'Are you speaking to me as my Lord Merlin or as my son?'

'A little of both, really.'

Margaret Fry's pale eyes lost a fraction of their sparkle. She was not the most maternal of mothers, but she knew her son better than any other human being on this planet and at this moment he was behaving most oddly. Furthermore, she detected an unusual agitation in his psychic aura which, while it caused no great alarm, did excite her curiosity.

'Well Michael, what is this problem?'

Fry stroked the stem of his champagne flute moodily, then nodded towards the semi-distant crowd. 'It crosses my mind that among our guests this evening we have a full Council of Five and a goodly cross section of the most senior bards and priestesses in Britain. Also, one of our most talented clairvoyants is present... Before everyone goes tomorrow morning, I would like to hold an unofficial gathering of a Council of Five, along with some of our elders and including Helen. Do you think you could arrange it?'

'Unofficially?'

'Yes. I thought the music room rather than the temple.'

'May one enquire for what purpose?'

'I've not done too badly these past six years, have I Margaret?'

'My dear, you are the most powerful and highly respected Merlin that we have had in two hundred and fifty years and you know it as well as I do.'

'Thank you for the vote of confidence, even though you are my mother.'

'That hasn't anything to do with it. You asked me a direct question and i gave you a direct answer which, incidentally, is more than you gave me.'

'Yes. Very well...' Fry chose his words carefully. 'Something very unusual might be happening that *might* cause a major catastrophe to our faith. At this point in time, because the whole thing is without precedent, I need a sounding board and I need advice... And also possibly Helen's services before I officially call a convocation of The Council of Thirteen.'

'Yes, all right,' Margaret Fry responded. 'I understand that, buy why this unofficial approach?'

'Because what I have to discuss really is quite incredible and I might do myself harm by even broaching the subject. If I am wrong in a certain opinion, I would be seriously jeopardising both my credibility and my authority as The

Merlin, but if I am right and do nothing, our entire faith, our organisation, all the hard work we've done over these last years could be destroyed within months and we wouldn't be alone.'

Margaret Fry's senses were pickling. A hollow knot of tension was beginning to build in her solar plexus and someone was running an icy cold finger up and down her spine.

'What do you mean? We would not be alone?'

Fry looked at her shrewdly across the top of his champagne glass, wondering how much he should tell her. 'We might, and I do most strongly emphasise might, be facing a threat that could bring about the fall of Druidism... and if that happens then Christianity and Islam would also fall, along with the Buddhist faith and any other world religion you might care to think of.'

She blanched. 'Michael, are you being serious?'

'Yes, I'm afraid I am rather and if it's going to happen, I think it's going to start happening soon. Certainly this year...'

Margaret struggled to bring her reeling senses under control, very much aware that she was being closely scrutinised by her son. The look on his face, now that he had allowed his mask to slip just a little, told her that this was no jest and that he was deeply worried.

'How long have you carried this on your own?' she asked astutely.

How long indeed. Did he measure it from the first time Mage had come to see him, the second time, or the third time? Did he measure it from his own frightening trance probes in the astral, or from the time he'd started picking Mage up in his dreams? Or did he measure it from long before then when he'd begun to correlate his own unfocused visions of some forthcoming nameless horror, visions that had prompted him to pay special heed to some of the disturbing reports that had started trickling in, not only from his own people, but also from some of his contacts in the Wiccan movement? Where did anything begin?

He gave his mother a rare half smile and shrugged his shoulders in mocking self depreciation. 'For a little while,' he admitted. 'Certainly for a few weeks. Perhaps I should have brought it up earlier, but I was no more sure then than I am now. As your Merlin, I am asking you to arrange this unofficial council, and as your son I have told you what I have told you, and you'll keep it to yourself for just a little while, please.'

'Leave it with me,' Margaret said with firmness, suppressing the desire to ask further questions. 'What time would you like to sit?'

'Oh not too early. Say ten o'clock? Morning coffee.'

'Who do you want from among the elders?'

Fry looked beyond his mother. 'Thomas,' he said quietly. 'Martin of Glastonbury, and I think our Lady Mary.'

Margaret's eyes narrowed. 'They are all three, very strong traditionalists.'

'Yes I know. They'd give me a hard time and pull me to pieces. Frankly, I rather hope they're successful. If nothing else, they'll keep me on terra firma... And mother, one thing more... Not a word to any of them with regard to what this is all about, least of all Helen?'

'I understand. What about me? Do you want me present?'

'No I don't,' Fry said bluntly, 'but you are our administrator and like it or not, I'll need you there.'

The Reverend John Light woke from a sequence of terrible nightmares. He could not remember the dreams but the aftershock of their images disturbed him both on a conscious and subconscious level. The bright California sunshine flooded reassuringly through the bedroom windows and later, after he'd dressed, he ate a spartan breakfast sitting by the side of his swimming pool. Tamara sat with him, long legs dangling duskily in the shimmering water, matching her mood to his own. He looked at her thoughtfully, wondering why she stayed with him. She had money of her own, was competitively intelligent and was half his age. He did not treat her well... Not that he treated her badly, mind you... But he knew himself well enough to know that he was a difficult man to live with. Sometimes they would talk, sometimes they would have sex and sometimes he would ignore her for days. And yet she was always there, if not in his bed, certainly in his aura of influence, coming close when he needed her, keeping her distance when he needed his space.

There was never any talk of love and there was never any talk of commitment or of what they might be doing tomorrow or next week or next year... Perhaps it was this lack of anything solid, this rare quality of freedom, that bound her to him. She was beautiful and she was black and she was his, and yet if she got up and walked out of his life for ever, he doubted that he would feel much one way or the other, despite the fact that they'd been together now for what, twelve years? Yes, it must have been all of that. She'd come to him a virgin of fourteen – a gift from someone who'd needed a big favour badly – and she'd had her twenty sixth birthday three weeks ago. He'd bought her a Cartier watch and a Suzuki Jeep... The watch remained in its presentation box and the Jeep hadn't been out of the garage since they'd driven down the boulevard on a first day's test drive. Stupidly – he thought it was stupid anyway – the birthday card he'd given her still had pride of place on the dressing table in her bedroom.

Tamara had her own room. It worked best that way. It kept things straight.

'Can I get you some more coffee?' she asked quietly.

'No.'

'Anything?'

'No. I'm fine...' His eyes defocused on the shimmering water, the dream memories dancing tantalisingly out of reach. He became aware of an ache behind his eyes and a hollowness in his belly that made him uncomfortable; he put it down to tiredness and the stress of the pounding schedule that had been part of his life for these last few months: his television audience was growing weekly and seldom a month passed without one of the West Coast papers publishing a major spread on the new age gospel of light according to the larger than life Reverend John. Hundreds of letters poured in every day, both to his Church Headquarters in downtown LA and also via the TV station. Some of them were begging letters, others were filled with praise. Some contained death threats, while many others contained unsolicited financial donations. It had been going on like this for three years and the flood of reaction became ever stronger.

He was now a rich man, and while he lived well in some respects he also lived frugally. His Church was worth more than several millions of dollars, but the money was genuinely tied up in charitable trust. He himself lived on quite a modest salary that he paid himself on a monthly basis and although he owned the house and the Cadillac and could afford to buy Cartier watches, there was never more than fifty thousand dollars in his personal checking account at any one time. His accountants liked it that way and for a nigger who had been born with nothing but fear and bed bugs, he was well content... But sweet Jesus, he was tired now and restless. He needed a break and he needed a rest. Some time and space where he could just sit and relax and think and get his head straight. Maybe do some fishing, maybe a little reading... The memory of a place eased its way into his mind and he pushed it straight out again. Anywhere but there! No, definitely not there!

'Tammy babe, can I change my mind. I need a drink.'

'Sure. What do you want?'

'Southern Comfort, orange and ice, and while you're in the house would you mind bringing the diary from the office...'

With one mental eyebrow raised, Tamara disappeared into the shade of the large single story building. Even though it was not yet nine thirty, the heat of the day was building and the air conditioning had switched itself on automatically in reaction to the rising mercury. She shivered at the sudden change of temperature then had to bite back the smile. It would help, of course, if she put on some clothes. But she knew that John, and she always thought of him as John, never Johnny or Jonty or The Reverend, liked to see her naked. Even if he was not always sexually motivated, she knew that he liked her walking around the house in the nude. She was beautiful and she knew that she was beautiful, and she also knew that he appreciated her beauty asexually for that beauty's own sake. There was never a problem when other people were around – then she would wear clothes from her extensive wardrobe that befitted the occasion – but when they were alone, either watching the TV or sitting by the pool, or if she was reading while he was working on a speech or a sermon, as often as not she'd be undressed.

Sometimes she would be aware of him watching her and would pretend not to notice. Sometimes because his look was different, she'd make it clear that she had noticed. Frequently they would couple in bouts of wild frenzy after half a day's foreplay. Other times a single look would be enough to bring them roughly together for the sake of his sexual release. This might have given other women a problem – she knew that – but basically that was what she had been trained for. She may have been a virgin before being given to John Light, but there was nothing about sex that she didn't know. She'd been born in a brothel and had grown up in a brothel, and from the age of eleven had been scrupulously tutored in the physical arts of man pleasing. There had been other children in that Memphis Delta hell, but she'd been the best.

She mixed the drink, thinking vaguely of Mamma Bet. Four girls between nine and twelve sprawled across the sweet smelling bed and Mamma Bet sitting on the basket work chair near the window. "When you's on top your man and his thing is right up inside you, don't you go thinking you gotta move up an' down like a jitterbug at a firefly's ball. You go real slow and grab him hard with your pussy muscles. That'll bring him coming into you like an express train, an' it's a lot less tiring work for you too!" She wondered what had happened to the old madam and wondered also about her three child companions. What had happened to them, where had they gone? If they'd done as well as she had, they'd have no cause to complain.

Leaving the drink in the kitchen, she walked panther-like into John's study and retrieved the heavy red diary from his desk. Her thoughts flashed back to her man and she glanced casually through the curtained window to see him standing at the pool side, hands thrust deeply into his pockets as he stared into the middle distance. He was in a strange mood. The fact that he had asked for a drink was in itself unusual and the fact that he had asked her nicely was more unusual still. She knew that he had slept badly... Twice she'd been woken by his shouts and when she'd gone in to sit at his bedside just before dawn, his face had been covered with perspiration, the lines of his forehead drawn into a frown. She'd stayed with him a while, soothing his brow, until he'd dropped into a more peaceful sleep pattern... But she'd lived with him for too long not to know that there was something else troubling him this morning. She didn't know what it was, but if it was important, he'd tell her eventually. He always did.

She took him the drink and the diary and he sat with both beneath the Ambre Solair umbrella, taking a mouthful and opening the diary at the relevant page. 'Thank you,' he said, absently.

Tamara's mental eyebrow went up another notch. *Thank you?* Usually, it was "thanks babe", or "great", or just "okay"... Sometimes she might get nothing more than a nod and frequently not even that. He looked up from the diary and caught her watching him. 'Better slip into some clothes. Vern and Paris are due in the next ten minutes or so.'

'Anything special you want me to wear?'

'Anything you like, but I've got to tell you Tam, you look just great as you are.'

Tamara went back into the house to dress, more confused than she would care to admit. She wasn't used to compliments.

They sat around the poolside table. John, Tamara, Vern and Paris. The latter couple were attractive black Americans in their early thirties, well dressed in expensive clothes. They'd been married for ten years, but had no children. They were both lawyers by training, but committed followers of John Light's church by vocation. Not only did they function respectively as business managers, but also as Arch Deacon and Deaconess. That morning both of them were worried and neither was in a frame of mind to conceal their agitation. Vern was doing the talking while his wife, Paris – stupid fucking name, John Light frequently thought disparagingly – sat listening intently.

'We have a number of problems that have to be dealt with fairly immediately,' Vern said vehemently. 'One is that the TV company is threatening to embargo any further broadcasts unless (a) they get a transcript of exactly what you're going to say before you say it, and (b) you absolutely guarantee to stick to the script. The bad language – for God's sake you can't accuse people of being motherfuckers on live prime time television – is in direct contravention of their morality clause. It doesn't matter that its making you a household name the length and breadth of the West Coast, it doesn't matter that we and they are getting floods of very positive reaction. They're terrified of the orthodox lobby and they're even more terrified of jeopardising their precious public broadcast licences. The people in the street may be supporting us but the advertising agencies are not. Revenue is down and Joey Leadbetter really put it on the line to me last night.

'Our second problem is less easily resolved. We've got people queuing up to join our ranks but we simply don't have the venues or the facilities to deal with them all. Either we have to tone things down rapidly until we're in a position to take on hoards of new converts, or we have to expand rapidly. If we're talking about expanding, then we have got to take on more admin staff pronto because, apart from anything else, we've already got the IRS breathing down our necks. I've already disclosed the books to them and, although they can see where every damn penny we makes goes, they're still not satisfied. They think we're running a scam and because we're not, they can't damn well find it. Because they can't find it convinces them that it's got to be there and they're looking harder every day, and those boys in blue suits are not making things easy.

'Now what we need from you John is a very clear and unambiguous sense of direction. We need you to tell us exactly what you want and we need a commitment that next time you go live on TV, you're going to play it by their rules. If we don't get that, we could find ourselves in some very deep shit before the end of the year!'

If there is an end of the year...

The thought came unbidden, popping into Light's mind so suddenly that even he himself was surprised by it. Now what the hell had made him think like that? Immediately the Englishman's face swan into view and his mouth puckered into a scowl. That fucking Colin Mage was the cause of all this, wasn't he, him with all his scare mongering stories about openings and things that went bump into the night! He tried to erase Mage's image from his brain, but it wasn't easy. Oh, he'd sent him packing all right, but the Englishman had scratched a raw nerve and had cracked open a memory from Light's earlier life that he would much have preferred to forget about. Yes well too fucking late for that!

'You want a clear and unambiguous sense of direction, do you?' Light sat a little straighter in his chair and laid his huge hands palms down on the table. 'Okay, well here it is. First of all, the TV company. You write to them today or call our pal Leadbetter and tell them that I exclusively reserve the right to say whatever I want to say however I want to say it. You can also tell 'em that from now on we intend to double our fees and that, furthermore, we want those fees up front. You can also tell 'em that if they don't like it, I don't give a shit and they can take their precious cameras and prime time slots and shove 'em right up their asses. As for the IRS, show 'em everything and let them worry about it. We know we don't have anything to hide and they can discover that themselves at the taxpayers' expense. As for everything else, you sort it out, because for a little while, I'm out of here. I'm gone for maybe two or three weeks. I'm gonna take a holiday.'

His words fell like bombshells around the table. John Light take a holiday? The word wasn't in the man's vocabulary! Vern Rimmer looked aghast, first at Light than at his wife, then back to Light.

'Are you fucking crazy or what?' he exclaimed. 'The TV boys won't buy it, the IRS won't buy it, and I don't buy it! A fucking holiday? Now of all times? You couldn't pick a worse time and, apart from that, you never take holidays!'

'Vern,' there was almost an avuncular tone in Light's voice, 'I don't care if the TV and the IRS don't buy it. I don't care if you don't buy it. I'm out of here either this afternoon or this evening and I'll ring you from wherever I'm going, to let you know when I'll be back. Paris,' he turned to the other man's wife. 'Be an angel and just cancel all my appointments. Tell people I've got a bad throat or something. Tell them anything you like.'

He stood up, towering his full six and a half feet over them. 'And that,' he said in a self satisfied tone, 'is my clear and unambiguous direction for the day.'

Later, Tamara came and stood behind him as he threw things into a soft leather holdall. He felt her presence, but said nothing. Not only did he sense her presence, he also tuned in to the confusion that surrounded her psychic aura. Well, that was to be expected. He was pretty damn confused himself. In the end, it was she who broke the silence.

'Where you going?'

He straightened but didn't turn to look at her. 'South. Deep south.' He laughed ironically. 'Back to the land of my birth, babe. Back to those roots these nigger novelists keep writing about.' There was a bitterness in his voice that was scarcely concealed by the self depreciating sarcasm. 'Swore I'd never go back, but now I think I've got to... Fucking damn dreams,' he added as an afterthought.

'You want me to come with you?'

Then Light did turn, and Tamara, who thought she knew most things about this giant of a man, was startled by the haunted look in his eyes. She'd seen that look before, but very rarely and only in their early days together, when he'd been smoking dope or drinking heavily.

'To tell you the truth Tam, yes I do... But I'm going to leave it up to you to decide. We're not going sight seeing and it ain't pretty down there in that part of the world...'

'Then if it's my choice, I'm coming.'

... And even as she began her own packing she knew that after twelve years of cohabitation, something was beginning to change – no, in the space of a few minutes, had already *changed* in this most curious and unorthodox of relationships.

Eight thousand miles away in the fortified desert town of Beer Sheba, the old man called Herschal ate cheap falafel in an austere cafe near the bus station. He was not happy. For one thing, the place was full of IDF boarder guards – children in scruffy camouflage suits with loaded rifles who looked at him as though he was a piece of shit... Which he supposed he was in their eyes, but it didn't make him feel any the better. They had their crosses to carry and he had his (and odd thought for a Jew) and as far as he was concerned, his cross was significantly heavier than theirs. Also he loathed being in the town. After the clean, fresh purity of the desert, it stank of grime and he felt oppressed by the surrounding breeze block buildings...

Beer Sheba! What wonderful images the name conjured up. Once the encampment of a noble priestess queen three thousand and more years ago – and even just fifty years ago he remembered it as it had been; a beautiful, natural oasis with verdant palms and clean white sand. Now it was a fortress, built and occupied by the Israeli Defence Forces. Barbed wire, machine gun posts, tank traps and, of course, the mines. He hated being here, and he'd hate it even more if he had to go to Jerusalem. Yes well, with luck that could be avoided. If he used the right words and dangled the right bait, Shapiro would come to him. First he'd have to talk to Shapiro and that meant an expensive phone call, which brought him to the first of his problems. The money for the call. He'd literally spent his last half shekel on the gritty falafel.

He swallowed the last of the falafel and wiped greasy hands along the threadbare seems of filthy trousers. Sighing, he stood up from the fly strewn table and shuffled out of the bus depot in the direction of the town centre. Night had fallen and the streets were filled with bustling soldiers and sabras moving from bar to cafe and cafe to bar, many with guns, some in although most out of uniform. The lights, bright and white, made his rheumy eyes blink and the noise of a thousand conversations shouted in competition with the strident blasts of modern music that seemed to emanate from every other doorway, assaulted his ears. He grimaced and tried to close his senses to the discordant intrusion.

There was solitude in the desert and he'd liked it that way until the dreams and visions had begun – and after that there'd been no peace of mind. He'd not been surprised when the Englishman had found him. In fact, he'd been expecting something or someone for days. And after the Englishman had gone, things had become progressively worse...

Herschal found the entrance he was looking for and entered the money lender's shop. It was lit by strip lights. Cold, unfriendly, spartan. A fat man of fifty slouched behind a bare counter. Behind him were cupboards and shelves. The shelves held religious ornaments, the cupboards, lots of box like drawers, were enigmatically shut.

'I want some money,' Herschal said bluntly.

'So do we all,' said the fat man, looking up briefly from the newspaper he was reading. 'And I lend it, but not without sound collateral and not to tramps like you.'

'Tramp am I?' Herschal said with a voice that dripped with scorn and contempt. 'Well, what will you give me for this?'

Dipping his hand into the canvas money bag he wore strapped to his chest beneath a loose and ill-fitting jalaba, he pulled out a coin and slapped it on the counter. The money lender picked it up suspiciously, his suspicion rapidly turning to incredulity.

'Do you know what this is, old man?'

'Of course I do,' Herschal snapped. 'It's a British gold sovereign minted in 1887 and probably worth more shekels than you've got in this soulless dump. The point is, what will you give me for it?'

Ten minutes later, Herschal left the money lender's with a wry smile tugging at the corners of his leathery mouth. He'd got a bad price, but what did it matter? He now had a bundle of usable currency which was more than adequate for his needs – and there were still another eleven gold sovereigns in the canvas bag with twice as many still stashed in the cave in the desert.

He bought clothes and a few toiletries then used the public washroom to make himself marginally more presentable, then took a room in a hostal three streets west of Ben Gurian Prospect. The concierge, a humourless twig of a middle aged woman, had not wanted to accommodate him, but his ability to pay in advance strapped with a healthy bribe had tipped the scales in his favour. The room was austere. A cot, a sink, a bedside table, an open wardrobe, all in utilitarian grey breeze block, but at least it was clean and more importantly, quiet.

After showering in the small cubicle provided five doors down the corridor, he went to bed and tried to sleep. In truth, he was exhausted but sleep didn't come easily. He'd walked more than twenty miles that day and his ancient old feet throbbed painfully. Also, his mind was alive with vivid thoughts, most of them worries, some about the past, most about the future. Sleep finally took him, but it was light and fitful and full of anxiety.

Armed with loose change, he stood in the telephone kiosk beneath the palm tree in the silent sun-drenched square. Cafe owners hosed their dusty pavements, a few unstacked red plastic chairs. The air was sharp, almost cool. The temperature would rise over the next hour or so, but now it was relatively early and the desert breeze teased Beer Sheba's littered streets.

Perhaps it was too early to make the call? No – he was just looking for excuses. He could have made the call last night, but had put it off until now and even that had been one excuse too many.

He picked up the receiver, fed some money into the slot and, with spindly fingers, punched in the digits of a telephone number that was known to very few and was most definitely not listed in any directory. After only three short rings the line was opened.

'Identification code,' said an impersonal male voice.

'This is Megiddo One,' Herschal replied equally impersonally.

'Hold for clearance please.'

Herschal held, feeding more coins into the slot. He fretted with impatience, but controlled it, knowing full well that this procedure could not be rushed. After fifteen or twenty seconds the telephone clicked and whirred and then another voice said:

'Megiddo One. Second stage code access please.'

'The Lion of Judah sleeps at Megiddo,' Herschal answered formally.

This time the response came more quickly. 'Code is confirmed. Is your line secure?'

'Of course it isn't,' Herschal's impatience was wearing thin. 'I'm in a public kiosk in Beer Sheba.'

'Give me the number then hang up. We'll call you back.'

Herschal did as he was told and had to wait a full minute before the telephone rang shrilly. He picked it up and immediately noticed the difference in the tonal quality of the other man's voice. Obviously they had employed a scrambling device.

'Very well Megiddo One. You're cleared through to Mossad Jerusalem. I have to tell you that we have an immediate problem. We have your code name on screen, but we don't know who you are or anything about you...'

'That's exactly as it should be,' Herschal snapped testily. 'Put me through to Shapiro and let's stop wasting time.'

'Hold...'

Herschal held, more relaxed now that someone else was paying for the call. It was a long hold this time before a different voice came on the line. 'Shapiro,' it said curtly.

Herschal breathed a sigh of relief. 'Hello Max. It's me. We've got to talk. I'm in Beer Sheba. Come and meet me here as soon as you possibly can.'

'Just a minute,' said a voice. 'Did you say Max? You want to talk to *Max* Shapiro?'

'If I'm not talking to Max Shapiro, then who am I talking to?' Herschal was immediately on guard.

'I'm very sorry but Max Shapiro died two years ago.'

Herschal felt a lead balloon slowly begin to inflate beneath his ribcage. Max dead? How was that possible? Why, the last time he'd seen Max he'd been hale and well, a picture of health and that was only when... Herschal did his sums and his spirits sank a little lower; it had been twelve years since he'd last seen his old friend and he'd have been well into his sixties then. Now, if he'd been alive, he'd have been in his mid seventies... Obviously he'd not made it that far and Herschal suppressed his fury and frustration with old age.

'I'm sorry to hear that,' Herschal managed to say, swallowing his grief. 'Now, in answer to my other question, who are you?'

'I'm Leon Shapiro. Max's son.'

Leon Shapiro... Yes, of course Max had had a son. Herschal had met him once when he'd been about fourteen years old... A thin pale faced child with thick owl-like glasses. Where had it been? Herschal sifted through his memory. Yes, it had been the boy's Bar Mitzvah. There'd been an open air party on the quayside in old Jaffa... Dancing and singing with lots of wine and, of course, Max's wife Rebecca had still been alive in those days... And then there'd been a bomb alert and the party had broken up to be re-vitalised later on in Tel Aviv, even if some of the spirit had been sapped from it.

'Can I take it,' Herschal spoke carefully, 'that the son has followed in the father's footsteps?'

There was a chuckle down the line. 'Yes, you may take it that way sir, but as my colleague may have told you, we have a problem. We have a code name and password for you, but other than that our screens are blank. Before we can proceed further with any kind of conversation, I shall need further identification.'

'No you won't young man.' Herschal retorted. 'It is quite enough that I've accessed you and that I'm now requesting a direct meeting in the field. There are not that many One suffixes on your files or whatever it is you're using for files these days.'

'It isn't as easy as that,' Leon Shapiro's voice answered without rancour. 'Your coding is one that has not been used in this office for a very long time. You know who you are talking to, but all we know is that we have a voice claiming to be Megiddo One. Frankly sir, you could be anyone who's come by this access code by any number of nefarious means.'

Herschal felt himself getting cross. He breathed deeply to control the surging tides of temper and tried to see the situation from Mossad's point of view.

'Listen to me carefully then, Leon Shapiro. My name, or at least the name I'm going to give you, is Herschal. Dip into your memory and see if it conjures anything up. If it doesn't, then somewhere in your organisation there is something called the Elijah File which was compiled by your father over a great number of years. It had the highest priority of secrecy and only a few members of Mossad and a few senior members of the Knesset knew of its existence. May I suggest you find that file and read it. In the meantime, there is a small cafe about twenty yards away. I'm going to have some breakfast and will come back to this telephone exactly one hour from now when I'll expect you to ring me again with arrangements for a meeting within the next twenty four hours. I assume that this conversation is being recorded, so let me tell you again that I am Megiddo One and I am contacting you now on a most important matter of Israeli State security. Let that be registered on the record.'

Herschal slammed the phone down on the cradle and marched over to the cafe. He took a table in the shade and ordered mint tea and honey cake, mourning not only his dead friend but also his own lost youth. He set about the business of waiting – something, he reflected wryly, that he was very good at. He'd spent most of his life waiting for something, one way or another, and on this occasion another hour wasn't going to make too much difference.

A hundred miles away in Jerusalem, Leon Shapiro sat holding the dead phone, thoughtfully drumming his fingers on the formica table top. He wondered what he ought to do next.

He was a tall lanky man in his mid thirties with black curly hair and thick horn rimmed glasses. He had firm but sensitive features and dark olive green eyes. A wide and mobile mouth gave him an easy smile but it was a smile that became a cruel wolf-like grin if you caught it at the wrong angle.

He looked owlishly at his younger companion, an obese twenty five year old with a sallow complexion and thick greasy hair pushed carelessly beneath a hamulka that was at least two sizes too small.

'Well, what do you make of all that, Irvin?'

'Haven't got a clue,' said his junior, who had been privy to the whole conversation. 'Have you ever heard of The Elijah File?'

Shapiro shook his head, as much in frustration as answering in the negative. 'No, I haven't, but it doesn't mean that it doesn't exist. My father played a few things very close to his chest in his time and if this Herschal, this Megiddo One, is one of his old operatives, that might explain why we haven't got a profile on him.' He pursed his lips. 'Either way, I think this is one for our beloved director to sort out.' He stood up impulsively. 'You'd better come with me and bring the recording with you. I'm sure he'll want to hear it.'

Three minutes later Shapiro and Irvin were ushered into the unremarkably plain office of Mossad's Director General. There were a few black and white photographs on the walls, a filing cabinet in one corner, a window covered by a Venetian blind made of metal and an office table with three telephones. The walls were painted grey and there was a pale Persian rug scattered across the floor.

Gideon Lemski was Mossad's third director in forty eight years of the service's history. The first had been Menachim Begin, while the second had been Max Shapiro. He was craggy man with iron grey hair. Well into his sixties, there wasn't an ounce of spare flesh on his stocky frame and apart from his feet, he was in excellent health. The feet were the problem. Ever since a small skirmish with a land mine in the six day war, he'd had recurring chronic gout. His feet were swollen that morning and he was not in the best of tempers.

He cast Irvin a passing glance and felt a waving curl of contempt at the fat boy's slovenly appearance. My God, if this was what they were giving him to work with these days, little wonder Mossad was no longer the finest secret intelligence service in the world! Gideon Lemski was an old soldier. What he wanted were slim, battle hardened commandos, and instead they were giving him chubby children with PhDs in computer technology. Fucking computers.

His eyes came to rest on Shapiro. 'All right. What's this all about then?' At least Shapiro looked a little more presentable, and even if he hadn't, there was still a natural warmth in Gideon's heart for the son of his old friend and mentor. He never let it show in the office, but out of the office they socialised a lot despite the difference in age and, of course, the families had always been close.

Shapiro shifted uncomfortably, wishing that there was a chair to sit on. But there were no chairs and he stood uncomfortably at loose attention in front of his director's desk, feeling, and not for the first time, like an errant school boy brought up before an unsympathetic headmaster.

'Well,' he cleared his throat. 'We had contact this morning, only a few minutes ago actually, from a field operative called Herschal using the codename Megiddo One. He used a valid pass phrase, even though it was one we hadn't used in years. He's phoned in from a public kiosk in Beer Sheba and is demanding a face to face on what he refers to as a matter of national security. We challenged him on his authenticity and he told us to refer to the Elijah File. Then he hung up, after telling us to phone back in an hour – with the fairly clear indication that if we didn't he wasn't going to wait around much longer. Our problem is that we don't know who this agent is or what he's doing in Beer Sheba. We have no record of him, full stop, and we have no idea what this Elijah File is... He first thought that I was my father... So I thought you might know something that we don't, or at least might be able to give us a sense of direction on this one.'

Something sick and unhappy uncoiled in the pit of Lemski's stomach. Acidic juices coalesced making his cheeks feel hollow. Herschal. Megiddo One. The Elijah File.

Oh, he knew all about the Elijah File, but it was a file that had never been opened and looked at in any detail for at least the last fifteen years. It was a file that only a handful of men – and one woman – had ever known about and it was not a file that had ever been filed or micro dotted for the benefit of Mossad's ubiquitous computers. It stayed in the safe sunk into the teflon and concrete beneath the floor of the Knesset bunker... Coming out only occasionally to be shown to each of Israel's new prime ministers whenever there was a change of government, and only then if that person had difficulty in accepting what the department minister and the director general of Mossad had to tell them. Golda Meir had taken it very seriously as had Menachim Begin... Others had had to be convinced.

The file had been opened in 1933 by Max Shapiro and, although the last addendum to the file had been made early in 1992, it had never been closed. Almost fifteen years of silence... Fifteen turbulent years of uneasy coexistence with the Arab world, wherein little by little Arab and Jew had come fractionally closer together in search of some rapport and compromise. Now, when things were more hopeful than they'd ever been in Israel's chequered history, now Megiddo One had made contact and the Elijah File beckoned with the black flapping wings of disaster. Why *now* of all times?

Part of him was amazed that Herschal was still alive. It was the same part of him that had quietly hoped that the Elijah File would never again be opened. And that was the same part of him that miserably wished that Herschal was dead. No news was good news and Herschal was always bad news.

He was aware of the scrutiny he was under from his two agents and knew that this whole affair was going to have to be handled very carefully indeed. He trusted Shapiro implicitly, but the university whiz kid was another matter all together.

'The Elijah File exists,' he told them both quietly. 'In most circumstances, you would never had heard about it, but what is done cannot be undone. A warning, however... you will now both immediately forget that you've ever heard of such a file and everything subsequently concerning Megiddo One will be channelled directly through me. If either of you cock-up or there is even the hint of this being mentioned outside of this office, you'll both spend the rest of your careers in a slit trench on the Golan Heights. Is that very clearly understood?'

Irvin had gone pale while Shapiro looked on quizzically.

'Tell me it is clearly understood,' Lermski insisted and the two other men indicated that it was. 'Good. Now, you will telephone Megiddo One at the appointed time and you will tell him to remain where he is until he's been collected.

I want him quietly and courteously picked up before noon today, and...' he thought for a moment 'deposit him in the safe accommodation in Ashquelon. You may tell him that I shall talk to him in person within the next twenty four hours. I want all this done quietly and without any fuss and without anyone else in this department or any other department knowing. You may pass all your other duties on to colleagues and you are both seconded to me for the duration.'

'Er... Do we have a code name for this operation sir?' asked Irvin tentatively.

'No we do not, for there is no operation running here.' Gideon's voice was terse. 'I presume you have a recording of this morning's conversation? Please hand it over and...' He looked at Irvin balefully in the eye 'kindly forget that it ever happened.'

He turned back to Shapiro. 'Get on to whoever we've got in Beer Sheba. Tell them to locate the kiosk where the phone call was made from and to make contact with Megiddo One... Surveillance only and very covert. They're looking for an incredibly old man who'll be as scruffy as hell. If he doesn't fit that description, I'll need to know immediately and there'll probably have to be a change of plans...'

'He sounded quite old,' Shapiro said thoughtfully, 'so he's probably our man...' He looked for further enlightenment but none was forthcoming.'

'Get on with it then,' Gideon said, and the two younger men left the room, leaving the director alone with his thoughts. He wondered if he should call the prime minister's office, then decided against it. He would see what Herschal had to say first... No point in panicking them over in the Knesset any more than they were panicking already. After all, this might yet turn out to be nothing of importance. He shivered involuntarily and wondered if he could be so lucky.

8.

Calle Sombra

Calle Sombra – The Street of Shadow. It was aptly named. Mage stood at the end of the road, hands on hips, looking at the house that faced him some fifty yards away. The street ran south to north, a narrow pavement to the right, fronting small neglected cottages, while on the left, half a dozen small trees clung to the imposing east wall of the Santa Clara convent. The wall, a bleak edifice of whitewashed stone with peeling paint and crumbling mortar, must have been at least sixty feet high, causing the street to dwell permanently in its shade. Even in the height of the summer when the sun would be at its peak, this street would still exist in the shadows of the convent church.

The house that engaged his attention was large by Spanish village standards. A single door, painted the ubiquitous dark green, with four ground floor windows, two to the left and two to the right. On the second story, five windows - all of them shuttered - ran in a straight line. The roof was the usual lichen covered tile. The walls, once white, had suffered the same neglect as the rest of the street and were now an uninviting shade of grey.

He walked slowly down the centre of the narrow road, feeling slightly sick in his stomach. The house repelled him for what it represented but at the same time beckoned him forward, teasing his morbid curiosity. And yet it was more than that. On a deep psychic level within his soul he was able to pick up an emanation from the building which, to say the least, wasn't good. There was another feeling – the feeling of being under observation, of being watched by unseen eyes and although the day was not cold, icy tendrils trickled up and down his spine.

Finally, he came to stand before the door. He tried to focus his mind on what might be beyond the threshold, but in this area his senses were dead. Knowing that the house was empty, he banged on the door with his fist just the same... Perhaps out of frustration, perhaps just for the sake of hearing the satisfyingly empty echo.

To his left a flight of steps led up to a small square; The Plaza de Santa Clara. It was a poor place, with a few scattered shrubs and plants, but at least there was some sunlight and a sense of life. There were houses facing inwards, a couple of old Andalucian lamp posts and the main entrance to the convent church.

With the house behind him, he walked slowly across the square towards a dingy bar with a dirty brown door. Santa Clara was to his left and gave off its own dark emission of negative energy. Leaning against the bar counter he ordered coffee and watched as an enormous cockroach scuttled across the sawdust that was liberally sprinkled over the filthy floor. The place stank of sweat and old beer and the barman who served him was unkempt with thick greasy hair and a badly stained denim shirt. Taking the small coffee cup, and aware of the barman's eyes following him, he went and sat on the wall outside, taking a tentative sip of the thick black liquid (which, surprisingly enough, tasted reasonably good). He lit a cigarette and studied the lay out of the square, checking to see if there was any rear access to the house. Non was apparent, but that didn't mean that one didn't exist. Checking the map of his memory, he knew that another street, Calle Vasquez, ran west to east just north of Plaza de Santa Clara: there might be access from there or an alley way or something like that...

He didn't particularly want to look in the house, but felt that he had to, like it or not. If it was Dolorean's property, it if was where he'd be bringing Alexandra, then Mage felt he had a vested interest to pry open the house's secrets.

Mage dragged hard on the Marlboro and not for the first time wondered if he might have got it all wrong. What evidence did he have to suggest that they'd be coming here other than what Alexandra had told him? Might she not have been lying or deliberately laying down a smoke screen to throw him off the scent... Yes, of course it was possible, but when he thought of *how* Alexandra had told him, he knew he was on the right track. This village, this house, his own deeply rooted feelings, both as a magician and a man, told him he was in the right place. They would be coming: he didn't know exactly when, of course, but all that he'd learned told him that it would have to be well before June and the longest day...

We're going to a place in Spain called Castillo, she had told him in a flat cold voice that was alien to her. *We're going to live there and be very happy*... But then her voice had changed into one of rising panic and he'd detected the old Alexandra in the extremes of her distress. *Oh God, there's going to be something called The Opening. He can't do it without me and, oh God, I think I'm going to die! Help me Colin... Please help me...*

The gall of anger and dispair rose in his throat and he tossed the half smoked cigarette to one side. They were by no means the last words Alexandra had spoken to him, but her plea for help was the last time she had spoken to him as Alexandra – as his wife. On the two occasions he'd spoken to her after that, Alexandra had gone and she'd become someone else. Some*thing* else.

He'd wanted to kill then and it had been a wild unbridled passion based on the human desires of revenge and remorse. He wanted to kill now, but now it was different. He was balanced and controlled – trained and educated. He'd been taken across the threshold of credibility and had been given sufficient evidence to enable him to believe in the unbelievable. To believe in the impossible. In the strength of that belief, he knew he would have to kill the thing that masqueraded as a human being called Jack Dolorean - and he would do so or die trying with a battle cry of pure joy upon his lips.

The question was, and his eyes narrowed as he squinted across the square seeing the house in a slightly different light, could he also kill his wife?

Ignatious stared out of the small window of the vestibule. He could see Mage sitting on his wall, studying the house in Calle Sombra and he felt a thrill of fear temper his earlier mood of excitement and expectancy. How dare he, this English, come into Santa Clara's holy shadow in the broad light of day, scrutinising The Master's sacred home with such loathing and obvious contempt? It was not to be tolerated for very much longer. He turned to the pock marked young Spaniard who stood languidly across the room... He was little more than eighteen, but had the aura and composure of someone much older. He was slim with thick curly hair and had the deep black eyes of the Andalucian gypsy. Thin lips and the scars of childhood chicken pox marred his beauty... Which hardly mattered, for the last thing on Ignatious's mind right then were sexual aesthetics.

'Come Lorenzo...' the priest beckoned with a podgy finger. 'The very man we have been speaking of sits drinking coffee in our square.'

Lorenzo Matan edged over to the small window and looked down into the square. Earlier he had been uncomfortable in the presence of the fat priest, but now such discomfort departed as his mind was distracted into more important and obsessive lines of thought.

'That is the man who killed my father?' he asked slowly.

'Not exactly,' Ignatious answered truthfully enough. 'Not in the sense that he stabbed him with a knife or shot him with a gun. But that is the man who is responsible for your father's death. He is a wicked evil man, a bruho, a witch, an abomination against Mother Church. He has the power of dark magic and it was with that magic that he caused Don Diego's heart to stop beating. And if you ask me why this English should do such a thing, then I shall tell you. He has come to bring trouble to our village. Your father knew this and tried to stop him...' He let it hang, watching with deep satisfaction as Diego's son nodded thoughtfully in acceptance of all that he had been told.

'He must be stopped,' Ignatious said pontifically. 'Even if it means killing him... And if you were to kill him Lorenzo, this would not be a sin... Oh dear no! It would be a most pious act of salvation and Mother Church would bless you for it...'

'I will kill him then...'

'You must be careful, he has power and he is strong!'

'I will kill him,' Lorenzo said again, ignoring the warning, 'but not for your precious church. I do it to avenge my father and for the necessary honour of my family.'

'The church will still bless you,' Ignatious told him. 'And listen, my friend, it is best done quickly. Each day this bruho is among us, it is the worse for us.'

'It shall be done this might,' Lorenzo said formally.

'We can't afford too many questions,' the priest said thoughtfully. 'Take his wallet. Make it look like a robbery.'

'I do not want this extranjero's money!' Lorenzo snorted.

'No, of course you don't, but you don't want Jaime Gomez mounting another of what he calls his major investigations. This business has nothing to do with the police, it is between the church and this English witch.'

Lorenzo looked at the fat priest with a mixture of suspicion and contempt. 'Just what were you and my father up to?' he asked astutely.

'We were up to nothing,' the priest snapped. 'Unlike you, your father was a most religious man with a great love and respect for his church. When he saw that the sanctity of his faith was being threatened, he tried to do something about it and he died for his troubles. The witch killed him just the same as if he'd stabbed him in the back or put a gun to his head.'

Lorenzo moved towards the door. As far as he was concerned, this interview was over. 'Don't worry. The extranjero is dead. His eyes will never see tomorrow morning.'

Rubbing his hands gleefully, well satisfied with the way things had gone, Ignatious went back to the window. The Englishman had left the square and was no longer anywhere to be seen – and with a little bit of luck, by the following day, he wouldn't be seen at all ever again.

Mage walked down Calle Vasquez counting off the yards in his head and trying to find some access to the rear of the house that he knew to be only a few yards away in Calle Sombra. This was bloody stupid, he told himself angrily. He should have pressed the previous owner for more details about the house when he'd had the chance. That chance had gone now, but he made a mental note to talk to Pepe Ortega again as soon as he could. God, the old man might even have a spare key and what a lot of hassle that would save! Whether Señor Ortega might give him such a key, ah well, that was a different matter altogether.

He turned right at the bottom of Vasquez which brought him into Calle Quieros and right again at the end of Quieros which brought him to Calle Ubrique. The blue Land Rover sat against the curb on the corner of Calle Sombra. Mage climbed into the cab, but rather than turning on the ignition, sat there pondering for a while.

During this second week of his time in Castillo, he had not been idle. First of all he had thoroughly quartered the village, exploring every courtyard and alleyway at least once and sometimes twice and three times. Alert to anomalies and hidden meanings in street names, he had not been too surprised to discover a Calle de Luz – The Street of Light – that backed on to the church of Santa Maria down in the southern barrio of the village. There was a Calle Sacrificio and a Calle Vaca – Sacrifice Street and Cow Street – and even a little square behind the correos called Plaza de los Angeles – The Place of the Angels. Certainly such names were ambiguous if not entirely out of place. Other names such as Plaza Zodiaco, Caminette de Bruhas Blancos, Calle Otros Mundos were, in Mage's view, not at all ambiguous. There were totally out of place and out of sympathy with all that he knew of Spanish culture and the enclosed and supposedly Catholic nature of an Andalucian hill village. A Place of the Zodiac? The Passage of White Witches? The Street of Other Worlds? – these were far from normal names for a place such as Castillo and yet, when he'd tentatively questioned Hector about the derivation of such titles, Hector had failed to see the negative connotation. When speaking with older residents of the village, they had simply shrugged. Those names had always been those names. What was odd or peculiar about them?

Mage had deliberately cultivated his friendship with Hector Sanchez although, as if by some tacit agreement, neither had spoken about the events on the night of the storm out in the campo. It was as if both knew that they would have to talk about it sooner or later, but that the time was not there and then. He'd had lunch at Calle Santana twice and, in return for their hospitality, he'd insisted on taking them out for an evening meal: they'd gone to a small bodega a few miles out of Castillo. Anna had worn a new dress and had seemed to enjoy the treat enormously. Hector had had one bottle of wine too many and had laughed a lot, but Mage had been aware of the subliminal vibration of tiredness and tension that emanated from the doctor's aura and it had seemed to Mage's trained and sober mind, that tiredness and tension were but the tip of an iceberg that delved far more deeply into the doctor's soul.

In quiet ways, Mage had also made a mark on other people in the village. He spoke their language, was never loud or impolite, always paid for his food and drink promptly and always added a fair tip. The fact that he was renting Antonia's house and was obviously a good friend of the doctor seemed to give him a passport to peoples' acceptance and goodwill rather than the natural suspicion that many new foreigners met with when they first arrived in Castillo.

He was frequently aware of being – well, not exactly watched, but certainly under a degree of observation. It worried him that he could never seem to identify the observers and there were times when he felt that the village itself was a living organism and one that monitored his every more and thought – not necessarily with malevolence, but definitely with sentience. There was something distinctly unusual about the different moods and vibrations associated with different parts of the village. The northern quadrant of Castillo, where he sat now on the corner of Calle Sombra, was always alien and detached, making him feel like an interloper and an intruder. And yet, as one crested the brow of the hill and headed down past the town hall towards El Paseo and the streets around the Hotel Miraflores, the atmosphere immediately lightened, becoming more welcoming and hospitable.

The eastern quadrant of the village was static and devoid of any kind of atmosphere until one clearly came closer to the north south divide. It was something he could not easily put into words, but even without landmarks from the higher part of Castillo, he always seemed to know when he'd crossed some kind of invisible dividing line between north and south. One street, Calle Llanette, on the easternmost periphery, had an unusual energy all of its own and Mage was mindful of the fact that according to his dowser's map, this was where two ley lines actually met and crossed. In his mind, he'd marked Calle Llanette down for closer scrutiny and investigation.

The western quadrant, incorporating the castle, was in some ways the most curious inasmuch that there always seemed to be a mood of tension in the air. Here in the oldest part of the village, Castillo seemed to be at its most sentient. Irrespective of the weather, there was always that breathlessness in the air, that atmosphere which precedes a thunder storm. Mage had walked up the long road called Calle Misericordia to explore the castle on at least half a dozen occasions, and here the north south divide was at its strongest. The Christian keep perched in a positive way as he circumnavigated the tall round tower. Three hundred and fifty yards away, the Moorish citadel was irretrievably in the north. Here Mage did not feel so well at ease. The squat square ruin with its fallen arches and faded cracked mosaics repelled him in much the same subliminal way that the Christian keep attracted him. As a Pagan he'd smiled at that thought

Midway between the two ruins, the hard packed ground rose in a slight hump. Twice Mage had stood there at the very centre of the mound, feeling the opposing forces – pulling at his awareness. To talk of good and evil or black and white was to oversimplify the situation, but there was no doubt in Mage's mind that the Christian keep pulsed out the positive while the Moorish citadel seemed to suck in the negativity. Striving hard not to oversimplify, it was still inevitable that Mage be drawn into seeing the whole fortified hill top as some sort of giant battery with the two ruins as the positive and negative terminals.

That there should be such variation and dichotomy of atmosphere in a place as small as Castillo was in itself quite remarkable but what gave Mage even further cause for concern was the way in which the mood of the village changed after dark. Castillo in the night, especially in the late of the night when the bars had closed and the streets were empty... Ah, well that Castillo was a very different place to be. It seemed bigger. Less distinct. More alive, and yet uncannily more silent.

Mage had taken to walking the village at least once a night, sometimes close to midnight, other times in the late dark just before the dawn. He always wore dark clothes and soft shoes, moving as silently and as discreetly as possible, sense on full alert for anything, anything at all that might impinge upon his psychic awareness. On these walks, he met few other nocturnal wanderers, but the sense of being under observation was always so much stronger at these times.

The break – if indeed it could be called that – had come that morning when Henry Holloway had introduced him to Pepe Ortega, a dignified Spaniard of advancing years with a face like the bark of an olive tree and a leonine main of snow white hair.

Mage had fallen into the habit of taking at least a coffee if not breakfast each morning in The Miraflores. The ambience suited him and as it was a place much patronised by Castillo's expatriate community, he felt that sooner or later he might come into contact with some useful piece of gossip or information.

The conversation that morning had been on the subject of property speculation – something, which by all accounts, Henry was dead set against.

'I don't mind when somebody comes to the village, buys a house and settles down here, but when somebody buys a house, does it up a bit then flogs it on again less than a year later for twice the price, it makes my blood boil!'

'Does it happen often?' Mage had asked over the rim of his cup.

'No not really, but often enough. You take Pepe, here. Sold his house behind the church in Calle Sombra to Peter Cortez, who's a nasty bugger at the best of times. Half English, half Spanish and the worst of both breeds. Anyway, Cortez gives Pepe half a million euros and everyone's happy, but then damn me, a month later, Cortez sells it on to an English couple for a cool straight million, which if you ask me is not just plain greedy, it's downright bloody dishonest. Cortez must have had that couple tucked away in his back pocket all along.'

'It would not have been so bad had I liked the Englishman,' Pepe Ortega had added. 'but I did not. Already he had tried to buy my house on a number of occasions, but because I did not like him I told him it was not for sale. Obviously Señor Dolorean was determined to have it at any price and my only consolation is that if he paid Pedro Cortez a million euros for it, he paid half a million too much.'

Mage's bowels felt as though they'd turned to water. 'Excuse me, but what was the Englishman's name again?'

'Dolorean,' Henry had chipped in. 'Easy name to remember because it's the same as that sports car bloke who went broke in Ireland a few years ago, which wouldn't mean a thing to you unless you were heavily into sports cars. I actually met that Dolorean once at Earls Court in 1986 and he was a great fellow, not like this other spastic turdburglar that's bought Pepe's place.'

'You met him?' Mage had asked carefully.

'Yes, he stayed here for a night about eighteen months ago. A very cold fish and the only reason that I remember him so well is that he was so bloody humourless. We were having an impromptu party here in the bar and although he never complained directly, you could see he wasn't too pleased with all the noise... Oh yes, and the other thing is, he scared one of my girls!'

'How did he do that?' Mage had kept his voice very neutral, suppressing all emotion.

'Silly bitch's fault more than his, I suspect. She said that he looked at her in a funny way. Looked right through her, she said. Made her feel dirty. Don't remember all the details, you know, more than a year ago and all that, but she told me that unless I threw him out right there and then she was leaving. Well, we weren't that busy and the guy was a paying guest and frankly I thought she was making a fuss over nothing so I called her bluff.'

'What happened?'

'She left. Packed her bags and was gone in half and hour. Silly cow went to her mother's in Algerciras and, damn me, a couple of weeks later she'd gone into a convent somewhere near Huelva. Shame really because 'till then Teresa had always been a good little girl. A good little worker.'

'What about Mr Dolorean?'

'Shit, he just stayed that one night and I never saw him after that. When I think back on it now I wish I'd told him to go and that I'd hung on to Teresa... Just wasn't taking her seriously and than there was the principle of the thing.'

'So, did Mr Dolorean stay in the village?' Mage had asked, already knowing the answer to his question.

'No.' Pepe had shaken his head. 'He came and went and went and came maybe three of four times in the year – although I do not think he has been here this year. I sold my house to Señor Cortez in October and Dolorean was here to buy it from him in December. But that was nearly five months ago. Perhaps...' There had been a subtle shift in the old Spaniard's tone. 'Perhaps he will visit Castillo again soon.'

'What did you think of him?' Mage had prompted. 'What was it that made you not want to sell him your property?'

Pepe Ortega had finished his drink with a flourish then had met Mage's inquisitive look defiantly, daring him to laugh or be dismissive. 'It is as the girl Teresa said. He had dirty eyes. He looked at me and made *me* feel dirty also.'

'Yes Pepe,' Henry had come to Mage's rescue, 'but what exactly do you mean by dirty?'

'Just dirty.' Pepe Ortega had pulled on an old cloth cap, nodded politely to Mage and Henry, then had turned and walked out of the bar.

Mage had found him half an hour later. The old man was sitting in a quiet corner of Jacinto's staring moodily into any empty brandy glass. Mage had brought a fresh drink from the bar and placing it next to the old man's glass, had sat opposite the Spaniard and waited.

Clean morning sunshine had filtered in from the street causing harsh shadows. In the distance, somewhere beyond the kitchen, a radio had been playing Sevillanas. In the lightest of ways, a gossamer touch of reassurance, Mage had reached out and stroked the old man's mind. *It is all right Pepe Ortega. I understand you. I am friend, not foe. Help me. Trust me.*

Ortega had looked up, eyes hard and cold, mouth set in a grim line. 'I knew that you would follow me, but until now I did not know why.'

'Why, Señor Ortega?'

'Why?' Pepe Ortega's voice had dripped with contempt. 'You already know why! Do not play games with me, extranjero! You are the same as the other one!'

'Oh no, Señor Pepe, no, no, no...' Mage had breathed fervently, leaning across the table. 'Please believe me, my friend, I'm not like him at all! I beg you, let me show you. Let me prove it to you...'

Ortega had looked doubtful, but obviously impressed by Mage's sincerity, nodded slightly.

Mage had opened himself and had drawn the old man in. *Come on Señor Pepe, see me as a child, see my grandmother, Elsie Maud – you'd have liked her had you ever been able to meet her. See butterflies and wild flowers and beautiful songs and poems. See my strengths and also my weaknesses. See the work I've done over the years trying to help people. See my spirit, feel my fears, and know that this other man who also touched your mind is my bitterest and deadly enemy.*

He touched my mind too, and he even robbed me of my mind for a while, and he robbed me of something even more precious than that. I am not like him Don Pepe, and I do not make you feel dirty, do I...?

After a moment Pepe Ortega had lowered his eyes. 'No Señor,' he had spoken very quietly. 'You do not make me feel dirty. You make me feel very frightened.'

'That is because I also am very frightened,' Mage had said soberly. 'I'm frightened of the man called Dolorean and I am frightened about what is going to happen when he comes here again – and you were right. He is coming soon.'

Ortega had nodded thoughtfully, then had got up and had gone to the bar returning with another small balloon of brandy and a cafe solo.

'I need to ask questions,' he'd said flatly.

'I will try to answer honestly,' Mage had responded.

'I will know if you don't, won't I?' There had been just a shadow of humour in his voice. 'Perhaps in the same way that I knew it would be all right to bring myself more brandy while for you it must be coffee. How do I know that you will not drink brandy, Señor Mage? Tell me, how do I know that?'

The afternoon shadows began to lengthen as Mage sat motionless on the squeaky plastic seat. Calle Sombra took on deeper hues as shades of – menace? – edged along the street towards him. He wondered if there really would be any point in going back to Pepe Ortega in search of a key? After a conversation that had lasted for more than an hour on the complex subjects of clairvoyance and psychism, a conversation that had stretched his command of the Spanish language to breaking point, he reflected that tact might be the better part of valour. He might ask when next they met and he'd make sure that it was soon, if there was a rear entrance and would judge the advisability of any further requests on the old man's response to that. As for Calle Sombra, he would return later that night or in the early hours and put a hex upon the door. He might as well make things as difficult for Dolorean as he could. Allowing that thought to bring a tight smile of small satisfaction to his lips, he turned on the ignition and putting the Land Rover into gear, drove off in a cloud of blue smoke towards Calle Granadillos, some meditation and preparation for his for forthcoming night's work.

Angel lay stretched out on the tiny balcony, naked but for a pair of shorts. The late afternoon sun was pleasantly warm on his skin and he dozed in that half state between sleep and wakefulness. The siesta was valuable, for these last three nights had been full of dreams and he'd woken each morning just as tired as he'd been the night before. He could not remember the dreams, at least none of the details, but they'd been filled with a sense of threat and excitement and all seemed to revolve around the Englishman, his El Moreno, this Colin Mage.

By nature, Angel was neither secretive nor shy, but he held his privacy closely to him like a cloak and either by accident or design, did not associate with other groups of his age in and around the village. He took some small romantic delight in seeing himself as a mysterious lone wolf, but suspected that the truth of the matter was that he was just a loner – which was something very different indeed.

But Angel knew that he was *different*. He could neither verbalise that difference nor identify it to his own satisfaction, but it was there and had always been there, even before his parents had been killed. That such an intangible thing could draw an invisible fine line that separated him from other people, was a mystery in itself. Certainly he'd had friends as a child and while he was at school, indeed, he had friends now – but not *close* friends, not *groups* of friends that provided a sense of camaraderie. No girl friend with whom he could share intimacies and secrets.

If he had to put his finger on any one thing that represented this difference, it was that he knew things. He didn't know how he knew, he just did. For example, he knew that Colin Mage, the Englishman, was good, while Jaime Gomez, the policeman, was bad. That Señor Mage was in some unfathomable way important, while Jaime Gomez only thought he was important. He'd known that there was going to be an accident the day that his parents had been killed – he'd tried to warn them but as might have been expected, they'd paid no attention and he'd sat in the back seat of the old Fiat all the way from Ubrique waiting for it to happen - and, of course, it had happened.

He knew that Anna Sanchez wasn't very well and that he father the doctor was very worried about something other than his daughter's health. He'd known that his Grandfather Jacobo was going to die two days before the old man's heart had suddenly stopped beating. For two days the old man had carried a dark cloud across his shoulders that had spelt death in soft and gentle letters. Angel had said nothing. What was there to say? Who would have believed him had he spoken out and what difference would it have made? Death was death and if death was coming, then there was nothing he could do to stop it.

He knew that most of the drugs that came into Castillo from La Linea and Algerciras came through Lorenzo Bautista Matan and his two brothers; he knew that Jaime Gomez also knew this, but chose not to do anything about it. He'd known that the prostitute in Campamento had been dirty even as she'd been opening her legs for him, and he knew that one day he'd had venereal disease – at the best a bad case of herpes – and the next day he hadn't. This was impossible. He knew that it was impossible and Doctor Sanchez had told him it was impossible, but it had happened just the same.

Angel was young and his academic education had left much to be desired, but he was a bright boy and nobody's fool. He had his eyes and his ears, and other senses, all of which told him that there was something wrong in his village of Castillo de la Frontera, something indefinable that had been subtly changing degree by degree over many weeks and months and that whatever it was, it had something to do with El Moreno's presence in his grandmother's house up on Calle Granadillos. He had no idea how he was able to make this link, but in his mind the link was firmly made and he did not fear it for he strongly sensed that El Moreno was here to help rather than to do harm or damage.

To say that Angel had become somewhat obsessed with Colin Mage might be something of an overstatement, but there was something and, oh yes, it might be a wild fantasy, but if he felt it to be real then who was to say that it was not real, at least to him? Something that made him feel that he and El Moreno were two of a kind. Two lone wolves who knew things! He had not forgotten the circumstances of their first meeting a fortnight past and, oh yes, Señor Mage knew a few things all right!

His thoughts became hazy and he drifted off into a deeper sleep, lulled by the springtime breeze and the sound of his grandmother's gentle snoring from the patio below. Antonia had been sitting in their small garden, trying to read, but like her grandson she'd been wooed by the first real summer's day of the year and now the book was pushed to one side and her head had fallen backwards, coming to rest on the edge of her chair.

Angel dreamed of a pure young girl who delighted in doing sexual things to his body – and woke to the sound of chairs being drawn up around the patio table. There was the murmur of voices and the clink of glasses.

'Forgive me for interrupting your siesta...' A male voice, familiar.

'Give it no thought. We all sleep too much at our age! Will you take beer or juice, or shall I make tea?'

'Just a little water, thank you.'

Angel listened to the sound of liquid gurgling into a glass.

'Now Pepe, what brings you to see me on this fine afternoon?'

Ah, so it was Pepe Ortega...

'Antonia, I need to ask you about this extranjero who rents your house...'

Angel's ears pricked up and he was instantly alert.

'Oh?' his grandmother's voice was quizzical. 'What is it that you want to know and why do you need to know it?'

'I cannot explain my need... At least, not easily, and not in a way that you might understand...' Ortega sounded uncomfortable. 'I had hoped that on the strength of our many years of friendship you might answer some questions for me...'

'Well yes, that is fair enough, but tell me, what are these questions?'

'Señor Mage, your tenant. What do you know about him?'

'Not a great deal. He arrived in the village two weeks ago looking for somewhere to rent. Angel met him in Jacinto's and took him to see Granadillos. He liked it and money changed hands and that is where he now lives. He has paid me a fair price and he has paid in advance. Apparently he is a writer and now writes a book about psychology. More than that, I do not know what to tell you...'

'You yourself have met him?' Ortega asked.

'Yes, I have met him three times, I think. Angel brought him to see me the second day and then we shared a drink on market day at the Paseo Bar and, the last time, we talked for a while at the corner of Calle Santana...about the storm of last week and the weather... Nothing of great consequence.'

'Antonia, tell me, what do you think about this man? What do you feel about him.'

'I'm not sure I understand your question Pepe, but in trying to answer as best I can, then I must tell you that I like this extranjero. I like him very much. He is polite and there is a good feel to him and I certainly have no qualms about him living in my house. Now Pepe, you must tell me what all these questions are about.'

'How are you feeling these days, Antonia?'

'I'm well, thank you, but what does that have to do with it?'

'Antonia, you and I drank wine not three weeks ago at the wedding of Nieve Agutierez and Estaban Redondo. Not only did you look ill on that day, you told me that you felt ill. That the arthritis was getting worse in your hands and your legs and your hips, and that you had to go very slowly to get anywhere, and that you never travelled far without your walking sticks... And yet, Antonia, here you are today looking fresher and healthier than I can remember seeing you since Jacobo died and I watched you this morning walking up the hill from Tobias the ironmonger – true, you had one stick with you and you were not running, but you were walking well and without the accompanying stiffness that has been with you these last few years...'

'Yes,' Antonia sounded exasperated, 'these things are true. I do feel really quite fit and healthy and a lot of the arthritic pain has eased off and gone away, but I still don't know what this has to do with my renting my old house to an Englishman!'

'Has he ever held your hand, Antonia?'

'Yes, I'm sure he must have done. It is the custom to shake hands with people you know.'

'No, no, Antonia. I do not ask if you have shaken hands with this man, but if he has ever actually held your hand – and you have felt something pass between you?'

There was a pause before Antonia said, 'You had better tell me where this is all leading to, Pepe Ortega.'

Angel was immediately aware that there was now a different note to his grandmother's tone – and also that she had not answered Ortega's question.

'Very well, I shall tell you, but you must promise that you will not laugh at me and that you will keep what I tell you to yourself.'

'This is all very mysterious, but yes I promise what you ask.'

'Good, then listen... This extranjero and I were talking this morning about a number of things... We were actually talking about my house in Calle Sombra and your Señor Mage was very very interested in its new owner, another extranjero, who apparently is Señor Mage's enemy. The new owner comes soon and, when he does, I think that there is going to be a terrible fight between these two men, but it will not be an ordinary fight, because both of these men are powerful witches and they will use their magic against each other!'

'Pepe, this is impossible! I've never heard so much rubbish!'

'No, you must *listen*,' Ortega insisted. 'Both men have the evil eye and I know this because I have met both men and I have seen it in both men... The man called Dolorean who bought my house is the truly evil one, but your Señor Mage has this power too, although I know he can use it for good as well as for bad and I know this to be true for he gave me a demonstration of his power this very day, and I am grateful to him for the pain he saves me...

'Antonia, we were in Jacinto's talking about things psychological and he was explaining to me how, if it is trained properly, one mind can reach out and touch another mind without there having to be any words. I told him I didn't believe him and he said he could prove it to me if I so wished. I challenged him to do so, and he asked if he could hold my hand for a moment and when I gave him my hand he told me all about Isabella and how she had died, and he told me all about little Pablito and how he was happy in his new home in Ronda and how much he had liked the rocking horse present I had given him at Christmas and The Three Kings. He also told me about the pain of fire I have in my belly and, just as Sanchez has also told me, he has told me that this pain in caused by an ulcer and that I must stop drinking alcohol and avoid any kind of citrus in both my food and my drink. And then, and this is the most important thing, he told me that he would take away some of the pain and start the healing process, but that it wouldn't work for very long unless I did something more to help myself. Antonia, what could I say... I simply nodded and allowed him to take my other hand and... I do not know how to say this, but something came into me from him through one hand, and something went out of me into him through the other hand, and immediately, *immediately* Antonia, the fire in my belly eased off. Almost as though someone had poured a bucket of water over a campfire in the forest. My belly is still sore and it feels like it's been kicked by a mule, but that sharp fire pain has gone... And so I have come to you to talk about this, to alert you to the fact that your extranjero has this great power and also to warn you that there is some enormous trouble ahead. Now I am very confused. I do not know what to think and I do not know what to do!'

'Then Pepe Ortega, I shall tell you. First, you do as Señor Mage has told you and you stop drinking and you stop eating citrus in your food. Secondly, you thank God that there is someone in this world who can take away pain. Thirdly, you remember your debt to this man and return a favour if he asks for it. And fourthly, you keep you mouth shut and speak of this business to no-one. Tell no-one what you have told me and let kindness be repaid with kindness. If others might have reason to fear Señor Mage, it is between them and Señor Mage. You and I Pepe, we have nothing to fear, but much to be grateful and thankful fore, so I say to you again, say nothing.'

There was the sound of chairs being scraped back from the table. 'Antonia,' there was a note of pleading in Ortega's voice. 'Antonia, of course I will do as you say, but please God tell me one thing. Tell me that I am not imagining this. Tell me that you also have felt this man's power.'

There was a short pause. Angel held his breath, and then: 'I have felt it,' his grandmother said.

Angel was confused. Something strange was happening. He'd been following El Moreno at a very discreet distance all over the village. The Englishman had followed a very circuitous route, criss crossing his own pathway backwards and forwards all around the northern part of Castillo, frequently pausing at street corners and lowering his head as if in prayer while pressing his hands against the walls. It was almost three o'clock in the morning, they'd been walking since just after midnight and Angel was getting tired. What kept him awake and very much alert was the fact that he knew something important was happening and that he in some small way was a part of it. What intensified Angel's wild sense of excitement was the knowledge that someone else was also following Mage! It became like a game of spies or cops and robbers...Angel following the follower who followed El Moreno. It was too dark to see faces, but the other shadow that had slipped between himself and the Englishman had emerged from behind Cita Contrabando, The Smuggler's Bar, at the bottom of Calle Loba. Cita Contrabando had a bad reputation and people who frequented that place also had a bad reputation and Angel hung further back, on the premise that anyone who had furtively come out of Cita Contrabando was up to no good.

Now, there was a pause in the proceedings. Mage sat in the middle of Plaza de Santa Clara, almost looking straight at Angel, who stood watching from the shadows of Calle Sombra. Eighty metres beyond Mage the other shadow melted against the north west corner of the church. What was happening here? Did El Moreno know he was being watched? Was he waiting now for his followers to make a mistake?

Angel stood stock still, wishing that Calle Sombra offered more cover and concealment and was caught unawares when Mage suddenly got to his feet and started marching purposefully towards him. Angel took an involuntary step backwards and stumbled against the door of the house that he'd been leaning against. The door creaked open just enough to enable Angel to squeeze inside and he thanked his stars that these few small cottage houses in Calle Sombra were mostly derelict or empty.

Taking care not to kick anything over, Angel eased the door shut and tiptoed to the window. Here he had a clear view out into part of the street, confident that he himself could not be seen. A lamp, about thirty metres away in the square cast a pool of very dim light over the short flight of steps down into Calle Sombra enabling him to see something of the big house a few metres away at the end of the street.

Colin Mage came silently down the steps and stopped immediately outside the front door of the big house. Casting a cautious look around him, he then took something from the inside pocket of his jacket and laid it on the front step. A half second later, there was a spark of flame from a match, and Angel watched as the Englishman ignited a small bundle of candles, five or six of them, slim and no more than four inches long, seemingly bound together with cotton or twine. Angel strained for a better view. Yes, now in the light of the candles, he could see that there were five of them... Four white ones with a dark one in the middle. Then El Moreno raised his arms like the Christos and said something in a language that wasn't Spanish and Angel didn't think it was English either. The intonation sounded like a prayer, but what kind of prayer was said out in the street at three o'clock in the morning in front of an empty house and to the flame of a black candle even if there were four other white candles burning all around it?

Mage lowered his arms, then taking a pace of two forwards, rested his hands first on the door jars, then on the lintel, and then on the door itself. 'Cursed and restrained may all be who cross this threshold,' he spoke quietly repeating the line three times...Then summoning the gall of his ire, he spat profusely, watching with a degree of vicious satisfaction as his spittle dribbled down the old green wood. Then he took three steps backwards, raising his arms again briefly, palms up in supplication to the night sky, before lowering hands and arms to his sides.

From the corner of his left eye Angel saw something move quickly towards the Englishman from the long and empty street behind. A flash of steel in the street light was but a fleeting impression. Without any indication that he was aware of the impending attack, the Englishman suddenly turned to face his assailant, standing easy and still, legs slightly splayed. Lorenzo Bautista emerged into Angel's line of vision, a long switch blade knife held menacingly blade up in his right hand. His face was pulled into one of the most evil smiles Angel had ever seen as he slowly closed on his victim. To Angel's eyes, it was a poor match. Lorenzo was tall and lithe and young while El Moreno was older, shorter and unarmed.

'Can I help you?' Mage asked quietly.

'You can help me by dying,' Lorenzo spat at him.

'We all have to do that some time,' Mage offered conversationally.

'You will die now, for me!' Lorenzo moved closer, to within knife striking distance.

'Why should I do that?' Mage had not moved and seemed genuinely unruffled by the whole proceedings.

'You have killed my father!'

'Ah...' A long sigh escaped Mage's lips. 'And would, by any chance, your father be a gentleman called Diego who was taken ill at the Hotel Miraflores a couple of weeks ago? And would you...' Mage paused, and to Angel's ears, it almost seemed as though the Englishman was playing with the Spaniard, '...And would you then be that gentleman's son? Shall I call you Lorenzo?'

'Yes, I am Lorenzo and my father was Diego. You killed him and now you will die for it.'

'Ah, so you think I killed your father do you? Now I wonder who can have put that idea into your silly head...' Mage laughed. 'Okay, you think I killed your daddy. I promise you that I didn't, but I can see nothing is going to convince you otherwise. So come on, my friend. Kill me if you can.'

With a small cry, Lorenzo lunged. In a fluid movement, Mage swayed to one side and, as the switchblade went three feet wide of where Mage's head should have been, Mage's right foot came up faster than lightening and crashed upwards between the Spaniard's open and unbalanced legs. No cry escaped Lorenzo's mouth for even as he gasped for air to shriek with pain, the heel of Mage's right hand smashed into his nose, breaking it at once; a split millisecond later the fingers of Mage's left hand jabbed deeply into his assailant's throat. With a sigh, Lorenzo began to topple, but not before Mage had grabbed the knife arm, twisting it as the Spaniard fell and causing it to crack with broken bone, midway between the elbow and the wrist.

It was all over in less than two seconds. Angel watched from his hiding place, not believing what he had seen. But it was not over yet. Mage towered above Lorenzo, who was now flat on his back, and the Englishman still had firm hold of the Spaniard's wrist. 'Who sent you?' he asked. 'Who told you that I was responsible for your father's death?'

'You go to hell...' Lorenzo managed to gasp between breathless bloody sobs.

Mage reached over with his other hand and gently embraced Lorenzo's first and second finger. With a sharp backwards snap, he dislocated the fingers at the knuckle bone, bringing his foot down across Lorenzo's mouth the stifle the scream and allowing it to emerge as a gagging gargle.

Mage took the other two fingers. 'Now I'll ask you again. Who sent you. Tell me quickly but tell me no lie because I *know* who sent you and I simply want to hear it from your own lips.'

'You...'

Mage broke the Spaniard's other two fingers and kicked him hard in the side of the face. 'You tell me now my little one, or...' Mage knelt and rested his left thumb against Lorenzo's right eye. '... or I'll take your eyes from you.'

'It was the priest,' Lorenzo managed to whisper in a desperate whimper.

'Which priest...' Mage increased the pressure on the eyeball.

'Ignatious... It was Ignatious...' The fear in Lorenzo's voice rasped against the silence of the convent wall and Mage let him go.

'Yes, Ignatious the priest it is...' Mage's voice sounded hard and devoid of emotion. 'Well, you go back to your priest and tell him that if he wants me dead, next time he's not to send a boy with a knife. Tell him to send a spirit or a genie or the Djinn. Tell him to send Jadoc Dolorean. No man can end my life at this time and no man can move me from this place. Now, can you remember all that, Little Lorenzo?'

'Yes... Yes...' Lorenzo was now weeping as much as gagging with the waves of excruciating pain that engulfed his bruised and badly damaged body.

'Good.' Mage stood up. 'And I'm sorry that I hurt you, but if I see you again Lorenzo Bautista, especially anywhere near this village, I'll have your eyes. Remember that, my friend. Next time we meet I shall take your eyes.'

Mage looked back at the house. The five candles were flickering brightly on the doorstep and were burning down quickly into a coagulating mass of hot grey wax – just as they were meant to do. Then he looked once directly at Angel's window, rooting Angel – Angel who had seen everything and had heard everything – to the spot with the heart pounding fear of discovery. Finally, with a sad half smile the Englishman turned and strode off into the shadows of Calle Sombra, his foot falls echoing in counterpoint to Lorenzo's muffled and semi conscious moans that echoed upwards from the blood stained pavement.

9.

Evaluations

Jaime Gomez looked at his notebook and tried to find a pattern to some of the tales he'd been told. Lorenzo Matan was in the clinic at La Linea with an impressive list of injuries; someone had done a good job of giving him a long overdue beating – but Lorenzo wasn't saying who.

The list, Jaime mused, was a long one. Broken nose, broken teeth, broken arm, four broken fingers, one sprained wrist and two very badly bruised testicles. It would be a while before this strutting little peacock of a bully boy returned to Castillo – if indeed he ever did. Hs pride and street credibility were irreparably damaged for ever and Lorenzo would be in no hurry to hang his head in shame before his brothers and other village cronies.

As to who had attacked him, Jaime neither knew nor particularly cared. It had probably been a couple of middle men from Algerciras responding to some internecine strife between Lorenzo and the big boys down on the coast. Either way, they'd done a very professional job and he was thankful for it. At least it might halt the flow of drugs coming into the village for a while – unless Lorenzo's two dim-witted brothers thought they could do something on their own. Unfortunately neither Curo nor Rubio Matan had the brains they were born with: Lorenzo had the brains whilst his two brothers had the brawn.

Jaime reviewed the sequence of events. Apparently, the Guadiaro boy had been out walking his dog...

At half past four in the morning? Jaime didn't like that. It didn't ring true. Angel Guadiaro had said that he couldn't sleep so he'd taken the dog out for a pre-dawn stroll around the village. Instinctively Jaime knew this was a lie, but it was what the boy was saying and because Jaime didn't have any evidence to suggest otherwise, then he'd have to accept it at its face value for the time being.

According to Angel, he'd found Lorenzo lying on the pavement in Calle Sombra, bleeding and barely conscious. So, Angel had gone to the Matan house and had roused the family. Curo and Rubio had gone to Calle Sombra for their brother and, while Angel had returned to his own home, the two brothers had driven Lorenzo the twenty miles to the clinic in La Linea...

Why hadn't they taken him to Sanchez?

Rubio and Curo had said that Lorenzo had insisted on being taken to the clinic, and that besides, they themselves could see that it was too big a thing for Doctor Sanchez to sort out on his own. And who had done this thing to their brother? They didn't know – and Jaime, who prided himself on being able to spot a lie a fifty paces, had believed them. Oh, he'd get to the bottom of it all sooner or later, but for now he was content to collate the details. Details were everything. You got one version of details from one person, then another version from someone else, then a third variation from a third. Then you mixed everything together and got the overall picture seeing not so much what was there but what was missing. In pursuit of that which was missing, you found the ultimate truth, discovered who was lying and why, and cracked the case on that basis. It was not a foolproof formula, but it had worked well enough for him for more than twenty odd years.

Selecting a cigarette from the crumpled blue and white packet of Ducados, he lit it and walked over to the open window. The town hall clock was just chiming eleven and the bright morning sunshine threw the street below into a freeze of dancing shadows. The air was cool and clear and willingly took his smoke plumes up into the impenetrable blue of the wide Spanish sky.

In any country, any police force, you had to have a lucky break sometimes. His break had come that morning when the physician from La Linea had telephoned: "Got one of your village lads here, Jefe. Taken a beating... Name of Lorenzo Bautista Matan. You know him?... Yes, thought you might... No, he isn't going anywhere for a few days... Right. I'll expect you..."

Jaime had driven down to the clinic and had interviewed a bandage swathed Lorenzo at his bedside and the two brothers as well: then he'd come back to Castillo and had rousted Angel Guadiaro from his bed and got his story, and had been back in his own office and all before ten o'clock and in enough time to put that old bitch Marushi Matan in her place.

She'd come barging in a little after ten. 'My son has been beaten and nearly killed and you, you fat pig, you sit here drinking coffee as though nothing has happened. You should get out and catch the bastards who have done this thing to my sweet and innocent boy.'

Jaime Gomez had not been kind. 'Sweet and innocent little shit. The boy's a thug. A criminal. A hoodlum. He is a thief and he brings drugs into this village with the help of your other two precious sons and some mutual friends in the docklands of Algerciras!'

'It is a lie!' Marushi had screeched.

'It is not a lie! How else do you think those boys of yours pay for their cigarettes and their drinks, not to mention their car and their expensive jeans and shoes! You know they are an evil trio, just as your husband knew before he died. Looking at the three little shitheads he spawned, no wonder he died. I dare say he probably died of shame!'

'Cunjo!' Marushi had snarled at him.

'Cunja!' Jaime had snarled back.

'If this is true,' she'd towered above the table smelling of sweat and garlic, her ample bosoms quivering with rage. 'If this is true, why have you not arrested my children, hah! Answer me that one, you fat Catalonian fascist!'

'Because, you stupid Andalucian cow, while the Bautistas bring the drugs into the village, I know who brings it. I know where it comes from and I know where it goes. If they don't bring it is someone else will and that way I'll have to start all over again trying to control the flow of hard stuff!'

'My boys don't deal in it,' Marushi had bellowed. 'And even if they do, what harm does a little marijuana or hashish do to anyone? Who in Spain does not enjoy a little smoke now and then!'

'Marijuana and cannabis is one thing, cocaine and crack is another. Now get out of here Marushi Bautista because you're annoying me and if you annoy me any more I'm liable to use the evidence that I've got to put your three little bastards into jail for a lot of long years.'

White and frightened but still furious, Marushi had gone, leaving the policeman alone to savour the pleasure of her discomfort. God, he hated these Andalucian peasants! The women in particular! It was all a far cry from his days in Barcelona and Madrid and even in Marbella there had been a sense of metropolitan life; he was a city man who appreciated big cities. That was where policemen were real, where there was real police work to be done. But out here in the campo, it was a joke! How the fuck in hell had he ended up in this dump of a mountain village? – he remembered, but not liking the memories, forced his thoughts to race on. How wonderful it might be to live in America, or even South Africa. The police in those places at least got to use their guns occasionally and at least they were respected by the majority of the populace.

Once it had even been like that in Spain, when El Caudillo Franco had been alive! There hadn't been a drugs problem then, had there! Holy Saints, you even had to work hard to see a drunken Spaniard out on the pavements in those days! Young girls had had chaperones and you certainly never saw them smoking and drinking and cavorting in public the way they did now. Restaurants and bars closed at proper times, the beaches were free of nudity and sex was a thing that happened in the sanctity of the bedroom for the sake of procreation – and if you were lucky, just a little physical pleasure and release for two people who were in love and formally bound to each other with the blessings of God state and family. Those were the days when there had been a dignity to the Spanish character and a state of order. A rule of law.

That had been the police force he had joined as a raw recruit in 1962. Ten years later Franco had died and the whole thing had gone to put! There'd been one brief flicker of hope in 1982, but that insipid weak idiot Juan Carlos had come down in favour of the modernists and Jefe Tejero had gone to jail – along with a number of his most ardent and active supporters, of which Jaime Gomez had been one. He supposed he'd been lucky. He'd missed out on a prison sentence, but had been drummed out of the Guardia Civil and had ended up sticking molta tickets on car windscreens in Marbella.

It had taken four long years to get his sergeant's stripes back, but even then, a sergeant in the municipal police was a world away from being a sergeant lieutenant in the Guardia. Another four years of hard slog had got him his captaincy, but instead of sending him back to Barcelona, he'd ended up as Chief of Police in this crummy dump... And that also was a joke, wasn't it. Chief of Police! He was nominally in charge of two youngsters who didn't know their arse from their elbow, both of whom were closely related to the mayor, and a mayor who was virtually, if not quite, a fucking communist!

With a loathing born of the deepest contempt, Jaime Gomez hated the village of Castillo and if anything, he hated the Castillatos even more. The only thing that incensed him more than that were the extranjeros. The foreigners. There were far too many of them – in Spain at large and in this village in particular. If he could have his way, he'd expel the lot of them tomorrow!

He was fifty nine years old and he knew that unless something very important came along to change things, he would spend the next six years of his life stuck on the Godforsaken hill top with very little to look forward to after that. He prayed for a miracle... And although he had no real belief in such things, felt that there might – just might – be one in the offing. He did not believe in God, the saints, Christ, or The Virgin Mary – but something, someone who'd *said* she was The Virgin Mary, had come to him the other day in a dream or a vision – he didn't know what to call it really – and had told him to be ready. A miracle of change was at hand.

Jaime Gomez was the most level headed and practical of men. Spirits and visions were not a part of his world... But he'd seen something that night, one week ago, that had been extra ordinary... A phantom like female figure swathed in a pale blue mesmerising light that told him things were going to change and that he must be ready for the changes. By the time he'd got out of his chair and had marched across the room, the apparition had disappeared, but the visions still haunted his eyes and the voice still whispered teasingly in his ears.

One part of Jaime said that because this could not have happened it therefore did not happen and he had imagined it – but another part of him said that because he was not given to wild imaginings, he had seen exactly what he'd seen and that it was real. This dichotomy of mental attitude gave Jaime a problem and one that was not easily resolved. Thus, he chose to react to it in a policeman's way. He would wait for more evidence... But in the meantime that part of him that longed for change was reassured by the memory of the voice that had promised that change was on its way. There was little doubt in Jaime's mind that he would be ready for it when it came. If it came.

A little before noon Lorenzo woke from a light and frightening sleep. The extranjero's face danced in front of him and again he remembered the Englishman's words and the expression on his face when he'd said them. 'I shall take you eyes, Lorenzo: I shall have your eyes.'

There was not a fragment of doubt in Lorenzo's mind that this was not the truth and although there was a yearning desire for justice and revenge that fermented below the threshold of his physical pain, the fear of the English witch's threat was ten times greater.

'Do you want anything Lorenzo?' Curo asked from the bedside chair.

'Go and get the priest,' Lorenzo wheezed with some difficulty.

'Why, you're not dying or anything, are you?' There was alarm in the younger brother's voice.

'No but I want you to fetch the priest. Ignatious. From Santa Clara.'

'What if he won't come?' the other asked.

'Just tell him I'm here – and he'll come,' Lorenzo muttered confidently.

Lorenzo's confidence was misplaced, however, for by the time Curo had driven back to Castillo and located the priest, it was well into the afternoon. Not only had Ignatious already heard of Lorenzo's demise, it had caused him to miss his lunch with worry. Not for the well-being of Lorenzo Bautista Matan, but over what he should do now. He was both irritated and dismissive of Curo.

'Tell you brother to come and talk to me when he returns to Castillo,' he said shortly.

'Okay – but I don't think Lorenzo's going to be pleased about that. He said to come and fetch you.'

'I am far too busy to leave right now – maybe I'll try and get down there this evening, or for goodness sake, there must be a telephone at the clinic. Tell Lorenzo to phone me if he needs to talk. Here, I'll write the number down for you.'

'So you're not coming then?'

'I've already told you that I can't. I have other things to do which are, quite frankly, more important.'

Curo left, scrap of paper in hand, wondering what he was going to tell Lorenzo, and Ignatious watched him go, also wondering about Lorenzo. He fervently hoped that Lorenzo would not be in too much of a hurry to return home and realised that he would have to talk to him before he did, just to make sure that he would keep his mouth shut. He'd threaten him with excommunication if he had to – anything to make sure that he, Ignatious, was kept out of it all. He also wondered what had gone wrong. Lorenzo was strong and savage in his desire to avenge Diego's death... and yet here he was now, languishing in the clinic with all kinds of ailments. Obviously the Englishman had done this to him; there was no one else that it could be and this also worried Ignatious, for clearly the Englishman was more powerful than he'd first thought and – dare he think this? – had been led to believe.

He walked up the aisle of the church, and passing through the vestry, entered his own private apartments. He locked the doors and drew the curtains, then, sitting at his desk, brought out a large rough hewn stone from the cupboard of the desk and placed it on the desk in front of him. The stone, about the size of a small loaf of bread, was fundamentally dark grey with striated seams of some shiny crystal ore criss-crossing its craggy surface. Ignatious had never seen a stone like it before and it had taken some time for him to believe in all that it could do... Ah yes, now it was dull and lifeless, but if he placed his hands upon it and prayed, thinking of the master and using some of the key words that the master had taught him, then the stone came to life! The crystals shone and the stone vibrated with a subtle thrum of energy that was a life force in its own right.

He had used the stone sparingly, realising that its power was not of this earth but came directly from God and the master: the last time he had used it had been when he and Diego, along with Pedro Cortez and his wife Miriam, had all sat around the table together, fingers pressed against the glowing crystals, thinking of the English witch, this enemy Colin Mage, and had directed the darkness of illness and sorrow against him. And had the Englishman not been ill! Indeed he had, for four days he had suffered with a great fever!

Ignatious had not known what might happen... Perhaps the witch would die, or perhaps he'd just leave Castillo... And yet neither of these things had happened. The master had said that the witch must be killed, but he had not said how. Ignatious's recruitment of Lorenzo had seemed like a masterstroke, but now that had failed and Ignatious was at a loss for fresh ideas. The thought of telephoning England to report failure filled him with dismay and so he sat, quietly in the darkened room, stroking the stone absently in search of divine inspiration.

Inevitably his thoughts drifted back to his first catalystic meeting with the master. It had been almost two years ago to the week in the quiet time just after Semana Santa. He had been celebrating the usual Sunday morning mass to a half empty church. Spain's religious fervour had burned itself out the week before and now all but the most faithful were taking a holiday from the pain of the early morning Eucharist. Half way through the ceremony he'd watched the door open slightly and the figure, haloed with light from the entrance, had quietly slipped into the back row of the pews. The service had continued, but his eyes kept being drawn to the solitary figure at the rear of the church. Even though the late arrival had carefully closed the door behind him, a light still seemed to emanate from where he sat... Warm, haloed and radiant, and as the service progressed the light became ever stronger.

Later, at the end of the mass when the church had emptied, the slim figure had walked up the side of the knave and when Ignatious had turned from bidding the last of his flock farewell and good morning, the master had been waiting for him on the steps of the high altar. Only then, of course, Ignatious had not known that it was the master.

'Can I help you, my son?' he'd asked.

Indeed you can, Father Ignatious of Castillo, but not nearly as much as I can help you...

The master had not spoken. His lips had remained closed. But the words were loud and commanding in the priest's mind.

'What is this? I don't understand!' Ignatious had faltered, then the master had come a step closer to him and out of the glowing haze of light that filtered in through the stained glass windows depicting images of Christ on the cross and the Holy Mother Mary with Her infant son, and Ignatious had seen him properly for the first time. A slight slim man with a receding hair line and a curiously plain, almost flat face. He'd worn unremarkable glasses, but from behind the lenses, the eyes had been genuinely friendly.

His hands had reached towards Ignatious. *You are a priest of God as I also* am a priest of God. I come now from another realm to bring you gifts and to bid you be about the business of The Coming...Here, take my hands, and let the first of many gifts be given to you...*

Tentatively, Ignatious had reached out and the master had taken a hold of both his hands. And a surge of raw beautiful power had charged into Ignatious, making him feel ten feet tall and omnipotently strong. His enormously portly belly seemed to shrink and become taut and tight, muscles flexed involuntarily in his arms and legs. Something faded and clicked within his mind and he knew he was in the presence of an angel.

No, not an angel, the master had chuckled lovingly. *More than that. I am Master of The Realms and I am well loved by The Lord of the Other World. I come to tell you now that the prophecies of your books are real and the day of their fulfilment is but a short time away. Mankind will meet with its God face to face and you, my friend, are chosen to help effect The Opening that The Coming may be completed. In return for your labour and your loyalty, great reward will be given to you. You shall have the gift of sight and the power of life and these things are but a beginning of your ministry. Now, are you ready to serve, Ignatious? Are you ready to serve?*

Ignatious looked beyond the master and from the stained glass window Christ was smiling in encouragement. Mary the mother was weeping with pride for him.

'Oh yes Lord, I am most ready to serve.'

There had been other meetings over the intervening two years. Each time the master had brought gifts and promises and inevitably the promises had been fulfilled. The priest's prostate cancer had gone into remission without the need of surgery, Santa Clara had flourished with growing congregations, Ignatious's personal coffers had swollen with generous donations and he had basked in the approval of his superiors. Most important, he had been released from the terrible burden of chastity and had become a whole man in the service of his God.

But also the master had brought warnings and instructions. *The world of man is dying. Soon there is to be a new order, and on the final day of judgement the Lord of The Other World will again march across this earth. The churches will be full again and it will fall to a few well chosen men to be the priests and leaders of this new era. You, Ignatious, are one of those chosen!*

There had been the gift of psychic sentience – the ability to project one's mind and know what others were thinking and doing. Ignatious wasn't very good at it yet, although he'd been trying hard to master the technique for more than a year.

Gather a few select people around you. They will help. Occasionally I will send you friends to aid you in your quest. But keep the secret of the new era safe and, to those who you judge worthy, I will also give gifts...

Well, there had been Diego and Pedro and Miriam, and half a dozen others that Ignatious had surreptitiously drawn to himself: people with whom he had shared his great secret and, true to his word, the master had visited them all and had touched them with his spirit. The new era was coming and, when it did, he, Ignatious, and his close circle of disciples would be responsible for helping the master with the transition. They did not know *exactly* what was going to happen or even how or when – but it would be soon now, this year, and they were to be part of it all.

One of the master's more recent gifts had been the stone... The priest's fingers trailed across it weird and rocky formation and a deep sense of peace and calm came into him. Lorenzo was of no consequence. He had tried and failed to rid the village of the master's enemy, but there were other ways. Yes, there had to be other ways.

Unbidden, the mental image of Miriam Cortez flooded into the priest's mind. He did not particularly like this woman, but undoubtedly she had a unique power. He wondered if this power might not be harnessed and used against the English witch? At least it was an avenue of thought and, if this what the master's stone was giving him, this was the next obvious pathway to follow.

Angel sat drinking a rum and coke in The Bodega – the last bar on the left on the road that led north out of the village. During the evening the place was alive with youngsters and what Angel thought of as being the arty set of the foreigners, for the food was good and even by Spanish standards, the wine was cheap. During the day, however, and especially in the siesta, The Bodega was quiet and but for a few old men playing dominoes at a table near the bar, he had the place to himself. He sat on a rough hewn wooden bench out on the terrace, surrounded by unripe grapevine and wild jasmine; here in the shadows he felt cool and secure, which was good because he needed time to think without interruption.

He'd had very little sleep and although his body was tired his mind was jumpingly awake and alive with ideas. He worked hard, sipping at the long strong drink which he felt that he needed as much as deserved, to bring his jumbled thoughts into some semblance of order.

One: two weeks ago Señor Mage had arrived in the village and right from that first day it had been clear that there was something very special about him. Apart from anything else, he knew what you were thinking. He could read minds.

Two: when Señor Mage had arrived in Castillo, he, Angel, had had the herpes. One day later, he had not!

Three: Pepe Ortega had a painful ulcer and, according to Pepe's own words, El Moreno had been able to reach into the old man and take the pain away.

Four: on a number of occasions, at least two or three times now, he had seen Señor Mage holding his grandmother's hands and what Pepe had implied was true. In the last two weeks Antonia's joints were a lot less stiff than they had been and she was moving with an ease and agility that Angel had not seen for at least a year – and thus he did not think that this change in his grandmother's constitution had anything to do with the seasonal change in the weather.

Five: El Moreno had unusual nocturnal habits. He walked the village streets at night and had burned candles in front of an empty house. He had made mysterious movements with his hands in the air and had spat on the door...

Six: he was a warrior. Not just a quiet man in a black hat, but an aggressive and merciless fighter. In the space of one heartbeat (at the most, two) he had thwarted a knife attack and had laid Lorenzo low to the ground, inflicting terrible injuries. Angel had seen his fair share of marshal arts on the TV and at the movies, but never in real life. Nothing had prepared him for the sheer speed of it all!

He took another sip of the drink, grinning gleefully. There were quite a few other boys in Castillo (girls as well, come to think of it) who were far from sorry to hear of Lorenzo's downfall.

If Angel had been interested in Colin Mage before the business with Lorenzo, that interest had now become something more closely akin to hero worship. And so what if he was a witch? Well, it hardly mattered. After all, there were good witches and bad witches and obviously his El Moreno was one of the good ones. In any case, the whole concept of "witch" was a little grey in the Spanish language and especially down here in Southern Andalucia. Spaniards tended to lump everything from psychic awareness to spiritual healing beneath the banner of witchcraft – but he, Angel, had read some books during the last year or so, partly in search of his own identity and partially because the subject fascinated him – and he felt that he knew different to what most people thought.

The thing was, and this was the big thing, what was Señor Mage doing here, of all places? Why had he come to Castillo de la Frontera?

Angel knew, or felt he knew, that there had to be a reason and he very much wanted to know what that reason was. How, though, could he find out? He could hardly walk up to El Moreno and say 'Hello Señor Mage, I think you are someone very special and I need to know what you are doing in my village.' No, of course, he couldn't do that...

But then a thought entered Angel's head. Why couldn't he? Why couldn't he do that? And what would El Moreno say if he did?

His train of thought was broken by the squeaking of the rustic metal gate. He looked up as two people came out onto the terrace carrying tinto veranos; red wine with lemonade and lime and lots of ice, and laughing at some private joke. It was the American couple, loaded down with cameras and lenses – he wearing denims, but she in the tightest pair of white shorts imaginable and a loosely fitting halter top that left little to the imagination.

Angel's eyes had been vaguely roaming around the panoramic view of the distant mountains. Now, despite his own blushing embarrassment, they locked on to the girl as the couple drifted across the patio and sat only two tables away.

'Hi – ' The big fair man grinned at him.

'Buenas tardis...' This from the girl, carefully enunciating every syllable. She too flashed him a dazzlingly golden smile and he was glad that he was sitting down. His limbs had suddenly gone limp. Every time he'd seen them around the village during the month or so that they'd been here, he had thought she was beautiful. Each time more beautiful than the last.

'Buenas tardis...' he managed a weak smile and then, just a carefully as the girl... 'Good afternoon.'

'Hey...' the big man beamed. 'You speak English?'

Angel shook his head sadly. 'No. Muy poco. A few words.'

'More than my Spanish – you wanna drink?'

'Pardon?' Angel was floundering.

'Quieres ousted una bebida?' The girl asked, closing her eyes and counting each word off on her fingers. She hadn't got it quite right, but it was close enough.

'Gracias... No...' He looked at the quarter inch of liquid mingling with the melting ice in the bottom of his glass; 'Si! Gracias... Thank-you-very-much... Rum y Cola por favour.'

'One rum and coke coming up...' The American got up and went across to the entrance of the bar, leaving him, Angel The Confused, alone with the girl. He was awed and embarrassed to be in her presence, so much so that rather than looking at her, he stared fixedly at the table top.

'Gee, you really are a shy one,' the girl mused out loud.

'Pardon?'

'Er... Como nombre, por favour...?'

Her Spanish was dreadful, but it made him smile just the same. Her words were music to his ears.

'Angel - y tu?'

'Yo Christina,' she said proudly pointing to herself. 'Y mi amigo es Tom!'

Amigo? So she wasn't married to him then? It was stupid and illogical but he felt a flutter of relief double de clutch down in the lower regions of his belly.

Tom creaked through the gate and placed Angel's fresh drink on the table before him. 'Here you go, feller, and cheers to you.'

Angel didn't understand the words but caught the drift of their meaning. He raised his glass and said 'Salud.'

'Salud,' the two Americans spoke in unison.

'Ustedes le gustas Castillo?' Angel asked nervously – and tried it again very carefully in broken English. 'My village, Castillo. You like?'

'Great!' The American, Tom, was enthusiastic. 'Wonderful light for photography.'

'Muy bueno luz para fotografias,' Christina recited slowly with great concentration – the concentration turning to delight as she successfully completed the phrase. And then; 'Tom es uno fotografo y yo estoy la modela.'

Tom was the photographer and Christina was his model. That made enough sense – and Angel wondered what kind of photographs Tom took of his beautiful girl friend. His mind conjured up amazing pictures and again he was glad of the fact that he was sitting down.

Tom swung one of the cameras to his eye and shot off a couple of frames of the bodega and the wide panoramic view of the mountains. Then he shot Christina sitting at the table with her drink and then, not in the way of professional photographers but in the way of all tourists, he passed the camera and intimated that he should photograph Christina and himself sitting together. Angel was happy to oblige. He thought Christina looked even more lovely through the lens and he revelled in the feel of holding the expensive SLR in his untrained hands. It sure as hell beat the stuffing out of his 1961 model Braun Paxette!

Then Tom took another camera out of his bag, bigger, and curiously shaped. 'Hey Christina baby, let's get a couple of shots of you and Angel sitting together in the shade...'

Christina dutifully went and sat next to Angel and, so electrified was he by her physical proximity... she smelt of cinnamon and when she leaned just a little forwards he could see the black lace of her bra... that he failed to notice when Tom plugged a slim coaxial lead into the base of the camera, a lead that meandered casually and disappeared into the voluminous folds and compartments of his camera bag.

Christina struck several poses. In one she put her arm around Angel's shoulders and in her halting Spanish, told him to smile. In another she leaned back and draped one of her long long legs across his knees: this would be "muy bueno" for the fashion editor back in LA. Angel was on overload. There was a magnet on top of Christina's thigh that drew his eyes upwards inch by inch until they were riveted on the tight white material of the shorts between her slightly opened legs. The shorts were so tight he could even see how they cut into her sex.

Angel was totally unaware of the fact that rather than photographing Christina, Tom was focusing the curious camera exclusively on him.

Some forty five minutes later back in their hotel room at the Miraflores, the two Americans studied the five infrared polaroids that Tom had taken of Angel on his seriously modified camera.
In the pictures Angel's head and shoulders were little more than a dark silhouette, but around him shone a kirlian halo, principally a bright golden yellow with a few deep fiery red bands at the base of the coruna.

'What do you think, Tom?'

'I think the poor little bastard was so turned on that he didn't know whether he was coming or going. You really are a naughty girl playing up to him like that, but,' he studied the pictures thoughtfully. 'I also think we have a very actively psychic young man on our hands. No wonder he seems to hang around the Englishman so much.'

'What we need is a few shots of our mysterious Mr Mage himself,' she said.

'Fine. We both know it, but I just don't see how it's feasible. The POL has a fixed wide angle lens and it only works when the light is right. I don't see how we can shoot the Brit without him knowing about it and I don't think he'd pose for us without asking a lot of questions we wouldn't be able to answer.'

'How many pictures do we have now? I mean altogether?'

'Couple of hundred... And the amount of auric sensitivity among these villagers is way too high, way out of proportion to what you'd expect. Anyway, we'll put young Angel on top of our pile. He's definitely one of the front runners.'

'I liked him,' she mused. 'He was nice.'

'Baby snatcher,' he teased.

'Look who's talking!' She retorted with alacrity. 'He's more my age than you are!'

'True, but he's no more than sixteen or seventeen. You're twenty four and I'm forty two. The odds, baby, are all in my favour.' He slipped his arms around her and, cupping her breasts with his hands, nuzzled his face against the side of her neck.

'Yes, but what do we do now?' she asked, firmly wriggling out of his embrace.

'We could go to bed,' he suggested jokingly. Half hopingly.

'Uh huh. Not in the mood.'

'In that case,' he pulled back not at all put out by the rejection. 'Maybe I'd better put a call through to The States and talk to The Man. You got any change in your purse?'

'Use the mobile.'

'You know they don't work very well up here in these mountains. Give me some euros and I'll go and use the public phone in the bar.'

Miriam Cortez sat in the semi darkness of the shadows. Two hundred yards away at the bottom of the garden, Peter sawed wood while their daughter Lena played listlessly among the wood chips and shavings. The living room of the Cortez home was a spacious affair with numerous black beams and tall French windows: with the solid antique furniture and cluttered shelves and surfaces it was a gloomy union of shade and imaginary caverns, rather than the marriage of light and air that had originally been visualised by the architect and designer.

But the way it was was the way Miriam liked it. The shadows brought her a sense of warmth and safety and she leaned forwards now across the work table watching the candle flicker in harmony with the mirror behind it, feeling not only safe and secure, but also elated and excited – and vindicated! The priest had been to visit her. He'd finally admitted defeat and came looking now for her help and efforts. His way hadn't worked, just as she'd said that it wouldn't.

You had to fight fire with fire, and if this Colin Mage was a magician, he wasn't going to be thwarted by a boy with a knife or by vague energies directed at him through a lump of old stone... Curious though the stone might be. She paused in her reverie. You couldn't just dismiss that stone out of hand. Look what it – and it's original owner – had done for her!

She was forty years old. A year ago she'd looked like she was forty years old, but now, almost a year on, she could say she was thirty three and nobody would disbelieve her. Slowly but surely the premature grey in her hair had disappeared and now her hair was long and shiny black with more life and body than perhaps it had ever had. Her skin was smoother: wrinkles had quietly vanished, and her breasts, flat and saggy for seven years after the birth of her daughter, had swollen and had again become thrustingly firm. The same with her bottom. It hadn't happened over night, of course, but gradually, imperceptibly and with a discernible sense of momentum, especially during the last three months or so.

Nor was this all, for her mental powers of perception and telepathy had moved into an entirely new dimension...Just as Master Dolorean had promised. But this was a double edged sword.

She'd met Dolorean four times over twenty months and on each occasion the sense of wrongness about the man had been more intense. She knew that Ignatious the priest saw him as some angelic Christ-like figure who was a personification of the second coming – but that was not how she saw him at all. Well, maybe angelic in a very dark way, but there was nothing Christ-like about him, that was for sure! That he had great power, *very* great power, was indisputable and it was the source of that power that confused and intrigued her.

Miriam shuffled a deck of well worn Tarot cards and, not for the first time during the winter months of the last half year, thought of "The Master" and selected a card at random from the pack.

As always, and it *was* always, she turned the card and found it to be The Devil.

Her lips pulled into a secret smile. Let's see then, she thought, if things are running true to form. Turning another card, she thought of Colin Mage – now formally her adversary in craft and magic – and was not surprised to find that the card was The Magician. Every time she'd turned a card for Mage these past two weeks, it had always and without fail, been The Magician.

'Who then am I?' she muttered out loud and pulled back in some surprise when the card turned was The Queen of Swords and not The High Priestess as she had expected. She *was* The High Priestess and inevitably her Tarot symbol was always The High Priestess – but not so now.

Perplexed and put out but obeying the set rules of Tarot scrying, she asked her next question. 'What is my role of destiny with Colin Mage?'

She nodded to herself in satisfaction when the card selected was The Knight of Swords. This meant combat, so she was still on the right track.

'What will be the result of the combat?' she asked, and smiled broadly when the card turned was Major Arcana number thirteen. Death. She was to be victorious. Either Colin Mage was to literally die at her hands, which he might well do if she decided to use poison – but even if not, he was to be defeated and she would be successful in bringing about the death of the situation which threatened them.

She sat back from the table in satisfaction, quietly confident that her powers and abilities in the way of witchcraft were more than adequate to bring about the downfall of this interloper from England.

And yet she was far from entirely happy.

Miriam Cortez had been born a pagan from a dark and devious bloodline stretching back over many generations to the Romany tribes of Eastern Europe. She'd been introduced to the Wiccan pathway at birth and was consecrated Priestess in her own right at thirteen years old. By the time she was twenty five she'd been the High Priestess of thirteen covens in the South East of England. For many years she had earned a living, and a good living at that, using her psychic skills with The Tarot and palmistry – in the beginning on the corner by Southend Pier and in the end before she'd come to Spain and had met Peter, at the elite soirees and private gatherings of London's chic society.

She was a shrewd and clever woman and had seen much of the left hand path of life. Her body told her all was well and her mind was clearly focused and confident – but something lurked nervously and uncomfortably in the depths of her intuition. Who was this English magician and why was he here? Why, furthermore, was he Master Dolorean's enemy?

She wasn't surprised that Dolorean had enemies. Anyone with as much power as he had was bound to have them in abundance... Which brought her to the centre of her unease. Namely, Dolorean himself.

She had spent most of her working life getting into the minds of her numerous and very varied clients, but Dolorean was a closed book. On two occasions she had tried to penetrate his screens and both times had failed and on the latter occasion not without some pain. It was as though Dolorean had been playing with her psychic probe and then had slapped it away with a flick of his mind. She'd had a migraine for two days and a headache for more than a week.

The thing that puzzled her was Dolorean's aura: oh certainly on the charismatic levels of personality and presence, he demanded attention and filled the room but on a psychic level, there was nothing there. No spiritual vibration, no emotional sentience, no energy field putting out the personality pulse that all humans gave out and which all psychics and clairvoyants tried to tune into... And did so most of the time either on a conscious or subliminal level.

So whoever Master Dolorean was, it was clear to her that he was an adept, a master of the very highest magics. Her own physical retro-metamorphosis was proof enough of that. But, and here was another key question, what did Castillo in Southern Spain hold for an adept such as this? She dismissed the priest's mumbo jumbo as little more than that. He could believe whatever he liked! Dolorean was no more a reincarnation of Jesus Christ than she was herself and, while she firmly believed that his interests in Castillo had a purpose, something to do with all this bullshit about an Opening and a Coming, she did not know, had not been told, and could not even begin to sense what these words meant.

Ignatious and some of his Spanish friends, including the late Diego Matan and also including her own husband – fool – had it fixed in their minds that The Opening was to be something of great religious significance and she agreed with them, it was going to be very religious... But not, she suspected, in the Christian sense of the word. Master Dolorean was here to perform some high magical rite – of that she was sure. Powerful as he was, he couldn't do it alone, which was why he had recruited Ignatious and the rest of the holy coven on the promise of wonderful things to come. He had even made down payment. The subtle reversal of her ageing process, Peter's recent business successes, Ignatious's good health and energy after many months of what had been regarded as a terminal illness – were but forerunners of better things ahead. She savoured the taste of those "better things" not knowing what they might be, but certain in her own mind that they'd be more than worthwhile.

Even so, she still felt uneasy about Dolorean.

The cards danced through her hands again and she asked The Tarot a final question: 'What is The Opening?' And as always before the answer came in the form of The Tower of God. The destruction of the established order. The fire that caused the ashes from which the Phoenix would rise. Although she recognised some of the cause of her fear – what if some of that fire burned her? – she was quite determined that when that mythical bird of prophesy did rise, she'd be flying with it all the way!

But first, Mr Colin Mage, enemy incognito, witch to some, magician to others... Had to be dealt with. If it made it possible for Dolorean to give her what she wanted, she would have no compunction about dealing with the ubiquitous Mr Mage! She scooped The Tarot into their silken cloth and began to formulate a rough battle plan for her psychic attack.

After sleeping late into the morning, Mage had enjoyed a tapa lunch at Jacinto's bar. Here he had heard the Spanish version of Lorenzo's beating (for which he felt not one jot of regret) and had spent some time thinking about what, if anything, he ought to do about the priest. He'd come to no conclusion and had decided to let the matter rest in his mind for a while. It couldn't be left indefinitely, of course, not if this Father Ignatious was so close to Dolorean that he'd tried to get rid of him by means of physical violence. The question was how he should respond to the challenge. It wasn't enough just to neutralise one specific threat. A lesson had to be taught. A response carefully considered.

From Jacinto's he'd walked up to the castle. The place continued to intrigue him and he was all too well aware that he knew very little of the castle's history. The local historian, not a Spaniard but an émigré Scott called Hamish Hamilton, was visiting friends in Alicante and wasn't expected back for another week. The local Spanish potted history went backwards from Hidalgos to Christians to Moors to Romans and Shrugs; there were no clear dates and Mage felt more than just frustrated.

Now, late in the afternoon, the sun was low in the western sky throwing the sharp crags of the Hozgarganta valley into stark relief. A blue haze of mist hung low in the ravines and the more distant mountains that stretched inexorably towards Cadiz were shrouded in mist and mystery of their own. The air, while not cold, had cooled and caused him to hoist up the zip of his jacket.

He stood four hundred metres to the west of the castle, the village out of sight on the far side of the hill. From this perspective he had learned something new, namely that the crest of the crag upon which the castle stood was not as level as it appeared to be from the eastern perspective. From this view it was obvious that the crag inclined upwards towards the south, with the Christian keep on a noticeably higher elevation than the Moorish citadel.

Mage was a well read and reasonably learned man, but his knowledge of medieval Spanish history was at best sketchy. He knew that once upon a time the Moorish empire had ruled more than half of Spain until, in reaction to the hostile ambitions of the Moroccan, Ben Yusuf, the Castillian king Alfonso, with a little help from one Rodrigo de Bivarre, had begun the conquest and expulsion of the Moorish invaders. This, Mage thought, had been early in the twelfth century and, although the Moors were long gone, much of their culture and architecture still remained.

He began the severe upwards trudge back towards the keep, mindful of what he had found within the circular tower when he'd climbed inside the turret a few hours earlier.

It had not been easy to get in. The door had long since been blocked and filled with rubble, but by carefully negotiating the external edifice, he'd managed to climb the ten feet or so up to the first of several portals. From there he'd dropped to the hard packed earth inside. Light had slanted in from half a dozen other such portals which were spaced equidistantly but at varying heights around the tower. It created a cathedral-like effect, albeit minus the presence of stained glass. The upper floors (Mage could see there had been two) had long since collapsed, the rubble removed God alone knew where. Looking upwards, the tower was open to the sky.

And here was a curious thing.

Forty feet above his head, with a diameter of at least fifteen feet, the roof of the tower gaped open to the weather and yet the packed earth of the floor had been dusty and dry. With the hole above his head, not to mention the portals, the ground should have had at least some dampness in it and yet when he'd squatted down, rifling his hands through the top soil, it had been as dry as a bone.

The other thing that his senses had immediately latched onto was the stillness and calm serenity of his environment. Almost without thinking about what he was doing, he'd sat in the middle of the floor and raising and closing his eyes, had gone down into a long and deeply satisfying transcendental meditation. Closing his mind to all external thought, the irresistible sentience of the keep touched him with feelings of profound warmth and security, bathing him with an aura of peace and something else that might almost have been called love. This was a good place. A *right* place... And an hour later he'd come up from the meditation with a beatific smile on his face and humming the sacred ohm on a resoundingly resonant bass D vibration.

With the prescient awareness that always came with deep meditation, he'd realised that if the Christian keep was this positive, then the Moorish citadel, three hundred metres to the north, would probably be just as negative. He'd already felt some of that negativity from the outside and guessed that it would be twice as bad on the inside. Sooner or later, he'd have to find a way in and put his opinion to the test – but not this day. He'd wanted nothing to spoil the epiphany of this past hour in the Christian keep.

He'd allowed himself a few moments of analytical contemplation and again his thoughts had drifted back to the events of the early hours, to the young man he'd hurt and the priest – a bloody priest for God's sake – who'd sent him on his mission of murder. Although Mage had yet to meet the man, it came as no great surprise to learn that this Father Ignatious was the pastor of Santa Clara, that brooding Catholic structure that was virtually next door to the Dolorean house and formed such an integral part of Calle Sombra.

Lorenzo was out of it. Like all bullies he was a coward at heart and Mage knew that he'd put the very fear of God in him – but this Father Ignatious was another matter. Any Catholic priest in an Andalucian hill village was a potent force to be reckoned with and if Dolorean had managed to turn the village priest, of all people, it was dark testimony to the persuasiveness of his adversary's power!

His thoughts had then moved on to Anna Sanchez and he'd smiled bitterly to himself. Now here was an unexpected complication! As a man, Mage knew himself well enough to recognise that he was very attracted to Hector's daughter and that in other circumstances, despite their vast difference in age, he'd be enjoying the fantasy of some kind of union with the girl and, no doubt, would have been doing something to make the fantasy a reality. As it was, she was so incredibly vulnerable and he was and had to remain so sharply focused on Dolorean and Alexandra, that anything other than friendship seemed totally out of the question. And yet he could not deny the attraction, even though at times he was resentful of it when it side-tracked his thoughts from his purpose and raison d'être. Furthermore, he was mindful of his promise to himself to do something about her eyes and the greater terror that lay beyond the impending loss of vision.

He didn't know for certain that he could do anything to help, but he *felt* that he could, even if he wasn't sure precisely how. He didn't think it could be done through the process of absent healing; in this case there would have to be a laying on of hands and some active co-operation from the patient herself. But would she, and her father for that matter, agree to this? Would it not jeopardise things on a broader level, ie his position in the village? And what if he failed to help Anna? Would that not just add more disappointment to the rising tide of her despair? No, he couldn't allow that to happen and therefore before he tried to help, he had to be reasonably confident of success... and that would mean time and energy and practice. Well, that was all right. Any practice at sharpening his powers would be a good thing... Whether he used those powers to help Anna or to destroy Dolorean.

He'd climbed out of the keep, regretful at leaving, aware of its magic and also of its enigmatism, knowing that now he had found it, he would return many times. If there was to be a battle for mankind, where better to make preparation – and where better, if he failed, to make a last stand?

He'd strolled over to the western edge of the fortifications, suddenly prickling with sentience, aware that once again he was under observation. He'd turned casually... and several hundred metres away to his right saw a figure lounging against the arch that led to the cobbled path down to the village. At this distance it was impossible to identify his watcher, although he'd thought male rather than female. Shrugging – Spain was a free country and he had no right to assume that the castle was exclusively his own domain, he'd wandered down the steep slope towards the first chaotic rock formations that littered the mountainside all the way down to the Hozgarganta River, half a mile away in the distance.

Although not exactly out of breath, he was breathing heavily by the time he climbed over the broken wall and once again stood in the castle precinct. He was immediately aware of the figure, no longer lounging against the archway, but sitting on the wall next to it. Detaching itself from its perch, the figure walked purposefully towards him.

Now what was all this, Mage wondered? He began to walk towards the figure, not in a confrontational way, but determined the stand his ground if challenged.

A few seconds later he recognised Angel Guadiaro and relaxed. He'd half expected a visitation from another of the priest's emissaries or one of Lorenzo's henchman... Angel fell into the category of friend. Or at least, he thought he did. Right now he wasn't so sure. The boy looked flustered and intense. Highly excited and determined.

'Afternoon Angel,' Mage opened casually.

' Señor Mage!' The boy looked him straight in the eye. 'I wish to speak with you. I wish to ask you a question.'

'Fine.' Mage nodded in a friendly manner, but was on his guard again. There was something wrong here.

Angel took a deep breath. ' Señor Mage, I think you are a very special, most unusual man and I want to know why you have come to my village of Castillo de la Frontera!'

Mage had been prepared for a challenge, but had relaxed when he'd recognised Angel. And yet there was challenge here and a very definite one. Angel was not intimidating but nor was he backing down. He was fired up about something and Mage didn't think he could be fobbed off lightly – leastways, not without the loss of a lot of goodwill and a potential ally. Not for the first time he was mindful of Father Paul's prophesy on the island of Cael... *Go to Castillo and you will find an angel to help you.* And, of course, who had been the first person he'd met in Castillo? None other than Angel himself! Mage had spent enough time with the boy over the past two weeks to be well aware of the young Spaniard's own latent psychic sensitivity. Perhaps he'd underestimated it, or had even been the catalyst of some significant enhancement of Angel's gift. Like attracted like and psychic energy was always intensified in the presence of similar energy.

Which was all very well – but what to tell the boy? Certainly not the truth, at least not the whole truth, for who in their right mind would believe it anyway? Some of the truth then? Not a plausible lie, but enough of the truth to judge the boy's reaction? And besides, would it be such a bad thing to have Angel more bound to his side?

'All right,' Mage said after long seconds. 'But let's go somewhere and sit down for a while and I'll tell you some things that you might not believe and, if you do believe them, maybe you'll wish I hadn't told you!'

Angel followed Mage down the narrow cobbled pathway and then through the tight labyrinth of streets until they came to the house at Calle Granadillos. The sun had gone now and the temperature had dropped quite radically. The first fires of the evening were being lit in a hundred Spanish homes and the sharp air was filled with the smell of wood smoke that tingled the olfactory senses as it mingled with the springtime scent of eucalyptus and jasmine.

Mage took Angel into the kitchen and lit the gas bombona. He made tea, weak and pale, and added springs of fresh mint. Angel wrinkled his nose, but Mage told him to try it anyway and together they sat facing each other across the broad table where they'd sat two weeks previously to the day and had negotiated their transaction for the lease of the house.

Angel was tense and silent and filled with a bright excitement of expectancy.

He had not known how El Moreno would react, but obviously something was going to happen now that would assuage his youthful curiosity.

Mage lit a cigarette and looked at him evenly. 'Do you know what a secret is?' he asked.

Angel was indignant. 'Yes Señor, of course I do. It is when you tell me something very private and I do not ever tell that thing to another living soul.'

Mage smiled thinly at the accuracy and simplicity of Angel's appreciation of the concept. 'Then listen, my young friend, and I will tell you a very great secret. You might not believe what I tell you, but even if you disbelieve, you must still keep the secret. I promise that even if you don't, I shall not harm you in anyway... But sooner or later great harm would befall you for your betrayal.'

'I understand, Señor Mage, but you must also understand that I do not betray secrets!'

'Good,' Mage said promptly. 'I'm pleased to hear it.'

Then he talked to Angel Guadiaro for over an hour, sharing with him one of the oldest and best kept secrets the world had ever known. Angel did not believe what he was told – at least, not then – but he promised to keep the secret anyway, realising that whether El Moreno was right or wrong, he would soon find out for himself one way or the other. He desperately wanted Mage to be wrong. He had to make himself believe that El Moreno was wrong, for if he was not, it brought an entirely new meaning to the word terror.

10.

Michael Fry

In Calcutta, the woman called Kiku completed a complicated transaction. Money changed hands and certain family favours were pledged. The end result was that the boy, Rajad, became her legal property.

In Cael, the funeral wake for Father Paul was long since over, but now, standing by the cairn of stones that was his tomb among the tombs of more than a dozen others in the mouth of the huge cave above the beach, another, more curious ceremony took place wherein a short sword of beaten gold and a long staff of willow wood were placed into a young monk's waiting hands.

'Do you accept this guardianship of your own free will and pledge to protect The World Of Light against The Legions Of Darkness, and this to be your task for the rest of your days?'

The presiding priest awaited the answer patiently. It was good and necessary that one should contemplate the importance of a commitment such as this. Once given, the commitment would bind the giver to this tiny Irish atoll for the rest of his life.

'I do accept the guardianship and make the pledge,' the young monk finally spoke, and when he did speak it was more with humility and resignation than with the pride of being the recipient of the honour that had been bestowed upon him.

In Jerusalem Gideon Lemski re-read The Elijah File and in Ashquelon Herschal fretted impatiently, waiting for someone from Mossad to come and talk to him.

In a small but upmarket hotel room three miles west of Jackson, The Reverend John Light woke from a nightmare. In the dream he dreamed that he had walked between two trees and had been sucked into another world, a world full of demons and phantoms that followed him back into the reality of his own world even as he woke.

In Britain Michael Fry drove hard and fast through a dark night of pouring rain. He'd left The Oaks at four in the morning more on impulse than premeditation and by six o'clock was fast approaching of the border between England and Scotland. The rain had been his driving companion throughout the journey, the wiper arms of the black BMW in constant motion. He'd felt cocooned within the confines of the large luxurious car, and had driven quickly, seldom dropping below seventy miles an hour and frequently cruising nearer ninety... Which, he freely admitted to himself, was far too fast for the prevailing weather conditions. But he drove fast anyway, the speed and adrenaline acting as a catharthis to his impatience and his sleeplessness.

By eight o'clock he was running into Edinburgh, a city painted in bleary rainscape as the dawn struggled to lighten the lowering sky. What good he might do in coming to this city on this day, was debatable, but he had to do something to combat the creeping inertia of impotency – an inertia that was compounded by an increasing sense of frustration and impending danger. From Michael Fry's point of view, it had not been a good week in the world of Druidism.

He eased the car through the building breakfast traffic and finally found a reasonably convenient car park just off The Royal Mile. He cut the engine and sat there for long minutes, listening to the cooling tick and the pattering of the persistent raindrops. It was a drear and dreak Scottish morning, more reminiscent of the Ides of March than the end of April. He felt tired and dispirited. The tiredness was natural enough; he'd been working eighteen hour days that last week and when he had slept he had not rested well. The low spiritual energy was inevitable and also more worrying, and he realised that he had become obsessive – possibly even a little paranoid – about the Colin Mage business. It wasn't often Michael Fry made a mistake, but he'd certainly made one the previous weekend at The Oaks when he'd called his unofficial cabal of senior bards. He bitterly regretted his lack of judgement. It should have been something he'd handled independently rather than trying to share the responsibility of his knowledge with others who were so locked into the traditions of permanence and continuing order that they lacked the vision and wisdom to even contemplate an alternative pathway of probability because it was so totally unpalatable that, for the sake of their own egos, they chose to dismiss it as impossible. Druids, bards and supposedly advanced spirits they may have been, but beneath the trappings of their white robes and varying positions of power and influence, they were still only men, cursed with Man's fears and weaknesses.

What, then, Fry wondered, did that make of him? And what of the girl, Helen? The girl he'd driven to Edinburgh to see? She'd seen something of the impending horror and she'd paid a price for it. How would she react when she found him on her doorstep? He wouldn't blame her if she slammed the door in his face... Indeed, he reflected dryly, that was probably exactly what she would do. But at least he had to try.

That morning at The Oaks a scant six days ago, had begun well enough. He'd slept well and had breakfasted lightly before strolling into the extensive gardens at the back of the house. He'd found Helen by the ornate fountain behind the gazebo and together they had walked through the fresh English grass, allowing the scents of Springtime to fill their senses. A weak but trying sun had offered a modicum of warmth and there was that unique freshness and excitement that confirmed the birth of new life after an interminably long winter.

At first she had been shy and deferential and Fry had been made aware of how much distance there still was between the leadership and the grass roots of the Druidic movement in Britain. He'd tried so hard to reduce this distance and by and large he'd done well, even though he'd have been the first to admit that there was still a long way to go. He'd known Helen Ross for a number of years and had actively encouraged her activities in Druidism, to which she had come from a Wiccan background. Indeed, she had resolutely refused to give up her links with that other pagan interest, choosing to live with them jointly. If people from either camp had protested, she'd reminded them tartly that she was her own person and that if Wiccan or Druid wanted her in their camp, it would be on her own terms or not at all.

The thing which gave Helen Ross her power of selection was the fact that she was a highly accurate clairvoyant blessed with the ability to focus her gift in an aggressive and investigative way. Not for her the passive waiting game of seances or the hopeless congregations of small back street churches! Her abilities were further significantly enhanced by the gift of divination, both through the hidden truths of The Tarot and the I Ching, and also through dowsing – either diagnostically in the medical sense, or exploratively in the process of location and discovery.

And yet, Fry remembered, she was still very young. Thirty? Thirty two? And that *was* young to have harnessed so many diverse and powerful talents. Fry thought it was a blessing more than a curse that he was an asexual man, but even so, he did have an appreciation of beautiful and natural things and he conceded that Helen Ross had both of these qualities in abundance. She was small and petit, barely five feet and two inches in her shoes and yet had a curvaceous body with noticeable breasts, a tight waist and graceful hips. She walked well, like a dancer, poised and finely balanced. Her voice was soft with the lyrical lilting accent of the Scottish lowlands.

'I'm honoured to be here,' she'd said. 'But curious as to why I have been asked to attend.'

'You are very good at what you do,' Fry had said. 'The meeting this morning is informal and unofficial. I need some advice, some insight, some objective opinions before deciding on a particular course of action. I asked for you to be here for two reasons. Firstly, I might need to call upon your powers of psychometry and, secondly, to gauge your reactions to certain information I shall divulge. The three prime members of this morning's council of five are very traditional in their faith, with well established views and opinions. You, on the other hand, represent the new kind of Druid.' He'd smiled cautiously. 'You will give me my grass roots reaction.'

She'd nodded, accepting it in part, reserving her judgement on the rest. Clearly, there was much she wasn't being told.

Together they finished their circuit of the garden and, ascending the wide steps of the mansion's rear entrance, entered the library through French windows.

Margaret Fry had been creative in her arrangement of the seating plan. Sitting at a desk with his back to the windows, The Merlin faced into the room, Margaret on his right, Helen on his left. In front of him, at either end of a long sofa, were Thomas of Wales and Martyn of Glastonbury: to their left, and ensconced in a high backed wing chair, was Lady Mary Donahoe. Margaret served coffee in small white bone china cups and for the first few moments the conversation had been casual and convivial. Then Fry had brought the council to order.

'First of all may I stress the informal and unofficial nature of this morning's gathering and extend my thanks to you for agreeing to attend. I know that your time is most precious, so I'll get straight to the point.

'Some five months ago, and by his own petition, I had an interview with a man called Colin Mage. He is a professional occultist with remarkable healing abilities and a most thorough grounding in both the theory and the practice of magic. Some of you may have read his books in which, it must be said, he deals fairly and accurately with the ritual side of our Druidic faith.

'Mr Mage wanted to know if I had any knowledge of a specific magical ritual called The Opening, or if I had any reference to such a ritual. Although I told him that I had not, it did ring a bell at the back of my mind and I later ascertained that there was a grimoire written in 1767 by a French occultist called Martin Blanc Villiers. It had quite recently been published in modern French, in 1967 to be precise – and was a book that ran to almost a thousand pages, giving a detailed resume of a parallel world to our own that was full of malefic demons and making oblique reference to a ceremony which, should it be performed, would break down the barriers between these two worlds and give these demonic legions free range of conquest over our planet.

'Frankly I considered it to be nothing more than romantic drivel, written at a time when such grimoires were prolific in France and published to catch the wave of interest that was beginning to prevail in the mid nineteen sixties. But I was intrigued to learn why Colin Mage was so interested in the grimoire, so I sent him a note telling him I'd located the book and he duly came back and read it, over four days, sitting in this very room.

'I must tell you that I was, and indeed am, very impressed with this gentleman. Although not a Druid, he carries himself with the dignity of our church and in sympathy with our beliefs and ways. It was clear to me during his stay at this house that he was in some deep psychic distress and was in need of spiritual healing. This was given without his knowledge by certain members of the household and during the fourth and final day of that second visit, I learned that he believed that there was to be a performance of this opening ritual and that he very much feared that what I had regarded as romantic drivel was, in fact, a possible reality.

'It was left that he would report back to me with the result of his continuing investigations. While I was sceptical of his opinions, I felt it expedient to offer him some encouragement and moral support. I received a telephone call some two weeks later informing me that he was travelling to Ireland to interview the abbot of a monastic order on the island of Cael. In the interim he'd been to Paris and had located the publisher of the obscure grimoire to which I have previously referred. The publisher, Bernard Villiers, who is descended directly from the original author, firmly believes in this parallel world theory and put Mr Mage in contact with one Father Paul O'Connor who had written an occult thesis on parallel worlds back in 1935.

'It seems that this order of monks is Christian in name only. They have powers of clairvoyance and telepathy and, according to Mage, one or two of the more adept members of the order have mastered the art of levitation. Mage says that he saw it with his own eyes on two separate occasions and I have no reason to disbelieve him. Apparently this monastic order has been in situ on Cael since the time of Saint Patrick. The order was commissioned by the saint himself to guard what was perceived to be an opening between two worlds. This monastic order has amassed a wealth of evidence spanning over fifteen hundred years to indicate the presence of a parallel world which is fundamentally hostile towards our own time space continuum and during the last few decades has served as a repository and clearing house for all manner of international references to anything which confirms the order's own charter and mandate...

'From this Father O'Connor, Mage acquired two further contacts. A man called John Light in the United States and someone called Herschal in Israel. The former, a one time Satanist now turned Christian evangelist, had written what he called The Book of Black Revelation. This was twelve years ago, but certain references in that work corresponded to Paul O'Connor's belief and visualisations of a parallel world. The other man, the Jew, Herschal, was more mysterious. O'Connor had never met him, had never read anything that he had published, but had heard of him as being a mystic who lived a hermetic existence in The Negev Desert and who had the reputation of being able to move between two worlds.

'Cutting what is a very long and complicated story short, Mage travelled to Israel and, the Oaks know how, managed to locate this man in the middle of The Negev. Mage stayed with him for a number of weeks and came away with what he considered to be hard evidence to support his theory. His next port of call was California and a single interview with John Light.

'Mage reported that this meeting did not go at all well and that Light was far from helpful, denying that he'd ever been a Satanist and professing no knowledge of The Book of Black Revelation. Mage felt certain that he was lying and not only that, but also that Mage had frightened and distressed him by his visit. He was able to read Light's mind to some extent and picked up some terrifying memory patterns that indicated that Light had had some paranormal contact with the other world at some time in the past, and that the experience had caused sufficient shock and trauma to turn Light away from his Satanic way of life and push him into the arms of the Christian god.

'Colin Mage collated his information and has become convinced that there is a parallel world to our own. That this other world is and always has been aware of our world, although we have not been aware of it. That for thousands of years and increasingly throughout the nineteenth and twentieth centuries, this other world has been trying to effect a breakthrough and acquire control of our planet. That the inhabitants of this parallel world are not human, but take on the form of Djinn – a creature well established in Moslem legend as a demonic shapechanger with powers far greater than Man's own – and that these Djinn are both very envious of Man and also greatly hostile towards him.

'Mage believes that there are certain places on the face of our planet where the veil between the two worlds is particularly thin, and he refers to these places as openings. In the past the Djinn have tried to force access to our world through these various openings, but thus far have always been thwarted by men who, having become aware of the threat, have taken it upon themselves to mount guard over these openings and by the power of binding prayer and applied magic, have kept the openings closed and have contained the threat.

'Some of the openings have been identified but it seems that with the tides of time that govern our planet, certain openings can be more relevant and more volatile than others. A thousand years ago and beyond, the majority of these openings was within the crescent of Islam which is why Arabic legend is full of tales about Djinn. Once an opening has been closed – it stays that way and thus the Djinn have sought other places in the world where the walls of partition are thin. In our present day there is, Mage believes, at least one opening in the USA, one in Ireland, one in Spain, one in Israel and one in India. There may, of course, be more but these are the ones which are known and recognised. Each opening has its guardian... Light in America, Paul O'Connor in Ireland, Herschal in Israel... Some woman known only as Kiku in India. Mage believes that an attack is imminent and, indeed, has already begun in a small way at the Spanish opening and, as this opening in undefended, that is where Mage has gone now, to do what he can to identify the opening and neutralise the threat. He believes that at least one Shapechanger has already slipped through the veil and is abroad in our world preparing the way for its brethren.

'If this should occur, our planet will soon be filled with alien entities bent upon the destruction of Man and Man's world. One can only speculate as to what physical form these entities might take, but the nearest approximation might be that of the traditional Djinn, as handed down through Moslem literature – a large goblinesque creature with a demonic personality, able to change and shift shape at will, taking on both human and animal form and frequently a mixture of both at the same time... Emanating a most powerful and negative, not to mention destructive, spiritual vibration that would contaminate and corrupt all that it touched. If such an entity exists and if access to our world is forced, the resulting chaos and destruction of our world would be both immediate and cataclysmic. Man would have no weaponry with which to fight back. The invasion would be swift and deadly and what few humans did survive would be relegated to a cast of slaves in service to a stronger, if much lower spiritual hierarchy. It would represent the end of this world in a more apocalyptic way than any nuclear holocaust.

'You will notice that I have used the word "if". I fully accept that this theory is wild and far fetched. Almost beyond belief. And yet, Colin Mage believes it to be true and the people Mage has talked to believe it to be true and some of the evidence Mage has amassed clearly suggests that it *could* be true. I have studied and meditated on this matter for many long hours and freely admit that I am swayed by some of the evidence and also by my liking of Mr Mage and my respect for his integrity and his body of work. Against this, his theories and findings are most difficult to accept.

'The problem that faces me is a simple one. Do I write Colin Mage off as a misguided mad man and ignore the warnings that I have been given? Or do I, if only in part, accept that he might be right, and mobilise our forces to help him, at the same time protecting ourselves from whatever darkness might come our way? And if indeed the latter course seems appropriate, what, in specific terms, are we able to do? It is with these thoughts in mind that I seek your advice and wise counsel this morning.'

At first there'd been no reaction. The five other people had sat quietly, listening to The Merlin's introduction without interruption, absorbing his words into their own thoughts. Now, as he'd looked at them for some response, it was slow in coming.

Lady Mary Donahoe was the first to break the silence. She was a large but well proportioned woman, late in her fifties and not renowned for her tact and diplomacy. Indeed, she had the reputation of getting to the heart of a matter quickly. Even so, on this April morning, even she was careful.

'There are things you are not telling us, my Lord Merlin,' she had said astutely.

'Not much,' Fry had responded. 'Some of the background of how Colin Mage initially became involved and perhaps some of the details of the things that I have learned. But these are not important factors right now. What I need is your considered reaction to the salient questions. One, is it possible that there is another world existing in a different dimension which nonetheless shares the territory of our planet? Two, if that world is populated by a race of beings who are operating in a different time and space continuum and that race of beings is hostile towards us, what do we do about it? These are the relevant points and, as much as your scholarship, I want your emotional gut reactions.'

'In that case,' Mary Donahoe had said promptly. 'I think the whole thing is totally preposterous. I don't accept it and I don't believe it. Whatever evidence your Mr Mage has found is seriously flawed and inaccurate and, if I may say so, I am surprised that you have taken it seriously.'

'Fair enough.' Fry had smiled thinly. 'Thomas?' he'd turned to the rotund arch druid from Wales. 'What are your thoughts, please?'

'I'm afraid I'm inclined to agree with our Lady Mary,' Thomas Llewelyn had answered dourly. 'Years ago people believed in fairies and hobgoblins, but these are enlightened times and I think that if there were such beings we'd have felt their presence in our world before now. Of course, we don't have all the evidence that perhaps you and your Mage boyo might have, but if you're asking for my gut reaction, then I'd have to say it was impossible. No group of people more so than ourselves has its ear tuned to the pulse of our planet. If anything of this nature was happening, then I'd have thought we'd have picked it up first before an outside magician, or an ex-Satanist, not to mention some mysterious wild man in an Israeli desert!'

Fry had felt a flash of anger at the older man's arrogance and was secretly glad that he had not divulged anything of Mage's personal link with this affair. It would only have made the situation more implausible.

'Margaret?' He'd turned to his mother. 'Your views, please?'

'You put me in a difficult position,' Margaret Fry had answered thoughtfully. 'On the one hand I am your mother and I feel duty bound to support you whether you are right or wrong, but on the other hand I am here this morning not as your mother but as part of a council of five and as co-ordinator of the Druidic Order of All Britain – and it that role I must tell you that I share the Bard Thomas's view that this all sounds highly unlikely and that if any of it were true, we, as Druids, would be the first to know of it. Against that, however,' she'd rallied in an attempt to be supportive, 'I know this is something that has been worrying you deeply and, as The Merlin, you would have been remiss in your duties not to have given it some consideration. You have certainly done the right thing in deciding to consult us with this matter and it is to be hoped that the counsel of this gathering can do something to put your mind at rest.'

Fry had hidden his disappointment and, thanking his mother, had turned to Helen who'd been sitting in the corner of the salon staring reflectively into space. He'd had to speak her name twice before she'd looked up, startled. 'I'm so sorry,' she'd murmured. 'I was miles away and just thinking really, that nothing is impossible, is it? Other than that, I have no opinion, one way or the other.'

'Well I have an opinion,' said Martyn of Glastonbury and Fry's heart had sunk. Martyn was a prune of a man with a shock of white hair. He was well into his eighties and not only one of Druidism's most traditional bards, but also one of Fry's most vociferous critics. Fry had expected no support from this wiry old octogenarian and yet he was to be surprised.

'Helen Ross is right. Nothing is impossible and we, as Druids, should never forget that fact. And in any case, what might be impossible, or be seen as being impossible today, can so easily become possible by tomorrow. Our world is accelerating. Changes are occurring with disproportionate rapidity to any earlier time in our history. Just within the last few years we have seen the ending of the cold war, the collapse of the Soviet Empire, the reunification of Germany. For the first time in millennia, we see the possibility of a reconciliation between Jew and Arab and never in man's modern history has man been more ecologically aware. Although we have newspapers and new bulletins full of woe and strife, we are steadily moving towards less threatening and, as Thomas has said, more enlightened times. The Age of Pisces is ending and The Age of Aquarius is upon us and frankly, I would expect there to be some cataclysmic revelation or revolution within these next few years to finally put the coffin nail in the lid of the old age.

'As for this parallel world theory, well, why not? There isn't anything new about the idea. Albert Einstein speculated on the theory more than sixty years ago and Hubbard and his scientologists have it at the core of their unwritten creed and dogma. Brunner and Zelazney have written authoritative novels wrapped around the concept. There has been enough loose evidence over the years to suggest that there might be some truth in it and, while I don't believe in fairies, I am by no means convinced that once upon a long time ago they did not exist. We all have our legends surrounding the theorem of different life forms and different planes of existence. The English fairy, the Irish leprechaun, the Scandinavian troll, the North American sasquatch, the Himalayan yeti – and, of course, the Arabian Djinn. I have always found that where there is smoke there's fire and wherever there is legend there is always a grain of truth, no matter how diluted and discrepant it might be.

'If I was an alien entity who'd been watching the evolution of this planet for the last two or three thousand years, I'd think that now might be a very good time indeed to put in a take-over bid. Half the world is starving while the other half doesn't give a damn. Everyone is hell-bent on feathering his own nest one way or the other. As a race, we have become complacent with our sense of omnipotence – and yet we are all desperately looking for a change.

'We scream in protest when it does come, be it in the form of a new motor way or the restructuring of our hospitals, whether it is in the form of cutbacks in our armed forces at a time when we no longer need the military flexibility of a bygone age – we cry out for peace and yet are unwilling to disarm – or whether it's the admission of women priests to the Anglican clergy. Yet still we say we want change...

'Maybe we say it because we all know that major world change is coming!' He'd glared around the room defiantly. 'We've talked about it, speculated about it, we've given it a convenient new age title, but none of us knows what exactly that change will be, although we've all felt it coming for years. Who is to say that this change will be for the better? Change, as we have frequently found to our great cost, does not always equate with improvement.

'I do not say that there *will* be an invasion from another dimension, but I do say that we are both stupid and short sighted to blithely assume that it couldn't happen – and therefore, my advice to you My Lord Merlin, is to keep an open mind and monitor this ongoing business most carefully. As for what we could do if there were such an event,' he'd shrugged, '... well, I suspect that the answer is very little, but forewarned is forearmed and we could do worse than try to be a little more open minded and spiritually on guard.

'And that,' he'd ended abruptly, 'for what it's worth, is my opinion. But just let me add this... You say that as Druids we would be the first to know if something were amiss with our planet and I happen to think your right in that assessment and all I can tell you is that there has been a tremendous shift in earth energy in Glastonbury over the past half year that has not been to my liking and nor to any of our borothers in that part of the world. Some of us have had the jitters for quite a few weeks and that makes me think that we should not be totally dismissive of this yarn.'

Fry had felt like applauding the old man from Glastonbury, but even before he'd had the chance to thank him properly, Lady Mary and Thomas of Wales had jumped back into the fray and a heated three way argument had ensued that had done little to clarify anything and had simply caused the protagonists to become more polarised in the dichotomy of their views.

In the end, Fry had drawn the council to a close, thanking the elder Druids for their thoughts and indicating that he would take no action at this time other than to consider the matter further.

As Margaret had ushered the three Druids out of the room Fry had quietly indicated that Helen should remain. He'd opened the French windows allowing the fragrance of the morning to sweep inside and purge the negative ambience from the room. 'I didn't handle that one very well, did I?' he'd mused out loud.

'I think you did the best you could in the circumstances,' Helen had offered. 'Basically, they didn't want to listen. Even Martyn, who was, to be fair, supportive, used the opportunity to ride his pet hobby horse again and his advice was hardly constructive.'

'And you have no opinion? No advice for me?'

'Not really. It's out of my league. I have no terms of reference. I feel that you are holding a lot back, but if this is the case you must have your reasons. In principle it's quite easy to accept the existence of a parallel world, I mean, one could argue that the astral plane is a good example of that very thing – but without any specific evidence it's very hard to come down one way or the other. While there's ample evidence for the astral plane, this isn't what you're talking about, is it?'

'No,' Fry had said. 'I'm afraid that it's not.'

Margaret had quietly re-entered the room, looking irritated and perplexed. 'I rather think you've stirred up a bit of a hornet's nest among our three elders,' she'd told him. 'I don't know how much confidentiality you can expect from them.'

'It doesn't really matter does it,' Fry had countered. 'Especially if I am right.'

'Michael, are you sure about all this?' she'd looked at him wonderingly. 'You are usually the most practical and down to earth of men. What you have told us this morning suspends belief. I'm sorry I couldn't be more supportive but...'

'It's quite all right,' Fry had interrupted gently. 'You were not invited as my mother but as my counsellor.'

'But how do you feel now that you have been counselled?'

'Not very good because I still don't know what to do. On the strength of this morning's conversations it seems I should do nothing and yet all of my instincts tell me I should be doing something and doing it quickly. Frankly, I'd hoped for more from this morning, although in good conscience I didn't really expect it.'

He'd lapsed into a thoughtful silence and for a full half minute before suddenly becoming alert and meeting Helen Ross's eyes. 'Helen, will you do a psychometric reading for me?'

'Of course,' the Scottish priestess had nodded with a faint smile. 'That's why I was invited this morning after all. What is it you wish me to read?'

With Margaret reclining regally on the sofa and Michael Fry studying her intently from behind the small desk, Helen had sat on the edge of her own chair, playing with the plain white gold wedding band Fry had given her. Obviously a man's ring. Too large to be a woman's... And yet there was a woman connected with this ring, and not just in the obvious way. The ring felt cold in her hand and as she closed her eyes she was overwhelmed by a deep feeling of sadness. She'd quietly told Fry what she'd felt, fumbling for the right words to express the confusion of her feelings.

'A man's ring, given to the man by his woman... Their relationship has ended... A lot of pain and sadness and a sense of loss and emotional grief that is extremely profound...' A face had swum into vision. '... A man's face. In his early forties? Brown hair, brown beard, brown eyes. Lots of confused emotions. Heartache... But beneath the heartache something much deeper...' Helen Ross had shuddered. '... There is anger and rage and fury and the deepest of deep hurts... and something else as well...'

She'd begun to sway very gently from side to side as the sentient psychometric memory patterns of the ring began to take hold of her. '... Oh God, this man... He is so hurt and confused. So lonely. Hurting so much. But beneath it all, he'd icy cold. He's incensed with the desire for justice and revenge... He's very very strong on a psychic level and very very powerful... and I think... I think he's planning to kill someone!'

She had started to breathe very deeply, eyes locked tightly shut. One part of her mind had been up and flying on the wings of clairvoyant trance, but the other part of her mind was well in control and aware of her surroundings. She was also aware that she knew who the owner of the ring was. '... This ring belongs to your friend Colin Mage. The man who's gone to Spain...'

The wedding band had still been uncommonly cold in the palm of her hand. This was unusual. It should have been glowingly warm by now with the energies passing through it. The coldness of the ring seemed to seep into her hands and then creep up her arms until it clutched at her heart, causing a balloon of tension to inflate within her solar plexus. In the eye of her mind she saw her man standing alone... It seemed to be on the battlements of a castle... Surrounded by menacing cyclones of swirling black cloud. She'd sensed the presence of, but had not actually seen the dark malefic faces that teased and taunted from within that broiling mass of malignancy.

'He's in very great danger,' she'd said sharply. 'He faces it with confidence and determination, but...' A shiver had coursed through her. '... it's far far worse than he imagines.' From the cloud a hooked talon had curved towards him, horrific and unearthly. Involuntarily she'd recoiled from the vision, sickened by the sudden stench that had assailed her olfactory senses. 'This is getting very heavy and very scary,' she'd murmured.

She'd tried to focus on something else and without realising that she'd done it, transferred the wedding band from her right hand to her left. 'Ugh,' she'd muttered. 'That's pretty disgusting.'

'What do you see?' Michael Fry's voice had echoed distantly from a thousand miles away.

'A woman,' Helen had said slowly. 'Very tall. Good looking. Long reddish hair. But there's something wrong with her body. It's covered with stuff. A bit like fur? No, more like, well... Fungus? It seems to be moving on her... On no! It... It isn't just moving on her, it's feeding on her!' Helen had gulped. 'And the woman's watching it happen and, oh for God's sake, she's actually enjoying it! Oh I can't believe this. This is obscene!'

She'd taken a huge lungful of air and both Fry and his mother had been aware of the beads of perspiration that covered the Scottish girl's brow.

'Other pictures.' Helen Ross had said slowly. 'All blurred and disconnected. Two men, fighting in a dark street. A church with stained glass and a, well, a catholicky feel to it. Tarot cards... The Magician, The Priestess, The Devil... A tall man, glasses, receding hair. He's got a funny kind of gun and he's shooting at something... Another man, very big, very heavy. A negro. His chest is cut wide open and he's bleeding badly. A girl. Very young... Short black hair. Wearing black patches over both her eyes. A hill with a tower on top if it... Looks like Glastonbury Tor. Is Glastonbury Tor. Two people talking. A man and a woman. The man is your man and I think that the woman must be his wife. They're arguing and she's hitting him. And there's someone else watching from the bottom of the hill and he's smiling... It's all very blurred...'

Calmer now that the visions were less grotesque, Helen had leaned back into her chair, cradling the wedding ring in both her hands. Her head had fallen forwards, her words becoming more hesitant and slurred as the trance took her more deeply out of her own state of consciousness, plunging her into the uncharted seas of the psychic realms.

'Walking back to happiness, whoompah oh yea yea,' she'd sung softly beneath her breath. 'Helen Shapiro. I'm Helen... So there's someone else connected with this ring called Shapiro... No happiness for Shapiro and no happiness in the ring. Might have been once but not any more. The marriage is dead and so is the wife. The magician called Mage grieves for his dead wife... Only she isn't quite dead yet...' She'd giggled and it was an alien sound, not from her own voice box. 'Fry The Druid...' Her voice had taken on a guttural tone. 'I'll fry you and your little white faith if you interfere. I am Jadoc I am Djinn I'll open up and enter in...'

'Michael, what's going on?' Margaret had whispered tersely. 'She's going down far too deep and picking up something quite nasty. Bring her out of it.'

'Not yet,' Fry had snapped. 'I'll...'

'Candles,' Helen had mused, her voice changing back to something more normal. 'Dozens of them in concentric circles. A black circle, a green circle, a red circle, one within the other... In the middle... Oh, this is weird... There's nothing there at all. A void. An open space, but suspended in there, there's the woman, on her back, legs wide... and, yes I see, she'd having a baby... She's very big and pregnant and there's a man there with her in among the candles... There's an altar and as the woman's having the child he's performing some sort of ritual. Can't hear any of the words, but it's all very intense. Why isn't he helping her? He should be helping her...'

She'd paused, shrinking more deeply into the protection of the chair. 'There's a swimming pool and palm trees and deck chairs and a funny looking man who is all wrong. His eyes are odd and he wears thin glasses with funny lenses to hide them. He's smiling and he's got jagged teeth. His hair is sort of tufty... and he'd got very big ears... I... I don't like him. He's repellent. There's something inside him that isn't true. But he likes me. He wants me and he's thinking dirty, no, not just dirty but evil things about me... Ah...' She'd turned her face to one side, screwing up her mouth as if to avoid a most unwanted kiss. 'God, it smells foul...

'I'm somewhere else now... A high cave, red sandstone and lots of loose shale and dust. I... I don't like it here at all. It's not an ordinary place. It's full of magic... Candle stumps, marks and sigils cut into the walls, lots of crystals embedded in the sand... They've been put there on purpose. They all point towards the back of the cave. There's something very awful down there. It wants to get out but it can't. The crystals are stopping it. There are lights, shades of light, dark green and mauve. I can't see the lights but I can feel the vibrations. They're wrapped round something that hides behind them...'

Then she'd suddenly moaned and her stomach had bulged in muscular spasm. 'Back at the candles. Baby's coming. The lights are here too. Purple. Green. Oh *God* the pain is awful...' She lurched forward, bending double and grabbing at her abdomen.

'Michael, I think you've got to stop this now,' Margaret Fry said urgently, not bothering to lower her voice. 'This is getting dangerous.'

Fry had nodded, and moving round from the desk had knelt at the side of Helen's chair. 'Come back to The Oaks, Helen,' he'd said firmly. 'Break the link with where ever you are and come back to The Oaks. I'll count you back from five... Five, four, three...'

But Helen Ross was gone, flying into the abyss of psychic maelstrom and the vortex of precognition. The sound of buffeting wind and guttural chanting in an unknown tongue.

She was there, in among the candle flames... A dark place filled with flickering shadows and tense, shuddering noise. There were presences, human and not human... The thing which officiated at the altar certainly wasn't human, not with those bent and scaled legs and stumpy switching tale. When it turned and looked at her, she cringed, looking for escape from it hideous countenance: pig like, with a snout and tusks and rows of serrated teeth. It's eyes were baleful and black and it emanated a dark and powerful aura of pure malevolence.

Beyond the circles of candles another figure moved cautiously... This was a man carrying some kind of clumsy weapon and she felt that if she could but cross the room to his side she would be safe, or at least as safe as she could be in this shade of hell.

The room itself was strange. Low stone ceiling and stone walls, hewn out of the living rock and covered with strange sigils and markings that she did not recognise. The floor of this place was also stone until she looked into the middle of the room and here there was no floor at all, but a gaping circular hole... An aperture that was filled with turbulent energy and that awful green and purple light that came inexplicably from below.

If the thing at the altar had terrified her, then the creature that hovered in that space, defying all laws of gravity and seemingly buoyed up by the energies that swirled beneath it, was twice as sickening. It was obviously female, and a female in its last hours, possibly even last minutes of pregnancy. Its belly heaved with contractions and its open legs beat a soundless tattoo in the ether. It had some semblance of human form, long hair, sagging breasts, recognisable facial features... but there the similarities ended. Rather than skin, it was covered in a scaly membrane like sheen that seemed to glow and pulse in the candle light. Its head turned and it half screamed, half roared when it saw her. Something darted out of its mouth... a tongue, nearly six inches long, that spat at her, before curling back and slapping against its face. It bellowed again in pain as another contraction made its belly heave and then it squealed and wriggled, almost as though in sexual pleasure.

She wanted to be sick. She wanted to get out of here. She wanted to be with the man on the far side of the room but he was too far away. To get to him she'd either have to cross the candles or edge around the walls. If she edged to the right, that would bring her to the altar and the beast that was grinning wickedly at her from that point... But if she went left, that would take her into the shadows where no light penetrated and she was desperately afraid of those shadows. Something lurked within them. Something she could not see, but that could see her... That wanted to enfold her in its darkness. Something that wanted her, full stop.

Something cold and slimy wrapped itself around her legs. She looked down and screamed in shock. A thick scaly tentacle, the thickness of a man's arm had her by the ankles... A tentacle that disappeared into the shadows on her left, and was pulling her towards the darkness. She bent to try and free herself, lost her balance and toppled backwards onto hard stone. The pressure around her ankles intensified and she was dragged, then jerked violently into the stygian shadow. Electrical static crackled above her head as the candles faded and a new light began to emanate all around her... Bile green and misty, chokingly fetid.

The tentacle released its grip, coiled backwards upon itself, disappearing into the sulphurous smoke. Dazed and disorientated, she scrambled to her knees, eyes darting left and right in search of some reference point. Surely she was still in the room, but if so, where were the candles, where was the hole in the floor? Where were the two alien creatures? Where was the man? She cried out in fear and frustration and her cry became a wail of new terror and disbelief as a figure lumbered towards her out of the fumy vortex.

Webbed feet, each with five sharply barbed claws. Wide bent legs supporting a thick and muscular torso, both legs and torso covered in that same slimy fish scale substance. A distended and disgustingly large navel, with something snakelike coiled within it. Broad shoulders protected by some bony carapace, a short neck and a huge head... A clone of the creature by the altar, but so much worse. Saliva trickled down its jowls as the rows of razor teeth gnashed together; something flesh like and turgid hung loosely to one of its upthrusting tusks and its deep gimlitty black eyes glowed with malevolent intelligence.

What worried her – no, it didn't just worry her, it paralysed her with the most awful fear – was the entity's maleness. A phallic protuberance jutted out from its loins, fully a foot long, black and shining with greasy wetness. She had no doubt what it was and with a dawning awareness of what was about to happen, was overwhelmed with an even greater sense of panic.

The thing threw its snout back and emitted a sound that was half roar, half squeal. She flung herself backwards, scrambling madly to put some distance between herself and this abomination of masculinity, but without warning the snakelike coil in the creature's navel lashed out like a bull whip, wrapping itself around her throat in a grip of umbilical strangulation and the creature was upon her, ripping and tearing at her clothes with long claws that were insensitive to flesh, with its long quivering phallus forcing its way up between her legs. Her screams had echoed mutely into the swirling fog of chaos and pain...

... and had rattled the French windows of Michael Fry's library. Fry had pulled her up from the floor, slapping her face, then cradling her in his arms, oblivious to the bile and vomit that cascaded from her mouth all over his expensive silk suit and the even more expensive Wilton carpet.

Within a very short while Helen Ross had been ensconced in her bedroom with two of The Oak's resident healers in attendance. Fry had explained the sequence of events – the psychometric reading, the fading speech, the lapse into unconsciousness and then the spasms and screams. Neither of the healers was unduly unruffled. This kind of occult accident was common to them and they were well versed in the arts of psychic rescue. While one applied herbal remedy through a pipette, the other began an acupressure massage. It was quietly suggested that The Merlin should leave them in peace to get on with it. Fry had acquiesced but demanded to be called the moment she regained consciousness.

That call didn't come until late in the afternoon. Fry was told that Helen had suffered severe psychic trauma, but was out of her trance and sleeping naturally. Giving instructions that someone should be at her bedside at all times, Fry had got on with the business of being The Merlin... but it wasn't easy that day. His mind lingered on the memory of Helen's words and he needed to cross examine some of the things that she's said. Further, he'd wanted to know what had happened and where she'd gone when the trance he taken her down too deeply to some place of terror that had scared her into shock and catatonia.

He had discussed the incident at some length with his mother.

'I presume that the ring *does* belong to this Colin Mage?' she'd asked.

'Yes... but Helen didn't know that. Something quite shocking happened to that girl this morning. I think she picked up on what was happening down there in Spain and, whatever it is, it's caused her major psychological distress.'

'You... you didn't tell her anything you haven't told the rest of us?'

'No Margaret. Absolutely not...' *But I think I might well have to, later, when she wakes up. If I want her help, I'm going to have to tell her a lot more.*

That Sunday had been a long day and an even longer night for the Druid. He'd not been able to relax or settle to anything. Margaret, with a few troubled thoughts of her own, had sensed her son's mood and had deliberately given him a wide birth. In the sumptuous bedroom with the panelled walls and Queen Anne bed, Helen Ross had slept soundly and dreamlessly, primarily thanks to the occasional ministrations of the medical herbalist. When she had awoken it had been a little before eight o'clock on the Monday morning and Michael Fry had been at her bedside within minutes and had shared her frugal breakfast.

She'd looked wan and pale, but at least her eyes had been clear and alert; indeed, they'd seldom been still for more than a few seconds at a time, darting hither and thither with nervous apprehension, as though she'd been expecting to see something that wasn't there.

She'd also been embarrassed to find herself still at The Oaks when she'd fully expected to have been back in Scotland the previous afternoon, but both Fry and the herbalist, a serene man called Leonardo Santorini, had insisted that she remain where she was until she felt fully fit. The herbalist had administered an infusion of camomile tea laced with vervain and a mixture of Bach flowers, then at a sign from Fry, had withdrawn, leaving The Merlin and the priestess alone in some discomfort with each other's company.

'I'm sorry I made a mess of your suit,' she'd said, finally.

'You remember that?' Fry had asked, surprised.

A distant look had clouded her frightened eyes. 'I remember everything,' she'd said in a small voice. 'I wish that I didn't, but I do. All of it.'

In a move that was much out of character, Fry had reached across the linen bedspread and had lightly taken hold of her hand. 'I'm sorry to have to ask you this,' he'd spoken gently. 'But I have to know what happened. I need to know what you saw.'

She had closed her eyes and had swallowed, teeth tugging at her bottom lip in pensive contemplation as she relived the memories of her vision. She'd opened her mouth to say something, but no words had ventured forth, only a long shuddering sigh.

'I'm sorry,' she'd said, '... I can't. I really can't. At least not yet. You... you can have no idea how horrible it was... Still is, because I've still got it so clearly imprinted in my mind.'

'That's why I have to talk to you about it now,' Fry had insisted. 'While it's still fresh.'

'I've been travelling out on the astral for more than fifteen years, ever since I was fourteen,' she'd told him. 'But I've never ever had to deal with anything like this before.' Then her eyes had hardened and she'd looked at him coldly. 'You knew, didn't you? You knew that something like this might happen, yet still you let me take that man's ring, full well knowing that I might be travelling into danger!'

'No...' It had been Fry's turn to be embarrassed. 'No, I didn't really know what might happen, please believe me.' And then, quizzically and inquisitively... 'If Bard Thomas and Lady Mary Donahoe were right, then there was nothing to fear.'

'Well, they were wrong,' Helen had said flatly. 'I can't talk to you about... about what I saw and what happened, but I'll put your mind at rest about one thing. These creatures, the Djinn or whatever they're called, they're not a figment of someone's imagination. They're very real and your Colin Mage is right. They want us and they're coming through to get us.'

Then without warming she'd dissolved into floods of tears and, at a loss for what to do next, Michael Fry had sat on the edge of the bed, cradling the girl within his arms until the sobs had gradually subsided.

She had caught the train back to Scotland later that afternoon. Fry had telephoned the following morning and again on Thursday evening... There were things he *had* to ask her and things she *had* to tell him, but in their conversations, which had been formal and stilted, she'd shown no inclination to assuage his need for information.

Apart from his worries about Helen Ross and Colin Mage, the week had been fraught with other problems. Margaret had been consistently tense and uncommunicative and indeed had been so ever since he'd brought up the subject of a possible parallel world. Bard Thomas had been nothing if not sly with an excessively over confident bonhomie when Fry had met with him in Cardiff on Wednesday afternoon to discuss the forthcoming May Festival Eisteddford... And by Friday morning he'd heard three separate rumours from three separate sources, one that said he'd had a vision of the end of the world, another that he was having a homo sexual relationship with a man in Spain, and a third that said there might – just might – be a leadership challenge at the Summer Solstice Council of Thirteen!

With a gesture of impatience, he swung open the car door and stepped out onto the cold damp tarmac of the carpark. Edinburgh's chill wind ruffled through his hair, whipping him across the face with its cold clingy tendrils and as much to keep the chill at bay as his determination to get on with any unpleasantness that might face him, he marched briskly out onto the street and up the hill of the Royal Mile until he came to the address and number he was looking for. Without thinking too much about the consequences, he rammed his finger down on the bell push and was satisfied to hear the jangling summons on the other side of the door.

He didn't have to wait long. The door opened and he was confronted by a red haired giant of a man wearing a kilt and a frown.

'You'll be Mr Fry, then,' the giant spoke in a heavy brogue. 'Well, I'll tell you now, my instructions are to let you in, but I warn you, Druid or no bloody Druid, you upset yonder lassie upstairs and you'll be making your exit a sodding sight faster than your entrance.'

'I'm expected?' Fry asked quietly, totally ignoring the other man's veiled threat.

'Aye, since last night as a matter of fact.'

'I see. May I ask... how is she?'

'Better than she was last Monday, but no as good as she should be, no thanks to you and your lot of white robed weirdoes.'

'May I come in then?'

'Not if I had my way, laddie. Not if I had my way!' But nonetheless, he stood to one side and Michael Fry crossed the threshold and preceded him up the narrow staircase to Helen Ross's apartment.

The staircase led into a large open plan room full of light and pale furnishings. A raised dias in one corner provided a kitchen and dining area while the rest of the room, filled with a generous sofa and half a dozen large scatter cushions, was given over to a living room. There were many tall green plants and pots and vases filled with daffodils and wild flowers. The walls were pale cream, decorated simply with a few small water colours. The main source of illumination came from two large North facing windows that gave impressive views of the Edinburgh skyline.

Helen Ross stood with her back to the windows. She wore an uncomplicated skirt and matching blouse in dark beige. Fry thought she still looked pale and also that she'd lost some weight. He found himself wondering how well she'd been sleeping. Little better than him, by the look of it.

'Good morning My Lord Merlin.'

He was grateful to realise that there was no hostility in her voice.

'Good morning. I gather I'm expected.'

'You had to come sooner or later. I thought it might be last night – so, no, I'm not too surprised to see you here at this hour. You have been much in my thoughts, My Lord.'

'As you have been in mine,' Fry countered. 'But Helen, I am not here this morning as The Merlin, so may we drop some of the formalities?'

'As you wish. Will Michael do, or would you prefer Mr Fry?'

Was she taunting him? He wasn't sure... 'Michael will be quite all right.'

She nodded. 'I suppose it's time for us to talk, isn't it?'

'I very much need to talk to you,' he confirmed, seriously.

Her eyes looked past him at the other man. 'All right Macgregor, you can leave us now. I'll need a few hours alone with my guest. You may call back at lunch time if you so wish. I may be free by then.'

'I'll no leave you alone wi' this man,' the kilted man shot back angrily.

'You'll do exactly as I ask,' she replied icily. 'First of all this gentleman is my guest and secondly he is the High Bard of All Britain. You will show him the courtesy and respect that befits him on both counts. Now, please leave us.'

The man called Macgregor left in a huff of resentment at the put-down and Fry was reminded of Helen's own authority. She may have been allied to Druidism, but she had her own loyal following among the Wiccan fraternity.

'I'm sorry about that,' she said without rancour. 'It hasn't been an easy week. Some of my friends have become a little over-protective – for which I bless them.' For the first time Fry saw the trace of a smile. 'And how goes it with The Merlin?' she asked.

He laughed shortly. 'It has been a difficult week for me also.' He raised an eyebrow. 'Have you not heard the rumours? My mother thinks that I might be gay and Thomas Llewelyn thinks he might topple me at the Mid Summer Thirteen.

Martyn of Glastonbury is ecstatic that I have at last come to accept his Age of Aquarius theories. Believe me, my telephones have not stopped ringing.'

''Have you - ' she hesitated. 'Have you heard anything from Spain?'

'No I haven't, but then nor have I expected to. My only direct contact was through you last Sunday. Needless to say, the man and the place have been much on my mind, along with you and the events of last weekend.'

'Have you had breakfast?' she asked, suddenly changing tack.

'No.'

'Tea or coffee? Perhaps some cinnamon toast?'

'Tea and toast sounds most inviting. Thank you.'

She led him into the dining area and he sat at the kitchen table, an old farmhouse piece in natural antique pine and, while she deftly prepared the refreshments, he watched her thoughtfully. She was full of tension, but was dealing with it in a calm and professional way. Eventually she sat opposite him, pouring Earl Grey into bone china mugs and placing the sweet smelling plate of toast between them. Realising that he was hungry, he ate with appreciative gusto, noting that she only nibbled. A token gesture of appetite to keep him company.

When they had finished he appraised her frankly. 'When we spoke at The Oaks on Monday morning, you said that you remembered everything with clarity...'

'I still do.'

'I need you to tell me,' he said. 'I appreciate that it might be hard for you, but I have to know. So very much might depend on it.'

She lowered her eyes for a moment, then looked up to meet his gaze. 'Yes, I think I understand that...' She hesitated a moment longer and then began to tell him all that she could remember with as much detail as she could muster. At first it was painfully difficult, but eventually she found her stride and Fry listened in silence for more than forty minutes while Helen relived and unburdened her experience of six days before.

Finally she came to a faltering stop. 'That's about it really. My last clear memory is of that thing strangling me to death with what I can only describe as its umbilical cord and forcing itself between my legs hell-bent on an act of rape. Then I was back in your library, vomiting all over your suit and carpet... After that it gets shaky. I don't remember much until we talked the following morning. But that creature... Its still in my head, hanging on to my every waking thought like a big spider with its long furry legs wrapped around my mind. Needless to say, I haven't been sleeping very well and even though I have gone through an in depth cleansing ritual every day, it's still there inside my skull. I feel dirty and contaminated.'

Fry closed his eyes, thinking hard. Distressed and alarmed by all that he had heard he was aware that no small degree of damage had been inflicted upon Helen Ross's psyche. He had an excellent memory and an analytical mind and sat for a number of minutes sifting through the information he had been given. In the end he looked up.

'May I ask some questions?'

She nodded.

'First, there is the awkward problem of tense. Are the things you have witnessed from the past, the present, or the future? From what Colin Mage has told me, I clearly recognise some of your visions as being patterns from the past, but I wonder if you have any thoughts and feelings on the subject?'

She shook her head slowly. 'No, not really... But I suppose, when I think about it, the bit about Glastonbury Tor and seeing that weird man under the palm trees... that was all a bit vague and distant. The two men fighting and the bleeding black man, well, that was all very blurred, as was the bit about the man with the strange gun I told you about. On the other hand, the vision of the man on the castle battlements with all those swirling clouds around his head, that was crystal clear. Very close and immediate. As for the part with those, those *aliens*, in the place with all the candles... Frankly, it was so surreal and I've never experienced anything like that before.' She studied him bleakly. 'And I never want to again,' she added.

Fry pondered and then asked her to describe the man on the battlements in more detail. This she did, even down to the small green braid bracelet he'd been wearing. Fry was in no doubt that she'd made psychometric contact with Colin Mage.

'Do you think,' he said thoughtfully, 'that the man you saw on the castle wall was the same man who was down there with you in that room... The man with some sort of weapon?'

'It could have been. In fact, I'm sure that it was, although I never saw his face properly in the candle light. He was certainly the same man that I saw at Glastonbury Tor with the woman.'

'Think about that woman for a moment and tell me what she looked like.'

Helen shrugged. 'Tall, statuesque. Long auburn hair. Not what most men would call beautiful, but very striking. She was very cold and angry. More than that I don't know. It was only a brief impression, after all. But there's one thing I have a very dark feeling about...'

'Yes?' Fry prompted gently, almost knowing what was coming next.

'The woman on Glastonbury Tor and the woman that was covered with that slimy stuff that was feeding on her – and that thing that was giving birth in the middle of the candles... Well...'

'Was the same person?' Fry finished for her.

'Yes!' Helen looked relieved. 'Except by the time she got to those candles, she wasn't a person any more. She'd become one of those other things!' Her eyes, filled with wild pagan light, bore into Michael Fry. 'You knew, didn't you? Even before I told you?'

'Let's say that I guessed,' Fry admitted. 'But combining what you are telling me with what I have already been told, it wasn't a difficult guess.'

She stared at The Druid, challengingly. '... And you know who this woman is, don't you?'

Fry nodded sadly. 'Yes, I think so. She's Colin Mage's wife.'

She sat in silence for a long moment, digesting the implications of what she'd been told and weighing up her own feelings and reactions to the information.

In the end, she stood up. 'I'm going to make another pot of tea and I'll phone Macgregor and keep him at bay for the rest of the day. Then I suggest we go and sit in the living room and you can tell me everything. The whole story. I promise I'll try and be rather more receptive and constructive than you Council of Five.'

'That won't be difficult,' he riposted with some feeling. 'Helen, I really am most grateful to you for your time and consideration.'

'You're welcome,' she replied. And then, 'After all, since last weekend I'm as deeply involved in this mess as you are, aren't I?'

'Yes,' he answered reflectively. 'I rather suppose you are.'

11.

Helen

In Ashquelon, Herschal began to feel far from well and Leon Shapiro steeled himself for a difficult debriefing. In the United States, John Light and Tamara crossed into the state of Louisiana, heading through a maze of black roads that led them ever more deeply into the poor black south of the Mississippi delta. In Calcutta, Kiku prepared the boy, Rajad, for a long overland journey that only she knew would be his last. In Castillo, Colin Mage called on Anna Sanchez at her home in Calle Santana and asked if she would like to go with him to the fair in the neighbouring village of San Pablo, the following week. Mage was nervous, for if she said yes this would be their first proper "date" rather than some accidental or spontaneous meeting. Also in Castillo, Miriam Cortez swept out her special room – a room that not even Peter Cortez ever dared to enter and thought about the dark spell of magic that she would unleash against the English witch later that night. In England, Michael Fry had a private conversation with Leonardo Santorini and, in Scotland, Helen Ross sat down to dinner with three friends in Edinburgh's famous Witchery Restaurant.

The food, as always, was superb, but while her friends tried hard to be witty and entertaining, she was not in harmony with them. A dinner party had seemed like a good idea when it had been suggested, but in the reality of the experience she realised that what she really wanted and most needed was some space and silence, some thoughtful meditation and the privacy of her own company. Although her mind went frequently wandering off at tangents, she put on a brave face and a convincing act and was heartily relieved when the evening drew to a natural close. Declining the invitation to join her friends for a night-cap and making certain that nothing she said could be misconstrued as her making any invitations of her own, she parted company with them at the door of her flat and was glad to shut the door behind her.

In a gesture of defiance she flicked on the television in time to catch the last thirty seconds of The News at Ten... Daring the set to produce anything that might capture her restless mind. She need not have worried, for nothing did.

Kicking off her shoes, she curled up on the large sofa and tried to read one of the books she had bought earlier that afternoon. There were four of them; two hard back and two paper backs, all by the same author. His picture stared candidly at her from both the back cover and the fly leaf, a face she recognised. The man on the battlements. Colin Mage.

The Druid had not left until well after lunch, by which time her head had been buzzing with the very strange story she'd been told. More to clear her mind than anything else, she'd walked the mile across Edinburgh to her friend's book shop in Stockbridge and had had to wait a good fifteen minutes before Frances had found the time to chat. It was Saturday, and both Edinburgh and the book shop – an emporium that specialised in arcane and esoteric literature – had been busy.

'Hi Fran. You got anything by a guy called Colin Mage?'

'Sure.' The other girl had wrinkled her brow. 'There's "The Psychology of Seerism",' she counted one finger, then held up another, 'or there's "The Anatomy of Magick". These are his two well known books. Hard back only, I'm afraid, and not cheap. In paper back I've got "Healing Through Magick" and "Prophesy Through Magick". Very good solid stuff, all of it.'

'You've heard of him then?'

'Of course! It'd been an odd occult book seller who hadn't. I'm surprised you haven't come across him yourself. But then again, he's writing on pure magic and you've become a bit more spiritual and specialist these last few years, haven't you?'

Helen had been sheepish. 'Yes I suppose so. It's a bit difficult to keep up with every new book. Usually it's just a rehash of the same old theory... I thought I'd read everything worth reading...'

'I dare say you have, but Mage is new. Four books in the last six years. Very bright. Very refreshing. Strips away a load of the crap and mumbo jumbo. Brings the whole thing into the twenty first century. You've been on your own pathway for a fair bit longer than six years though, so I suppose you've got a good excuse.'

'Have you read him?' Helen had wanted to know. 'And if you have, what's he like? I mean, where is he coming from?'

'Well, as a writer, nice clear English. Doesn't use too many long words but still takes you in deep and gets you to the heart of the matter quickly. As for where he's coming from, well, I'm not exactly sure what you're asking me, but it seems like he knows his stuff and writes with the authority of a lot of practical experience. I'd say he was a fairly adept magician. Anyway, can I interest you in one of his books?' She'd grinned wickedly. 'It would be nice if I could. I'll be the first book I've actually sold you in years.'

'Oh yes of course... sorry. I'll take whatever you've got.'

'All four?'

'All four.'

'Hey, why the sudden interest, Hel? You know this guy or something?'

'No,' Helen had said weakly. 'But I've got a feeling I'm going to before long.'

She glanced at her watch. Almost eleven o'clock. She dismissed the thought of going to bed. There was no way she could sleep yet. Instead, she made a flask of coffee and, grabbing an old leather jacket, left the flat by the rear exit and descended the long flight of trip stairs that led down to the cobbled mews. Fumbling with keys, she opened the garage door, glad of the automatic light that immediately came on as the door swung open.

Her face broke into a smile as she slid into the cockpit of her old MGB roadster. It was a 1972 model in British Racing Green, with chrome bumpers and wire spoked wheels. Although elderly it was in concourse condition, mainly thanks to the labours of Duncan Macgregor, and the engine throbbed into life with the first turn of the key. She contemplated lowering the hood but even as she eased out into the mews, drops of springtime rain splashed against the windscreen and she thought better of it.

The car had come to her on her father's death in 1985 and she chose to run the car, keeping it in pristine condition, more as a memorial to his memory than as a mode of transport. This said, she loved the vehicle in its own right, seeing it as an extension and reflection of her own personality. She'd never been tempted to buy something more modern. Euroboxes and the plasticky panache of Japan left her traditional soul unmoved.

The MGB was as near to original as it could be, the one concession to modernism being the Blaupunct radio cassette player. As she cruised down the Royal Mile towards Holyrood House, she slid a cassette into the machine and the car was filled with the hauntingly enigmatic sounds of Enya. Good music to drive to. It filled the senses but did not distract the mind.

At first she didn't really know where she was going, content to cruise and criss cross the city, frequently travelling the same roads twice. Then she found herself heading towards the Forth Road Bridge and the smile crept back upon her face. She might not have had a specific destination in mind but the car obviously did.

Turning East on the Northern shore of the Firth of Forth, she headed towards Kirkcaldy but turned off to the right long before coming to that place and twenty minutes later was driving into the somnambulant little seaside village of Aberdour. The streetlights were luminescent in ther light rain and with the time fast approaching one in the morning, the tiny hamlet was as quiet as she hoped and expected it would be.

She turned right before the bend that curved the road up towards the railway station and allowed the car to burble down the long narrow hill towards the sea front and the harbour. Here she turned left and brought the MGB to a halt a few yards from the harbour wall. With the sea to her right and the rising hill of sleeping Victorian houses to her left, she sat there thinking quietly, taking a sense of peace and pleasure from her surroundings. Aberdour had been the home of her childhood and her father's home too for the many years he'd lived alone after the death of her mother, back when she'd still been a little girl. Both parents slept in the same churchyard, not a quarter mile from where she now sat, and although she'd been long gone from this place of childhood memory, it was ever present in her consciousness and a place that she frequently returned to, especially at times like this, in the dead of the night when her mind was so full of thoughts that sleep was denied its rightful role until those thoughts were brought into some semblance of harmony and order.

Three times in the last three years she had come to this harbour of retreat. Once when a relationship had ended in great anguish and acrimony. Once when she'd discovered that she was pregnant and had not known what to do about it... And the third time, almost a year ago, shortly after the termination of her pregnancy in an expensive Edinburgh clinic. An inconsequential physical process that had caused a deeply consequential emotional scar.

Taking the flask of coffee she slid out of the car, surprised at the mildness of the night. There was a warm buffeting breeze that carried the occasional heavy drop of rain. But it was not cold. She walked into the harbour, little more than a single concrete quay that gave a degree of man made protection to a natural cove, and strolled along the damp cobbles, looking absently at the dozen or so small yachts that clanked and clinked at their moorings. In the distance, from across the Firth, the lights of Edinburgh cast an amber shadow against the low scudding cloud. She leaned against the stone parapet, looking out across the water. She poured herself some coffee from the flask and wondered what she should do.

'What will you do now?' she'd asked Michael Fry towards the end of their very long conversation.

'I don't know,' he'd answered. 'Obviously I have no mandate and no support from my immediate council. I could call an emergency session of the full Council of Thirteen, but in the light of last Sunday's fiasco, I'm reticent to do so... At least not without a lot more hard facts and information. I have no direct contact with Colin Mage, although I'm sure he will make a point of speaking with me when he has something to report. In the meantime, I shall be very much on my guard and may well initiate some private proceedings at The Oaks that might provide a measure of protection and warning if the worse should happen...'

'Of course,' he'd looked at her expectantly. 'What I really need is an agent in place. Someone in Castillo who can give Mage some back up and at the same time report directly to me as to what is happening down there...'

'Oh no...' Helen had immediately caught his drift. 'Oh no. Forget it! As far as I'm concerned, it's impossible. That's the very last place I want to be in the world right now. Apart from anything else, it would be walking straight into the arms of self fulfilling prophesy!'

Fry had demurred. 'It was just a thought,' he'd said. 'After all, you are the most logical candidate.'

'No,' Helen had said sharply. 'It's not on. You must find someone else.'

The coffee tasted good and the night wind filled her senses with the smell of rain and the scent of the sea. Her thoughts turned back to The Druid's tale... and while her memory was not photographic, like most people working within the realms of the paranormal, she had an excellent degree of recall. Weird though the story may have been, Michael Fry had obviously accepted it at its face value, even though it had only been from Colin Mage's own subjective point of view. The Druid had not embellished anything, Helen was certain of that, and told it as it had been told to him.

'Colin Mage is forty two years old,' Fry had told her. 'He's Scorpio with Leo rising and a moon in Taurus, which should give you some insight to his mood and character. His early training in life was as a journalist, but being naturally clairvoyant from birth it was perhaps inevitable that his journalistic skills were directed more and more towards the occult. By the time he was twenty three he was well aware of his psychic abilities and delved ever more deeply into the learning curve that enhanced them. By the time he was twenty seven journalism was very much on the back burner and he was earning the better part of his living as a professional psychic. To all intents and purposes, he was doing a very good job of it.

'He met Alexandra Parish in 1987 and they married the following year. This was a major turning point in Mage's life and not only was their marriage a perfect match, it was also a very logical and natural union. Like Colin, Alexandra was a practising clairvoyant and their relationship functioned on a number of different levels, spiritual as well as sexual and emotional. After two years of living together they had achieved total rapport, could read each others minds at will and make telepathic contact even if one of them was out of the country on another continent.

'They were an attractive couple and they were very happy with their lot. Their working relationship flourished with Alexandra doing rather more of the clairvoyant consultations which allowed Mage to concentrate on his studies of high magic and healing and also, of course, his book writing. An enviable pair, and I tell you this to impress upon you this closeness and the incredibly tight bond of their union.

'I suppose no two people's lives can ever be perfect and their own dark cloud of sorrow came from their inability to have children. Rather than pushing them apart, if anything, it drew them even more closely together. One important point to make here, Helen, is that the result of the various tests they both subjected themselves to, clearly indicated that the problem lay not with Mage but with his wife.

'Eighteen months ago, partly in celebration of Mage's latest book being published and partly because they were both in need of a break after what had been a long and busy winter, they took themselves off to Spain for a much deserved holiday. An up-market package deal in an exclusive resort just outside Marbella. Lots of sun, sea, sand and sex.

'Their first week was pleasantly relaxing and uneventful but, sadly, alas, not so their second.'

'What happened?' Helen had asked, now completely absorbed by the story.

'To use Mage's own words, they got "latched onto" by this strange little man called Jadoc Dolorean. Apparently Mage and Alexandra were sitting by the swimming pool beneath the palm trees minding their own business, when out of the blue, they were approached by this man who introduced himself as Dolorean. He told them that he was holidaying alone and would they care to join him for a drink? He was, so he said, very psychic and had been attracted to them by their own very powerful psychic aura.

'Mage admits that it would have been churlish to turn him away, but he also says that even from that very first encounter he disliked the man quite intensely. Mage describes him as being somewhat skinny and scrawny with receding tufty hair and glasses. Very uneven teeth and unusually pale skin. His limbs seemed to be overly disjointed and there was something very odd and unpleasant about him that Mage couldn't quite put his finger on. Whatever it was, he didn't like it at all... This ringing any bells with you?'

'Yes,' Helen had nodded. 'It sounds very much like the man in my vision – and the palm trees would be right, wouldn't they?'

'Yes, I think it's a sound connection. Anyway, the three of them had their first social drink and after that the Mages couldn't get rid of him. Everywhere they went, he either turned up a few minutes after them or was already in situ waiting for them to arrive. He was quite a gifted psychic reader and impressed them both with his accuracy, pinpointing a number of things that only they could have known about. He honed in on their childlessness and quite openly told Alexandra that despite all the odds and the medical prognostications, she would nonetheless have a baby within the next couple of years and that the child would have a most important role to play in the salvation of the world.

'It was around this time that Mage began to loathe and detest Dolorean and this provoked one of the very few, extremely rare arguments he'd ever had with his wife. Alexandra was quite enchanted by their new found friend and deeply moved by the prophesy of her pregnancy. Mage felt that Dolorean had done no more than latch onto the desire factor and, in his attempts to please and impress, had amplified it dangerously out of proportion, raising a host of false hopes.

'Mage tells me that from his point of view Dolorean's interlopation completely ruined the second half of the holiday. Alexandra, however, seemed more than content to share time with him and every time Mage protested it led to an argument of one sort of another. Mage says that he felt hurt and bewildered by his wife's uncharacteristic attitude and that it was almost as though someone had worked a magic spell against the union of their marriage. He thought it then and is convinced of it now. To his credit, he didn't say much about it at the time. Alexandra had already accused him of being excessively Scorpionic and overly jealous.

'Two days before the end of their holiday Mage's patience finally snapped. He took Dolorean to one side and warned him off in no uncertain terms. Dolorean apologised, said that he had not meant to cause any distress and, by the next morning, had checked out of the hotel and had disappeared... Little good that did

Mage because Alexandra was furious with him when she found out and their last thirty six hours in Spain was a day and a half of cold moody silence.

'Mage thought that things would improve once they got back to England, which they did, but only up to a point. By tacit agreement their Spanish holiday was not discussed. They continued to enjoy the trappings of their marriage, but Mage says he felt as though something had been stolen from it. Some of the closeness, the spirituality – and he was in no doubt as to the cause.

'By the end of July Alexandra was behaving rather strangely and quite out of character. She'd become moody and secretive and Mage became increasingly worried and concerned. Their sex life was virtually non-existent and their psychic rapport was virtually in tatters. He says that he tried talking to her about it at least half a dozen times, but never got very far at all. The spiritual bond that had always bound them so closely together and that had made communications so easy and natural between them – had departed along with the sex and the psychic links.

'Quite by accident, on July 29th, he intercepted a phone call. He'd picked up the phone in his study to make an outgoing call, only to find Alexandra talking to someone on the bedroom extension. She was talking to Dolorean and by the sound of what was being said, it was clear that they had been in contact ever since Spain. Mage was hurt, but he was also furious. He challenged his wife and there was a very bad fight wherein he accused her of being dishonest and she accused him of being distrustful. The fight ended with Alexandra storming out of the house – and she never came back.

'Mage assumed that she'd gone to any one of half a different mutual friends, but when she hadn't returned by the following evening and he'd phoned everyone he could think of to phone, it was apparent that she'd gone elsewhere. He tried in vain to contact her on the astral and even got some of his people to sit in a search circle with him, but wherever Alexandra Mage had gone, it was obvious that she did not want to be found.

'By the beginning of August Mage was going frantic. He'd already contacted the police and every hospital in the North of England. By August 10th he'd been in touch with the Salvation Army listing his wife as a missing person and it must be said that he got a lot more sympathy and support from them than he'd got from the law. By the 15th, through his links with the media, there'd been a number of appeals on local radio and Yorkshire Television. Also, by then, he'd become quite convinced that Alexandra was with Dolorean somewhere. It may have been irrational, but from his point of view it was totally logical and thus a search for Dolorean was initiated. But that was a slow process. He'd not paid too much attention to the man in Spain and only remembered him saying that he had homes in Spain and England. Mage thought that it had been flannel designed to impress, but a phone call to the hotel in Marbella did bring to light an address in a place called Sotogrande.

'When a couple of Mage's Spanish friends dropped everything and drove down from Seville to check it out, all they found was a building site with a few breeze block foundation stones. To give them their due, they did do some digging and turned up a purchaser's address in the UK, but when Mage chased that one up it turned out to be a post office box in a small sub post office in Hinckley, Leicestershire.

'At that point Mage went back to the police and they promised to look into things more deeply but, of course, from their stand point they had little incentive and little to go on. There'd been a domestic fight and a wife had walked out on her husband. True, they had the registration number of her car, but nothing had been stolen, no crime had been committed. This kind of thing happened all over the country a hundred times a day. One can see why it was hardly on top of their list of priorities.'

'Wasn't he able to pick up anything at all on the astral?' Helen had asked. 'Obviously from his background and experience, he must have had a lot of different occult techniques at his disposal. If he wasn't getting any help from the law, why didn't he resort to using some of his professional skills?'

'I think this was what must have caused him the most pain,' Fry had mused. 'As I've said, he did try to forge telepathic linkage on the astral, but there was nothing there. Not an acorn. Not a sniff... Despite the fact that he was constantly projecting his thoughts in an attempt to make contact. And yet, on a number of occasions he was sure Alexandra was trying to get through to him and that she was in some distress. He says that he's aware that it could have been his subjective imagination, but by then he was clutching at every straw and it was literally tearing him apart.

'Perhaps that influenced his next move. Either way, it turned out to be a bad one. Rather than just probing into the astral he prepared and performed a major ritual of magick in an attempt to discover the whereabouts of his wife. Initially all went well. He's a careful and methodical practitioner and he certainly would not have been careless, even if he was emotionally in extremis. Towards the end though, something went drastically wrong. He remembers only that without warning he suddenly picked up his wife's aura and went chasing after it. Then he was above Glastonbury Tor fighting off the most savage psychic attack and battling for his life. He couldn't get back to the safety of his own circle and, the way he describes it, it was as though he walked straight into a trap someone had set for him, using Alexandra as the bait. He describes doing battle with all kind of malefic entities, but has no clear memory of the precise nature of his adversaries, only that they were very very powerful and he was swamped by them.

'Anyway,' Fry had paused for effect. 'He woke up two weeks later in a local mental hospital, as weak as a kitten and with a totally scrambled mind. A lot of his memories were gone and he described feeling as though someone had carved away a slice of his soul.

'Apparently a couple of good friends had found him collapsed on the floor of his home and they'd had the sense to remove the evidence of his occultism before getting him to the medical authorities. Mage remained in the hospital for another ten days. His memories came back slowly but he was severely traumatised and was frequently on the receiving end of nightly psychic attacks. Vivid dreams and hallucinations that might, in part, have been caused by the medication he was on, although I'm prepared to give him the benefit of the doubt. It was only when the same friends who'd found him got him discharged into their care that the attacks abated. They realised what was going on and built some very strong healing circles around him. They might not have saved his life but they certainly preserved his sanity.'

'Good to have friends like that,' Helen had commented. 'He's lucky.'

'They are two very elderly people blessed with great kindness and wisdom,' Fry had confirmed.

'You've met them?'

'No. Mage told me much about them and I did make a point of talking with them over the telephone. They confirm that when he first came to them from the clinic his aura was in shreds and that the psychic attacks that did occasionally erupt in their home during that first week of having Colin with them were not illusory. There was quite a bit of poltergeist activity including olfactory phenomena. It was not a pleasant time, but they fought the battle for their friend and finally won.

'At the end of September, quite a few things happened all at once. The psychic attacks started again, but this time with the support of his friends, Mage was ready for them. Not only did he resist them, he fought back, getting the clear picture of Glastonbury Tor on the two or three occasions he was able to trace the attack back to its source.

'Then the police contacted him to say that they had located Alexandra living near the village of Hobden in Somerset – not five miles from Glastonbury. A local constable had been doing a routine roadside speed check and had pulled her over, not because she was speeding but because he recognised the number plate of her car as something on his missing persons' list. Mrs Mage told the officer that she was not a missing person. She'd simply left her husband and was staying with a friend in the Glastonbury area.

'The third thing that happened was that Mage's lawyers were contacted by a firm acting on behalf of Alexandra, a legal practice in Glastonbury, petitioning for divorce on the basis of Mage's mental cruelty, an admission of her own adultery and irretrievable breakdown of marriage. Before Mage had time to react properly, it became apparent that she'd cleaned out their joint bank and building society accounts and had slapped a restriction order on their home, effectively freezing most of Mage's cash assets until such time as he agreed to a speedy divorce and a divorce settlement.

'Oddly enough, this all had quite a curious effect on Mage. He says that part of him relaxed, knowing that Alexandra was alive and knowing vaguely where she was. He was still mentally screwed up, physically weak and financially crippled, but says that he felt stronger and more focused then than at any other time since his wife had walked out of their home three months before.

'He told his lawyer to contest the divorce, got into his car and drove down to Glastonbury and, after quite a considerable feat of detective work, found out where his wife was staying – and sure enough, she was in residence with this Jadoc Dolorean fellow. Curious name, isn't it, by the way. Supposed to be Hungarian, or at least, so the man said.

'There was a doorstep confrontation and Mage was told flatly and firmly that Alexandra regarded her relationship with him as being over and that she was happy to be building a fresh life with her new partner.'

'What a shitty way of doing it,' Helen had muttered.

'Just so. Mage must have been very hurt and confused, but there was something that puzzled him a lot more than just the method of his rejection. He said that his wife spoke to him in a flat and toneless voice, as though she were reading from a script almost and that her eyes were completely dead, as though she was drugged or under some deep hypnosis... Reciting the words that someone had prepared for her. Also he said that the house reeked with evil and that he felt very frightened and threatened the whole time he was there.

'Alexandra shut the door in his face and that was the end of that interview... but it had given him food for thought and he became increasingly convinced that Dolorean was responsible for his wife's seduction and abduction... that he had her under some sort of spell or enchantment and that if the strength of the psychic attacks were anything to go by, Dolorean was probably a very powerful magician of the worst possible kind. So Mage changed tactics and went after Dolorean. He hired a private detective, quite a good one I believe, and within a couple of weeks some very interesting facts had come to light. First of all, there was no income tax or social security record for anyone of that name. There was no immigration record and there was no passport issued either by the British or the Spanish governments. Legally and officially the man did not exist. Not under that name, anyway.

'Mage and the detective went back to the police with this information and, although the police did pick up some interest at this point, they also pointed out that it was more a case for the inland revenue or the DHSS. Mage subsequently made depositions to both those departments, but we all know how those people can drag their feet sometimes and Mage was understandably very impatient. So back he went to Glastonbury for another doorstep confrontation and was amazed and dismayed by the deterioration in his wife's condition. She was quite slovenly and unkempt and seemed to be spaced out on drugs or something. Mage said she could hardly string two words together with any degree of articulation. Her speech was slurred and her eyes couldn't focus.

'Rather inevitably in the circumstances, Mage lost his temper and intent on confronting Dolorean, barged into the house – Mage says it was like a pig sty – to find Dolorean involved with some sort of alchemical work in one of the back rooms. Mage called him every name under the sun and Dolorean simply laughed at him, saying that Alexandra had made her choice and that there was nothing Mage could do about it. The law was on their side.

'Mage saw red and lost control. He swung a punch, but instead of knocking Dolorean senseless, it was like hitting a brick wall. He says that Dolorean's eyes changed from brown to a dirty yellow and that they became elliptical, and then he was lifted and thrown through the window into the back garden without the other chap even so much as lifting a finger.'

'Is that kind of telekinetic power really possible?' Helen had queried.

The Druid has hesitated. 'Yes,' he'd said shortly. 'I have actually seen it, but the energy is rare. Very rare indeed. And I've never seen it used aggressively in a combat situation.'

'And what about this Dolorean man's eyes changing shape and colour? Is this possible?'

'No, it's not, but it's what Mage says he saw – and it frightened him badly. It was enough to make him keep his distance for a while anyway. He started watching the house. Apparently it's quite isolated and there was plenty of cover. To all intents and purposes he virtually camped in a clump of bushes for the better part of a fortnight armed with packs of sandwiches and a pair of binoculars. Alexandra hardly ever appeared either in the garden or at any of the windows, but Dolorean was always in and out, sometimes at all hours of the night.

'I suspect that Mage wasn't quite balanced during this time. He tells me that he was wild with anger and not always rational in his thinking. The one thing that kept him going was the thought that Alexandra was being held against her free will, thus it was quite natural to hatch the idea of kidnapping her as soon as an opportunity presented itself. He felt certain that he could break her out of her fugue-like state if only he had a little time. He recognised that he would have to be very careful, realising that whatever Dolorean was, he was very very dangerous.

'Towards the end of the second week an opportunity did occur. Dolorean left by car, carrying a number of heavy looking suitcases and about an hour later Alexandra emerged from the house and cut across the fields on foot. She was wearing outdoor clothes and Mage assumed she was just out for a walk. Seeing this as his chance, he cut across the fields after her but she'd had a good head start and by the time Mage finally caught up with her she was almost at the foot of Glastonbury Tor. She walked straight up the bank without stopping and, if you know the Tor, Helen, you'll know that that was quite an achievement.

'Mage scrambled up after her and approached her under the arch of St Michael's Tower. He said she was simply standing there, looking North, eyes defocused and seemingly oblivious to her surroundings. She looked pale and dangerously undernourished... and very much in need of medical and psychiatric attention. The other thing that Mage noticed was the smell that hung to her. The nearest he got to describing it was that it was something like rotting seaweed...

'He intended getting her off the Tor, down into Glastonbury. They'd get a taxi to where Mage had parked his car, then he'd have her away back to Yorkshire. The trouble was, she wouldn't move. He tried pushing her, pulling, coaxing, leading, whatever, and then realised that she *couldn't* move. When he tried picking her up, he couldn't even get her heals off the floor. This was extremely unnatural but he felt that he didn't have too much time to question it just then. The whole business was unnatural and this phenomena on top of Glastonbury Tor was just the tip of the iceberg.

'So he stood directly in front of her, tried to make eye contact and went into a rescue ritual... The same kind of thing that Leonardo did for you last week at The Oaks. After about ten minutes he began to get some response, albeit only on a physical level. He started talking to her and her eyes cleared a little and she started talking back... Said that her name was Alexandra Dolorean, that she was deeply in love with her partner Jack, and that they were going to live in Spain together where they would breed horses and have lots of lovely children and live happily ever after. She said it all in a little girl's voice, as though she was about four years old.

'Mage carried on trying to get through to her and was aware that she was in a lot of psychological distress. He was also aware of impending danger. The Tor was deserted and it was a clear day, but the atmosphere was very tense and emotional. He tried slapping her face, but that did nothing to help. He tried lifting her again, but she simply wouldn't budge. In the end, he gave up trying. He broke down in tears, wrapped his arms around her and hung on while he sobbed his heart out.

'He hadn't planned it or anticipated it, but that did seem to have some effect and after a little while he heard her speak his name in something like her old voice. When he pulled back and looked at her it was as though she was waking slowly from a long dream. Her eyes were rolling all over the place and she was very disorientated. It didn't last long. She told him that Dolorean was taking her to a place called Castillo – but that it wouldn't be until the time was right, sometime the following year. That there was to be a magical ritual called The Opening or An Opening that she was to be a necessary part of. She pleaded with Mage to help her and said she thought she was going to die.

'This was all very stilted and disjointed, but before Mage could respond, all hell broke loose. Alexandra started screaming and the top of the Tor was suddenly surrounded by black thunder clouds and flashes of lightening. A huge gust of wind blew Mage fifteen feet towards the edge of the Tor and when he looked up he saw Alexandra still rooted to the spot, her hair flying all over the place, her whole body surrounded by lightening that struck out of the ether. He says there was a swirling mass of black cloud filled with flickering lights – green and mauve lights...' Fry had paused to make sure that Helen recognised the significance of the colours. 'Colin fought his way back to his wife, but he says that it was like swimming through treacle. He used all of his power to break through the barrier that had sprung up around her and by the time he got there he was bleeding from both his ears and his nose. By this time Alexandra was – well, the word Mage used was different, but I don't think that says the half of it. Her hair was almost on end, her eyes had become elliptical and amber and her face was contorted into a visage of evil. Mage says that she was screaming and smiling at the same time and, when he reached out to grab at her, she spat at him. He says that her tongue was impossibly long. That it wasn't a human tongue. He caught at her wrist but she pushed him away with such incredible strength that he went flying backwards again, and this time did topple over the edge of the Tor. He stopped rolling about twenty or thirty feet down from the summit and here the air was mild and clear even though the crest of the Tor was still being lashed by the storm. He was dazed from a bang on the head and three cracked ribs, but even allowing for this, he says it was the strangest thing... being able to look down and see Glastonbury and the surrounding countryside quite clearly while a few metres above him it seemed like the world was coming to an end. He says that it was not a natural weather cyclone. The green and mauve lights and the way in which the lightening became static energy around Alexandra defied all naturalness. Also he was very aware of that stale seaweedy smell which had become a lot stronger since the storm had broken loose.

'He watched as Alexandra moved out of the storm and began to descend the steps cut into the Tor. As she did this the tempest died as quickly as it had arisen. After about a minute Alexandra had moved out of his line of sight. He remembers trying to stand up... and doesn't remember anything else until he wakes up later that night in a strange bed aching like glory from a dozen different bruises and with a big white bandage wrapped around his head.

'He was lucky to have been found by a certain Mrs Livingstone who'd been out with her dogs, investigating what she later described to Mage as being strange lights on top of the Tor. When he questioned her about this, that was all she'd seen. Just strange dancing lights. Certainly no storm with black clouds and lightening... Mrs Livingstone runs quite a well known healing centre in Glastonbury and as her property virtually backs on to the Tor it wasn't difficult for her to rustle up some help and get Colin off the hillside down to the centre. Mage owes her a lot.

'By this time, he was completely strung out, verging on a nervous breakdown and no longer sure what was real any more. He knew how bad a state he was in, and it was no great effort to stay on at the healing centre for something getting on for three weeks until he regained some of his physical strength and mental equilibrium. The healers at the centre, and principally Mrs Livingstone herself, did an excellent job of putting him back together. His two close friends came down from York and as good as took up residence. As you may have gathered, these two friends are not without occult power and they did much to prevent any further incoming psychic attack.

'We must not forget the fact that Colin Mage is quite an extraordinary man with a vast reservoir of occult knowledge. As you can imagine, he did quite a lot of thinking and meditating during his three weeks of seclusion and recuperation.

'It was at this time, especially in light of his experience on top of the Tor, that he inevitably came to the conclusion that what he was trying to deal with here was not just the case of an errant wife having become bewitched by a powerful black wizard. There was something more. Something far more dark and sinister with decidedly demonic connotations. He'd met the full force of his adversary both in his dreams and on the Tor and he came to realise that there might be more at stake in this business than just the sanctity of his marriage.

'He made some discreet enquiries and learned that Alexandra and Dolorean had left the house in Hobden for God alone knew where. So, he contacted the private detective again with a locating brief and returned to York. He scoured his own library in search of any reference to a ritual called The Opening... As you know, there are a number of rituals that could be described as opening rituals – the opening of the third eye, the opening to the astral, the opening to self awareness – but he felt that he was looking for something more specific and dramatic that this. He went through his friends' collections of grimoires and even tried a number of antiquarian book shops in search of a clue. He drew a blank. To make matters worse, he was served with a court order preventing him from seeing or talking to

Alexandra on the strength of her accusation that he had assaulted her. In a degree of desperation, that was when he first came to see me at The Oaks.

'If you can think back to what I told you last Sunday, you will remember the rest of the story.' Fry had fallen silent while he'd contemplated his next thoughts. 'It would be conveniently expedient to dismiss Colin Mage as a man so obsessed with his grief that he has become paranoid in his beliefs... To say that his quest is born from the wild imaginings of a man who cannot come to terms with the loss of his wife and the termination of what he believed to be an extremely sound marriage. And yet, Helen, I have talked to this man quite extensively. I have channelled healing power into him and feel that I have seen the shape of his inner being. I have read his books, I have cross examined him under deep hypnosis and, although I accept that he may have become obsessive and will acknowledge that he does still grieve for the loss of his wife, I do not think he is paranoid. I do not think he is insane or unbalanced. I *do* think that he has latched onto something that may have devastating consequences for us all. Your own reading, last weekend, of Colin Mage's wedding ring confirms my feelings and excites my fear.'

Helen pulled the old leather jacket more tightly around her shoulders and gave in to the shiver that made her turn back along the quay. She'd been there for more than half an hour, gazing sightlessly across the Firth, and now the rain was falling more heavily than she'd realised. Yet much of her coldness came not from the weather but from the memory of Michael Fry's words. She didn't know this Colin Mage but she did know Michael Fry and if Michael Fry was worried enough to admit his fear to her, then she supposed she ought to be more than a little worried herself.

She wondered what magnetic qualities Colin Mage might have to make Michael Fry, who was after all The Merlin of All Britain, take him so seriously – and it was abundantly clear that Fry was taking him seriously, to the extent that he had checked and confirmed the existence and background of John Light's movement in California and Paul O'Connor's sect in Ireland. She had questioned him on this.

'Yes,' Fry had confessed, 'I think it's fair to say that Mage does have some magnetism and charisma about him... But it's a quiet thing, neither flashy nor flamboyant. In truth, I'd known of him long before I'd actually met him and, if you remember, he was approached some time ago to see if he might be interested in joining with the Order of Bards. On a different level, I suppose I just felt very sorry for the man. I was impressed both by his sincerity and by his persistence and, at the same time, fascinated – and worried – by his discoveries. Although fantastic, his words had the ring of truth about them.' He'd smiled. 'Helen, you know what it is like when you attain our level of psychic awareness. You develop an instinct for truth, both the obvious varieties and the hidden soul truths of a given thing. Mage may have been through the mangle, but I am certain that he was not lying or distorting the truth, either to me or to himself.

'But it isn't just Colin Mage's story that bothers me. Frankly, without any of the things I've told you, I'd still be feeling a little nervous and worried right now. I sense...' He'd groped for the words... 'I sense something in the air, in the ether, even in the astral, some aspect of tension that is building towards an explosive detonation. I have felt like this for more than a year now and so perhaps Colin Mage has simply focused some of these rather jittery premonitions I've been having. I think that Martyn of Glastonbury possibly put his finger more succinctly on the spot last week than even he himself realises.'

Helen turned on the ignition and the MGB purred into life. She let out the clutch and executed a perfect three point turn before blipping the throttle and driving off up the hill the way she'd come. She paused, engine idling, outside the cemetery where both her parents were buried... Just for a minute to say hello and goodbye. You're not forgotten and I love you... then she'd accelerated out of Aberdour back towards Edinburgh.

She arrived back at her flat just before three and was in bed by a little after. But even then sleep did not come automatically and it was nearer four before she finally dozed off.

She spent the better part of the following day, a wet and grey Scottish Sunday, reading Colin Mage's book "The Anatomy of Magick" and although the day was calm enough in most respects, she was aware of the undercurrents of tension and restlessness that thrummed away deep down within her subconscious. She acted an excellent part for various visitors when they called, including the aggressively protective Duncan Macgregor, and yet in truth she was frustrated by the invasion of her privacy.

She slept for a couple of hours in the late afternoon which, she realised later, was a mistake because it left her alert and awake during the evening when a little natural tiredness would have been welcome. Michael Fry telephoned a little after nine and she was glad of the call. They talked for fifteen minutes and although nothing new was discussed she appreciated being able to speak with someone who was tuned into her wavelength and knew how she was feeling.

Neither had sought it, but there was a strong if ill-defined bond between them. Fry, through Mage, had precognition of impending disaster, while she had had visions of the very nature of the beast. When he tentatively suggested that she might like to spend more time at The Oaks, she thanked him for the invitation and was not dismissive of it.

The following day, the Monday, was not a good day for her. She had a number of appointments with people seeking her help and counsel... She found these draining and unrewarding, experiencing frustration at the way in which so many people abrogated their own responsibilities, constantly looking either for the easy way when there was no easy way, the short cut when there was no short cut, for leadership when clearly the responsibility to lead rested upon their own shoulders. The frail she had deep sympathy and compassion for, but not the dullards and the lazy bones... at least, not that day!

The evening was worse. She took part in a local radio discussion programme, dealing with the increasing numbers of young people who were turning to the occult in search of direction and spiritual guidance. Her's was the explanatory voice of paganism and she came in for a vitriolic and bigoted earful of verbal abuse from the other two members of the panel; a minister of the Church of Scotland and a social worker with a degree in child psychology.

She arrived back at the flat feeling tired and depressed. She made a cup of tea and went straight to bed. Sleep came swiftly that night, but so did the dreams. She woke from the last fragment of a nightmare, for a moment disorientated and very glad that she'd left a small light on in the bedroom... Oh wonderful Helen, wonderful! High Priestess, expert on the occult, preserver of the pagan faith, and scared to sleep with the light off!

She felt vulnerably alone, aware of her loneliness and the emptiness of the big double bed. She chose to sleep alone these days, but there were times (too many times) when she missed the strength and protection of a man's arms. And yet it was easier and less complicated this way. For her the price of a man's presence in her bed was paid in the currency of commitment and always in the past that commitment had led to heart ache and pain. The strength in those arms was inconsistent, the protection illusory.

The bedside clock said four am. She was awake and distrustful of further sleep. She did not relish the thought of being transported back to that place of shadows and candle flames wherein dwelled alien entities who were bent upon the possession of her body and sought to snatch away her soul. She slipped on her robe and, making some tea, sat huddled in an armchair by the bay window watching the first grey flush of dawn break across the Edinburgh skyline.

One hour later she was dressed and driving out of Edinburgh along the A68. It was still not yet six o'clock, the traffic was negligible and she gave the MGB its head, driving it as it had been designed to be driven. Mist clung to the tips of the trees but shards of low sunlight lanced through diagonally from the east and the speed of her passage through this kaleidoscope of light created a surreal, almost Wagnerian effect which influenced her choice of music. She accelerated around Jedburgh with The Ride Of The Valkyries ringing in her ears.

Pushing eighty miles an hour along the stretch between Jedburgh and Otterburn, she began to feel good. She didn't quite know what she was doing, but she knew she was doing something and that this was infinitely better than doing nothing. She recalled a passage from Mage's book: *"The Power Of Magick manifests itself in many different ways,"* he had written. *"When faced with inertia and indecision, the magick within pushes the adept into action. It is often an impulsive and unguided action but if the adept can let go of all restraint and follow the pathway of impulse and intuition, inevitably the action leads to achievement. The achievement in question is rarely a goal in itself but is a stepping stone towards a more important destination and suffices to break the paralysis of stasis that inhibits the magician, releasing him from the restraints of his inhibitions and placing him fairly and squarely in the hands of fate and karmic destiny. The philosophy of "when in doubt do nothing" is not the way of the spiritual warrior."*

Helen had liked what she'd read. As far as she was concerned, Mage was preaching to the converted. Even so his words had found the mark within her and had done something to galvanise her into action.

With the majestic strains of The Tanhauser Overture filling the cramped cockpit she began her run in on Newcastle. She was making excellent time. Nature and the need of caffeine brought her to a halt at a Little Chef just south of Durham. It was now past eight o'clock and she availed herself of the opportunity to make a number of telephone calls... Three to Edinburgh, cancelling various appointments, and one to Michael Fry at The Oaks.

'You're up early,' he commented, and then as a large juggernaut lorry rumbled past rattling the glass of the phone booth – 'Where are you?'

'On the A1 near Durham, I need some information. Colin Mage's house in York. Where is it? What's the address?'

Fry supplied her with the information. 'Is that where you're heading?'

'Yes. Don't ask why because I'm simply working on instinct.'

'Of course. Will you find your way to The Oaks later on?'

'I'd have thought so. Can I just arrive without specifying a time?'

'I'll be here all day.'

They hung up and Helen resumed her journey south. She'd have been disconcerted at The Druid's reaction to her call, had she been aware of it. Michael Fry had returned the receiver to the cradle, smiling a smile of quiet self satisfaction. Leonardo Santorini had raised an àesthetic white eyebrow inquisitively.

'The Priestess?' he asked.

Fry nodded. 'Yes. She's on her way down to York. Going to have a look at Mage's house.'

'It seems to be working then.'

'It would seem so, although we must not congratulate ourselves prematurely. Let's keep our people at it, Leon. Nothing must break the circle, but you may feel free to inform them that something positive has just fallen into place.'

'A coincidence?' Leonardo raised the other eyebrow questioningly – saw Fry's look of response and lowered it. 'No,' he said, smiling and answering his own question. 'Of course not.'

Helen pulled the car over to the side of the road and sat looking at the house – a large Victorian end terrace with a small square of front garden and a path which led down the left half side bordered by a high privet hedge. The house stared back at her enigmatically, holding onto its secrets and mysteries. The front patch of garden was a mess, overgrown with weeds and indeed the whole edifice of the house looked sadly neglected.

She got out of the car and pushing open a creaking iron gate, negotiated the narrow passage, brushing the privet to one side as it threatened to swipe at her face and pluck at her clothes. If the front garden was bad, then the back garden was even worse. Once there had been a lawn and flower beds, but now rose and lilac bushes ran wild, enveloped in encroaching rhododendron. The grass had grown tall and weeds and twigs of dead branches from a geriatric apple tree had over powered the places where once bright flowers had grown in neat and healthy splendour.

A sense of loneliness and desolation stole over her as she peeped through a grimy rear window. In the kitchen there were unwashed cups and plates and in the dining room a large table was covered with newspapers and piles of photographs. There were books too, some open at a page, most of them closed and scattered haphazardly. Through a partition door she caught a glimpse of the front room. A red sofa, a dead fireplace, a dusty mirror, dead or dying evergreen plants...

She put one hand against the window and another against the rough brick of the wall. A lump rose in her throat and her eyes misted with tears. Once this house had been light with love and laughter, but now it was shrouded in a veil of deepest sorrow. The heart and soul was long gone from it and now it was no more than a shell, the repository of a man's tears and broken dreams. The ghost shape of happy times had been strangled and wrung out by more recent grief and great despair.

With the house acting as conduit her psychic mind reached across time and space and made gossamer contact with the mind of its owner. So much sadness. So much rejection and anger. So much confusion and fury and fear. She had heard Fry's story about Colin and Alexandra Mage and now it was as though she'd tuned in, first hand. She had speculated how Mage must have felt, not knowing whether his wife was dead or alive and then learning that she was alive, but seemingly lost to him through the interdiction of another. Now she didn't need to speculate. Now she knew! The horror of the emotion made her pull back involuntarily with a gasp as the full weight of the house's stored memory hit her like a sledge hammer, making her senses reel.

Beneath the apple tree there was an old rustic bench. It was covered with mildew stain and a few bird droppings, but she went and sat on it anyway, trying hard to collect her thoughts and still her troubled emotions. It was there, a good hour later, that Michael Fry found her. She wasn't too surprised to see him.
He sat on the bench next to her, noting her red eyes and realising that she had been crying.

'Well?' he said quietly, resting his hand upon her hand.

'All right,' she said flatly. And then more defiantly. 'All right! I'll go! But I want some guarantees!'

'I'll give you all that I can,' he replied softly, squeezing her hand more tightly than before.

12.

Magic

It had, by any standards, been a convivial evening, made successful by its spontaneity rather than by any form of preplanning. The day has been hot, the evening warm, and for the first time that year Jacinto had put tables and chairs out in the street. Mage had sat there with Angel. They had been joined by Antonia and, shortly after that, by Pepe Ortega. Only a few minutes had passed before Hector Sanchez drew up a chair and pulled out his pipe. Hot on his heels, but from the other direction, had come the American couple, who'd insisted on buying drinks for the ensemble, seemingly as their passport to join the informal gathering.

Mage noted that Angel seemed nervous, but that those nerves had only surfaced with the arrival of the Americans. Antonia had been sprightly and there'd been a twinkle in Ortega's eyes that had not been there the last time they'd talked. Once, their eyes met, and Mage had been gratified to receive the old man's cordial nod. Nothing needed to be said. The imperceptible inclination of the head had said it all. Hector had been on top form, but Mage noticed that he drank little. At one point, when the conversations involved neither of them directly, he'd leaned across the table to help himself to one of Mage's cigarettes.

'Anna tells me you have invited her to the feria at San Pablo,' he'd begun cautiously.

Mage had laughed. 'Yes, I did ask her, but alas she said neither yes or no, only that she would think about it.'

'Well, she's thought about it and I'll tell you now that she is going with you. I dare say she'll tell you herself later.'

'I'm pleased,' said Mage, not quite sure where this conversation was going. 'Hector, this doesn't give you a problem, does it?'

Sanchez had rubbed his chin. 'No, the fact that my daughter seems happier than she has done in weeks does not give me a problem. The fact that her headaches seem to be getting a little better does not give me a problem. The fact that she has actually decided to go out with someone and have some fun does not give me a problem...'

'But you'd be much happier if I were some nice ordinary Spanish boy a lot nearer her own age!' Mage had laughed again and it had been an easy laugh. 'Hector, please don't worry. We are only going to the fair at San Pablo. I asked Anna to come with me because I thought she might enjoy a night out. I dare say you'll be there too along with half of Castillo. She will have no shortage of chaperones.'

Hector had looked sheepish and slightly embarrassed. 'You just take care of her,' he'd said in a friendly manner... and Mage had known there was much being left unsaid. They had still not discussed the matter of Dolores' baby and perhaps it had to be discussed soon. The thing which caused the bond between them was also a barrier and Mage desperately wanted that barrier down.

Jacinto had brought out trays of sandwiches. Unordered and unasked for, but provided just the same, and by eleven o'clock the pavement was crowded with chairs spilling out onto the road. A party atmosphere prevailed, although no-one seemed to know what they were celebrating. Mage had felt uncommonly relaxed... He was among people who were living and laughing at the simplest of pleasures. Good company, a drink, a yarn and a tale, local gossip... He had to remind himself that beneath this social bonhomie dark chasms yawned. A girl up the hill, possibly going blind. A catholic priest who wanted him dead. Streets with strange names that were full of shadows that should not be there...

Sitting with his back to the wall of Jacinto's bar, he'd stolen a glance to his right, looking down the road beyond the three old taxis to where it wound its way down into the folds of Spanish pines and eucalyptus trees... Almost waiting, detached from his present company, for someone to come marching up that road towards him. Friend or foe. To help or to harm. One day, and it would have to be one day soon before the longest day of the year, it would be Dolorean and Alexandra. What would he do when they came? More to the point, what would he do if they didn't come?

No, that had been an impossible thought. They were coming. They had to come. It was merely a question of time.

His mood broken, he'd quietly excused himself from his new found friends and had walked down across the village square to stand beneath the orange trees, hidden by the shadows, protected by the darkness of the night. The village of Castillo danced before his eyes, the snug white houses, the warm glow from open windows, the sound of a thousand distant conversations, the clatter of a hundred dominoes. Dogs barked and a shooting star ricocheted across the sky, North to South, directly above the battlements of the castle that stood high and brooding over all at the top of the hill. What portent to read into a mote of interstellar debris making brief contact with planet Earth's unwelcoming atmosphere? An accident of cosmic design or a warning augury of things to come?

Yet might it not be a good omen? The star had been flying from the North, and although his enemies were in the North, so too were his friends.

He was not alone in the village square. Children played freely despite the late hour. Old men sat in groups and talked softly of the girls they'd known when they were young. A gaggle of old women sat in one corner complaining about their husbands, while a trio of young girls crossed the square left to right in a predatory way in search of whatever adventure the late night might bring. And there were couples, too... Some strolling arm in arm, others sitting in romantic isolation and yet another locked into a lip bruising kiss.

Mage's earlier mood was all but gone. Now he felt the loneliness of his own solitude and pulled back further into the shadows until he came to the low wall and railings that surrounded El Paseo. It made a natural seat and, with the railings as a back rest, he sat down, stretching his legs out in front of him and pulling the brim of his hat down over his eyes.

He thought about this place Castillo. It was two faced and Geminesque. A coin that had two sides. One side shone with all the vibrancy of the Andalucian joie de vivre, but the other side contained mystery and suspense and ever present sentient threat.

His mind switched to Anna Sanchez and the brief exchange of words he'd had with Hector. He hoped he'd put Hector's mind at rest and wished he could do the same for his own. He was presenting himself to both Anna and her father as a friend. He told himself that he was interested in Anna because he wanted to help heal the wounds that would spoil her life and might yet even end it – and yet, whenever her image came into his mind he experienced a sexual thrill of response. He could deny this as much as he liked to everyone else, but could not deny it to himself. He was enough of a psychologist to work out the machinations. He'd been celibate for many many months and had been travelling through the darkest tunnels of emotional chaos: Anna Sanchez symbolised a light at the end of that tunnel. She was young, beautiful and fresh and tragically in need of his abilities, while he in turn was desperately in need of being needed.

He sighed and reached for a cigarette. The old brass Zippo flamed and, as it did so, he caught movement out of the corner of his eye. From beneath the trailing branches of the orange trees Angel emerged, paused, then walked over determinedly to where Mage sat.

'If you wish to be alone Señor Mage, please say so and I shall go. But if not – there is something I must ask. A favour, if you can grant it.'

'Come into my office,' Mage said wryly, moving up the wall a few inches, giving Angel enough room to sit down.

Angel sat, holding his hands together, seemingly agitated and excited at the same time. He did not look up when he began to speak. 'When we talked the other day you told me many things, some which were easy to accept, others which were hard to believe. You talked to me about the powers of good and evil, of light and dark... You spoke of this man Dolorean who is coming here to make some very bad magic and that you were here to try and stop him. I asked you about magic and you told me that, like this other man, you also have the power to make it. That if your power is stronger than his all will be well and, if it is not, then there will be many problems for many people...'

Mage sucked on the Marlboro and let the boy get round to it in his own time.

'Since our conversation I have looked again at the many books that I have, in search of the knowledge of how to make this magic you spoke of. Perhaps I have the wrong books, or perhaps the people who have written them do not know as much as they think they do, but the information I look for is not there...

'Señor Colin, there is something that I want very badly, but I do not think I can get it. Not even if I worked all my life and lived to be a hundred years old. And yet this something that I want is so important that it is driving me crazy. I wish you, if you will, to show me how to learn the magic to make this thing happen for me, or if this is not possible, to intercede on my behalf with a little of your own.'

Mage put two and two together, got three and guessed the rest. 'What's her name?' he asked softly.

Angel looked up abruptly in surprise. 'How did you know that...?'

'Magic,' Mage smiled whimsically in the darkness, not feeling too bad about letting Angel jump to his own conclusions, even if in this case they were wrong. And then – 'Her name, Angel...?' which was unfair because he'd already guessed the answer.

'It is Christina, la Americana,' Angel said miserably. 'I want her so very badly and I think she may like me a little bit too, but she is with her friend Tom and I do not think I stand any chance with her. Even if Tom was a million miles away, I do not think that Christina would favour someone like me. She is so beautiful. She could take her pick from everybody.'

'Yes she is very pretty,' Mage mused, thinking of the vivacious blond. He could understand Angel's attraction. Christina was the kind of girl who turned heads and he guessed that half the male population of Castillo lusted after her to one degree or another. Angel was probably right. She *could* take her pick and Angel's chances were minimal to zero.

But it would be an interesting experiment, wouldn't it?

Mage wondered about the American couple. They were attractive together and not out of place with their friendly smiles and expensive cameras. Mage had seen them round the village on a number of occasions, although he had not actually exchanged words with them until that evening. They seemed genuine enough and yet there was something that nagged at the back of his mind that suggested they were not all, or were perhaps more, than they appeared to be. He was mindful of the fact that they had been there that day in the Miraflores bar when the old man Diego had collapsed. He'd been aware of their presence then, but had only given them a cursory inspection, his attentions having become more focused on the policeman. Perhaps he ought to pay them a little more attention now? Angel was well placed to be of assistance.

'Tell me,' he said, 'all that you know about Christina and Tom.'

Angel talked eagerly and quickly, passing on all the information he had... which was only as much as he'd been told. In the end, he looked at Mage expectantly. 'You will do something to help, Señor Colin?'

'Yes Angel, I'll try... but not a word to anyone about this. It's strictly between you and me. No one else must know.'

'On my parents' graves, I shall not breathe a word!'

'Okay, come to the house tomorrow, sometime in the afternoon. There are some things you will need to get. First of all, I'll need something belonging to Christina... any small thing, a handkerchief, an old letter...' Mage grinned in the darkness. 'A lock of her hair or one of her finger nails, but I dare say that's asking for too much. If you can, bring me a photograph of her...'

'I have that already,' Angel exclaimed.

'Good. Well bring it... and the other thing I'll need to know is her birthday. Think you can find that out?'

'I'll try, but I'm not sure how...'

'They're still probably sitting outside Jacinto's, so go back. Buy them a drink. Be friendly. Talk about birthdays or horoscopes or whatever. Just do it a bit carefully and tactfully, okay?'

'I shall try... And I come to Granadillos tomorrow afternoon!'

'Fine. Make it about three o'clock. Before the siesta.'

Full of silent gratitude, Angel raced back across the Paseo and Mage, pulling himself to his feet, strolled off at a tangent towards the maze of narrow streets that led up to Calle Granadillos. His thoughts played with various ideas of what he might be able to do for Angel; if nothing else it would give him a chance to flex a few muscles and who knew what might not come from a illicit peep into the curvaceous Christina's soul. If there *was* anything more to her than met the eye, he would find out the following afternoon, providing, of course, Angel was able to procure something, anything, that belonged to her of a personal nature. Anything to make the psychometric link. The chances of him actually obtaining a lock of her hair or a nail clipping were really fairly slim, but he might be able to come up with an old sock, or something.

The vision of a small pink sock would not go away and Mage cocked his head, pausing in his stride. 'Be damned,' he murmured beneath his breath. 'Little bugger's going to bring me on of her socks!'

He turned the key in the lock and entered the house.   And froze.

Something was wrong. The atmosphere was impaled upon an aura of intrusion. Someone was either in the building, or had been and gone, but in going had left their spore hanging in the ether like a dark veil.

Swiftly and silently he slipped the jacket from his shoulders, took off his hat and eased his feet from his shoes. Wrapping the imaginary silver pentagrams around himself and centring the Ch'i energy within his solar plexus, he moved cautiously and cat-like into the building.

And found nothing.

The place was empty, his belongings undisturbed. The more he moved into the house, the more the feeling or intrusion evaporated – but back at the front door it was as strong as ever. It was only when he lifted his coat from where he'd discarded it in the hall, that he noticed the small brown manila envelope wedged up against the wall where the opening door had pushed it. The dark feelings he was experiencing were emanating from this.

Not knowing what the envelope contained, he was very careful. He went upstairs to the living room, returning a few seconds later with his carpet bag.

Kneeling by the envelope, he produced a flat brown box from the bag, flicked the hidden spring on the box so that it popped up into its true form – a box of mirrors... Weathered old oak on the outside, mirrored on the inside, the base of the box, the underside of the lid, and the four containing walls. With a long pair of tweezers he lifted the envelope from the floor, depositing it in the box and deftly closing the lid.

Box in one hand, bag in the other, he retreated back upstairs and placed the box in the middle of the circular table that dominated one corner of the salon. Sitting at the table, the carpet bag well within reach, he concentrated on building a measure of protection. First, still working with the solar plexus energy, he balanced his chakras and formalised the placing of the pentagrams, reciting the names of the four prime Guardian Angels. Taking the circular flask from the bag, he anointed his forehead and the crown of his head with the rich aromatic liquid, feeling as always the vibrant charge of vital energies that were inevitably catalysed by the oil's exposure to the air. To the left of the mirror box he placed his athame, the sharp sacrificial dagger, and to the right, the crystal tipped willow wand. Penultimately, he lit sandalwood incense as an act of ritual cleansing and, as the final act of his preparation, he lit a single tall white candle.

Only then did he open the box and carefully using the tweezers and the blade of the dagger, extracted the contents of the envelope.

It was a small square of yellow hide parchment, covered by a mandala of reddish brown lines of various thickness. He studied it carefully, taking in every detail and allowing it to touch to rim of his psychic aura in an extremely controlled way. He knew vaguely what it was – and it was nasty – a Wiccan hexcurse of dark intent. But a vague appreciation was not good enough. He had to know exactly what was intended by its presentation and the precise nature of its purpose.

The fact that the thing had been inscribed with blood – probably from an animal – made it clear that it was not a healing hex. That fact apart, the mandala vibrated with negativity and, when he looked closely, he found the pagan sigils for Hecate – the black manifestation of the Wiccan Goddess.

There were also astrological sigils for the planet and archetypal energy of Mars, the god of war. Furthermore, the maze of tortuous mandalic lines wound ever inwards on themselves, ending inevitably in self strangulation around the coded occult signature for The Devil.

So, what did he have? It was clearly a spell taken from the discipline of witchcraft – a dark spell that did not wish him well but wished him dead or gone from this place with the open threat of diabolical intervention should he refuse to die at will or leave in haste.

He had no intention of doing either, but that was the message sent by the sender.

And what of the person who had sent him this bane? Obviously they had knowledge of the craft. The mandala was expertly drawn and anyone with the knowledge of The Devil's True Name was more than a first year beginner.

There was something that he could not easily define that told him that this had come from a woman, rather than from a man. The style of the hex came in an old and traditional form, sharp and precise, more akin to the feminine principle than the more expansive and careless egocentricity of the male.

Whoever had sent it – what had they hoped to achieve? Did they think that this scrap of paper could scare him off? Had they assumed that the power they had invested in the hex would be sufficient to taint him and contaminate his temporary home? Even if he'd been careless and had handled the hex with his hands, there was not enough power in it to do any lasting harm.

Whoever the guilty party was, they'd been very confident or very stupid. Perhaps they'd even been both. They'd overestimated the potency of their own power and had seriously underestimated his.

Another thing he was reasonably sure of was that whoever had sent the hex was not Spanish, but more probably English. The concept of mandalic hexes was not in the Spanish tradition, and this piece of diabolism had a distinctly Anglo Saxon feel to it. So, how many Anglo Saxon witches were there in a place like Castillo de la Frontera? He smiled, and on this occasion his face was not without its own Satanic expression. It shouldn't be too difficult to find the answer to that one and whoever they were, by showing their hand in such an unsubtle way, had played right into his own hands.

He'd asked Angel to provide a lock of Christina's hair to forge the magical link for that forthcoming exercise... But whoever had sent him the hex had provided him with something far more powerful. They'd given him a psychic signature written in the fabric of time and space with each tortured circle of the mandala. They'd given him a clear target to strike back at whenever he chose to launch his counter offensive.

And he would have to retaliate, he thought grimly. There was no way he could let this one pass. He'd come to Castillo to fight a battle against dark forces and while Jadoc Dolorean may have been his prime target, he knew that there were others allied to Dolorean, one of whom, acting on Dolorean's behalf, had worked the hex.

He balanced his anger. He could strike back now or wait until he had identified the witch. On the one hand the knowledge would bring added power, which was an argument in favour of waiting for a while. But his present anger was a natural energy waiting to be unleashed against his foes and as the time fast approached midnight he was all keyed up and raring to go. This was the right time to apply a little black magic of his own.

He reached towards the bag, then paused reflectively. No, he would not act now. The anger could be contained. The force of the hex had now been neutralised. It was safe in his box of mirrors and could do no harm. They sender would not expect immediate results, but logically they would be on guard at that moment against some form of counter strike. Better to retaliate at a time when they might not expect it. Tradition, especially the Anglo Saxon tradition, had it that dark magic was crafted in the hours of darkness but Mage had long since learned that there was no great advantage in this proposition. Magic was magic and providing the ritual was correct and the intent clearly focused, it was a force that could be used at any time.

He closed the lid of the box, collapsing it inwards upon itself and trapping the mandala between the reflective surfaces. The box was then deposited in the carpet bag and Mage walked all around the house opening the doors and windows, blowing away the last vestiges of the mandala's negative vibrations.

He felt good. If all they could send against him was a boy with a knife and a witch with an ineffectual curse, perhaps he had a chance of coming out of this in one piece after all!

The morning sunshine cascaded through the grapevines and other foliage of The Miraflores terrace. Tom and Christina sat in a secluded corner talking earnestly. They were not arguing but their conversation was heated and intense.

'Look Christina, I don't think there's any alternative. John's gone walkabout and nobody knows where he's gone. Vern is running things in his absence, but he doesn't know why we're here so there's no point in reporting to him, even if we had anything to report which, of course, we don't.'

'I agree with what you're saying,' Christina acquiesced, 'but John's instructions were as clear as day. We're to stay here until he personally says otherwise. We both made that commitment and just because we can't contact John through normal channels, it doesn't mean to say that he can't contact us if he needs to. He's got our number and he knows where we are. He's provided us with an open line of credit to stay here as long as we need to and I don't think we can up stakes and fly back to The States just because you've taken all the pictures you want to take or because you're bored with this place.'

'Hey, it isn't like that at all!' Tom protested. 'Sure I'm bored, but the reason why I'm bored is that there just isn't anything happening in this dump. All we're doing is wasting our time and John's money. If John was aware of that I guest he'd tell us to haul our asses out of here pronto.'

'But we don't know that,' Christina insisted. 'It's just you surmising to justify your own arguments. We don't even know why John sent us here – not the real reason anyway and I can see him being pretty pissed off if he phones us tomorrow night, say, and finds that instead of being here where we're supposed to be, where he needs us to be, we're half way across the Atlantic ocean cruising at thirty thousand feet.'

'Jesus!' Tom slammed the palm of his hand down on the table making the breakfast things rattle. 'Jesus Chris! Anyone would think you actually like this godforsaken hole!'

She looked at him oddly and her voice took on a slightly different edge. 'I don't think it's a godforsaken hole and, yes, as a matter of fact, I do rather like being here.'

'Oh for God's sake, it's the end of the fucking world. Pitsville! The Boonies!'

'And our beloved Los Angeles is the centre of civilisation, yes? Well, it might be a bit on the quiet side in little old Castillo, but at least the air is clean and there's no crime and no violence. I don't hear a constant chorus of police sirens and I'm free of egotistical photographers and bull shitting agents who keep telling me what to do and how this shot and that shot will be so much better if only I'll take off a few more clothes and give them a better flash of my pussy!

'Tom, you go if you want to, but until I hear the words of recall from John Light's own mouth, I'm staying put, okay!'

He looked at her coldly, and then stood up. 'There's a flight to New York from Madrid at ten o'clock tonight and we're booked on it.'

'No,' she said softly. 'You're booked on it.'

Miriam Cortez sat in the sun trap of her back garden. She sipped at a drink appreciating the clink of the ice cubes and listening dreamily to the sound of running water that gushed forth from the small fountain. Eyes closed, she picked out the location of a chicada and followed the progress of a humming bee. The sun warmed her skin and she felt sleepy and deliciously relaxed. It was always thus after what she referred to as "a working".

All of the tension she'd built up within herself over the weekend had been discharged against her adversary; she'd found the peak of that energy in the early hours of Sunday morning and had spent the following twelve hours binding her curse within the mandalic hieroglyphics of the hex... And had written it in her own blood. The cut on her wrist itched beneath the dressing she had applied, but it was a healing, satisfying itch.

She'd delivered the curse to the magician's house the previous evening, amazed by the lack of protective energies that had emanated from the building. The Englishman was a fool. If he had come here to wage an occult war, he should have protected his home with some sort of psychic screen or barrier.

She had slept lightly through the night, never for more than a few minutes at a time and tuned to pick up any nuance of reaction, held in tension to oppose any form of retaliation. None was forthcoming, however, and she contented herself in pouring negative energy into the airwaves, directing them against the man in Calle Granadillos.

It was too much to hope that he'd drop dead on the spot – although something like that had happened once a few years before. It was not a fair comparison, however, for that other recipient of her curse had been a frail old soul of seventy, already scared half to death by the flickering of their own shadow. Mage obviously did not fall into that category but she was confident that her "working" would have its desired effect sooner rather than later. Of course, she didn't know *exactly* what would happen... You couldn't always be that specific with spellcraft. To be sure, you had to be very specific in the stating of your aims and desires, but after that the Higher Energies had to be left to work in their own ways. She'd demanded that Colin Mage be totally neutralised and so, on past experience, one of two or three things might occur. Either he'd suddenly die of natural causes or be the victim of some freak and totally unforeseen accident, or he'd fall into a lethargy of sickness from which he could not recover without her first removing and unbinding her curse. Of course, he might just decide to pack his bags and leave... She giggled sensuously to herself. He wouldn't be the first Englishman to do that, now would he!

The thought that Colin Mage might be rather more powerful than she was in the command of high magic was a thought that never once entered her head. Although she'd never actually spoken to him, she'd seen him wandering round the village being so polite and ingratiatingly nice to everyone and he hardly cut a dashing figure. She saw him as soft and weak and the fact that he'd trounced the Matan boy meant nothing. A lucky fluke, which in any case, had nothing to do with real power, the kind of power she knew she had running through her and available at her finger tips.

She smiled a slow and wicked smile. No, it would only be a matter of hours, a day or two at the most, before she could tell the fat old priest that the threat had been eliminated – and she would make very sure that the Master Dolorean came to know of exactly how it had been done.

Angel saw only what his eyes told him.

Turning the corner of Calle Consuelo, he darted back into the shadows of a shop doorway and watched as Tom and Christina emerged from the entrance of the Miraflores. He was too far away to hear what they were saying and saw only that they embraced, holding each other tightly and kissing deeply. Tom broke away and caressing her cheek with intimate familiarity, turned and walked away down the hill, disappearing from sight as he turned the sharp corner at the bottom of the steep incline.

Angel's heart ached, but it would have ached far less if he'd seen Tom climb into the taxi that was waiting out of sight in Calle Blanco – a taxi that was loaded with suitcases and camera bags, and which spirited Tom away from Castillo towards the N340 and in the general direction of Malaga airport.

With a sick churning in his gut he cut through the narrow passage that linked Consuelo with Granadillos and, filled with dubious thoughts, made his way up to number fourteen. Could El Moreno do this thing for him? If he could, it would be more than magic. It would be a miracle.

Hector had had a busy Monday morning surgery. Mondays were always heavy after the extravagances of an Andalucian weekend. The last patient on his list was Juanita Lopez and as Anna showed her into his small office, he was already thinking about his lunch.

Dressed in the traditional black, Juanita was a woman in her late forties who looked near sixty in her severe garb and with her stooped figure and greying hair. The Spanish sun had not been kind to her complexion, covering her face with a latticework of lines and wrinkles. Hector remembered the last time he had seen her, which had been almost three years ago: like many of her peers she had chronic back problems caused by too many long hours bending over in the fields. He had on that occasion been blunt. The back pain would not get better, it could only get worse. This was the price of being a campera. If she wished to see some improvement, she must get off the land. Find different work that did not demand so much bending and lifting.

She had shrugged her shoulders in resignation, for what other work was there in these parts for a woman such as she? Predictably the back problems had got worse until she'd been forced to give up the fields, but then fortune had smiled upon her, for the new young priest in Castillo who had come to look after the church of Santa Maria – well, he needed a housekeeper and as she was the most devout of women and lived only two doors from the church, she was the logical choice. The fact that the new work was poorly paid mattered not a jot. She had just enough to live on and being housekeeper to young Father Francisco gave her some new standing in the village.

'Good afternoon Juanita,' Hector beamed at her, thinking of the swordfish steak that awaited his attention in the kitchen. 'How's the back?'

'The back is good,' she said, holding herself to stiff attention in the chair. 'I come today with a different problem.'

'Fine. What exactly is the trouble?'

'It is not with me,' she said hastily, 'but with Father Francisco. I think you must come and do something for him.'

'Can he not come to the surgery himself?'

'No.'

'Well what ails him?'

'He has taken himself to his bed and will not rise from it.'

'He has a fever?'

'No.'

'A cold, then?' Hector was becoming slightly exasperated.

'No. More than a cold. I think you must come now. I change his sheets every day, but each day it is worse. I have said to him three days ago that I should fetch you, but each time he has refused. I come today without his consent. Today it is more serious than before.'

Hector noted the reference to the bed linen. 'He has the flux?'

'No.'

'Then what is so wrong with Francisco of Santa Maria that is so important that I should forego my lunch to come rushing down the hill to put it right?'

'He bleeds,' she said. 'Maybe he bleeds to death. You must come and see for yourself.'

Something in the woman's voice registered in Hector's awareness, alerting him to the fact that there was more to this situation than met the ear. Obviously there was something that was making Juanita act in such an obtuse way – something she was not telling him. He was tempted to say that he'd come after he'd had his lunch, but if he did that his lunch would be spoiled by worry and curiosity. Better to stroll down to Santa Maria first, find out what was wrong and try to put it right, then enjoy his lunch at leisure afterwards. And if Francisco de Santa Maria was bleeding – what did she mean, *bleeding?* – better see him now than later anyway. He called through to Anna, telling her he had to go out on a house call and, picking up his doctor's bag, followed Juanita Lopez out into the street.

A warm dry wind gusted along Santana blowing a sheet of newspaper where it would and causing dust devils to dance beside the pavement. It was very hot, far too hot for Spain, even in May and there was an odd scent on the wind that he couldn't quite identify which uncannily made him feel nervous and on edge. There was no explanation for this feeling, it was simply there, teasing in the breeze. The sky had a metallic sheen to it and he wondered if there was another storm on the way? It would certainly explain away some of this piano wire tension, so unsubtley woven within the strands of the atmosphere.

As they walked along Santana, cutting up through Calle Cisne then trekking down the steep hill of Calle Consuelo, Hector tried to engage Juanita in conversation, but she was having none of it, answering in monosyllables and offering no more than she'd already given.

They arrived at the priest's house which was little more than a two room appendage to the church. Here Juanita hung back. 'You go in first,' she said. 'He is in the upstairs room.'

Hector nodded and pushed his way before her into the priest's abode. The ground floor was a cluttered place that served as a kitchen and general living area. A door in one wall led through to the vestry of the church and slightly beyond the door an open stone staircase led to the upper room... small, white and cool with a basic shower unit in one corner, decorated sparsely. Black olive wood cross on one wall and to the left of it, an icon of the Virgin Mary. On the opposite wall a framed print of the pope hung in company with a pictogram of the Sacred Heart of Christ. There was a window, shutters closed, that filtered in a minimal amount of light and beneath the shutters was a low cot bed. Supine on the bed, covered in a white sheet – or at least, a partially white sheet – lay the still figure of the young priest. Hector pulled the only chair over to the bedside and opened the shutters a few inches to allow more light into the room.

'Now Father Francisco,' Hector used his gentlest bedside manner. 'What seems to be the trouble?'

It was in part a rhetorical question for Hector was immediately aware of the blood stains that were liberally dotted across the white linen. He could even smell the blood that had caused the stains. Father Francisco's eyes, dark and shining with fever or fervour against the pale white skin of his face, looked up at him dreamily.

'Old Juanita brought you after all then?' His voice emerged as a low murmur. 'Well Doctor, she has wasted your time. By the grace of God I am dying and there is nothing that you or anyone else can do about it.'

'I will not argue with the grace of God,' Hector said, 'but now that I am here, let me at least see if there is anything that I can do to help.'

The priest, no more than twenty six or so, so Hector guessed, closed his eyes in submission and Hector carefully drew back the sheet that covered his pale emaciated body... And sat staring at the sight that met his eyes, not quite believing what he was seeing – and even when he did recognise the truth of what his eyes were telling him, not understanding it and not knowing what to do about it.

Trickles of blood dribbled slowly from what appeared to be a cut in the priest's left side, just beneath the rib cage. There were open wounds on the backs of his hands, and a few inches higher on the backs of his wrists. When Hector nervously turned the priest's arms there were corresponding wounds on the man's palms and the undersides of his wrists. Discarding the sheet and looking downwards, there were similar wounds on the priest's feet, red weals that suppurated and looked sore.

Hector brought his eyes back to the young man's face, feeling dumbfounded and lost for words, to see the priest watching him quizzically. With some effort he raising his right hand and brushed the quiff of thick dark hair away from where it had fallen across his pallid forehead, to reveal a line of irregular red marks that crossed his brow, a millimetre below the hairline. He managed a wan smile before his hand fell languidly back across his chest.

'I do not think you medicines can do much to help me, Doctor Sanchez.'

'How... how long have you...'

'Been like this? It began one week ago. There is no pain, only some discomfort. But I am very weak. I cannot take food and can drink only little. Juanita has worked hard to keep me clean.' The priest managed another dreamy half smile. 'It has not always been easy.'

'You should have sent for me days ago,' Hector said gruffly, trying to cover his confusion.

'And what could you have done?' the priest chided gently.

'What I'm about to do now,' the doctor retorted and reached for his bag.

Half an hour later he had cleaned Father Pablo's wounds, inspecting them with infinite care before applying thick smears of antiseptic cream and covering them with clean white dressings. While his pulse was a little on the weak side his heart beat and blood pressure were quite normal and there did not seem to be any high temperature. Nevertheless, Hector took a blood sample and gave him a couple of shots, one of anti-tetanus, the other antibiotic. He was working in the dark and relying on instinct and intuition, along with the philosophy that said a clean patient was a healthier patient. While it was true that Father Pablo was weak, he put this down to lack of food rather than to loss of blood. Thus above the protests of the priest, he instructed Juanita to make hot broth and together they coaxed a few mouthfuls down their patient's throat, along with some weak tea, liberally laced with brandy and fresh honey. Hector took a certain satisfaction in seeing some colour, albeit not much, return to Father Francisco's cheeks after these administrations.

'Is there anyone I should speak to about this?' He asked after Juanita had gone back down the stairs. 'Do you want me to bring Father Ignatious from Santa Clara, or contact your Bishop in Seville?'

'By the saints I pray you no, do not breathe a word to anyone,' Pablo implored with noticeably a little more strength in his voice than there'd been before. 'I beg you, Doctor Sanchez, let me die in peace.'

'Fine,' Hector said flatly. 'The problem is that you're not dying. The weakness and probably any delirium you've been experiencing is through malnutrition.'

'But the wounds... These are the stigmata of Christ...'

'That's as may be,' Hector retorted, not unkindly. 'But while stigmata is something that I know very little about, I do know that you are not the first to suffer this experience and I have yet to hear of anyone dying from such a condition. Granted, there is a mystery here that is beyond my medical knowledge... I have examined your wounds and have never seen anything quite like them in my life before and, even if you had inflicted them upon yourself which I am quite sure you have not done, then I do not know how you can have done it...' Hector hesitated. 'In truth, I would expect someone such as yourself to have more understanding about this sort of thing than I... Usually stigmata is associated with religious and spiritual experiences...?'

Hector formed it somewhat uncomfortably as a question and the priest nodded slowly, indicating that he understood what the doctor was driving at. 'And you want to know if I've had any such experience? If I have spoken with Christ or have seen the face of the Virgin Mary? Alas no, Doctor Sanchez. These visions have been denied me... But there is another vision and one that is with me constantly...' It was becoming an effort for the young priest to speak and he had to rest for a moment before continuing.

He closed his eyes and opened them again, locking them onto Hector's own. 'My vision is of God's final day of judgement. That day is at hand. The earth will open up and all the spirits of the damned shall ascend into Heaven to be judged by Our Father.' He reached out a bandaged hand and took Hector's wrist in a surprisingly firm grip. 'On that day I shall die. On that day all shall die. My vision is of the end of the world and it is coming soon!'

Hector stood halfway up the hill where Calle Consuelo split into a fork, becoming in part Calle Sanfransisco. His head ached and his mouth was dry and a well spring of turbulent confusion trembled in his gut, leaving a hollow emptiness in the place of his heart. His visit to Father Pablo had unnerved him and the young priest's words unnerved him even more.

A year ago he'd have written off the priest's warning as religious drivel brought on, no doubt, by the curious stigmata, in itself no more than a psychosomatic manifestation of some deeply spiritual or psychological trauma. But that would have been a year ago and since then this village had become a different place. A place where a healthy young woman had started going blind, where children were being born with the most appalling deformities, where the suicide rate had suddenly quadrupled, where there had been a spate of killings and mutilations so totally out of character with the ambience of this land... Where viruses mutated overnight, where some crops failed while others flourished in unreasonable abundance... Where, beneath all, there was a thrumming under-current of subliminal tension that made a man eat less and drink a lot more.

Now, into this cauldron, toss one catholic priest who bled from wounds in his hands, wrists and feet, not to mention that nasty graze on his left side, who spoke about the coming of the end of the world... And Hector Sanchez was not prepared to write it off as the psychotic ramblings of religious fervour.

It was part of everything else that was happening in Castillo.

Hector looked upwards as a vulture, paragliding on the hot thermals that wafted up from North Africa, swooped low over the rooftops. Its enormous wingspan momentarily cast Hector's corner of the street into fleeting dark shadow, then the shadow was gone and Hector was left gazing at the brightly metallic sky. A hot gust of unrefreshing wind caused a dust devil to dash across the cobbles, then, like the vulture, it was also gone leaving only the devils of doubt and uncertainty tumbling over one another in the seat of Hector's soul.

As Angel raised a hand to bang on the door, the door opened before him, causing his heart to skip a beat. At first, for one fleeting second, he thought the door had opened on its own, but then in the shadow of the lintel he saw El Moreno watching him with a crooked smile on his face.

'I saw you walking up the hill,' the magician explained, standing to one side and beckoning Angel in.

For another fleeting second, Angel hesitated, wondering whether or not he really wanted to pursue this matter. Then, the vision of Christina dancing before his eyes and squirming in his belly, he stepped into the cool shade of the house.

El Moreno was somehow different this afternoon. He seemed smaller, tighter, more compact... and instead of wearing his usual earth colours, he was today dressed in black. Angel suppressed a shiver, wondering if there was any special significance to this.

Mage led him to the foot of the stairs, then halting in his stride, turned and looked at him with great penetration. 'You understand that what happens here this afternoon is strictly between ourselves. You do not speak of this to anyone, not to anyone at all. This is firmly understood?'

'Yes Señor, I understand...'

In Angel's mind there was the memory of El Moreno gazing down at the bloodied Lorenzo. *I shall have your eyes* he'd said. Angel was in no doubt that a similar threat might be directed towards himself were he to breach El Moreno's confidence in any way.

'Follow me up the stairs then,' Mage said, 'but do not enter the room. Wait at the top step.'

Angel followed the Englishman up the flight of stairs and duly waiting on the top step, senses assaulted by the strangeness of the ambience that filled this once so familiar but now totally different room. The window shutters were firmly closed and the room was bathed in soft yellow light from a dozen burning candles. In the middle of the room was the old round oak table, upon which were a number of different things: Angel could see a knife and a flask, a square box, many beautiful crystals and maybe another half dozen candles, as yet unlit.

Then El Moreno positioned himself so that the table was obscured. 'Angel before we start there is a question I need to ask you. Assume for a moment that I had never come to Castillo, is there anyone else you might have gone to for help in this matter? Is there anyone else who might have worked some magic for you? Is there anyone in this village, especially among the extranjeros, who has the reputation of being a witch?'

Angel furrowed his brow. 'There is old Immaculada in Calle Loba,' he said reflectively. 'She collects herbs and makes poultices, but I do not think she has magic, even though as children we would call her La Bruja de Loba. Some of the girls still go to her for love potions, but from what I have heard they don't seem to work very well. I think that Immaculada might be good at getting rid of a few warts and things like that, but not much else.

'There used to be an extranjero called Christopher. He lived here for a while and made horoscopes for people on his computer and read the palms of the people down in Gibraltar and the Costa del Sol, but he has been gone from Castillo for more than a year...'

'Anyone else?' Mage encouraged.

Angel shrugged. 'There is Miriam Cortez,' he said. 'Everybody *says* that she is a witch, although I do not know this is a certain fact. It is only what I have heard.'

'Then tell me what you have heard,' Mage insisted, remembering immediately where he'd heard the name Cortez before. It had been something to do with the sale of Pepe Ortega's house, hadn't it? In that transaction someone called Cortez had acted as Dolorean's agent.

'What have I heard? Only that Señora Cortez is not such a very nice lade and people who she doesn't like seem to have a lot of bad luck from time to time. Felipe Diaz says that she puts spells on people. Felipe worked with the Señora's husband Pedro and Señor Cortez is not a very nice man either... And yet, as Felipe once pointed out to me, he has done very well these last few years with his work and his business, while much more talented men have done far worse. Felipe says that the Señora gave her husband a spell for success and that it worked! He also told me of an argument they were having one day, Señor Cortez told Felipe that he'd better not do anything to offend him or his wife would turn him into a frog. Sure, it was only a joke but Felipe worried about it all the same.

'I also remember that when they first came to Castillo Señora Cortez was very friendly with old Immaculada and the man called Christopher. They would frequently drink together in each others' homes. Then, I don't know. Maybe there was an argument or something, Señor Christopher left Castillo and now Immaculada and Señora Cortez never meet.'

To Mage's ears this was interesting stuff. What had happened to the Brit and why had he left in such a hurry? What might Immaculada tell him if he asked her nicely?

'This Señora Cortez... What does she look like?'

'She is tall and very thin... She has long black hair... A pointed sort of face... I am sorry Señor Colin, I do not know what to tell you.'

'Would you have gone to her if I hadn't been around?'

'No,' Angel said shortly. 'I do not like her.'

'Where does she live?'

'In Calle Quieros.'

Mage dug into his memory... He couldn't quite place the street, but it was quite close to Calle Sombra in the area of Santa Clara. It wasn't enough to launch an attack on but it did give him some food for thought. When he got round to that part of the proceedings he was sure he'd be able to confirm or deny his own suspicions regarding the identity of his craft adversary. There was one other snippet of information provided by Angel that told him he was on the right track.

'Over these past few months Señora Cortez has spent much time with the priest, Father Ignatious. It has become the source of some amusement and speculation. Is the witch becoming a nun, or is the priest becoming a witch, or are they having an affair... These are whispers I have heard.'

'Thank you Angel, you have been very helpful. Now, to change the subject, did you discover the date of Christina's birth?'

'Yes Señor Colin. She is born on August 5th... But I do not know what year.'

'No matter.' Mage moved to stand behind the round table. He took a long yellow candle from a bundle of many different colours and, with the dagger, began to carve Christina's name in the wax. When he had done this he laid the candle on the table. 'And your own birthday, Angel? When is that?'

'The 18th of March, Señor...'

'Ummm, Pisces,' Mage mused out loud, selecting another candle, this one pale silver in colour and again carving into the wax with the blade of the knife, this time inscribing Angel's name in bold letters. When he'd finished, he looked up.

'You have a photograph of the girl?'

'Yes, I have it here in my pocket.'

'And something personal that belongs to her?'

'Yes. At Jacinto's last night she had kicked her socks and shoes off under the table and I managed to steal a sock without anybody seeing...' Angel wasn't sure why El Moreno was smiling in such a way and he felt it inappropriate to ask. Instead he reached out, offering both the sock and the picture, and El Moreno walked across the room and took the items from him.

'And Angel, tell me exactly what you want from this girl.'

'I do not understand what you mean, Señor Colin...'

Mage looked at him with a degree of sympathy. 'Tell me exactly what you want of Christina. Do you, for example, want her as your wife for the rest of all time or will you settle for one night in her bed, sharing and knowing all of the secret sexual delights of her body? They are two different things and require two very different kinds of magic. The first is harder than the second to provide, the second much easier than the first.'

'Oh if I could have her for just one night!' Angel almost cried in melodramatic anguish. 'Then this would be enough! If only you can give me this thing!'

'Just one night?' Mage looked at him shrewdly. 'Very well, I shall bring you together for just one night and whatever you achieve with this lady after that, you achieve on your own. Now, lean forward and bow your head...'

Angel did as he was told and for the first time noticed the line of white powder that curved around the room in a perfect circle. El Moreno and the table were within this circle, while he, standing as he was on the top step, was without. He felt a sharp tug as Mage paired a lock of hair from his head with the dagger, then El Moreno was looking at him sternly again.

'Very well my young friend, this will take some time, so sit and be silent and observe.'

Angel lowered himself to the tiled floor and resting his back against the wall, watched as the Englishman went back to the round table.

Wearing black trousers and a black shirt, but with bare feet and nothing on his head, El Moreno stood silently for many long minutes, arms stretched straight out from his shoulders, one palm turned upwards the other facing down. He began to chant sonorous words in a language Angel could not recognise and, after a while, it seemed as though El Moreno was swaying slightly from side to side. Then abruptly he leaned over the table and with a single taper lit five of the candles which had been prepositioned among the pieces of crystal. For what seemed an age he stood staring at these five sources of light before lighting the other two candles that had been inscribed with Angel's and Christina's names. These two candles, the silver and the gold, Mage brought together in the middle of the table so that their melting waxes coalesced and, still muttering in an intelligible tongue, he began to bind them together with a find strand of red cord. Soon the cord had a number of knots in it, seven in all, and the melting wax dripped onto cord and knots alike.

Occasionally Angel heard his own name mentioned and that also of Christina and, unless he was much mistaken, either the candles burning around the room were suddenly much dimmer or the candles burning on the magician's table were burning that much more brightly. This mystery was partially resolved when Mage dipped the blade of the dagger into the flames of the inscribed candles – Angel felt a sudden hollowness in his guts and all the hairs on the back of his head seemed to stand on end – and lifting the dagger towards the shadows of the beamed ceiling, drew the twin flames up to an impossible height, maybe fifteen centimetres, no, nearer twenty five, from the wicks! This was impossible, but it was happening, impossible or not. Mage teased the flames with his blade making them dance to the ancient tune he was singing...

With his free hand he deposited Angel's hair, along with the small photograph and a few strands of cotton from Christina's sock, into a heavy silver chalice, then without warning he dipped the blade of the knife into the bowl and there was a flash of light and flying sparks followed by plumes and billows of incense that hovered and clung around the table before eddying gently around the room and inevitably rising to the rafters. Carefully, Mage tilted the silver and gold candles so that the wax dribbled into the silver chalice and then stood back in silent repose with his eyes firmly shut.

After what seemed an eternity, Mage opened his eyes and snuffed out the two inscribed candles with an antique instrument designed specifically for the purpose. Then he spent some time stirring the contents of the chalice before packing them into a small leather pouch that he closed firmly by its draw string. Only then did he turn and look at Angel.

'Four days,' he said quietly. 'She will be yours within four days, for one night only...' He crossed the room and Angel stumbled to his feet, his brain and senses numbed by the ritual he had witnessed.

Mage handed him the pouch. 'Keep this with you constantly. When you lay with her, you will be strong and you will remember all that has happened here today, but again I warn you... Not a word to anyone.'

Or you will have my eyes! Angel took the pouch and with as much respect, thanks and decorum that he could muster, fled.

Mage heard the front door click shut and, with an amused half smile, moved back to the table, drawing with him a chair upon which he sat for many long minutes in silent meditation.

As the town hall clock chimed five he brought the mirror box from the carpet bag and placed it upon the altar cloth. He discarded the old candles and lit fresh ones – this time five long black tallows. In the chalice, now freshly cleaned, he nurtured glowing charcoal until the black briquettes burned white with mounting heat. Stripping his clothes off he stood naked before his makeshift altar and raised his arms in supplication.

Now for the other business he thought. *Now for another kind of magic!*

With the point of the dagger he pricked the end of his finger and watched dispassionately as tiny globules of blood dropped into the chalice and fizzled on the white hot coals. He focused his eyes on the fireblood and closed off his senses to everything else. After – how long? – the coals lost their sharp edges and he was staring into a shimmering cup of white heat; blurred picture of distant visions began to swim up at him, faces and memories from his turbulent past...

Michael Fry wrapping the green bracelet around his wrist... His Grandmother patiently teaching and explaining the potency of the words of power... Alexandra as she had been in the early days and Alexandra again as she'd been after the change and transition... Dolorean, malefically corrupt and gloatingly wicked in his gleeful triumph. There was Herschal, the old man of the desert and Paul O'Connor in Ireland, both of them in their different ways explaining how the impossible was not only possible but real... He saw the faces and heard the words of friends back in England, people who had taken him on trust and had helped him regardless of their own misgivings: Josh Tetworth, the detective, saying "Colin, this Dolorean guy! Really weird. Doesn't legally exist!"

Then there were faces of people he'd met in Castillo, principally Angel, Hector and Anna... and as the semi-trance took him into the lower realms of the astral, he reached out for Anna Sanchez and laid a blessing on her eyes.

Angel again, this time in association with Christina, and as he thought of Christina, John Light's black face swung into view. Was there a link here or was it circumstantial autosuggestion caused by the American factor?

There was a tingling, tearing sensation and Mage lifted out of his body and looked down at himself hunched over the table surrounded by the enveloping corunnas of candlelight – and with the lifting came the stillness that brought the soulcalm and the awareness of his own strength. Pulsing magnificently into the astral were his symbols of power and protection, the interlocking silver pentagrams which in one sense were finite, holding him in stasis in the room that had become his temple, acting as his body armour and becoming the creative energy for his offensive strike and in another sense, infinite, towering into the realms of the astral like a beacon, magnetising to him the cascading energies from all points of the planet, focused and held by the four prime angelic entities that were the anchor points of his pentagramic matrix. Rapheal in the east, Michael in the south, Gabriel in the west and Uriel in the north. *Show me, my lords, show me...*

Within the haze of heat a face swam into view and a name for the face echoed through the temples of his mind. Cortez. Miriam Cortez! And no, this was not autosuggestion born of Angel's information. This came from a different source and as if to prove it the corners of the mandalic hex began to curl within the confines of the mirror box and the squirls of the bloodlines shimmered within the cone of power he was creating.

From where his mind hovered, just beneath the ceiling, he watched his own right hand reach out and take the square of hide parchment from the box of mirrors, then place it in the centre of the glowing coals.

'Be damned.' He heard his own voice say. 'And may this curse be returned to you, the sender, with tenfold retribution. May that which has been visited on me be visited upon you. Here and now, in this very moment. So mote it be.'

The hex did not just burst, it *exploded* into flames and he felt a surge of power flow out of him like a long held and pent up orgasm.

Colin Mage had the anger of magic in his soul. The Hurting was upon him in all its dark glory. For months he had been battered by incoming psychic attack and for many many weeks he had travelled the pathway of the spiritual warrior, learning healing, acquiring energy, conserving... Now The Hurting and the frustration of passivity boiled over and he lashed out at his adversaries, at those who sought to harm him, at those who sought to destroy all that was sweet and good in his world.

There was the sender of the hex. If it was Miriam Cortez, she would now suffer the wrath of his retaliation, and if it was not, then no real harm would befall her. There was also the priest, fat Ignatious of Santa Clara. Well, let him too be aware of a magician's spite and maybe find some succour and comfort from juvenile thugs with knives, or prayers to whichever particular version of God he pretended to worship.

Another spasm wracked Mage's body as again a bolt of energy discharged itself from his being... This time directed towards the wayward priest.

But above all there was Dolorean. There was always Dolorean!

Focusing all the force of his fury he discharged a thunderbolt of raw mental energy against his enemy. He didn't know exactly where Dolorean was but he was confident that this counter attack would find him through his two acolytes, the witch and the priest.

Again there was the sensation of tearing fabric, but this time the process was reversed and Mage found himself back in his body, feeling dazed and empty now that the psychic and magical energies had been drawn from him. Now he was at his most vulnerable. Fumbling for the chair, he allowed himself to sit and closing his eyes against the sting of the heat and smoke fumes, began to recite the closing mantras of protection and preservation, regulating his breathing and bringing his senses back to reality.

Despite the heat of the room and the late afternoon, his body was cold, covered in a sheen of perspiration. Methodically he closed his circle, dousing the candles one by one in the order in which he'd lit them. Only then did he allow himself the luxury of moving away from the table and wrapping a rug around himself, stretched out full length of the sofa. Even then, tired though he was, he could not allow himself the sleep that his exhausted being craved. He was fighting a war. A major attack had been launched. Not knowing his enemy's strength, he had to remain vigilant.

Miriam Cortez woke from a light sleep, disorientated by not realising that she'd dozed off and wondering for a split second where she was. Early evening sunshine poured in through lattice shutters casting long slanting shadows across her opulent bedroom. She tried to push herself up from her pillow and fell back with a small groan. Her head was pounding with the most colossal headache she'd had in years, worse even than the memory of her pubescent migraines. Indeed, the room seemed slightly out of focus and the walls and ceiling appeared oddly distorted.

She became aware of the wetness between her legs and was immediately alert. Her period had been as regular as clockwork for twenty years and she was not due for another eight days. And yet there was no doubt about it, she was in full and heavy flow. Her thighs and the bed were awash. With a snort of disgust she pushed herself up onto her elbows – and with firm and gentle pressure, something pushed her back again.

She lay there dazed and confused, wondering what was going on. This was ridiculous! With an impatient gesture she pulled the sheet from her body, horrified by the smell that assailed her and also by the stain that spread out beneath her thighs and buttocks. How could she have slept through this?

Again she pushed herself up onto her elbows and again came into contact with an invisible barrier of pressure that would not let her rise further and indeed, gently forced her back to the pillows. She tried turning, both left and right, but there was a subtle weight upon her shoulders that made it impossible for her to shift more than a few inches in either direction. Next she tried swinging her legs over the side of the bed and to her horror, recognised that her legs would not move at all.

'I'm paralysed,' she thought in mounting panic. 'I'm fucking well paralysed!'

Calming her pounding heart, she thought back to earlier in the day. She'd been reading a book, sipping red wine. Lena had come home from school around three then had gone off with Peter to Sotogrande around four. She'd felt drowsily tired and had transferred from the veranda to her bed a little after five. There'd been no problem then, had there? Just a little tiredness that made a formal siesta look like an attractive proposition. What time was it now? Seven fifteen by the bedside clock, so she'd been asleep for a little under two hours and in that time something had gone seriously wrong.

Yet again she tried to rise and yet again that wall of pressure pushed her back. In frustration she screamed out her husband's name at the top of her voice, but her cry was curiously weak and even to her own ears sounded oddly muffled.

She wondered just how long she'd been bleeding and then came a more sobering thought. Just how much blood had she lost?

Ignatious de Santa Clara did not like spiders. In fact he was disgusted and terrified by them. Thus when he looked up from his prayerful reverie in front of the high altar to find a large tarantula resting on the knuckles of his clasped hands, he let out a screech of pure horror and, flailing his hands apart, fell backwards off the small prayer stool and went sprawling across the floor of the church. Watching the eight legged monster – it wasn't really a tarantula, it just looked like one and that was quite bad enough – scuttle off into the shadows beneath the first row of pews, he felt beads of perspiration form on his face and in the small of his back. His arachnaphobia was acute and the shock of actually finding a spider on his hands while he'd been praying to The Master was an abomination of all that was good and holy.

Panting slowly, he climbed to his knees then fell forwards again, doubled over by the sharp jagged pain that lanced upwards from his bowels to his stomach. It made him cry out in agony, a single cry that echoed around the lofty vaults of the church. The pain was shocking in its intensity, made all the more horrific by its unexpectedness. And yet the pain was no stranger. He'd lived with it for many months until The Master had come and had taken the pain away. The cancer of the colon that had been no so slowly killing the priest had gone into strange and immediate remission and the pain had become a distant memory. Now it was back in all its miserable splendour and, as another vicious spasm clutched at his gut, his sphincter ruptured and he felt the hot rush of wet shit discharge from his bowels with the putrid stench of something far worse than ordinary diarrhoea.

He fell flat on his face, his forehead banging against the unforgiving stone causing the world to tilt with a different kind of dizzying pain. He didn't lose consciousness, but lay there dazed and unable to move.

A minute became an eternity of passing seconds. Ignatious didn't even *try* to move – but something else did. He caught it out of the corner of his eye, a flurry in the dark shadow beneath the front row of pews. A flurry of something furry.

Slowly the spider emerged from the gloom... The same one that had been on his hands, black and malignant, fully three centimetres across in the body, with those eight incredibly bent and hairy legs. Ignatious whimpered with fright and then nearly gagged on his own vomit as he realised that the spider was not alone. There was another monstrosity behind it, spindly and grey with a smaller body but with legs that were so very much longer... And then there was another to the left of that, squat and dark brown with a single white stripe down its back.

Even as he watched, four more eight legged horrors emerged from beneath the bench, a little to the left, and then another three were chittering across the floor towards him from the right, one of them quite enormous with something sticky and glutinous attached to one of its mandibles.

The phalanx of spiders moved inexorably towards him with cold deliberation. Ramming his fist into his mouth to stifle the scream that threatened to escape taking all logic and reason with it, Ignatious rolled over onto his back – and came face to face with the biggest spider he'd ever seen in his life. It hovered ten centimetres above his face suspended by a single strand of web that seemed to fall endlessly from the roof of the church some forty feet above him.

How? How was it possible that a spider could be so big? How was it possible that it could drop such an incredible distance? These thoughts flitted fleetingly through his mind and then it all became academic. The giant from the roof dropped the last short distance onto his face and Ignatious began screaming in earnest.

In the La Linea medical centre Lorenzo Bautista Matan woke from a terrible dream and vowed to himself that he was *never* going back to Castillo. In his dream, something had been eating his eyes.

In Calle Santana, Anna Sanchez's eyes filled with moisture. She was not crying and the moisture was not a flow of tears. Her limited vision became even more misty and opaque and yet the crushing headache that had been making her feel sick and dizzy all day, was suddenly and inexplicably gone. 'Papa,' she called nervously. 'Papa? Are you there?'

Peter Cortez approached the curve in the road with a subconscious degree of respect. The bend had the reputation of being a killer, but he'd driven this road a thousand times and in any case he prided himself on being an excellent driver.

He dropped down into third gear and played the wheel to the left, preparing to take the curve at a safe and steady thirty. The car, however, veered violently to the right, careered off the road and ploughed through a thick bush of wild yellow gorse before crumpling into a solid stone wall.

Cortez's head banged against the windscreen – he'd not been belted – then he fell back in his seat, out cold with the impact and concussion. A smudge of blood was smeared across the glass and more blood welled up and dripped from a nasty gash above his right eye.

Lena Cortez, who had been stretched out asleep in the back, woke as the impact threw her against the front seats. It took her a few seconds to realise what had happened and even when she did, this eight year old girl's reactions were curious.

There was no panic, no concern, no apparent worry. Some curiosity, yes, as she got out of the car and inspected the damage, but certainly little more than that. She glanced both ways up and down the road, but the road was deserted.
Wrapping her small hands around the handle of the front door, she pulled it open and clambered in next to her father... Only he wasn't her father, of course. She knew it even if he didn't. Even her mother, who'd never said anything to either of them, could not be sure. She eyed Cortez solemnly and with unblinking eyes. She knew he wasn't dead because she could see the rise and fall of his chest.

Hesitantly she reached out her hand and trailed her fingers through the blood that fell down the side of his cheek. Then she put her fingers into her mouth to taste, and it was sweet and warm – not like some of the stuff she'd tried from dead birds and other small animals. Yes, this was sweet and warm... She dipped her fingers in for another taste... And really rather nice.

In England, at The Oaks, Michael Fry stopped mid-sentence in his conversation with Helen Ross. He cocked his head to one side as though listening to a one sided conversation. There was a subtle hollowness in his solar plexus caused by the tension of jumping nerve ends and a feeling of exultant excitement coursed through him bringing tears to his eyes and causing a lump to rise in his throat.

'Michael? What's happening?' Helen's voice was full of concern. 'Are you all right?'

'Picking up Mage,' Fry said shortly. 'He's gone over to the offensive. He's attacking.'

Helen's eyes opened wide with wonder. 'You have this strong a link with him?'

'Yes.' Fry's voice sounded strained. 'Yes, I have.'

Also in England, but 200 miles south of where Fry sat with Helen Ross, Jadoc Dolorean looked down at his incubator. The female was unconscious, of course, as indeed was the norm these days. He monitored her progress and condition every two hours by telepathic link and psychic probe and maintained her physical strength by regular transfusions of his own blood and liberal dosings of the herbs and unguents he'd brought over with him from the Homeworld. She was sufficiently into the state of transition for him to manipulate her body shape and texture and he had her covered now with a light down of body fur that insured the Newlife's comfort and well-being within her.

He resented the time spent during this incubation period and dreamed idly of the time when the bridge would be formed between worlds, when the opening would be complete and he would be reunited with his kind who would pour through for The Taking... And he was not unaware of the power and authority that would be his at that point. After all, it was he who had been chosen from the many to perform this task.

He much preferred the warmth of that other place close to the opening, but security and the need for a cooler climate for the incubation coincided with the culture of the woman he had stolen, and also the tradition of his kind demanded that the female should always incubate on her own soil. Soon the time would come when she could be moved and the Newlife would be birthed into the breach of the opening, its first cries of life forging the link between worlds and opening the door for The Hoard. Just another few short weeks and the transition would be complete, the Newlife ready to emerge.

Beneath him on the bed the female stirred, her lips stretching to form a single word that was whispered half as a question, half as a supplication... 'Colin?'

Jadoc Dolorean pressed down immediately with his will sending the female into the deepest level of sleepfugue. A minor chill tugged at him. It was wrong that after all this time the female still had link memories to what had gone before... That somewhere deep in her subconscious there still dwelled the name of her manmate. That should have long since been expunged and eradicated.

Another chill tremoured through him, marginally more noticeable than the first. He felt muscles twitch and noted a trembling sensation in the skin of his face and forehead. Turning from the bed he looked at his reflection in the wall mirror. For a moment, all was well and the alien human face gazed back at him blandly from the bevelled surface of the glass... Then the chill took him a third time, not just a chill but an icy blast that made his head ring with unexpected pain. The mirrored reflection danced before his eyes, becoming misty and ill-defined, and for a brief second, a single heartbeat in time, the shapechanger's visage slipped, the features of his face coalescing into a blur of scale and tusk.

Through the veil of pain he fought for control – and found it. The face fell back into the regular human features of Jadoc Dolorean, but the shapechanger was breathing hard with the effort. The pain gradually stilled and diminished to be replaced with an ice cold anger. There was no doubt in his mind that the lapse in his disguise had been caused by a psychic attack from the female's manmate and this was worrisome. The manmate, this poor magician, was supposed to have been dealt with and neutralised long ago and yet here he was, waiting for them in Spain, unleashing challenging thunderbolts across the astral plane that was common to both their worlds.

The shapechanger again looked down at the incubating female and thought that despite the risk, he might have to move her to the opening a little earlier than expected.

Back in Castillo, Miriam Cortez lay supine on her bed. Twice more she had tried to rise and twice more she had been firmly pressed back. There was no pain. In fact there was not much of anything... She drifted on a tide of semi consciousness, slipping ever more gently towards death as the lifeblood drained from her. She knew now that she was dying and thought in abstract terms about Lena and Peter and realised with unique clarity that she didn't really care, either about leaving them or what might happen to them after she'd gone. They would survive – or at least Lena would, and as for Peter, well, he didn't really matter very much anyway.

She felt cool as the room dimmed ever more deeply into shadow, but it was not unpleasant. Occasionally she lifted a little way out of her body and saw herself lying in the ever growing puddle of dark red blood that now dripped through the thick mattress of the bed and stained the pale white wood of the floor.

As the town hall clock struck eight, a low sonorous roll of thunder rumbled interminably along the Castillato valley and she became aware of a tingling breaking sensation within her as the nerve endings let go of the spirit that bound them to the flesh of her being. Even as the thunder echoed towards the mountains, Miriam Cortez's spirit left her body.

Not once had she given Colin Mage so much as a passing thought or wondered what part he might have had to play in her downfall.

13.

John Light

Tamara drove the Cadillac down the length of the main street before pulling into the parking lot in front of the general store. It wasn't much of a street, and nor was it much of a store. Come to think of it, Demsville Louisiana was not much of a town. One street with a few side yards and alleys, a drug store, a gas station, three bars and a post office. Population three thousand and something and most of that population living out on small holdings and border line farms.

There was a small motel three hundred yards up the road from the gas station. They'd spent a night there when they'd first arrived, but it had been hot without air conditioning and buzzy with mosquitoes. Their room had stank of stale sweat and dirty socks and she was glad that they were staying out at the cabin now. For one thing it was cleaner, even though there were no utilities like running water or electricity, and for another, Light seemed much calmer now that they'd finally arrived at their destination. He was still moody, but in other ways far more relaxed than he'd been on what had seemed to be an interminable cross country journey from LA.

This last day or so he'd talked to her, telling her things about himself, especially about his childhood, that she'd not known. He'd grown up in these parts, around Demsville, and even when he'd left at the age of sixteen for the bigger towns and cities he'd always returned to Demsville on a very regular basis, sometimes for weeks and months at a time.

The Lord knew why. She got out of the Caddy and looked down the length of the town. There was nothing, absolutely nothing she could see to commend it. Even the outlying countryside was poor and scraggy. They'd driven for more than half a day along dusty back roads, occasionally passing through small ramshackle hamlets with lean-to wooden huts. Here were sullen niggers that time and society had forgotten and the poor white trash with their thin women and beer-gutted men. There had been dangerous looks of envy and malice as the expensive car had cut a swathe through them, but Light had looked straight ahead, either not seeing them or not noticing.

For her part, Tamara had taken some reassurance from the presence of the loaded pistol that was cleverly concealed and clipped beneath the inner edge of the passenger seat, equally accessible to passenger and driver alike in an emergency. That emergency had never arisen but there had been a couple of times when her hand had strayed down beside her left leg and she'd found herself travelling with her fingers brushing against the pearl handled smoothness of the heavy Colt Python.

... There'd been a Grandmother and an Aunt. Both dead now, who together had worked hard to give Jonty Golightly whatever upbringing and education he'd had. There'd been an extensive smallholding constructed from clapboard and corrugated iron which had long since gone, leaving no trace of its long but temporary existence. The cabin shack was still there, but that had been built much later and Light had built it himself out of solid seasoned wood. It stood on the edge of a small lake, maybe three miles from where the farm had been, in a small dip of land that was made attractive by the thick foliage of heavy undergrowth and a few modest trees. She would not have chosen it as a rural weekend retreat, but Light still nominally owned this meagre patch of land and she supposed that he wanted to retain some contact with the place of his childhood. If the original farm had gone and he'd actually built the cabin with his own sweat and effort, she guessed that it made a degree of sense.

Tamara entered the store and purchased the items on her list. Several litres of bottled water, a twenty four pack of beer, canned food and an assortment of anything that could be cooked on an open fire. She had to make two journeys before the stuff was loaded and secured in the Cadillac's spacious boot. She slammed the lid shut and all but jumped with surprise to find the old man standing next to her. Even at three feet she could smell the dirt and cheap drink fumes that emanated from him and she recoiled from his ugliness.

His face was mutilated by a long scar that cut down from the bridge of his flattened nose to the jawline beneath an ear that was minus its lobe and outer rim. His negroid skin was particularly black, made more so by the shock of erratic white hair and the prickly white stubble that covered his face. He wore an eye patch, a cheap home-made thing, over one eye and the other, deep muddy brown, sized her up warily.

'Yo wid de man?' he finally asked.

Tamara had heard John Light referred to as The Man since she was fourteen. True, there were other "men" but she nodded her head just the same. 'Yeah. I'm with The Man.'

The old negro shuffled and maybe he wasn't so old as she'd first thought... it was difficult to tell beneath that white hair and whiskers and the flapping old coat, full of voluminous folds and covered with stains without number.

'Yo tell him you've talked to Old Rugby. Yo tell de man dat it's still there, but mo powerful 'an befoe. Yo tell him to be careful and not to go messin' again. Yo tell him Ole Rugby's still sufferin' from dat las'time.' The white haired negro turned and shuffled away. 'Yo jess tell him, y'hear.' Then he was round the corner and out of sight and Tamara climbed into the car feeling thoroughly contaminated by the encounter.

Light listened thoughtfully as she passed on the message but offered no explanation. She didn't immediately pursue the matter, marvelling instead at the amount of work Light had got done in her absence. The cabin, no more than a wooden hut eight feet by ten, had been scrupulously cleaned and it had also been repaired; the door now hung straight on its hinges and the gaping hole in the roof had been boarded over. There was a substantial pile of firewood and kindling and he had dug a fire pit and had already laid a fire. Drying on a rock were two small fish that he'd taken from the lake.

The lake itself, maybe fifty yards across and nearly three times as long, fed a small stream over to the right of the hut, while in the distance, over on the left amid a cluster of boulders, the surface of the water was disturbed by the splashing cascade of a natural spring. Tamara had tasted the spring water on their first day and had found it surprisingly cold and fresh... Unusual for the Mississippi delta country where even fast flowing streams tended to be brackish and polluted.

But then again, this whole area was a little unusual. For one thing it was uncommonly calm and still, to such an extent that even the birdsong was muted. There should have been midges and the lake shore should have been alive with mosquitoes, but she'd slept in the cabin for two nights now and hadn't so much as heard a whine or a buzz. She'd also been fearful of spiders and anything else that crawled, slithered, chittered or bit, but after two nights of sleeping on hard boards wrapped in travel blankets with car cushions for pillows, she'd not been disturbed or alarmed once.

The biggest mystery was the change in John Light. There'd been two nights free of nightmares. He'd slept soundly and now that they were actually here he seemed significantly less subdued and noticeably more alert. In retrospect, the road journey had been something of a trial. Long moody hours of silent driving punctuated by noisy nights filled with the shouts of his violent dreams – and even when he'd slept in the car while she had driven, his sleep had been restless, full of grunts and moans.

He'd lost some weight. Enough to be noticed, but he looked better for it and his speech patterns had also gone through a subtle metamorphosis. Gone was the black jive of the west coast negro, gone the thundering pontifications of the evangelistic reverend, and in their place were the neutral, almost cultured tones of any reasonably well educated American. She noticed the difference in how he addressed her: she was frequently Tam or Hon or Babe or Tammy – but he'd also got into the habit of calling her by her full name, Tamara, and although she couldn't figure out exactly why, she realised that she like this very much indeed.

Light had never treated her badly. He'd never hit her and had never abused her – had never taken her against her will and had always respected her need for a little privacy every fourth week or so. But there had been times, times without number, when she'd felt ignored – when her own identity had been overwhelmed and submerged beneath the powerhouse personality of "The Man". She'd been an appendage, an addendum, a courtier and as such, frequently superfluous to requirements. She'd accepted it, but had not always liked it.

This also was something that had subtly changed and continued to change almost on a daily basis. In one way it made her nervous for this was something she'd never had to deal with before and didn't know how to deal with it. But in other ways it was the most welcome and wonderful thing that had ever happened to her. She didn't know if she loved John Light, indeed, with her background she wasn't even sure she knew what love was. But she knew that she liked him and in many ways, although his faults and shortcomings were legion, she admired and respected him. She'd always been his woman, but now, over these last few days, it seemed that he, or at least part of him, was becoming her man.

He lit the fire and they cooked and ate the fish, washing it down with warm beer. They sunk the other cans and water bottles in the lake in an attempt to keep them half cool and for a while they sat in companionable silence. And yet there was a coiled spring of tension within him and she noticed how his eyes kept gravitating towards the far side of the lake. It wasn't as though he was staring mindlessly into space, more that he was looking for something. Looking *at* something, keeping it under constant observation.

After about half an hour, towards late afternoon when the sun was low in the sky and some of the heat was just beginning to fade from the day, he turned and eyed her cautiously.

'If I could read minds,' he mused thoughtfully and then grinned, 'and let's face it babe, sometimes I can... I'd say that one of the thoughts going round in your mind right now is just what the hell are we doing here, right?'

Tamara nodded and Light eased himself to his feet. 'Okay. I want to show you something. Go get the gun from the car.'

While Tamara dutifully went and fetched the Colt, Light threw more branches on the fire. Then, taking the gun from her hand, he led her gently round the end of the lake. They crossed the stream and strolled along the lakeside until they were almost opposite the cabin. Light turned her away from the lake and they walked a few yards towards a gentle rise in the land before Light stopped.

'Okay, Tamara, I want you to look ahead of you and tell me exactly what you see.'

Nonplussed, she studied the terrain and wondered what she was supposed to be looking for. 'Grass,' she said with a self conscious giggle. 'Plenty of grass... A hill, some bushes, a few boulders, a couple of dead trees...'

'Concentrate on the trees, Tam. Concentrate on the trees.'

The trees were stunted and at some distant time had been destroyed by fire. Maybe they'd even been stuck by lightening. The boles, once silver white, were now blackened, the skeletal fingers of the branches pointing accusingly skywards. They stood maybe ten or fifteen feet apart and twenty or thirty feet beyond them was a long low boulder. Between boulder and trees the land dipped into a small and ill-defined hollow.

'Okay John, I'm concentrating on the trees, but I still don't see anything.

What am I looking for?'

'Be patient,' he said. 'Look a little while longer. Not so much at the trees themselves...' His voice lowered a couple of notes. 'Look between the trees.'

Tamara stood for fully five minutes before a small 'Oh!' escaped her lips. And then a minute or so later: 'What *is* it?'

At first she'd seen nothing, then the air had shimmered briefly, rather like a heat haze. Then it had happened again with a greater degree of distortion. A thin filament of rippling light danced from tree to tree, over in a millisecond but enough to record on the retina of the eye. Then for a handful of heartbeats the air took on a liquid effect, defocusing the boulder in the background to no more than an oval blur, before flicking back into the sharp focus of normality. The whole process was vague and incredibly subtle, so much so that she wasn't absolutely sure of what she was seeing.

She took a step forwards and felt Light's restraining hand on her shoulder. 'No,' he said. 'It's dangerous.'

'Dangerous?' she echoed. 'John, it's *beautiful!*'

'Yeah, well it's still dangerous. Watch.'

He picked up a piece of fallen timber, fully three feet long and four inches in diameter at the heavy end. He threw it forcefully between the trees in an arching parabellum. She watched it flail end over end until it disappeared.
In mid-air.

One second it was there, the next second not, simply snapping out of existence before their eyes. She blinked.

'What happened?' she asked.

'You tell me,' he retorted grimly.

'It's a trick!' she exclaimed.

'Is it?' he countered. 'Okay...' he picked up a smaller, stumpier branch and held it out towards her. 'You try then.'

Tamara took the stump of old root and drawing back her arm, launched it in pursuit of the first branch. It was not a graceful lob and the missile entered the space between the trees barely three feet above the ground. Nonetheless it too vanished into thin air.

'This is impossible, John!'

'Ain't it just,' he replied laconically.

There were many small rocks around their feet. He picked one up and pitched it to the left of the left hand tree. She watched the stone bounce off the thin scrub grass twenty feet beyond the trees.

'You can go to the left,' he said, then pitching another stone on the other tangent, 'and you can go to the right.' He took a third stone, a little larger than the first two and heaved it above the blackened branches, watching it drop like a mortar bomb on the rocky outcrop beyond the sunken dell. 'If you can fly, you can go over the top... But...'

He picked up a fourth rock, three times the size of a baseball. '... But you sure as hell don't go through the middle!'

He hurled the stone with all the strength of his arm and in a fast flat trajectory it flew between the trees. Like the two wooden projectiles before it, it simply dematerialised and snapped out of sight.

'John,' a note of nervousness entered Tamara's voice. 'John, this is really weird.'

'Weird?' he echoed with a humourless laugh. 'Tamara, I tell you baby that this is the most fucking scariest thing I've come across in all my life!'

She looked at him then and saw the strain in his face and the fear in his eyes. 'You gonna tell me about this John?'

'Sure,' he grimaced. 'But later. Not now.'

Together they headed back towards the cabin, neither of them looking behind them, both of them wanting to, in search of some reassurance that wasn't there.

He didn't know exactly what it was or how long it had been there, although with regard to the latter he suspected that the answer was a very very long time. What complicated matters was that it was not a constant phenomenon. There'd been times when it wasn't there and times when it was.

He'd first found it thirty five years before. He'd been stalking a jackrabbit with his new gun – his *first* gun! It was a .410 buckshot special acquired tenth hand and presented to him by Old Nance and Aunt Epiphany half as a twelfth birthday present, half as a bribe.

'You learn the juju magic, you get the gun,' Aunt Epiphany had said a few weeks before. 'You don't learn the juju, then you make do with new pants!'

He needed the pants but wanted the gun so much more and had entered willingly into the contract. Now on this hot August day, barely a year after an American president had been shot to death in Dallas, Jonty Golightly was pleased with his prize. It may only have been an old light gauge shot gun but to him it was a coming of age talisman, more potent and powerful than anything his Grandmother and Aunt could concoct with their potions and chantings.

He drew a bead on the jackrabbit as it ran beside the lake and, almost as if sensing the finger pressure building on the trigger, the animal veered to the right and disappeared between two trees.

Literally.

Young Jonty Golightly rubbed his eyes. There was nothing wrong with his eyesight but jackrabbits didn't just disappear like that.

'Must've gone down some friggin' hole,' he muttered to himself and cautiously moved towards the area between the two leafy green and densely foliated trees.

The rippling folds of light that suddenly but subtly blurred his vision made him pull back – way back, at least ten feet, where he sat on his haunches and watched with fascination.

This part of the lakeside had always attracted him and even as a small boy he'd played here for countless hours. He couldn't actually remember playing among these two trees though – although he subconsciously recognised that they'd always been there. He didn't know exactly what he was looking at now, but he knew that it was something different that he'd never seen before, he also sensed that it was something powerful... A fact confirmed when a blue jay swept out of the sky, aiming for a landing on the distant boulder, and like the jackrabbit before it, flipped soundlessly into non-existence. Even at twelve years old and despite his upbringing, perhaps even because of it, he recognised the odd power of this place.

Tentatively, he found a solid stick and tossing it between the tree trunks, was not surprised when it too performed an impossible vanishing act. 'Be damned,' he murmured and brought the .410 back up to his shoulder, lining the sights against the left hand tree. He squeezed the trigger and felt no small degree of satisfaction as part of the bark exploded beneath the buckshot. He reloaded and repeated the performance with the right hand tree, again satisfied that his aim was spot on. Now he aimed between the trees, lining up on the boulder behind them and again squeezed the trigger.

Nothing. No puff of dust, no whine of pellets, no scuff or rock chippings. Buckshot, like bird and jackrabbit, simply evaporated. Undeterred, he approached the anomaly from another angle. He hunted around till he found what he was looking for... A long thin branch, maybe eight feet from end to willowy end. Branch in hands, he slowly advanced towards what he thought of as some kind of freaky force field, holding the branch out ahead of him like an antenna. The end of the branch danced up to the area between the trees and faded from view: he eased it in another few inches, then eased it out again. It emerged readily enough but brought with it a sick cloying stink that he couldn't begin to identify. Not to be thwarted, he eased it inwards again, this time two or three feet: the smell became stronger and he was aware of a vibration rippling down the branch towards his hands. This time when he tried to pull backwards, the branch would not move... Then without warning the wooden probe leapt from his hands with such violence that it took some of the skin off his palms and was immediately sucked up into the vortex, leaving Jonty flat on his backside feeling puzzled, excited and bewildered.

And also frightened, for as the branch had gone, there'd been a distant sound, something like a muted angry roar and he'd got the clear impression that someone, or something, had pulled the branch through the barrier and was more than pissed off that he, twelve year old Jonty Golightly, was not still hanging on to the end of it. The boy drew back hastily and retrieving the gun, quickly slipped another shell into the breach, although what a single round of .410 buckshot might do against something that might choose to emerge from between the trees to get him, was highly debatable. Either way, he didn't want to hang around to find out.

Later on, over supper, he carefully questioned Old Nance and Aunt Epiphany and it became glaringly apparent that they had no terms of reference to what he was talking about and that they had no knowledge of two special trees and a force field that buzzed between them and swallowed things whole. For reasons best known to himself, Jonty chose not to enlighten them. It was his secret and his place, a place that pulled him back to the shores of the lake times without number during his early years.

Sometimes there was nothing there and you could walk between those two trees like any two trees in the world. Other times the light was wrong and the air was ruffled and on those times he kept well backed away, looking, watching, studying, half waiting for something to happen... Waiting for something on the other side of that barrier to find its way through to this side of the barrier. With the acquisition of a more arcane education than either Aunt or Grandmother could provide, a specialist knowledge that was not on the curriculum of any school he attended, he came to recognise the importance of the place by the lake and in a time of motor cycles and black leather jackets and girls that needed to be impressed, he built the cabin by the shore – even *then* careful to put fifty yards of water between it and the trees.

By the time he was nineteen years old, Jonty Golightly was a physical giant and with a personality and will to match. His occult power was growing with the seasons, this made possible by his recognition of that power and his awareness of its flaws and limitations. Others were not aware of the limitations and recognised only the power. In pursuit of that power, Jonty became their natural leader, heading the thirty strong pack of black jacketed bikers through the backroads of Louisiana and making paler Angels of Hell pull quickly to one side in deference to the black masters of the south. Jonty, no longer calling himself Jonty, preferring the ambiguous title of 'Lightly' took a perverse pleasure in calling his chapter The Black Masters and growing up in the time and place of his years, saw it as his holy quest to wage war against the whites. Not all whites – only the whites of his world, the underworld of drugs and gang fights and road rumbles.

There were occasional incursions from other counties and states... Long haired angels on Harley Davisons, armed with knives and clubs and sawn offs... That didn't stand much chance against heavy calibre automatics and the brilliant tactics of the black general from the Mississippi delta. Oddly, there was little hassle and interference from the police, who by tacit agreement stood to one side as one element of a sub-human culture annihilated and reduced the ranks of several other elements who created more than enough problems for ordinary folk in their own territories. Indeed, more than twenty percent of Light's armoury came indirectly from police stores and the intelligence of his battle tactics came from more than one police control room. By the time he was twenty two, 'Lightly' was more than man to those who knew of him. He was Legend.

In the summer of 1978, a number of things coalesced that were destined to bring John Light to one of the most crucial turning points in his life. First, a new state governor elected on a law and order bill, authorised a crack down on what had come to be euphemistically known as the Angel Wars. In the space of a few weeks The Black Masters' supply of arms and information were reduced to a trickle. The Louisiana State Police were given licence to arrest with all force necessary anything that looked remotely aggressive on two wheels.

Secondly, not giving a damn for governors or state cops, a long list of biking chapters decided that Lightly's dominance had to be broken once and for all: there were a hundred old scores and injustices to be resolved and settled, and the fact that some no good nigger was beating the shit out of whites was enough to unify what amounted to a veritable army of adversaries. For the whole of June and July of that year there were war councils in places as far flung as Shreveport to Baton Rouge, New Orleans to Alexandria and Lake Charles. A date was set and the word went out.

Thirdly, there was Juliette.

Light had lost his virginity at fourteen years old. Aunt Epiphany had seen to that with tact and compassion. His twelfth birthday present may have been a .410 shot gun, but his fourteenth was a doe eyed hooker who looked a lot younger than her twenty two years and who specialised in breaking in virgins. In the interim period he was never short of a woman, indeed, sometimes had as many as three or four in tow at any one time, but Juliette was different. A mulatto with Cajun blood... creamy dark skin, negroid features softened by cross breeding and fair, almost white blond hair. She was six years older than he was and she came to him not as his concubine, but as his equal. Her own knowledge of magic and the voodoo juju of the deep south learned from her own womenfolk made her more than his equal in this respect. Light was besotted and she became not only his mistress but an avatar that showed him the way into a deeper level of understanding of mysteries he'd been exposed to since childhood but had never really understood.

Had he not been so involved, he may have picked up the warning signals at least a little earlier than he did. As it was, it wasn't until the last week of July that he began to feel uneasy about something he couldn't define. The change of tactics by the Louisiana State Police had caused some of the brothers to be a little more circumspect in their behaviour, but as Captain Kitson had reassured him up in the county seat of Avon, it would be all over in a couple of months after the new governor had made his point. It may take a few arrests, but things would be back to normal by fall. On July 31st, Light phoned Kitson on the Captain's restricted number up at Avon County Police Department.

Henry Kitson was a career cop whose career had stopped moving a good eight years before. At forty years old he wasn't getting any younger and nor was he getting any richer. He wasn't, in essence, a bad man but he had become a bad policeman... At first making a point of being somewhere else when a marijuana deal went down and collecting a couple of hundred dollars for his trouble and lack of vision. Then it became a couple of thousand dollars to be on the other side of the county when something heavier than a little pot was going through the pipeline. Lightly had found him fertile soil to till and from Lightly there came not only the cash, but also the black pussy which gave Henry more thrills than he could get from any harsh white hooker in the dusty rooms of Baton Rouge. From Henry's point of view, it was a golden deal because Lightly wanted so little in return. Just the occasional snippet of information. On that night of July 31st, Lightly wanted something more.

'Henry, my man, what's happening? My juices tell me somethin' big an' nasty is coming down hard from a great height that ain't got nuthin' to do with no clean up campaign pioneered by the governor's office.'

The policeman had looked blankly into the phone. 'Hey man, I've not heard nothing... Nothing you don't already know about anyway.'

'You sure about that now, Henry?'

'Sure I'm sure.'

'So there's nuthin' I need to know?'

Kitson was totally perplexed. 'Not a damn thing I can think of... Hey listen, we know each other, right? If there was something you needed to know, I'd be on the phone to you straight away...'

'Ummm...' Lightly had paused in the conversation, reviewing his own feelings, 'Okay, well listen Henry, I'm out at Aunt Epiphany's place and I guess I'm going to be here for the next coupla days, so if you *do* hear anything, you know exactly where to get me.'

'Yeah, yeah, I got it – but listen man, what am I supposed to be listening for?'

That was the bummer. Lightly didn't know. 'Anything at all,' he said ambiguously and hung up.

By the following morning, August 1st, the feeling of unease had not gone away. If anything, it was even stronger. He phoned Kitson again in the early afternoon, but again Kitson had nothing to report. He made a few other phone calls to the list of numbers that he had, brothers in outlying chapters of The Black Masters, and to them all his message was the same. 'I ain't happy. Somethin's comin' down. So arm up, mount up an' be alert, okay?'

If he'd been able to talk to every number on his list, or even if he'd been able to be more specific about his concerns, things might, even then, have turned out differently and directed John Light away from his forthcoming nemesis. As it was, he walked out into the afternoon sun letting his eyes roll over the lines of bikes that were parked in and around the farm yard and outbuildings. Here at Epiphany's – he thought of the place as being hers now that Old Nance had died – were the thirty or so riders of what he called his Praetorian Guard. There were maybe another two hundred Black Masters all over the county who owed their allegiance to him and it was for these brothers that he worried more.

Making a snap decision, he beckoned his two lieutenants over, giving the nod to Juliette also. The four of them congregated in Aunt Epiphany's small kitchen where his aunt, silent and almost fugue like, brought fresh beer from the freezer.

'Rugby, Leroy... I dunno what it is, but my psychic hackles are fuckin' well drivin' me mad, an' I ain't happy sittin' here round the farm waiting for somethin' to happen that I ain't got no control over. I bin talkin' to Kitson on the phone an' he says there ain't nuthin' to worry about, but I don't trust him no further than I can spit an' if somethin' is gonna happen, too many folk know we're here, or leastwise, know where to find us...' He paused, thinking even as he spoke. 'So, I want to move us out a ways. Not far. Just over to the lake, but you spread the word an' spread it good, everyone's got to stay on the cabin side, okay? No wanderin' off!'

'An' Leroy, I want you to take Max an' Micky and Sammyjo and Knutter. Take one of the mobile phones and hang around Demsville. Anything even squeaks down there, you get on the wire...'

He turned and looked at his aunt. 'I'm gonna take one of the mobiles as well, an' if anyone calls me you let me know straight away an' I'll get back to 'em from the cabin.'

Epiphany looked at him and nodded. 'I got it – but I don't like it. You all goin' down to the lake, have a little swim, have a little smoke, maybe eat a little fish, do some screwin' in the long grass behind the rocks, fine! Just fine! But what happens if someone comes here lookin' fo you and you ain't here. Gonna take it out on me if I'm all on my own, ain't they!'

'No-one's gonna come here lookin' for us and no-one's gonna do you no harm,' Lightly answered with a rare case of blind sight.

'What do you want me to do?' Juliette asked quietly.

'Just stay with me babe,' Lightly grinned.

Later that afternoon they made love on the springy soft grass well beyond the rock behind the trees. In the distance above the sighing sounds of the wind and the chirruping cicadas he could hear the occasional laugh and the sound of a bike being revved up and once the sound of a bottle breaking. The sounds were reassuring. They meant that his boys were doing as they were told and staying on their side of the lake: he'd verbalised what was amount to a death threat on anybody who violated the boundaries that he'd outlined. His disquiet had been muted by their love making but now after the climax or orgasm, his thoughts again turned towards the doubts that teased uncomfortably in the back of his mind. Juliette, either picking up on his mood, or acquiring one of her own, was also quiet. She rubbed her hand along the length of his flaccid penis, squeezing the last juices from it and rubbing them into the hairs of his belly. Then she pushed herself up onto one elbow and looked at him quizzically.

'Where do you reckon you'll be five years from now?' she asked out of the blue.

'Probably right here, making love to you,' he responded, grinning slightly with his eyes closed.

'Is that a thought or a dream?' she asked.

He opened his eyes and looked at her. 'No reason why it shouldn't be both.'

'Uh huh,' she shook her head slowly. '*You* might be here, but not me,' she retorted.

A small thrill of fear skewered Lightly's guts. 'Why?' he asked. 'Where you gonna be?'

'I'm gonna be dead,' she said. 'Mama always said I was gonna die young. An' she was right, I guess. I feel it. In here.' She pointed to her solar plexus.

'Bullshit,' Lightly shot back. 'That's just Cajun crap. People like us, people like you, don't die. We live for ever!'

'That a promise?' she asked.

'We-ell,' he wheedled evasively, 'maybe not for ever, but sure as hell for a fuckin' long time! Five years from now...' He pondered... 'Yeah well okay, I'll be sellin' cars in Alexandria and you'll be pregnant. We'll have settled down like ordinary normal folk do!'

She laughed out loud. 'I don't believe that you believe that,' she said.

'Well, maybe not the bit about settlin' down an' selling cars, but the rest should be right enough!'

'You want that? For us?'

'Damn right I do!'

'Can you tell me something then?'

'Sure. What?'

'That you love me?'

'Sure I do!'

'But can you tell me that? Can you look in my eyes and actually say the words?'

Now he also propped himself up on his elbow and their eyes met only inches apart. He found that it was a lot more difficult to do than he thought it would be, but from somewhere he found the words, words that she wanted to hear but words that were also the deepest truth, and for the first – and last – time in his life, he said:

'I love you.'

At 11pm on the night of August 1st, six hundred and eighty two white bikers, most of them loaded with booze or drugs, all of them looking for blood and battle, crossed the borders into Avon County. Over many days previously they had filtered surreptitiously through the back roads of Southern Louisiana in ones and twos, sometimes threes and fours, hiding up well off the roads by day, riding carefully and diligently avoiding any kind of trouble by night. They came south from Shreveport, east from Lake Charles and some of the more further afield Texan border towns. Chapters from Arkansas had sidled down the eastern banks of The Mississippi joining with other white chapters from New Orleans, before cutting west and north west across the swamplands of the Mississippi delta. Carefully and methodically they had skirted the major towns of Lafayette and Alexandria and Baton Rouge. With a synchronisation of watches dictated by a well laid battle plan, the wraps came off all pretence of guile and deceit and six hundred and eighty two riders belonging to no fewer than thirteen different chapters of Hell's Angels, armed with axes, knives, a few hand guns and a preponderance of sawn off shotguns, invaded Avon County with the express purpose of destroying the all powerful Black Masters Chapters that had dominated the southern part of the state for so long... It was a serious intent, but many reasoned that if a little fun could be had along the way, well, that was all a part of it, wasn't it?

A few riders were aware of the import of what they were doing. In the eyes of government and state, this was pure anarchy and they knew that there was a very good chance that they would be doing battle with the national guard before morning. That was accepted, albeit with worry, and even the most conservative Angel had been fired and inspired by the concept of the scale of the forthcoming battle. Thirteen Chapters! Over six hundred riders!

For the Black Masters it was a night of rout and chaos. Despite Lightly's warning, the out of county incursion took many by surprise and the sheer weight of numbers arraigned against them brought confusion and mandatory flight. But Avon was a small county and flight was restricted to the limited infrastructure of narrow black tops and dusty back roads, and retreat from one troubled cross roads led The Masters into ambush as another.

Throughout the midnight hours the still of the Louisiana countryside was

shattered by roaring motor cycle engines, banshee howls that cut through the slumbering hamlets and townships: in Pexton half a dozen Black Masters were beaten to death at the railway crossing by the timber yard and in Scaife and Moony molotov cocktails were hurled through the doors of black bars burning another twenty. In the small shanty town of Normandy, The Masters fought back against odds of four to one and were eventually slaughtered at the roadside, while in the larger village of Hampton a pitch battle raged in the streets for more than half an hour before Lightly's brothers finally fled for their lives into the trees.
In Studeville two discotheques with bikes lined up outside them were put to the torch and a police patrol car overturned – the officers rousted out of the wreckage and clubbed unconscious with gun buts and axe handles. In the small town of Childerston, population just over four thousand, over a hundred bikers met in the main square and in the riotous battle that followed shop fronts and windows were indiscriminately smashed and splattered with blood from both black and white combatants alike.

The Childerston Sheriff's Office had three patrol cars. One had already been called out to an unspecified emergency half an hour earlier, another failed to start when the young deputy flooded the carburettor in his fear and excitement, and only the sheriff's vehicle managed to make it to the town centre, by which time it was all over bar the shouting. Three dozen wounded figures lay dazed or dead around what had once been an attractive tree lined boulevard, while another sixty riders surged towards the sheriff's car with whoops of glee and wild yells full of blood lust.

The Angels cut a swathe around the patrol car as they roared out of town and while bricks rained down on the roof and shotgun pellets scored the paint work, Sheriff Phil Hewitson and his deputy ducked beneath the dashboard, powerless to respond. And yet Sheriff Hewitson had a crucial role to play in the night's proceedings for he was the first to telephone the Avon County Police Department to warn them of the unprecedented wave of violence that was heading their way.

At first Henry Kitson did not believe what he was hearing, but when over the following half hour another four dozen telephone calls jammed his switchboards, he realised in something of a panic that he had to act. He made three impulsive decisions, of which two were the wrong ones.

The one *right* decision was to go through the somewhat complex procedure of calling in the Louisiana National Guard – although even then it would be another ninety minutes before the first guardsmen would be deploying on the roads and byways of Avon County, by which time the worst of the death and damage would have been done.

His second decision was to despatch, and incidentally, also to disperse his meagre reserves of patrol cars and manpower in arbitrary cross country sweeps in a futile attempt to detail and arrest any of the marauding incursors that came his way. It was a stupid move that was to cost a number of policemen their lives and cause thousands of dollars worth of damage to police vehicles. Also, it left the county seat, the town of Avon, virtually undefended.

His third decision was to be his most costly, for instead of sitting tight in his control room and directing matters from there, he chose to take a car out himself and direct his troops from the front line.

That was what he told himself and the deputy he dragged along with him, anyway. In fact there wasn't any such thing as a "front line", just a constantly moving wave of bloody skirmishes that cascaded across the county creating havoc in a dozen places with quaint, almost English sounding names.

Piercebridge, death toll fifteen. Ironside, fourteen dead, fifteen wounded. Newmarket, twenty two dead, twice as many wounded, a gas station and half a block of wooden shops on fire. Crosbytown and Marthawood, only three and four dead respectively, but two of these victims were Highway Patrol offices who'd been vectored into the area from their usual beat along Route Ninety... The list was a long one, and growing.

The other reason for Henry Kitson taking to the roads was the considered safety of his own neck! He was into The Black Masters and their leader in no small way. Twice he had been asked if anything was coming down and twice he had answered, honestly from his point of view, that there was not. If Lightly and his people survived this night, they would be looking for him with a vengeance. Better, he thought, to be miles away from where they would expect to find him... Somewhere close to the county line with a clearly defined escape route if he needed it. If The Masters got creamed – and from what he was hearing, they were getting creamed all the way up to their black asses, then he had nothing to worry about (providing Lightly got creamed with them!). And if they didn't, well, he'd make his way back in the morning with reinforcements from Carter County and with maybe a couple of platoons from the National Guard and finish the job himself!

His eyes gleamed with rare excitement. He was going to miss the bucks and the pussy, but if he played this one right he might find himself in a no lose situation. Out of deal with The Masters, and therefore out of threat, and out of Avon County on the cresting wings of promotion and commendation that he'd long given up any hope of getting. Until now. If he handled it right.

Lightly received his first warning call at eleven fifteen from the small town of Pexton. Five more calls came in as many minutes after that from border towns and crossings all around the county, which, taking an intuitive leap, gave him a vague idea of what was happening, if not the true scale of it.

Remaining quietly calm, although his heart pounded with excitement, not least because his premonitions had been proved to be correct – and he also registered in one cold mote of his mind that there had been no warning call from Henry Kitson – he gave his orders with a clarity that brooked no argument.

'Rugby, take Juliette and five of the boys – Nicko, Tango, Harris, Jimbo and Macey. Get over to the farm and dig in. Make sure Aunt Epiphany is okay and shoot anyone that comes near if they ain't black. Danno, you take your family down to Demsville and reinforce Leroy and Sammyjo. The rest o' you guys mount up an' follow me. We'll take the back tracks across to Coltonville and join up with the brothers over there.'

'What's comin' down man?' came a querulous voice from the back ranks.

'We're gettin' hit, that's what,' Lightly told everyone present. There was no point sending a brother in combat blind. 'Scores of white boys comin' at us from all sides of the county at the same time. Someone's bin plannin' this one for weeks. Word's out that after tonight The Black Masters ain't gonna exist no more...' He kicked his motorcycle into life, standing high on the pedals, grinning and shouting at his shoulders. '... So let's go kick white ass an' rewrite the script!'

Twenty three motor cycles, some of them carrying pillion riders, roared into life and burned away from the lakeside sending up clouds of dry summer dust that drifted across the still waters of the lake towards two sentinel trees. If anyone had looked in that direction they'd have seen dim eddies of curious mauve and green light that seemed to drift enigmatically around the lower branches.

'What happened then?' Tamara asked.

Light shot her a sad laconic grin and tossed another substantial branch onto the fire causing a shower of sparks to fly upwards into the purple sky that still clung tenaciously to the last traces of the day before the rapidly encroaching night finally claimed it as her own.

'It was a total fuck-up,' he said simply. 'If you count The Black Masters, there were more than eight hundred fighters riding around the county, killing and wounding, burning, raping and sometimes running at virtually every little village and cross-roads and yet we rode around for nearly four hours, clocking up more than two hundred and fifty miles, and we didn't get involved in one single fight. Either got there half an hour too early or ten minutes too late. We chased some guys along route ninety, but by three o'clock a lot of out of county police had filtered in and the National Guard had helicopters up in the air with search lights and long rifles... You know, marksmen, snipers with night scopes. Whatever orders they'd been given I'll never know but their bottom line was if it was a bike, shoot it off the road.

'What with the cops and the National Guard and all those white guys riding in from out of county, we really did get creamed. More than a hundred bikes busted or burned, ninety dead, another fifty so fucked up that they were in hospital for weeks afterwards... Sure, we took a load of white trash down with us and I guess their casualties were about as bad as ours, but there were three times as many of them then there were of us and they'd got the high ground of surprise...'

By three thirty most of the white chapters were streaming out of Avon County, some fighting rear guard actions with the police or National Guard, some just speeding for their lives, rictus grins of victory etched across their tired faces, even though blood covered many a hand grip and dripped from splattered petrol tanks and black plastic seats to mix and sizzle with hot oil and engine grease.

It was only now that the enormity of the night's events began to dawn on the protagonists and state authorities and now, in counterpoint to the high staccato howl of bike engines, there was the ever present wail of police and ambulance sirens, the clanging of fire bells and the steady whirring thump of helicopter rotor blades. On the great stage of world affairs, a world obsessed with the price of oil, the events of the night of August 1st rated many front pages in local Louisiana papers but scored less than five paragraphs in the national daily giants who were more concerned with the comings and goings of a certain Sheikh Omani in the Persian Gulf. The story of Avon County's Angel Wars was a nine day wonder, overshadowed by edicts out of OPEC... Unless one happened to be a resident of Avon County. To those who lived there, the events of that night were to be remembered for many years to come.

By three fifteen, a dusty and dishevelled Praetorian Guard was heading back towards Demsville from the river crossing where they'd wheeled their bikes off the road for a council of war. They were tired and thirsty and fuming with frustration.

'We ain't achievin' nuthin',' Lightly yelled above the revving engines. 'Let's get back closer to base and link up with Danno and Leroy!'

But in Demsville Danno and Leroy and the other Black Masters were not in visible attendance. They were found, eventually, on the stretch of wasteland between the gas station and the motel, amid a wrecked tangle of mangled motor bikes. Bones were broken, skin ruptured and torn, flesh burned by exploding fuel tanks. None was less than seriously hurt, many were dead, among them Leroy and Danny.

Lightly looked at the burning fires. They were almost burned out now, having consumed all that was combustible. Whoever had caused this carnage had caused it some time ago while he, great black not so fucking clever general, had been chasing phantoms on every back track and black tom between Demsville and the Texas border.

A hollowness stole through his bowels and icy tendrils clutched at his heart. Very suddenly he felt the most urgent need to be back at the farm. It was a good half hour from Demsville and Rugby and the others were good soldiers... But dozens of good soldiers had fallen that night and nowhere in Avon County was sacred.

Even before they got to the farm he knew it had been hit. Even before they'd seen the dull glow in the sky, his psychic sentience told him to be prepared for the worst.

'There were about a dozen white guys,' he told her quietly. 'They must have been there for quite a while because the barn and the outhouses were burned almost to the ground. Five of the brothers were dead and Rugby, the guy you talked to this afternoon, was three quarters that way gone. They'd raped the women, of course, and they were dead too... Death by fucking and beating and mutilation...' Light spoke with deep bitterness, a testimony to the pain he'd carried with him over the years.

'They were stoned and they weren't expecting us, so we took them easily enough. My guys went wild. They were like tigers and six of the whites were dead before the others gave up and it was all over... And we had ourselves six prisoners...'

'What do you wanna do with these boys?' one of The Masters asked, newly appointed to the role of lieutenant now that Leroy and Rugby were out of it.

Lightly had just come out of the house, eyes stinging with tears that could not fall, belly heaving with vomit that would not rise. His heartbeat was erratic, the soul of his love, that hallowed place within his being, shattered and defiled and scarred for ever.

Epiphany had been strapped to the kitchen table, her body violated and cut. And she'd been old and ugly. What they'd done to Juliette in the bedroom was so much worse. So very much worse. They hadn't just raped and beaten her, or cut her up a little, they'd carved her. *Carved* her, for fuck's sake.

'What do you want us to do, man?' the lieutenant, a thin kid called Tobias whined again, and the ears of other Black Masters hung on Lightly's reply.

'Take 'em round to the back of the house,' he said in a tight voice. 'Strip 'em and stake 'em to the ground. Get 'em cleaned up. Someone make 'em some coffee.'

'Make 'em coffee?' a voice echoed from the back of the ranks. 'After what they done? You fuckin' crazy man?'

'No I ain't crazy,' Lightly spoke, fighting to keep his voice under control. 'I just want these motherfuckers alive and sober when I kill 'em.'

While six terrified white bikers were taken to the plot of waste ground behind the farm, Lightly went back inside the house. He took Epiphany from the kitchen and laid her on the bed with Juliette. He wanted to clean their wounds and make them look decent, returning to them some of the dignity that had been so brutally torn from them, but where to start? The two carcasses were just that... caricatures of the people they'd once been, mutilated and dehumanised by the barbarism of the torture that had preceded their deaths.

In the distance of his distracted mind he heard the sound of fresh engines approaching the farm. Maybe five or ten bikes and also a car. If they were friends they could wait and if they were enemies there were enough Praetorians outside to deal with the situation.

He doused the room with petrol, stacking a couple of gallon cans next to the bed. There would be no burial – how did you bury *bits* of people? – but there would be a funeral pyre and by the light of that fire he would take a terrible revenge. He was no stranger to death and had already taken human life on more than one occasion, although always in the heat of battle when it had been a case of kill or be killed. What had to happen now was going to be different. He would not be killing in cold blood, for his blood was boiling with silent screams of rage that demanded release, but this next piece of killing would be dispassionate and full of old testament ritual. The eye for the eye, the cutting of that which offended, the punishment premeditated to fit the crime.

He drenched the rest of the house with gas and paraffin, then walked out onto the back porch, his nostrils flared against the powerful stink of blood and burning. The first grey tinge of dawn was lightening the sky to the east and although he was not to be rushed he knew that his time in this place was finite.

The babble of shouting voices died to a whisper and then to silence as all eyes turned upon their leader. Tobias hurried up to him, nervous and on edge, but as much in control as anyone could be at a time like this.

'We got the white boys staked out like you said,' he reported. 'They ain't entirely sober but they're clued up enough to know they're fucked and they's shittin' themselves... An' somethin' else man. Richie's just rode in from Opelousas with some of his boys. Seems they got themselves a coupla prisoners. Richie figured you might want to talk to 'em so he's brought 'em here...'

Lightly scanned the gathering. Ahead of him, some forty yards away, he saw the six naked figures stretched and pegged to the ground and over to his right between the house and the barn there was a grey sedan surrounded by bikers. In the middle of the huddle he noted two white men in soiled and crumpled uniforms. Henry Kitson – who'd pissed himself twice since being grabbed on his run to the Texas border – and a young deputy who looked as though he ought still to be in school. Lightly beckoned them over and Richie and three of his boys dragged the two struggling policemen over to the foot of the veranda.

Lightly turned to Tobias. 'I want a sharp axe,' he said, 'and a gallon of gas.'

As his lieutenant nodded and dashed off in search, Lightly nodded his appreciation to Richie. 'Thanks man. Owe you one for this. Where'd you pick up this scum?'

'Racing out of Plum Valley like the devil himself was on their tail. Ran slap into us and we're just taken a mauling ourselves from some fuckin' Texas boys and we was in no mood to argue. Din' recognise the dude at first and probably wouldn't done till he told us who he was an' because he was fuckin' important and your friend, we had to let him go. Didn't sound right to us man, so we brung him to you...'

'Listen!' Kitson yelled at the top of his voice, 'it wasn't my fault. I didn't know anything. I swear, none of us knew anything. I tried to phone you man, I really did, as soon as it all started happening, but no-one answered the phones, man. Nobody answered the phones...'

'Shut the fuck up!' Lightly snapped at him contemptuously and the police captain fell to whimpering silence.

Lightly looked at the young deputy. 'How old are you, boy?' he asked.

'I'll be twenty two next month... Sir.'

The deputy was obviously a very scared young man, but Lightly gave him his due. He was holding his shit together better than his boss.

'You got a name?'

'Marvin. Marvin Walker, sir.'

'Well you just hang on in there Marvin Walker and maybe you'll live to see twenty three. Henry...' he turned his attention back to the police Captain. 'Henry, I'm gonna leave you till later. Right now I've got some executions to attend to.' His eyes went back to the deputy. 'Marvin, you're gonna have to watch this too and when you're making out your report about this incident, be very mindful that those guys staked out down there are the same guys that killed my friends, that raped and killed my women and after they'd done that they cut off their tits and stuffed 'em in their mouths and they cut off the pricks of the black boys they'd killed and shoved them up their pussies with a load of other stuff you don't even want to know about... You gonna remember that for me, Marvin?'

The deputy looked as though he was going to vomit... And did vomit... and after he'd puked all over his shoes looked up to see the coals of Lightly's eyes still boring into him.

'You gonna remember it, Marvin?' Lightly asked again with such malice and menace that even two of the boys from Opelousas found themselves suppressing shudders and for once thanking the God that made them that He'd made them black.

'Yes sir... I'm gonna remember it.'

'Good.' And then turning to the waiting brothers, raised his voice. 'Okay you guys. Stand clear of the house. Move your bikes. She's goin' up.'

Masters rushed to move their machines then stood back in expectation as their leader turned his back on them and with slow deliberation tossed a burning box of matches through the back door. The building went up with a whoosh and whumpf of flame and Lightly stood there for several minutes watching it before turning and striding out towards the staked prisoners.

John Light looked into the flames of the fire, remembering and reliving every nuance of that night as he'd done a thousand times since and would do a thousand times yet to come. 'I'm not sure you want to know the rest of it, Tam?'

'John, I want to know it all. You got to tell me. You need to tell me... What did you do to them. The white boys?'

'I chopped off their pricks and their balls and, while they were still screaming and bleeding to death, I poured petrol over their bellies... poured it into the holes where their pricks had been and I set it alight, and I watched them burn. They didn't take too long to die, but for them it must've been a very long death. Ten minutes, I guess. No more than that. And they all knew why they were dying.'

A lot of brothers witnessed the six executions. The tale would be retold many times over many years and with an inordinate amount of detail, some of it embellished, although most of it not. Nobody left Epiphany's farm without being deeply affected by what they'd seen. Some told stories of how Lightly had stood there, stripped to the waist and covered with blood, bellowing like a wounded bull in the smoke and breaking dawnlight, axe in one hand firebrand in the other... Others remembers his words, or at least *said* they remembered them, an insult of curses against God... Words that were later to add to an already awful reputation. All agreed that in that space of time, the man was not sane. Some even were to say that he was not human. Deputy Marvin Walker tried many times to write the report that was required of him, but never actually did so. After some time in a mental institution he was to quit the police force and, as such, no official record of the events at Epiphany's farm was ever put on file

It had always been known among The Black Masters that their leader had the power of juju but it was on this early morning that they were to be given a demonstration of his true power of magic... or at least, what they perceived as being his power.

Lightly turned from the line of dead flesh, dropping both the axe and the firebrand. Richie and Tobias were closest to him, close enough for him to see the fear and respect in their eyes. Beyond these two lieutenants was the wider ring of watching riders, and among them an ashen Police Captain Kitson and his fainting deputy. Lightly's eyes came to rest upon them and, even from twenty feet away, he heard Henry Kitson's moan.

'What you gonna to do the cops?' Richie asked.

'The deputy lives,' Lightly replied. 'I want the word to go round the white circles 'bout what's happened here. As for his boss... There's been enough killing here to last a fuckin' lifetime an' if that white ass over there had been a bit more on the ball in delivering his half of a bargain, maybe a lot of tonight's mess could've bin avoided. But I can't just let him be. Guy's gotta be punished...' He looked over to the brothers and raised his voice. 'Everyone outa here,' he shouted. 'But listen good. We're going over to the lake... The far side of the lake, but I don't want anyone moving more than a yard or two from the water's edge. We'll deal with our fuckin' friend from the Avon Police Department there, you got it?'

Twenty minutes later, Lightly walked out in front of his people, all who watched silently in expectation, their backs to the lake, their eyes upon the space in front of them. Henry Kitson was dragged out and flung at Lightly's feet.

'Stand up, man,' Lightly commanded.

The police captain obeyed, but it was not straight forward. He was quivering in fear, words of apology mingling with trembling pleas for mercy and in the end Lightly had to help him by dragging him to his feet and shouting.

'I ain't gonna kill you, man!'

Taking some reassurance from his persecutor's words, Henry Kitson managed to acquire some sense of presence and came nervously close to some degree of self control.

'No, I ain't gonna kill you...' Lightly raised his voice so that even the furthest away member of his pack heard every word. '... But a lot o' my people are dead because you didn't do what you'd bin paid in advance to do. You disgust me and you offend me and, man, I curse you to hell for it. What you're gonna to is simply disappear from my sight and from the sight of my brothers here, and wherever you go, you just remember a lot of folk died these last few hours because o'you. An' just you remember, all o'you, an' especially you Deputy Marvin Walker, that while I could've executed this white shitbag same as them others, I've shown him clemency an' mercy!' He turned and glared at Kitson, no-one, not even Kitson himself, aware of the dark gleam at the back of Lightly's eyes. 'Now Captain, I want you to walk away from here... Go on, out between them two trees and what happens to you after that ain't nuthin to do with me. I want you to disappear man. Just disappear...'

Hardly believing that he'd been spared, Kitson looked first of all at his captor, then at the trees and the open space beyond... Maybe they were going to shoot him in the back once he'd made a break for it, but then again, maybe they wouldn't. At least the way that had been offered presented him with a chance, a *good* chance of survival. Kitson nodded and bolted in a rambling gait.

Between the trees.

And vanished.

There was no scream, no cry; one second he was there in full view of forty pairs of eyes and the next second he was gone. The only sound that ruffled the waters of the lake was an indrawn gasp of breath and a few "where the fuck's..." or "Holy shits..."

Lightly turned again to his brethren.

'I never laid a finger on him. I told him to disappear... an' the guy has disappeared. He ain't coming back. The same thing happens to anyone who crosses me in future. The same thing happens to anyone who comes sniffin' around this lake o'mine without my permission or without me bein' here. Don't any o'you guys forget it!'

Light took Tamara in from the lakeside and they made themselves as comfortable as they could be on the hard boards of the cabin floor. He lit a candle and, with the single flame casting shadows against the bare walls, took the girl in the crook of his arm and they lay there in silence. He wasn't sure how she would react... Wouldn't have been surprised if she'd pulled away from him in revulsion... But there was no reticence or reserve on her part and she snuggled up close to him, her body language saying more than mere words.

Sleep was elusive for them both and Tamara's curiosity was still far from assuaged. He found himself telling her the other part of his story... Of his days in the delta as some kind of voodoo prince, not a title that he had chosen for himself but one that was bequeathed upon him just the same... Of his constant travels between New Orleans and Memphis, Memphis to Dallas, Dallas across into Florida, two weeks in one city, three months in another, but wherever he went, never that far from Demsville Louisiana.

The Black Masters fell to the wayside and became a thing of the past and in their place came two other congregations, one of supplicants and petitioners eager to share or use the juju magic that seemed to be so powerful within him, the others more cynically, and with Lightly's tacit understanding and co-operation, in search of a middle man for a thousand and one deals that required a middle man.

Tamara pushed gently on the matter of magic. She'd always known that this was an essential part of his background and, indeed, when she had first come into his world it had been the world of secret ceremonies and bizarre midnight meetings in dark and dangerous places. The reverency and the evangelism had come much later and, despite her close proximity to the man over the years, she'd never really known what Light had truly felt about these subjects. Her own observations suggested that much of the time he was simply playing the part rather than being the real thing deep down inside... Although give him his due, he played the parts well, fooling all of the people all of the time. The thought that he had never fooled himself was in interesting one, not easily dismissed, especially in the light of this evening's revelations.

He laughed quietly when she told him what she was thinking.

'Oh yes, babe, the magic's there all right and it sure as hell works. But listen Tam, there's all kinds of different magic depending on the understanding of the mind that looks at it. I flick my lighter in front of some bozo who rubs two sticks together to make fire and he's going to call that magic even though you and I know it's just modern technology.

'Say you've got a sore throat and there isn't a doctor around for a hundred miles and say I give you some belladonna tea. Your throat is soothed and you feel okay again. If you didn't know better you might say that was magic when really it's just basic herbal medicine. Say I've got a guy who comes to me because no matter what he does, he just can't get it up. I give him some lycopodium and next time he gets into bed with a woman he's got a prick as hard as the rocky mountains... he might think it's magic, but again it's just another ticket on the herbal remedies train.

'Now, let's expand this a bit. Say someone comes to me because they're deaf and I make them hear, or someone's got back pains that the doctors can't do anything to improve and I take the pain away and in effect, give the guy a new back... This still isn't magic. It's *healing* and although some folks are going to call it magic, they're calling it wrong. It might be *magical*, but that's something else, entirely down to your own perceptions of what's going on. Healing is just a channelling and focusing of energies; not everyone can do it but you don't have to be a magician to dip into that healing power.

'But there are other kinds of magic. I can go into a room full of a hundred people who all think they're right and I'm wrong and I'll talk to them for an hour and have 'em believing that my way is not only the right way, it's the *only* way and it's what they really believed all along. But Tam, there's nothing mystical about that. It's crowd control, will power and personal magnetism.'

'Okay,' Tamara said. 'But what about that time when Vern and Paris broke up and you made that charm to bring them back together again?'

'Aw hell, that's simple,' Light chuckled in the darkness. 'They *wanted* to get back together again and were both looking for ways to get around their pride. That old juju charm, well, it was just a catalyst.'

'All right, but what about the guy from North Dakota who wanted you to put a curse on his two business partners because they were blackmailing him and cheating him blind? You did some stuff for him and within a week both the other two guys were dead, one from a coronary and the other in a car smash. Is that just coincidence or what?'

'Ah, no, Tam. I was coming round to that kind of thing. That's *real* magic and it never ceases to amaze me the way people always want to write off that kind of thing as coincidence or some kind of heaven sent miracle, while at the same time regarding what is no more than natural law as something magical and mysterious. The whole thing about real magic is that it goes against all the rules of natural law. Wouldn't be magic if it didn't... But I've got to say what we're talking about here is our very limited perceptions of what natural law really is.'

'So how do you do that?' she mused.

'What? Knock two guys off without getting my black hands dirty? Yeah, well Tamara, this is where it starts getting complicated...'

He fell silent, thinking how to verbalise something that was essentially so pure and simple, but so impossibly difficult to put into words. He cupped his hands, heel to heel, fingers lightly touching.

'We've got this world of ours, a planet full of people, all of them with minds, each mind full of a million different thoughts, a million different dreams and desires. Now all of those minds create an energy. We can't see that energy, just like we can't see the wind, but we do feel it and we do see its effects... Some minds are stronger than others, or maybe a different way of saying it is that some people have got a lot more willpower than others. Either they're born with it or they come to realise that the power is there and they work to get it... And this process of working to get it is as much as part of magic as is the using of the power once you've got it.

'So, say you've got this mindpower running through you, this extra energy. Next question is, how do you use it? Well babe, it's simply a question of tuning your mind into the buzz of all that other mental energy that's floating around looking for someplace to go and using your willpower to shape and bend things the way you want them to be. I make it sound easy and it's not. You got to work like hell to build up your own mental energies and you've got to work even harder to *focus* those energies, which is what all the rituals and ceremonies are in aid of.

'Because you're focusing, channelling your energies into a very tight band of power, you can't influence big broad things like governments or wars or starvation and poverty, you can only influence very narrow specifics like a single person's thoughts or their actions or their feelings.'

Tamara saw the obvious flaw in this argument. 'Okay, but what's to stop you working on the president of the United States and getting him to bring in a chunk of your favourite legislation?'

Light guffawed. 'Don't think it hasn't been tried! Trouble is to make that work you've also got to work on Congress and the senate and the various committees and it would take far too much time and far too much energy.'

'Well, what if a whole group of people like you got together and tried it that way?'

'Good theory. Probably would work. The problem is that there just aren't enough people like me around in the world to do it...' It wasn't a boastful statement, but in case she thought it was, he added: 'Maybe twenty, twenty five and most of them not in The States. A lot in Europe, maybe a few in Russia and quite a few more in India and China. The problem is we don't know who we are. We sense each other in our dreams, but that's about it.'

It was Tamara's turn to fall silent for a while. After a time she asked: 'Okay, but what about God? Where does He figure in all of this?'

'God?' Light echoed. 'Tammy, I don't think God figures anywhere in anything, leastwise not as some cranky old guy with a white beard sitting on a celestial throne surrounded by chittering little things with bow lips and Botticelli bottoms. I don't believe in God and, despite all the shit that was written about me a few years ago, I don't believe in the Devil either. What I *do* believe is that there are two opposing energies, call 'em whatever you like, good and evil, black and white, although I'm happier thinking of them as negative and positive. I've played with these energies almost all of my life and as such I reckon I know more about them than most.

'Initially the negative energy is more attractive. There's more of it about and it's easier to tap into. The positive is much harder to get hold of and harder to hold once you've got it. It's more volatile and more unpredictable and it takes a damn sight more out of you than the other does. Its rewards are fewer and more modest, but it does have one crucial thing in its favour... It keeps you separate from the negative and gives you a measure of protection against it.

'During the late seventies and early eighties, I was as black and negative as any human being you're likely to meet on this planet and I did some pretty terrible things. I was the nearest thing to God that I'd ever discovered and I revelled in it. So what if I killed a couple of bad guys up in North Dakota? Thousands of good guys had been killed in 'Nam, so what price two more casualties who were worth a fuck sight less than some of our soldiers north of Saigon? And if I'm going to be honest with you Tamara, those two fellows up in North Dakota were only the tip of the iceberg!

'Then, a few years ago, something happened and I got scared. Really scared... And in the space of a couple of weeks I gave up the juju and started talking about God and about being good...'

'But you said you didn't believe in God!' Tamara protested.

'I don't,' Light replied. 'But I do believe in good and if you want to make other people move from a negative vibration to a positive vibration, you've got to give them a symbol, something with a handle they can grab hold of and identify with. The God ID is as good as any and better than most.'

'But why?' Tamara was still puzzled. 'Why the sudden switch?'

'I told you,' he replied. 'I got scared. I got to see the full power of what controlled negative energy can do and I swear to the God that I don't particularly believe in that it frightened the living shits out of me. That's why John Light's evangelical message gets across and works so well. It's sincere and from the heart. People have got to change how they feel and what they do. They've got to embrace the good and the positive to counter balance the negative. They've got to see the light, because if they don't, all that's dark and dirty, all that's destructive and negative, will reach across the scales of balance and destroy them all. Destroy *us* all...'

He propped himself up on one elbow and in the candle light she could see the sheen of sweat that covered his skin. The agitation in his voice was clearly written across his face and, unless the candle light lied, there was a fever of fear in his eyes.

'Where do you think that jackrabbit went?' he asked her. 'And where did our sticks and stones go? The ones that disappeared on us this afternoon? What do you think happened to poor old Henry Kitson after he dissolved into nothing that morning twenty years ago? I told you earlier that there are two prime energies and those energies are not restricted to the human mind. They hold the world together. The positive energy is here with us, with humanity and all that's good in the world of man, but there's another energy abroad in our world, just as tangible, just as real, even if we can't see it. It's a world that starts on the other side of those trees, Tammy, pulsing and throbbing and gaining strength every season, every year, soaking up like a sponge all the negative energies that we create and God knows we create enough of them, don't we, just waiting for the day that the weight of energy tips finally into its favour and then it'll spill over and spoil us all!'

Tamara saw that he believed what he was saying, although she herself couldn't fully understand it and found it hard to accept the little she did understand. In an attempt to soothe and placate she reached up and eased his head down onto her breast.

'Hey John, it's one helluva theory, but come on man, how can you be so sure that you're right about all this?'

He pulled away from her and stared at her ferociously. 'How do I know that I'm right? Okay, I'll tell you Tamara. It's because I've been through the trees. *I've been through the fucking trees and I've seen what's on the other side!* And believe me lady, it's not very nice. *It's not very nice at all.*

14.

The Elijah File

It was raining in Ashquelon. Herschal sat on the back veranda of the small hotel and stared across the green and saturated garden towards the row of cyprus trees and beyond the trees the flat grey puddle of the sea. The air was pungent with different smells, among them the tang of wet sand and the dank of rotting vegetation. Somewhere, interwoven within this symphony of olfactory depression, was the whiff of cooking beetroot and sizzling salt beef sausages. Herschal was depressed, made more so by his inability to see a way out of the mess that he'd got himself into.

They'd picked him up in Beer Sheba, polite, cool, official and distant and had driven him to Ashquelon. The hotel stood to the side of the town, a polyglot collection of characterless houses with insignificant gardens and a featureless "let's copy the Americans" shopping mall and it had been his prison ever since. Oh, he was free to wander through the gardens and along the beach if he wanted to, but not without three toy soldiers in distant attendance, bulges under their arm pits, walkie talkies never far from their mouths. If he wanted to go into the town centre he was met with implacable smiles. *Just tell Frank or Bruno or Lou what you want and we'll have it for you within the hour...*

He said he'd wanted to walk into the town for the exercise... *Better stick to the gardens or the beach, Mr Herschal. General Lemski's orders...*

Gideon Lemski! Herschal felt like spitting. The hotel was no more a hotel than he was a sabra. It was a Mossad safe house in which he did not feel safe, only restricted and frustrated. He wanted to blame somebody and Lemski was the obvious candidate, although he was well aware of the fact that much of this was his own fault.

He'd been checked into the hotel and shown to his room. He'd slept for a while then had bathed and climbed into the clean clothes that had been provided. They didn't fit, but at least they'd been clean. He'd eaten a sparse meal then had demanded to see the director of Israel's secret service.

'We are the director's deputies,' Max Shapiro's son had said politely. 'And...'

'And bullshit,' Herschal had snapped back. 'I'm going to talk to the Director General of Mossad himself, or I'm not going to talk to anyone at all.'

Not in the least put out by the old man's rudeness, Leon Shapiro had nodded politely. 'Can you give us any indication as to what this matter is about, sir?'

'Yes. It's about the security of the State of Israel.'

'I see. Well, I shall communicate your comments to Director Lemski and in the meantime, enjoy your stay.'

Gideon Lemski had arrived three days later. It might have been sooner had it not been for the fact that Herschal came down with a heavy cold that carried a high fever and that Lemski himself was suffering from an acute attack of gout in both feet. When he finally did limp into Herschal's room, it was with the aid of two stout walking sticks and he'd flopped down into a convenient arm chair with a gasp of relief. 'Gout,' he'd explained gruffly. 'Like walking on broken bottles.'

'Painful,' Herschal had agreed, his eyes drifting over to the bespectacled Leon Shapiro who was leaning languidly against the wall by the window and the chubby Irvin Rosenblum who had sat himself down on the edge of the bed. 'Perhaps it would be better if you and I spoke alone,' he'd said to Lemski. 'So,' he'd nodded towards Leon and Irvin, '... if you two young gentlemen will excuse us?'

'Just a minute,' Lemski had said, holding up a hand as Leon had uncurled from the wall and Irvin had half risen from the bed. 'These two special agents are my personal aides and they are also the case officers assigned to your debriefing. Anything you have to say to me, Mr Herschal, you can also say in front of them.'

Leon and Irvin had resumed their positions and Herschal had experienced a feeling of dismay. The fact that Lemski had called him Mr Herschal and not Megiddo One was a clear indication that he was not being taken seriously. All right – he tried to see if from their point of view – so he'd been out of active service for more a great many years, but against that, surely they'd referred to The Elijah File?

'You are aware of my record in the service of Mossad and in the service of the State of Israel long before Mossad ever came into existence?' He'd asked testily.

'Yes I am, and that's why I'm here,' Lemski had replied crisply. 'Your record is a remarkable one, but the world, our world, has changed much since you were last involved with our department and, with great respect, nobody even knew that you were still alive until your phone call of four days ago...'

Three pairs of eyes bore into the old man and his feeling of dismay had deepened. Oh yes, the world had changed all right! He'd got older and Mossad had got softer, more polite, more bureaucratic. The sharp edge of elitism, the preparedness to act with spontaneity on hunch and intuition that had made it the creme de la creme of intelligence agencies the world over, was noticeable in its absence in his three visitors.

He'd studied them individually. Lemski, the old soldier, an old soldier with political ambitions, who did things by the book. Herschal had been responsible, in part, for the writing of that book, but Lemski was obviously reading from the pages of a later edition.

Irvin Rosenblum, obese and crafty. A mummy's boy with a handful of college diplomas. He'd never seen combat and his hands had never come anywhere near an Uzi or a Davidka. His weapon of war was a fucking computer! Herschal didn't know anything about computers and he distrusted anything of which he had no knowledge. Thus he automatically distrusted, and in principle disliked the fat boy from Jerusalem.

And what about Leon Shapiro, son of his dear dead friend Max – Max, who all those years before when he'd been even younger than his son was now, had designated Herschal with the code name Megiddo One... Herschal had probed into Leon's persona and had found feeling and sensitivity, a mixture of hardness and softness that made him ill-suited to be a warrior in the service of Israel and in Herschal's mind, ill-suited for anything else. Shapiro had shifted uneasily, almost as though he could feel the old man plucking at his secrets, and oh yes, here was a young man who certainly had a few of those. *I wonder if Lemski knows?*

A deep sorrow descended over Herschal. He'd made a mistake. He should have stayed in the desert. These people, the soldier, the coward and the queer, they would not believe him if he told them what he'd come all this way to tell them. Worse, from their technological world of computers and common sense, they would either laugh at him or think he was senile or insane. If Max had been alive that would have been different. Max had understood, had *known* how it was done, but Max was not here and these three others were here in his place. Like it or not, they were all Herschal had.

He'd been tempted to apologise for wasting their time, to say he'd been mistaken and to ask them to take him back to Beer Sheba, but whatever else Herschal was, he was an Israeli and a Jew and very much in that order and he owed it to his country, the country he'd served for all his life, to give it some kind of warning.

He'd stalled for time by looking Leon Shapiro in the eye and asking him outright: 'Did you father ever talk to you about me? Not officially, but in a personal way?'

'I'm not sure I understand your question,' Leon had answered carefully. 'My father certainly spoke of you on a number of occasions. He regarded you as his friend and his number one agent, but he never told me anything about you or about any of the things you did together. We never *discussed* you, if that's what you're asking me.'

'Yes, that's what I'm asking you and more's the pity he didn't tell you a bit more, but thank you. You have answered my question. Now, let me ask you another. Have you read the Elijah File yet?'

Leon had looked uncomfortable and Lemski had come to his rescue. 'Mr Shapiro has not read the file, nor will he, and nor will anybody else until such time as I see fit to release that file and that certainly won't be until after I know what this is all about. Forgive me Mr Herschal, but my feet are hurting and I have pressing business in Jerusalem. Can we get to the point of why you have found it necessary to contact Mossad again after all these years and what is so important that my ears must be the first to hear it.'

All right, Herschal had thought. All right! I'll tell them enough to clear my conscience and then we can all go home!

'What's today's date?' he'd asked.

'Friday, April 29th,' Leon had answered quietly from the window.

'April 29th is it,' Herschal had said. 'Well, there's no immediate worry, but any time after June 21st you can expect a major attack to be launched against Israel. I would have thought it might be nearer the end of June or the beginning of July before you're really aware of what you're up against because it will be an insidious assault that will cause Israel to crumble from within, but by then it'll be all over anyway and you won't be able to do anything about it.'

'And may I ask who is to be responsible for launching this attack?' Lemski had asked sceptically.

'An old enemy,' Herschal had answered promptly. 'A very old enemy.'

'You mean the Arabs?' Irvin had asked nervously and incredulously.

Herschal, who'd promised himself that he was going to tell them as much of the truth as he could without leaving himself wide open to ridicule, pondered the question carefully before answering.

'Yes. In a way, but not in the way you might expect.'

'What nonsensical guessing game is this?' Lemski had snapped. 'It might interest you to know that while we do still have a few problems with our Arab neighbours and while our Palestinian problem is far from resolved, at no time has Israel been safer and more secure in its relationship with the Arab world. The Gaza Strip has autonomy now and we're working on deals for the West Bank, and we're actually talking sensibly to people like the PLO and the Syrians. We sat still while that madman in Iraq threw Scud missiles at us and if anyone else ever pulls a stunt like that again they know, as do the Americans, we will retaliate by going Nuclear. Believe me, it's an effective deterrent. I say again, Israel has never been safer, and here you are walking in from the desert like a prophet of doom, saying that all we've worked for is in jeopardy from an unspecified threat from an unspecified enemy.'

'Prophet of doom,' Herschal had mused theatrically before looking at the Mossad boss with a measured degree of scorn and contempt. 'Yes, well, you'd do well to ponder that title, wouldn't you? And ponder it a little more deeply when next you read The Elijah File. But I suggest you do it quickly because the chances are that there'll be nothing left to ponder by summer's end. Now, I've told you what I came to tell you. You don't believe me, all right, but I've told you, and what you do with the information is up to you. As for me, I've got nothing else to say, so I shall stay here for tonight and go back where I came from tomorrow and you can sort it all out for yourselves!'

He'd glared balefully at the trio, each in turn, before continuing with his diatribe. 'But when everything's crumbling down around your ears...' He'd looked at Gideon Lemski witheringly. '... When you can't feel the pain in your feet because your feet aren't there any more... When your computers are blowing up in your face...' He'd cast Irvin a disparaging glance before scowling at Leon. '...When you don't have to worry about Tel Aviv because Tel Aviv will just be a charnel house of rotting corpses... Just *don't* say that Megiddo One didn't give you all fair warning!'

Of course it had not been as easy as that. Later that evening his temperature had soared into the low hundreds again and the doctor who had been summoned diagnosed bronchitis giving strict orders that Herschal should remain in bed and finish the course of strong anti-biotics he'd provided. In any case, Lemski gave strict instructions that Herschal was not to be released until he gave his personal consent, and that was something he didn't intend to do in a hurry. Certainly, he'd lost his temper, which had been a stupid thing to do, but unlike his two deputies, he was very familiar with the contents of The Elijah File and, while he wanted to write them off as the ramblings of a senile old man – a *very* old man, The Elijah File dictated that at least some time be spent examining what meaning might dwell within Herschal's words. The question was how to go about it?

    The following morning, April 30th, Irvin Rosenblum was officially been detailed to other duties and Leon Shapiro was been called to an early meeting with Gideon Lemski; they met, not at Mossad HQ, but in a stylish restaurant close to the Knesset Building, much favoured by numerous politicians of all persuasions. Lemski poured coffee for them both and without preamble asked the younger man what he'd made of the previous day's meeting.

    'Seriously?' Leon asked and when the director nodded, 'Well, I think the man might have been a good agent in his time, I know my father thought very highly of him. But he'd obviously past it now. I suspect he's not well and he'd getting his past mixed up with his present. If he's been stuck in some water hole in the Negev for the last God knows how many years, maybe he's having hallucinations or visions or something.'

    'Visions?' Lemski asked sharply. 'Why do you say visions?'

    'No reason,' Leon retorted mildly. 'But old people do get a bit fuzzy, don't they?'

    'How old do you think he is?'

    'Difficult to tell with all that hair and suntan, and I've never been good at guessing ages anyway. But somewhere around sixty five? Seventy maybe?'

    'He's ninety eight,' Lemski said shortly, taking some small pleasure from Leon's surprised reaction. 'And as for being fuzzy, curious how he knew that Rosenblum works with computers and that you worry a lot about Tel Aviv... And before you start getting defensive and hot under the collar, I know all about your friend in Hayarkon Street and it doesn't give me a problem and it doesn't give Mossad a problem, and so it shouldn't give you a problem... But how did the old bastard know that you worry about Tel Aviv more than, say, Jerusalem? Or Haifa, or Nazareth or Jericho?'

    'I don't know.' Leon worked hard to keep his voice neutral. Lemski's knowledge concerning his friend in Hayarkon Street had come like a bolt out of the blue and had shaken him more than he'd care to admit. On the one hand he was enormously relieved to learn that Lemski *did* know and that there was to be no censure or criticism, but on the other hand he was alarmed. The question was *how* did Lemski know? Shapiro had been paranoid in his discretion. To cover his uncertainly he kept the conversation focused on Herschal. Ninety eight! That was totally incredible! There had to be some mistake, surely?

'What happens to him now?' he asked.

'Nothing. He stays where he is. Has lots of good food and takes lots of exercise and if he's going to be ill, then there are plenty of worse places that he could be sick in. I want a permanent but very low key guard mounted and I don't want him slipping back into the Negev until I'm ready to let him go.'

'You're not taking what he said yesterday seriously, are you?'

'It's difficult,' Lemski replied evasively. 'I know I didn't handle the interview very well and I'll agree that the old fool is probably unhinged, but I can't afford to dismiss him entirely out of hand. I've read The Elijah File, and you have not, which brings me directly to the point of this meeting...' He pushed over a slim black leather briefcase. 'You've got maximum security clearance as of midnight last night, so you read the file and see what you make of it. At least, when you've done that, you might understand the shape of the potential problem we might have here. Needless to say this matter is not to be discussed with anyone, and after you've read the file it comes straight back to me. It won't answer all your questions but it will tell you why our elderly friend is going to be staying in Ashquelon for a while. And another thing. He was your father's friend. They were as thick as thieves and I suspect that your father had good reason for making sure this dossier remained incomplete in certain key areas. Your job over these next few days, or however long it takes, is to get close to the old man and fill in the blanks for us. While you're doing that, and I want you to report directly to me every twelve hours whether you've got anything to report or not. I'll be having a look at a few other things. If we are faced with a threat some time after June 21st, I want to know exactly what it is and where it's coming from.'

Later that day, and indeed over the following two days, Leon Shapiro studied The Elijah File with an ever increasing sense of incredulity and disbelief. It was an amazing document, and certainly, as Lemski had told him, incomplete, but nonetheless intriguing for all of that.

He opened the briefcase in the privacy of his own small flat, drink in hand with some light classical music playing quietly in the background. Rather than the usual stapled and typed document that he'd been accustomed to seeing as the regular Mossad form of file presentation, here was a loose ring binder with a collection of letters, some of them typewritten though most of them, certainly in the early part of the file, scrawled by hand in heavy black ink on old and yellowing paper. The first was dated June 7th 1930 and was addressed to the Chairman of the Jewish Agency in Palestine.

> *"Sir - I write to inform you that within the next two years Adolf Hitler will become chancellor of Germany, at which time a programme*

of unprecedented violence will be directed against the Jewish community within this country. The Nazi party is not the short term reaction that so many choose to see it as being, but a most powerful force that is destined to become more entrenched and evil with every year of its long ascendancy. It is most strongly recommended that every Jew resident in Germany be alerted to the forthcoming threat and provision be made for their removal to a State that offers a greater degree of safety..."

There were another four letters in a similar vein dated at regular intervals over the following three years, the tone of each becoming more agitated than the one before. Leon's eyes had dwelled on such a missive dated November 11th 1933.

"Sir - As I have prophesied, The Nazis are now burning books and are beating women and children in the streets. The pogrom has begun but there is far worse to come. Within the next ten years there will be another world war far more costly and heinous than the one that went before. I have written to other people in other countries alerting them of the coming holocaust and they, like you, have not written back. Something must be done to save the Jews, not only in Germany but in the whole of Europe, and plans must be laid now. In another few years it will be too late..."

Leon scanned the words carefully, his eyes lingering on the word *prophesied* and again on the word *holocaust*. Holocaust was a very familiar word within the vocabulary and the consciousness of the Jewish mind, but it was usually used in the past tense... The holocaust of what had happened in Europe between 1939 and 1945. It was curious to see it used in the future tense. The coming holocaust... He read on, pausing to look at a typewritten note on a piece of faded Jewish Agency note paper.

For the attention of The Committee on European Jewry.
Haifa, Palestine 22nd October 1938.

Gentlemen – Over the last few years we have received a number of letters from someone who signs himself simply as Herschal describing the plight of Jewish communities in Nazi Germany. His letters have consistently predicted most accurately the evolution of events in Europe and in studying this correspondence I have become convinced that the writer of these letters is neither a crank nor a madman, but someone who has the ability to see a general event some significant time before it has happened. Eg. please see items 1 through 12, reference Hitler's chancellorship, the burning of The Reichstag, book burnings, torchlit parades, the re-arming of the nation and the consistent pogrom against our people. We have all been concerned about the situation in Austria and I direct your attention to "Herschal's" letter to us, received by this office on January 19th wherein he mentions this event along with a number of other items which I feel ought to be given some consideration. I have written to our correspondent (copy enclosed) and will inform this committee of any further developments as they occur – Yours, etc. M Shapiro.

Leon scrutinised the signature and had recognised it clearly as his father's hand. 1938! The association between Max Shapiro and Herschal went that far back! If Lemski was right, Herschal had been forty two years old and his father, what? Early twenties? He'd avidly read Herschal's letter of January 19th, noting that the sender's address was now different. Previously he had written from Berlin, now he wrote from Paris.

> "My friends, as you can see I have left Germany. We have suffered so much in that ill-starred place. Already half a million Jews have been killed by the Nazis and millions more, yes, millions! are yet destined to die in places the world has not yet heard of but will never forget once it does. How lucky you are to be safe in Palestine and how lucky I am to have friends in France. I shall be safe here for a while – maybe two years, but there will come a time when even France, a divided France, will feel the weight of the German jackboot!
>
> In the meantime I write to warn you that before the end of this year the Third Reich will have annexed Austria without a shot being fired and what has befallen the Jews of Germany will also befall the Austrian Jews. In Germany it is already too late. The borders and escape routes are already closed or are closing even as I write. If our people in Austria can get out they should do so now while there is still time. There are no more than a few months left before the Austrian borders will be closed to the fleeing Jew. Let them, while they can, escape to England or Switzerland. Only these two countries will be able to offer our people safe haven in the dark years ahead. Can you not help our people get to Israel?"

Leon read the short note, typed on an old and irregular typewriter, that his father had sent in return.

> Dear Mr Herschal,
> We write to thank you for your informative letters. Unfortunately our influence is insufficient to bring about the changes you advocate for European Jewry and is incapable of altering the tide of events now sweeping across the continent. We value your views and information and wonder if you might enlighten us as to your source?
> Yours sincerely, M. Shapiro, Jewish Agency in Palestine.

Herschal's letter of October 1938 was addressed directly to Maximillian Shapiro. Leon had hunted around for any correspondence in between and could find nothing. If there had not been any further correspondence, how had Herschal known his father's first name? Max's note of earlier in the year had been signed simply M Shapiro.

> "Dear Mr Shapiro - As I warned you, Austria is now a part of The Fatherland. The Anshluss is complete and our people are trapped. Oh why could you not have acted? Done something to warn them? Next year it will be worse! The Germans will invade Checkoslovakia and no-one will lift a finger to help the people there. Adolf Hitler will enter into a pact with Josef Stalin and later in the year will invade Poland. After much prevarication England and France will declare war on Germany and in 1940 Germany will invade France. France will be defeated and divided. England will not fall but it will be about four years before they are able to return and fight on European soil and, in those four years, the Jews of Europe will be destroyed. More than six million - yes Mr Shapiro, six million! will die in camps especially constructed for this sole purpose. Can you imagine anything so awful!"

Leon's blood was running. Either this was an elaborate hoax, in which case it was a hoax that his father as much as the other man was a perpetrator of, or Herschal had been having detailed visions... There, that word visions again... Involving European history months and years before it had actually taken place. How was this possible? How could this come about? Herschal was reporting things even before the policy that brought those things to fruition had been agreed and thrashed out in the cabinet rooms of Europe! Leon had started looking for the line that led to evidence of the hoax – but had failed to find it.

There had been letters between Max Shapiro and The Jewish Agency in Haifa and two further letters from Herschal to Max, dated July and October 1939 in which he described the mood in France at that time, going on to reiterate many of his earlier warnings and for the first time mentioning place names like Auswitz, Belsen, Birkenau and Dachau...

There were minutes of meetings held by The Jewish Agency and in one of them an instruction to Max to contact a Monsieur M, one of the very few Jews in the French Government of the day, directing him to effect a meeting between Monsieur M. and Herschal. Subsequently, there was a letter dated 20th December 1939 from the French politician who had met and talked with Herschal that very same day in a Paris cafe:

> "He is a slight man," The Frenchman wrote. "Not frail, but wiry. His hair recedes and he wears glasses. The atmosphere in his presence is one of tension and suppressed excitement. He fidgets and finds it hard to sit still. He is intellectual and speaks several languages

fluently – German, French, English, Hebrew and Aramaic. He switches languages easily and if, as his name implies, he is a natural born German, his accents and speech patterns disguise this fact. He is clearly a Jew.

He refused point blank to reveal the source or sources of his information but did so openly without guile or craft. He is convinced that France will fall next year, that The Maginot Line will not hold. He says the Boche will simply go round our defences through Luxembourg and the Benelux countries and that our defence is to be a most feeble affair. France is to be divided, half occupied by the Germans, half run as a puppet state beneath the leadership of a man called Petain – which is a name well known to most French ears. France will eventually be liberated in 1944 or 1945 – he was not sure which year precisely, by an invading army of British and American troops aided by soldiers from all over the world. Free Frenchmen, he says, will fight beneath the banner of one they call "The Gaul" and this "Gaul" is to be the leader of France for many years after what he calls The Holocaust of Europe.

While I find all of the above impossible to believe, the point is that Monsieur Herschal believes it implicitly. It would be most tempting to dismiss him as deranged and yet his manner and demeanour suggest this is not the case. He is polite, sincere and serious – and it is to be hoped seriously wrong in his assessment of France's future. As for millions of Jews being systematically killed by the Nazis, this, of course, is preposterous. I have no doubt that there will be pogroms and scourges, but nothing on the scale that Monsieur Herschal visualises.

Yours, etc. Marcel Macon"

Leon sat back and rubbed his eyes. This letter from Marcel Macon had been written on French Ministry of The Interior note paper. It was thin and faded and if it was a fake it was a damn good one. Furthermore, the letter was not addressed to his father, but to the chairman of The Jewish Agency and thus, if this was a fraud, many other people far more important than his father had been in on it from the beginning.

He filled his glass and had carried on reading. From the gist of the correspondence Herschal had left France a week before the Germans had invaded. There was a letter from Lisbon that spoke of the Iberian peninsula's neutrality... And another letter several months later from the city of Fez in central Morocco. Here, he said, he felt truly safe (a Jew in a country full of Moslems?) living and studying with friends, although he didn't say who the friends were or what it was that he was studying.

There were half a dozen more letters despatched every six months or so, accurately plotting the course of the war in Europe. Were it not for his father's reports and comments, he would have been suspicious of the dates, but Max

Shapiro's involvement gave the process a degree of credibility that would not otherwise have been there. Leon had never been close to his father, certainly not emotionally, but he'd known the man well enough and had always respected him for his honesty and integrity. He'd been an exceptionally clever man and could not in any circumstances have been fooled easily.

His eyes rested at random on a few key sentences that leaped out from the mass of tightly filed letters. *"Spring 1941 – Hitler will attack Russia later this year and will reach the suburbs of Moscow before he is finally turned. This is the beginning of a long end in which millions more will die. Watch for a battle at a place called Stalingrad. This should be perceived as most crucial..."* And... *"December 1941 – America is destined to enter this unholy war. The Japanese will catch her by surprise. England will become a fortress island upon which the Americans will build up their reserves in preparation for the assault on Europe. British bombers will pound what Hitler calls his one thousand year the Reich by night and American bombers will attack by daylight; the Russians will push from the east and the allies from the west and finally The Reich will be defeated. Only then will the horrors committed against the Jews come to light for all to see and even then there are those who will deny it for ever after..."*

There was a letter dated February 1st 1944 which, to Leon's eyes, had seemed to be notably more specific. *"Mr Shapiro, I write today to tell you of secret weapons that will change the face of the world. The Germans experiment with rockets while the Americans seek to discover how to harness the power of the atom. Both will be successful and, while rockets descend on England, atomic bombs will eventually fall on Japan. The irony comes after the war when Americans will attach their bombs to German rockets which will be a necessary defence against the ever growing threat of Russia. Only Mr Churchill in England is really aware of the threat that Russia poses – and nobody is listening to him either!"*

Leon wandered through a number of other items pausing when he came across a note from his father. In all earlier correspondence Max Shapiro's communiques had been addressed to The Jewish Agency in Haifa. This item was not. Instead – and Leon had noted that there were no addresses, only names – the memo was designated for circulation to: David Ben Gurian, The Jewish Agency. Menachim Begin, Irgun. Aaron Steiner, Palmach. Micky Rizzo, Jewish Defence League. It was dated May 21st 1944 and was formal and to the point.

"Gentlemen – You will be aware that for a number of years we have been in receipt of valuable and highly accurate information from an agent called Herschal. Please find attached detailed file and a copy of his latest report which states:
  (a) The allies will invade France during the first week of June, this year 1944.
  (b) That eleven months later the war in Europe will end with Adolf Hitler's suicide. Allied and Soviet armies will divide the continent and take an aggressive stance against each other.

(c) That a million displaced Jews, many of them survivors from the death camps, will be trying to reach Israel. That this move will be blocked by the British in an attempt to appease their Arab allies. Notwithstanding there will be a massive exodus of European Jewry into Israel.
(d) During the following three years, Israel will be split by warring factions. Jew will fight Jew on Israeli soil.
(e) In 1948, the British will relinquish their Palestinian mandate. In May of that year David Ben Gurian will proclaim the establishment of The State of Israel which will be recognised (initially) only by The United States of America.
(f) In May of 1948, Israel will be attacked by the joint forces of Lebanon, Syria, Jordan and Egypt.

Our agent Herschal ends his report by saying that only if Israel fights as a cohesive unit with all internecine factions pulling together in the face of a common enemy, will we survive the Arab onslaught.

While you may be sceptical and tempted to ignore this information may we draw your attention to the reports received from this agent over the last fourteen years.

Respectfully, M Shapiro."

Leon had read this particular missive from his father with great care and curiosity. It was interesting to note that even as early as 1944 organisations such as The Palmach, later to become the IDF were already in place, and that The Haganah, later to become Mossad, was not on his father's list and therefore it was safe to assume that this was where the memo had originated.

Leon ploughed on.

It was all there. How Max had brought Herschal to Israel in 1946 and the long inventory of information provided by Megiddo One, as he was now called, from that time right the way through until 1983. As in all previous reports, the information was broad and vague, but devastatingly relevant and never less than totally accurate.

December 1948...Next year, a parliament will meet for the first time... and Mr Chaim Weitzman will be elected our first president. Thank God for The Americans. By May of next year they will have helped us join The United Nations. Then we may have good reason to feel a little more secure.

January 1956... This will be a critical year for us. Nasser, the Egyptian, will nationalise the Suez Canal. France and Britain will protest and there will be military action. War will also come for Israel. We shall be on the attack, for once, and will occupy much territory including Gaza and parts of the Sinai Peninsula.

December 1957... The United Nations will end the war this year. We will have to give up our occupied territories but will gain something of importance in return. Let us look to Aqaba.

December 1966... Beware. Our enemies plan to mobilise their armies again. Let us look to Egypt and Syria as being our prime enemies. There will be a war in 1967: it will be fierce and bloody but will only last for six days. If we are to survive this war we must strike first! We must be ruthless! We have a one eyed General called Dyan who will lead our troops into battle (if the politicians let him!) and by the end of it all we shall have the Sinai up to the canal. The Golan Heights, The Gaza Strip, East Jerusalem and much of West Jordan. What a prize!

August 1967... The politicians will wrangle about the Palestinians but nothing concrete will come from it. They (The Palestinians) will launch commando style raids into our nation. Their targets will be indiscriminate. We shall have no choice other than to retaliate with direct military action.

... And so it continued, year after year, warning after warning, stratagem after stratagem, always months and sometimes as much as a year in advance. Herschal mentioned The Rogers Plan of 1970 and dismissed it as unworkable. In 1972 he warned of the forthcoming Yom Kippur war in 1973. He was ignored by his country's new leaders and Israel got a very bloody nose. He provided clear commentaries upon political situations long before those situations actually came into being and was accurate in predicting Israel's wildly fluctuating economy almost on a month by month basis.

One very spooky aspect of the file was the way in which Herschal predicted the death of certain individuals and the ensuing power struggles that followed to fill the departed's shoes. Writing in 1980 about 1981, Herschal made more than passing reference to the murder of Abu Rabia, predicted for the month of January. There was a three page document relevant to the assassination of Anwar Sadat, scheduled to take place in the autumn, probably around September. General Moshe Dyan, Herschal reported sadly, would die a short while after, towards the end of October, but from natural causes.

One of the strongest bees in Herschal's bonnet was the concept of Arab nuclear power. He wrote in 1980 that *within a decade Arab missiles will fall on Tel Aviv, launched almost certainly from Iraq. Unless something is done to curtail the Iraqi nuclear programme, those missiles most assuredly will be armed with atomic warheads.* Indeed, Herschal's warnings with regard to Iraq's nuclear potential had been picked up on by Mossad fully a year before and, as a direct result of that, the situation had been carefully monitored for two years until in the June of 1981 it was considered that the Iraqis were too close for comfort in the process of building their bomb and a squadron of Israeli Air Force fighter bombers had broken every international law in the book by carrying out a very illicit but eminently successful strike against the Iraqi nuclear plant at Osirak. The whole world screamed trespass but there was much relief and quiet applause in the war rooms of Whitehall and The Pentagon.

The file read like a latter day version of the prophesies of Nostrodamus but in this case with the seer's eyes focused firmly on the State of Israel and the fate of the Jewish people.

There was no indication as to the source of Herschal's material, not even in Max Shapiro's footnote to the file, dated March 1986, in which he stated that Megiddo One was taking extended leave of absence to do some personal research in The Negev and that he would contact Mossad at some unspecified time in the future if the need arose.

Leon was been aware that the file was far from complete, but even so it had taken him all of the day and most of the evening to sieve through it. By ten o'clock his eyes were crossing, his head buzzing and locking the file in his safe, he went out for a walk.

The Jerusalem night was soft and scented with a gentle breeze, becoming dusty and oppressive as he ambled through the old Jewish quarter of the city. He drank poor coffee and ate a cheap meal and finally found himself sitting on a rock not a stone's throw from The Wailing Wall, still trying to digest the significance of the knowledge he'd acquired.

The important issue was Herschal's source! Where did this mine of information come from – and yet, *did* that really matter in the light of the man's amazing accuracy over so many years, even down to pinpointing the month of someone's death? Either way, he' was able to see why Gideon Lemski could not afford to dismiss Herschal's words as the ramblings of a half baked old desert nomad. All right, he may have gone AWOL for twenty five years and he *might* have lost his marbles – but with that track record stretching all the way back to 1930, could Lemski, or anyone else for that matter, afford to take the risk?

Although it was late, he took the mobile phone from his jacket pocket and punched a call through to Lemski on his home number.

'Yes?' his superior answered.

'Leon Shapiro – I've read the file.'

'And?'

'And I'm sitting here on a rock near The Western Wall trying to decide whether I should put in for a couple of months' extended leave and find some distant relatives to visit as far away from Israel as possible, or whether Mossad's been the victim of the most enormous hoax in Israel's history perpetrated over the last sixty years and involving some very prominent people, including my own father.'

'And what do you think?'

'I don't know what to think. I need to know what *you* think. I need to know the source of our man's information.'

Lemski had chuckled. 'No, that isn't in the file, is it. I'd hoped you might have been able to work it out for yourself. Your father did eventually, but it took him years to believe it and to be convinced.'

'Give me a clue?' Leon suggested hopefully.

'Why do you think the fucking thing is called The Elijah File?' Lemski replied tiredly. 'The man's a fucking prophet, or so your father said, anyway. He has these dreams, these visions of the future, all neatly laid out in his head and when he wakes up he writes it all down and sends it to us in the form of an intelligence report.'

'Are you serious?' Leon was staggered.

'Yes – and I know how you feel.' There was some sympathy in Lemski's voice. 'It sucks, but that's the bottom line. Maybe we shouldn't be so surprised. This country's been breeding prophets for millennia. Maybe we should just be thankful that this one's on our side.'

'So do you believe what he said?'

'No. Not without something else to back it up. But I can't afford to ignore it and now that you've read the file I'm sure you can understand why. What I *am* going to do is pull a full overview survey on every damn thing I can think of that might pose any kind of threat and you're going back to Ashquelon in the morning. I want you to become his baby sitter, his best friend, his mother and father and if necessary even his arswiper. Your father was his friend so you become his friend. I think there's something he's holding back on, something he isn't telling us and I want to know exactly what it is. I want him milked dry and I want to know exactly what's going to happen or what he thinks is going to happen, no matter how bizarre it might sound... But Leon, very much on a my ears only basis. No written reports, but you talk to me every twelve hours regardless, got it?'

'Yes,' Leon had answered thoughtfully, his mind already racing. 'Leave it with me. I'll see what I can do.'

Two days later Herschal was feeling fit enough to take a short walk around the garden. Then he ate a light lunch and mooched around the hotel. He was the only guest and had the place to himself. Although comfortable enough it was a little on the Spartan side with pale cream walls and occasional imitation wood panels. The white wood furniture was relatively new and at least the place was clean. Completely out of character, which was not difficult for there was no character, the walls had been decorated with a series of cheap prints of Parisian street scenes – and half way along the corridor that led to his room there was a picture of Pont du Saint Michelle with Notre Dame Cathedral in the background. He'd not noticed the picture before but he noticed it now.

The print, more of an artist's impression that an exact rendering, caused Herschal to stare at it intently for many long moments, absorbing the detail. To the right of centre, guiding the eye along the melee of the bridge towards the spires of the church, was the cafe... How ironic, he'd thought, that he should be dumped in this two star establishment, a place that fancied itself a slice of Epoc de Belle France and that he should have found this particular picture! He'd moved a step closer, focusing his eyes on the detail of the cafe but at this distance, only inches away, the artist's hand was reduced to impressionistic daubs of colour.

What quirk of serendipity, he wondered, had caused this picture of all pictures to be hung on his prison wall? He blinked his eyes rapidly, incredibly holding back a tear, and with very little imagination was able to remember the meetings around those same cafe tables back in the 1930s – and how odd, how incredibly odd, that the meeting the Englishman had told him about that had taken place only the previous year with Villiers had also been in that very establishment. Well, perhaps not so odd really. Villiers had also been a creature of habit and he'd always been drawn to Saint Michele even when Herschal had known him as an intense and gawky young boy all those years before when Paris had been a very different city to the city it was today.

Without thinking, he reached up to lift the picture from the wall. It was surprisingly heavy and he had to lower it to the carpet more quickly than he'd anticipated with a sharp exhalation of breath.

'Want a hand?' Leon asked quietly from where he'd been watching unobserved from the T junction of the corridor.

'Of course I do!' Herschal snapped – and then in a milder tone – 'Do you think you could bring it to my room?'

Leon carried the picture into Herschal's bedroom and at the old man's bidding propped it on top of the dressing table leaning at an angle of fifteen degrees against the wall. Herschal had sat on a chair studying the print intently, while Leon had perched on the end of the bed.

'Is it that good a picture?' he asked.

'The picture is rubbish,' Herschal had snorted derisively, '... but this cafe on the corner, oh this brings back so many old memories.'

The Elijah File fresh in his mind enabled Leon to make an intuitive leap. 'Is that where you met Marcel Macon back in 1939?'

Herschal laughed and when he turned to look at Leon, his rheumy old eyes were twinkling with delight. 'So that fool Lemski showed you the file after all, did he! I thought that he'd have to. And yes, that's the cafe where I met Monsieur Macon, and he was a fool as well. So much faith, he had, in his precious Maginot line and so much faith in man's basic goodness that he could not visualise the horrors which even then were being unleashed against us by the Nazis. But there were other meetings with other people over many previous years. It was a rendezvous for certain fraternities that flourished in the thirties.'

'Artists?' Leon asked innocently.

'Piss artists!' The old man guffawed, his cackle then becoming a chuckle and falling into a moment's silence. 'No, young Shapiro, not artists. Even then they preferred Montmarte and Montparnasse... My lot were dreamers, visionaries, philosophers, occultists. *We* knew that there would be a European war as early as 1932. Once Hitler acquired the chancellorship, it became inevitable. We tried to warn everybody, but nobody really listened and those that did, did nothing.'

Leon remained silent, not knowing quite what to say. In any case, after a half minute Herschal had rambled on. 'And there was another meeting that took place in that cafe only last year which was probably more important that any of our old get togethers all those years ago. I wasn't there, of course, but I heard all about it from a man who was. Shame you couldn't meet him. He's probably the only person in the world who can change what's going to happen after the 21st.'

'Ah,' Leon was quick to respond. 'So it's by no means certain that what is supposed to happen after June 21st is going to happen at all?'

Herschal looked at him frankly. 'How old are you?' He'd asked abruptly.

'I'm thirty three,' Leon had replied. 'What's that got to do with anything?'

'Nothing much, only that you should be old enough to know that absolutely nothing in this life is certain. I tell you two things. One is that Israel is in great danger, two is that there is one man working hard to prevent this danger from manifesting itself, although he will most probably fail. You and your boss don't believe the first part of what I have told you, so why should you believe the second?'

'Gideon Lemski is not a fool,' Leon countered defensively. 'What he said to you the other day is quite true. Never in Israel's history has our future been so secure.'

'Hah!' Herschal had been scornful. 'You think that just because you have conceded some autonomous territory to the Palestinians all your troubles are over! Yasser Arafat may be as dead as a door nail but it won't be long before some new Mahdi will be preaching his holy war on Jewish soil demanding rights of access to Jerusalem. The Arab's aims have not changed. Only his tactics. Mind you...' And Herschal chuckled wickedly, 'after June 21st the chances are that the Jewish Arab problem will be a thing of the past. We may find ourselves on the same side against something far nastier than those dirty little bastards from Hamas!'

'So the threat you have spoken of doesn't come from Hamas or the PLO?' Leon jumped in quickly.

'No... The Arabs will suffer the same fate as the Jews. I told you before that we will be facing a very old enemy and it is so old that both Jewish and Arabian cultures are young by comparison. It is everyone's enemy, although true to say the Arabs have a better chance of surviving its onslaught than the rest of us.'

'You're talking in riddles, Mr Herschal!' Leon complained reproachfully. 'Could you not be more precise as to the identity of this old enemy you speak of?'

'And have you lock me up in some mental asylum? No fear! And yet, you know, back in the Negev I thought it would be so easy... That I'd be able to tell your father what was going to happen and then simply go back to the desert and let him worry about what to do.'

'My father's been dead a long time,' Leon said softly, 'but I'm alive and kicking. Can you not tell me what you would have told Max and let me do the worrying?'

'It's difficult,' Herschal had responded slowly. 'Your father knew certain things. If he did not tell you then he must have had good reason. Because of what he knew it would have been possible for him to understand the information I possess, but how can I explain things to you? You have no terms of reference. I do not doubt that you are a very clever and intelligent young man, but I suspect that in so many areas you are still basically ignorant.'

'Oh come on!' Leon protested. 'You're being arrogant and you're condemning me without trial!'

'Am I?' Herschal pondered. 'Then in the spirit of our conversation, answer me this. What was the religious faith of the Arab world before the prophet Mohammed rode out of the desert and created Islam?'

Leon opened his mouth to answer then realised that he actually didn't know the answer and shut it again.

'Hah! That got you, didn't it!' Herschal had grinned triumphantly. 'But I wouldn't worry about it too much. Seven out of ten Arabs wouldn't know the answer either! Got any cigarettes?'

'I don't smoke.'

'Then why don't you wander down to the reception office and pinch a couple from one of my guards. They're bound to have some and if not, well you could go and have a rummage behind the bar or somewhere.'

'You shouldn't be smoking,' Leon protested. 'I mean, you've got bronchitis and...'

'Listen, I'm ninety God knows how many years old and at my age I shouldn't even be living! Now be a good boy and go and find me something to smoke and let me do some thinking. When you come back I might have a proposition for you.'

Later that day, Leon had phoned Gideon Lemski on a secure line.

'How's it going?' Lemski wanted to know.

'Difficult to tell,' Leon responded. 'The threat Herschal refers to isn't coming from the PLO or Hamas or Al Quiada, although he infers that the Arabs will be preaching a peace process with one lip and demanding Jerusalem with the other. The impression I got was that this threat is not just directed against the Jews and Israel, but against everybody, including the Arabs. He even says that Jew and Arab may yet fight side by side against a common enemy, but what that enemy might be I haven't got a clue and he's definitely not saying.

'He does say that there is someone working to prevent it all from happening but he's not saying who, where or what. He also indicates that my father knew a lot more than ever went down in the file...'

'That doesn't surprise me.'

'... And he's offered me a deal!'

'Oh yes, and what's that?' Lemski's interest suddenly quickened.

'He says that if we're prepared to take him back to the Negev, and I go with him, he'd tell me everything I want to know – but only in the Negev. There's something I'm supposed to see.'

'Forget it,' Gideon Lemski retorted emphatically.

'Yes I thought you'd say that, but don't dismiss the idea altogether. It might be worth considering, even if only as a carrot to dangle. But you're right about one thing. He definitely knows a lot more than what he's told us. I think he got completely phased by the fact that Max wasn't around to de-brief him. He looked at you and me and Irvin and completely chickened out.'

'All right,' Lemski said shortly. 'You can tell him I'm considering it.'

'Have you got any idea what my father might have known that we don't know?'

'No. No offence meant, but your old man was a tight old bugger and very weird in some of his ways. Megiddo One and The Elijah File were his personal projects. No one else ever got a look in. We all knew of Megiddo One, or at least some of us did, but your father took damn good care to make sure that none of us ever met him. Kept him under very close wraps.'

'Ummm... All right, one other thing. Do you know what the Arabian religion was before Islam?'

'Yes, it was – Shapiro, what is this? A quiz show or twenty questions?'

'No, it was just a question he asked me and I didn't know the answer. I just wondered if you did.'

'Zoroastrian,' Lemski said after a long pause. 'Don't know how you spell it, don't even know if I'm pronouncing it right, but what's it got to do with anything?'

'I don't know, but I'd appreciate it if someone could send me some stuff on the subject, just in case.'

'In case of what?'

'In case it's important. One thing I can tell you is that our guest in Ashquelon is neither senile nor insane. He's as bright as a button and he's playing games with me!'

If Herschal was playing games with Leon Shapiro, four days later there was still no obvious winner and he sat on the veranda wrapped in a shawl watching the rain squall move north from south across the distant horizon. It would be raining in Tel Aviv by tea time. The chest infection still had not cleared up entirely and he felt weak and aching in every bone in his body: there was a constant nag in his left arm that he'd not told anybody about and an ever present hollowness in his stomach that might have been a side effect of the anti-biotics and then again might have been something entirely different. Peering out into the rain swept horizon, he caught a glimpse of his own death, realising that it was closer now than he'd ever thought possible and the chances were that he'd never know, at least not from this world, whether his prophesy was going to be right or wrong. He had no fear of death. Ninety eight years was long enough for any man. But given a choice, he'd prefer to die in the warmth of the desert cocooned by the things that had become so familiar over these last few years and not in this poor hotel, so cold and impersonal and damp with the mists that rolled in from the sea.

He'd worked on Leon and Leon had worked on him, each to no avail. In the end they'd played chess together and had talked on a host of uncontroversial matters; a bond of sorts had formed between them, and why not? For after all, was this not Max's son? But he'd refused to be drawn... Oh yes, he'd told Leon, there were many things he could tell him and *would* tell him, but get me home to the desert first. Leon, he felt sure, would have complied willingly enough but it was that old gout ridden bastard in Jerusalem who was putting the mockers on things. *No, Mr Herschal. You tell us what you have to tell us and then, when you're well, we'll get you back to where you belong!* Well as far as Herschal was concerned, Gideon Lemski could go and suck his own piles, and would damn well have to before Herschal spoke to him again! A lump formed in his throat and his eyes moistened. God, but this was no way to go out! No way for a life to end... He looked longingly at the sea and wondered how much energy it would take to get to the beach and if, once he got there, what the chances might be of wading out into the ocean and drowning before his three toy soldiers leaped in and hauled him out? It was an interesting thought, and if by tomorrow he was feeling just a little stronger and there were no nice words from Jerusalem, he might well be tempted to put it to the test!

The door creaked behind him and a footstep fell on the boards. 'Well, what did your boss say this time?' he muttered resentfully full well suspecting he knew the answer already.

'He says you can go home,' Leon said quietly. 'Whenever you feel well enough to travel.'

15.

Venta Cristobal

On Thursday the fifth of May, especially during the late afternoon and evening, a gentle migration began to take place from Castillo towards the neighbouring village of San Pablo. A festive mood was in the air and people paraded their fine Sunday clothes, many of the girls wearing their traditional feria dresses made from many metres of fine lace and tiered ruffs. They wore mantillas in their hair and carried fans and castanets. Some walked the dusty twelve kilometre road, others travelled in the backs of carts or in dangerously overcrowded cars. There was a determined mood to have a good time, to relax and unwind, to dance and to drink; personal concerns and individual worries could be forgotten about and put to one side for a while, for it was carnival time in San Pablo! The first of the summer's ferias that would begin that evening and carry on almost unabated until Sunday night when there would be the usual pyrotechnic display of fireworks.

The Andalucian tradition of each village having an annual fair was not new and stretched back into antiquity, but the concept of each village holding its carnival in sequential rotation – San Pablo in May, Tessorillo In June, Gaucin in July, Castillo in August, San Roque in September – was a modern innovation craftily and surreptitiously encouraged by the Falangist government of the 1950s. This way, there was always a carnival to look forward to during the long summer months, each well within distance of wherever one lived. It kept people in work and gave those who worked hard and grumbled much something to focus on. In a subtle way it subdued political criticism and in the minds of cynical politicians, it kept the peasants happy. Whether "the peasants" were ever aware of this manipulation was something of a moot point, but either way by the 1990s the point was well and truly lost. The feria was the feria and even if it was a modern tradition, the first of the summer's carnivals in this part of the province was always in San Pablo!

Perhaps this particular year there was an even greater determination among Castillatos to go to the feria in search of some fun and festivity. At the best of times the majority would have needed no urging, but there were a good few who also saw the carnival in San Pablo as a good excuse to get out of Castillo for a while to escape the very strange atmosphere that had descended upon the village over the last few days, cloaking it in a veil of tension that everybody felt on one level or another whether they recognised it or not.

One of the few who had noticed the very odd vibration was Jaime Gomez. As afternoon turned to early evening, he sat on the terrace of the Bar España smoking a Ducados and pulling thoughtfully at his lower lip. The entrance of the bar, one of the oldest in the village, faced onto the main street, only fifty yards or so up the hill from The Ayuntamiento and Jaime's office. It was a spartan place with a stainless steel counter and a few stools but Jaime liked it because when you went out onto the terrace it seemed that the village was far behind you; you could sit and look across the valley as he did now, watching the mountain peaks turn to gold and deep orange with the setting sun and visibly measuring the encroaching shadows as they crept up from the foothills and inevitably flooded the lush meadows and the Ronda road. This evening the road was busy and would become even busier as the night grew long. Cars, from this distance the size of matchbox toys, hurried to and fro, streamers trailing back from bent aerials with music blasting from open windows. It went without saying that each car was illegally overloaded and more than one vehicle would be carrying contraband from Gibraltar or small quantities of drugs from Algerciras... But he wasn't in the mood to be conscientious or vigilant: the mayor's nephews could look after things for a while. He was technically off duty for another two hours and he wanted this time to think. Also, and he glanced at his watch, he was supposed to be meeting someone in the next few minutes who might, he hoped, be able to answer one or two nagging questions. Indeed, he hoped that Doctor Sanchez might go one further and give him some indication as to what questions he, Jaime Gomez, as Chief of Police, should himself be asking at this time.

It had been impulse that had made Jaime phone Hector earlier that afternoon and suggest that they meet for "a quiet drink away from prying eyes and flapping ears to talk about a few things". Sanchez was not a friend for Jaime had no friends, but their professional association was one that worked and he had a loose affinity with the doctor for they were both refugees from other worlds. Neither of them had been born a Castillato. Both of them, in their own way, were men of the world.

At the appointed time of seven o'clock, Hector arrived at the Bar España. Like the policeman, he'd had a disturbing few days and was more than a little tired and disgruntled. He'd been called to the Cortez house late on the Monday evening and had signed the required death certificate. It was clear that Miriam had died through a massive haemorrhage, but there was no indication as to what had caused it. Jaime had gone to the house from the scene of the accident on the Sotogrande road; Peter Cortez and Lena had been dispatched to the clinic in La Linea, although it seemed that neither had been that badly hurt – which was more than could be said for the wife and mother.

Together they had surveyed the blood-soaked room. Hector had said that without an autopsy it was impossible to say what had caused the bleeding and this had caused Jaime Gomez to be thoughtful.

'She has no close friends in the village,' he'd said, 'and at this point in time, both members of her family are in the clinic at La Linea. This gives us two choices. We can say that we are satisfied that this woman has died of natural causes, in which case it falls upon us to clean her up and bury her – or, as the doctor, you can say that you're not satisfied and the police from La Linea will have to take her and they'll have to sort it all out. It's up to you.'

Hector had nodded. In different circumstances he may have reacted differently, but that particular Monday night he wanted none of it. 'Make the phone call Jaime. Let's get her out of Castillo. I think that will be best for everyone.'

Jaime had smiled approvingly and Miriam's corpse had been on the La Linea mortuary slab before midnight.

Hector poured a bottle of San Miguel into a frosted glass and downed half of it in a few long swallows before resting the glass on the table. 'Have we heard anything about Señora Cortez?' he asked.

Jaime Gomez nodded. 'They are mystified. As you said, she died from loss of blood, almost all she had in her as a matter of fact. But there is nothing to indicate why. It is a most peculiar death. They say we did the right thing in letting them handle it.'

'What about her family?'

'Ummm, there is something peculiar here also. When the ambulance came to the crash site Pedro Cortez was badly dazed, but certainly coming round from the blow to his head. He had a bad cut, but I did not think there was any serious damage. The child seemed to be in some state of shock... But now they say that Cortez has gone into a coma and that the child is suffering from catatonia. There is some talk of transferring her to the mental institution in Algerciras if she doesn't show any signs of improvement over the next few days. They are both being watched carefully and so far neither of them know about Señora Cortez. She will probably be buried tomorrow, by the way, mystery or no mystery, and in La Linea, thank God. Not here.'

Hector took another mouthful of San Miguel, digesting Jaime's information with the cutting edge of the ice cold beer. 'It's a messy business,' he offered. And then: 'What else did you want to talk about Jaime? I mean, we could have discussed Señora Cortez over the phone...'

Jaime drew another Ducados from the blue and white packet and let his eyes wander over the Castillato valley before bringing them back to the table.

'You and I have both lived in this place for a long time,' he began carefully. 'The difference between us is that you like it here and you are well liked, while I hate it here – and nobody likes me.' He smiled thinly, fat lips pulling back across stained yellow teeth. 'I accept that I am probably not a very likeable person, but Hector, I am a good policeman and I do my job here as best I can and although I do not like this village, I know it very well. I know its people. I know what most of them are up to at any one time and I know how they think. Sometimes,' he drew hard on the cigarette, 'sometimes you see more when you are always on the outside, looking in.'

'True enough,' Hector agreed, not very comfortable with this conversation, not knowing where it was going or what it was leading up to, and yet curious despite himself.

'I think,' Jaime continued just as carefully, 'that there are some very unusual things happening in this village. I think they've been happening for quite a while. And I wondered what you might think. You are much closer to people than I am.'

'What unusual things in particular?' Hector asked, suddenly feeling nervous.

'Don't you think it a little odd that suddenly both our priests are stricken with illness at the same time? Don't you think there was something odd in the death of Señora Cortez? Nobody just bleeds to death without cause and isn't it strange that while the señora lays dying her husband and her daughter are involved in some inexplicable car accident. I also think it a little odd that one of our village boys has taken a very bad beating but is not saying who did it. At first, I thought there might be an obvious link with some of the people down in Algerciras, but the word I get from my colleagues down there is that the suppliers know nothing about it and are as mystified as I am.'

'Maybe he was in a fight over a girl,' Hector offered feebly. 'As for Pedro Cortez, it's a very bad road from Sotogrande and maybe him going off the road the way that he did is just one of life's coincidences. Father Ignatious has been sick for years. It is common knowledge that he has cancer so I break no confidences in telling you this. He has enjoyed a period of remission, but was taken ill again on Monday...'

'Another curious coincidence,' Jaime interjected. 'A lot of things happened on Monday, didn't they? And what about our young priest Father Fransisco? Can you speak of that without compromising yourself?'

Hector finished his beer. 'He is sick. In the head. Some kind of nervous disorder. I see him every day, but can't give you any real prognosis – but I think it might be a while before either of our padres are back on their feet.'

'Another drink?'

'Thank you, yes.' Hector breathed a silent sigh of relief as Jaime went to the bar. He hoped his distortion of the truth regarding Fransisco de Santa Maria had escaped the policeman's inquisition. And with some amazement realised that history was being made. Jaime Gomez was actually buying him a drink! Jaime was renowned for his miserliness and if he was putting his hand in his pocket now, there had to be good reason. In truth Jaime had been correct in his self appraisal. Nobody liked him... and yet, Hector squirmed uneasily, it was also true that nobody had ever really made an effort to like the man. His visage and attitude were unpleasant, to be sure, and no Chief of Police could ever be popular, but in that moment he found himself wondering just how much Jaime actually deserved the reputation he'd obviously had to learn to live with. Hector took his friendships, although never his friends, for granted. How difficult might it be, he mused, to live in a place like Castillo without friends? To be respected, yes, but at the same time universally loathed?

Jaime placed two fresh bottles on the table and resumed his seat. 'I was just thinking,' he said, pouring the beer in the glasses. 'Yes, I was just thinking what a *violent* little place our Castillo has become. We have had more sudden deaths and suicides in the last ten months than the last ten years put together. You have been a part of this, so you know what I mean. I think of the Torres knifing the other week... we always have fights, but knifings? I think of Rosaria Pina's death... what a way to die. Drinking battery acid the way she did! And Alonso Pina mutilating her corpse like that before hanging himself with barbed wire! This is not the Castillo I came to a few years ago! And I think of all the people, especially the farmers, who have left this place over the last twelve months even though their crops have been good. Gone to Gaucin or Tessorillo for no real reason... I look for explanations, but Hector, I do not find them! Do you know the Aguila boys? You know the way they loved that stupid dog of theirs?' Hector nodded. 'Well the little bastards tied it to the rail track and the Ronda express splattered it all over the Marchenillas crossing... Hector this is not normal behaviour, even for boys who might have been smoking too much marajuana!'

'Yes,' Hector agreed. 'I'd heard about that. Messy business. Totally mindless.'

'And last autumn,' Jaime continued, 'we had those two boys drowning in the Hozgarganta although they'd been swimming in it safely for years. We had two rapes and, Doctor, I ask you, how common is rape in this corner of Spain?'

'More common than you'd think if you define rape as intercourse without consent. It happens all the time between married couples. But I take your point. It is rare for a single girl to be assaulted the way that Angelica and Constancia were.'

'And there's another thing...' Jaime had looked at Hector shrewdly. 'I don't know the exact numbers, but a lot of babies seem to be dying at birth. One month a woman is heavy with child and the next month she is heavy with grief, and not a suckling babe in sight... Although I dare say you know more about that than I do,' he added as an afterthought.

Hector sighed and met the other man's eyes. 'You're not wrong,' he admitted. And then, coming to a decision: 'Many babies – and forgive me, but I cannot tell you which ones – are being born badly deformed. One way or another they do not last very long.' Hector's face was grim as he remembered the last occasion he'd attended such a birth.

'You need say no more. I understand your meaning most perfectly.'

Jaime fell silent and Hector felt disinclined to prompt him. There was obviously more to come and Gomez would get there in his own time.

'I am not an imaginative man,' Jaime said slowly. 'Policemen seldom are except in the books and the movies. I plod along, watching everything and everybody; I take notes and make up files and all things being equal, I don't miss very much. And yet...'

'Yes?' Hector asked, aware that Jaime Gomez was acutely embarrassed about something – which was another minor revelation. Hector hadn't thought Jaime had it in him to be embarrassed about anything.

'And yet, I sense an atmosphere in Castillo these days. On the surface people seem the same, but beneath the surface it is almost as though they are waiting for something to happen. Something bad. You may think I am stupid to speak of such things as atmospheres... We are, after all, both men of the modern world with scientific minds and we should not concern ourselves with things such as moods and atmospheres. This sort of thing is for young girls and superstitious old women and...'

'It's all right.' Hector held up a reassuring hand. 'This atmosphere that you speak of is something that I myself have also felt, especially these last few days. It's real enough Jaime. You're not imagining it.'

Jaime looked relieved, and indeed Hector also experienced a sense of relief. It was one thing to feel something, and another entirely to have that feeling put into words by a third party who, independently, had also experienced what you yourself had experienced. It gave substance to your own perceptions and evaluations and that was important when those evaluations were built on something so elusive and intangible.

'I am pleased to hear what you say,' Jaime said solemnly, looking down at his nicotine stained finger nails. 'I thought that I alone...'

'Well, you're not alone.' Hector said generously. 'The question is, what do we do about it?'

'Do? I'm not sure there is anything we can do other than watch and wait and see what happens... But I am very glad we have had this conversation and I would ask that we keep our thoughts to ourselves for a while... Also, if there is anything you hear, providing you do not have to break your Hippocratic oath, I hope you will keep me informed...'

'Yes, I can certainly promise to do that,' Hector confirmed.

'Thank you. Good. Now, there is one other small matter I need to ask you about.' A curious note of enforced professionalism entered Jaime's voice and Hector was alert to the sudden change of mood. 'If someone, someone in this village, said they were having visions of the Virgin Mary, what would you, as a doctor, advise them to do?'

Hector completely failed to recognise the fact that it was a loaded question, but he answered it honestly enough. 'I'd advise them to go and talk to a priest,' he said seriously. '... but that of course would be rather difficult for them to do in Castillo right now, wouldn't it?'

As Hector and Jaime sat drinking and talking on the terrace of the Bar España, Angel sat sipping a coke on the terrace at the Hotel Miraflores. He had been deeply shocked by the news of Miriam Cortez's death and was extremely mindful of the conversation he'd had with El Moreno on the Sunday afternoon. He had no evidence, of course, but he felt certain that the two things were inextricably linked and could not get over feeling a degree of guilt. It was as though he had pointed a finger... A finger based on hearsay and now Señora Miriam was dead. He did not believe that Mage had played any *physical* role in her demise, but he could not dismiss the persistently nagging thought that El Moreno was mixed up in it somewhere. Angel had given Mage a wide birth since Monday night and part of him was deeply beginning to wish he'd never become involved with the business of magic spells in the first place.

There was another reason why he was feeling disenchanted. El Moreno had said that Christina would be his within four days and that deadline had passed more than three hours ago. Indeed, he'd not so much set eyes on Christina since Sunday lunch time. Someone had told him she'd gone to Colmenar for a few days and someone else had told him she'd left the village full stop. Not knowing where she was made him angry and upset and he'd already resolved that he would go to the carnival in San Pablo later on that night and get blinding drunk.

In fact he might as well start getting drunk now for all the good his sobriety was doing him. Coke always tasted better with brandy or bacardi in it anyway.

Pushing away from the table beneath the vine leaves he strode purposefully into the bar and almost cannoned straight into Christina who was in the process of climbing up onto one of Henry's tall bar stools.

'Hi Angel, como esta?'

'Muy bien,' Angel responded automatically, desperately trying to hide his confusion at the sudden unexpectedness of this meeting.

'Here we go, Christina,' Henry beamed from the other side of the bar. 'One tinto verano special, as ordered... Buenos tardis Angel, que quieres por favor?'

'Bacardi cola.' Angel muttered spontaneously, digging his hand into his pocket.

'Hey no,' Christina chipped in. 'Let me get this one. On my tab, okay Henry.'

Angel, having lost track of the exchange in English, looked confused until Henry patiently explained in Spanish that Christina was inviting him to the drink. Angel's confusion turned to embarrassment and he said that it would be more appropriate if he bought Christina a drink. Christina, using Henry as interpreter, said that he shouldn't be so silly and if there was a problem, then he could buy her a drink later. Angel brightened up at that and said he thought that would be all right and that it was a very good idea.

Trying desperately to master his minuscule reserve of English, he raised his glass and said: 'Cheers... You have been away from the village, yes?'

'Yeah. I had to go to Malaga. Tom couldn't get all of his gear on the plane so I had to send it on after him.'

'Tom, he is not here?' Angel asked.

'Nope! He's vamoosed back the The States and I guess that's the end of another beautiful friendship.'

'So you and Señor Tom – you no longer friends?' Angel was finding it hard to contain his excitement.

'Sure we're still friends, but no longer *good* friends, if you know what I mean.'

Angel looked helplessly at Henry, the subtleties of Christina's choice of words completely lost on him.

'They had a bust up,' Henry spoke swiftly and neutrally. 'He wanted to go back home, she wanted to stay here. He went, she stayed. No hard feelings on either side.'

Angel wanted to smile, but knew that it might be better not to. Even so a gleeful shout of laughter rocked him from the soles of his feet to the top of his head. Keeping his face solemn, he said: 'I am most sorry to hear your problem.'

'No problem,' Christina shrugged. 'These things happen all the time.' And then, 'Hey, you know there's a fair at San Pablo tonight?'

'Yes, I know. Everyone is going.'

'Are you going?' She pressed.

'Yes, I think so.'

'That's great!' Christina's face lit up in a radiant smile. 'What say we go together? I was going on my own, but I guess it's so much nicer to go with someone you know. At least you got someone to talk to and to dance with and have a good time with and... Oh gee, I guess I should have asked... I mean, will it be okay to go together or have you got a date with someone else...?'

Again Angel's eyes turned beseechingly to Henry

'Basically,' Henry said, 'she's asking if you'd mind taking her to the feria. She's lonely and she doesn't want to go on her own.'

Angel felt his knees knocking and rubbed his sweating palms against the side of his jeans. Despite the sweet bacardi his mouth was unaccountably dry. 'Señorita,' he spoke almost formally, perhaps to hide the tremor in his voice. 'It would be a big... Henry, rapido, como dice placer en ingles?'

'Pleasure,' said Henry.

'...A big pleasure!' said Angel de Guadiaro.

'Well that's terrific!' Christina exclaimed, not quite sure why she was suddenly so happy. 'You hang on here while I go and change my dress and then watch out San Pablo because it's party time!'

At one minute to eight, Colin Mage brought the Land Rover to a halt outside house number fifty in Calle Santana. Feeling stupidly nervous but keeping those nerves well under control, at eight o'clock sharp he knocked on the door of the Sanchez house... Hector opened the door and welcomed him into the living room.

'You are right on time, but of course by Spanish standards, and by a Spanish *woman's* standards, that means you are early.'

The part of Hector Sanchez that was Anna's father duly noted that Mage looked clean and smart and, despite the fact that he had a beard, he'd obviously used some expensive shaving lotion. Also it looked as though the Land Rover had not only been cleaned but also polished. This was good, for despite the many misgivings he had in his heart, it showed that at least Mage was going to the trouble to make an effort for Anna – which, of course, was just as it should be.

'Anna will be a few moments yet, which is convenient, because it gives us an opportunity to talk... Can I offer you a drink? A soft drink perhaps?'

Christ thought Mage. *He's more nervous than I am!*

'No, I'm fine thanks.'

Hector reached for his pipe and went through the usual ritual, in half sentences between sucks and puffs. 'Colin, my friend, we must have a talk... A proper talk... Soon...' The doctor was partially disappearing in a thick fog of blue smoke. '... About the night of the storm and what happened... and about some of the things we started to discuss. Also,' he paused, finally having got the pipe going to his satisfaction, 'about some of the things that have happened since.'

'I heard about the death of the Cortez woman,' Mage said blandly, wondering how the doctor might feel it he knew he was entrusting his daughter that evening into the care of the man who had cursed Miriam Cortez to an early grave. Mage, along with the rest of the village, had heard the news on Tuesday morning. Perhaps, he'd thought, he should feel some remorse, some responsibility, but instead there'd only been a sensation of sadness and an awareness of the fact that the battle lines of the forthcoming confrontation had been subtley redrawn in his own favour.

'Yes,' Hector was saying. 'An unhappy business. Candidly, she was not a woman who was particularly well liked... In fact there were many whispers that hinted that she was quite an evil woman, some even said she was a witch, although how they worked that one out considering her close friendship with Father Ignatious up at Santa Clara, I'm not quite sure! Although people are always shocked by death, especially in a small place like this, even now there are some who are saying good riddance to bad rubbish! But Colin, there are other things happening. Other things I must discuss with you. You and I are not alone in our feelings about Castillo. I've just come from talking with Jaime Gomez, our Chief of Police, not twenty minutes ago and he is most ill at ease. He also feels the things we feel. Things are not right in the village any more. Jaime even tells me there is a man having visions on the Virgin Mary!

'And on another level, tell me what, if anything, do you know about the phenomena of stigmata?'

'There is someone in the village with stigmata? Christian stigmata? Wounds in the hands and feet?' There was suddenly a sharp edge to Mage's voice.

'Not only hands and feet, but also across the forehead and,' Hector placed his hand against the side, 'here, beneath the ribs.'

'And this person is also having visions of the virgin?'

'No. From what Jaime has said, and he only referred to it in passing, this is someone else.'

Mage's mind went on back peddle. He remembered what he'd read in Maton Blanc Villiers' grimoire all those months ago – something which had been doubly confirmed by his conversations with Herschal and Father Paul O'Connor.

'There's always psychic and spiritual disturbance before an attempted transition,' Herschal had said. *'It can go on for weeks! Even the most heathen of souls find themselves thinking of God. People who've never been near a church in their life suddenly start getting very religious.'*

Paul O'Connor had been even more erudite. It had been at the end of a long day's meditation and mental exercise and Mage's muscles had been aching in reaction to the unaccustomed physical disciplines they'd been subjected to.

They'd sat on a rock with the sea at their backs, looking up at the yonic gash of the cave mouth half way up the cliff. It had been bitterly cold and their breath had frozen to vapour the moment it reached the frosty air. Father Paul's thick Irish brogue had lilted in counterpoint to the crashing of the Atlantic waves on the shingle beach behind them.

'May God and Saint Patrick preserve us if they ever find a way of coming through in any numbers or if they can find a way of forcing entry to our world without warning. As it is I suspect that the psychic energy required to effect the teleportation takes quite a while to build up and is so great that we do get a degree of forewarning. I am only speculating, of course, but I suspect that there is a process of psychic seepage from the other side which manifests itself in all kinds of different ways over here. Irregularity in crop harvests, stillborn children, a tremendous degree of aggression and agitation among the local population providing there's a population to be agitated. Perhaps it's no accident that the majority of what we call "the veils" are in places such as this. Were it not for our presence here The Djinn would be relatively free to come and go as they pleased and we couldn't have that! Oh dear me no! The other thing to watch out for is any kind of poltergeist activity and any form of religious stigmata. In 1804, which was the last time anything tried to force its way through here, at least half the guardian brothers were manifesting some sign of The Christ's suffering on the cross and our whole community took on quite a mood of religious fervour and frenzy.'

Mage looked up and met Hector's eyes. 'Yes. We must talk about this, and perhaps urgently. Preferably tonight, but if not tonight, tomorrow after your morning surgery. Are you coming to the feria?'

'Perhaps. I don't know. God knows I'm tired!'

'Come if you can.' Mage forced a smile. 'A little unwinding will do us all some good. But if we miss our chance tonight, tomorrow will do just as well.'

'Good! I had hoped you might say something like this!' Hector thrust out his hand and Mage grasped it firmly with both of his own. 'And tonight you will look after my Anna? Make sure she has some fun? Give her a good meal and see that she does not drink too much?'

'You can rely on it!' Mage grinned.

As if on cue the door opened and Anna Sanchez walked into the room. She wore a white silk blouse and a burgundy red skirt that fell in swathes of a hundred narrow pleats that flowed like liquid around her legs as she walked towards the two men.

'Colin. I did not know you were here until I heard your voices. I have kept you waiting! Papa, you should have called me!'

'Honestly, I've only just arrived...' Mage's grin for Hector turned into a full blooded smile for the man's daughter. She looked lovely! A perfect symbiosis of svelte sophistication and the simple freshness born of youth. He looked at her with lingering appreciation and approval and she blushed.

Hector went with them to the roadside and nodded approvingly as Mage opened the truck door for her and helped her up onto the high bench seat. He remembered the times when the spotty boy from the next village had come calling, sitting arrogantly behind the wheel of his aggressive little car, beeping the horn and revving the engine impatiently. Every time she had gone off with him Hector's heart had been in his mouth and he'd sat and counted the hours and minutes until she'd arrived home safely. Watching his daughter depart this evening with Colin Mage, Hector experienced none of these feelings! Indeed, earlier misgivings about this "date" had suddenly evaporated And he was man enough to admit to himself that yes, he'd certainly had a few of them. Now his mood was one of constrained excitement. It was good that Anna liked Colin for he somehow knew that with Colin's help and also that of Jaime Gomez, he might yet get to the bottom of Castillo's many ills.

Mage navigated the Land Rover out of the village past the bodega and a few minutes later they were out on the rolling and winding Ronda road that would bring them to San Pablo. They had to raise their voices to be heard above the low thrumming drone of the engine.

'The Land Rover... You have made her very smart and clean!' she called.

'In honour of a special occasion!' he called back. 'It's not every day we get to take a beautiful girl out to a carnival.'

Anna blushed some more, but behind the smoky lenses of her glasses her dark eyes sparkled in the last rays of the evening sun. 'You needn't have gone to so much trouble. Even if she was very dirty, I would still have come with you!'

Well, thought Mage. That was reassuring! The trouble was that after the magic came the exhaustion, and after the exhaustion the jittery energies that demanded physical action to counter balance the mental state of mind. So yes, most mindful of this Thursday's appointment, he'd washed, waxed and cleaned every square inch of the vehicle, removing every speck of dust and smudge of grease... But he'd also cleaned the house top to bottom and had tidied Antonia's garden and had taken several long aggressive walks into the countryside beyond the castle. Even so, he was childishly pleased that she had noticed and, glancing at her now as she sat to his left, he felt a small thrill of pride.

Was pride the right word? He looked at it, teased it, played with it, and decided that it was. The psychology behind the emotion was both simple and complex and inevitably centred around his relationship with Alexandra. Whatever the reasons, whatever the temptations and enchantments, whatever the guile and craft of magic practised by Jadoc Dolorean, his wife had left him for another man. Mage's masculinity, his male ego and his self esteem had been shattered by this fact. While his mind, his knowledge, his common sense, his deepest fundamental *belief* all said the same thing – that she had not gone on her own accord... She'd been tempted, enticed, enchanted, fucking well *stolen* for Christ's sake, the child within him raged with resentment and rejection. The bottom line was that she'd gone. *Couldn't she have fought back harder?* The manchild asked. *And just how hard did she fight? Just how hard was it to walk away from everything we'd worked to build up over the years? Had Dolorean's petition been resisted at all, or had it been secretly welcomed?*

He realised that he was gripping the wheel too tightly and that their speed had crept up to an unwarranted fifty miles an hour. He eased back on both the peddle and the wheel.

'Are you hungry?' he asked cheerfully.

'A little... No... I tell you the truth. A lot!'

'That's good. So am I!'

There'd been too much time on his own. Too many worries and recriminations. Too many journeys across the oceans of despair and self denial. He'd folded in on himself, found the core of his being and had wrapped himself around that island in a desperate quest for strength and survival. There'd been no time for anything other than the basic requirements of social intercourse and as for pretty girls and parties... They were things of the past, unseen and undesired when he'd looked into his own vague and indeterminate future.

And yet here he was, driving to the local fair with an exceptionally beautiful young woman who seemed more than pleased to be in his company. It was enough to remind him not only of his natural masculinity but also of his humanity. He would walk the streets of San Pablo with Anna Sanchez on his arm and he'd damn the man who said he didn't have the right to do it. If he could laugh for an hour and make Anna happy in the process, well there was achievement in that, and if strangers looked and thought that here was a girl out with her father or a man with his young mistress, well that was fine by him! Either way they'd be seeing him *with* someone rather than standing silently alone or skulking along the dark shadows of solitude.

'Why are you smiling?' she shouted.

'Was I smiling?' he shouted back.

'Yes you were smiling!'

He cast her another glance – and yes, pride was definitely the right word! She was watching him intently, her own generous mouth pulled into a mischievous grin.

'You're smiling too!' he told her.

'It is because I am happy.'

'Then there's your answer,' he riposted, glad to have found a way to get off the hook.

The road from Castillo wound tortuously through fertile green fields full of orange groves and grapevines, the terrain of the land soft and undulating, the elevation constantly rising. San Pablo rested to the right of the main road, a fat flat squabble of white houses pushing out in all directions from the single phallic spire of the church. Instead of taking the slip road that led directly to the town, Mage carried on towards Gaucin and Ronda for another kilometre before turning off to the left and entering the courtyard of a small roadside restaurant called Venta Cristobal.

'This place okay?' he asked.

Anna looked worried. 'The food is wonderful, but it is very expensive.'

'Then it's exactly the right place. I'm feeling very expensive tonight.'

He jumped out of the cab and was there to help Anna down the steep step to the ground. He hesitated... Should he offer her his arm, take her hand, or maybe throw his arm across her shoulders? God knew he had no desire to jump all over her bones but he did desperately crave the intimacy of some light physical contact.

In the end Anna solved the problem for him by slipping her arm through his own and flashing him that wickedly mischievous grin.

'Come then, my rich Mr Englishman and let us hope that your wallet can match my appetite!'

They ate in a small enclosed courtyard, open to the sky but with high walls made from old stone which were covered with a profusion of trailing plants and ivy, some in ironwork baskets, others clinging naturally to the rock. The tables, about a dozen of them, were made from rustic oak and were illuminated by countless candles and a series of pseudo medieval coach lamps. Two strings of modest fairly lights were looped corner to corner and in the centre of the courtyard a small fountain created a gentle lullaby of cascading water that seemed to harmonise perfectly with the soft guitar music that played unobtrusively in the background. There were large terracotta pots filled with plants and palms and exotic flowers that filled the evening air with a dozen mingling scents and perfumes. The restaurant was reasonably full, but the tables were well spaced and the leaves of small trees and the meanderings of the biggest grapevine Mage had ever seen in his life, gave more than an illusion of privacy. The low buzz of muted conversations added to the ambience rather than detracted from it.

They started their meal with fresh prawns in avocado and graduated to a main course of chicken breasts delicately cooked in ginger and served with a piquant lime sauce on a bed of fresh al dente vegetables. For desert their choice was again unanimous and they virtually inhaled the creme caramels that came in flambé of dark rum.

Mage had already broken his self imposed ban on alcohol when he'd ordered a bottle of Freixenet Black Label – perhaps the finest of Spain's sparkling white wines. It was smooth and as dry as any French Chablis and yet had the added zest of the spritz with the superiority of the more full bodied flavour of the Spanish grape. Even so, he had drunk most sparingly, his one and a half glasses to Anna's three of four, which did not go unnoticed or unremarked upon.

'You are trying to get me drunk!' she exclaimed as he topped her glass for the fourth time.

'No I'm not. It's just that I don't drink very much and yet this is such a good wine. It seems a shame to waste it.'

'No, you do not normally drink at all, do you? In fact, in all the time I have known you, this is the first time I have seen you drink anything other than coffee or lemonade.' She looked at him candidly. 'Why is this?'

'Well,' he said casually and vaguely, deliberately misunderstanding the question. 'Tonight is a special occasion. It's a long time since I've taken a beautiful girl out to dinner.'

'I thank you for the compliment, but that is not what I meant. Of course, if I am prying and you do not wish to tell me...'

It would have been easy to lie but the last thing he wanted to do in the world was to be less than honest with this woman. So he told her as much of the truth as he could.

'Oh I enjoy a drink as much as the next man,' he said casually, 'although I have never been what you might call a heavy drinker... the occasional beer with a friend, or like this evening, some good wine with a nice dinner. The trouble is that alcohol, even very small amounts, can sometimes distort the senses and in some of the work that I do it is very important that those senses are not distorted.'

'Are these senses so important to the writing of books?' she asked.

'No not really,' Mage laughed, realising that he'd walked head first into a trap of his own making. 'I sometimes like to think that they are, but that's not quite the same thing, is it!'

Anna waited patiently and he realised that he was by no means out of the woods just yet. Their conversation over dinner had been light and uncontentious. They'd talked with easy familiarity about a host of inconsequentialities, everything from the food to Ein Geddi, the weather, the Spanish way of life... He'd told her something of what England was like, especially the North of England, and he'd made her smile, even laugh once or twice when he'd tried to draw parallels between the dour stoicism of Yorkshire folk and the people of Southern Andalucia. His initial nervousness had long since departed and he felt that she was as comfortable in his company as he was in hers. Perhaps it might not be such a bad idea to steer their conversation into some deeper waters.'

'I do write books,' he said slowly. 'But I have other work as well and it is this other work that discourages the alcohol.' He paused, then asked her directly. 'Anna, do you know what it means to be psychic?'

She furrowed her brow. 'Yes, I think so. There is a woman in the village who reads tea leaves and sometimes she sees things in playing cards... And there was a very old man at Ein Geddi who could see things about people when he stared into the embers of the fire or held their hand for a while... Is this the sort of thing you mean?'

'Sort of... the old man at the kibbutz... I suppose you could say that I am a little like him.'

'You?' Anna raised her eyebrows, looking for the punch line of a joke.

Mage nodded. 'Me.'

'But Colin... The old man, I think he just made things up to please people or he said things that were so vague that they could have applied to anyone.'

Mage nodded again. 'Yes but with me it is a little different. I do see things and know things about people – and I don't have to stare into a fire or hold their hands. I just know it in here,' he tapped the side of his head, 'and in here.' He rested his palm against the top of his stomach. 'By seeing things and knowing things, I can sometimes reach into those people and help them solve their problems... Help them find a pathway to some happiness when all they can see is unhappiness and darkness. It doesn't make me extra special in any way, because there are so many other things I cannot do. If a fuse blows in the house, I will light a candle and send for the electrician. If the Land Rover's engine is sick, I don't know how to mend it and must take the car to the garage...'

'So you can tell what another person is thinking?' Anna asked very cautiously.

Mage noted that she was not smiling now and the caution in her voice rang alarm bells in his head. 'No,' he said emphatically. 'I can't read minds, not in the way you mean anyway. I can sometimes tune in to how a person is feeling though and sometimes I know what they are going to do before they do it, even before they've thought about doing it. It works in reverse as well. I can sometimes know what a person has done, even if they don't want me to know that thing. The point is that I have no right to intrude and I certainly don't go round looking into people unless they ask me to... But when they *do* ask me to, it's very important that my own mind – and those senses we were talking about a few minutes ago – are absolutely crystal clear. Like your father, in fact very much like your father, people rely on me not to make mistakes.'

'And have you been reading peoples' feelings in Castillo?'

'Only when I've been asked,' he responded gently.

A half smile – oh so tenuous and enveloped with layers or suspicion and curiosity – began to play across her face. 'Could you do this with me?' she asked.

'Yes I could, but there'd by a problem wouldn't there? Anything I said about you I could have learned by having previously asked your father or I could have spoken to people in Castillo who know you... And you'd never be sure whether I was really doing it or whether I was cheating...' Mage desperately wanted to avoid getting trapped into doing any kind of serious work with Anna that night. It could come later – would have to come later if he was to do anything about her eyes – but for now he needed to gain her trust, to assert the fact that he was absolutely no threat and to inspire her with some confidence. Having broached the subject, however, and having come thus far, he knew he could not back out without some kind of evidential demonstration... but it had to be kept light, in keeping with the party mood of the evening. Almost as though reading his mind Anna leaned across the table. 'You must do something for me,' she insisted. 'What you say is hard to believe – I do not say that I do not believe you, but I want some evidence!' There was challenge in her attitude but also the childish excitement of expectancy.

'All right.' Mage was happy to oblige. 'Let's think of an appropriate experiment... have you got a pen or a pencil?'

Anna said that she had and groped in her purse while Mage passed over a clean paper napkin. 'Okay Anna, you write down any five numbers between one and ten, and in any order you like. Do it behind the menu card so that I can't possibly see what you're writing, then screw the paper up into a very tight ball and place it in my left hand.'

Anna did as she was asked and Mage noticed just how far she had to lower her head to see what she was writing. He accepted the crumpled ball of paper and held it tightly in his fist. 'There's no way I can possibly know what you've written here, is there?' he asked lightly.

'No way,' Anna agreed.

Mage reached over and took the pen from her and, taking another napkin, closed his eyes in concentration before scribbling down a sequence of numbers. When he'd finished he pushed both napkins back across the table.

'Keep my napkin to one side for a moment and just have a look at the numbers you wrote down. In fact, read them out loud if you like...'

Anna unfolded her napkin and read 'Five, Nine, Three, Eight, Two.'

'Okay, now take a look at my numbers.'

Anna picked up his napkin and held it up to the light. 'Five, Nine, Three, Two, Eight... Colin, this is amazing! How did you do it?'

'The fact of the matter is that I'm not exactly certain,' he replied ruefully and truthfully. 'I just thought about you and let my senses wrap themselves around the napkin and the pen did the rest.'

'It's a trick!' she exclaimed in delight. 'A very good one to be sure, but still a trick!'

Mage shook his head softly. 'No,' he said. 'Not really.'

'Then you must do something else,' she said eagerly. 'Show me something else. Do something more.'

'Very well – but this is at your invitation. You are asking me to do this. I'm not prying, okay?'

'Okay!'

'Then reach across the table and take my hand and let's see if I can find you some proper proof.'

More than willingly, he noticed, Anna took his hand and again he allowed his eyes to close. 'We have to find something that absolutely nobody else could know about... Something that is secret to you... Something that I could not possibly have any knowledge of...'

And something small and insignificant, something that would prove the point without opening Pandora's box. He felt her fear from the other side of the table and it was almost as though she was willing him to reveal the darkness of her single great secret... Well, he knew what that was, but it would be so much better if she spoke to him of it first. In the meantime...

'All right, I think we might have something here... You're wearing a white blouse and a red skirt, but it was a difficult choice for you. Only a short while before I arrived to pick you up this evening you still hadn't decided what to wear. I can see you holding up clothes... There is a dark green dress made of some silky stuff, but one of the straps in broken, so you discard it and next you're looking at a black dress, but it is too formal... You're wondering if it will be all right to wear a trouser suit... It's pale in colour and you try it on, but you've lost weight since you bought it and it no longer hangs well. In the end you choose the clothes you are wearing now – and very lovely you look in them too!'

'These things are true,' she said very slowly in a bewildered, disbelieving voice. 'You could not have known and yet it is as though you were there in the room with me. I am impressed... but I am very nervous about this... and also intrigued. How, Colin? How can you do this?'

Mage ordered coffee and for the next forty minutes told her many things about his childhood and his early life... About Elsie Maud, her influence on him and what he knew of her life and times. He explained the gift of psychism as best he could, making it a gentle thing with soft edges rather than anything dramatic... How, if you lived with a thing as the norm then it became the norm. He spoke to her of some of the people he'd known, how they'd helped him learn and understand, and he spoke in modest terms of some of the people he thought he might have helped over the years. Very deliberately he made mention of his work in healing and was gratified to notice Anna's quickening interest – not that she was not interested already. Indeed it seemed that she hung to his every word.

He explained, or at least tried to explain, how the process of channelling worked, but recognised that he probably didn't do a very good job of it. He'd written a book on the subject and after a hundred thousand words and ten chapters, he knew he'd only scratched the surface of the matter. Thus he looked for simpler analogies to explain how the channelling of healing energies worked.

'Say you cut your finger,' he suggested. 'It bleeds because it is meant to bleed. The white blood cells rush to the wounded area to combat any invading bacteria, there is localised pressure in the blood system and because there is a lesion in the skin, out comes the blood... A totally natural physiological process, which is as it should be. But let's say you're in pain... Now the reason why you're in pain is because the nerve endings in your finger have been damaged. This registers in the brain and the brain reacts by causing the pain. If we can interrupt this energy flow and convince the brain that all is well, then you've still cut your finger and it still bleeds, but because there is no pain and discomfort to get in the way, the healing process is speeded up beyond all recognition. In olden days this might have been thought of as magic, but today it's simply seen as a natural channelling of energies... Is this making any sense to you Anna?'

'Yes I think so – but it is a very difficult concept to accept. If everyone could do what you say you can do then there would be no need for people like Papa, would there?'

The "what you *say* you can do" was not lost on Mage and he glanced frustratedly around the restaurant. It was quieter now and he felt secure enough in their quiet corner to do what he did next.

He pulled the candle over and placed it in the middle of the table between them. 'Put your palm over the candle flame and keep it there for as long as you comfortably can,' he told her.

Anna look dubious but nonetheless brought her palm over the candle and held it about six inches above the flame for all of three seconds before pulling it away with a gentle 'Ouch!'

'Fine' said Mage, 'but now let's try it again – just a little differently this time.' He took her left hand across the table. 'Give me a few seconds,' he said, 'and when I say "go" put your right hand back over the flame and see how long you can keep it there this time round.'

He channelled into her, using the opportunity to blow away the nagging headache that was beginning to build up behind her eyes and stilling the qualms of nervousness that he sensed churning away in her solar plexus. He focused on her mind and her right hand fully aware of the fact that he would not be doing this now were it not for a glass and a half of dry white wine and the overwhelming need to prove and impress.

'Go,' he said.

Anna lowered her hand over the candle. She felt the warmth, but no great heat. There was a pins and needles feeling, not just in her hand but also in both of her arms. Before her palm had hovered six inches above the flame... Now she tentatively lowered it to five and then four and a half and registered no appreciable difference in either temperature or sensation. As the seconds ticked away she found her eyes darting between her hand, which by now should have been blistering but was not – and the serene face of the man, this man of great strength, of mystery, and yes, even of magic, who sat opposite. She felt his aura, his very presence, wash over her like a great wave. He was all around her, within her, actually a part of her. Never had she felt closer to another human being, not even her father. Never had she felt anything *like* this ever before. No longer was she a single unit of one, but a totally melded half of a unit of two. She wanted to weep and shout for joy at the same time...

She withdrew her hand from the flame, bringing the palm up before her eyes, staring at it with bewilderment and disbelief. The flesh should have been burned... Even now there should be blisters... and yet there was no blemish on her skin, no puckering flesh, no cindering scar. The tingling sensation continued for fully half a minute until Mage slowly opened his eyes, at which time it inexplicably faded away.

'No pain,' he spoke in a low voice. 'And because the brain felt no pain, no wound, no scar...'

'If... If you can do this...' her heart was pounding and she was glad of the dark glasses for her eyes were full of tears, not of pain but pure emotion brought to the surface by the discharge of psychic energy that had taken place. '... if you can do this... in God's name, what else can you do?'

'Lots of things,' Mage said and it seemed that his voice was incredibly tender. She felt the pressure of his touch and had no desire to remove her hand from his grasp. Not for the first time she found herself feeling very very safe in this strange man's pressure.

Mage paid the bill – expensive by Spanish standards but laughably cheap compared to what he would have expected to pay anywhere else. They walked, not touching, to where he'd parked the Land Rover and stood for a moment allowing the night to brush them with its warmth and protective darkness. In the sky above them a million stars shone from a background of blue black velvet; the cicadas chattered incessantly and in the distance the sound of the San Pablo carnival drifted tantalisingly across the open fields and orange groves – the rhythms and Sevillanas and flamenco, the occasional whoosh of a rocket and the crack of a firecracker; the deep resonant thrum of powerful generators... A muted cheer and a scattering of applause.

'It was a wonderful dinner,' she said. 'Thank you for bringing me to such a good place.'

'You're welcome,' Mage replied easily. 'I'm glad you enjoyed it, although I'm sorry if things got a bit heavy with all the talk about being psychic and the healing stuff. How's your hand, by the way?'

'Fine... as though nothing had happened... And I promise you, nothing got "heavy" as you put it...' She searched for the right words. 'This has been one of the most unusual, most exciting nights I can ever remember.' She turned to look at him. '... You are a most extraordinary man, Señor Mage, and although I say this clumsily, I wish you to know that I am most pleased to be with you.'

Mage preened himself. These words were music to his ears. His ego was flattered and his self esteem went up several notches on the Richter scales of congratulation and self confidence. He might not have been quite so pleased with himself, however, had he realised that in that hour Anna Sanchez had begun to fall quite seriously in love with him – which was not so difficult for her to do as she'd been half way there already.

'Party time in San Pablo?' he suggested.

'Party time in San Pablo!' she confirmed, and much to her own surprise as well as his, she leaned up and kissed him lightly on the cheek.

16.

Carnival

Mage parked the Land Rover and they walked the last few hundred yards into the village, heading towards the main square along a narrow whitewashed street which was festooned with ribbons and streamers. Doors were open with families sitting upon the steps, drinking and laughing or talking quietly among themselves. Despite the lateness of the hour, young children and toddlers played in the road and babies suckled on their mothers' breasts. When they finally arrived at the Plaza Principal, it was to be assaulted by a blaze of colour, bright sounds and delicious smells.

Unlike Castillo, San Pablo de Buciete was built on level ground with the numerous streets of the pueblo branching off in all directions from a single central plaza which also served as the main street. It was a good thirty yards wide and as much as two hundred yards in length. At one end, in front of Saint Paul's tall white church, a band played for fifty or sixty dancing couples and all along the boulevards on both sides of the square, there were mature orange trees with fairy lights strung up imaginatively in their branches. Beneath these trees were rows of food stalls, coconut shies, lucky dips, gift tables, a marionette theatre and even a tombola tent. Set back in one street there was a ghost train ride and, in another, a roundabout for young children. In a third street there was a hall of mirrors and in a fourth a bouncy castle. At the opposite end of the square from the church stood the convent, in front of which was a modest arena of dodgem cars.

Every other building seemed to be a bar, with tables and chairs flowing out over the pavement and into the road. Many such establishments had their own small bands of musicians who battled manfully against each other and vainly against the professional eight piece in front of the church. It was a case of enthusiasm and exuberance versus loud amplifiers and there were no outright winners...

The place was alive with merry making people – old men with starched white shirts and the ubiquitous Spanish pin striped trouser, young men with sombreros, some wearing cummerbunds and riding boots, although a majority of the younger boys had settled for skin tight jeans that looked as though they'd been sprayed on with a can. And yet it was the women who were the most eye catching with their mantillas and fans and the multi-coloured feria dresses that fell to the ground and swished along grass verges like slim crinolines from a bygone age. There were yellow dresses with black spots, black dresses with yellow spots, red frocks edged in gold, green gowns edged in white lace... The combination of colours was almost infinite, wrapped around a single traditional style. Everywhere were the red and orange flags of Spain and the green and white flag of Andalucia.

Mage stood on the corner where the street they had followed joined with the plaza and its boisterously happy throng. He was surprised by the numbers of people present and was delighted by the vista that opened up before his eyes. This, it seemed, was the real Spain, sought elusively by so many and actually found by so few. A trio of laughing boys brushed past them, each carrying an almost full bottle of wine and a car honked an ancient horn from somewhere behind them. Children, some carrying flags, others balloons on long strings, darted underfoot. One threw a firecracker that detonated only a few feet distant and Mage felt Anna jump. He edged her to one side and they stood beneath one of the orange trees for a few minutes, savouring the atmosphere, soaking it up and as far as he was concerned, revelling in it. Anna, however, seemed less enamoured and she looked up at him nervously.

'Colin, this is awkward, but I need to ask a favour of you.'

'Of course.' He was immediately attentive. 'Anything you want.'

She bit her lower lip apprehensively. 'Would you take my arm, or perhaps put your arm around me and if we are to walk around the carnival, would you sort of guide me a little bit... I haven't spoken to you of this, but as you must have realised, I have something of a problem with my eyes. I do not always see things clearly, especially at night when I am in unfamiliar surroundings...'

He responded quickly. 'Don't worry about a thing,' he said reassuringly and slipped his right arm around her narrow waist. 'I'll be with you every step of the way. Now, what would you like to do first?'

'Can we make our way towards the music – and maybe we could dance for a while?'

'Sure. How's your passa doble?'

'Very good.' She managed a half smile. 'How's yours?'

'My dear young lady,' Mage retorted in a superior tone, 'I'll have you know that my passa doble is the talk and envy of North Yorkshire!' He tightened his grip around her and she reached her left arm around his back, resting her hand upon his shoulder. A glass of white wine in his belly and the devil in his mouth, he leaned close to her ear and whispered: 'Don't worry about your eyes, Anna. You're with me now and everything's going to be okay, I promise!'

Then he led them out into the jostling throngs of people heading towards the distant bandstand and the pulsating rhythms of the Spanish night.

Christina was turned on. What exactly was doing the turning, she wasn't sure and frankly she didn't care. It was enough for her to recognise the carnal craving in her body. She wanted sex and she wanted it badly and she wanted it soon.

Tom might have been an asshole of a human being, but he'd been damned good in bed. She did not miss him at all, she realised, but she was certainly missing the sex and those deliciously decadent feelings of satiation and satisfaction that came afterwards. It had been six days since she'd last made love and the way she was feeling now, that was six days too long. The question was, if she was going to get laid, who was going to do the laying?

There was only one candidate really and it came down to Angel. She was not particularly attracted to him, but he was sweet and it would be refreshing to be with someone so young... She wondered if he was a virgin and felt her juices flow at the thought. Hey, wouldn't that be a hoot! Either way it was obvious that he was very inexperienced and even more obvious that she would have no difficulty in seducing him. He'd hung on to her every word all night dancing attendance to her every whim and following her everywhere with those big brown Andalucian eyes, so full of soul and worship. In many ways he was rather like a loveable little Spanish puppy. She knew that he wanted her – it was there in every look and moonstruck glance, but she also suspected that he realised he had absolutely no chance of having her and it was this, more than anything, that *did* make him attractive in a peculiar way. Most other men – who was she kidding? *All* the other men she'd ever known would have done a polite and sometimes not so polite disappearing act once it became apparent that they were not going to get anything and, to his credit, it appeared that Angel was not like that at all.

They had arrived in San Pablo quite early and had drunk their way round every bar in the square before eating something from one of the stalls. Then the band had struck up and they'd danced for a while before drinking their way back around the square in the other direction. Then she'd wanted to dance again and they'd found themselves in this little back street bar with this most *amazing* juke box that had all the old Sinatra hits and Billy Eckstein and Sarah Vaughan and Ella Fitzgerald. They'd smooched around the floor occasionally cannoning into other couples, most of them in their fifties or sixties and it had been here, dancing with their bodies pressed against each other in the crush, that the desire had suddenly risen within her.

'Hey,' she pulled at his hand. 'Let's get out of here and get some air.'

Angel was happy to let her lead him out of the tiny bar – he was happy to let her lead him anywhere! He was in love and lust and his senses were precariously close to overloading. Dancing with her, feeling her body move against his own beneath the flimsy silk of the short yellow dress she was wearing had taken his breath away and had caused an uncomfortable bulge in the front of his tight blue jeans, which had caused acute embarrassment! She must have felt it pressing against her. Must have known what was happening. Was she embarrassed too? Was she offended? Was this why she was pulling away from him now and dragging him outside?

Once they were out in the street she allayed some of his fears by putting her arm round him and telling him he was cute.

'No entiendez,' he mumbled. 'What is this "cute"?'

'It means that I like you,' she said and he understood that well enough to blush deeply.

'I like you also,' he stammered.

'Let's find somewhere real quiet, you know, un citio muy tranquilo, where we can be alone for a while, okay?'

'Okay,' Angel agreed, not sure that he was reading this situation right, but deeply hoping that he was.

They walked down the street, away from the parties and festivities, and within a few minutes were coming to the outskirts of the village. They turned a corner and came to a low wall beyond which were the open fields of the campo. There was a broken gate and Christina pushed through it, running into the field. Angel, worried slightly about grass snakes, bulls and cowpats – he was wearing new shoes! – had little choice but to follow after her.

Fifty yards into the meadow there was an old wooden hay cart filled with dusty straw. She hauled herself onto the edge of the cart and patted the place next to her. Angel swung himself up and wondered what he was supposed to do next.

'You want to make out?' she asked.

'Christina... I am so sorry... what is this "make out"?'

'This is make out,' she said, leaning towards him and bringing her mouth down firmly on his unsuspecting lips. She found his hand and brought it up to cover her breast, at the same time pushing her tongue between his teeth.

Pulled by the gravity which influences most lovers they lay back in the straw amid a tangle of arms and legs and rapidly discarded clothes, and it was here that Angel was cruelly struck down with the revenge of The God of Booze and Bacardi in particular. As he rolled between Christina's widespread legs his rampant erection suddenly died an incomprehensible death.

'Mierda!' his shout of frustration echoed across the empty field.

To give Christina her due, she handled it all very well. Indeed, she'd anticipated this scenario and would have been surprised if something like this had not happened. He was so young, for Heaven's sake!

'Hey baby, don't worry,' she soothed. 'C'mon, just lay next to me and let's look at the stars for a while... You don't have to worry about a thing. You just trust your old Auntie Chrissy and everything's gonna work out just fine.'

Angel didn't understand the words but their tone was a soothing balm to his shattered pride and his limp prick. He stretched out on his back next to her, one arm beneath her neck, trying desperately hard to control his contorted emotions. Christina worked on him slowly, kissing his lips and eyes, nibbling his ear and rubbing her hand in slow languid movements across his chest and belly. When he began to moan softly she lowered her mouth to his nipples and allowed her hand to glide down and stroke his member. He was far from hard but at least there were some signs of life down there.

Her tongue traced patterns along his body, moving ever downwards until she was licking his semi erect penis. *Getting better all the time*, she thought, taking his manhood fully into her mouth. Angel squirmed in ecstasy as she teased him ever closer to his full potential.

When she lifted up from him he took this as a sign but she pushed him back down onto the rough bed of straw. 'No not just yet... Tranquilo Angel. Tranquilo. Mia turno... My turn...'

She reared up above him, making the cart rock, then straddling him she lowered her sex to his face, stroking him with her wetness and rubbing her aching clitoris against the bridge of his nose. *If he loses it now I'll murder the little bastard.* Reaching behind her she wrapped her hand around Angel's erection which was now full blown and throbbing for release.

As Angel's tongue got the idea of what Angel's tongue was supposed to do, she calculated that he'd probably not last more than a few seconds once he was inside her and thus she brought herself to near climax before suddenly swinging her hips backwards. *Christina, baby, you've got one chance at this. Fuck it up and there goes your fuck!*

She lowered herself – made contact, pressed down firmly, and bless his little Spanish socks, he squelched in right up to the hilt. She managed to hold him for all of fourteen seconds and then he spasmed and ejaculated into her in one long flowing stream. That did it for her and her drawn out gasp of pleasure – okay, so some guys got a scream – mingled with Angel's whimpering moans.

She collapsed over him with a degree of satisfaction It hadn't been the best fuck she'd ever had but he'd lasted about three seconds and four thrusts longer than she'd expected. As for Angel, he clung to her as though it was the end of the world that had come rather than he himself, and why not, for as far as he was concerned this was the single most important thing that had ever happened to him in the whole of his life! And now he did see the stars, millions and billions of them in one kaleidoscope vortex as broad and as long as the sky was high... And in the distance above the muted sounds of dance bands and dodgem cars, the old clock of San Pablo's parish church struck midnight.

In Castillo, the town hall clock also struck midnight as Immaculada Morro struggled towards the taxi rank lugging a heavy suitcase. She was an old woman and the walk down from Calle Loba had been arduous. With most of Castillo revelling in San Pablo the small square was deserted and only Jacinto who had had a belly full of ferias over the years had kept his bar open. He was leaning on the corner of the doorway just thinking that he might as well close, when Immaculada wobbled into sight.

'Where are you off to at this time of night?' he asked incredulously.

'None of your business,' Immaculada grumbled unsociably. 'Where are all the taxis?'

'San Pablo,' Jacinto said. 'But if you're in no rush there'll be one here in a minute.'

'And what if I am in a rush?' she snapped back.

'Well, I'll call Antonio Morales and see if he's gone to bed yet.'

'Do it.'

'All right... Where do you want to go to?'

She shuffled. 'To my sister's house. In Torre Guadiaro.'

'A bit late to go visiting, isn't it?'

'None of your business Jacinto. Just phone Antonio and tell him to be quick.'

She sat down on one of the white plastic chairs and listened with half an ear as Jacinto made the call. She gritted her teeth. Who'd ever have thought she'd ever leave Castillo after all of these long years and like this! Like a thief in the night! But she'd made up her mind. She was going and that was that. Her sister's boy could come back in the morning and collect the rest of her things in that old van of his and then she would sell the house in Calle Loba and split the profit, if there was any, with Evangelica. Her sister wouldn't worry about giving her a room in her big house if she sniffed money in it. Either way Immaculada was done with Castillo. She was going and wasn't coming back. Really, she should have left months ago, but she was old and set in her ways and why should she leave? This was her home, wasn't it? Well it might have been, but not any more. Not after this last week.

It had started with Miriam's death – there was no loss there for the woman had been an evil bitch – but the manner of her passing had been shocking. Nobody was saying anything, of course, but Immaculada's instincts born of seventeen generations of gypsy breeding, told her that Miriam Cortez had died from no purely natural cause. There was dark magic abroad in Castillo – always had been and always would be. It was that kind of place.

And then The English had come knocking on her door. She had been afraid but he had been very powerful and she'd allowed him into her parlour. Wanted his palm read, or so he said, and because she'd wanted the money, she'd read it and never had she seen a hand that held so much death and pain and violence. But he'd known that anyway... And although it had taken her a while to realise, while she had been reading him *he* had been reading *her*. When it was all over she'd felt even more afraid and confused.

'Go to your sister's,' he'd told her.

'How do you know I have a sister?' she'd replied querulously.

'You have a sister in Torre Guadiaro,' he'd replied wearily. 'You don't like each other much but she has a house that is too big now that her husband is dead and the children have gone. You need some company and she will use your money fairly for the good of you both. In any case things will become very bad here in Castillo. It will be dangerous if you stay... I come today as a friend. To warn you.'

Two psychic minds had met across her small table and then she'd known real fear. 'You killed Cortez!'

'No. But I wished her ill and turned her curse.'

Immaculada had paused for a second receiving the aura he'd allowed her to absorb. She'd begun to tremble. 'The Other One is coming back, isn't he?'

'Yes, and I shall be here to meet him when he returns.'

'I think he is stronger than you,' she'd said slyly. 'You won't win.'

'All the better for you to be with your sister if I lose,' he'd retorted mildly.

He'd gone then but she'd played the conversation over and over again in her mind, mindful of all things thought and unsaid as well as words actually spoken.

Even then she might have stayed were it not for the lights up at the castle. She'd seen them first on the Tuesday, looking out of her bedroom window late at night, watching them dance along the battlements and the arches of the Moorish ruin. Small orbs, sometimes blue, sometimes pale green, occasionally a purpley mauve colour... Never still for a second and so thin and frail that you couldn't be sure you were seeing them at all. But they were there. She knew they were there, and she knew there was something dark and unholy behind them that glowered sentiently down upon the sleeping village. A Satanic mass of something evil that hid behind the rocks and bushes, flirting with the ruins, directing those little blue and green fireflies. She'd strained her old eyes and despite her fear had opened the window in hope of a better view. It had been a warm night but she'd been pierced by the lance of ice cold energy that had passed through her... She'd wanted to turn from her gaze but had found that she could not and she'd fought against her own rising panic as one by one the strange lights flickered out and the dark mass of something vaporous and intangible flowed over the battlements in swirling fog-like tendrils that snaked like wisps of smoke directly towards her window.

Breaking the fugue, she'd slammed the window shut, bolted it and had drawn both the shutters and the curtains, leaning against the wall with an ache in her heart, that heart in her mouth, waiting for something – may the saints preserve her from whatever it was – to come and get her and carry her back to whatever crypt it had crawled from.

Nothing had happened. No ghost had rattled its chains at her door. No phantom sought to suck her soul through the hole in the roof where the rain leaked in during the winter. Fully half an hour had passed before her heart beat had returned to anything near normal but then she'd been alerted by another very earthly kerfuffle that emanated from outside her home, a snuffling sound and a squealing. She'd peeped through the shutters and had seen small shapes scurrying all over the steep hillside that led up to the battlements. At first she'd had to strive to interpret what she was seeing, but eventually it had dawned on her.

'Alvaro's pigs,' she'd muttered to herself, thinking of the sties that Alvaro Alvarez carefully maintained at the bottom of the hill between the end of the castle and the cemetery. 'Must've got out somehow...' Then she'd cackled at the thought of Old Alvaro's face when he realised what had happened. 'All hell to pay in the morning!'

That had been on the Tuesday night and sure enough, on the Wednesday morning they'd been a wonderful show with Alvaro and his fat wife and his two dim witted sons running all over the place, gathering as best they could their scattered herd.

Wednesday night had passed without incident, but not tonight, not this Thursday night. Oh dear me no, you couldn't say that this night had passed without incident. The lights had been back, brighter and more agitated than before and the cloud of swirling blackness that was like smoke but wasn't smoke, was much more aggressive in its billowing and eddying, trailing over the battlements and spiralling its way down the hill towards the village, actually touching some of the houses at the northern end of the street with wispy tendrils and massing with menace above the cemetery and Alvaro's pig sties. Even now she could close her eyes and still hear the pigs squealing in her head. Not a happy sound and one that had been filled with fear and distress.

But the thing that had finally made her pack her suitcase and had sent her marching from her house had been the ghost of her old enemy, Miriam Cortez. It had stood there, half way down the hill, marble white and eerily illuminated by those strange little balls of luminescence, the black mists swirling around its feet and ankles like an angry tide. Miriam had raised a hand, finger pointing directly at where Immaculada stood transfixed in her window, so paralysed with fear she didn't even have the strength to pull the curtains across and shut out the horrific scene of pure malevolence.

You're next and apparition had whispered coldly inside her head. *I'm coming for you and you're next.*

On no I'm not, Immaculada had thought. They might call me Mad Macu from Calle Loba but I'm not totally stupid. I'm leaving. Right now! And ten minutes later she'd been trudging down the main street, suitcase scraping against the silent road.

'Antonio's on his way,' Jacinto called cheerfully and emerged from the bar with a small glass of fino which she gratefully downed in one swift swallow.

'You should leave too,' she said shortly.

'Leave?' Jacinto echoed. 'Why should I leave? I live here! Where should I go?'

'There's going to be trouble,' Immaculada warned.

'Trouble? What kind of trouble?'

'You'll know it when it comes,' she said darkly.

When, a few minutes later, Antonio's old diesel car chugged to a half outside the bar and Antonio put her suitcase in the boot while Jacinto helped her into the back of the cab, she leaned out of the open door and grabbed the bar owner by the arm.

'Thank you for the drink and thank you for your kindness. Just remember there is going to be trouble here. When it comes The English will help!'

'The extranjeros? How will they help and what is this trouble you keep speaking of? Macu, I'm sorry, but you're not making any sense.'

'No not the extranjeros,' Immaculada sighed in exasperation. 'The English...'

The taxi pulled away leaving Jacinto scratching his head in perplexity. Nutty old fruit cake, he thought. These old folk were all the same. Then he dismissed the incident from his mind and went about the business of closing down his bar.

He wiped a handful of glasses and gave the aluminium counter a cursory going over, then stacked the chairs on top of the tables leaving the detritus of litter for his wife to sort out in the morning. He was in the process of putting up the shutters when, to his surprise, a car pulled up outside and he heard the bar door being rattled.

'Go away,' he shouted. 'I'm closed.'

'It's me, Antonio... Jacinto, open the door. Please. Something's happened.'

Jacinto opened the door to find a pale faced Antonio Morales hopping on one foot and wringing his hands. The car stood a few feet away but of Old Macu there was no sign.

'What's up?' he asked. 'Where's the old woman?'

'She's in the back.' Antonio said hesitantly. 'I think she's dead.'

'She can't be dead,' Jacinto said blankly. 'She was alive and well and as bright as a button polishing off my fino like a good one, not ten minutes ago.'

'Yes, well I think she's dead now,' Antonio retorted stubbornly. 'We were driving out of Estacion and about a hundred metres before we got to the cork oaks, she just gave this little gaspy sort of moan and keeled over. I pulled the car over to the side of the road and had a look and she's not breathing and I think she's dead.'

'Let's have a look,' Jacinto said pulling the car door open. 'She's probably just got some indigestion or she's fallen asleep. At worst she's probably just fainted.'

But when Jacinto leaned into the back of the taxi, saw her pallor, listened for a non existent heartbeat and looked for an absent pulse, it was clearly apparent that Antonio was right and that Immaculada Morro also known as Mad Macu from Calle Loba was indeed a very dead old lady.

Oh shit, thought Jacinto. Now what am I supposed to do?

They had danced two bright passa dobles in a row and then a brisk Spanish waltz. Moving fluidly together, Mage had kept the steps unambiguously simple and Anna had been happy to follow where he'd led. Neither of them were well educated dancers, but both had a sense of rhythm and both were light on their feet... They'd laughed in each others arms as they'd whirled around the floor but both were silently pleased and relieved when the band launched into a selection of slower numbers, latinesque rumbas and tango style rock ballads, which gave them chance to catch their breath and move more closely together. They were not exactly smooching but it was near enough the next best thing to make no difference. Mage's arms circled Anna's waist and she hung on with both hands clasped around the back of his neck. There was nothing overtly sexual in their behaviour, but they were both very aware of each other's physical presence.

He could feel her breasts pressing lightly against his chest, her thighs brushing against the material of his brown cotton chinos. The thin silk of her blouse teased his fingers and every time they made accidental contact with the strap of her bra, a small electric shock thrilled through his mind, causing a feeling of butterflies in the pit of his stomach and stimulating the long dormant energies of the kundalini.

For her part, Anna was on an all time high. The warm night, the wine, the wonderful feeling of just being alive, all combined to dim the worry concerning her failing vision. For the first time in many months her fear of the future was overshadowed by the pleasure of the present. Whatever his feelings or motives, she was eternally grateful to this curious Englishman for reminding her that whatever the prognosis was concerning her eyes, she still had a life... and also a body.

She was just as aware of Mage as he was of her, equally conscious of each finger of his hand as it made contact with her back... Aware also of the hardness of her nipples and the ache of excitement that twisted and turned in her tummy. She may have been a virgin but she was mature enough to recognise the deep fire of desire when she felt it. Unconsciously she pressed a little closer to him, feeling incredibly safe and content within his embrace, wondering for a moment how she might feel if he were to hold her like this in some other place, away from the music, away from the brightly coloured lights, away from the security of a thousand laughing people? She hung on to him, aware of his musky scent that reminded her of spices and old oak casks, and was both tantalised and terrified by the thought...

From the opaque corner of her eye, she recognised the shape and features of Pedro Martinez as he danced by with Marie Hesther Alarcon – was aware of him watching her and could not prevent the small smirk of satisfaction from creeping across her face. Let him look! Let him wonder! Let him regret his hasty retreat.

It was difficult for Anna not to draw comparisons between Pedro of San Pablo and Colin Mage. Mage treated her as a friend, as a mature adult. He talked to her as an equal, was polite, and in all ways a gentleman... None of which could be said for Pedro.

And yet, and here she had to be honest with herself, she'd liked Pedro well enough at the time. He'd been good looking and fun to be with. There had always been a party or a barbecue to go to, and the fact that he'd had a car had opened up the scope of their social lives with trips to discotheques on the Costa de Sol and frequent outings to places like Seville and Jerez and Malaga.

But the car had also caused problems, for Pedro had seen its back seat as a bed on wheels and he'd for ever tried to get Anna into that position of commitment... She'd enjoyed some of his kisses but for the better part had not welcomed his clumsy fumblings up her skirt and inside her blouse – rejecting outright his insistence of any further intimacy. She remembered, with hot flushes of shame and distaste, the times when she'd been pressed into providing him with a degree of physical relief – that much she had done, full well knowing that if her hand did not provide it then another's would. She'd accepted this as the social norm of her time and place, but this didn't mean that she'd had to like it. In fact, if the truth be known, she'd positively hated it, but had put up with the situation full well knowing that she'd soon be part of Pedro's history should she decline.

She doubted that her friendship with him would have gone on for much longer anyway, but he'd nominally been her boyfriend, or at least the closest she'd ever come to having a proper boyfriend, and when she'd got ill with the headaches and the blurring vision and she'd told him what she herself had been told, their relationship had ended within the month. She despised herself for getting ill, but despised Pedro even more for his reaction. Rather than being her friend, he'd turned and run. Maybe it would have been naive to expect anything else, but even so, it still hurt.

Well, Pedro was a thing of the past and here she was now, dancing with her Englishman, and she knew who had got the best part of the deal! She silently wished Pedro luck with Marie Hesther – and unless Marie Hesther had changed religions since she'd last spoken to her, Pedro would need it. Marie Hesther Alarcon was about as Catholic as they came and if Pedro thought he was going to get inside her knickers, well, he might, but he'd have to put a ring on her finger first.

Even if the good looking boy, and let's face it, she thought, that's all he was and probably was all he ever would be – even if he'd offered her a ring, she might have been flattered but she'd still have declined. The ring would have been worthless if its sole purpose was a passport to sex. Better if good sex with the right person led to the giving of the ring! This might not have been a Spanish attitude, but she'd spent too many of her early years out of Spain for the restrictive philosophies of the Catholic church to totally corrupt her common sense. Also having Hector for a father helped enormously.

She wondered how she might react – and it was an alarming thought – if she ever found herself in that situation with Colin? She forced the thought away. Colin was an exciting new friend and it would be wrong to see him at this stage as anything other than that.

At this stage...

That was the tantalising thought that would not be stilled. Was there to be a next stage? And if so, what form might it take?

Enough, she told herself firmly. Enough of these silly notions and romantic daydreams! Let me enjoy the magic of this moment, the happiness of this one night. Let me walk before I can run and before anything else happens between us...

What? When?

... let us see how he reacts when I tell him what I told Pedro last autumn! Yes, let me tell him about my eyes and see how he reacts to that!

They danced for another few minutes but when the music became more aggressively upbeat by tacit agreement they left the floor and, forcing a passage through the milling crowds, found sanctuary at a small bar table, sheltered beneath an orange tree and a candy striped awning. The table was already taken but the man whose space they were invading stood and made them welcome, deferring to Mage and calling him Jefe... That loose Spanish term that could mean anything from Boss to Sir or even Master, depending upon how it was used.

Anna squinted as she sat down and recognised the sprightly frame of Pepe Ortega. Now here was a curiosity. Pepe was one of Castillo's most senior and highly respected citizens, a wealthy man, and one not noted for his generosity, either of pocket or spirit. Indeed, his reputation for irascibility and haughty disdain preceded him, as did his contemptuous loathing and profound dislike of extranjeros. Pepe Ortega's xenophobia was legend and yet here he was, greeting a much younger man, and a foreigner at that, with a notable degree of pleasure and respect, making a great show of calling the waiter over and ordering drinks. Yes, Anna thought, this was very odd behaviour indeed and something that added another chapter of mystery to the enigmatic book of the man she'd just been dancing with.

'How are you, Señor Ortega?' she asked politely.

'Oh, I'm *very* well, thank you Anna. I'm very well indeed...' The old man spoke to Anna, but his eyes looked past her towards Mage and it was almost as though he was talking to Colin rather than to her. She sensed that there was something here that she was missing, something passing between these two men that she was not privy to. '... and may I say,' Ortega beamed at her, 'how good it is to see you here, out and about and enjoying yourself!'

'I would not have come had Colin not invited me,' she admitted, and then, turning to Mage, 'and thank you so much for asking me, Colin. It has been a splendid evening.'

'And not over yet!' Pepe Ortega chuckled. 'The night is yet young! Have you seen your father, by the way? He's around here somewhere.'

'He's here now.' A familiar voice boomed behind them and Hector Sanchez lowered his frame into the one remaining free chair, precariously balancing a full glass of San Miguel on the edge of the rickety table. He leaned over and shook Colin's hand, kissing Anna affectionately on the top of her head as he did so. 'This Englishman, he has fed you well and made you dance?'

'Yes Papa, he has fed me very well and I have made him demonstrate his English version of our passa doble. He acquits himself very well...'

The waiter arrived with a coke for Mage and a tinto verano for Anna, and a few seconds later three other people pulled chairs up around their table, namely Henry Holloway and his wife Vivienne and a tall lanky man with brown hair and a wispy moustache. He was in his early thirties and wore huge horn rimmed glasses over a broken beak of a nose. Henry introduced him as Hamish Hamilton, Castillo's unofficial historian and amateur archaeologist.

'Henry tells me you're very interested in our castle,' he said in a thick Scottish highland brogue. 'Anything you need to know I'll be pleased to help as much as I can...'

'Thanks,' Mage shook his hand, eager to talk to him but not wanting his attention distracted from Anna... And yet Anna was in cheerful conversation with her father and perhaps it was enough that she sat close to him, her knee touching his own beneath the table. It seemed that this lightest of contacts contained a message – *we are with others now and our privacy is compromised. Don't worry. We are still here together and we can afford to spend a little time socialising and sharing conversations. Nothing is lost. Soon we will be on our own again and nothing will have changed...*

To test this theory, Mage allowed his left hand to fall between their two chairs, his fingers gently caressing Anna's right hand. Their fingers touched but lightly and yet the contact, once made, was willingly maintained. Whether he held her hand or she held his was both debatable and immaterial. Neither pulled away from this most innocent of physical links and Mage was more than happy to accept this as confirmation of his prime thought. They had been together and were still together despite the proximity of a father and a gathering of friends. She was telling Hector of the dinner they had enjoyed at Venta Cristobal and her face was alive with animation... A beautiful face with a perfect profile. Mage realised that he was staring and turned his attention back towards the archaeologist.

Hamilton was one of those men who bubbled with youthful enthusiasm, his natural energy making it difficult for him to be still or silent. He used his hands in wide expressive gestures and his eyes were constantly moving, monitoring all that went on around him.

'So what can you tell me?' Mage asked.

'Potted history, right?'

'Fine.'

'Okay, well we've got excellent Paleolithic remains more than twenty five thousand years old... Some marvellous cave paintings if you go a little way up the Hozgarganta. It's a track, but well worth it if you're interested...'

Mage remembered his first day up at the castle. Somehow he'd known that there would have to be caves.

'Indications suggest an Iberian encampment circa 1000 BC through till around 100 AD... Then the Romans arrived and they built extensive fortifications all over the place. Dug up some marvellous stuff when I first arrived here a few years ago. Lamps, buckles, sword hilts, clay jars... You name it, I found it. Anyway, Rome started spiralling into its Grand Decline around 300 AD with the invasion of the Vandals and for a while our castle gets lost in the murky depths of the dark ages.

'The Moors started filtering over from North Africa as early as the beginning of the eighth century, 710 AD to be precise, and by the end of the 11th century they held pretty much the whole of Spain in a pretty tight vise. Round about then, the Christians, under the banner of King Ferdinand The Third, started kicking their arses in a fairly serious way. Ali Omar Ben Yusef landed from Morocco in 1236 with a heavy contingent of Moorish reinforcements, but Ferdinand clobbered him at Valencia in 1239, along with a little help from his pal, one Rodrigo de Bivarre – and to you and me, that's El Cid, by the way. When Granada finally fell to the Christians it was all over bar the shouting.

'Bringing this back to our own little castle, the Moorish citadel dates back to circa 800 to 850 or there abouts and the Christian keep and castle to around 1495 to 1505. There aren't many written records so what I'm giving you, I'm giving you piecemeal from the bits that I've read and researched and the bits and pieces I've dug up. If you're looking at the castle's more modern history, well this is where I lose interest, but there isn't really all that much anyway. It would have been used as a garrison by regular Spanish forces against smugglers, bandits and any other incursors and it came in useful as a bomb factory during the peninsular wars. There was a bit of a battle in 1806 when British dragoons and sappers attacked from Gibraltar and effectively sacked the place. It's been allowed to crumble into ruins ever since, which is a shame. Should be cleaned up and designated as a national monument... Christ knows I've written to Madrid about it enough times, but like everything else it all comes down to money. It if was on one of the costas and could be utilised as a tourist attraction I dare say that would be rather different, but everything in government these days revolves around the euro.

'Anyway, I don't know if any of this helps... I mean, what are you looking for? What's your precise area of interest?'

'None, really,' Mage said thoughtfully, 'except that it's an unusual old ruin, especially with the juxtaposition of the two cultures...'

'Och no, you'll find that all over southern Spain if you know what to look for...'

'But there's one thing that does puzzle me a bit,' Mage continued. ' – and that's the location of the Moorish citadel. I mean, if the Moors were there first, why didn't they build their citadel on the highest point of the mountain? Looking at the cliff, and especially from the far side, it's obvious that the Christian keep is built on the higher ground...'

'Very observant of you! I had a party of students from Malaga doing a dig four years ago and none of them caught on. You got any idea?'

'None at all, I'm afraid.'

'Water!' Hamilton exclaimed triumphantly. 'That's the answer. The Moors would certainly have had a watch tower where the keep is now, but they built their principle fortifications over the well. If you've got billions of gallons of H2O in your basement, it throws a whole new light on siege mentality, doesn't it?'

'There's a well up there?' Mage asked, not bothering to conceal his surprise.

'Sure is,' Hamilton confirmed. 'Goes right the way down into the core of the mountain. Fed from the river, of course. The whole bloody hill is volcanic in origin and what you've got here is a perfect fumer hole straight the way down through the bedrock.'

'It must be incredibly deep,' Mage mused out loud, beginning to think of other things.

'About six hundred feet,' Hamilton agreed. 'At least, it's six hundred feet down to the water level of the river, but when the river is in winter flood, the well level rises about five hundred feet under pressure. Even so,' he grinned expansively, 'they'd have needed a bloody long bit of rope for their bucket, wouldn't they?'

Mage gave a half smile in response. 'You've actually been inside the citadel? You've measured the depth of the well?'

'Yes, like I said, we were doing a thorough root around in 1990 with a little bit of funding from the ayuntamiento and I don't mind telling you that the well came as a bit of a surprise. But anyway, we plumbed it, twice as a matter of fact. Once in September when the river was no more than a trickle and again in October after the first heavy rains of the season. I'd guess that the whole mountain is riddled with caves and reservoirs that would take a fair bit of the overspill, so even when the river went down again, the drain-off factor would be quite significant. You'd be sitting pretty with that amount of water under your arse.'

'When the Christians arrived, why didn't they employ the same tactics?' Mage wanted to know. 'Why not just pull down the citadel and build their keep over the well?'

'You've got me there,' Hamilton admitted. 'Would have been the logical thing to do, but for whatever reason, they didn't do it.'

Mage pondered what he'd been told and absently lit a cigarette. 'How do you actually get into the citadel?' he asked. 'I've walked around the place a dozen times and there are no obvious means of access.'

'What you've got to remember is that an awful lot of muck and debris has gathered around the place over the years. What you're actually seeing is only the top two floors. The ground floor and the cellar with the well is buried under five hundred years of accumulated crap. We found the main entrance but had to dig fifteen feet down to get in and, after the excavation, the town hall insisted it be all filled in again... And I can see their point. Without an awful lot of work it would have been one helluva safety hazard. Any wee kiddie could go wandering in and break his neck of fall through the hole in the floor in next to no time. I dare say there might be other ways in... If you were a good climber and had a head for heights, you could try the roof, but make sure our local coppers don't see you. You'd have to force entry, because from what I can remember, that roof is pretty solid. With a bit of luck, you might find one of the tunnels, but here I'm only speculating...'

'Tunnels,' Mage echoed. 'Tell me about the tunnels.'

'As I say, I'm only speculating. I don't actually know of any tunnels, but I do know my Moors. They were great diggers. Marvellous engineers. Natural tunnelers. Most of their serious fortresses, and make no mistake Castillo would have most definitely fallen into that category, would have had two or three secret exits and entrances. Christ, they'd have had to have some way off that mountain. Water may have been no problem, but you've got to remember a man's still got to eat... And it's interesting to remember when they tried to get some modern plumbing into Castillo, and we're only talking about the 1920s for crying out loud, they found that the whole village was riddled with tunnels. Made their job mega easy. But if you're going to be around here for any length of time by far the easiest way would be to go up and ask Alfonso at the ayuntamiento for an excavation permit and dig your way down to the door. It'd only take a couple of days' hard labour, and less if you had a team of diggers.

'I mean, are you planning to be around for any length of time or are you just passing through?'

There was the most imperceptible pressure as Anna's fingers tightened around his own. She'd obviously heard the question. Her eyes might have been a problem but there was certainly nothing wrong with her ears.

'No,' Mage said. 'I'm not just passing through. I'll be here for quite a while.'

The pressure round his fingers eased and Hamish Hamilton smiled brightly. 'That's great! In which case, Alfonso's your man and if you need any help from me just give me a shout.'

While Colin Mage sat digesting what he'd just been told, while Jacinto and Antonio wondered what they ought to do with Immaculada's corpse and while Angel and Christina lay semi naked in their hay rick counting the stars, Jaime Gomez was parking his patrol car at the top end of Calle Misericordia. The street did a sharp uphill S bend then flattened out into what served as a car park for those who were too lazy to walk up to the castle.

Well, this was as far as they got! Jaime was resigned to walking up the rest of the way, but walk there he would. He had little choice, really... Stupid old Alvarez had phoned to say his pigs were having hysterics and there was something up at the castle that was frightening them, but this was not the only reason for his nocturnal sortie. He, like Immaculada Morro, had seen those same subtle reflections of light that danced elusively along the battlements. Unlike Immaculada, he'd come up with a highly temporal theory of explanation.

Kids doing drugs, he thought. Someone stepping into Lorenzo Bautista's shoes already. Probably one of the brothers.

Taking the heavy torch from the back seat, he slammed the car door shut and surveyed his surroundings. Beneath him the village fell away down the side of the hill towards the valley, looking quiet, serene almost, but at the same time mysteriously without form or dimension, lit only by the intermittent street lights. A shadowy place, full of mewling cats, barking dogs and a million secrets. A car's headlights cut a swathe along the Ronda road and there was a distant thump of disco music from the apology of a night-club down behind Cuenca's bar. They wouldn't be doing much business tonight, he thought. Everyone who could walk or who had wheels was drinking the cheaper drink over in San Pablo.

He turned and looked up at the castle, dark and towering above him. No lights now, just an amalgam of brooding stone. There was no moon and the stars did little to illuminate the ruin. A steep cobbled path cut up from the car park, curving first to the right, then turning back on itself to the left, where it disappeared beneath the Moorish arch. Over to the left, the circular keep jutted upwards, while over to the right the Moorish citadel seemed to squat, half hidden by the battlements. He thought about using the torch, then dismissed the idea. No point in giving whoever was up there advance warning of his presence. Pushing his peaked hat a little further back on his head, he started up the cobbled path, going slowly and making efforts not to make too much noise.

By the time he passed through the Moorish arch, he'd climbed three hundred feet. The night was warm and even though he was wearing his lightweight summer uniform, he found himself sweating profusely. With the arch at the back, he paused to mop his brown and to gather his bearings. Here the cobbles petered out, giving way to scrub and hard packed earth, but there were still two definable pathways. One curved over to the right leading towards, and subsequently around, the citadel. He knew that if he walked beyond the citadel he'd come to the northern rampart that would give him a fine view down over the cemetery and Alvaro's pig pens. The pathway to the left was an uphill trudge to the Christian ruins and it was here that he focused his attention. There were many nooks and crannies and quiet corners that could easily conceal a conclave of druggies, and it was the most logical place to hold a clandestine meeting. The area around the square citadel was far too open and offered no cover at all. He forced his eyes to pierce the gloom around the base of the distant keep, but there was nothing to see but layer upon layer of thick shadow. He stilled his breathing and tuned his ears to pick up any nuance of sound, and yet there was nothing... Not even a sighing whisper of night breeze, no high pitched thrill of cicada, not even the faintest buzz of airborne insect. The oddity and unnaturalness of the silence did not register on Jaime's consciousness. At least, it didn't right then. It would do so a little later, but for the time being he was so engrossed in the business of being a policeman that anything that distracted him from his mission was dismissed to the back of his mind.

Jaime moved off in the direction of the keep, staying close to the eastern wall and taking great care to be quiet. As far as he was concerned, he had all the time in the world.

A good half hour later he'd carefully covered all the ground around the ruins of the Christian castle, even risking occasional flashes of his torch, and still had come up with nothing. There wasn't even a courting couple, not so much as a single whiff of hashish and no sign that anything untoward was amiss. Feeling cheated and disgruntled he leaned with his back against the stump of an old olive tree and smoked a Ducados, allowing his attention to wander across the stretch of earth towards the Moorish citadel. There didn't appear to be anything there either, but having come this far he thought he might as well wander over and have a look anyway. It was only a small detour from the cobbled way that led down to the car park.

He still exercised a degree of caution, for while, in his opinion at least, a drugs transaction was more likely to have taken place in the Christian part of the ruin, he was also mindful of Alvaro's complaint. Something was disturbing his pigs, he'd said, and as the crow flew, the pig pens were not two hundred metres from the citadel. Jaime Gomez thought that Alvaro Alvarez was three pesetas short of a duro, but it wouldn't hurt to take a look anyway.

It was only as he approached the citadel that he became aware of the soundlessness of the night – oh, to be sure, there were noises drifting up from the village; the distant disco beat from Cuenca's, a car door slamming, the shriek of female laughter – but they came from another world. Up here, the night was still and silent and in some unfathomable way, sentient with watchfulness.

His pace slowed as the pale stone and marble edifice rose above him and, feeling unaccountably nervous, he moved the torch to his left hand, unbuckling the holster stud with the fingers of his right. The smooth butt of the nine millimetre Beretta was reassuring to his touch.

He circumnavigated the citadel twice before he began to relax and even then it was only a marginal thing. He *knew* he was alone and yet at the same time he also knew that he was being watched. If anyone had asked him by whom or what, he'd have been at a loss to answer. It was painfully obvious that he was the only living soul moving around the crest of Castillo's craggy hill that night and yet he was jittery and very much ill at ease.

Leaning over the parapet he played the powerful beam of the torch over the cemetery and the pig pens. Nothing moved. Nothing stirred and whatever had upset Alvaro's swine, well, it wasn't doing so now. Turning, he ran the torch beam along the northern face of the citadel. The light bounced back off the pale wall and disappeared into the dark impenetrable cuts of the arrow slits. Was there someone up there, observing him and laughing at him behind his back? It was impossible, of course, for there was no way into the interior of the citadel – but that's what it felt like all the same.

Jaime stepped off the narrow foot ledge of the parapet and stood on something soft and pliant that squelched beneath his boot. It completely threw his balance and he went sprawling headlong in the dust. He jarred his elbow and bit his tongue. His hat went flying as he grazed his head on a sharp stone. Dazed and furious at the indignity, he swung the torch over and looked down the length of his body to see what he'd tripped on.

His heart skipped three beats in a row and he recoiled in revulsion at the sight.

Nominally, he was looking at what he assumed had once been one of Alvaro's pigs. At least, it might have been one of Alvaro's pigs a few days ago, but it certainly wasn't any more. Something grotesque and inexplicable had happened to it that made him want to vomit.

Feeling the blood trickle down his forehead he wiped it away with the back of his hand, swinging around on his haunches and rising to his knees so that he could get a better look... The beast was obviously dead, but that was only the half of it. Its body was covered in a silvery membrane, beneath which there appeared to be tiny scales... Furthermore, the dead animal's body was curiously twisted and elongated, as though something had tried to stretch it and pull it apart. It was twice its natural length and shoved up against the right angle of the parapet ledge, there was little wonder that Jaime hadn't seen it until he'd actually stepped on the thing.

Something had happened to its face... For that, like the body, was also twisted and distended. The mouth was wide open, its tongue lolling, almost buried in the hard sand. Its eyes were open, glazed opaque and amber in death.

What in the name of Jesus happened to it? Jaime wondered. What killed it? What's all this scaley silvery stuff?

He shuffled a few inches closer, looking for some obvious wound that might be designated as the cause of death: it was difficult to see for the pig was buried up to its belly in the hard earth – and that in itself was a curiosity. How in the name of all the saints had that happened? And there was something else, Jaime realised. There wasn't any smell. No stench of dried blood or rotting flesh... There were no flies buzzing around either... which made him wonder just how long ago this had happened.

Groggily he came to his feet and stood there for a minute letting his head clear before striding over to retrieve his hat. He beat the dust off his tunic and stood staring down at the dead thing at his feet. Christ, Alvaro was going to have forty fits when he found out... But then fuck Alvaro. This wasn't his business any more. The health and safety people from Algerciras would want to have a look at this and, when they did, maybe old Alvaro would find that he had a few awkward questions to answer. No animal ended up like this through natural causes. Someone had *done* something to it and as Alvaro was the only pigman in Castillo... Well, that's where the first line of questioning should start anyway.

There was nothing more he could do up here, he decided, and turned to go. Something vague caught his eye over to the right of the citadel and he swung the torch over in that direction. At first he couldn't make out what was wrong, but then came to realise that the torch beam wasn't doing anything. An area of darkness between the citadel wall and the western parapet simply seemed to swallow up the light. If he played the beam on the wall of the parapet, or the wall of the citadel, or indeed on the earth in front of him, then its light shone brightly enough. But when he lifted the torch to light his way back along the path, it petered into nothing. It was as though a great black absorbent blanket had been dropped in his way.

He took a couple of cautious steps towards the phenomena... He thought of it as a cloud but it was unlike any cloud he'd ever seen before... but nothing gave clue or indication to what it was or what was causing it. It was simply a black hole or nothingness that sat between citadel and battlement... The torch beam *should* have illuminated the dirt path along to the cobble way. It should have illuminated the western wall of the citadel and the eastern face of the parapet. It should have illuminated the Moorish arch some hundred metres to the north – and yet it did none of these things.

Jaime was not a superstitious man and nor was he prone to letting his imagination get the better of his common sense. While a lesser man might have retreated in the face of this phenomena, Jaime Gomez edged forwards, determined to penetrate the mystery.

When he thought about it afterwards, he had no real recollection of taking that last step that suddenly plunged him into the darkness. One second he was in the warmth of the Spanish night, and in the next he was lost in the vortex of total sensory deprivation. There was no sight, no sound and no feeling other than within the temple of his own being. He felt his hand withdraw the gun from its holster, yet even when he brought it up to his chin, could not see so much as his arm. He blinked his eyes furiously, knowing only that his eyes were shut by virtue of the lightening of the abstract image caused by the retinal pressure.

He half turned, half stepped backwards, but now the darkness was all around and he no longer knew which way was backwards or forwards. He opened his mouth to breathe but the darkness was without air and he gagged before stumbling over to the left – at least he thought it was his left – and collapsing to his knees. Again he fought for oxygen and again there was none forthcoming. In a rising wave of panic he began scrabbling about on all fours before he started falling into the chasm of choking unconsciousness.

...From a point in space somewhere above his sprawled body, he looked down in a calm and detached manner upon his crumpled form. Now there was no need to breathe and in a curiously disseminated way he was comfortable within his own presence. Now he saw shapes of light and shade within the darkness and although he could discern no specific form or feature, he was nonetheless aware of a deep sense of threat and menace... Of alien wrongness about this whole performance of impossibility.

His discarnate identity willed his unconscious body to move but it remained motionless. Aware that a body could not live if a body couldn't breathe and mindful of what had caused the body's initial collapse, he found himself screaming at his own corpse, becoming increasingly fearful and distressed. Then, to his mental eye, it seemed that the ground around his body was beginning to ripple, and then not only ripple but crumble, and from the earth white worm like strands emerged, wrapping themselves around his wrists and ankles and – oh God forbid – they were trying to pull him down beneath the soil. Now he suddenly knew why Alvaro's pig had been so stretched, its belly so deeply embedded in the ground.

Even without the physical restraints of his body, Jaime's mind screamed in protest. He cast around for some means of escape but within the stygian folds of blackness no escape route beckoned. Indeed the darkness pressed ever inwards upon his spirit and he became more aware than ever of the malevolent entities that writhed without form within the envelope of his plight. He could not see them and yet he knew they were there – could feel their presence as they rubbed and brushed against him.

He looked down and realised that his body was becoming smaller and dimmer... There was no sensation of lifting but he knew he must be rising. Now he looked upwards, and there, thank Christ, there was a smudge of something. A diaphanous shade of blue. He struggled towards it, knowing that if he could but reach it, he would be safe and free.

Then he was aware of hurtling upwards and he burst into the light, a pale blue incandescent coruna that covered The Virgin's head like a halo and flowed over his being like a waterfall.

This is it, he thought. I must be dead.

The Virgin smiled. *Not yet, for you have much work to do before your time is come. Now, breathe – and live!*

And Jaime breathed a gasping ragged breath and was rolling on his back staring up at the velvet sky, pinpointed with a billion burst of starlight. He spat out the soil that had filtered into his mouth and breathed again, drawing lungfulls of air into his hammering chest.

Wondering what the hell had happened, he slowly dragged himself up into a sitting position, feeling an itchy pain around both wrists and ankles and looking around cautiously for the cause of his nemesis. The darkness, that black void of pure negation, was still there, hanging over the parapet of the north wall, obscuring it from sight. It also covered the place where he'd found the twisted pig and although there was nothing to be seen, he heard a distant scuffing. Something was going on over there. He didn't know what and he didn't care what. Alert to the fact that he was alive when he fully expected to be dead, and ever mindful of the breathless horror he'd experienced when the void had covered him, he crawled away in the direction of the cobbles and the Moorish arch, determined to put as much distance between himself and this place as he possibly could.

His mind groped for the questions that would bring him the answers he had to have, but for now it was sufficient to know that The Holy Virgin had saved him from death and possibly even from a fate worse than death. He did not ask why or what for. That would come later.

It was well after one before Mage and Anna left San Pablo. He drove slowly back towards Castillo not wanting the night to end. The Land Rover's engine purred reasuringly and he felt that if necessary he could go on driving 'till dawn. He mind was vitally alive although Anna was visibly tired now. She'd agreed readily enough that it was time to go home when he'd tentatively suggested it after a half hour long session on the dodgem cars.

And that, he grinned at the memory, had been fun! He and Anna had been in one car, Hector and Hamish in another, Henry and Vivienne Holloway in a third. They'd rumbled around the small arena laughing and jeering between bumps and shunts, with the steady thump of 1970s rock and roll music pounding in their ears. After a while a fourth car had joined in their private circus and Mage had seen Angel, one arm around Christina, the other waving in wild elation. It had been clear from the look of pure joy written across the boy's face that he had achieved the reality of the magician's visualisation.

He hoped that Angel enjoyed his happiness while it lasted, for unless Mage's assessment of Christina was very wrong, it might not last for very long.

After they'd run out of tokens for the dodgems they'd taken a table at a chiringuito bar, sitting in the open air with their backs to the convent wall.

'One last drink and back to Castillo?' Mage had asked.

Anna had nodded. 'Sadly I think that might be a wise idea. It has been a wonderful evening, but someone must be up in the morning to make sure my father is fit for his surgery. It will be a long session. Many sore heads looking for excuses to cheat a day off work and, by the look of it, Papa might be one of them himself.'

Hector laughed at something Hamish Hamilton had said and Mage had noted that while nowhere near drunk, the doctor was definitely in a merry mood... but then, why not? A merry mood prevailed throughout San Pablo that evening and certainly there was something of a party atmosphere around their table. Bottles and glasses clinked almost in time with the music from a wondering caballero band of musicians who played gypsy melodies on guitars and concertinas. Girls danced with their young man with swirls of gaily coloured silk and linen. The smell of roasting meat did succulent battle with the perfume of night stocks and blooming oleandser. The conversation was convivial and animated and as Mage had leaned with his back against ther warm stone wall, he'd felt deeply relaxed and very much a part of this small group of people. The horrors and the tensions of the previous months had suddenly seemed distant and remote, visions and memories of dark magic no more than an echo from his past. The demons of doubt and disharmony born of fear and rejection belonged to a different world and it was all too easy for him to forget his reasons for being here.

And yet, like a barb, another thought had struck him. Unless he was able to avert the opening, gatherings such as this might soon become a thing of the past. Hector's extra beer, Angel's carnal desires, the Garths' concern for the future of the Miraflores, Anna's precious eyes... Would all fade into inconsequence. If the Djinn broke through in Castillo this part of Spain would be the first region to fall beneath their yoke. What then might happen to people like Hector and Anna? He had scant knowledge to work on, only what he'd learned in Ireland and Israel and what he'd read in Blanc Villiers' grimoire.

- And thus, by most devious workings of the highest and blackest magicks on both sides of the great divide between mankind and its oldest enemy, shall the curtains between the two worlds be torn apart and with the tearing Djinn and Demon shall spew forth their presence and their venom to destroy and enslave the world of Man which is their greatest desire and ambition. They shall be unstopppable and will corrupt both the flesh and the spirit with their poisons -

Heavy reading but words well remembered. Initially it had been easy to dismiss them as fantasy, published to catch the eye of increasing interest in things occult and metaphysical by a generation of minds that rejected the absolute doctrines of church, state, science and solipsism. But the teaching of Herschall and Paul O'Connor had breathed life into the words making them all too possibly real, and when grimoire and teachings were confirmed by his own senses and experiences, it made him shudder with fear and revulsion. The fear was palpable and he fought it most of his waking moments on a subconscious if not always a conscious level. He knew his life was forfeit to his quest, as indeed it had been right from the beginning. It was disconcerting to feel the way he was feeling now and he'd disciplined himself to be mindful of his mission. New friends and Anna Sanchez in particular were a delightful diversion when he needed no distraction from his purpose and he would, he'd realised, have to be more on guard against this mood of complacency.

Even so – he dropped into third gear to take a sharp left hand bend – it had been a rewarding and satisfying evening that had served well to remind him what he was fighting for. It had also served him well in the sense that, wanted or not, it had been a joyful and lighthearted occasion that had made him feel a little more like a member of the human race rather than the constant outsider, always distant and set apart, ever looking inwards, ever looking in. The Land Rover contained a full tank of gas, the engine sounded sweet and the night was clear. Sleep would contaminate the memory of these last hours of freedom, so let sleep be denied. He would take Anna home then drive on somewhere until the tank ran dry or the dawn brought natural tiredness and the reality of the daylight. That way the illusion of this special night could be preserved a little longer.

Anna sat quietly in her corner of the cab and, like Mage, nor did she want this night to end. Certainly, she was tired, but it was a healthy tiredness and if necessary sleep could wait a while if it had to. She was glad to be out of the noise and bustle of San Pablo and to be free of the crowds of people and what she really wanted now was some quiet time where she and Colin could be alone – where they could sit and talk without fear of interruption and where, if it felt right and if she could find the courage, she could tell him about her eyes.

Her problem was in knowing how to bring this about. She could invite him in for coffee when they got back to Santana and although she knew this to be a breach of Spanish etiquette, she was confident that Colin would not take advantage of, or misinterpret the invitation. She was conscious of the fact that her father might not entirely approve, but was more worried about being interrupted at a crucial point. Within seconds Hector's presence would dominate. He would want to do all the talking and Anna out of habit and Colin out of politeness, would have to do the listening.

There were places she knew of where it would be possible to park the Land Rover, where they could sit and talk in private – but these were places she'd been to with Pedro and even if that wasn't a problem – which it was! – the question still remained... How to suggest such an idea without seeming to be excessively bold and forward? Either way she had to say something soon. One last bend and they would be running down the hill towards the turn off for Castillo. Once they'd turned off the Ronda road, it would be too late.

Taking a deep breath she turned to face him. 'Colin, I wish to show you something. When we go around the next corner there is a dirt track to the left hand that leads up through the trees to the top of the hill. If you take it, it is well worth the short detour...'

Mage was more than happy to oblige and a moment or so later they were four wheeling up a steep and bumpy incline with pine cones and eucalyptus leaves brushing at their side screens. At the top of the track the trees thinned out and there was a small parcel of land where it was possible to back up, turn and reverse. Here there was a dynamic side-on view of Castillo, stretching south to north upon its spiny ridge, less than a kilometre away in the near distance. To Anna it was just a blur of myriad lightpoints, to Mage it was quite spectacular.

He cut the engine and the silence of the hillside settled upon them like a welcome blanket. Pushing the side panel forwards he inhaled the warm night air, redolent with the scent of pine and soft fertile soil. In the circumstances it seemed sacrilegious to light a cigarette, but he lit one anyway, dangling his arm out of the window so that Anna would not be troubled by the smoke.

'It's a beautiful place,' he said. ' – and it's been a beautiful night. Thank you very much for coming with me.'

She didn't answer for a moment, doing silent battle with her inner feelings, balancing desire against upbringing and breeding. 'I have enjoyed it also... And there is something I wish to ask you, which is very difficult for me for no matter what words I use, it will probably sound wrong and you will think very badly of me.'

'I doubt it,' he replied. 'So just ask what you want and don't worry about how it sounds.'

Fear clutched at her stomach, for despite Colin's words, this was still far from easy. 'If we have both enjoyed tonight, do you... I mean, would you want me to go out with you again?'

Mage registered every word and realised that there was hidden motive behind her question. This was not just some shy Spanish girl being coquettish. It was a fair and direct question with a hundred peripheral connotations. The peripherals aside, it deserved a direct and honest answer.'

'Yes Anna, I would like that very much indeed.'

He felt her relax just a little but she was still wound up with tension and suspense. He felt her struggling, but on this occasion had to let her get there on her own. He had a fairly good idea of what was coming, however.

'I would also like to be with you,' she said slowly, feeling her cheeks flush crimson and glad of the darkness. 'But there is something you must know. Something I need to tell you... The view of Castillo is beautiful from up here, yes?'

'Yes it is.'

'...Colin, I know that it is beautiful because I remember it as being beautiful, but the truth is that I cannot really see it at all. It is just a blur of shapes. I have this problem with my eyesight. You must have wondered why I have to wear these horrible glasses all the time? Well, the reason is that for the last ten months or so I've been going blind. The doctors in Madrid say I might have another year before my eyesight fails completely – and I wanted to tell you this now rather than later. I would not wish there to be any misunderstandings between us. I mean, if... if... Oh please Colin, this is not easy for me to say, but if you came to find that you had feelings for me, then you have to know from the beginning what you are getting yourself into.'

There, she'd said it and she'd said it all, and more besides, leaving herself wide open to rejection and ridicule. She had, even if not in so many words, told him that he was important to her and although this went against the grain of her character and her culture, instinct and intuition told her that this was the way to proceed. Colin was an Englishman, not a Spaniard, and the rules that governed the Spanish rituals of courtship were null and void. She clasped her hands tightly together wondering what his reactions might be. Wondering what he must think of her for being so brazen.

'Come here,' he said, reaching his hand towards her. Nervously she slid along the bench seat. His arm went around her shoulders and he pulled her beneath his wing of protection. 'First of all, thank you for telling me what you have told me. Secondly I'd be happy to be with you whether your eyes were perfect or whether you were as blind as the proverbial bat. Thirdly, and right now most importantly, what makes you think you're going to lose your sight?'

He sat and listened as she told him about the dizzy spells and the headaches that had become her constant companions over the previous year. Of the routine eye test in Marbella that had detected the glaucoma and of the three trips to see the specialists in Madrid. She told him of the cat scan and the final diagnosis. She also found herself telling him about Pedro, but she made no mention of the brain tumour, which was hardly surprising in the circumstances. Mage remembered that Hector had not told her about it and therefore Anna had no knowledge of its existence.

Maybe Hector should have told her. It might have helped had she had something tangible to blame. Mage respected Hector's reasons for remaining silent. Blindness was one thing to deal with, but death was another.

He cradled her in his arms, holding her protectively and wondering what he should say. Realistically it should perhaps be *don't worry about a thing Anna because the chances are we'll all be dead by the end of June anyway* which would serve no purpose at all! Could he in good conscience tell her that she would *not* go blind? That he would prevent it from happening? What if he wasn't around the fulfil the promise, or what if he was and he tried and failed? That wouldn't help

Anna Sanchez one single jot. In fact, it would do her great harm.

'Listen,' he said carefully, 'maybe you've been told you're going to be blind but even the best of doctors can sometimes get it wrong and make mistakes.'

'Three doctors?' Anna countered. 'Three different doctors?'

'Yes,' Mage insisted firmly. 'Even three different doctors! But now let's assume that they haven't made a mistake. Let's assume that they can't put what's wrong right by surgery. There are still other ways in which you might be helped...'

He could not say more without saying more than he was able. Understandably Anna couldn't let it go at that. 'But how, Colin? I do not understand how!'

Mage floundered, looking for another angle of attack. In the end, he said: 'Let me ask you something Anna, and think about it before you answer. You don't know me very well and you know very little about me, but on the strength of what you do know – do you trust me?'

She did not need to think for very long. 'Yes, I trust you.'

'Then on that trust I want you to believe me when I say I think I can help you with your problem. I can't give any guarantees and it's important that you remember that. I don't want you seeing me as some kind of miracle man. I don't want you getting your hopes up only to be disappointed if I fail you. But if I am to help at all it means that you carry on trusting me for a little while longer, and that for the time being you say nothing to Hector about this, okay?'

'Yes... I understand what you are asking me, but Colin forgive me, I do not understand how you can help me when the doctors in Madrid and even my father can do nothing.'

Mage thought for a moment. 'You've spoken of your headaches,' he said easily. 'And yet, I don't think you were troubled earlier this evening at the Venta or in San Pablo, right?'

'Yes,' she said in a small voice, '...but...'

'But you have a very bad headache right now, haven't you?'

'Yes I have, but how can you know this?'

'Let's leave that for a while, shall we?' he suggested. 'And instead, let's see if we can get rid of that headache for you. Will you let me try? Will you help me?'

Anna, whose head was actually pounding, nodded in the dash board light. 'Yes, of course. What do you want me to do?'

Mage removed her glasses then brought her back into the crook of his arm. She shut her eyes when he told her to and felt the pressure of his finger tips as they pressed against her forehead. She breathed deeply as instructed and tried to see the pale blue colour he was asking her to visualise. At first his fingers felt warm, but then increasingly they became cool, then cold, then absolutely icy. With an odd tingling sensation the ice crept into her head and wrapped itself around the dull red epicentre of her pain. Very gradually, almost imperceptibly the headache began to diminish. First it became a cavern of tenderness and tension and then even that sensation died and she was left with a with a feeling of coolness gently weaving its way through her head like a clear mountain stream bringing refreshment to parched earth on a hot day. In the space on a few minutes her head became clear, free of pain and discomfort.

'How?' she whispered, totally bewildered.

'Hush. Don't ask.'

'But...?'

'Hush,' he increased the pressure of his arm, bringing her head down onto his chest. 'Hush... and I will tell you things that are my secrets and then they will be your secrets too and you are bound to their keeping...'

Anna felt silent, aware of their hearts beating in steady unison. She listened to his words, but did not understand them all – which was his intention – but understanding enough to find total faith in this man... This man who was unlike any other she'd ever met. This man who could heal and take away pain, who could make her feel safe and who gave her things to hope for... Dreams of a future which until now had been denied. He spoke to her softly, tenderly stroking her hair and soon she slipped into sleep, which was also his intention, and knowing that she was asleep he carried on talking, placing the power words of defence deep within her subconscious and igniting the all powerful self healing mechanisms that dwelt deep within her psyche. In the morning she would remember little. Only that he had taken the headache away. But she would awake with fresh will to survive, her body focused on fighting against the inevitability of her illness.

She would not remember the drive back down the hill into Castillo, but she would cling valiantly to the memory of their kiss beneath the orange tree outside her home in Calle Santana. It would be like a dream and she would not remember if he kissed her or whether it was she who gave the kiss. She would only recall that it was the kiss that changed her life... that changed *her* at the very core of her being.

Sitting on the small terrace of the house in Calle Granadillos, he sipped iced water and watched the first lightening of the sky which heralded the dawn. He'd been there for hours, daring sleep to seduce him, neither resisting nor looking for the journey that would take him away from wakefulness and the crowding thoughts of confusion that cavalcaded through his tired mind. True, he could have meditated, but that would have been too easy... almost cheating. In any case, meditation never solved a problem but only gave the meditator the opportunity to see the problem in clear enough perspective to select the appropriate solution. It was a discipline he did not wish to impose upon himself at this time, preferring to give his thoughts and feelings free reign – and if sleep wanted him that badly, it would have to fight for him and take him naturally and in his own time.

Behind him, in the bedroom, a single small candle burned, throwing just enough light to see by and also casting long shadows. The moths and the occasional droning mosquito headed for the flame, leaving him in comparative and contemplative peace. Very quietly, almost below the level of hearing, Samuel Barber's Adagio For Strings played on a small radio cassette; each time it had finished he'd lit another cigarette and had rewound the tape back to the beginning, letting it run over again and again, each sweeping sequence of violins and cellos carrying him to a point once removed from the central self.

He'd gazed steadfastly at the castle. It was up there somewhere, this opening he'd come so far to find and destroy. Every instinct told him this truth and he'd suspected the truth long before Hamish Hamilton had offered him the last and crucial pieces of the complex jigsaw puzzle. Water. The Djinn liked water. Had to have it as part of their ritual of metamorphosis... And caves and tunnels hidden in the bedrock of the hillside... Yes, that would make perfect sense, wouldn't it! Somewhere there would be one tunnel that twisted and turned, defying man's perception of natural law, with each of its two entrances in different worlds. Somewhere along that tunnel there would be a dividing line between the world of man and the world of Djinn. He did not relish the thought but he knew that sooner or later he would have to descend into that labyrinth.

How to force access? Hamilton had said that the obvious entrance was through the citadel... So, if necessary he would acquire the required permit and start digging, but he guessed that there would be other ways. If there were tunnels coming out there would have to be tunnels leading in. Wouldn't it, he speculated, recognising that it might be actually more than idle speculation... Wouldn't it be wonderfully convenient if there was a tunnel that ran from the citadel to the Dolorean house in Calle Sombra! If there was, it would explain Dolorean's determination to have that particular house at any cost!

He made a mental note to talk again with Pepe Ortega. It was imperative that he examined the inside of that house as soon as possible and if he could do it with Ortega's help and co-operation, so much the better. Without it, he'd simply have to force a window or a roof tile and risk discovery.

His thoughts turned to Alexandra. She still haunted his dreams on a regular basis, albeit without the intensity and the ferocity that had once been the case. Maybe it was because his system was becoming immune to the ongoing psychological onslaught, or maybe it was because his presence in Castillo had given him other things to focus on and occupy his mind. Even so, it didn't take much to push the barriers to one side, opening up the floodgates of old memories and past events. There was a computer tape of key memories that filtered through his head, which once begun was impossible to stop.

...Seeing her for the first time at one of his lectures. She'd asked questions afterwards with acute perception that had demanded detailed and concise answers. She'd been wearing a pale green suit and he'd been instantly attracted to her.

Their first date – dinner at a local Indian restaurant where she'd worn tight black pants tucked into black leather boots and had seduced him with her vivacious smile and razor sharp mind.

Their first night of lovemaking that had taken place nervously in her crumbling rustic cottage in the middle of the West Yorkshire countryside. It had been raining and the roof had a serious leak. Neither had noticed nor cared as they'd careened along the pathway towards sexual climax and emotional commitment.

He remembered his wedding day and their wedding night and their less than comfortable honeymoon in Ireland; the weather had been appalling, not that they'd noticed or cared overmuch. Gusts of cold rain blowing against their hotel window had encouraged them to stay in bed, sometimes for whole days at a time. It had not been difficult. Their sexual appetite for each other had been insatiable.

He remembered the first time they'd seen the house in York. It had been ramshackle and in need of much repair, but they had set to with a will and enthusiasm and he saw her sitting on top of an aluminium step ladder, white paint splattered over her jeans and speckled in her dark red hair.

There were quiet nights, listening to music. Party nights when the house had rocked with laughter. Tearful nights as they'd accepted their inability to have a child. Celebratory nights as first one book and then another had been accepted for publication. Throughout all there were wild nights of sexual delight and soft nights of gentle words and tender loving.

He remembered the last time they'd made love – not a hundred miles from where he now sat. She had ridden him like a valkyrie, red main tossing in the ecstasy of her orgasm. It had been a scant fourteen months ago and it might have been ten years.

Then came the dark visions. The bitter reflections of their painful words. Alexandra's fury at his dismissal of Dolorean, the horror of their doorstep confrontations, the agony and the anguish of their last encounter at Glastonbury when he'd been permitted one last fleeting glimpse of the wife he'd once loved before she'd succumbed and slipped beneath the power of her captor and seducer.

Then there was the Alexandra of his most awful nightmares. The fanged crone who sought to claw out his heart. This was the cutting edge, the killing blade of his opponent's psychic attack. But here someone had miscalculated. They'd made a mistake. He'd not been expected to fight back. It had been assumed that he would crumble and capitulate, and although for a while it had been a close run thing, he'd emerged from the ordeal with a new strength and victory and the challenge had served to ignite his zeal and determination to fight back until the bitter end.

He sipped at the water, lit another cigarette and watched the dawn light creep over the village and bounce off the old stone of the castle. Somewhere to the north a dog barked and a cock crowed in the east. To counter the intrusion he reached out with his toe and turned to dial on the radio cassette, causing the Adagio to swell in volume, and with the evocative poignancy of the music, he again found himself thinking of Anna Sanchez.

He was excited and enchanted by her sudden presence in his life and yet also he was deeply afraid. He could not afford emotional entanglements on any level and he clearly recognised Anna as a threat in this respect. He was not free to pursue her. For one thing, he was still technically and legally married to Alexandra. He'd told his lawyer to stall and his lawyer had employed a variety of delaying tactics to ensure that the litigation proceeded at a snail's pace. Michael Fry had told him to regard Alexandra as being dead, and in his heart of hearts he knew this to be the case; it had to be seen as such to ensure his own emotional survival. But in the eyes of the law and by society's standards, he still had a wife.

For another thing, he was here in Castillo for a purpose and nothing must be allowed to distract him from that purpose, not even and least of all a beautiful and vulnerable young girl half his age whom it would be difficult to enjoy a relationship with even if he *was* free to pursue it. Anna may have made him feel needed and wanted, she may have reminded him of his sexuality and his humanity, but in other ways she also served to remind him of just how far he'd strayed from the collective identity of the human herd, which was something that had absolutely nothing to do with the twenty year discrepancy in their ages. He and Anna came from two different worlds. She was a virgin, for Christ's sake, and he was... Well, he wasn't sure what he was, but wherever, he knew he couldn't possibly be right for someone like Anna. Right now she needed him to give her healing and hope, but what would happen after the healing? Or after all hope had finally disappeared? How might they fare then, as Virgin and Magician?

And yet, and yet, and yet... Her open trusting face danced before his eyes. Her voice filled his ears, her perfume and the scent of her hair assailed his nostrils. He closed his eyes and could visualise her every feature, the multiple nuances of her every expression. It was too late to say he must be on guard against the persuasiveness of this distraction for unwittingly he had already allowed her to penetrate his defensive screens. She was there inside his consciousness with an uneasy and ill-defined presence in his heart, and if he was to fight a battle in Castillo, he realised that it would not only be to prevent the invasion of the Djinn, not only to release the trapped spirit of his dead wife, but also to protect the heart and mind of Anna Sanchez.

17.

Negev

They stopped in Beer Sheba and Leon filled the Toyota Land Cruiser with things he thought they might need. It was difficult to know what to buy. Herschal was maddeningly vague about what he had at his desert retreat and Leon had no real idea just how long his sojourn into The Negev might last. He had been surprised at Gideon Lemski's decision to let Herschal go, but he didn't question it too deeply. It was obvious that they weren't going to get anything out of the old man in Ashquelon, so maybe there would be more information forthcoming once the prophet was back on his home turf. The Toyota was equipped with state of the art mobile telecommunications, so if he did learn anything of value, Lemski would be the first to know.

The improvement in Herschal's health once he'd learned he was going home had been miraculous to behold and when they'd finally driven out of Ashquelon that morning, he'd been wide awake and bright with excitement. But as they road had unwound before them he'd fallen into a wheezy slumber and Leon had realised that he was far from being totally fit. But then, for God's sake, what did you expect from someone who was ninety eight years old? Leon had cast him a number of serupticious glances trying to be objective with regard to Herschal's aging process, and even after some hard study, he would *still* have put the old man on the under side of seventy!

Leon stacked the boxes of canned and dried goods behind the back seats, Herschal barely grunting acknowledgement and they resumed their journey southwards.
They took route 86 as far as Bor Mashash then cut across route 84, picking up route 86 again at Beer Mashabhim. Here they headed due south again, bypassing the village of Sede Boqer. He drove steadily through the early afternoon and finally pulled over onto the hard shoulder when he came within sight of the Elat pipeline that crossed the road, supported on a spidery gantry bridge. They were now deep

within The Negev. His eyes searched across the barren scrub land seeking out any sign of life or any dot of colour that might alleviate the monotony of the desert. There was nothing and, but for the pipeline and the black road, both of which shimmered in the heat, they might have been on a different planet.

He shook the old man gently. 'We're at the pipeline,' he said. 'You told me to wake you at the pipeline!'

Herschal stretched, scratched and yawned himself into wakefulness. They got out of the Toyota to urinate and exercise their legs and were blasted by the furnace of heat that the vehicle's air conditioning had hitherto held at bay.

'It's hot,' Leon said shortly. 'Do we have much further to go?'

'Not too far – and it will be cooler once we're off the road.' Herschal fastened his trousers. 'Carry on south for another five kilometres. The road is straight but there are one or two potholes, so don't go too fast. Call out when you see the sixty kilometre sign. We turn off a few metres after that.'

They climbed back into the Land Cruiser, their clothes clinging to their bodies. Leon started the engine and wound the air conditioning up another notch to compensate. At the K60 sign he slowed down and crawled in first gear at a walking pace.

'That was the sixty kilometre sign,' he said. 'What am I looking for?'

'I'll let you know. We're coming up to it soon. Go slower or we'll miss it.'

'If I go much slower we'll stall.'

'Then stall... Never mind, we're here. Turn off the road where that old beer can is stuck on top of the bush stump.. You see it?'

Leon saw the beer can but little else. There was just a vast expanse of shingle and shale and hard packed sand. Nothing at all that looked like a path or a track. Engaging 4WD he nonetheless eased the heavy vehicle off the road and for more than an hour they headed due east until miracle of miracles, they came to something that might once have been a little used goat track.

'Which way?' he asked.

'Turn right. Head south.'

Herschal was smiling now, as he had every good reason to. They may have had another few kilometres to negotiate but as far as he was concerned, this was his back yard.

The goat track wound its way around stones and boulders, and unless Leon's imagination was playing tricks on him, the ground seemed to be rising gently. In the distance there was a long low escarpment, which turned out to be much closer then he first thought. Within a short while it marched to their right, rising abruptly out of the desert to a height of three of four metres. The goat track wandered along the base of this small cliff and they followed it for a while until Herschal directed Leon through a narrow cut in the rocks and they emerged into a small arena.

It was obvious that this was their destination. There was a substantial tent, a small latted hut, a fire pit and the scattered belongings of an old man who'd been away from home too long. Next to the fire pit there were a couple of wooden crates and a jerry can. A makeshift table, covered with an Arab blanket and weighted down with heavy stones, stood to one side. What caught Leon's astonished eye, however, was the tiny spring of crystal clear water that trickled merrily from a lichen covered hole in the wall. It formed a small damp puddle in the sand and here grew a dozen small green plants and three or four clutches of attractive wild flowers.

Two other things registered. One was the cave... a gaping oval of darkness cut in the face of the rock by whatever God had created this part of the planet. The rock was worn smooth by passing aeons of sand carried by the desert wind and the cave looked curiously out of place with the rest of the oasis. And then there were the tyre tracks of another vehicle that had sometime in the not too distant past found its way to this desert retreat. Outside the encampment the winds would have obliterated the tracks within hours, but inside the natural enclosure the rocks and cliffs preserved and gave protection.

'Amazing,' he murmured, jumping down from the cab. 'Too fucking amazing!'

Just as Herschal had said it would be, it was cooler here and there was an almost unnatural silence. A warm breeze eddied over the edge of the escarpment but it was not unpleasant. With the sheer cliff there was plenty of shade. Not a bad place to retreat to, he thought, if you wanted escape and solitude. Not a bad place to call home if you were sick of the world and could enjoy your own company.

Later, after they had unloaded some of their things and Leon had moved the Toyota into an area of shade near the escarpment wall, they sat near the spring, drinking iced tea from the Land Cruiser's small refrigerator. There was a finite supply of such luxuries and once they were gone, well, they were gone. They were at least forty kilometres from the nearest habitation and Leon was certain he'd never find this place again on his own. He marvelled that Herschal had been able to survive out here for so many years and marvelled also at the effort he must have made, getting himself from this camp to that phone box in Beer Sheba. He gave voice to his thoughts and Herschal had nodded, choosing, as the prerogative of the very old, to accept Leon's words as praise and compliments.

There were always wild bird to be caught, he explained, and locusts tasted fine if they were properly cooked. Occasionally he would kill a lamed goat. No, of course it wasn't kosher, but it was food. There was always fresh water from the spring and during the winter months there were berries on the bushes. Sometimes The Bedouin would pass along the bluff. They would leave offerings, for although they were Arab and he was Jew, he was regarded as a holy man and a holy man was one of God's Chosen, in any faith or language. Leon was surprised to learn that the Bedouin still wandered The Negev. Why not, Herschal countered...? After all, they were here before the Jews! Leon was uncomfortable with this thought, but kept his discomfort to himself, recognising it as a reaction of his own upbringing and political conditioning.

On more than one occasion his eyes lingered on the cave. Herschal noticed this with a degree of satisfaction. For the lessons he intended to teach it was first necessary that his pupil's curiosity should be aroused. Right now the only truly rising factor was Leon's sleepiness; it had been a long hot drive and the natural warmth of the soft sand combined with the light splashing of the water was enough to make his eyelids heavy. It wasn't long before they closed completely and within a short while he was sleeping deeply in a heavy slumber.

With his back against a convenient boulder, Herschal allowed his eyes to roam across the familiarity of his home. Already the memories of his captivity in Ashquelon had begun to fade and other memories took their place. He case a glance at the Mossad agent, wondering how easy it was going to be to convince him of the horror that might yet be unleashed upon an unsuspecting world. With the other man, the Englishman, it had not been difficult at all. Indeed, he'd been preaching to the converted.

For three days he'd been twitchy with expectancy and on the afternoon when Colin Mage's yellow Suzuki jeep had finally crested the top of the escarpment, it had come as no great surprise. Mage had scrambled down the steep embankment, gratefully accepting the tin mug of spring water that Herschal had offered. The traveller's eyes had been tired, his beard matted with sand and desert dust. Their eyes had met and they'd unashamedly studied each other for long seconds.

'You're Herschal,' Mage had said.

'How long have you been looking for me?' Herschal had responded.

'A week. Eight days.'

'How'd you find me?'

Mage had smiled uncannily and Herschal, even then, had sensed his power and authority. He'd dipped his hand into his pocket and had produced a lead crystal pendulum. 'With this,' he'd answered.

'I'm very impressed.'

'You shouldn't be. It took long enough. I've put more than a thousand kilometres on the jeep's odometer.'

'Why?'

Mage had passed back the tin mug. 'The Djinn,' he'd said... And Herschal had nodded in understanding. Why else would anyone go to so much time and trouble to seek him out?

'Drive your jeep along the cliff top for half a kilometre. There's a path that winds down and brings you to the end of the bluff. Double back on yourself and I'll meet you over there.' Herschal had jerked his thumb in the direction of the defile.

An hour later the Englishman had been sitting almost where Leon Shapiro now slept. His eyes had surveyed his surroundings and had alighted on the cave.

'In there?' he'd asked.

'Sometimes. Very rarely. And even then, only if you go deep enough. Tell me how much you know.'

'Really I know very little. That's why I'm here. I need to learn more.'

'If you know about The Djinn you know more than most.' Herschal had responded dryly. 'You're privy to a secret that's as old as Man's time on Earth. What I want to know is, how did you find out about me?'

Mage had started by telling him about the people in Ireland, and then as night had fallen, he'd told him the rest of it, about his wife and their strange estrangement. About a man with superhuman strength whose eyes could change shape and colour. He told him about all that he'd learned from an occult book publisher in a Paris cafe.

Herschal had cooked goat meat in a well used pan over the flames of an open fire. 'It sounds about right,' he's said thoughtfully when Mage had finished his story. 'They can't come through unless there's one of their kind already on this side who can open the door for them. Two magics. A small magic to transfer their catalyst, and a major magic, using their catalyst, to open the gates of hell.'

'Has it ever been done?' Mage had asked.

Herschal had shrugged. 'On a grand scale, obviously not, or we wouldn't be sitting here now, would we? On a minor level, who knows? All of the world's great leaders – and I don't mean today's puny politicians – and especially the aggressors, all had knowledge of High Magic. You can start with the Egyptian Pharaohs, graduate through Alexandra and Charlemagne, and end up with Adolf Hitler... They all had it. Who's to say they didn't tap into The Djinn, or that The Djinn didn't tap into them? I have no proof, but it's an interesting theory.

'One thing I can tell you though is that they know we're here and they want what we've got. They have walked among us over the centuries, albeit in ones and twos. They've always brought pain and conflict. There's never been an offer of peace or alliance. Fundamentally, they're a hostile bunch of bastards. Fortunately, from our point of view, their greatest strength is also their greatest weakness. Because they emanate on such an intense psychic level they inevitably attract the attention of those humans who are able to tune into psychic vibrations. They attract us to them as they themselves are attracted to us. It's Man's basic instinct to protect his territory and so there is always conflict and, thus far, thank God, Man has always won... At least to the extent that he's been able to deflect and defer a full scale invasion. And this, by the way, is another Djinn weakness. There are many men and very few Djinn! We outnumber them and we seem to be able to combat them one at a time, but if they're ever successful in creating a conduit and cross into our world in any strength of numbers, our goose will be well and truly cooked.

'To our advantage there are very few places on the face of our globe where The Djinn can force entry. Their psychic vibration has always alerted us – has always alerted *somebody* – and therefore we've always been in place to nip the threat in the bud, so to speak. At least, that's the way it's worked up until now. From what you've told me it would seem that whether you like it or not you've been elected as Guardian of The Spanish Gate. I wish you luck. You're going to need it!'

'I need more than luck,' Mage had said urgently. 'I need facts. Information. Knowledge. I need to know everything that you know.'

Herschal had laughed his cackling laugh. 'That'll take more than one night of conversation around a desert camp fire. How long can you stay.'

'As long as it takes. You will help me, then?'

'Oh yes, I'll help you all right. Haven't got much choice in the matter, have

I?'

...And thinking of camp fires, Herschal stirred himself and laid some broom and kindling in the fire pit. He gathered roots and dried lichen, which burned like peat. He wasn't particularly hungry but the day was fading. When night fell the temperature would drop like a stone. His bones were old and in need of warmth and the time he'd spent in Ashquelon had not served him well, softening his stamina with comfortable beds and constant hot water. Apart from that, Mossad would wake soon and it was a foregone conclusion that when he did, he'd be hungry.

Now their roles were reversed. Herschal slept in his black Bedouin tent and Leon tossed restlessly in his blanket in the back of the Toyota. It was totally quite and after the noise of modern Israel, the silence was unnerving. He tried turning the radio on and got nothing for his trouble but a crackling hiss on static. Likewise the mobile telephone. Thankfully there was nothing wrong with the cassette player and he managed to doze for a while with the somnambulant strains of Saint-Saens' Samson and Dalila playing in the background. Then the music ended and he was awake again with a full bladder and a heavy stomach. They'd eaten canned kosher sausages for dinner and now each sausage sat like a leaden weight in his gut. He grabbed his jacket and climbed out into the night.

It was cool and crisp without being unbearably cold, even so, he was glad of the coat. The stars shone in startling brilliance, filling the campsite with a shadowy dark blue light. He followed his memory and found the latrine, and was not at all comfortable with the primitive arrangements. He may have been a member of Mossad but he was no field agent and he was not accustomed to roughing it. The experience in the latrine made him hope that he wouldn't be here for too long.

Three days. Three days maximum, then he was out of here and back to proper food and hygienic sanitation. It the old man hadn't opened up to him by then, well too damn bad because it would be too damn late!

Standing in the middle of the campsite, feeling frustrated and resentful, he nonetheless took stock of his surroundings and became aware of the symmetry of the topography. The arena was almost circular. The spring was a little over to the right and the mouth of the cave was precisely opposite the defile in the rocks that lead out into the open desert. It was almost as though the place had been man made, which of course was impossible.

His attention focused on the cave mouth. Even in the daylight there had been something faintly repellent about it. Now, in the dark starlight, it was positively malignant. And yet, even though it was much against his will, he found himself strolling towards it for a closer look.

The entrance to the cave was not large. A man's standing height and perhaps three metres wide at the base, narrowing to about a metre at the height of its natural arch. The rock face around the entrance was incredibly smooth and cold to the touch. Surprisingly cold. He withdrew his hand quickly and took a step backwards.

Something tugged away at Leon's consciousness and he recognised it as fear. It was irrational and illogical but it was not to be denied. It's only a cave, he told himself. If there'd been anything dangerous about it, surely Herschal would have warned him? His vision was unable to penetrate the gloom and rather than allowing his imagination to start playing tricks on him, he turned away and walked back to the Land Cruiser. He looked back at the cave once and a shiver ran down his spine that had nothing to do with the temperature of the night.

Herschal ate a hearty breakfast while Leon settled for coffee. When he'd finally slept it had been fitfully and he'd awoken unrefreshed with stiff joints and a serious headache. He drank the coffee moodily, casting occasional glances over his shoulder at the dark aperture behind him.

'What's in the cave?' he asked Herschal abruptly.

Herschal looked up from his messy plate. 'What makes you think there's anything in there at all?' he asked mildly.

Leon glared at the old man, feeling out of place and embarrassed. Words wound themselves around his tongue but he was hard pressed to find the right ones to express his feelings.

'I don't know,' he said finally. 'I was looking at it last night – and I just felt that there was something inside. Probably just my imagination.'

'Probably,' Herschal agrred. 'After all, it must have been dark. You couldn't have seen anything.'

'No,' Leon agreed, and then, almost blurting it out, 'but I just thought that I *felt* something.'

'Ah well, that's not quite the same thing at all. What did you feel?'

'Oh this is stupid!' Leon snapped.

'Not at all. You felt something. What was it that you felt? Feelings are as important as visualisations.'

'Well, if you must know, I felt that there was something inside the cave that knew I was on the outside!'

'And why is that so impossible, just because you couldn't *see* it?'

'Stop playing games,' Leon squared up to him, his voice full of challenge. 'Is there anything in that cave or not?'

'Why don't we go and have a look?' Herschal countered.

'All right, why don't we?' Leon retorted, furious with himself for having come so close to blowing his cool and losing his composure.

The mouth of the cave faced due east and the early morning sun shone directly into it. In the daylight it didn't seem nearly so intimidating. Once inside and armed with a spotlight he'd brought from the Toyota, Leon realised that the cave was far deeper than he'd first imagined. The soft sand at the entrance gave way to harder footing and, walking in a little way, he could see that the cave became a downwards turning tunnel that disappeared from sight twenty metres into the bedrock.

'How deep does it go?' Leon asked.

'How deep does it go?' Colin Mage had asked the very same question.

'A very long way down,' Herschal told Leon. *How far can you imagine?* He'd asked Colin Mage.

Leon shone the light against the walls. They were covered with pictograms and sigils and flowing Arabic script. 'You the artist?' he asked.

'I'm old but I'm not *that* old,' Herschal replied sardonically. 'The sigils go back many thousands of years, the pictograms come a little later, circa 3500 by our Jewish calendar. The script, well, that's more modern. Written about the time Mohammed rode out of the mountains.'

'People have been using this cave for that long?' Leon marvelled.

'Yes they have.'

'But,' Leon flashed the light around again. 'What do all these signs mean?'

Colin Mage had known. He'd taken one look and had turned to Herschal. 'Binding Rituals?'

Herschal had nodded approvingly. 'Yes. Three sets, created at three different times by three different cultures... Indicating, of course, that The Djinn have tried to force passage through this particular opening on three different occasions.'

'What about your own work?' Mage had asked.

'Deeper in the cave.' Herschal had told him. 'Impregnated crystals mostly, embedded in the sand and wedged into the walls. Also there is the air of the oasis itself. Prayer and purity are very effective.'

'Have you ever seen one of them?'

'In the flesh? No, thank God. But in my mind, yes, many times. The cave stretches back for about a hundred metres before things start getting difficult. There's a rock fall and a pool of what passes for water. You couldn't drink from it. It's totally turgid. But look into the pool for long enough, and if you have the focus and the state of mind, you'll find something glaring back at you that's not just your own reflection. Before you attempt it you have to be working on an extremely high vibration. It took me the better part of a year, but I don't suppose you can afford to stay with me that long, can you? No, of course you can't. In any case, there's no guarantee that you'd pick anything up anyway. The phenomena in not consistent. Even so, I'll take you down there and let you find out for yourself... But I'd suggest some rest and preparation first...

'Come on Herschal, what does it all mean?' Leon asked as Herschal led him back out into the morning sunshine.

'That's what you're here to find out,' Herschal replied enigmatically. 'But the student cannot run before he walks and you cannot describe the colour red to a man who has been blind from birth... Come, take me to my tent. There are things I will show you...'

It was the first time that Leon had been inside the tent. He wasn't sure what he'd expected, but was still surprised by the opulence. Thick Arabian rugs covered the soft sand and there was a scattering of cushions. Intricate tapestries adorned the black fabric of the walls. There was a low coffee table, expertly carved from olive wood and next to it a highly ornate chest which would not have looked out of place in the treasure hold of some ancient Spanish galleon. There was a hint of incense and the air was pleasantly cool and fragrant.

'You may as well sit yourself down and be comfortable,' Herschal said, opening the lid of the chest and delving into the contents. 'We might be here for a while. Now, tell me, what do you make of this?'

He handed over a wafer thin plate of what appeared to be beaten copper. One side was shiny and smooth, but upon the other was etched the picture of a face surrounded by written script that Leon found impossible to decipher. At first glance it was not dissimilar to some of the writing in the cave, but he couldn't be sure. The face, however, was easy to react to. Half man, half pig, it stared at him challengingly from the burnished metal with gimlet eyes, pig like snout and glinting tusks that thrust upwards and outwards from the maw of the mouth. It had a low Neanderthal forehead from which two short horns jutted like stubby scimitars, one almost above each eye.

'It's pretty damn ugly, whatever it is,' Leon said. And then: 'What is it?'

Herschal took the artefact from him but did not put it away, leaving it in full view on the rug. 'That, my friend, is the face of your enemy. It's the face of the Djinn!'

'The Djinn?' Leon echoed blankly. 'Look, I'm sorry Herschal, but I have no terms of reference. I haven't got a clue who or what you're talking about.'

'No, I know you don't and that's my problem. Where do I start in teaching you what you need to know to believe what you need to believe? You're a product of your time and the training of your mind will make it hard for you to accept what I have to tell you... Do you believe in God, Leon?'

'Yes, I suppose so, in an abstract sort of way. I've never given it much thought, really.'

'Well think about it now and think about The Talmud, The Bible and The Koran. Think about the beginning of the world and how it might have happened!'

Leon grinned. 'Why not tell me what you think and I'll sit and listen.'

Herschal nodded his head. 'No, I'll not tell you what I think. I'll tell you what I *know!* First of all you need to take both the Darwinian and religious theories of Man's evolution and throw them on the scrap heap. This world began with an explosion of cosmic energy and out of that energy, not one, but two spiritual life forms emerged. At the dawn of time these two life forms – they were abstract but extremely sentient – battled for supremacy. One won and one lost. We, the species of Man, were the winners and we emerged as the dominant species, but our victory was not total. Our adversaries, The Djinn, were not dismissed from this world, rather they were locked into a different continuum of time and space.

'I understand that the concept of a separate time-space continuum will be hard for you to come to grips with, but for now just accept it as fact. It will make things easier as we progress.

'So, Man, and here I'm talking about the spiritual chemistry of Man's soul, is triumphant over The Djinn. He develops through his physical and physiological evolution, while The Djinn, locked in their own dimension of existence, develop along their own evolutionary pathway. Now, while Man eventually forgot about The Djinn, The Djinn, as the imprisoned sub-species, never once forgot about the existence of Man. The jailer may forget his prisoner, but the prisoner is always aware of his jailer!

'For millennia they've been trying to break their bonds of exile in an attempt to take what they consider to be their rightful place on the physical earth plane of our planet. Man, or more accurately a very few special men, have always managed to stop them, but in the modern ages of science and reason, it has become increasingly difficult.

'The Djinn's greatest strength has been in their awareness of us in comparison to our ignorance of them... And yet deep within Man's subconscious there has always been that awareness. Whenever Man has striven to acquire spirituality or even to find the power of magic, he has always found The Djinn or a trace memory of their spore.

'Man has found other names and identities for his enemy. Look at the picture again... It's Sumerian. More than eight thousand years old and it pre-dates the earliest evidence of the Jewish race. The Sumerians were great occultists and they certainly had some contact with The Djinn. The writing says in words to the effect: "Behold Man's enemy. Let all magicks be employed to keep him contained within his own world. Let those who have truck with him be killed and dismembered with great magicks performed to destroy their very souls."

'The Sumerians fought against The Djinn, not as individuals but as an entire culture. If you study the arcane writings of the Chaldeans and the very early Egyptians you will realise that they did the same. Time, however, dulls senses. More secrets are buried and forgotten than are ever revealed, and by the time of the Greco-Roman civilisations The Djinn had passed into the myth of folk tale and legend.

'But in Man's deepest subconscious The Djinn have never been totally forgotten and their influence is at the root of our every fear and superstition... Vampires, werewolves, goblins, demons, even the devil himself – all owe their existence to our folk memory of another race of alien beings!'

Herschal tapped the artefact. 'Look at this! Is it any wonder that half the ancient world including the modern Jewish and Mohammedan religions refuses to eat pork? Is it any wonder that the Christian depiction of The Devil is a beast with horns? These are but two obvious examples of our enemy's subliminal influence over us.

'Now, let us speak more of our enemy. We know so little but we are not entirely ignorant of his power and his prowess. For many centuries he has been monitored by wizards and magicians, psychics and seers, some of whom have sensed his presence and have sought him out, others who have stumbled across him by accident as I myself did fifty years ago. We have their writings and grimoires to help us and these things we know...'

Herschal began counting on his fingers. 'One – as I've already told you, they know we're here. Somehow they are able to tune into our world and they are as familiar with it as we are ourselves.

'Two – The Djinn have very strong psychic abilities and they are powerful in the craft of magic; remember, they have followed a different evolutionary pathway. They are shapechangers, or at least, those who have found their way into this world have certainly had this ability. They can assume human identity, although how exactly they do it, how long they can maintain it and whether they can do it en mass, these are all unknown factors.

'Three – to gain access to our world there has to be a ritual opening at a place where the fabric between the two worlds is very thin. One such place is here, in this very oasis. There is another place in America, one in Ireland, another in Spain and another in Northern India. There may be many more and certainly in the past there have been many more, but these are the places that we know of today. For the ritual to work there has to be a Djinn Shapechanger already in place in our world to work the ritual from this side – a door that can only be opened by two keys turning in the same lock at the same time. And Leon, listen very carefully! A Shapechanger is already here! He's already crossed over and I...'

'Oh for fuck's sake!' Leon exploded, flashing and flushed with uncharacteristic anger. 'Shapechangers, Djinn, Magic! Wizards and Other Worlds! You expect me to believe in all this... this garbage? You've dragged me out to this Godforsaken hole in The Negev to tell me fairy stories? Herschal, you're out of your mind! You've been in the desert too long. Had too much sun. The only demons and devils in this world are the ones floating around in your ancient old head. You don't need a debriefing by Mossad, you need a fucking mental hospital!'

Leon stood and stared angrily down at the old man and Herschal was mindful of the difference in the reactions between this young cosseted Jew and the frightened Englishman to whom he'd told a very similar story not such a long time ago. Mage had hung on to his every word and when, after many hours of conversation, Herschal had told him not only everything he knew but also that which he suspected and all that he'd ever heard spoken on the subject, there had been little doubt that Mage had believed. The Englishman had wrapped him in an embrace of thanks and gratitude and Herschal had felt Mage's tears brushing against the stubble of his own rough cheek.

More in sadness than rancour, Herschal studied the furious face of Max Shapiro's only son. What would Max have thought, he wondered? How might Max have responded? He might have been dismissive, but he wouldn't have got angry about it... And come to that, why was Leon so angry? It wasn't just anger, either, was it? There seemed to be a rage sweeping through the younger man. Even if he'd been thoroughly pissed off at having been dragged into the desert on a wild goose chase, this anger was totally disproportionate to the cause.

'There's no need to be rude,' Herschal said quietly. 'I'm sorry you don't believe me and, being realistic about it, perhaps I should have expected your disbelief. But for the record, just so that you can never say you were not warned, let me assure you that all I have told you is true. Let me also tell you that I have told this tale to another man who *did* believe me, and at this very moment he is preparing to do battle with The Djinn in Spain... Certainly for his own sake, but also for ours' as well. The longest day in the Western Hemisphere is June 21st and our longest day is Djinn's longest night – when his strengths are at their greatest. Whenever there has been transition between the worlds it has always been in the summer months, irrespective of which continent the transition may be taking place upon. If the man in Spain wins his battle, then we will be safe for a while longer. But if he doesn't, and there is a very great chance that he will not, chaos will descend on Israel – and also the rest of the world – within a few very short weeks.

You can't...'

'Herschal, I'm sorry, but this is the biggest load of crap I've ever heard in all my life,' Leon snorted derisively.

'Is it?' Herschal retorted mildly. 'Well, if it is... if there is no such thing as Djinn, demons and magick, if Vampires and other such stuff are just the fodder of fairy tales, if all of what I've told you is no more than the contents of a deranged old man's mind, answer me this... Why are you so frightened of that cave over there? Why did you have to force yourself into it and even then not without a huge flashlight, and why was it that you couldn't get outside again fast enough?'

Leon looked down at him blankly. 'You've got a screw loose. There was nothing in the cave that frightened me. I was just curious, that's all... And in any case, whatever I felt about the cave has got nothing to do with this other rubbish you've been spouting on about.'

'Oh but it has!' Herschal assured him vehemently. 'The cave leads to a veil between dimensions. Three times The Djinn have tried to escape into our world through that cave and three times they've been repulsed. Your subconscious picked up on those energies and it scared the living shit out of you.'

'Herschal, I'm out of here,' Leon said almost formally, then turning his back on the tent, he marched out into the sunlight and headed for the Land Cruiser. He wasn't sure he could find his way back to route 86 the way he'd come, but all he had to do was keep it steady and head due west and he'd pick up the road sooner or later. Gideon Lemski might not be amused at the waste of time, but at least he could be reassured with regard to the prophet's impending threat. Look out Gideon, we're going to be attacked by an old man's heebie jeebies! He grinned to himself at the thought.

Back in the tent Herschal quickly considered his options... It might be easier if he simply allowed Leon to leave. He'd given his warnings and really, that was all he'd set out to do. But on the other hand he felt riled and rankled. There was a point to be proved and a matter of principle at stake and Leon Shapiro might still be useful if not essential to Herschal's future plans. With a sigh he delved again into the chest and, producing a heavy gauge Remington pump action shotgun, which he always kept well oiled and *always* kept loaded, he followed the Mossad agent out into the daylight.

Leon was in the process of opening the Land Cruiser's door when the explosion came, shredding the Toyota's front tyre in an instant. The vehicle lurched and Leon fell backwards, not comprehending what had happened until he turned to see Herschal standing a few metres away, the smoking Remington still pointing precariously in his direction.

'You fucking maniac!' he screamed. 'You could have killed me!'

'If I'd wanted to kill you I'd have aimed at you and not at the tyre,' Herschal retorted waspishly. 'As it is, I just wanted to slow you down and, as you haven't liked the words you've been hearing today, I thought I might as well talk to you in words you can understand. You might not know anything about myth and magick, and you certainly don't know anything about PR and tact and diplomacy, and your interrogation technique stinks. It's to be hoped that as a member of Mossad you do know something about guns! I've just blown your tyre away and if you don't sit and listen, I'll blow away another and you can walk to Beer Sheba just as I did a little while ago.'

To Leon's eyes, Herschal cut a comical figure in his baggy khaki clothes and with his flying mane of wild hair – but the shot gun was held firmly and was pointed in his direction, and that wasn't comical at all. Leon was mindful of the fact that for many years Herschal had been a field agent whereas he himself was without experience. The heavy gauge shotgun looked lethal and despite his great age, Herschal seemed to be handling it very professionally.

'You kept me in Ashquelon for near as damn it two weeks and I think the least you can do is stay here for another twenty four hours. If I can prove to you in that time that I'm not mad and that The Djinn really do exist, then you might want to rethink your attitude – and if I can't, then I'll help you change that wheel and you can be out of here by this time tomorrow. So –' the barrel of the Remington didn't waver a millimetre. 'What do you think?'

'You don't seem to be giving me much choice, do you?' Leon countered.

'Oh. Sorry.' Herschal immediately lowered the barrel of the gun so that the muzzle faced the sand. 'Well, what about it?'

'Twenty four hours?'

'That should do it if you're willing to co-operate. Providing you follow my instructions, I reckon there's a chance, only a chance mind you, that I can prove I'm not crazy. I'll take that chance if you will.'

'What are you going to do in twenty four hours?' Leon asked – and immediately wished he hadn't.

'Why, take you down to the bottom of the cave, of course,' Herschal answered lightly.

Once they turned the first corner it became very dark indeed. Leon used the flashlight to guide the way while Herschal carried two thick altar candles with the Remington and a heavy satchel bag strapped across his shoulders. Their footfalls made no sound on the smooth earth and with each step Leon found himself becoming more tense and nervous. The rock face was pitted and black with numerous jutting outcrops that created impenetrable shadows and the air, while cool, was stale. The thing that really registered, however, was the silence. He could hear Herschal's steady breathing, the creak of the leather straps that held both gun and satchel and even the swishing of the material of their clothes seemed deafening in this claustrophobically enclosed space. He would have killed for the sound of human laughter or a Tel Aviv taxi's noisey honking horn. Occasionally there were niches in the walls and here there were other examples of ancient script bound up with indecipherable hieroglyphics. On more than one occasion he saw similar faces to the one depicted on the copper plate, carved into the stone and then covered with ancient colour. It was a detestable countenance just as this was a totally detestable place, but he'd given his word. Twenty four hours and it would be all over and he could be on his way back to Jerusalem with a clear conscience.

The tunnel zigged first left and then right... Leon counted three lefts and two rights before Herschal stopped him at a point where a thick red cord hung, suspended from the ceiling. Leon shone the light upward and saw that the cord disappeared into a deep crevice above his head.

'What's this?' he asked.

'I'm just about to tell you...' Herschal stared at him steadily. 'Just in case something goes wrong and you've got to leave this place in a hurry, no matter how terrified you might be, for God's sake, don't forget to give this chord a good hard pull. Then you've got exactly twenty five seconds to get as far from the cave as you can.'

'What have you got up there, a bomb?'

'About eighty kilos of semtex,' Herschal said levelly.

'*What!*' Leon's' jaw dropped. 'Are you *serious?*'

'Eighty kilos of semtex,' Herschal repeated soberly. 'Enough to seal this opening for ever.'

'But where the hell did you get it from?'

'Stole it.' Then Herschal grinned. 'From your lot, as a matter of fact.'

'I simply don't believe all this!' Leon spluttered.

'Umm, well, you wouldn't, would you. Let's hope nothing comes along to change your mind.'

They executed another right turn and emerged into a low cavern. It was about five or six metres wide and almost as long. At some time there had been a rock fall that effectively cut off the continuation of the tunnel and between the rocks and where they stood there was a substantial pool of flat black water. At first Leon thought that it might be tar, but Herschal assured him otherwise.

The narrowest of ledges ran around both sides of the pool, providing a barely navigable walkway which Herschal negotiated with practised skill, lighting a number of white candles that were equidistantly spaced. Soon the cavern was illuminated by the candle flames, but there was no warmth in the light. The flames burned dully, causing glinting reflections from – what?

Leon shone the torch around the cave within a cave and became aware of the crystals. There were dozens of them, some amethyst, others clear quartz, set into every conceivable nook and cranny of the walls and even embedded in the sand next to his feet.

'You've done all this?' he asked, and in the enclosed space his voice sounded curiously muted and flat. There should have been an echo and it was noticeable by its absence.

'Yes.' Herschal jumped down onto the sand next to him and again Leon had to admire his geriatric athleticism that would put many younger men to shame. 'Each crystal is focused and each contains a blessing and a curse and a binding ritual. Some openings that The Djinn have used in the past, especially the very old ones, are dead. Others, such as this place, are only dormant. What I've done here is to cap the volcano and one never knows how successful one has been in such a process until it is put to the test.' He shot a glance at Leon. 'So maybe it's about time we did put it to the test. Now, if The Djinn don't exist you've got nothing to fear other than a long night of boredom, but if something does come through, then there are a few precautions that have to be observed. You listening?'

'I'm listening.'

'Notice the placement of the crystals in the sand and especially those at the water's edge. Don't disturb them. If anything goes wrong and I say run, then run like hell, but *between* the crystals. To you they're just pieces of funny glass, but to The Djinn they're like mines. If something does escape the opening then the crystals will contain it within this cavern for a while, hopefully giving you chance to get out and ring that red bell rope I showed you. You may think that I'm just a cracked old man, but if something does manifest itself here it will be incredibly dangerous and they'll be no room for bravery or heroics. There are only three men, possibly four, in the whole of the Middle East and Western Hemisphere who are qualified to fight The Djinn, and Leon, you're not one of them. If something does occur, then I doubt you'll want any further convincing that all that I've told you is true. It will be your job and also your responsibility to get out of here and then do whatever you think you've got to do.

'But listen, if for whatever reason I don't get out of here, then go to the man in Spain. His name is Colin Mage and you'll find him in the Andalucian hill village of Castillo. You will tell him all that happened, all that you saw.' There was a glint of something unfathomable in Herschal's eyes. 'The intelligence you will be able to give him will be invaluable and at least he will believe all you might have to say – which is probably a damn sight more than your boss will. Now, have you got all that?'

'Yes, I've got it all, but I think you're being incredibly melodramatic. This place is, well, yes, it's spooky and it's weird, but nothing's going to happen here other than what we might conjure up with our own imagination.'

'Maybe I sound melodramatic to your ears, but just so that you understand... Anything that you do see here tonight, and all right, all right, you might see nothing, but anything you *do* see, will be real. Don't fob it off as a figment of your imagination. It might cost you your life. I know it's very atmospheric down here, but don't be tempted to think that atmospherics cause an event. Inevitably it's always the other way round.

'Now, by way of an experiment, see if you can find a nice heavy stone then lob it into the middle of the pool and observe what happens.'

Leon picked up a fair sized lump of rock.

'Throw it upwards,' Herschal commanded, 'so that it actually drops into the water.'

Leon did as he was told. The stone, weighing all of half a kilo, left his hand, arced upwards towards the roof of the cave and fell into the middle of the pool with a resounding plop. Eddies and ripples lapped against the sand.

'So what?' Leon asked.

'So nothing,' Herschal replied. 'Just remember what you've done and what happened when you did it. You threw a stone in a pool of water and all was as it should have been. Remember it.'

'Okay, but what do we do now?'

'We sit and wait,' Herschal eased himself down onto the sand, 'and in case we do not wait in vain...'

He went through the process of ejecting the cartridges from the Remington and placing them securely in the satchel bag, reloaded with brass cartridges that had solid heads. The enormously big bullets glinted dull silver in the subdued light and Herschal grinned mischievously at his companion.

'Yes, solid elephant shot from Purdey's of London, and yes, they're made from pure silver. Don't know if it will do any good, but tradition has it that silver is effective against shapechangers.'

'And werewolves?' Leon added with sarcasm.

'And werewolves,' Herschal laughed, 'which may or may not exist but,' he jabbed a finger in Leon's direction, 'what certainly does exist is the medical condition of lycanthropism which is symptomised by the unusual growth of excess hair on the human body and severe mental disorder at the time of the full moon. Talk to anyone who works in a mental hospital anywhere in the world and they'll tell you all about lycanthropy. Interestingly enough the standard medication for this condition is fulminate of silver, either taken homeopathically or, in severe cases, diluted and injected directly into the bloodstream!'

'Now, let's just sit and wait and be alert if you can – and don't worry too much if you can't. I'll stir you if anything happens.'

'What are you expecting?'

'Perhaps something, although probably nothing. I sat here for many nights with The Englishman and his mind was more in tune with all of this than either yours or mine, and together we came up with nothing. Tonight may be different. If it isn't, I'll have egg on my face, and if it is, you'll have it on yours. I've worked in this cave every other day for the last twenty years binding the place with every trick of magic that I know – but I've been absent for the last two weeks and I've lit the candles of attraction... The Djinn are like moths and they're forever attracted to the light.'

Herschal sat cross legged with a ramrod straight back, hands resting on his knees, one palm turned upwards, the other down. Leon, without the discipline of Herschal's training, lounged more casually in the sand and stifled the occasional yawns, which were more of boredom than tiredness. It was obvious that the old man truly believed all that he'd told him and equally obvious that he was off his trolley. And yet, the easiest way out of this ridiculous scenario was to humour him for this one night. Better this way than go up against an ancient lunatic with a 12 bore shotgun loaded with that crazy ammunition. Silver bullets, indeed!

The thought that Herschal might actually do him some bodily harm had crossed his mind and yet no matter how hard he tried, he couldn't see the old man hurting him deliberately. By accident, yes, well, that was another story!

He grinned to himself and imagined that he was sitting in their favourite restaurant around the back of The Sheraton Hotel. He would order shrimps and champagne and Dov would look at him lovingly across the table.

'Well, what's my favourite secret agent been up to this week?' he would tease.

'Normally I couldn't tell you,' Leon would smile back mysteriously. 'But this week has been a real raver! I've been debriefing Israel's only living prophet, ninety eight years old and looks like sixty... Went with him to his place down in The Negev and the bastard shot up my car because I wouldn't believe his tales about magick and ghosts and demons... Anyway to cut a long story short, I agreed to go down this old cave in search of these things that he calls The Djinn, which according to him are hell-bent on conquering the world! Anyway, there was this pool and all these candles, straight out of a B feature horror movie...'

Leon slipped into a light doze but the conversation with Dov carried on in the dream state, only they were no longer in the restaurant but in the big double bed at the apartment in Hayarkon Street.

'Well he must have had some magic,' Dov was saying quite seriously.

'How do you work that one out?' Leon asked curiously.

'Age cell degeneration. Learned it first year at medical school. If the guy looked sixty and acted sixty...'

'More like forty on a few occasions!' Leon laughed.

'Then he couldn't... simply *couldn't* have been ninety eight...'

Even though his eyes were shut all of Herschal's senses were on red alert. He felt Leon Shapiro fall into his slumber and wrestled alone with the problem that filled his mind. If Leon wouldn't do anything to help Israel or Colin Mage, then he, Herschal, would have to travel to Spain and help Mage himself. But...

But he was suddenly feeling very old and weak. The nagging chest pain was still there and his body felt hot and hollow. He knew that he had limited time left on this good planet Earth, which was fair enough... He'd lived a very long time and if there was now an end in sight he could accept it without wails and tears. In his heart of hearts, he knew that the chances of his getting to Spain were minimal to non-existent and therefore it would *have* to be Leon.

But Leon didn't believe him and the only thing that might make him believe was the very thing that would probably rob him of his last few months or weeks, maybe it might only be days! of life – and also put Leon's life at some considerable risk. Indeed, if Herschal executed the plan he was now forming in his mind, he might even be signing Leon's death warrant.

Odd. He'd spent all these years trying to contain the genie in the bottle and now here he was, actually contemplating pulling the cork out instead. It would, he mused, serve a valuable purpose – or at least it might if the Shapiro boy got his shit together – and also it would assuage his own curiosity. Maybe it was his final challenge, his last act of ego. A number of men had contained The Djinn over the long centuries, but few, maybe only four in the last half thousand years, had been successful in actually conjuring one up!

The thought that he might actually win a contest of strength with a shapechanger excited him enormously. What a tale to tell when he arrived in heaven! But it was an earthly curiosity that edged him ever further towards his final decision. All his precautions, the incantations, the rituals of defence and offence – would they, could they actually work? Was he, Herschal of Germany and France, Herschal of Fez and Morocco, Herschal, Jew of Europe and Israel, Herschal the seer and Herschal the prophet – was he just human, the batty old man that Shapiro thought him to be, or had he in all the years of his travels and searches become more than human... The True Soul? The True Spiritual Warrior?

His decision still only half made he opened his eyes briefly. All was as it should be. Nothing had changed. The candles burned, the son of his friend slept, the waters of the black pool were still.

He slowly dipped his hand into the satchel bag and brought out a twisted lump of dark metal. More than twisted, it was fused and misshapen as though once having been subjugated to some great heat – which, more than a thousand years before, it had. Given to him by Mahmoud Nazaar of Fez for services rendered in 1944 and 1945 it had been a most powerful talisman even then. In the intervening years it had gained energy as an object of reverence and through never having been used for its only purpose.

Allah knows why, Mahmoud Nazaar had said, *but there may come a time when you need to summon our common enemy to destroy him, which, of course, is easier said than done! And yet with this, which was once a part of the casket owned by the greatest magician before the Prophet Mohammed – and I speak of the great Ali Al Hadin himself! – you, as Al Hadin once did, may summon The Djinn to this world. But if you do, be most careful. Summoning The Djinn is one thing, controlling him once summoned is another matter. Even Al Hadin only had limited success with that ambition!*

Herschal had told the story to Colin Mage on one of the many nights they had sat, trying abortively to penetrate the unfathomable depths of the glossy black pool. Mage had held the lump of tortured metal and found it impossibly heavy for its diminutive size.

'Ali Al Hadin,' he'd mused. 'The name sounds familiar but...'

Herschal had rocked with merry laughter. 'Oh yes Colin you have heard of him many times. Anglicise the name and you'll find the great magician's identity easily enough!'

'Al Hadin – Aladdin? Oh come on, you can't be serious?' Mage had been incredulous.

'Yes that is how you would know him, but his story was twisted out of truth and turned into fable a full four hundred years before Scheherazade told the tale to The Great Caliph. Today he has a small chapter in a book of Arabian fairy tales, you see him in your curiously English pantomimes and the Disney people have turned him into a cartoon hero and yet twelve hundred years ago Ali Al Hadin was as real as you and I are today. Not as some poor peasant boy looking for a lucky break, but as a powerful Prince of Persia who could trace his lineage back over thousands of years to The Sumerian dynasties. He had contact with The Djinn and such was the strength of his knowledge that he actually managed to master some degree of control over one of them for a while. Forget about magical lamps! This ingot is all that is left of the lead casket, supposedly made from a band of the same stuff that bound the arc of the covenant, which was the repository of his spells and grimoires. Believe me Colin, it is very very powerful!

Mage had been impressed just as Herschal had been impressed nearly sixty years before. Now the ingot throbbed in Herschal's hand almost in time with the beat of his heart. It had an energy all of its own, pulsing like a beacon. Holding it in both hands at eye level he muttered the incantation of summoning then threw the ingot from him and watched as it disappeared soundlessly beneath the surface of the water causing not so much as the faintest of ripples. Herschal's sense of loss was profound, but so also was his determination.

Right, he thought, narrowing his eyes to slits. Let's see what happens now.

Leon woke, not knowing what had woken him, not even realising that he'd been asleep. In the dream he and Dov had been sitting on their favourite stretch of moonlit beach, dangling their feet in the warm waters of a benign sea. But then the sea had become cold as dark menacing clouds had obscured the moon and he awoke to the awareness that he was freezing.

Something was different. Within the cavern the atmosphere had changed and it wasn't just a question of temperature. He cast around to discern the cause and his eyes immediately fell upon the pool. Before the water had been black but now it seemed to be grey – the greyness caused by a thin film of opaque mist that clung to the surface.

Herschal still sat cross legged, but now the big Remington rested across his knees and the old man emanated an aura of tension.

'What's happening?' Leon asked anxiously.

'Nothing... yet.' Herschal answered tersely. 'It's been like this for two or three minutes.'

'But what is it?' Leon demanded. 'And why is it so cold?'

'Let's wait a while and see, shall we.'

'But you must know *something*.'

'You don't accept or believe what I know,' Herschal retorted, 'so let's just wait and see what happens.'

They did not have to wait very long. After only a moment a mauve light began to glow weakly from within the mist, a gentle inconsistent pulse that never lingered in the same place for longer than a second.

'Well what's this?' Leon wanted to know.

'Take another rock and as you did with the first one, throw it into the middle of the pool.'

Fascinated by the turn of events and with a growing sense of unease, Leon lobbed a rock into the pool and blinked with disbelief as the rock sparked and flashed out of vision a good metre above the mist that covered the water.

'I don't believe I just saw that!' he exclaimed.

'But you did see it?'

Leon shot Herschal a sideways glance. 'Of course I saw it. We both saw it, didn't we?'

'I most certainly saw it,' Herschal agreed. 'I just wanted to make sure that you had!'

Leon picked up another rock, bigger and heavier, something of the calibre of a small canon ball. Coming to his feet and using both arms, he heaved it into the pool – and, like the smaller rock before it, it snapped out of vision with a crackle of sparks just above the line of the mist.

'This is weird!' Leon said, and there was a hollowness in his voice that signalled alarm. Indeed, the Mossad man was feeling decidedly unnerved and apprehensive. He hadn't liked this cave right from the very beginning and he was liking it less and less with every passing minute. Something was happening here: the atmospheric pressure within the cavern was changing. He swallowed and felt his ears pop as the pressure in his head equilibrated And, damn it all, the quality of light was changing too. The odd mauve reflection within the mist was getting substantially stronger – either that or the light from the burning candles was growing significantly weaker.

He picked up the flashlight and directed the high powered beam across the pool. It should have thrown the distant rocks into bright relief, but instead they were only blurred shapes, dimly apparent. Between the shore and the rocks there was a rippling effect in the air above the water, a phenomena that reached up like a column, actually brushing and becoming a part of the cavern roof...

Herschal came to his feet, noting with no small degree of satisfaction the look of fear in Leon Shapiro's inexperienced eyes.

'Herschal I don't know what's happening here, but don't you think we ought to leave?'

'Leave?' Herschal echoed. 'Where to? What for? This is what we came to see! On the other hand you don't believe in any of this stuff so you've got nothing to worry about.'

'But what is happening?'

'Not a hundred percent certain, but at a guess I'd say that there's a shapechanger trying to find its way through the veil... Look at all the crystals... The way they're shining! They work a bit like an early warning system and if they're anything to go by, there's something big, bad and nasty on its way to pay us a visit.'

'But what are you going to do?' Leon took a step backwards and to his left, bringing him closer to Herschal.

'The moment it shows its ugly face, I'm going to blow its fucking head off! That's what I'm going to do!'

'I still think we ought to leave,' Leon insisted.

'A bit late for that,' Herschal retorted. 'Because if we *are* to be visited by a shapechanger, something you don't believe in, let's never forget, then it's better we stop it here because if we can't stop it here, we sure as hell can't stop it out in the open at the other end of the tunnel.'

Leon swallowed again, this time only partially successful in clearing the pressure in his ears. There was a burbling noise like someone farting under water, which was a good analogy for now an unpleasant smell began to fill the cavern. Leon was hard pressed to describe it, but it was half way between hot sulphur and rotting seaweed.

The grey mist began to eddy and swirl in an anti-clockwise direction, gradually being drawn upwards into the disturbed folds of air above the pool. Now Leon could see the surface of the pool and it boiled and broiled like a hot cauldron – and yet rather than heat, coldness permeated throughout the cavern, making his teeth chatter, half in reaction to the coldness, half in fear. And Leon admitted to himself that he was frightened now. The temptation to turn and flee was very great within him, but as long as the old man stood his ground, he knew that he would have to do the same.

The rational side of his brain told him that there was nothing paranormal happening here, that this was just seismic activity caused by some long dormant thermal spring – *in which case why was he so bitterly cold and how did that explain disappearing rocks and boulders?* – or if not seismic and thermal, maybe it was volcanic, and if not volcanic, maybe it was just a projection of his own overtired mind. The thing to remember was that somewhere there simply had to be a rational explanation for all that was happening. The emotional side of his brain said all that was bullshit and that something very strange and dangerous was coming down.

As if to confirm his emotional assessment, a shape began to form within the column of mist that revolved with ever increasing velocity, and without any shadow of doubt it was the most horrendously disgusting thing he'd ever seen in his life. Squat barrel shaped torso, covered with scale and oozing a slimy silvery green substance... A head, half man, half boar, with razor sharp tusks and horns, rows of serrated teeth became a flattened snout and glimlitty amber eyes glowed – no, not glowed but actually *burned* with hatred and intelligence. Strong muscular arms – could he really call them arms? – clawed at the air between them. Razor sharp bill hooks protruding from webbed amphibianesque palms where hands and fingers should have been, scythed through the ether less than twenty feet in front of his eyes, and something liquid and serpent like seemed to be uncoiling from the beast's belly.

Leon trembled in horror, only marginally aware of the hot wetness soaking his trousers as he pissed in his pants. Jerkily he turned to Herschal who stood in a semi-crouch, the butt of the Remington pulled firmly back into his shoulder.

'Shoot!' Leon screeched. 'For God's sake shoot it!'

'Hah! You believe me now, do you?'

'Yes I believe you, now for God's sake, shoot the bastard thing.'

Herschal squeezed the trigger and in the small cavern the blast of the detonation was concussive. Even so Leon was still able to hear the beast's bellowing squeal of rage as Herschal's shot found its mark in the middle of its chest. Herschal fired twice more in rapid succession and Leon saw both bullets strike... or at least he thought that he did for now something very peculiar was happening. The monstrosity was loosing its sharp edge of shape, and flowing like a stream of liquid lava became a snakelike coil of scale and steam that came curving across the roof of the cavern straight towards Herschal and the upraised shotgun.

'Run Leon,' Herschal yelled at the top of his voice, then fired the gun into the fluid mass of malignancy that hovered above his head.

Leon, descending into a state of shock, tumbled three steps backwards and then three more as whatever it was dropped downwards from the ceiling and covered the top half of the old man's body. There was an alien squeal of victory and a human scream of agony. Leon had an impression of snapping jaws and bloody tusks and for one brief millisecond two baleful amber eyes glared directly at him from amid the maelstrom of movement.

As Leon took another backwards step the Remington twelve bore shotgun fell to the sand and Herschal's headless torso toppled forwards. Blood spurted upwards like a fountain and also cascaded downwards from the old man's severed head that was held in the grip of the hideous mouth that hovered half a metre beneath the roof of the cavern.

That was enough for Leon. He turned and ran in blind panic, protective waves of insanity descending over his fragmenting psyche. He heard the shrill squeal of rage behind him and ran that much harder as though the devil himself was in hot pursuit – which as far as Leon was concerned was near enough the truth to make no difference.

The part of him that was still functioning pulled viciously at the red cord as he fled past, while the other part of him that demanded flight and survival took no notice at all, concentrating only on gaining the freedom of the light and fresh air of the oasis.

He shot out of the cave like a cork from a bottle and not slowing one jot in his stride, pounded across the sand for all he was worth. The functioning part of his mind took note of the parked Toyota but it was also the functioning part of his mind that was counting off the seconds. In any case, the functioning part of Leon's psyche could not have exercised any control over the subliminal desire to put as much space as he could between himself and that thing down there in the cave that had bitten off Herschal's head. Leon's instincts for survival simply screamed at him to run and keep running.

He was half way through the defile with ten metres to go before he reached the open desert, when the escarpment behind him blew up. He felt the heat as the clothes were shredded from his back, then, as the shock wave caught him, he was lifted off his feet and carried into the air like a leaf before the wind.

As he turned somersaults in the air, his mind turned somersaults behind his eyes giving a blow by blow action replay of the events in the cavern... Then he felt himself falling, but was actually unconscious before coming into hard and shocking contact with terra firma some twenty or thirty metres distant from the entrance to Herschal's no longer existent desert retreat.

He was still unconscious when the IDF helicopter found him two hours later. He had a broken collar bone, three broken ribs, massive bruising and some minor first degree burns on his back. He remained unconscious for another three days, hovering on the borders of coma and it was a further four days before he was in a position to make a carefully edited verbal report to Gideon Lemski. Fully one week later, a fortnight after the encounter with The Djinn, he was released from hospital.

18.

Alliance

Hector cast his line into the deepest part of the river while Mage sat on a nearby rock quietly smoking a cigarette.

'To tell the truth there aren't any decent fish left in this stream,' Hector said sadly. 'Not that there ever were all that many. But a year or so ago you could usually be sure of pulling something out. Nobody's catching much these days though.'

It was Saturday morning and this, the time and place of their meeting, was twenty four hours later than expected. The previous day, the Friday, had become impossible.

First of all there had been another death and, although it had been a clear diagnosis of heart failure, the fact that old Immaculada Morro of all people should suddenly drop dead registered on his mind as being an odd coincidence. Miriam Cortez had had the reputation of being a witch and Mad Macu had been Castillo's unofficial seer and wise woman long before the Cortez family had taken up residence. Was there a link between these two deaths or was it, as his rational mind demanded, purely a matter of coincidence.

After the formalities of the death certificate and the interment order he'd run foul of Jaime Gomez who'd said he'd wanted to talk to him and yet, when he'd taken Jaime into his consulting room, Jaime had talked about nothing in particular but had insisted that he be given a thorough medical examination. Hector had obliged, but had found nothing particularly wrong. Jaime had drawn his attention to the odd pink weals on his wrists which were also there to a lesser extent around his ankles. He'd said that they itched but was evasive as to how he'd come by them. Hector gave him some anti-histamine, suggesting that it was probably an allergic reaction to something. Jaime readily agreed that this was probably the case and after he'd taken his leave, Hector had been left wondering about the police chief's nervous demeanour. This was unlike the Jaime Gomez the village had known and loathed all these years.

Then Juanita had summoned him to the church of Santa Maria where he'd found Father Francisco in an extremely sorry state. The priest had been bleeding quite copiously from his wounds and had fallen into a semi-conscious delirium. He'd changed the dressings and had vowed to himself that if there was no improvement within twenty four hours, like it or not, Francisco was going to hospital.

By this time, the best of the day had gone and Mage hadn't turned up at the surgery anyway...

Although he *had* turned up that morning suggesting that they might have a chat now that Hector had more time. What Hector wanted to know was how exactly Mage had known that he hadn't had any free time on the Friday!

Then there had been his conversation with Anna on the Friday evening. It had not gone well at all and he now berated himself for not having handled it with more tact and sensitivity. He didn't want to dwell on it but his memory of their words caused him to feel anger and most of that anger was directed towards the Englishman who sat behind him now puffing away at his cigarette without a care in the world.

There were things he wanted to say to this Colin Mage and things he wanted to know from him as well. The problem was in finding an opening for their conversation, a conversation that might end up being a heated argument if he didn't get what he wanted from it.

The opening he was looking for was to be found in the most surprising and unexpected of ways.

Hector's line went tight, the rod almost pulled from his hands, now bending and whipping as he fought with the fish that had taken his bait. It had to be a sizeable beauty to cause all this commotion the surface of the river was patterned by the underwater struggle and for a second he thought that the line would snap beneath the pressure.

Mage, who knew nothing of fishing, came and stood next to him.

'What have you got?' he asked easily.

'Don't know till I get it out – but whatever it is, it's big...' he released and played the line then started winding it in again. 'Out of my fishing box. The knife and the club. This thing's going to be alive and kicking when I land it – if I land it!'

Mage took the items requested from the box and watched in fascination and admiration as Hector played with the fish, slowly drawing in the line until whatever he'd caught on his hook was now only a few feet away at the water's edge. Then the fish – if that was what it was – came out of the water, flying towards its captor. Taken totally by surprise Hector fell backwards and the silver monster, trussed up in weed and fishing line, landed on his lap. It would have been funny but for the fact that the thing was still very much alive with snapping jaws that caught Hector firmly around the wrist causing the doctor to cry out, not just in surprise and outrage, but also in very real pain.

He tried to throw the fish off and succeeded only in splashing blood across the front of his trousers. He didn't need to call for Mage, for Mage was already there, prizing the fish's jaws apart and flinging it to one side before bringing the club down resoundingly on its head, not just once but three or four times before the thing ceased its writhings and gave in to death.

'By all the saints what is that thing?' Hector gasped, grasping his injured wrist and staring with incomprehension at the dead fish.

'You're the fisherman, so you tell me,' Mage said quietly.

Together they studied the bludgeoned carcass. It was half a meter in length and about the same in girth. The head, bulbous eyes and mouth, accounted for more than a third of its presence, while the other two thirds, rotund and scaly, was covered with scabaceous protuberances. A single ridged fin ran along its back and the two gill fins were more like two small horizontal sales. Upon closer examination, the mouth was filled with dual lines of sharp teeth with downwards thrusting fangs that interlinked with a short pair of upwards thrusting tusks.

'For all the world I'd say it was some sort of catfish, but it's unlike any specimen I've ever seen before. The shape, the size... all wrong... and in all my years of spinning lines, I've never known a fish to attack a man before... Leastwise, not like this thing went for me!' Hector gingerly took his hand away from his injured wrist and inspected the damage. There were two small puncture marks below, which had drawn some blood but had not caused any real harm. On top of the doctor's arm, however, there was a nasty horseshoe of a gash where the fish's teeth had torn the flesh. 'Christ,' Hector muttered. 'This hurts. Need some anti-tetanus and a dozen stitches I shouldn't wonder.'

'I'll bring your bag,' Mage said and retrieved the doctor's black briefcase from the Renault that was parked a few yards back in the bushes. As an afterthought he also brought the bottle of drinking water that was tucked behind the driver's seat.

Hector fumbled with the bag, but with Mage's help, found the hypodermic and a phial of anti-tetanus solution. With swift confidence he injected the drug into his left arm above the elbow. 'Let's get this cleaned up,' he said, looking dubiously at the wound and realising that it was deeper and more serious than he'd first thought. 'Sorry Colin, but I'll have to get down to La Linea. Don't think I can sew this up myself.' A wave of pain shot up his arm and he winced, looking balefully at the perpetrator of the injury.

'Sure. I'll drive you, but let's see what we can do here first.' Mage took the water bottle and washed the wound thoroughly. 'Got a bandage in that bag of yours?'

Hector nodded and, with his free hand, produced the required item. Meanwhile Mage had broken a leaf from a nearby Aloe Vera plant and proceeded to anoint the serrated wound with the plant's discharge. Hector was about to protest, but as the Englishman smeared the stuff lightly into the wound the doctor became immediately aware of the diminishing pain – *he put his fingers on my forehead, Papa, and took away the headache* – and was prompted to remain silent.

Hector watched as Mage did a fair to middling job of applying the bandage. When he'd finished Mage grinned at him apologetically. 'Best I can do, I'm afraid. How does it feel?'

'Damn fish must have bruised the bone or got its teeth into a tendon. It hurts like the devil.'

'Okay, well let's see if we can help a little...'

Mage took Hector's wrist in both his hands and immediately the hector felt a tingling sensation wrap itself around his forearm. A numbing coolness embalmed the heat of the cuts and the pain began to subside even further.

A blue jay hurtled across the river, skimming the surface of the water before angling upwards through the branches of the weeping willows and eucalyptus trees towards the distant village and the western ramparts of the castle. The waters of the Rio Hozgarganta murmured in the background in counterpoint to the chirping of crickets and the occasional hum of early summer insects. For a moment he was overwhelmed with the desire to stretch out and sleep... Indeed, as his forearm became numb, his eyelids closed and he felt the warmth of the sun penetrating the cotton of his shirt and warming through to the muscles of his broad back.

Did he, just for a few seconds, drop off into a doze? Either way when Mage finally let go of his wrist he eased back into wakefulness, aware of the fact the he'd drifted off somewhere and also aware of the fact that he was now without pain.

'You realise,' he said slowly, 'that if there were more people like you, medicine and the medical profession would soon become redundant and superfluous to Man's requirements?'

'I hardly think so,' Mage laughed quietly. 'And apart from anything else there aren't too many people around quite like me.'

'You have the power to take away pain,' Hector said sombrely. 'You've just proved that to me here on this river bank. You can put people into deep trances as you did with Dolores. I can't prove it, but I suspect that you have a beneficial effect on things like herpes, rheumatism and ulcers... It seems an odd coincidence that a number of people you have been associated with since you've been among us are suddenly healthier than they have any reasonable right to be. The Guadiaro boy, Old Antonia, Pepe Ortega... They're all my patients, you know, and I've got eyes in my head. I *know* that you can take away headaches...' He looked at Mage meaningfully. 'The question is, what else can you do? I mean, for example,' and an angry note crept into Hector's voice, 'what are you like with blindness? Can you take away brain tumours?'

Mage chose his words carefully. 'The honest God's truth is that I'm not certain just how far these abilities of mine do go... Sometimes people call me a healer which isn't quite right. All I do is act as a channel for those healing powers that are around us all and are within us all. I think I might be able to help Anna a lot but I can't guarantee it and I wouldn't want to raise any false hopes, either within her or within you. I'd like to *try* to help, but I'd rather do this without her knowledge. At least, at this stage.'

Hector fought hard to control his emotions. 'Can it actually be done?' he asked. '*Has* it ever been done?'

'Yes and yes, but the question is can *I* do it? I've had some successes over the years that have confounded a number of rather cynical doctors that I've had dealings with, but that isn't the same as guaranteeing a cure for every person that I touch. In fact, the successes that I *have* had have been with people that I've liked and have had an affinity with.'

'And you have this *affinity* with Anna?' Hector asked with just the trace of a barb.

'Yes, Hector, I have. I like her very much. But that's as far as it goes.'

'Have you told Anna that?' the doctor asked dryly.

'I haven't told Anna anything much,' Mage said evasively. 'She had a bad headache on Thursday night and I was able to take it away. I've told her that I'm her friend and that I'll do anything I can to help. It was *she* who told *me* about her eyes and my only response was to say that even if the medical prognostication isn't wrong, nothing is ever certain in this life. There are always miracles.'

'So now you have my daughter praying for a miracle, is that it?'

'No. Now I have your daughter fighting against something she has hitherto believed is inevitable. This way she'll never be able to say that she succumbed to it without a fight! I've known people who have contracted awful illnesses. They've given in to them and the illnesses have taken them through the ultimate doorway. But I've known others who fought back, who have gained remission and who fight to retain that remission every waking day of their lives. You could say that they're living on borrowed time, but at least they're living rather than just waiting for an inevitable end. We all have to die some time, Hector, you of all people know this. Dying itself isn't important. It is how we die that counts.'

'What about the others?' Hector asked, tactfully changing the direction of their conversation.

'Yes. I've done what I can at a distance to help them... at least that's true as far as Angel and Antonia are concerned. With Pepe it was a bit different. I needed something from him and gave him something in return as a gesture of goodwill.'

'Pepe's got a gastric ulcer that's caused him a lot of grief over the last two years.'

'He hasn't got it now,' Mage said softly. 'Haul him in. Take a couple of x-rays or whatever. Examine him. He *had* an ulcer when I first met him, but when I was with him two nights ago it wasn't there then.'

Hector pounced. 'So what you can do for Pepe Ortega can you not also do for my Anna?'

'Hector, I can try. I will try. I want to try. All I did with Pepe was reach into his belly with some healing energy and he has done the rest for himself. No two people react the same way to it. I've no guarantee that it would work for Anna, but listen to me, my friend, *I do want to try!*'

Mollified somewhat, Hector sat thinking and clumsily filled his pipe. The wrist was beginning to itch but not uncomfortably. 'I understand what you are saying,' he said. 'And you have my goodwill and co-operation... I'll bet that surprises you, doesn't it, coming from a doctor... but it is as a doctor that I know the limitations of medicine. And with you,' he looked up slowly, 'there are no limitations, are there?'

'In principle, no, there are not. In practice...' Mage shrugged, '...in practice, there are always the limitations of the person who is channelling the healing and believe me Hector, I am a man of many limitations.'

Hector puffed a plume of blue smoke up into the branches of the magnolia tree that shaded their stretch of the river. 'You realise that with Anna you may have bitten off more than you can chew, albeit in an entirely different area?'

Mage looked puzzled. 'Enlighten me.'

'I know my daughter very well indeed Colin. Unless I'm much mistaken and I know that I am not, the girl has fallen for you, hook line and sinker. You could call it a childish infatuation, but my daughter is not a child and to her it is all very real and romantic.'

'She has told you this?'

'Not in so many words... but we talked last night, as we have talked on a number of occasions these last two or three weeks and her one subject of conversation is you... Colin did this, Colin said this, Colin said the other. Colin, Colin, Colin... My ears ring with the sound of your name! So, in whatever dealings you have with her, be mindful of her feelings and respect her emotions. She is both vulnerable and fragile.'

Mage stared at the flowing river, thoughts confused, for indeed this was more than he had bargained for. He ran his memories over all of the times he and Anna had been together and there had not been many of them and most of them had been with Hector in attendance, wondering if he'd given the girl any opportunity to fall for him. In all honesty, he recognised that he had not. His own feelings were held in secrecy and stasis and he'd never once given Anna any encouragement or indication that he was anything more than a friend... At least he hadn't until tat magical kiss of Thursday night, but how much importance did one attach to a kiss?

'Yes,' Mage said thoughtfully, 'she is very young and very fragile and very vulnerable and very afraid, and I promise that I shall ever be mindful of it.'

There was something in the Englishman's words that told Hector that this part of their conversation was over. He did not know what might happen between this strange man and his so very precious daughter, if indeed anything might happen at all, but in some unfathomable way he felt reassured by Mage's reaction and was happy to leave it there for the time being.

Hector kicked the dead fish, rolling it over onto its side and exposing its belly. 'It looks, at first glance, like a case of mercury poisoning. After that big spillage in Japan a few years ago there were all sorts of repercussions in the evolutionary chain... Not just with the fish in the sea but also with those poor buggers who ate them on the shore... but,' and he looked at Colin shrewdly, 'I don't think there is any mercury polluting this river. I think it is something else entirely. I think it's the same thing that affected Dolores' baby and all those other children that have been badly born this year. It's the same thing that contaminates this whole mountainside... that causes violence and agitation in our village, that causes one of our priests to be bleeding like the very Christ. It's the same thing that's making our stalwart chief of police behave like a skittish virgin and it's the same thing that's causing all these sudden accidents and deaths. Miriam Cortez last week, Diego Moreno the week before, old Immaculada Morro just within this last thirty six hours. I also think that you are a part of it.'

'I am,' Mage said openly. 'But I'm also here to stop it, if it can be stopped.'

'Thank you for your candour. Now tell me exactly what it is that you're going to try and stop.'

'In simple terms,' Mage began...

'In any damn terms you like!'

'...In simple terms, you have to accept that there are two energies abroad on this planet. If we are looking for titles, let's call them good and evil. The battle between these conflicting energies has been going on since the very beginning of sentient time and the two opposing forces usually balance each other out... but let us suppose that there are a few places on the fact of the earth, and I mean physical places, such as Castillo, where those opposing forces are not so finely balanced... Where there is an opening of opportunity for evil to gain the upper hand and to dominate all of the powers of good that are abroad in the world. But let us further speculate that this opening of opportunity is not a constant one, but one that is suddenly created or gradually contrived – and here you actually have this mountain and its village of Castillo.

'Right now, it has become the focal point of evil intent. It is here that darkness will try to overcome the power of light. As such all of the negative vibrations within this place and its people are brought to the surface... Here you will find bad genes mixing with dark moods and bad tempers. The violent beast-like quality within Man will inevitably be drawn to the surface and that which is the personification of evil and darkness will be drawn to this place just like iron filings to a magnet.

'There is a man... or more accurately, an evil being who has the power to impersonate a man, who is nonetheless real in this world, who has identified Castillo as being a place that teeters on the brink between light and dark. Indeed, over the last year, perhaps even longer, he has done much to contaminate that which is good in Castillo... Pushing it ever more towards the darkness. He has brought sickness and death with him and avarice and greed. I don't say that he has personally caused your daughter to fall sick, but I'm very certain that had this man never come to this village, there'd be nothing wrong with Anna's eyes, no nasty tumour lurking at the back of her skull.

'This man has come and gone from Castillo over the last dozen or more months... He's not here now but will be within another few weeks. When he returns it will be to perform a very specific magical rite, which if it is successful, will bring pain and chaos to everybody... and I don't mean everybody in Castillo, I mean everybody in the world.

'Hector, if I speak to you of magic, you will deride me, but believe me, there *is* great magic abroad in the land. You have in Spain the tradition of El Brujo – the Witch – and this man who is my enemy is a very powerful and very dangerous brujo. As I say, he will be here soon... but I am here before him. In the short time I have been here I've tried to undo some of the bad that he has brought with him to this place, which is only accidental to the fact that I am here to try and stop him from doing any more damage. There will be a battle between us and one of us will win and one of us will lose.

'There is no point in bringing in the authorities, for he has broken no law of this land. They could, therefore, do nothing. And yet I tell you this, and it is as much as I can tell you, this man is against all law and against all natural law and the true nature of our world. He has to be stopped and I'm here to stop him.'

'And does this man have a name?' Hector asked.

'Yes he does. He calls himself Dolorean. Jadoc Dolorean.'

'Then I know this man,' Hector said quietly.

Mage said nothing but his stomach felt hollow and his heart beat quickened.

'Yes I know your Mr Dolorean. He is the man who frightened one of Henry's girls so much that she had a fit of hysterics and her mother had to call me out quite late at night to give her a sedative. She said that he had the "evil eye" and out of curiosity I made a point of meeting him the following morning and although I have to say that I perceived no evil in him, I certainly did not warm to him... In fact I remember feeling that I disliked him quite intensely. It must be said that he gave me no cause to do so and that it was purely a gut reaction.

'And this, of course, is the same Mr Dolorean who was so insistent about buying Pepe Ortega's house in Calle Sombra. He ended up using Peter Cortez as a middle man, which caused Pepe a lot of grief, as I remember it. Pepe absolutely did not want to sell the house to Dolorean, although it had been on the market for a number of years and while I'm not sure of the reasons he was absolutely furious with Peter Cortez for his duplicity in the matter...'

A curious look crossed Hector's face as he made the connection. This Dolorean person had been involved with the Cortez family and now Miriam Cortez was dead, her husband and daughter still in the clinic at La Linea. Immaculada Morro had first been Miriam Cortez's friend then her bitterest enemy, and now she too was dead. Dolorean had frequently been seen in the company of Father Ignatious of Santa Clara and now Ignatious was out of his remission from cancer and was again a seriously sick man. Ignatious's right hand man when it came to matters temporal and practical had been Diego Matan and Diego was also dead – his eldest son badly beaten up and fled from the village.

Hector's mind flashed back over some of the other tragedies that had occurred over the past few months, looking for a further link between them. The only one he found was that they'd all been associated with Santa Clara's parishioners, rather than Santa Maria's. This did not take into account the horrendous pattern of bad births, but it did account for a disproportionately high percentage of other incidents of violence and savagery that had rocked the village over the last year, including the Torres knifing and the two recent suicides, one through hanging by barbed wire, the other through the deliberate drinking of battery acid. Even Carlos who had run amok in Calle Llanette with a sledge hammer had been a Santa Clara man!

Hector looked at Mage questioningly. 'I perceive a pattern of events that could quite easily be tied into your Mr Dolorean. I'm prepared to accept on the strength of your word and my own instincts that he is possibly a very evil man, but while I do not deride you, I must, as a rational man of science, hesitate over this business of magic. Brujos exist, of course, but do they have any real power other than in the imaginings of the mind?'

'How's your wrist?' Mage asked softly.

Fully twenty minutes had passed since Mage had applied the dressing and Hector looked down at the white bandage with a small sense of wonder. There was no pain, only that odd itchy feeling and in all truth he'd almost forgotten the fact that he'd been injured.

'It feels fine,' Hector admitted curiously.

'Let me have it back for a moment or so.'

Again Mage cupped Hectors wrist in his hands and closed his eyes in concentration. Before, Hector had felt a coldness but now warmth flooded into his arm... a pleasant sensation that again caused tingles and satisfyingly scratched the irritating itch. For fully three minutes Mage was immobile, then he pulled away with a long sigh, full of his own satisfaction. Then he passed Hector the fishing knife.

'Let's take the dressing off and have a look,' he suggested.

Hector removed the bandage and looked down at his wrist with a bewildered confusion of conflicting reactions.

'What has happened here?' he finally managed to speak.

'You're the doctor so you tell me,' Mage answered in a neutral tone.

Hector could not tear his eyes away from his wrist. There was a livid red mark where the gash had been but the skin had bonded and conjoined with a minimum of coagulation.

'About a dozen stitches, I think you said,' Mage remarked pointedly.

'The lesion could not have been as I first thought,' Hector muttered.

In response Mage said nothing but raised a sardonic eyebrow with a questioning look in his eyes.

'No. Of course. You are right...' Hector's shoulders sagged. 'I saw the damage with my own eyes and it would certainly have needed a number of stitches. But not now.' He looked at Mage wonderingly. 'But how, Colin? Just tell me how.'

'I can't because I don't really know how. It's a matter of channelling the healing energies through the centre of the soul power and then of course there is the human mind. It's infinitely more powerful that we give it credit for being, and once you've harnessed the mindpower and have learned how to focus it, then nothing, in theory, is impossible. The point is this. You can call this a demonstration of healing, but what would you call it if instead of healing your arm I caused it to wilt and wither with disease... if I caused you to feel pain and experience sickness? You wouldn't call it healing, would you? So what *would* you call it?'

'I'd call it evil. I'd call it a blasphemy! But surely you could not do this?' Hector protested.

'If I have the power to heal I also have the power to destroy,' Mage said patiently. 'While I would not do this, or at least I'd try very hard not to do this, *would* and *could* are two very different words. If I use whatever I've got to help you, that's one thing, but if I use it to harm you, it's not only magic, it's black magic, dark and evil... and believe me, Hector, Jadoc Dolorean has no love for mankind. He had no desire to heal. It's his mission to make contact with all that is negative and destructive and to draw it through the ritual opening that his magic will create here in this village of Castillo.

'Look, I don't really know how to say this to you, but this man's magic is so powerful that he can do things that are not humanly possible for the rest of us to do... He could pervert your mind and hypnotise you without you ever realising that he'd done it. Your own free will would be subject to Dolorean's will but the frightening thing is *you wouldn't know!* He could even change his shape if he wanted to...'

'Change his shape?'

Mage chose not to be diverted or checked in his stride. 'He has superhuman strength and if he wanted to impress you he could repeat all the miracles of Jesus Christ including the raising of the dead and walking on water.'

'Colin, you seriously believe all this?'

'I know it sounds incredible. One year ago, then no, I would not have believed it. But now? Yes Hector, I believe totally. In the last twelve months I've spent time with a man who has been successful in halting the ageing process. I've talked to another man who has seen demons and I've spent a number of weeks with a group of people who don't bother talking to each other. They don't need to. They've mastered the art of telepathy and the total symbiosis of mental energy. Not all of them by any means, but a few, have mastered the art of levitation and for many hours when they're in deep meditative trance, they are able to defy the laws of gravity. I wouldn't have believed any of these things had I not seen them first hand with my own eyes, but I have seen them and I do believe. I've also seen some of the awful power within Jadoc Dolorean and I know what he's capable of. He's coming back here soon Hector and this time when he returns all hell is going to break loose!'

Hectors' pipe had gone out. He stuffed it into his trouser pocket and for another second or so studied the miracle of his wounded wrist. 'Can you find some time to try and help my Anna?' he asked quietly without looking up.

'On my life I promise that I will.'

Now Hector did look up and met Mage's penetrating brown eyes. 'Then I am your friend and your ally and you will tell me what I have to do to help you.'

Mage reached out and took the doctor's hand. 'The first thing I must ask is that you say nothing to anyone of what has happened here this morning or discuss the matters that we have spoken of with anyone, not even Anna. And the next thing we'd better do is go and visit these two sick priests of yours.'

As they walked along the cool aisle of the empty church Mage felt that he was trespassing upon enemy territory, and yet standing in the corner of Ignatious's private apartment watching Hector and an attendant nun from the nearby convent go through the motions of making the semi-comatose priest more comfortable, it was hard for him to regard this fat old man as his enemy. It was only when he moved over to a narrow window and found himself looking down into Calle Sombra with Pepe Ortega's old house pulling at him like a magnet, that he was reminded of the more than tenuous link that bound the priest to Dolorean and

Alexandra.

Piecing together the snippets of information provided by Hector he realised that Ignatious of Santa Clara had been struck down by the same blast of psychic energy that had dismissed Miriam Cortez. The priest was Dolorean's man, of that there was no doubt, and as such he steeled himself to feel no pity.

'How is he?' he asked when Hector was finally done and they stood together in the small vestibule that separated the priest's quarters from the main body of the church.

'Basically, he's pretty sick. Cancer of the bowel is awful whichever way you look at it. I diagnosed it about two years ago...' Hector became thoughtful. 'He was waiting to die. It was too far gone for any kind of operation to be successful... and then, about eighteen months ago, about the first time we saw your Mr Dolorean in this village, Ignatious went into a state of remission. No reason, no cause, but it just happened and for the last year he's been as fit as a fiddle. The cancer was still there, of course, but it wasn't growing and it wasn't causing him any pain. And then all of a sudden you turn up in our midst and within a couple of weeks poor old Ignatious is right back where he started.' It was Hector's turn to raise an eyebrow. 'Do we make anything of that?' he asked diplomatically.

'Possibly,' was Mage's ambiguous reply. And then, 'how long would you give him, Hector?'

'Not much more than a couple of months.' Hector, who at this stage, know nothing of Ignatious's link with Dolorean, sounded sad. 'He's not the most endearing old soul I've ever met, but I can think of a dozen better ways to go.'

'What's the state of his mental health?' Mage asked.

'Odd you should state that. He's pretty confused and muddled, but that's only natural after having suffered from the small stroke that took him last weekend, but as well as that he's very agitated – almost as though he's scared to death about something that has nothing to do with his medical condition.'

'That figures,' Mage said moodily, stroking his beard. 'Is he sleeping now?'

'Should be. I've given him a strong enough draught.'

'Okay. Do you mind if we go and sit with him for a while?'

'I don't see why not...' Hector licked his lips. 'Are you going to...'

Mage shook his head. 'I doubt it... We'll see, but I don't think so. Our good Father Ignatious has almost certainly been touched and contaminated by Dolorean and I just want to see if I can slip into his head for a few moments to discover just how much damage has been done. Also I need the answers to some questions that he couldn't or wouldn't give me if I asked outright... Is this going to compromise your Hippocratic oath?'

Hector smiled thinly. 'Colin, it has already been compromised and in any case I think perhaps that there are some things which are more important than naive oaths taken in innocence and ignorance. I mean, you're not going to do him any harm, are you?'

No more than I've already done, Mage thought. 'No,' he said. 'Of course not.'

They moved back into the bedroom and stood either side of the sleeping clergyman. He looked pale and weak and seemingly posed no threat. Mage reached down and closing his eyes, made light fingertip contact with the back of the old priest's mottled hand. He may have been heavily sedated but Mage still covered him with somnambulant thought as a vanguard to his mental probe. Gently, without any visible indication, he slipped into the sick man's head, opening his own mind to receive the imprints of his mental patterns.

Slowly he began to unravel the old man's memories and amid flashing visions of the Christ that was not The Christ and the virgin that was no longer human let alone a virgin, he extracted the information that he sought.

A thousand miles to the north east a dark green Jaguar swerved off the road and came to rest in a grove of trees just outside the small French town of Amboise. The female in the left hand seat neither moved nor reacted to the sudden change in direction and velocity, but the driver rested his head against the rim of the steering wheel, struggling for vision as he sought to exorcise the alien presence that had suddenly entered his head.

His thoughts were magnetised towards his destination, towards The Place Of The Opening, and he found himself focusing upon his first disciple. All was not well.

The first disciple's face swan into vision before his hooded eyes... The priest was prostrate, supine on a sickbed, and he was not alone. Jadoc Dolorean sensed other presences around the bed – two powerful entities, although one much more so than the other. And then there was a melding of minds. Something inveigled its way into his brain and began to suck the energy from within it.

Dolorean was instantly alert. The Magician! The female's manmate!

With a growl that was far from entirely human, Jadoc Dolorean shook his oddly shaped head in pain and brought down the screens of mental self preservation. At the same time he lashed out in retaliation against the alarming and unexpected intrusion.

The images were coming thick and fast into Mage's consciousness... There was a floorboard that led to a narrow tunnel, somewhere vaguely to the left of Santa Clara's high altar. Then there was a stone, dark and craggy, striated with silver seams. It was hidden somewhere, but somewhere close. Then there was a sea of faces, some which he recognised others that he did not, sitting around a table, all concentrating on the curious piece of streaky ore. The scene changed and he saw Ignatious talking to the young boy who had attacked him in Calle Sombra...

Then there was a flare of yellow light and within the light he beheld the death mask of Alexandra's face – and behind it, lunging for him with jagged teeth and amber eyes, a travesty of the man who had already caused him so much grief and harm. For one fleeting second there was the smell of rich leather and the impression of a large car parked amid tall and swaying trees... and then Mage calmly broke the link, taking his fingers back from Ignatious's hand and stepping away from the edge of the bed.

He'd been aware of the dark aura of energy that emanated from the priest's body and would perhaps have spent some time looking at the extent of damage caused by the cancer, had not the image of Dolorean and Alexandra suddenly started to crown his mind, which at that point had been wide open and extremely vulnerable. Now, sensing an incoming counter offensive, he closed his mind and pushed out with his own formidable defensive shields.

'Something might happen here,' he said shortly.

'What...?' Hector began, but then fell silent as the priest's eyes snapped open. Hector mimicked Mage in taking a backwards step, for there was something not quite right about the look in those eyes. They were hard and shining with malevolent intelligence, as black as agates, and unbelonging to their owner. The eyes looked on to Hector and the doctor found himself staring into two black orbs or sentient hatred. Ignatious's lips pulled back across clenched teeth and a guttural voice emerged, not so much from the mouth but more, if this was possible – which it was not – from the actual vocal chords themselves.

'Meddler!' The voice grated at him...Then the priest's head was turning away and Hector breathed an inwards sigh of relief. It had been a brief (thank God) but weirdly unnerving experience for whoever had said that single word – *Meddler!* – whoever it had been, Hector was sure of one thing. *It hadn't been Ignatious!*

'Hector, over here please,' Mage spoke calmly and Hector moved around the end of the bed to stand at his friend's side. 'Keep well back, but look at our friend's eyes!'

'I know,' Hector muttered. 'They used to be baby blue and now they're as black as coal...'

'Black?' Mage echoed. 'Look again!'

And when Hector did look again the eyes were now no longer black but a dull and dirty orange... The irises, brighter and more luminescent, edging towards amber, had drawn themselves into slits. Cat's eyes in a man's head.

'Soon!' The guttural grating voice, seemingly coming from somewhere deep inside the priest, echoed around the room...

...And then the room was filled with flying cascades of green bile and yellow vomit that spewed forth from the priest's gagging mouth. A picture of The Virgin Mary shattered on the wall where it hung and a heavy crucifix detached itself from the back of the door and hurled itself across the room to crash against the narrow window, smashing the small panes of glass into even smaller smithereens. For a few seconds the priest's body quivered and vibrated, the bed trembling against the tiled floor, bed clothes flying in all directions in response to the priest's flailing arms and legs.

Then there was stillness and silence. Hector, suddenly five years older in as many seconds, stared at Mage speechlessly. Mage stared back.

'You didn't do any of this did you?' The doctor finally asked.

'No.'

'Then for God's sake what?'

'That part of Jadoc Dolorean that resides within the mind and body of the priest.'

'You're saying that in some way Ignatious is... possessed?'

Mage looked grim. 'Not exactly, but your analogy is near enough the truth to make little difference,' he conceded.

'What,' Hector began tentatively, 'do we do with him now?'

'I want him out of here,' Mage said tersely. 'Out of the village and into some nice safe hospital ward where there are always people on hand to monitor his progress or lack of it. As far away from Castillo as you can get him, as much for his own sake as ours.'

'There is the ecclesiastical hospice in Seville,' Hector mused. 'Is that far enough?'

'It sounds perfect,' Mage replied.

'It won't be difficult to effect such a transfer. Maybe it's something I should have done days ago. The Andalucian way, however, is that we look after our own for as long as we can.'

'I'm glad that you didn't,' Mage responded. 'Because despite the mess, an awful lot of good has come from this encounter. For one thing, you've had some first hand experience of what we're up against. Secondly, I've gleaned some important information. Ignatious wasn't the only one to be contaminated by Dolorean's power... There were others and I've got to find out who they are. They'll be people who've had particularly close dealings with Ignatious over the last year and perhaps they'll be people who've shown some odd behavioural patterns. Unless I'm mistaken, they'll be a list floating around somewhere. Also there's a lode stone hidden away which I must find and destroy.'

'A lode stone? What's a lode stone?'

'In this case it will be a lump of crystal ore that has been impregnated with sentient psychic energy. It acts like a beacon for negative vibrations, gathers them in and then, if you know how to control it, discharges those energies in an offensive manner against anything that is perceived by the controller to be a threat.

'More importantly, there is a secret passageway located somewhere that I'll have to find, even if only to see where it leads to. It'll be within a stone's throw of the altar...'

With hands that were far from calm or confident, Hector began stuffing his pipe with rich aromatic tobacco. 'And you got all this from reading Ignatious's mind?'

'Yes, and more besides, I'm afraid.' Mage lit a cigarette and passed Hector the flaming Zippo. 'I got the distinct impression that Dolorean has left his lair in England. He's on the move. Almost certainly on his way here.'

The dark green Jaguar cruised slowly through the sleepy French town of Amboise, negotiating the one way system no less than three times before Jadoc Dolorean found what he was looking for.

As he checked into the small but up-market private hotel, the receptionist, a thin woman with her hair in a tight bun, looked on with some sympathy. 'Your wife looks very tired monsieur... If there is anything we can do?'

Dolorean flashed her an easy grin. 'You're very kind,' he said in perfect French. 'The pregnancy... the long journey... I'm sure she'll be much brighter by tomorrow.'

The porter led them up to an old fashioned but well appointed room that gave an attractive view over the River Loire. Dolorean tipped him generously with firm instructions that they were not to be disturbed.

As soon as the bedroom door was shut and bolted and he was positive that no one could see into the room – he'd made certain they were on the third floor and not overlooked by any other building – he relaxed his shapehold and gradually reverted to his more natural form. The facial muscles fell into something humanoid, but most definitely not human and beneath the ridiculous garments he had to wear in his guise of homo sapien, his body shape also began to change. The body armour of scale and carapace was not called for in his circumstances and he was content to fall into a loose approximation of his naked self.

As his form metamorphosised so did that of the female. She sat on the edge of the bed, bulging beneath her smocklike pregnancy dress, staring vacantly into space. Now that he no longer had to maintain her shape and motion as well as his own, he was able to draw on fresh reserves of energy. Stripping the clothes from the female he eased her down on the bed, monitoring the life form that pulsed within her. At least all was well in this respect... for a few moments out there in the light he'd worried about the incubator's internal physiological mechanism. There'd certainly been some tension and distress when he'd had to deal with invading thoughtwaves from the manmate.

Needing rest himself he stretched out on his own bed and closed his eyes. Normally he only needed to sleep four hours in a forty hour cycle, but that was in his own environment. In the manworld, using his energies day in day out to shapehold for two, while constantly guarding and monitoring against discovery, eight hours in forty had soon become an absolute minimum.

He'd been active now on this side of the divide for two and a half man years. While the intelligence he had gathered had given him great strength and knowledge, his physical and mental reserves were dangerously low. This, however, was only to be expected and he'd been well prepared by his clanfather to endure the stress of long term residence in the manworld... indeed, not just prepared but *chosen!*

Even so, he was glad that his mission was nearing its final phase. Less than one and a half man moons and – thin lips pulled into what passed for a smile – they would no longer be man moons but The Moons Of The Dispossessed. The Moons Of The Djinn! While the most delicate part of his mission lay still ahead – the placing of the female at The Opening and the ritual magic crafted around the emergence of The Newlife that would create the reality of the other opening, giving his brethren and clan access to this green and sweet domain – the difficult part of his mission was over. The selection of the incubator and the long months of duality and subtefuge were behind him.

And yet he worried. The manmate magician was still active after all that had been thrown against him. It seemed that he had successfully overcome the First Disciple and all the powers that had been invested in him. Even now the manmate was at The Sacred Place, waiting for him and preparing for combat and confrontation. The Shapechanger did not know how he had managed to survive the psychic onslaught that had been focused against his life force, but the fact of the matter was that he had! What the Shapechanger did know, however, was that nothing could be allowed to jeopardise or delay The Opening and, therefore, before he even attempted the ritual, the manmate magician and any of those who might have allied themselves with his unholy cause would have to be neutralised once and for all. Destroyed and dismembered, their shards of rotting flesh discarded upon the four winds of oblivion.

In his building anger the shapechanger's body began to writhe as the scales of offense and defense found form on his hard and shining hide. He breathed deeply, found the control he sought and the scales disappeared as ambiguously as they had formed.

'Soon,' he whispered to himself in the barked squeel of his own tongue. 'Soon I shall destroy you. Not with the magic of my mind but with the claws of my own hands! You should have died months ago and by the time I've finished with you, you'll wish you had!'

Earlier that same day, but on the other side of the world, John and Tamara had booked into The Ambassador Hotel on the corner of Lafayette Street in the old quarter of New Orleans. Light had signed the register as Reverend and Mrs John Light of Los Angeles and had glared challengingly at the reservations clerk, daring her to take issue with anything. Tamara had noted the nature of the registration with a sense of profound pleasure and deep wonderment. The last days out at the Demsville cabin had not been altogether pleasant, but if this was the result of their sojourn, then as far as she was concerned, it had been more than well worth it.

Light had talked to her a lot more, telling her about the dark years of his involvement with black magic, years of powerful but highly illegal existence. He'd also told her, albeit without any detail, of the one incident which had in the space of a few short hours brought about the radical conversion from Satanism.

'I was in the shit,' he'd grinned at her mirthlessly. 'I had the FBI, the IRS and the Narcotics Bureau crawling up one half of my black ass and the Mafia along with a group of radical right wing terrorists climbing up the other half. Not one of them could touch me on their own, but then they decided to get their act together by co-operating with each other and I was suddenly target of the season and fall guy of the year. They chased me all across the States for the better part of three weeks and however much distance I managed to put between us, they seemed to catch me up just a little more with every Goddamn day. In the end, I ran to Demsville and holed up with Old Rugby for a while.

'I managed about two days of peace before they figured that's where I was then I was running again on Rugby's antique Harley, but with nowhere to run to. They had cars patrolling every road and they even had a couple of choppers up in the air. One of 'em spotted me and chased me all the way across the where the old farm used to be... There was a guy on a loud hailer saying to stop or they'd shoot and then the bastards started shooting at me and the guy on the loud hailer was saying they'd stop if I stopped, but Tam, I knew that if I stopped I was going to be stopped for good.'

He'd pointed to the track that led away from the lake. 'I came down that track doing eighty miles an hour with two police cars coming up fast behind me and this helicopter sitting right on my head. Reckoned that I'd rather be damned than dead or shut up in sing sing for twenty years so I drove that old Harley right between those two trees over there... and the cops never did find me.'

A glazed and veiled expression had crossed his face. 'Don't want to talk to you too much about what happened that day, Tam, but I'll tell you this. By my watch I was gone from this planet earth for exactly three hours and ten minutes, but by old Rugby's watch and by the time that passed in this world I was gone for the better part of three days and to tell you the truth Tammy, I've never been the same man since.'

They'd stayed in the cabin for another day and then in the space of an hour, Light had decided it was time to go. They'd done a minimal amount of packing and now, going from the ridiculous to the sublime in the space of four short hours, they were checking into one of The South's most prestigious hotels. As she sat in the bath, foam bubbles frothing above her chin, she reflected that life with John Light was nothing if not unpredictable.

A little while later, she found him standing by the window, studying the panoramic view of what was surely one of America's most characterful cities. He was naked and still. Thoughtful, but not particularly tense. Coming up behind him, she wrapped her arms around his enormous chest, resting her cheek against the hard edge of his shoulder blade. It was a while before he spoke.

'Got some decisions to make, I guess,' he said quietly.

'Want to tell me what they are?' she asked.

There was another moment of silence and then 'One of them concerns you. I know that you saw what I wrote on the registration form... You want to tell me how you feel about that.'

'I feel very good about it John – but I'm not asking you for anything.'

'I know. You never have. But what if I'm asking you for something?'

Tamara's heart was pounding and her legs felt weak. She could not believe that this conversation was actually taking place. 'Are you asking me what I think you're asking me?' she finally managed to ask, but unable to keep the quaver from her voice.

'I guess I am at that.'

'Then as sure as hell I ain't going to say no to you, John Light, but I am going to ask why?'

'Feels right. Feels necessary. Feels as though it might be part of a few other decisions that I've got to make...'

He turned and looked into her eyes and saw the love that was there, that had always been there and cursed himself for not having seen it and perceived its worth a long time before this. But this was just another thing that he'd been guilty of running from and now the time of running was coming to an end.

'What happens Tam, if there isn't any more cash and glamour? If you and me were just living quietly together, enjoying the same kind of things that everyone else enjoys? I've given up other lives in my past and I can give up being the evangelical reverend just as easily if I have to.'

'You do whatever you want to do John, and whatever it is, I'm happy to be there doing it with you.'

'You sure about that?'

'Damn sure, John.'

'Okay. I need to phone LA.'

The telephone call between John Light and Vern Osborn was stormy to say the least. Vern wanted to know where he was, where he'd been and when was he getting back to California. Everything was a mess, Vern said, from the waist paper baskets in the office to the negotiations with the radio and TV companies – who had agreed to John's terms, who would continue to agree to John's terms if only he'd turn up and keep to the contracted schedule of broadcasts. Everyone wanted to know where Light was and rumours were rife. One conviction was that he'd done a disappearing act as a huge publicity stunt, another idea was that he was having a nervous breakdown somewhere and there was even a third opinion that said he was dead.

'What do I tell people?' Vern yelled down the phone, anger getting the better part of good manners.

'You tell 'em whatever you want to tell them,' Light said calmly. 'I've got things to do and don't scream at me about being in the hot seat. You've earned a good living these last ten years while my ass has been the one that's been burned, so now earn your salary. I'm out of communication for the next few weeks at least and nobody needs to know why or what for. It's my own business. I'll phone you again when I know what's happening. Now, I've got a question for you. Have I had any message from a couple of people called Tom Lewis or Christina Carol?'

'Yeah. Tom Lewis arrived in LA from Spain two days ago. Says that there ain't nothing happening there and so he got bored and came home!'

'What about Christina Carol?' Light asked.

'Far as I know, she's still there. Tom said she wasn't ready to leave, so he left without her... For God's sake, John, what the fuck is this all about?'

'Can't tell you yet, Vern. Maybe I can never tell you. But thanks for holding the fort and just keep at it until I get back to you, okay. But there's one thing I *can* tell you that might come as a bit of a surprise...' He winked at Tamara. 'Tam and me are getting married in the morning!'

'You're what?'

Light hung up and then dialled the international operator. 'I want to make a person to person call to a Christina Carol in Spain,' he instructed, giving the number and settling down to wait. Tamara folded her body into the crook of his arm as they lay on the bed, three words ringing in her ears. *Married. Tomorrow morning.*

The ringing telephone dragged Christina from her hazy morninglight daydream. Angel stirred as she reached across the bed and lifted the antiquated receiver from its cradle. She became immediately alert when she realised the call was incoming long distance and from the States.

She was wide awake when she heard the unmistakable bass tones of John Light's voice speaking in her ear. He asked a number of questions to which she gave clear and direct answers. One of the questions in particular she found more than just a little interesting.

'Have you,' he asked her, 'come across the Englishman called Colin Mage?'

'Sure. He's resident here. Supposed to be writing a book on psychology. Shared bar space with him a few times and I'd say he was a very powerful honcho. Exudes energy like you wouldn't imagine. Never managed to get a picture of him though... We *might* have done if Tom hadn't been so impatient.'

'Tom Lewis is history,' Light told her. 'At least, as far as I'm concerned he is. He's back in LA and you're where I asked you to be. That's important, and I thank you for your faith... Now Christina, forget all the hard facts. Give me your gut reactions. Tell me about the village. What do your senses tell you?'

'There's something strange going on here. It's full of the weirdest energies and from the photographs that Tom did take, I can tell you that there are some very strange and powerful auras in this place...' Angel stirred out of his slumbers with a semi comatose yawn. '...Listen Reverend, I'm not exactly in a position where I can talk to you openly right now. Any chance you can phone me back in an hour or so?'

'I will phone again, but probably tomorrow or the day after. What I need you to do is simply stay put until I get there.'

'You're coming *here?*'

'Almost as good as on my way.'

He broke the connection and looked down at Tamara. 'Ever been to Spain, Tam?' he asked thoughtfully.

'John I've been with you since I was only fourteen years old and you *know* I've never been to Spain!'

'Well baby,' he leaned over and kissed her nose affectionately. 'That's where we're going. That's where *you're* going. For your honeymoon.'

19.

Sombra Revisited

Mage watched as the two medics transferred Ignatious into the back of the ambulance. The priest's skin was as white as their white coats, shining like alabaster in the mid afternoon sunshine. His head lolled to one side and although his eyes were open, they were vacant and unfocused. Mage knew he would not last anything like the two months Hector had given him – he'd be lucky if he managed two weeks! The shadow of death hung over the stretcher and despite the warmth of the day, a shiver curled up the middle of The Magician's spine.

Priest killer! A voice hissed in the back of his mind.

The ambulance finally pulled out of the plaza, watched by a hundred pairs of eyes. In true Spanish fashion, people had forsaken their siestas to come to their windows and open doors to watch the unfolding drama. There was a palpable sense of unease. Ignatious may not have been endearingly popular with his flock but he'd been their priest for the past twenty years and it bode ill for the congregation when its priest was being carted off to die.

'Where are they taking him, Doctor?' one distressed woman called shrilly from her doorway.

'To the church hospital in Seville,' Hector called back, aware that his words were being picked up by many other ears. 'You must not worry. I have spoken to the authorities and there will be another priest here to take mass in the morning.'

'What about Father Francisco from Santa Maria?' One man asked, his voice carrying across the sunbaked square. 'We hear that he also is very sick.'

'Oh, you mustn't worry about that either. He'll soon be back on his feet,' Hector responded with more cheerfulness and confidence than he felt. 'He's just come down with a rather nasty virus, that's all.'

The substantial crowd of onlookers was only partially mollified. There was, after all, something wrong with a village when *both* priests were ill at the same time.

'Christ,' Hector muttered to Mage. 'I need a drink.'

'Yes. Me too. But somewhere away from here, I think.'

They climbed into the doctor's pale green Renault Four and Hector drove in silence, pulling in to the side of the road at the bodega. They found a table on the terrace, hidden away from prying eyes behind a lattice screen that was adorned with a profusion of climbing plants. Mage sipped at a coke while Hector gulped thirstily from a glass of light beer.

The velvet bag with the mysterious lode stone sat on the floor between their feet. It had taken Mage less than five minutes to find it at the bottom of a cupboard in Ignatious's study, while Hector had been making his phone calls; two to Seville and one to the clinic in La Linea, Mage had almost gone straight to it.

'What are you going to do with it?' Hector asked after a minute.

'I'm in two minds,' Mage admitted. 'Every instinct demands that I throw it into the river and have done with it, but on the other hand it's an important weapon in the enemy's armoury. If it could be turned against him it might be very useful to us. Do you have any thoughts about the list?'

'I've got a lot of thoughts about your list,' Hector replied. 'None of them very good...'

Hector had watched while Mage had laid the stone upon the study desk then he'd sat in Ignatious's chair and closing his eyes had held his right hand palm down, a few centimetres above the curiously striated lump of quartz. After a few moments his brow had furrowed.

'Not many of them, thank God,' he'd murmured. 'Certainly less than a dozen. I'd expected more... There's an old man with a craggy face. Very lived in. A heart condition and an alcohol problem...'

'Diego Matan,' Hector said straight away.

'...Okay... Now I've got a tall woman. Long dark hair. Fine features. Very red lips... long red finger nails... she's not a Spaniard...'

'Miriam Cortez!'

'...Next to her is a man with a muddled mind... a moustache... I can see a birthmark or a tattoo on his hand and there's a kind of funny scar just above his right eye...'

Hector had been fascinated. 'That's Peter Cortez,' he'd confirmed.

'I've got a young man now... late teens or early twenties... plump, greasy hair, very curly... an awful lot of anger and violence in him...'

'This sounds like a boy called Miguel Torres.'

'...An old woman, very devout, but obsessively so. Eyesight is bad. Wears thick correctional lenses. Then there's a man. He's very much associated with the old woman. He's old too. Got a fat face and thinning hair and I can see liver spots on his scalp...'

'I know who you're seeing!'

'Women...' Mage carried on giving no indication that he'd heard Hector's comments. 'Two women. Both young, very young indeed... sisters, I think. There's a very tight bond that binds them together... they might even be twins... And another man. Very strong and vital, this one. Enormous hands. Wears a lot of gold jewellery... He enjoys killing and I have him with a rifle under his arm. Maybe he's a hunter or something...'

There had been a long sigh and Mage had opened his eyes. 'That's it. That's the magic circle... the secret cabal. But I don't know who they all are.'

'I think I do,' Hector had said evenly.

Their privacy had been suddenly broken as an elderly nun swept into the study. 'What is happening here?' she had asked imperiously. 'These are private apartments!'

'Your pardon, Mother Superior,' Hector had been charming and confident. 'Alas, our good Father Ignatious has suffered a serious decline in his health and I have just been telephoning the ecclesiastical authorities in Seville to arrange for his admission to their hospice. He needs to go there straight away... the medication and attention he requires can no longer be provided here... There will be an ambulance here within the hour to effect the transfer.'

'And who is this man?' she'd asked brusquely, nodding towards Mage, who had carefully placed himself between the investigating nun and the lode stone that still sat exposed on the desk.

'This gentleman is Señor Mage. A good friend of mine from England.'

'Is he a doctor too?'

'He does a wonderful job of healing people!' Hector had said enthusiastically, avoiding the question and denying the lie. 'As for our presence here, I'm afraid I'm having to check through some of the father's papers, looking for old prescriptions. The doctors in Seville will want to know what drugs he has been taking and in what quantities.'

It was a lame excuse but the Mother Superior had accepted it. Even so, she'd hovered in the hallway and although they'd had no time to search in any depth, Mage had, however, surreptitiously covered the stone with an old velvet bible bag and when they'd eventually left, he'd carried it out nonchalantly tucked beneath his arm.

'Your list.' Hector drummed his fingers thoughtfully on the gnarled old olive wood table. 'It is interesting. I know all of the people you have described and they all have one or two things in common. They've either recently gone missing from Castillo, or they've recently died.

'Diego Matan passed over with a heart attack, two weeks ago... Although to the best of my knowledge, and remembering that he'd been my patient for ten years, he did not have a heart condition as such. Certainly, his liver was playing up a fair old bit and he was wheezy with emphysema, but those conditions do not in themselves bring about heart failure.

'The woman you describe with the long hair and red nails and lips. This is without doubt Miriam Cortez. She died a week ago and her husband Peter, he has a moustache and a tattoo of a bird on his left hand, is in hospital with the weirdest case of concussion ever to register in Andalucian medical records.

'The violent young boy with the curly hair – this sounds very much like a lad called Miguel Torres. He's currently in Algerciras jail waiting to be tried on a case of malicious wounding. He was in a disco brawl a couple of weeks ago and the silly fool pulled a knife and all but killed Paco Camino with a very nasty stomach wound.

'The two young women, and here's a bit of a mystery, are Sisters Serafina and Isabella. Both novices at the convent. They're twins and they're alike as two peas in a pod. What's more, they also happen to be Ignatious's God daughters. Both these girls had an attack of religious hysterics last week, but there's nothing remarkable in that because these two silly children have been having visions of Christ and the Virgin Mother since they were six years old... This time was a bit different though because instead of having visions of God they said that they'd seen the devil. It was all over the top. In my opinion, a lot of unnatural sexual repression finding its own way to the surface. You shouldn't put pretty girls in dark places like convents. On the other hand, the Mother Superior – she's the old battle axe who barged in on us back in Santa Clara, by the way – she took it seriously enough to pack them off to a Carmelite sanctuary, one of the order's safe houses, up near Antiquera. I've not heard how they're getting on, but to the best of my knowledge they're still there.

'The last character on your list is a man called Raul Castro. He's an arrogant and an extremely violent man... certainly the hunter, as you so accurately described. He has a place half way between San Pablo and the river. Nominally he's a game warden for the National Park, which is an anomaly if ever there was one. I always thought that game wardens were employed to preserve our wild life but Raul tends to prefer killing it. If there's a venta or a bar around these parts serving venison or wild boar, you can bet your last duro they bought the carcass under the counter from Raul Castro! What on earth he's doing involved with Ignatious, I have no idea. He's probably the most irreligious man I've ever met in my life.'

'And where might he be now?' Mage asked quietly.

'I haven't a clue. I've not seen him round the village for the last few weeks, but that doesn't mean to say he hasn't been here. Even if he hasn't been in Castillo, that's not unusual. He's a man who does not like company and he spends much of his time out in the campo. I suppose in a way, Raul is our odd man out because he's the only one on your list who isn't dead, hasn't committed suicide, hasn't fallen sick or had an accident of any sort. At least, to the best of my knowledge he hasn't.'

'Maybe,' Mage mused, 'it wouldn't be a bad idea to drive out to his place sometime in the next day or so. Just to make sure he is still in one piece.'

'I take your point,' Hector concurred uneasily, 'because when you work it out the odds are nine to one that he's not!'

Mage leaned back enjoying the warmth of the terrace as it seeped into his body. He had to work hard not to allow his feeling of elation get out of hand. Hector's horror stories of other peoples' misfortunes were but one side of the coin. Flipping the mental penny and scrutinising the other face, he realised that in the space of four short weeks he had successfully destroyed Dolorean's inner circle of disciples and, indeed, without any real effort or concentration of energy. To all intents and purposes, his presence alone had been enough to create the havoc.

Certainly, Dolorean would still come to Castillo, bringing with him the full force of his power and his craft, but when he arrived he would find himself alone and without allies. That did not mean that he would not acquire new ones, but the circle he'd spent a year in the building of was irrevocably smashed. Mage did not know to what extent this might hurt the shapechanger, but the thought of any damage done to the Djinn was enough to cause him a profound feeling of satisfaction.

Hector found himself studying Mage's face and he was struck by the anomalous blending of the strength in the Englishman's features. The soft brown eyes – were they really so soft, or were they not just impenetrably deep with mystical sadness? If a man's eyes were the windows to his soul, Mage's soul went on forever! True, he had an easy smile but there were times when Hector had seen ice in that smile as well as gentle laughter. He wore his tightly cropped beard like a mummer's mask that concealed the identity of the true man beneath and although Hector was the most heterosexual of beings, he was still able to look at Colin Mage in that moment and clearly appreciate and understand why Anna might find him so magnetically attractive.

He exuded a powerful energy that made one unambiguously aware of being in his presence. Even though he may have done nothing to draw attention to himself, he commanded that attention in a way that was both inexplicable and unnerving. When he *did* do something to attract attention, rather than answering questions, it created a dozen more.

'I wonder what you're thinking, Hector Sanchez,' Mage said dreamily without opening his eyes.

'Don't you know?'

'No. As I told Anna, I can't read minds at will. With Ignatious it was different. An invasion of privacy and with very good cause, but in your case I have no good cause and therefore it would be extremely difficult and morally wrong... but I do sense your questions and your bewilderment. I sense that you need me to put your mind at rest about a dozen things you can't even begin to put into words and, until you can do that, I can't help you any more than I've already done.'

'Maybe we should just leave it where it is for the time being...' Hector looked almost shame faced into his empty glass, feeling not unlike the schoolboy caught out stealing apples.'

'That might be wise,' Mage agreed, 'but, Hector, just remember one thing. Whatever I am, whatever you *think* I am, I am no threat to you or to those you love. I'm here to help – if possible, to avert a threat – and if people around you like Diego and Señora Cortez have come to some grief, then to some very great extent it's all a part of what is happening here. They've been the cause of their own troubles.'

'Yes, I dare say that is true. We are all the cause of our own troubles, are we not?'

Mage opened his eyes. 'No, that's not always true,' he said firmly. 'I'm not, you're not, Anna isn't... but people like Diego and Miriam, even Ignatious... they are very different.'

A thoughtfully curious look found residence on Mage's face. 'Hector, do you know a small petite blond woman, very attractive, around her early thirties... not Spanish?'

The doctor shook his head. 'No, I don't think so. Why?'

'Odd. It's just that I have the impression of someone who fits that description standing very close to you. There's a bond between you and, for want of better words, I'd call it a lovebond.'

'Colin, my friend, the only lovebond that I have in my life is the one that I have with Anna. With my work and my daughter, frankly there's no room for anyone else.'

'Ummm,' Mage mused. 'That might be true and might have been true, but I'll tell you one thing, it isn't going to be like that for ever. There's someone coming into your life who is going to be very important to you and you're not going to travel along the avenues of your future just as Anna's papa and the village's doctor. There's a lovebond waiting around the corner and unless I'm much mistaken, it will be with a very pretty lady with short fair hair and freckles. If you don't know her now, you'll certainly know her when you meet her.'

Hector looked amused and not a little sceptical. 'It's a nice thought, but forgive me if I say I'll believe it only when it happens. The question is, what do we do now?'

'Go back to the church and look for that tunnel,' Mage said promptly.

'You are sure that there is such a tunnel?'

'I was right about the stone, wasn't I?'

'That, my friend,' Hector conceded, 'you most certainly were!'

The floor around the altar was made from solid cement and concrete. There could be no tunnel here – besides which Mage had had the clear impression of wooden planks and boards. His attention was drawn to a small door off to the left. It was unlocked and led to the vestry, which was a windowless box of a room without light or air but which *did* have plank floorboards, which were covered with an old square of faded carpet. Giving Hector a knowing look, Mage kicked the rug to one side with his boot and both men found themselves staring down at what was obviously a trap door.

'Well,' Hector said with a half hearted chuckle, 'That was easy enough.' Leaning down he took hold of the brass ring and heaved. The trap door swung up soundlessly on well oiled springs and the dim light from the vestry illuminated a set of wooden ladder rungs that disappeared into the shadows of the earth.

'We're going to need a light. I'll fetch the torch from the car.'

'Hang on...' Mage pulled out his Zippo and, igniting the flame, climbed down through the hole in the ground. Within a few seconds there was a small click and the tunnel was filled with harsh light from a single shadeless light bulb wedged into a socket next to the ladder rungs.

Hector looked down at Mage's grinning face two metres below. 'You knew that there'd be a light switch,' he said accusingly.

'No. I just guessed. Come on down and close that trap door behind you.'

Hector eased his considerable bulk over the edge and, lowering the lid, descended the rungs of the ladder. The loamy smell of earth assailed his nostrils and arriving at the bottom it was easy to see why. While there were duckboards on the floor and support timbers every few metres, the tunnel was cut through hard packed soil and thick clay.

It was narrow – the width of a single man – and he had to lower his head to avoid scraping it on the crumbling rough hewn roof and it was also very long. It disappeared into the distance as straight as an arrow. It was very hard to judge that distance, but he was able to discern the far end of the tunnel by another pool of light that beckoned them forwards along the intensely claustrophobic passageway.

'Well Hector, what do you make of this?'

'I'm not sure what to make of it, but have you noticed the timbers? The tunnel may be old but all this wood is new. Somebody has recently gone to a lot of trouble in making this tunnel usable. It will be very interesting to see where it leads us.'

'Hector, I'd be a liar if I said that I didn't already have a pretty good idea.'

Mage counted off almost two hundred paces before they arrived at a ladder, the exact replica of the one at the vestry end of the passage, that led up to its own easily definable trap door. Without hesitation, Mage ascended the steps and after some fiddling with a catch and bolt, swung the door open and upwards.

It had been hot in the tunnel but now a wave of damp coldness descended upon them like a thick blanket. No light penetrated the oblong aperture of stygian blackness and, although Hector scrambled up the ladder after Mage, following him into the unknown, he did so very much with his heart in his mouth.

Mage lit the Zippo again and Hector struck matches. Along with the glow coming up from the tunnel there was enough light for them to see that they were in a small featureless box of a room; bare wooden floor, mildewed walls and a single door. The atmosphere was chillingly oppressive and, as Mage tried the door, finding it locked, he was very aware that this was indeed the heart of enemy territory.

'You any good at picking locks?' he asked Hector conversationally.

'No,' the doctor replied. 'Are you?'

'Hopeless.'

'So what are we going to do?'

'I weigh in at around a hundred and eighty pounds,' Mage mused, 'and no offence meant, but you must be all of two hundred and fifty, which gives us the combined pushing power of over four hundred pounds – so let's push like hell and see what happens.'

'You're seriously going to break in?'

'Damn right I am.'

'What if there's somebody there?'

'Then they're in for a shock – but Hector, there isn't anyone there.'

The two men leaned their shoulders to the door and heaved. There was a splintering and a groaning of pressure but the door held fast, only bursting open with a loud crack of breaking wood when they applied a battering ram technique.

Mage did not hesitate. Holding the Zippo above his head he strode across the threshold and ran lightly up a flight of stone steps until he came to another door. This one was unlocked and swung open to his touch. He emerged into a long corridor with light filtering through from shuttered and curtained windows to both his left and his right. The air was full of the smell of age – old papers and ancient wood. Dust motes danced in the shafts of light and floorboards creaked beneath his feet as he moved towards the strongest source of daylight. Pulling back the latticed blind, he found himself looking along the length of Calle Sombra, with Santa Clara's sombre edifice over to his right.

'Surprise, surprise,' he spoke to himself with a note of profound satisfaction in his voice. 'Calle Sombra revisited!'

With Hector's help he searched and checked every room. The house was not dirty, but it was very dusty and had that unlived in feel to it. Both the electricity and the water supply were connected, and there was a basic degree of furnishing – a table and four chairs in the kitchen, beds in two of the three bedrooms and a three piece suite that had definitely seen better days in the main salon. Pictures of a bygone age enshrined in heavy frames adorned many of the walls. Mostly they were hunting scenes, the stag at bay, the beheading of the boar.

'Monuments to the very worst of Spanish bad taste,' Hector murmured. And then, 'what are we looking for, Colin? There doesn't seem to be anything here which is out of the ordinary.'

Mage pursed his lips. 'I don't know. I don't know what I expected to find. The atmosphere leaves much to be desired... cold and unwelcoming...'

'Colin, if I am to play Doctor Watson to your Sherlock Holmes, I must point out that the damp and cold comes from the fact that the house has been empty all winter and that the unwelcoming feeling might just have something to do with the fact that we are guilty of trespass and breaking and entering... but,' and Hector cast a cautious glance over his shoulder, 'it is also true to say that ever since we have been here I've felt very uncomfortable. It's almost as though the house knows we're here and I have to tell you, my friend, that I am not very happy with this feeling.'

'No, neither am I,' Mage agreed. 'But I suppose it's to be expected. This house is extremely important to Dolorean. He went to great expense and connivance to get it. There must be something here that...'

His words were cut off by a heavy thud that came from beneath their feet.

'What was that?' Hector exclaimed.

'It came from down in the cellar,' Mage said. 'The trap door...'

They hurried down the stone steps and, sure enough, the trap door was now firmly closed and no amount of pulling or prising would get it open again.'

'Did it fall or was it pushed?' Mage wondered.

'I beg your pardon?'

Mage grinned. 'Sorry. What I mean is, did the trap door close by itself or did someone close it? In the case of the latter option then *who* closed it? Maybe we'd better get back to the church and see if anyone has been messing around at that end of the tunnel.'

They moved back up onto the ground floor and here Mage paused for a few moments, pushing his mind out into every corner of the house, impregnating it with his psychic spore. Inevitably Dolorean would bring Alexandra to this place and he wanted it to be known to them both that this space had been penetrated.

'No way out at the front,' Hector informed him. 'But there's a garden at the back, so if we've got to break our way out, that's the way to go.'

As luck would have it there was no need to do any breaking for while the back door was firmly locked there was a fair sized window above a sink in the kitchen that swung open without resistance. It was a tight squeeze, especially for Hector, but within a very few minutes they were both standing, albeit a little dusty and bruised, on the small back porch of the house.

As Hector had said, there was a small garden, matted and overgrown by wild vegetation and surrounded by a high crumbling wall, remarkable not only for its height but also for want of a door. The sun was out of sight and low in the sky and the garden was in deep shadow, a brooding sentient shadow that made Mage's hackles rise and pushed his psychic defences up to a state of red alert.

Hector was immediately aware of the state of sudden tension in his companion but for the life of him could not see what was causing it. They were out of the house now and the danger, if indeed there had been any danger, was behind them, surely? And yet here was the Englishman, poised and coiled and sniffing at the wind like a hawk in search of its prey. Hector studied the younger man's eyes and saw that they were quartering the overgrown garden ahead of them, square metre by every square metre.

'What's wrong?' the doctor asked nervously.

Mage did not answer the question but instead asked one of his own.

'Where would you say was the easiest place to get over the wall?'

'Straight ahead of us, I suppose.' Hector thought out loud. 'Where the bricks and stones have fallen. We could climb up there easily enough, although I don't know about the drop on the other side.' He surveyed the roof tops. 'By the look of it we'll be dropping into the alleyway that runs behind Calle Vasquez and, if my memory serves me well, that must be four metres if it's one of your English inches.'

'Okay Hector, when I give the word, let's go for it. Through the garden and over the wall as fast as you can. Don't stop or pause in your stride no matter what happens or what you think might be happening. You got it?'

'Yes I've got it but I can't pretend that I understand it.'

'What I was looking for in the house isn't in the house at all. It's out here in the garden.'

'Yes, but what exactly is it?' Hector demanded.

'I'm not sure, but whatever it is, it isn't very nice. It will stop us from leaving if it can.'

The magician's eyes quartered the garden yet again. Down upon the soil beneath the shade of the broad leaves something slithered and moved. Half way between the porch and the wall, a little over the their left, were the ruins of a well; above the well and emanating from it was a rippling effect that Mage took special note of, sensing it rather than actually seeing it with his physical vision. Certain corners of the garden seemed to be darker than they had any right to be and within the shadows darker shadows moved without form, waiting greedily and full of menace.

He contemplated going back through the house and forcing exit through the front door and yet strongly sensed that if he did this would be walking into the greater trap and thus immediately thought better of the idea... And there was no doubt in Mage's mind that they had walked into a carefully prepared trap!

His eyes went back to the well. There was now a wall of unnatural shadow blurring it from clear vision and to Mage's mind it seemed that it was gloating, taunting, almost daring him to make a move.

The prime weapon in any occultist's armoury against darkness is light. Mage went through the ritual of surrounding himself – and also on this occasion, Hector – in bright halos of white fire, constructed in the familiar mental matrix of the interlocking pentagram. And then:

'Right Hector. Don't stop for anything, and let's go!'

Bemused by Mage's urgency, Hector stepped off the porch. Something – it might have been a spider's web ...brushed against his face and he found himself wading through a writhing mass of vegetation that wrapped itself around his ankles, whipped at his thighs and moved underfoot even as he tried to walk forwards. He staggered and lost his balance and had Mage not gripped him firmly by the arm, he would have fallen his length.

An obnoxious odour of rotting compost rose up to assail his nostrils and beneath this stench was another smell, one that was subtly familiar, although he could not quite place it. There was the strangest sensation of walking into a wall of thicker, heavier air. He found himself fighting for breath and although his lungs heaved deeply, very little oxygen was forthcoming – and that which there was, was tainted with the taste of corruption. His eyes watered and his head swam and yet even with his vision impaired it seemed that there were other things moving in the garden – things that were alive, that caressed his cheek with wet kisses and wrapped themselves around his will.

Vaguely he discerned the ruined well a metre or so over to his left. For all the world there seemed to be a discarnate face studying him from somewhere just above the heap of rubble – hideous and monstrous, leering and grinning. Then something hit him firmly on the side of the face, dragging his attention back to his objective. The trouble was, he no longer knew exactly what that objective was, where he was, where he was going or what he was supposed to be doing. All he wanted to do was to close his eyes and sleep as waves of tiredness and nausea coursed through his body... a body that felt increasingly like lead and which did not want to move at all. And yet something was dragging him forwards and although he knew that he had to keep moving, this dreamlike sensation of drowning in cement became more ardent with every heartbeat.

Something wet and slimy wormed its way up his trouser leg and he felt his scrotum tighten in revulsion. Then he tripped and found himself falling forwards against a pile of rubble.

'Climb, Hector!' A voice from many miles distant seemed to be called his name and studiously he began to climb the very obstruction that had tumbled him.

From the top of the wall, Mage, one hand in Hector's belt, heaved the doctor over the edge and half lowered, half dropped him into the sanctuary of the alley below. Before dropping down after him he cast one last distressed glance backwards at the psychic maelstrom of the garden. Plants and weeds writhed in unnatural motion, air eddied and folded inwards upon itself in opaque ripples and the whole area of the well was obscured in a veil of contorted shadow that emanated with evil intent.

'Fuck you,' Mage muttered, then dropped off the wall landing in a crouch next to Hector who, without Mage's measure of occult protection, had not escaped unscathed from the malevolent psychic forces that had sought to cause them harm. Slumped against the wall he was conscious but dazed. Sitting next to him, Mage cradled his head on his shoulder and pushed cleansing thoughts into his mind, knowing instinctively that the wall was a natural barrier against the negative energies contained within the garden.

He cast around him, half hoping that someone would arrive bringing help – and ardently praying that they would not. He and Hector cut an odd sight and better this be sorted out without the complication of unbelievable explanations for the benefit of third parties.

Thank the saints for sweet fresh air! Hector's sense returned slowly and just for a moment, as his eyes began to clear, it seemed that Mage's head was on fire with a pale golden light that hung to his face and beard.

For a second, Hector wondered what he was doing, sitting on cobbles with his back to the wall in a less than salubrious back alley, then his memory returned and he remembered the inexplicable experience in the garden behind him.

'Holy Mother, Colin! What happened back there?'

'Difficult to explain. Either we passed through a storm of negative psychic energy or we ran foul of a psychic defence net, deliberately laid down by Dolorean to deter nosy parkers and trespassers. If you'd been on your own, you'd have probably been okay, but you were with me and my own psychic energies acted as a catalyst. A child retrieving a lost ball would have come to no harm, or if you'd been chasing a butterfly, you'd have been allowed to pass in peace. A monk seeking solitude for prayer and meditation would have been turned away, but someone like me that it senses as a danger, triggers the defence mechanism and puts it into a mood of aggressive retaliation.'

'You talk about "it" but what exactly is "it"?'

'Energy. No more, no less, but in this case, a tightly focused negative energy, formed and crafted in the most alien of minds. In days gone by you might have said that a witch or a magician had put a curse on the garden, but that's being far too simplistic. Suffice to say that as the energy we ran into was born of the mind, it was our own minds and imaginations that it attacked.'

'You seem to have faired rather better than me,' Hector said with just a trace of petulance in his voice.

'Sorry,' Mage smiled apologetically. 'I suppose that I was more psychically prepared and on guard that you were. I should have warned you, but until we stepped off the porch, I really didn't know what to expect.'

Hector climbed unsteadily to his feet and looked thoughtfully at the old white wall. 'If somebody had said that I, Hector Sanchez, would be able to jump down from a wall this high, I would not have believed them. And,' he turned to look at Mage, 'if I told anybody what happened to me back in that godforsaken garden, they would not believe me, would they?'

'No,' Mage said enigmatically. 'I don't suppose they would.'

Evening descended upon Castillo like a soft dark blue veil. Lights came on at street corners and in the numerous shops and bars that dispensed simple food and cheap wine and an illusion of gaiety and good cheer. There was no breeze and little relief from the heat of the day. Castillatos went about their business talking about the unseasonable warmth and wondering if there might be another early summer thunder storm in the offing. Cicadas sang a noisy song and Anna Sanchez wrote a poem.

Jaime Gomez drove out of the village, heading for the municipal rubbish dump at San Martin de Tessorillo. In the back of his car there was an old suitcase and three cardboard boxes, each overflowing with his lifetime's collection of pornography. There were dozens of video tapes and hundreds of hard core magazines and, although part of him was loathe to let them go, for in truth they were the closest he'd come to ever having any kind of sexual relationship, The Virgin Mary had been adamant. They had to go. He had to be pure – had to be cleansed if he sought to enjoy the special blessings she was empowered to bestow upon him.

This was the same evening that Lorenzo Bautista Matan limped away from the clinic in La Linea, aided by his two wary and worried brothers. They were surprised when Lorenzo insisted that they take him to their aunt's house in Manilva and more surprised still by his absolute aversion to the idea of returning to Castillo.

It was also the same evening that the unusual and uncommunicative little girl called Lena Cortez went missing from the clinic. The staff mounted a cursory search, but were preoccupied by other, more pressing things. A coach had gone over the cliff at Aldea Burito and although no-one had been killed, there were some very serious injuries and if the death rate was the be held at zero, the medical staff would be working overtime through the long hours of the evening. One of the senior administrators did notify the police and then, although not entirely forgotten, the incident was certainly put to the back of everyone's mind.

It was also the evening that Christina received another transatlantic telephone call from the United States. The line was crackly but clear enough for her to be tremendously excited and gratified by what she heard. Also there was an instruction. Get close to Colin Mage.

Hector examined his wrist in the harsh light of the bathroom. The wound had closed and seemed to be healing well. No process of medical stitching could have done a better job. He washed and shaved, his mind a thousand miles elsewhere. If Colin could do for Anna's head when he had done for his arm... The thought was turbulent and full of wild imponderables.

Anna had a brain tumour. This was fact. The best surgeon in Madrid had said that an operation was impossible. This was also a fact. Anna would be blind within a year and dead within two... Señor Villafranco had been gentle but inflexible in his prognosis and had allowed for any advances that medical science might make.

But had he allowed for miracles? Had he allowed for someone like Colin Mage? What Mage had done that morning had been miraculous and what he had done out in the campo for Dolores, had that not also been miraculous?

Hector took a glass of sherry out on to the small terrace at the back of the house and, sitting in his usual rattan chair, filled his meershaum pipe and allowed his eyes to roam across the jumble of roof tops. He was to meet Mage a little later in the evening and together they would visit Father Francisco at Santa Maria. He pondered on that. What would Mage do to help Francisco? What could he do? Were there other miracles to behold?

...And what about this other thing? Colin "seeing" him with a small blond woman? Was this possible? In his heart he didn't really think so, but Mage's words combined with his own sense of loneliness in the mood of the moment made him acutely aware of his own isolation and solitary position. It was all very well being the popular village doctor, held in high esteem and appreciation by many caring friends and patients, but while this certainly satisfied the doctor within him, it left the man inside him rather out on a limb!

He'd been celibate for more years than he cared to remember and had long ago learned to control the longing for a woman's love... In the earlier days there had been occasional liaisons that he had deliberately kept light and casual; for one thing he'd been unable to make an emotional commitment to anyone after the death of his wife and, for another, his prime commitment had always been to Anna.

In a moment of rare insight and self honesty, he realised how he had used his loyalties towards Anna as a subliminal excuse for keeping faith with the memory of her mother... and perhaps, just perhaps, he had done himself no favours in this respect. Might it not have been better for Anna if he'd made a point of marrying again? Might not a step mother have been better than no mother at all?

Hector was tired and his emotions were scrambled after what had been a curious and eventful day. Now, relaxing for the first time in many hours, those emotions crept to the surface and he found that he was weeping silently – weeping for the lost years of his history and for the uncertainty of his future. Weeping for his daughter and weeping for all the suffering that seemed to be focused on this small Andalucian hill village of Castillo de la Frontera.

Anna's footfalls fell lightly on the patio behind him.

'Papa, what are you doing out here all by yourself?'

'Just sitting and thinking about a few things,' he said, quickly pulling himself together.

'You have been out all day... did you catch any fish?'

'Yes, I fished this morning, but no, I didn't catch any fish.' *One caught me though!* 'Then this afternoon Father Ignatious was taken ill and had to be shipped off to the hospital in Seville.'

'Poor Papa.' She began massaging the chords and knots in his shoulder and in the back of his neck. 'Not even able to enjoy a single day off without someone wanting you for something. You need an assistant. A young doctor fresh from medical school who could help you with your work.'

'Lovely idea, but you know how the ayuntamiento funding works as well as I do. They'd never wear it.'

'Well at least you can put your feet up and relax for a while now. I'll cook you some supper. I'd have done it earlier if I'd known you were home.'

'Sorry my sweet, but I have to go out again in a few minutes. Colin is anxious to meet Father Francisco. Apparently he has some experience in Francisco's ailment and if he can help then I am happy to accept that help.'

'You are meeting Colin this evening?' Anna asked with quickening interest.

Hector turned and looked at her candidly... 'Anna, I've been with Colin all day. We have talked of many things and have had an interesting adventure or two... and I owe you an apology. Some of the things I said last night were unwarranted and I hope you'll put them down to a father's natural concern for the welfare of his only daughter.'

Anna kissed the top of his head. 'Don't worry Papa. I know of your feelings and I know why you feel them. You've got nothing to worry about though. I like Colin very much but it's not as if I'm having an affair with him.'

Hector nearly said *yet* but thought better of it and held his peace.

'Anyway,' Anna continued, 'if you are meeting him this evening, is there any reason why I should not come with you and meet him also?'

'I don't think it would be a good idea for you to come with us to Francisco's' Hector said cagily. 'You know what priest's can be like... But there's no reason why you shouldn't join us for a drink at Jacinto's first... if you'd like that... if you're feeling well enough.'

'Papa, I'm feeling better than I've felt for weeks!'

Yes, Hector thought. *Just like Pepe Ortega and Antonia Guadiaro.*

Washed and showered, Mage sat on his own terrace allowing the night to cloak him with its darkness. As usual his eyes were focused on the castle, standing now in stark and jagged silhouette against the purple sky and more than ever he was aware of the positive/negative polarities that pulsed from the keep and the citadel. He'd felt them even more strongly when, after having left Hector, he'd gone up there to bury the lode stone in the ruins near the keep. He'd accepted that it might have been his imagination, but for all the world it felt as if the keep welcomed the responsibility and thrummed with a vibration of victory. The citadel, on the other hand, had seemed to be more negative than ever, reaching out to him and touching him with energies that had reminded him strongly of those which he had encountered in Dolorean's garden.

Wouldn't it, he'd wondered, be so very convenient, so very logical if the well in the garden, which had obviously been at the epicentre of the psychic disturbance, led into the labyrinth beneath the citadel? Without climbing down and having a look for himself, he would never know for certain and he knew that that would be a very difficult project. The forces in the garden were sharply focused and tightly concentrated. They would not let him enter the well without a battle and that was one battle he was by no means sure he could win. The well might even be a lure, a subtle trap. Far better, he'd thought, to do battle in daylight when you knew what you were fighting.

Other thoughts had filtered through his mind. He could gain access to the house in Calle Sombra through the tunnel from the church and set fire to it... but that would be a pointless exercise. The property was still Dolorean's and firing the house would not deny the shapechanger access to the well.

Okay then... he'd grinned to himself in the last soft light of the afternoon as his imagination had gone slightly overboard. What if...? He'd seen himself straddling the garden wall, igniting a stick of dynamite with a Clint Eastwood cheroot and lobbing the explosive into the well.

The problem was that he didn't have any dynamite and had no idea where to get any. In any case, the option was probably too melodramatic to be realistic. But his mind had twitched. What if, instead of dynamite, he used something else? Say the psychic equivalent of explosive? Something that would (hopefully) disperse or destroy the negative energies and at the same time deny Dolorean access to his hidey hole? Now here was an idea that was not without merit and was significantly more feasible than the Clint Eastwood option.

He'd allowed the idea to form in its own time, working out what he would use and how he could use it. He would act on it the following day and, as for this evening – he'd glanced at his watch and had realised that he was fast running out of time. There were appointments to be kept, one with Hector and another with a priest who was suffering from the stigmata of Christ... But even so, there was time to prepare and he'd spent a few moments searching around the base of the keep until he'd found what he was looking for in the form of an almost circular stone, smooth and flattened, and with a hole almost dead centre of middle; once upon a time it might have been a cog in a mill wheel apparatus, but now it was to become the missile that would carry his psychic nuclear warhead.

Back at the house in Granadillos, he'd worked thoughtfully for an hour with mantra and crystals, finding a piece of clear white crystal quartz that fitted snugly in the hole in the stone. Secured by the miracle of superglue he'd adorned the object with sigils and talismans before anointing it with oils and incense, then he'd surrounded it with five small white candles, offering prayers as the candles burned...

Moving from the terrace back into the house he went to the altar table in the living room and noticed with satisfaction that the candles had burned down a waxy mess that had coalesced around the stone. He would be late in meeting Hector, but nonetheless waited until the last small candles had puttered out naturally before leaving the house, methodically locking all the doors behind him as he went.

When he arrived in the square Hector was already sitting at one of Jacinto's tables – with Anna in attendance. Mage was pleased to see her but knew that he would have to be wary with his words. What he and Hector were up to was essentially a private undertaking and he didn't want to have to explain things to anyone and least of all to Anna. Even as he slid into a vacant seat and Jacinto, without being asked, placed a small glass of coffee in front of him, he caught Hector's apologetic glance that clearly indicated that Anna was here on her own account.

They barely had time to exchange greetings and pleasantries before Angel and Christina came and sat at the very next table. Mage noticed that Angel was still flushed with the victory of his conquest, although who had conquered whom might have been something of a moot point. He remembered the boy as he'd been that first time they'd met and marvelled at how much he'd changed in just a few weeks. Gone was the guitar and the attendant friendly dog, and gone also was some of the diffidence and shyness. In their place there was a cocky confidence, which in part was due to Mage's money in his pocket and Christina's body in his bed. For any young Spanish male it would have been a heady combination.

The two girls talked cheerfully, although Mage was aware that Christina was dominating the conversation. This created the opportunity for Hector to lean across the table and speak quietly.

'I'm sorry about this but Anna insisted upon coming. I've told her she cannot come to Santa Maria with us, but she has insisted that I bring you back to the house for supper afterwards. I hope you will say yes because my life won't be worth living if you say no.'

'My answer had better be yes, then,' Mage said affably. 'But if we can, let's give ourselves some leeway with the timing.'

He turned his attention towards Anna, appreciating the simple elegance of her outfit. She wore a white shirt with blue denim jeans tucked into soft brown leather boots. In comparison, Christina seemed overdressed for the occasion, but, Mage reasoned, maybe that went with the persona of being a professional model... If indeed that was all she was. He could not help feeling, and not for the first time, that there was more to this American girl than met the eye.

Since arriving in Castillo his mind had been crowded with a thousand thoughts and he'd never really probed into the reason for Christina and Tom's presence here in the village – and, talking of Tom, where had he suddenly disappeared to, and so quickly? Mage was not naive. He could not believe that his enchantment for Angel was the sole energy behind Tom's absence.

On the face of it their cover story was a good one; photographer and model exploring the locational possibilities of Southern Spain... He intuitively knew that it was a cover story, but a cover story for what? He tuned into Christina's psychic aura and detected an urgency of excitement – and was bemused and puzzled to find that although she was busy talking to Anna, her thoughts were actually focused upon himself.

She was enthusing about a car she'd hired for the following day and of a beach that she and Angel intended to visit at a place called La Bolonia where there was a "darling little beach bar and miles and miles of golden sand".

Any second now there's going to be an invitation. She's going to suggest that Anna and I go with them and make up a foursome!

'Hey!' Christina exclaimed delightedly, 'I've just had a fantastic idea! Why don't you and Colin come with us and make up a foursome?'

'Yes, I'd like that very much,' Anna said eagerly – just a little too eagerly – and then with a degree of trepidation, 'but, of course, I cannot speak for Colin.'

'It sounds like a very nice idea,' Mage said easily and was immediately aware of Anna's lifted spirits. 'What time do you want to leave?'

'As early as we can. Straight after breakfast? Say about nine o'clock?'

That would give him ample time to execute the plan he had formed and the idea of lying in the sun for a few hours, next to Anna and away from Castillo, did have a certain appeal. Furthermore it was apparent that Christina had some fairly powerful psychic screens. To be sure, he could penetrate them easily enough, but not, he suspected, without her knowing that he was doing it. Tomorrow, with the balmy effect of Ambre Solair and a litre of good lunch time wine, it would be much easier and the mystery would be solved.

'Sounds good to me,' he said. 'We'll meet you at the Miraflores. Nine o'clock sharp.'

The light in the room was soft, the illumination coming from a handful of altar candles and a small bedside table lamp. From outside in the street came the clatter and shouts of children playing; in the near distance two women argued about the price of fish and a television quiz show with canned laughter added to the buzz of noise. And yet there was a stillness around the priest, enhanced by his steady breathing and also, to Hector's eyes, by the very presence of Colin Mage, who knelt on the hard floor as though in prayer, gently holding Francisco's left hand in his own.

'Who is this extranjero?' Juanita had asked querulously when they had arrived.

'He is a friend of mine from England who has much experience in treating the kind of sickness that afflicts our young father,' Hector had told her. 'Now why not take yourself off and get some supper and let us see if we can do something for our patient, for if we can't he'll have to go off to the hospital in the morning.'

Juanita had not been too happy about going but the doctor was the doctor and if he'd told her to go, it was better that she went. She hoped that her charge would recover quickly, but if he didn't she was pleased to know that the responsibility for his welfare was to be taken out of her hands. The nature of the priest's wounds were truly remarkable and, if she'd had her way, not only the whole village but the whole world would know about them, but both Señor Hector and Father Francisco had made her promise to keep the secret and, once made, a promise was a promise. If he was to be hospitalised, however, the secret could not remain a secret for ever. Word was bound to get out, and in her opinion that would be good for everybody.

If Jesus Christ had arrived in Castillo, then as far as she was concerned, people should know about it!

Together Hector and Mage had examined the priest, who was either sleeping deeply or in some sort of trance. The blood still suppurated from his stigmata, which appeared to be more livid and pronounced than ever.

'From a purely medical point of view, how is he?' Mage had asked

'I'd say he was as right as rain. Heartbeat and pulse are both good and all the other vital signs are as they should be. I've checked his blood count and his urine and there's nothing amiss there... Physically the wounds are a mystery, and although I'm no expert, I'd say that they're caused by whatever is going on inside his head.'

'And you'd be right,' Mage acknowledged. '...And if we're going to help him we have to find out what exactly is going on inside his head. You've got no way of doing that, but I might have... Let me have a little time and space and let's see what we can discover.'

Hector had leaned on the door with his arms folded while Mage had gone and knelt by the side of the bed. Watching him now it seemed as though there was a halo of light around Mage's head and shoulders, which could quite easily have been the effect from the bedside lamp or the product of the doctor's imagination. While his vision may have been suspect, his other senses told him that there was something happening here; he could feel the tension in the room and on more than one occasion looked down at his forearm and studied the fine line scar that should have needed stitching, but now was obviously healed beyond all need of further medical attention.

Lightly stroking the priest's palm Mage slipped into his mind, taking with him salvoes of peace and calm and tranquillity. It wasn't a difficult operation for Francisco was without any form of defence. Indeed his mind was so wide open that the slightest of suggestions was accepted as absolute reality. In one breath he was playing pirates with the children out in the street, and in the next agreeing with the two women that the price of fresh fish was quite exorbitant; in a third he was answering all the quiz questions on the TV programme and becoming richer by the minute. Interestingly enough the money that he was winning would be spent on motor cars and nice clothes and luxury cruises on large liners and there would be beautiful women... No, not beautiful women but one beautiful woman who would love him for the man that he was and teach him all the delights of the flesh, introducing him stage by stage to the sin of wild passion...

...And beneath this vision of mental awareness there was another that screamed treason and betrayal, that flogged his weak spirit, a spirit that was now so corrupted by carnal desire that he no longer deserved to live, and was certainly no longer worthy to serve the God that he had once loved to the exclusion of all worldly temptation.

Good Christ, what on earth has caused this mess? Mage wondered. And the answer, when it came, was staggering in its simplicity. An act, a natural act of sexual release, executed by the priest's own hand in a moment of intense physical need, had been quite enough to tip the young man's mind over the edge and down into the labyrinth of guilt and self disgust.

He was a good looking boy who had probably been sailing close to the precipice for many months... The tensions and pressures of the many years spent in the seminary now supplemented by the temptations and pressures of the real world and the responsibilities that went with this his first, and thus in many ways, most important posting.

Mage fumed. This celibacy thing caused more harm than good. It was both hypocritical and unnatural and the sooner the catholic church got its act together the sooner the world might become a saner, better place. The pressures on the priesthood were enormous and in Mage's opinion the vow of celibacy should have been optional rather than compulsory.

Discarding his own feelings he probed more deeply into Francisco's psychosis and found an alarming pattern of visions. The priest was so wound up with the enormity of his sin that he'd quietly convinced himself that it had been the devil's work rather than a momentary lapse in his own self discipline. It was Francisco's version of the devil that caught Mage's attention for rather than being the usual icon offered by the church, it was more in keeping with Herschal's description of the Djinn and not a million miles away from the cave paintings he himself had seen in the cave in the Negev. Given that Francisco's mind had been spiralling down in mental collapse it was interesting that he had picked up on the actual description of the evil that threatened rather than Mother Church's more classical and stylised depiction. Surely this was an indication that the Djinn's psychic aura was already permeating through the atmosphere and ether of this place? Perhaps this was both natural and logical in the circumstances, but Mage still found it alarming.

Putting his thoughts behind him, he concentrated on the task in hand. *Francisco,* he thoughtspoke firmly and commandingly. *It's time for this nonsense to stop. It's time for you to come back to us. You have much work to do and you cannot do it while you are like this!*

'Who are you?' Francisco's subconscious whispered in reply. 'Who is this who speaks inside my mind?'

'Mine is the voice of love and justice. Mine is the voice of judgement. Mine is the voice of forgiveness that brings the message of forgiveness. Francisco Albeciete Toledo of the church of Santa Maria in the village of Castillo, I come to tell you that you are forgiven. That your wounds are healed. That you have been judged and in that judgement have not been found wanting. I also come to tell you that you are needed in this place of Castillo. A darkness of evil comes this way which I cannot fight alone. I need your help but for you to help me you must be fit and well, alert and on your feet. So let these wounds on your body and the wounds within your mind be healed.'

'Are you God?'

'I am the voice of my own God and speak the words that your God bids me speak to you.'

'And I am forgiven despite the magnitude of my crime?'

'You have committed no great crime, but that which needs forgiveness is freely forgiven by God. You must summon sufficient faith in your beliefs to forgive

yourself. This is the word and the command of spirit.'

'What would you have me do, Lord?'

'Sleep and sleep deeply without disturbance and wake in the morning with a clear bright mind and a body that is free from the stigmata of the Nazarene's suffering. And when you wake, healed and well, be about your God's business. Be well, be healed, be free from guilt, be at peace!

'Amen,' Francisco breathed with a silent sigh of obedience and contentment. 'Amen, Amen!'

Mage rocked back on his heals and climbed slowly to his feet. The healing energy had gone out from him and he now felt drained and incredibly tired. The tiredness would pass, but in that moment he felt as weak as the proverbial kitten. Hector saw him stagger and was at his side in an instant with a supporting arm.

'Colin, my friend... Are you all right?'

'Yes, I'm fine. Just a little weary. This has taken quite a lot out of me, I'm afraid.'

Hector licked his lips. 'Dare I ask... What of Father Francisco?'

'I think he'll be okay. He'll certainly sleep the night. Look in on him in the morning. If he's not much improved then we'll come back tomorrow evening and try again then.'

'Can I ask, I mean can you explain what it is that you have actually done?'

'Hard to explain, Hector. Let's just say that my conscious mind has made contact with his subconscious mind and that I've tried to unscramble some of the very scary and confusing thoughts that he's got locked away in there. Let's hope that I've done some good, but the fact of the matter is that we won't know until the morning, one way or the other. Anyway, right now, if you don't mind, I need some fresh air and some exercise, and I need something to eat. Let's hope that lovely daughter of yours has been busy in the kitchen. I don't care what she's concocted, I'll take it all!'

Forty minutes later Anna served a risotto of prawns and rice which Mage wolfed down ravenously. Hector then made coffee while he sat with Anna on the terrace counting the stars. Anna sat on the high backed rattan chair while Mage sprawled his length, swinging gently on a hammock. Long before the coffee was cold Mage had fallen fast asleep, much to the consternation of his hostess.

'Do you think we should wake him?' she asked her father tentatively.

'No,' Hector said firmly. 'No I don't. The man is exhausted and after some of the things that have happened today, I'm not in the least bit surprised. Fetch a blanket from the bedroom and cover him over and let him sleep for as long as he likes... And no, my darling, don't ask me any questions, at least not tonight, for I have no clear answers for you.'

Anna went and came back a few minutes later with a light quilt. She draped it across Mage's body, bemused and puzzled by the aura of mystery that emanated not only from this situation but also from her father's strange and unusual attitude.

Hector drained his glass of wine. 'I think I'm almost as tired as he is, so thank you for cooking a wonderful supper, and forgive me if I leave you for my bed.'

'I think I might stay here for a while, just in case he wakes up and needs anything – if you don't mind?'

'Mind? No, I don't mind,' Hector answered distractedly. 'In fact I think it's a rather nice gesture... Just try not to disturb him if you can help it.'

'No, of course not... I'll just sit here, and sort of keep watch...'

Both confused, albeit for different reasons, father and daughter parted company. Hector was asleep within seconds of his head touching the pillow, but it was a good two hours before Anna fell asleep, curled up in her chair. In all that time Mage did not stir once.

20.

La Bolonia

As always, the dream took him along the tunnel then propelled him through the circular opening, casting him into the void... But then the dream changed and he was standing in a busy street – not in this century but the one that had gone before. Horse drawn cabs clattered over cobbles, crinolines and cloaks swirled in the lamplight and all around there was the cacophony of conversation and laughter. In the distance a single trumpet sounded a haunting fanfare, while much closer at hand thrumming guitars played vibrant flamenco rhythms. From a nearby tavern at the corner of the street a roar of applause drowned out the sound of wildly clicking castanets.

He was standing in a square and so real was the dream that he could feel the cobbles beneath his feet and smell the smells of the place and time; horses, manure, old leather... crisp linen, strong black tobacco, the ordure of sewage and the mysterious tang of wine and blood.

Ahead of him was an arcade of shops, confined beneath a series of sandstone arches and lit by crude wrought iron chandeliers of lamps and lanterns. One shop beckoned him forwards. The Armouria of Juan Cordoba al Andaluz.

Then in the way of dreams he was inside the armouria, looking at display cabinets that contained fine swords from Toledo and long barrelled muskets from the gunsmiths of Madrid. Flights of arrows were displayed dustily on dimly lit walls, along with a variety of hunting bows that vied for space with old pistols and blunderbusses that were antiques even in their own time.

The wizened and leathery face of Juan Cordoba looked up from behind a cluttered counter. He was an old man, sly, with pinched features and narrow eyes.

'Ah, My Lord, you have come for it, then?'

'Yes,' he heard himself say. 'Is it ready?'

'It is, My Lord, it is!'

'And does it work?'

'Yes, My Lord, it most certainly does. We have tried it out in the campo this very morning. The sighting is accurate up to one hundred strides.'

'And trajectory?'

'Flat and hard and fast, undeviating and with tremendous velocity, but only up to the one hundred strides. As with all ballistics, one must sacrifice range for accuracy and striking power.'

'And the projectiles?'

'We have made six, My Lord, and this work has been the greater challenge. The weapon itself was simple to build, but the quarrels were another matter.'

'Show me.'

'Of course.'

The armourer stooped beneath his high counter and heaved a misshapen bundle of sacking into place. Pulling the covering to one side he handed his patron the weapon that had been built to his own design and specification.

Nominally it was a cross bow with polished olive wood providing the stock and support for the silver steel of the bow arm and the dully oiled metal of the firing mechanisms, but instead of there being a single grooved slot for the bolt, there were two, one mounted above the other. Not one, but two tightly corded bow strings rested out of tension across the launch rails and within the filigreed finger guard there were two triggers instead of the usual single device.

As he lifted it to his shoulder and sighted along the top quarrel groove he found the weapon to be heavy, but nonetheless exquisitely balanced.

'We have made you the six quarrels, My Lord, but offer gentle warning. Hit your target with the second bolt or miss it for ever! The process of reloading and retensioning the strings requires strength and patience. There will be no time for a third or fourth shot if you miss with the first and second.'

'Have no fear. I shall not miss. Show me the projectiles you have made.'

'Yes Lord, at once.'

The armourer presented him with a flat olive wood box looped and secured to a wide leather belt. By springing a catch the box opened like a case to reveal six quarrels that nestled side by side held in place by individual brackets. The projectiles were made of steel, steel which had been ground and polished to the smoothest of finishes, but instead of being barbed with the usual arrow heads, these bolts were simply tapered down to hollow points, about three or four millimetres in diameter.

'It will be a most delicate affair,' the armourer observed.

'What will be?'

'Why, the decanting of the poison into such a narrow phial.'

'What makes you think I intend to fill these bolts with poison?'

'Why else would you require the quarrels to be hollow?' The armourer was suddenly nervous, realising that he had tip toed a step too far. 'But fear not My Lord, for no word of this commission shall pass my lips.'

'No, no word shall for if such word does then I will know from where it originated and in response to one single whisper your life and the lives of your family shall be forfeit!'

The armourer swallowed hard, full well knowing that his patron's threat was not an idle one. 'You will take the weapon now, My Lord?'

'No. Payment shall I make as agreed but the weapon will be collected by my man at a later time. Now, I believe that the sum of four hundred pesetas was our agreed price?'

'It was, Lord, it was, but surely such a weapon, such a deadly work of art, is worth a hundred times more...'

A hundred times more...

A hundred times...

The dream faded and Mage awoke, displaced and disorientated, not just by the dream, but also by the oddity of his awakening. He was swinging gently in a hammock on Hector's patio, fully dressed and covered by a light blanket. The cool air of the early dawn brushed across his face as he swung off the hammock, standing still for a moment to gather his wits.

He'd been drained after the interview with Father Francisco, which had in itself come at the end of a particularly draining day. He remembered rocking in the hammock after having tucked in to Anna's delicious risotto, but he had no memory of having fallen into sleep. He did, however, remember the dream and he ran over it again in his mind ensuring that it would not fade with the encroachment of the day.

His watch said that it was twenty minutes after six, which gave him plenty of time to execute the plan he had formed the previous afternoon. Scribbling Anna and Hector a brief note, he left it propped on the hall stand and as quietly as he could, departed from the house by the front door and stepped out into the street.

As he walked up to Granadillos, light descended upon the village from the east. The air was crisp and clear and chased the last vestiges of sleep from his brain. Tendrils of mist whispered and clung to the tree tops and the meadows by the river down in the Castillato valley, and yet even as he paused on a high street corner to survey the scene and savour the moment, the first rays of the sun found their way through the complicated canyons of the Sierra Morenos and the mist began to retreat before the onslaught.

The sleepy village stood silent in these first few moments of full daylight. Buildings cast long shadows to the west, white walls shining in soft iridescence as the new sun kissed them with its presence. Mage breathed deeply, filling his lungs with the scent of pure morning and tasted the aroma of wild flowers and dew soaked grass. He was reminded of days from his childhood... Summer days and springtime mornings when his world was new, his spirits high... When a tree to climb spoke words of dare and challenge and a riverbank beckoned, begging to be explored, offering mystery and great adventure.

He closed his eyes and allowed the sensations to wash over him. In that moment, without the sound of people or the clamour of traffic, Castillo belonged to a different world and to another time... And then a dog barked and a car door slammed, destroying the spell and breaking into his reverie, reminding him that there was adventure enough in the here and the now with enough mysteries to last a lifetime.

He carried on walking up the hill and arriving at the house in Granadillos, showered and changed his clothes and, mindful of his programme for the day, threw a few beach things into a canvas bag. Then, lighting his meditation candles, he sat for half an hour nursing the circular stone he had prepared the previous afternoon, taking a certain power from it, amplifying it, then channelling it back with even greater force and focus. Finally, feeling clean and refreshed and as confident as he could be in the circumstances, he set out through the village, heading towards the northern barrio and the house in Calle Sombra.

The sun was warm on his body, and now, although it was still only eight o'clock on a Sunday morning, Castillo was beginning to show some signs of life. Snippets of conversations wafted out of windows, the smell of hot bread and coffee with the occasional crackle of bacon drifted out of doorways. In one street a child laughed and shouted, demanding that its parents wake to start the day, and in another street a baby cried, making much the same request.

He arrived in the alley behind Calle Vasquez without incident and with a little help from a tree which sprouted stuntedly from the corner of the passage, he climbed and sat astride the wall and found himself looking down into the Dolorean garden. It was still and silent and covered in dark blue shadow, and yet Mage still sensed its sentience and inherent negativity. He weighed the stone in his hand, reassured by the way in which the sun's early morning rays made the crystal sparkle like a brilliant uncut diamond, and mentally measured the distance from the wall to the well.

'Here goes nothing,' he muttered, and with a silent prayer, lobbed the impregnated stone towards its target. He watched it arc upwards and then drop with uncanny accuracy into the centre of the well. He waited for something to happen – a splash, a bang, a cry, a scream, a rumble of diabolical thunder – and yet there was nothing. No sound disturbed the tranquillity of the morning.

With a mental shrug of disappointment and anti-climax – he'd expected *something* for Christ's sake – he lowered himself back down into the alleyway and wondered what he ought to do next. It was too early to go for Anna, there was nothing more he could do here and there was certainly no point in returning to Calle Granadillos. He was playing with the idea of breakfast when imperceptibly he felt a tremor emanate from the cobbles beneath his feet. It was faint and intermittent, but for the duration of half a dozen heartbeats, it was definitely there. It might have gone unnoticed had his senses not been wide open and, as if to confirm the presence of seismic activity, a small triangle of plaster dislodged itself from the wall and fell to the ground, landing tremulously upon a clump of weed. And that was it – nothing more was forthcoming – but it was enough to tell him that his aim had been true and that his actions were not without effect and consequence, even if he was not exactly sure what they might be.

Suddenly feeling a lot better about this Sunday morning he strolled up into Calle Principal, and as the Bar España was the only bar open at that hour, chose it for his breakfast venue. Sitting on the terrace drinking strong coffee and eating warm churros, he put the time to good use by assessing his achievements and redefining his challenges and objectives... And yet the growing warmth of the sun in a cloudless blue sky, and indeed, the glorious vitality of the day, acted as a distraction. When it came to creative thought he could do little more than recognise how tired and jaded his mind had become; he needed a break, an opportunity to recharge his batteries. It could not be too much longer before Dolorean arrived... Mage felt sure that he was already on his way... and then the battle would begin in earnest. Thus, if he was to be given this day to rest and relax upon a sunny beach amid some youthful company, he fully intended to make the most of it. Certainly, there was a hidden agenda – to get closer to Anna and to solve the riddle posed by Christina, but – and he grinned to himself as he popped the last piece of coffee dunked churro into his mouth – these items were all he needed to justify taking a day off from his quest to secure the village against Dolorean's forthcoming incursion.

The light blue Fiat Panda bounced along the back road. To the right there were densely foliated hills, while on their left small farms and tiny silver streams flashed past as Christina drove with gay abandon, chattering incessantly to her captive audience. Angel sat white faced, closing his eyes every time they bounced over yet another pot hole or approached a blind corner. As a token gesture his hand rested lightly on Christina's naked leg, but his thoughts were more on survival than sex. In the back, blasted by the rush of air that entered through the open sun roof, Anna was constantly thrown against Mage. In the end, and it was no great sacrifice or inconvenience, he put his arm around her and held her close to him to prevent her from being thrown about as the car careened through the lush countryside. He'd already tactfully suggested that Christina should slow down a little, but his suggestion had fallen on deaf ears. He quietly resolved that on the return journey, either by fair means or foul, he would do the driving.

Looking at the map as they had congregated outside the Miraflores, it had seemed logical to take the cross country route that would cut out having to drive down to San Roque and then through Algerciras, but now Mage wasn't so sure. The back trail may have been the scenic route but the road surface was deplorable and the journey seemed interminable. The only bonus was his proximity to Anna, who looked fresh and lovely in a pale green summer dress and a wide brimmed yellow straw hat.

Their route, having turned off the main carraterra at Timbales, had led them along narrow winding lanes and after having been scared to death by Christina's appalling driving for more than an hour, Mage was now heartily wishing they had taken the longer route through Algerciras and Tarifa which would at least have provided them with much smoother roads. Furthermore, the wind from the open sun roof made conversation almost impossible in the back of the car, a fact that Christina had obviously failed to notice. Anna had managed to ask him how he'd slept and he'd shouted a reply of gratitude and apology.

Eventually they connected with the main highway to Cadiz and a few moments later, having turned off the smooth black top road in favour of what was little more than a cart track, they were driving through incredible fields of wild magnolias towards their destination. One final hairpin bend and then they were rewarded with the spectacular view of what was truly one of the most magnificent beaches Mage had ever seen. It stretched away for mile after mile into the hazy distance, rolling sand dunes to the right, pounding surf to the left.

The track led them to a cluster of houses, some made from stone although most of them were clinker built from solid planks of wood. Even as they parked behind a low stone wall towards the rear of the tiny hamlet, Mage could hear the pounding roar of the Atlantic breakers and smell the salty tang of the ocean.

They unloaded the car and walked along a narrow white walled lane, emerging at last on a sandy spur of land. The sea was fifty meters away, directly ahead of them, while to their left and right there were two bars. One was open, the other closed, and thus the decision as to where they might have a pre beach drink was made for them. They sat around a white plastic table shaded from the sun by a huge umbrella of dried palm leaves. Mage ordered coffee for himself, coke for Anna and bacardis for both Angel and Christina. It was early in the summer and early in the day and not only were they the only customers in the chiringuito beach bar, they were also the only people on the beach.

Fortified by their liquid refreshment they moved down to the water's edge about a hundred meters away from the bar, and spreading large towels around the portable parasol Christina had brought, they shrugged off their clothes and plunged into the bracing coldness of the waves.

They had all underdressed in their swimming gear and it was a quartet of different styles that splashed into the waiting sea. Mage's plain black trunks contrasted with Angel's brightly coloured Bermuda shorts and Christina wore a minuscule lime green bikini that revealed far more than it concealed. In comparison, Anna's plain white single piece swimsuit looked positively demure, but to Mage's eyes Anna's apparel was significantly more alluring, and watching her self consciously slip out of the pale green dress was nothing less than erotic.

Mage was neither a natural, nor stylish swimmer and he ploughed through the water in a dogged and persistent breast stroke. Anna, on the other hand, lithe lean and unfettered, cut through the waves in a powerful crawl. She wore a small pair of racing goggles to protect her eyes, but in this environment did not have to rely on her vision. The beach was on her right, the open sea to her left, and however strong the Atlantic currents might have been, she knew that she was stronger. She swam now in pursuit of freedom and to hide her embarrassment and feelings of inadequacy.

Seeing Christina in her skimpy bikini had made her very aware of her own incredibly boring costume, and while that was bad enough it was not the only cause of her discomfort. Watching Colin peel off his clothes to reveal his deeply tanned and muscular body had caused a flush of something warm to explode within her – and knowing that he had been watching her take off her dress, seeing every contour of her body, but in that awful swimsuit, made her deeply envious of Christina's curvaceous shape, and also of her confidence. If that lime green bikini was anything to go by her own white single piece was ten years out of fashion and a lifetime out of style.

Eventually she began to tire and made her way back towards the sound of Christina's shrill cries of laughter, noting with a small sense of satisfaction that while she had swum for fully a good half kilometre, Christina had yet to get her hair wet! The American girl splashed in the shallows with Angel – and that was an unlikely match, was it not? - but of Colin there was no sign.

With her feet on the sandy bottom she turned a full three hundred and sixty degrees looking for the Englishman but failing to locate him. This was hardly surprising, she thought grimly. There could have been a shark the size of a house bearing down on her from no more than twenty meters away, and she wouldn't have seen that either!

And then he was there, standing in front of her, hair slicked down and eyes sparkling merrily in the spray.

'You swim well,' he told her.

'Thank God I can do something well,' she retorted sharply. Perhaps a little too sharply, for she saw his eyes narrow at the way in which she rejected what had, in all truth, been a fair and honest compliment.

'And what is it,' he asked, his gaze never wavering, 'that you feel you don't do well?'

She lowered herself into the water, bringing the sea up to her neck. 'Colin, I do not see so well – and in comparison with Christina I do not think I look so well either.'

The sound of his laughter echoed above the waves and she looked at him reproachfully.

'You're laughing at me,' she said.

'Yes I'm laughing at you,' he agreed, 'for surely you can see well enough to see me standing here?'

'Yes...'

'And a little while back you could see me well enough to know that I couldn't take my eyes off you when you were getting undressed on the beach.'

'Colin, I...'

'And if you can see *those* things, then for the time being you can see well enough...' there was a delicious devil may care lightness in Mage's heart, '...well enough to know that I think you are totally gorgeous and long after Christina is fat and forty and that silly costume she's nearly wearing won't come anywhere near her, you'll still be totally gorgeous!'

'You really think these things?' she stammered, blushing pink in her cheeks despite the cold of the sea.

'I really think these things,' he said soberly and in such a way that she could not possibly doubt the sincerity of his words.

It was too much! She ducked her head beneath the surface and swam a few metres along the beach, rising again to stare vacantly towards a distant, and unseen by her, headland. He thought she was totally gorgeous! But what did that mean? He'd also told her, not once, but twice, and on two separate occasions that he thought she was beautiful, and what did *that* mean? Might it mean, *could* it mean that he felt the same way about her as she felt about him? What other meaning could there be?

Mage caught her up, and standing behind her and a little to one side, threw caution and common sense to the wind. He was intoxicated by a sense of freedom and excitement; his eyes took in the beauty of her face, the wide eyes, sensuous mouth, the high cheek bones... Made note of the long neck and graceful shoulders, lingered longingly upon the gentle curve of her breast and locked on to the hard nipple that thrust against the wet and clinging material of her costume. Not caring about the consequences, and despite Hector's warning... Not even *thinking* about the consequences or remembering what Hector's warning might have been, he slipped his arms around Anna's waist and pulling her back against his body, sank his face into the side of her neck.

He heard her moan but she made no effort to pull away. *God help me*, he thought – and brought his hands up to cup her breasts.

Anna felt her breasts pushing against his hands, her nipples (Holy Mother how they ached!) probing against his fingers. She felt his chest pressing against her back, the hardness of his sex up against her buttocks... Part of her demanded that she pull away, but another part of her, more aloof and in control, countermanded the instinct. This felt good. She was enjoying it... Scared out of her wits, yes, but definitely enjoying it. She had little doubt that if this was Christina with Angel, Christina would certainly not be tempted to retreat from the challenge like some shy coltish virgin, and besides... Anna dredged up a dirty basket of self honesty... She'd dreamed of something like this happening, hadn't she? How many nights during the last few weeks had she lain in her bed, imagining what it might be like, to have Colin hold her in this way? How many nights had she *not* thought of it? Mage was only the second man to feel her breasts. The first and other had been Pedro. She had not complained too much when Pedro had fumbled inside her blouse, and as she felt so very much more for Colin why should she resist the far greater pleasure of this man's embrace? True, she hardly knew him, and true, she had only known him for a short time, but she knew that she most desperately wanted him to want her. She also knew that she was going blind, and she knew that Colin knew it too, and yet as far as he was concerned, it did not seem to be important. If some benign sea god had emerged at her feet at that moment, she would have willingly done a deal. *Oh God give me this man and I'll happily go blind with gladness!*

Gingerly she brought her own hands up to cover his hands. 'I did not know you felt about me in this way,' she managed to say with a modicum of calm and control that was more of an illusory act than the real thing.

'Then know it now,' he said, and lowering his hands to her submerged hips, turned her to face him. 'Know it now!.'

His mouth found her lips, and as her arms wrapped themselves around his neck, he drew her ever more closely to him; now she could feel her breasts crushing against his chest, her legs pressing against his legs... Now she could feel the rigidity of his manhood nuzzling against her pubis. Again the inclination to pull away was dismissed by the woman within her, and she gave herself fully to the kiss, welcoming the hand that sought to caress her breast once more and opening her mouth to receive the passion of Mage's gently probing tongue.

As Hector Sanchez thoughtfully left the church of Santa Maria, heading for the Hotel Miraflores in search of some solitude and a stiff drink – as his daughter and her three friends made their way up the beach towards the chiringuito and an early lunch – as Michael Fry eased the black BMW to the side of the road just outside Glastonbury, feeling a thump in his stomach that told him she had landed safely – as John Light and Tamara boarded an aircraft in New Orleans bound for Madrid, flight GA 109 was landing on time at Gibraltar airport and twenty minutes later Helen Ross emerged from the small terminal building, suitcase in one hand and travelling bag thrown across one shoulder.

The warmth and light had hit her as she'd walked across the tarmac, ogling the omnipresent rock with a sense of awe; she'd been told that it was big, but hadn't expected anything quite so substantially massive. Now with the rock and the terminal building behind her, she hunted for a taxi.

'Sorry lady,' a swarthy Gibraltarian driver spoke to her carelessly in a curious patois accent. 'They're playing silly bastards on the border again. There's at least a two hour jam. You're better off walking across the frontier and finding a Spanish taxi on the other side.'

Unaware of the resentments caused by the intransigence of both the Gibraltarian and Spanish governments, she marched off towards what obviously the border crossing which was at least a hundred yards away, and found herself seriously wishing that she'd worn some lighter clothes. Five minutes later and far more easily than she'd expected she crossed into Spain where a large thermometer clock told her that it was three minutes past twelve and thirty two degrees centigrade. She began to perspire beneath the thick grey flannel dress and navy blazer.

There were ten or fifteen taxis to choose from. 'Castillo?' she spoke carefully in English to the first driver to catch her eye. 'The Hotel Miraflores?'

'Si Señorita. Hotel Miraflores, Castillo de la Frontera. Cinquenta euros...'

She had no idea whether or not it was a fair price, but at least the taxi driver seemed to know where she wanted to go, and that had to be seen as a step in the right direction. Besides, this was Michael Fry's money she was spending, and while that should not have made a difference, she found that it did. He'd not only provided her with her air tickets, but also with a thousand pounds in travellers cheques and a line of credit at the Royal Bank of Scotland in Gibraltar Town. While she had every intention of respecting his generosity it was still something of a novelty, knowing that she could travel first class without having to monitor every penny that she spent. She settled back in the taxi and prepared to enjoy the drive.

First they followed the southern shore of Algerciras Bay with the modern concrete ugliness of La Linea crowding in from their right, they negotiated the small town of Campamento before heading inland towards San Roque and passing one of the most antiquated and offensive oil refineries she'd ever seen. The belching smoke of pollution and the smell of burning chemicals made her frown in displeasure. *Come to sunny Spain and suffocate!* she thought disparagingly.

Beyond San Roque, a totally unmemorable town if ever there was one, the scenery changed from urban industrialisation to open countryside filled with rich fields full of cattle and rolling open meadows dotted with immaculately pristine farms and distant villages that sparkled enticingly in the brilliant Andalucian sunshine.

Then they started to climb through hills that were covered with forests of cork oak, pine and eucalyptus; as the hills became steeper, causing her driver to constantly shift gears, she caught occasional glimpses of distant mountains, cruel and jagged and most unlike the softer, more friendly peaks of her native Scotland. Her eyes constantly darted between these more distant vistas to the chaotic profusion of wild flowers and tall grasses that swept past in a blur at the side of the road.

At one point the road curved sharply to the left and they crossed a tumbling river full of white water that rushed over rocks causing cascades of spray to explode in the air. A series of small rainbows arched across the torrent pointing the way to a dozen pots of gold buried in the rich green foliage that lined the river banks, sometimes trailing into it and weaving downstream like braids of hair. The pagan in her smiled with delight for here surely was Elvan earth energy in abundance.

As they carried on driving, Helen found herself becoming increasingly enchanted by the character of the land. When the village of Castillo finally came into sight she studied it intently from the window of the taxi, searching for some clue that might begin to unravel the mystery and magnetism of the place, but was rewarded only by the extremely attractive view of huddled white houses with their multi-coloured roof tops and the campaniles of two churches and the magnificent edifice of the castle..

'Hotel Miraflores?' the driver asked as they entered the maze of narrow streets, carefully negotiating a route between three parked cars and an ancient mule, heavily laden down by panniers loaded with bails of straw and a collection of earthenware pots.

'Si, por favour,' Helen confirmed, using three of the dozen words of Spanish that she knew in one sentence. She'd tried looking through a phrase book on a number of occasions during the previous week but her schedule had been punishingly heavy and there hadn't been much time or energy to absorb more than the twelve or thirteen words that she'd mastered.

Two right turns and one sharp dog leg to the left down an impossibly steep hill, and the taxi shuddered to an insecure halt outside The Miraflores. Helen paid the driver and for a few seconds stood and studied the antiquated hotel in the picturesque street before picking up her suitcase and with a wave of thanks to the taxi man entered the small hallway and climbed up the stairs to the bar, which also, nine days out of ten, served as the hotel reception.

Delighted by the low beams of rich old wood she smiled hopefully at the craggy faced man behind the bar. 'I don't suppose there's any chance that you speak English, is there?' she asked.

Henry Holloway beamed at her and five minutes later she was being shown into a room with two neat single beds, brilliantly white walls and a window that provided an interesting view of the street below. The room was spotlessly clean and full of light and character. Changing out of the grey dress that had seemed appropriate for the rainswept skies above the M62 motorway but which was totally redundant now that she had arrived and had experienced her first blast of Spanish heat, she slipped into a pair of jeans and a T shirt, and after hanging up her clothes in a dark olive wood wardrobe, made her way back down to the bar, although not before making sure that a certain bag which contained a number of items she neither wanted seen nor disturbed was secured away at the bottom of a cupboard and the bedroom door was firmly locked behind her.

She'd told Henry that she'd be staying for one week with the option of a second week which she'd either confirm or cancel within the next few days. Sitting now at the bar drinking the delicious thick coffee and feeling the summer breeze waft through the building carrying the scent of musty oak and a dozen different perfumes from the gardened terrace – indeed, casting a glance out onto the terrace to have her eyes assaulted by scores of verdantly green plants with their profusion of flowers, all set against that impossibly perfect blue sky, it crossed her mind that if she had to stay here for the rest of her life, it would be no great hardship.

Casting around the bar, allowing her eyes to rest upon the clutter of ornaments and antiques collected from every part of the world along with bronzed mirrors, old bullfight posters and literally dozens of scaled model trains displayed with great care and pride in a number of strategically placed cabinets (they also rested on shelves and windowsills and even shared space with the bottles behind the bar) her eyes finally came to rest on the hotel's only other customer. He was a large man with mane of black curly hair streaked with grey and a luxuriantly bushy moustache. He was darkly tanned, and if his aura was anything to go by, deeply troubled by something that caused him to stare moodily into his glass with furrows and frowns of concentration. Not young, she thought... Fifty or fifty something, but strikingly attractive for all that.

Without realising that she'd been doling it, she'd been staring at him quite openly. Now he suddenly looked up and caught her eye.

She looked away guiltily, but now felt his eyes boring uncomfortably into her. Eventually she was forced to look up and as their eyes locked something elusive and indefinable passed between them.

'You are not Spanish,' he said abruptly in English.

'No. I'm from Scotland.'

The most curious complexity of expressions filtered across his face, and then very tentatively, almost as though he thought she might bite it, he held out his hand. 'Welcome to Castillo,' he said. 'I am Hector. Doctor Hector Sanchez.'

When he had entered Father Francisco's dormitory an hour or so earlier, he'd found it empty. The bed had been neatly made with clean sheets and old Juanita had been sweeping the plain concrete floor with a besom. She'd stopped when he'd entered the room and had eyed him with a knowing look that implied some secret knowledge.

Hector had returned her gaze measure for measure. 'Where is he?' he'd asked.

'In there.' She'd nodded in the direction of the church. 'Praying. The English has cured him – and I suppose that's something else I have to keep secret!'

'Indeed you must, Juanita. Indeed you must.'

Hector had found him kneeling before the altar. Instead of his usual surplice he'd been wearing faded jeans and an old blue shirt, looking more like a poet than a pastor. Sitting behind him in one of the right hand pews he'd studied the look of rapture on the young priest's face, noting that of the stigmata, at least on the forehead and the man's hands, there was no sign.

It had taken Francisco fully five minutes to become aware of the doctor's presence. When at last he had done so, he'd turned to look at Hector wonderingly.

'Good morning Doctor Sanchez.'

'Good morning to you Father Francisco. How are you feeling?'

'I've been ill,' the priest confided. 'But through the intervention of Jesus Christ I am well again now.'

'Jesus has healed you, then?'

'Not directly. He sent one of his angels.'

'Ah, so an angel has healed you! Who was this angel? What did it look like?'

The priest's eyes had clouded with confusion. I am not sure. I was flying through the realms of purgatory – both my body and my mind were afflicted – then the angel spoke to me and healed me of my wounds and when I woke this morning...' the priest had smiled shyly, 'I was well again.'

'Do you remember my visits to you? Hector had asked. 'Do you remember talking to me? Do you remember me dressing your wounds?'

'Yes – but only vaguely... The wounds... they were very unusual...'

'They were certainly that.'

'You saw them?'

'I certainly did.'

'And... they were real?'

'They were real.'

'You... you did not tell anyone else?'

'Yes. One man who is a good friend and who will say nothing... But what of the wounds? Are they totally gone?'

Francisco had held out his hands for Hector's inspection. It was as if the stigmata had never been there. There had been so sign of mark or blemish. 'It is the same with my side and my feet,' the priest had said.

Hector had departed a few minutes later. He'd wanted coffee and brandy and his pipe. He'd needed a silent corner in which to examine his own thoughts and feelings and had come to The |Miraflores where he'd met Helen Ross, who was petite, blond, pretty, about thirty years old and who was not Spanish – and who fitted Colin Mage's description in every way.

It was a long lunch. They ate paella and Mage made sure that the bacardi flowed freely. By two o'clock Christina and Angel were more than merry and Anna was also intoxicated – not by alcohol but by the happy ambience of the day and Mage's presence by her side. True, he had not kissed her again since they had emerged laughing from the waves, but he had held her hand and had never been more than a few centimetres distant. If she closed her eyes she could still feel his lips upon her mouth, his hands upon her body... And later, when they returned to the beach and she did close her eyes to sleep for a while beneath the shade of Christina's parasol, she did so with Mage's fingers interwoven within her own.

As Angel and Christina dozed off into a hazy sun and bacardi soaked siesta, Mage's mind remained wakefully alert. Feigning sleep himself he mentally used one of his familiar mantras to forge the psychic sword and insidiously brushed up against Christina's aura. There were several layers of awareness and he had to sift through them gently until he found what he was looking for. Beneath the vibration of Christina's libido that created erotic fantasies that did not, alas, revolve solely around Angel, he picked up other faces and thought forms. There was, for example, the departed photographer, Tom, and Mage became aware of the fact that their parting had been amicable enough, and also, more importantly, that they had not been in Castillo by accident or coincidence. They'd been there for a clandestine purpose, but now Tom was out of the picture. What was that purpose and why had Tom left so abruptly?

In the eye of his mind he saw Christina holding a telephone and masculine words echoed distantly in his ear. *Get close to Mage* the voice said, and the voice seemed oddly familiar. He ran it like a loop tape in the back of his mind, savouring it, tasting and touching it until familiarity gave way to sure foundation, and with that foundation John Light's black face swam into view, and like a dam breaking, the rest of the words burst forth and he became privy to the rest of their conversation – or at least, that part of it that Christina's memory cells had retained.

'I'll be damned!' Mage murmured under his breath as Christina stirred, causing him to withdraw from mental contact. *I'll be damned. She's not only here on his ticket, but he's actually on his way here now.*

Mage propped himself up on one elbow and reached for his cigarettes. Smoking thoughtfully, his eyes narrowed to focus on the horizon and he thought back to his first and only meeting with the American evangelist which had taken place earlier in the year at the sumptuous Los Angeles headquarters of The Church Of God's New Light.

The meeting had been prompted in part by Father Paul's conviction that it would be a worthwhile lead to follow up, and also in part by Mage's assessment of the Reverend John's book of Satanic Revelation. The book, a slim privately published volume, contained too many clues and veiled references to The Djinn for it to be ignored or dismissed. It formed the cornerstone of The New Church's philosophy, providing the foundation for its creed and doctrine. Key passages had pricked Mage's ears, causing his eyes to gleam. Light had obviously produced the work with mass readership and remunerative conversions in mind, and as such it was often written in an archaic and pseudo biblical style, but even so some of the script had not been without power...

"Following the pathway of Satan it was inevitable that I was drawn ever more

closely to his presence. On a day when all of my earthly enemies conspired and became united against me, I sought refuge and passed through the opening from the world of man to the world of hell. Only then did I become truly aware of the cruelty and the evil which stalks this planet. Only then did I see the tusk and scale of the Dark Ones who work unremittingly to bring about our downfall. Only then did I become sincerely afraid, not for my life but for my soul. The Other Side is a placed filled with goblins and shapechanging genies who welcomed me to their midst and sought to corrupt and contaminate me even more than I was already contaminated in my earthly existence. And thus I realised that as there was an even greater evil abroad in the world than my own Satanic deeds, there might yet be hope for my physical and spiritual salvation, but only if I renounced my own corruption... Only if I changed the meaning and purpose of my life. Only if I changed the direction of my life. Thus I resolved in those lost and painful hours of residence in that other most horrifying dimension, that should I be able to escape from it, I would bring warning to all men that there is not a single devil in hell, but hoards of them, able to mimic man and take on the most convincing human form, moving among men and spreading the true evil of a seed much darker and more dangerous than mere Satanism. The Other Side of the opening between worlds is dark and it is hot, and it is devoid of the familiar features that make it recognisable as any place on earth, and yet I was always aware that it was an intrinsic although unseen part of our own world. Thus, having escaped that awful place through application of wit, guile and determination, I am come to tell you that there is a hell, for I have seen it! I come to tell you that there are demons, for I have seen them with my own eyes. Their dwelling place is darkness and our only defence against this darkness which is for ever growing and encroaching, is not only to embrace The Light, but also to create it, both within ourselves and within the dimensions of our earthly and spiritual existence. I tell you, I have seen this darkness and it has offended everything within me that is human. I have renounced that darkness and now I am Light Within Light."

His references to scale and tusk, to dimensions and openings, genies and shapechangers, had excited Mage's interest and expectation. If the passage could be accepted literally it broadly indicated that its author had had personal contact with the Djinn – had crossed into their dimension, had been appalled by what he'd experienced, and by whatever means had managed to get out again, chastened and changed but at least alive to tell the tale. Here then was a man that Mage had felt he simply had to talk to.

Paul O'Connor had helped by accrediting him to his own Holy Order of Saint Patrick and by sending a number of trans Atlantic faxes to arrange the meeting. Thus, when Mage had finally been shown into John Light's sanctum sanctorum, a bright modern office with a notable absence of religious artefact or atmosphere, the evangelist had welcomed him as an emissary bringing fraternal greeting from an Irish holy order.

Mage had been immediately aware of the black American's prescient psychic aura and had brought up all the barriers of his own formidable defences. Initially it would do no harm for the evangelist to be kept in ignorance of Mage's true quest.

As they'd shaken hands he'd felt the powerful pushpulse of inquisition and had reflected it back to its source. Light, not unaware of the transition of the energy, had been immediately on his guard – although he'd given no visible sign of this altered state of awareness. Indeed, he'd been charmingly affable, calling for coffee and enquiring about Mage's impressions of California. After the refreshments had arrived the sparring had begun.

'I see you are from The Most Holy Celtic Order Of Saint Patrick The Protector,' Light had said genially. 'That's quite a title. The question is, of course, how can I help you? The fax we received from your Father O'Connor said that there was a matter to be discussed, a sensitive matter, I seem to recall, that was of our mutual interest and could be to our mutual advantage... Although forgive me for being blunt, but I can't for the life of me figure out what The Church of God's light might have in common with your Irish order.'

Mage had prepared his presentation reasonably well. He'd considered forgetting it and saying simply The Djinn... It might have been an effective short cut, but it might equally have brought the interview to an abrupt termination. He sensed that he was already on thin ice, so he'd proceeded with the carefully rehearsed plan A.

'The Order Of Saint Patrick is a rather curious one,' Mage had begun. 'It is funded principally by Vatican Trust, but while it is a spiritually very advanced order, its purpose and duties are singularly more secular. Basically it acts as an intelligence gathering unit for paranormal activity; a UFO sighting in Iowa will be recorded along with poltergeist activity in the South of France. The order acts as a repository and a clearing house for any reported or published occult activity across the world. If a priest in the jungles of Bolivia has a vision of Jesus Christ on Tuesday morning they'll know all about it in Ireland by Wednesday lunch time. Inevitably the order has an interest in all religious cults and sects and an even greater interest in the spiritual foundation of their existence.

'In theory, all the information which is gathered is held in the name of the papal authorities in Rome and is available to them on request, but in reality a rather different situation prevails. Rome is told what Rome needs to know and over the decades the Order of Saint Patrick has become something of a law and institution unto itself, which is fair enough in the circumstances, those circumstances being that it has been in existence for a lot longer than the Vatican has held authority in the Christian world and has been collating its intelligence since a time before the inquisition. Most of all, however, it is because its original holy orders and mandate came from Saint Patrick himself. The order's loyalties are fairly well defined along the lines of Saint Patrick's mandate first, then the will of God followed by the good of Man, and finally the needs of The Vatican and the catholic church.'

'This is all very interesting,' Light had said and Mage had seen that he was more than just interested. 'But I still fail to see what this has to do with my church here in California.'

'I'm coming to that, Reverend,' Mage had said politely. 'The secret of it is in Saint Patrick's prime directives to the order, which while they might sound melodramatic to most men's ears, probably will not do so to yours. On the island of Cael where the order is founded there is a cave and within that cave there is an area where the veil between two worlds is very thin. The inhabitants of that other world are shapechanging creatures called Djinn and The Order Of Saint Patrick The Protector has been in place for the past sixteen hundred and eighty years for the sole purpose of keeping The Djinn locked up in their own dimension on the other side of the divide.

'Twelve years ago you published your book of Satanic Revelation and from reading that book it is clear to us that you have had personal contact with the Djinn. That you have entered – and have returned from their dimension. That you are either as good as your word and are their enemy or quite the reverse – that you are their agent in place. I have travelled here today to find out which, and you're going to have to tell me Reverend, for just as my ability can block the psychic probes you've been directing against me ever since I walked into this office, then so also has your own psychic power been successful in blocking mine. If you are the enemy of the Djinn then I need you to help me stop them from breaking through into our world which they will surely try to do in Spain before or at midsummer, for there is a place there similar to the place in Ireland where the veil between our two dimensions is sickeningly thin... Similar, I suspect, to a place you encountered and explored some twelve or thirteen years ago...' Light's armour had cracked and Mage had received a flash vision. '...A place between two trees, perhaps, and close to the waters of a lake or river. Or if you are not the man of light you profess to be and are joined in unholy communion with the Djinn, I am here to serve notice that your machinations are known... The Djinn that is already among us has been identified and your intentions shall be thwarted.'

'This is fucking bullshit!' Light had exploded, giving Mage deep insight to the man's fear and rising panic.

'Is it? Mage had queried calmly. 'In that case how do you explain your own book of Satanic Revelation?'

'It's just a book and I don't have to explain a God damn thing to you!'

The American's psychic armour had disintegrated and Mage had been given clear vision of the trees and the lake and the rippling folds of alien light that had embraced the fleeing black man as he'd raced his motor cycle into the realms of none-existence. Mage had opened his mind and had drawn John Light into the reflection of his own memories, eliciting a startled cry not only of fear but also of horror and revulsion from the American's lips.

'Know this,' Mage had said coolly. 'The Djinn are active. They're on the move. They seek to force entry at a place called Castillo de la Frontera in Southern Andalucia. I shall be there to stop them and I need all the intelligence and information you can give me. You've got to help me, Mr Light, because if you don't, the very same thing that scared you shitless twelve years ago, that scares you shitless today when you think about it, is going to scare you even more shitless tomorrow when it comes physically knocking on your door looking for its old friends and aqaintences.'

'Get out of here!' Light had railed and raged at Mage, the disgust and terror clearly visible on his sweating ebony face. 'Get the fuck out of here and don't come the fuck back! Ever!'

Mage had left. Light had given him no choice...But at least he'd felt partially successful in the execution of his mission. What ever else John Light may have been, he was not acting on behalf of the Djinn. He'd certainly encountered them, of that Mage was quite positive, and they'd terrified him half to death...So much so that he'd sent Christina and Tom to Castillo to survey the lie of the land... And now for whatever reason, he was on his way here himself!

Mage stubbed his cigarette out in the sand. Both the girls were asleep of dozing but he was aware of Angel watching him, face propped in the cup of his hand.

'Everything all right?' he asked softly.

'Yes Señor Colin. Everything is good.'

'And is it good with Christina?' Mage nodded towards the tousled blond.

'Yes, it is good... Very good, but...' a shadow crossed the young Spaniard's saturnine face and in that single word "but" there were conversations clamouring for release.

Mage knew it and sighed, not wishing to be drawn into that particular dialogue. Even so, when he spoke, it was with sympathy and understanding. 'Listen Angel, women like Christina have many lovers. You are not the first and nor will you be the last.'

'I know Señor – and this knowledge, it tears away at my guts and it kills me!'

'Don't let it do that, my friend. Live for today, Angel, and let tomorrow take care of itself.'

Determined, at least for the next hour or so, to follow his own advice, Mage broke eye contact with the boy and reached for the bottle of Ambre Solair.

21.

The Arrivals

Hector arrived at The Miraflores just before nine that evening and ordered a gin and tonic. It was not his usual drink but this was what Helen had been drinking earlier that afternoon, and he put it down to subliminal auto suggestive influences. He'd been happy to show the attractive Scottish girl around the village and had even bought her lunch at the Bar España. He'd noticed that she wore a curiously woven bracelet made from green and gold fibres, tied around her right wrist – and he knew where there was another one just like it! On more than one occasion he'd felt like asking her if her presence in Castillo had anything to do with Colin Mage.

For her part Helen had welcomed the guided tour. It had given her the chance to get the feel of the place and to form some initial impressions. She would explore again later on her own, but for now this was a good opportunity for her to get her bearings. She'd tried hard to maintain her objectivity but had found it difficult to ignore all that she'd been told of the village, directly by Michael Fry, and indirectly through The Druid by Colin Mage.

Helen was a highly trained psychic and as she'd walked through the quiet Sunday streets, soaking up the ambience and chatting amiably with the doctor, two thoughts had become clear "facts" in her mind. The first was, just as Michael Fry had said there would be, there was a definite atmosphere here, a thrumming chord of tension which was hard to define but which reminded her of Stonehenge or Culloden Moor on the night of a solstice moon. Colin Mage was not wrong. There was a pregnancy of expectation that churned her stomach with that not always welcomed big dipper feeling. Something was happening here, and something else, something bigger, was going to happen soon.

The other thing was that she'd felt increasingly sure that Hector Sanchez knew Colin Mage. Not sure of her ground or what Hector might or might not know himself, she'd deliberately fought shy of saying anything that might compromise her. Like Mage, she had a "cover" story that could be as firm or as flexible as she needed it to be, but before she gave anything away, she'd have to talk to Mage first to find out what was going on.

In the end it had been the doctor who'd provided her with the evidence to prove she'd been right in thinking that he knew Mage. They'd been sitting on the terrace of the Bar España, she drinking a rare gin and tonic, Hector sipping at a beer. He'd commented, rather probingly, she'd thought, about the bracelet Michael Fry had given her.

'I have a friend who has one just like it,' he'd said, too casually for the remark to be casual at all.

'Really? That's quite surprising because there aren't too many of them about. They tend to be made specially, and you certainly can't buy them in the shops. They're usually given as gifts, by special people to special people.'

'And are you a special person, Miss Ross?'

'You bet I am!' she'd replied light heartedly, deliberately mocking herself. '... And if your friend has got one then he must be a very special person too.'

'He is. A very special person – but tell me, Miss Ross, how did you know that my friend is a man? He could just as easily have been a woman.'

Realising that although she might not have walked into a deliberate trap, she had successfully put her foot in it, Helen had waffled wonderfully. 'I suppose I just assumed,' she'd said gaily.

'No,' Hector had smiled at her, but there had been a brittleness in the smile. 'You knew.'

'How do you know that I knew?'

'Miss Ross,' there was a tired tone to the doctor's voice, 'my friend is, as we have both established, a very special man. He and I have all but lived in each others pockets for these last few weeks and I have been aware of some of his unusual gifts and talents. He carries with him a certain mystique – he would call it an aura, an energy, perhaps, and unless I am very much mistaken this same energy is something that you also carry with you. Even if these things were not true, only twenty four hours ago my friend told me that he "saw" me with someone who fits your description in every way... And now, out of the blue, here you are.'

'Would you care to name this friend of yours?' Helen had asked lightly. 'Then at least we'll know who we're talking about.'

No, Miss Ross. You name him.'

'Very well. I think your friend might be someone called Colin Mage.

'Spot on, Miss Ross, just as I thought you would be... And I thank you for your honesty. The thing is, are you his friend or his enemy?'

Something in the way he had asked the question had made her relax slightly. Obviously the doctor did know something, which made things a lot easier. 'Colin Mage has some dreadful enemies,' she'd said flatly. ' - But he also has some very powerful friends and I assure you, Doctor Sanchez, in fact I *promise* you, that I am one of the good guys.'

'You are a friend of Colin's?'

'I suppose that I must be, although to tell you the truth, I've never met him.

I know of his work and I know why he's here, and what I need to do is meet with him personally. I have messages from people in England who are his allies. I can see that you're worried but if you'd like to take me to him, I'm sure I'll be able to put your mind at rest.'

'I think you might have to wait for a few hours. He's out of the village at the moment – with my daughter, as a matter of fact – and I'm not expecting them back until well into the evening.'

'Fine - but can you tell me how much you know?'

'How much do I know?' Hector had echoed. 'I know enough to wish that I didn't know anything at all, and I know enough to know that before you and I discuss these matters any further, you must first speak with Colin...' Hector had rubbed the bowl of his meershaum against the side of his cheek. '...So I suggest that we mark time until this evening. I'm not sure when exactly they'll be back but if we're in the bar of The Miraflores for nine o'clock I dare say we'll make contact sooner or later.'

Helen had been more than happy with that. As far as she was concerned, although she'd yet to meet the magician, she'd already made an important contact.

***

At nine thirty that evening as the aircraft carrying John Light and Tamara from New Orleans began its long and gradual descent towards Madrid, Jadoc Dolorean and Alexandra Mage crossed the French border at San Sebastian and entered the land of Spain. Sticking to the motorway systems and making the most of the light traffic, Dolorean put his foot down and steeled himself to a long night drive. Providing there were no hold ups they would be bypassing Burgos by one o'clock the following morning and by noon they would be lunching well south of Madrid, somewhere on the road that ran as straight as an arrow through the table top flatlands of La Mancha. He intended being in Cordoba by early evening and Castillo for midnight.

It was also around nine thirty on that Sunday evening that Colin Mage and his small entourage trooped into the Hotel Miraflores in search of long cold drinks after their thirsty drive up from the coast. Mage turned the corner at the top of the stairs and paused with a small stab of surprise to see Hector sat at the bar with a shapely blond female who struck him as being oddly familiar even though he was fairly sure he'd never seen her before.

Anna, also taken by surprise, not so much by her father's presence but more by his company, wrapped her arms around his neck and gave him a dutiful kiss on the cheek.

'You smell of sea and sand and sun oil,' he joked. 'Have you had nice day, my darling?'

'Papa, we have had a wonderful day!' she exclaimed as Christina noisily pulled extra bar stools into place and Angel ordered drinks.

'That is good, and now you must meet a new friend of mine who has arrived in Castillo today from Scotland... Helen, this is my daughter Anna – the young man who is asking you what you would like to drink is Angel Guardiaro, this other young lady is Christina from the United States – and finally, the gentleman you've come looking for, Colin Mage.'

Helen shook hands all round, immediately noticing Anna's reserve that hid turbulations of jealousy and suspicion, and eventually coming into contact with the man she'd heard so much about and had travelled so far to meet. He was wearing old blue jeans and a faded denim shirt with a black hat pulled rakishly low over his eyes – eyes that studied her intently as she studied him. She was aware of his dark tan that made him look a lot more Spanish than English, and of the rimes of salt that matted his beard. Even more so, she was aware of the phenomenal power that exuded from his presence. As their hands touched in the handshake she received a sharp shock from the charge of psychic energy that he carried within him, and so strong was it that she involuntarily pulled her hand away from the physical touch.

Over the years she had come into contact with innumerable people who had been gifted with psychic ability and who carried the spark of magic with them in their auras. Michael Fry was a good example, but while Fry's energies were gentle and well rounded to the point of being quite refined, Colin Mage's energies were raw and straining, a reaction of atomic fission held in tight control... But if that control ever slipped, if ever he was pushed over the edge into a state of critical mass, or, God forbid, he chose to unleash the power within him on his own account, she marvelled and shuddered in contemplation of what the results might be.

Does he even know he's got it? she asked of herself – and then realised the literally quite awful truth. *Yes, he knows, and he's holding it within by a constant act of sheer will, and, my God, I'm not even seeing the half of it!*

'You've come looking for me?' he asked, echoing Hector's words of introduction.

Her pre-prepared speech crumbled along with any composure she thought she might have had. 'Michael Fry has sent me,' she said weakly.

Mage brushed his forefinger against the braiding of the green and gold bracelet. 'Yes,' he said softly. 'I can see that he has. The question is why?'

'He wants to know what's happening,' she blurted out, 'and he thought you might need some help.'

'And he's sent you.'

'Yes.'

'Where are you staying?'

'Here in the hotel.'

'Okay, I'll come to you later and we'll talk then... For now, I don't want to break up a nice party.'

As they moved out of the bar and on to the terrace, arranging themselves around a table beneath the pride of Henry Holloway's grapevines, Mage could detect the insecurity and hostility than emanated from Anna in measurable waves.

'This Miss Ross... She is an old girlfriend of yours who has come to check up on you?'

'No.' Mage forced the laugh to his lips. 'I promise you that I've never met her before this evening. As far as I know she's just here on holiday, but because she's in the same business as I am, we do have a number of mutual friends back in England. Someone has told her that I am staying here and she has brought me some messages and information that will help me with my work.'

Anna was mollified but Mage was troubled. As they sat beneath the vine and a canopy of early evening stars, he was aware of the subliminal tension around the table. Christina was being very American in her domination of the conversation, while Angel sat moodily silent, trying to come to grips with something that his youth and his Spanish machismo couldn't handle very well. Hector was his usual gregarious self, but even beneath the bonhomie Mage could detect another restless excitement that had much to do with Helen Ross's elfin presence by his side. Anna's grip on his own hand was propriatorally possessive and he wondered with some dismay and a number of misgivings how she would react when she learned that not only did he have a wife, even though they were legally separated with a divorce pending, but that the lady in question was probably on her way to Castillo at that very moment. Although his affection for Anna was strong and although the sexual attraction was powerful, he now none-the-less deeply regretted his earlier impulsiveness on the beach at La Bolonia.

The impromptu drinks party of the terrace broke up before eleven o'clock, but after having walked Anna home to Calle Santana it was close to midnight before Mage knocked quietly on Helen Ross's door. Not without a sense of trepidation Helen let him in and for more than an hour they sat talking on the edge of her bed. There was no doubt in his mind that she was an emissary from Michael Fry and he listened intently as she narrated the sequence of events that had caused her to make this journey. He was deeply grateful and very moved to learn that the Druid was so much on his side, but was not at all sure how he should deal with Helen. As tactfully as he could, he said as much.

Having regained much of her composure, Helen was more readily able to deal with the problem. 'We can handle it one of two ways,' she said in a brisk, business like tone. 'You can regard me as a friend of a friend who has a vested interest in your presence here, and can furnish me with any relevant information that might help him to help you. I'll act as go between, but will get on with the business of enjoying a holiday, making my own reports to Michael as and when I see fit. In other words, I'll hover in the background and act as your back up if you need me, but will fundamentally stay out of your hair – or you can bring me in on this and let me help you as much as I can. I know I didn't put on a very good show earlier this evening, but I'm not just some silly little acolyte who doesn't know a wand from a willy. I am Wiccan High Priestess to The Scottish Clans and I am Priestess To The Druidic Order Of Bards. I have a lot of knowledge and no small amount of power that I am pleased to place at your disposal.'

'Why?' Mage asked. 'Why would you do this? You must surely be aware that there's an awful lot of danger involved.'

'Have you ever actually seen the Djinn? In his true form?'

'No,' Mage admitted. 'I haven't.'

'Neither have I, but I've seen him in clairvoyant vision. I'm disgusted and I'm frightened and I want to do something to make sure your own fears are never realised.'

'Fair enough... How much has Hector told you about what's been happening here?'

'He hasn't told me anything directly,' she grinned faintly. ' – Other than the fact that he knows you and is aware of some of your powers. How much does he know himself?'

'Just about everything,' Mage said.

'Just about?'

'He doesn't know about the Djinn or anything about my personal involvement through Alexandra. Everything else, he knows.'

'And what of his daughter?'

'She knows nothing at all.'

'Then with respect, I dare say you might have a bit of a problem when your ex-wife turns up. That young lady has got her emotional claws well and truly hooked into you. She hated me at first sight.'

'No, I don't think Anna is capable of that kind of hate. Certainly she was suspicious of you, but we have to put that down to an awful lot of insecurity. She's going blind and is under sentence of death from a brain tumour – although she herself is ignorant of that latter piece of information, so please, don't breathe a word! She sees me as a lifeline, and for my sins I've encouraged it. I want to help her if I can, and I can't do that without gaining her trust and confidence. Any other emotions I may have generated within her are a very complicated bonus... But I do quite agree with you. I am going to have a problem.'

'By the sound of it, you've got one already,' she said not unkindly.

'Yes, I suppose I have,' he laughed bitterly, and moving over to the window, opened it and lit a cigarette.

'Are you in love with her?' Helen asked.

'I feel a lot of love for her,' Mage admitted, 'but, of course, that's not the same thing at all, is it?'

'No it isn't,' Helen said, joining him at the window and helping herself to one of his cigarettes. She hadn't smoked in years but all of a sudden it seemed like a good time to start again. 'But for what it's worth, I think you are. You just haven't realised it yet. One thing's for sure, she's crazy about you.'

Mage closed his eyes. 'I've found myself wondering a few times this last fortnight how things might have been if I'd come to this place as a free agent... If I'd never met Alexandra, or even if I had, if I'd got an ordinary divorce behind me – if there is such a thing. It would be so easy, so natural to build something with Anna in those circumstances. As it is...' He left the sentence unfinished and Helen's heart went out to him.

'I don't want to sound critical,' she said, 'but haven't you left yourself wide open? If the girl's got a brain tumour, then there isn't much you can do other than be supportive, and the more supportive you are, the more dependent upon you she's likely to become.'

'I can heal the tumour,' he said abruptly.

Helen chose her words carefully. She did not doubt that Mage *believed* he could do what he'd just said, but she'd moved in the world of magic for long enough to know that even the most sincere prayers of spiritual healing were unlikely to affect a malignant brain tumour that was sufficiently advanced to make a girl start going blind. Even metaphysical energies could not go against natural law.

'Colin, I'm not sure that spiritual healing could do a great deal of good in a case like this. Obviously it can help Anna and her state of mind in a holistic way, but...'

'I'm not talking about spiritual healing,' he interrupted her. 'I'm talking about psychic surgery.'

Now Helen had to be even more tactful. 'Colin, there's been so much experimentation on this subject over the years and either it hasn't worked, or worse, the psychics involved have been exposed as charlatans and frauds.'

'I'm neither a charlatan nor a fraud,' he said without rancour, 'and in the right circumstances I know that I can do it. I wasn't sure about it at first, but I am now. If it hadn't been for everything else that's going on here, I'd have probably done it already... But there isn't much point in healing Anna this week if by next week she's going to be dead anyway, impaled upon some bastard Djinn's tusks.'

'Is there... is there really a chance that it could come to that?'

'Yes, I'm afraid that there is. I know it is hard to believe, but I do believe it, and so must you if you are to be of any help to me at all.'

'I do want to help, so will you tell me what has been happening here?'

'Sure. I'll give you facts and figures first, then thoughts and impressions. Okay?'

Mage returned to the edge of the bed and started talking. He was still talking an hour later when the town hall clock chimed two.

At two a.m. Jadoc Dolorean was a hundred and fifty kilometres north of Madrid. The Jaguar ate up the distance carniverously, seldom dropping below seventy miles an hour and frequently cruising at over a hundred. As dawn streaked across the eastern skies he was south of Madrid and Toledo, but with the dawn came his first delay. The female began showing signs of agitation and distress and rather than risk the unthinkable he detoured by the small town of Manzanes and pulled the car discreetly off the road into a grove of olive trees. It took almost an hour to regulate the incubator and although he resented the loss of time, realised that it was a necessary investment. Nothing could be allowed to go wrong at this late stage and he was aware of the inexactitude of the science he was practising. Incubating a female of his own kind in the Homeworld was a routine procedure. Doing it with an Earthworld female in an alien environment requiring constant vigilance and monitoring. It was a delicate process and although he was not the first to attempt it, and indeed would not be the first to succeed, for every one who had succeeded a score had tried and failed.

The Jaguar's engine ticked in the silent grove. Now that the female was stable, Dolorean got out of the car and walked slowly around the stunted olives. It had been a long drive, virtually none stop from Ambois, and although he would not have admitted it to his brethren, he was glad of the break. It meant that he would be delayed in arriving at the Sacred Circle, but better to arrive a little late than to arrive incomplete. Even so, he fumed against the restrictions imposed by having to exist in this puny human body and looked forward to the day when he could assume his natural form.

He resumed driving but at a much more sedate pace and made a point of stopping more frequently during the growing heat of the day. He was delayed again at noon but made up time during the early afternoon. By four o'clock he was closing on Cordoba by which time the female was again becoming uncomfortable, which with the Newlife burgeoning inside her was hardly surprising. He bowed to the inevitable and pulled off the main highway again in search on an hotel. The Circle would have to wait for one more day.

As Dolorean and Alexandra were checking into the Hotel Alhambra on the outskirts of Cordoba, John Light and Tamara were checking into the Hotel Miraflores in Castillo. Henry Holloway wasn't exactly ringing his hands with glee, but he was feeling more than a little satisfied. The Miraflores had six rooms to let and to make any kind of profit the hotel had to run at fifty percent occupancy for at least half of any year. It had been a bleak and disastrous winter, but now things were certainly looking up. In the space of two days he'd let two rooms, and although he had another three which were unoccupied, the guests that he did have were good payers and long stayers, not just weekend wallies from Gibraltar. It was curious though, he mused as he rearranged one of his train set displays, how his three different parties of guests all seemed to know each other.

Mage had slept late that morning. The hours of sun and sea air that he had enjoyed the previous day combined with his late night conversation with Helen Ross that had gone on into the early hours, conspired against him and he did not meet up with Hector until well after noon.

'Where to and what to do first?' Hector had asked eagerly'

'We need to see if we can locate our friend Raul Castro,' Mage had said. 'We still don't know who shut the trap door on us in Calle Sombra and he's as good a candidate as any. But first, if you don't mind, I need to have a word with Hamish Hamilton.'

'Hamish? What do we need with Hamish?' Hector had asked.

'I've got a proposition for him,' Mage had replied.

They'd found the archaeologist washing a very rusty Seat Ibiza outside his front door in Calle Lanette. He'd immediately offered to make drinks but Mage had declined.

'Then what can I do for you?' Hamish had asked amiably.

'I've got to get into the citadel,' Mage had told him. '...But I need to do it quietly. I just wanted to be sure that there isn't a way in before going through the front door, so to speak.'

'Well, if there is, I don't know about it,' Hamish had mused, 'and I worked on the building long enough to find one if there was. As I said on Thursday, you can break down a wall or go through the roof, but you'll not do it quietly and not without half of Castillo watching on and wondering what you're doing. Easier by far to excavate the door.'

'How busy as you at the moment?'

'Not very. Why?'

'I'd like you to excavate the entrance for me,' Mage had said. 'Get the permit and hire the diggers in your own name, and I'll not only cover all the expenses, I'll also pay you well, both for your time – and for your discretion.'

'This sounds very interesting,' the archaeologist had grinned. 'When do you want me to start?'

'Now,' Mage had said. 'Today.'

Hamish had rubbed his chin thoughtfully. 'Well, let's see. I could walk up to the ayuntamiento in the next half hour and sort out the permit. It's a formality. They probably won't issue the permit for another day or so, but as long as I've got the receipt and they know what I'm doing, there won't be a problem. It might take me an hour or so, perhaps a wee bit longer, to recruit a couple of likely lads to act as diggers, but with a wee bit of luck I can probably start excavating after the siesta. If we put in a good morning tomorrow, then I dare say we'll have the door open for you by lunch time Say twenty four hours from now. That any good for you?'

'Absolutely excellent!'

'Want to tell me what this is all about?'

'No,' Mage had said. 'I don't. At least, not yet. But you get me into that Citadel, and if anything comes to light of an archaeological nature, it's all yours.'

'But there isn't anything there, man.' Hamish had said slowly. 'Just bare walls and floors and the old well in the dungeons. We spent hours looking for anything that might have been of interest but the place was as empty as a crofter's purse.'

'That was then,' Mage had said quietly. 'This is now.'

'But nothing will have changed!' Hamish had exclaimed. 'Since we finished working there the whole place has been sealed up as tight as a drum.'

Not from underneath, it hasn't, Mage had thought, but he'd kept the thought to himself, choosing instead to smile mysteriously as the lanky Scot. 'Let's just say that I might know something that you don't, and that if there's any gain to be had out of this business, then you'll benefit from it as much as I do. Now, have we got a deal?'

'Too damn right we have!' Hamish had thrust out a hand and Mage had shaken it warmly in confirmation of their contract.

Later he was to deeply regret having struck this bargain, wishing instead that he himself had done what he'd contracted the archaeologist to do on his behalf. By then, of course, it was much too late.

After having left Hamish counting a wad of euros that Mage had provided as a down payment they'd driven out to Raul Castro's finca in the foothills beyond San Pablo. The place had been deserted with no signs of habitation. The garden had been overgrown clearly indicating that nobody had worked in it recently, and although a layer of dust covered the rooms of the small stone built farm house, nothing had seemed particularly out of order. Of the finca's owner there'd been no sign, although curiously neither of the two doors or four windows had been locked or latched. There'd been wide tyre tracks gouged into the soft soil outside the front porch, but Mage had no means of knowing how fresh they may have been.

'What do you think?' Hector had asked.

'No one here,' Mage had responded, stating the obvious. '...And by the feel of the place, there's been no one here for quite a while... Although it's odd that the doors and windows are open.'

'Not really. We Andalucians are not door lockers by nature. What *is* a bit odd is the fact that are two loves in Raul's life... apart from killing, that is... and neither of them is here. I'm talking about his horse and his car. So, he's either stabled the horse somewhere and has gone off in the car, or he's garaged the car and gone off on the horse. Raul's not the kind of man who would trust others with either, however, so I guess that he's put Fidel in the horse box and has taken him with him wherever he's gone. The other thing is that Raul's a gun freak and yet there are no guns in the house, so he's taken them with him too. It all suggests that he isn't intending to come back immediately, although I suppose that depends on where he's gone and when he went.' Hector had looked sideways at Mage. 'Do you have any feelings about it?'

'You mean psychic feelings? No, none at all, I'm afraid, but would you accept a guess?'

'By all means.' Hector had been intrigued.

'He's either gone to La Linea or Antiquera, possibly even to Seville. Look at the situation from his point of view. He's been part of a circle, and has probably joined that circle in response to the promise of marvellous things to come. All of a sudden the circle is smashed. People are dead, so he'll want to make contact with the living. Cortez is in La Linea, still in a coma. Ignatious is in Seville, and to all intents and purposes is dying. The only other relatively healthy members of his team are in religious retreat in Antiquera and if that isn't where he's gone directly, I dare say that's where he'll end up going.'

'What can we do in the meantime?'

'Not a lot we can do, other than telephoning the Sisters' Mother Superior and making sure they're still in residence... Maybe we could warn her that there's a gun toting gun freak coming her way who's interest in her charges isn't particularly spiritual, but if we do that then I'd prefer to do it anonymously. For now,' Mage had glanced at his watch and it had been a little after three, 'let's get back to Castillo. Maybe I'll have some inspiration on the way, and if not, I'll let you buy me a drink in Jacinto's bar.' Then, as an afterthought; 'What is Anna up to this afternoon?'

'Trying to sort out my filing system and making excuses for me if anyone telephones,' Hector had chuckled, '...And seething with resentment that it's me who is with you this afternoon, and not her.'

'She had me all day yesterday,' Mage had quipped, a little too lightly, a little too glibly, causing a frown to furrow the doctor's face.

'That will cut little ice with my daughter. She's a strong willed young woman and when she's got a bee in her bonnet about something – when there's something she wants – she won't give up until she gets it.'

'What are you saying?' Mage had asked, swinging himself up into the cab of the Land Rover.

'Only what I told you on Saturday morning,' Hector had retorted, climbing up beside him. '...And after your day together yesterday I don't suppose Anna's feelings are any less strong than they were the day before. Colin, if I know my Anna, she's secretly dreaming of miracle cures, of marriage and babies, and of living for ever in her own little house somewhere on Castillo's mountain, cooking your dinner and darning your socks and living happily ever after with me, her dear old papa, half a mile away on the other side of the hill. Anna is a romantic but I am realistic. I don't think she can have those things, at least, not with you – and not with anybody if the worst comes to the worst. All I'm saying is that I do not wish to see her hurt or disappointed.'

Mage had turned on the engine but had hesitated before putting the vehicle into gear. 'We should all have some faith in our dreams,' he'd said. 'I don't know if I could make Anna's dreams come true, if indeed her dreams are what you say they are. But I'll tell you one thing, I won't let that fucking brain tumour kill her, and if she goes blind then it'll be over my dead body. In a worse case scenario I might break your daughter's heart, but in return I'll give her her sight and her life!'

Hector had been taken back by Mage's vehemence. 'Colin, how can you make such a statement? If it is the will of God that Anna is afflicted in this way, then...'

'Then I'll make God change his mind!' Mage had snapped back angrily

They'd driven back to Castillo, each man locked into his own thoughts. As they'd passed the bodega they'd encountered Helen strolling by the roadside. She'd been heading in the right direction and Mage had pulled the Land Rover over while Hector had opened the door for her.

'Hi, where are you guys heading?' she'd asked cheerfully.

'It is on the strength of where we have been that we now go to Jacinto's bar. It is early in the day to start drinking, but we feel justified. You will join us of course?' There'd been a hopeful note in Hector's voice and Helen didn't disappoint him.

'Sure. Love to, then you can tell me what you've been up to.'

Mage had parked in the square and in the bar, cool, and at this hour of the day relatively quiet, had ordered the drinks. A beer for Hector, the same for Helen, and a coke for himself. If there'd ever been an afternoon when he felt he needed something stronger then this was it. He'd resisted the temptation, however, full well knowing that in his present mood, one drink would have led to two or three.

It would be bloody typical, he'd thought, if in the moment Dolorean arrived he was rolling round pissed or trying to come to grips with a hangover!

He'd listened in desultory way as Hector had explained Raul Castro's link with Ignatious and through Ignatious with Dolorean, and while Helen had listened intently, full well knowing that she was only getting part of the story – that part which Hector knew – Mage had moved restlessly round the bar, chain smoking cigarettes and nursing his coke as he'd studied old posters and photographs, reading the fine print of council edicts that were sellotaped to the walls. On more than one occasion, he gone and leaned up against the door, allowing his eyes to roam down the street in search of .... of what? He'd not been sure, but there'd been a tension in his stomach and a tension in the atmosphere of the afternoon. Looking upwards he'd realised that the sky was no longer bright blue but a high celestial grey. The temperature had dropped a degree or two and it had looked as though the long and unseasonable heat wave might now be coming to an end. With a small shock, he'd realised just how long he'd been in Castillo and that if it did start raining soon, then he would welcome it. Something was needed to clean the dust from the streets and the cobwebs from his mind. The day at La Bolonia might have been restful in some ways and illuminating in others, but mindful of Hector's words, had not solved any of his problems. Indeed, if Hector was right, it had only added to them.

'Hey Colin, my friend, it is your turn to buy the drinks again!' Hector's voice had called along the bar counter.

Of course he's bloody well right! Mage had thought savagely – but he'd covered his emotions and had rejoined Helen and Hector and had made an effort to become involved in the conversation, although part of him was well aware of the fact that Hector would have probably been happier if he'd never met him... If he'd met Helen Ross quite by accident and in other circumstances, just as he, Mage, had earlier wished that he might have met Anna in different circumstances.

The rain, a gentle drizzle, had begun to fall around four o'clock. The afternoon had darkened and cooled rapidly. Jacinto had turned on the lights and Mage, weakening to an insidious internal pressure, had ordered a carajillo – black coffee and cognac. They'd been discussing whether or not there might be any mileage in phoning Antiquera and Seville, and Hector had been suggesting that it might not be a bad idea to ask Jaime Gomez to look into the whereabouts of Raul Castro, when the bar door opened and shut behind them and a booming bass voice, speaking in Spanish but with a very definite American accent, asked if anyone knew where The Hotel Miraflores might be. Hector had turned on his stool and in English had begun to give the required directions. Knowing exactly who the voice belonged to, Mage had also turned and had come face to face with John Light.

Helen had been assaulted by the charge of static electricity that was suddenly omnipresent in Jacinto's bar. One part of her had been aware of Hector's voice, of the slim dark girl who stood in the doorway, of Jacinto himself, frozen in the act of polishing a wine glass, but all of her senses had been magnetised and absorbed by the two men who'd stood facing each other, their auras mingling and coalescing

in psychic symbiosis. Colin Mage, the troubled and enigmatic magician had stood facing the newcomer, a veritable giant of a black man, all of six and a half feet tall, and as broad as he was high. Helen had not had to labour in search of the Negro's identity. This was obviously the reverend John Light that she'd heard of, both from Michael Fry and Colin Mage himself... The question was, what was he doing here? And furthermore what was happening between these two men? Even Hector had realised that there was something amiss; his words had trailed off mid-sentence as Mage and Light had locked eyes, their facial expressions and body language giving nothing else away. *It's almost as if they're deciding whether they're friends or enemies,* Helen had thought. *Each is waiting for a sign from the other, they're testing each others psychic willpower, and neither of them is prepared to make the first move. Neither is prepared to back down!*
In the end it had been Colin Mage's face that had cracked into half a smile and he'd tentatively held out his hand.

'Good afternoon John. Welcome to where it's all at.'

Light's own face had relaxed into the hint of a grin and there'd been a significant subsidence in the degree of tension, both in the bar and between the two men. 'You're one hell of a powerful motherfucker,' Light had said in a neutral tone of voice. Then he'd taken Mage's outstretched hand and the grin had broadened into a full smile. 'You knew I was coming!'

'Yes,' Mage had confirmed, 'but only since yesterday afternoon.'

'Christina?'

'Afraid so – but she doesn't know that I got through her defences. To your credit, you've trained her well.'

'Not well enough by the looks of it!.'

'She'd never have blown it if she hadn't been so keen to get close to me.'

'What the hell. I guess it doesn't matter now anyway.'

'I guess it doesn't. I'm very glad to see you here.'

'At the end of the day, I guess I didn't have much choice. You have a lot to answer for, Mr Colin Mage from The Holy Celtic Order Of Saint Patrick The Protector... A lot to answer for!'

Then he'd dropped Mage's hand, and as if by some tacit agreement, both men wrapped their arms around each other and clenched each other in a bear hug while the four spectators, a relieved Helen, a curious Hector, a blasé barman, a patiently silent Tamara, had looked on in bemusement.

***

They met in a quiet corner of the Miraflores at eight o'clock. Between the bar and the entrance to the terrace there was a small alcove with a narrow bench table and stools. Old black and white photographs of pre-war Castillo hung on white stone walls and an open window provided a view of the courtyard. Gentle evening rain pattered on the broad leaves of the palms and not even the smoke from John Light's Havana cigar or Mage's cigarettes could dispel the exotic scents that wafted in from the garden.

By tacit agreement the meeting was just between the three of them. Light sat with his back to the window facing Mage and Helen who sat with their backs to the wall. Mage spoke at great length about the situation in the village, and of all the events that had gone before. Light was a patient listener. He didn't interrupt, and Mage made a point of being as detailed as he could be in his briefing. It was, of course, familiar to Helen's ears, but Light was hearing it all for the first time.

After Mage had finished speaking, the American sat quietly for a moment, digesting the information, and applying it to his own formidable and unique knowledge. Eventually he looked up and made eye contact with his two companions.

'We have an awful lot of questions here,' he said slowly, 'and very few hard answers. What we *do* have is a handful of incontrovertible facts and lots of theory, speculation and supposition. We *do* know that the Djinn exist, we *do* know that they are hostile, and we *do* know that there is a parallel world... And if either of you have ever doubted it, put your doubts away. I've been there and I've seen the bastards, and although I know you're both as curious as hell, just bare with me for a little while and I'll get round to telling you the story in my own way and my own time. We *do* know that there are a number of openings... I've just come from one in The States, and I'm quite prepared to accept that there are others. This indirectly brings me to my first question. Given that there is an opening here in this village, do we know exactly where it is?'

'In or beneath the Moorish citadel up on the top of the hill,' Mage said promptly. 'At least, that's my best guess. I won't know for certain until I get inside and have a look, but I expect to be able to do that sometime later tomorrow.'

'Okay... Now, if your theory is right and the actual ritual of The Opening isn't scheduled to take place until June 21st we are blessed with some time to prepare our strategy an tactics. It seems to me that we have two obvious options. One is that we get to the opening and seal it before the Djinn gets to it, and the other option is that we simply kill the Djinn as soon as he gets here. No Djinn, no opening, no problem!'

'Do you have any idea how we might go about doing those things?' Mage asked wryly.

'Nope, but there's one thing I can tell you. Killing a Djinn ain't easy. For example, a point three five seven magnum bullet is a total waste of time. I pumped five rounds into one of them at five yards, and I watched those bullets simply bounce off the motherfucker. They've got some kind of armour plated scaling; it's not always apparent, but when they're pissed off or if they sense any kind of danger, it's immediately in place.. and if it'll stop a three fifty seven, then I guess it will stop most other things too.'

'They're magical creatures,' Mage observed, 'and if they conform to any kind of natural law, it isn't law which is natural to us. If we are to destroy the Djinn, and I don't mean the whole race of them, just the one who's on his way here, then I think it must be on a mental level and by the application of magic. But forgive me, I've been trying to get my head around this for months and I still haven't been able to come to grips with the mechanics of the thing. But I do take your point about the speed at which they're able to change forms. I threw a punch at mine, and literally in split seconds he'd undergone sufficient metamorphosis to be able to lift me with one hand and throw me a good ten or fifteen feet and through a kitchen window to boot.'

'Okay, let's change the subject for a minute. Who else in the village knows what we're up against?'

'No one, as far as I know. There's you, me, Helen, and possibly Tamara, depending upon what you've told her. The people here who have come into contact with Dolorean have not seen him as an alien entity. To Ignatious he's a messianic saviour, and I suspect that the same is true for the rest of Ignatious's lot, with perhaps the exception of Miriam Cortez, but whatever she saw him as being we'll never know now what it was. There are a couple of others who have partially seen through the Djinn's disguise, but because they haven't known what they've been seeing, they regard him as being everything from a not so very nice man with nasty eyes to a particularly evil black magician. At this stage I've chosen not to enlighten them further. But there are three people, Pepe Ortega, Angel Guardiaro and Hector Sanchez, who believe that Dolorean is primely responsible for this village's ills, and they all know that there are going to be problems when he arrives here... And they do know he's coming because I've told them he is. In Pepe Ortega's case I didn't need to tell him. He already knew, even though he didn't know how he knew. The number of people in Castillo with degrees of psychic energy, sometimes latent, sometimes very close to the surface of their consciousness, is remarkably high.'

'I know.' Light smiled guiltily. 'Tom and Christina managed to take more than four hundred kirlian and auric photographs, and although I've not seen them, I've had Tom's report, and their evidence supports your observations one hundred percent.'

'On the subject of Christina?' Mage raised an eyebrow.

'Clever girl but basically she doesn't know shit from shinola. She doesn't know what's really going on here, although I have told Tammy. Part of her mind rejects it, of course, but I haven't held anything back – except what I went through in the other dimension. This brings me to another issue. I think maybe we should restrict what we know to ourselves. The less people who know our secret, the better. I know that sounds contradictory, but if we did go blabbing our mouths or shouting what we know from the roof tops, we'd be locked away for being certifiably insane, or if folk did believe us, we'd cause real panic in the streets.'

'I think Hector should be told,' Helen said quietly.

'Why?' Mage was curious.

'A number of reasons... I can't give you all of them, so just put it down to instinct and intuition. But ever since you've been here, Colin, Hector has been a part of this. He's your secular link with the people of this village. He's a medical doctor, and although I pray to the Gods that we don't, we might yet need his professional services...' she deliberately failed to mention that part of her vision at The Oaks where she'd seen a large black man with his chest covered in blood. 'The other thing is that although he has been contaminated by exposure to you, he still retains a scientific mind and a degree of objectivity which might serve us all well in the days ahead.'

'Some pretty good reasons there,' Light said, 'but I still don't feel that it's a good idea. The last thing we need is anyone in authority trying to run the show or binding us with Hippocratic scruples.'

'I take your point, but Helen is right. I think we need the doctor... Or, if I'm to be totally truthful, I *want* Hector with us, fully armed with all the knowledge we can give him. He's a remarkable man John. He's already as good as thrown his lot in with me and I want to be able to tell him everything. He'll probably react the same way that Tamara has done, but if there's going to be a fight, I want the man by my side. But leave him to me, will you? I'll sort him out in my own way over the next couple of days.'

'Okay by me man,' Light held up his hands. 'This is your show. Your the general and I'm just one of the grunts.'

'That isn't the way it is at all,' Mage retorted, faintly irritated.

'No, I know it ain't,' Light's grin lit up his face. 'I was just making a point.'

Jet lag and the long fast drive from Madrid took Light to an early bed. Mage bought Helen some supper, over which they discussed everything that had already been discussed and also Light's arrival.

'Don't you think it's a bit odd, him arriving out of the blue like this?' Helen asked.

'Not really, no,' Mage answered. 'If his destiny says he's got to be here, then here he is, just as you are, just as I am. In a perfect world other people should be coming to join us from Ireland and Israel, but I have a feeling that we three are it. Father Paul won't weaken his position on Cael and I guess Herschal is a bit too old to get here all the way from the Negev... But don't misunderstand me Helen. You can have no idea how God-thanking glad that you and Light are here. You bring your own talents and the blessings of The Druid. Light brings his own information and experience, and as far as I know, he's unique inasmuch that he's actually come face to face with the shapechangers and has escaped to tell the tale... And when he's ready to give it to us that intelligence will be invaluable.'

'And what about Hector?'

Mage grinned wickedly. 'You like him, don't you?'

Helen blushed. 'I hardly know the man Colin, but yes, of course I like him. You'd have to be pretty weird not to like a guy like that! But that's got nothing to do with the question I asked.'

Mage glanced at his watch. It was nearly eleven. Not late to go calling by Spanish standards, but perhaps a little too late to go calling with the mission he had in mind.

'I'll leave Hector till tomorrow,' he said. 'He's already had to absorb an awful lot. Let's let his mind come to grips with what he already knows before we try expanding it any further... But listen, I want you to know that I picked up on what you were feeling back there in the hotel. Hector is important to us, and if you're serious about wanting to help me and providing it won't compromise either your principles or scruples, get a little closer to him. He likes you a lot, although I'm sure you don't need me to tell you that... And if you can open his mind just a wee bit more for me, I'd be very grateful.'

'Promise me a decent pagan burial if his daughter bites my head off?'

'Absolutely!.'

At three a.m. Hector was roused from his sleep by the jangling of the antiquated telephone bell. Twenty minutes later he was hovering over the sick bed of Alvaro Alvarez, Castillo's pig breeder and swineherd. Alvaro's temperature was over one hundred and three degrees Fahrenheit; he was flushed and foaming at the mouth with pale green bile. His muscles were locked in spasms of cramp that caused him to shout and scream with pain through the waves of his raging delirium and as far as Hector was concerned, it was the clearest case of rabies that he'd ever seen. He filled two syringes, one with twenty five millilitres of Ravoxin, the other with the same amount of anti-tetanus, and shot them unceremoniously into the pigman's blood stream. Forty minutes later, in response to his summons, Jaime Gomez arrived and shot the pig that had bitten Alvaro late the previous evening. The swineherd outlived the pig but only by a couple of hours, dying with one last enormous convulsion of the heart as the first grey light of the dawn crept across the eastern sky. Later, Hector would recall that it had been with an oddly intense degree of satisfaction that Jaime had dispatched the offending animal.

At four a.m. John Light woke sweating and shaking from the most violent nightmare he'd had since the ones he had experienced on the road from LA to Demsville. In the dream he had been dead, but something coiled and snakelike had been wrapped around his throat, making it impossible for the real John Light, a poor but pure nigger boy called Jonty Golightly, to escape in the last soul releasing scream of agony that welled up in his chest – a chest that was being clawed open by long barbed talons that were intent on ripping out his heart. *Always knew I'd get you in the end* said Police Captain Henry Kitson's voice. *Always knew I'd get you in the end!*

At around five minutes past four Helen Ross woke from her own nightmare. In it, she had been in bed with Hector Sanchez, and in the way of dreams, Hector's daughter Ann and Colin Mage had been in the bed with them. Hector was stiff and cold – as dead as the proverbial door nail – while Anna moaned softly as a putrescent growth of cancerous white fibres extended from the back of her head, mingling with and impregnating the folds of her pillow, white was not really a pillow at all, but a massive pulsating tumour with a mind of its own. She looked to Mage for help but when she did, she found him watching her wolfishly with glowing amber eyes, eyes that became twin orbs of crimson fire even as she watched. Then something wrapped itself around her wrist... it was one of the tentacular fibres from the tumour, and Anna's voice had giggled insanely in her ear. *He's mine!* it said. *He's mine so you must leave him alone!*

At four fifteen Mage woke from his own recurring horror. He put on the light, lit a cigarette and made a mug of strong tea. In the distance he heard two sharp cracks. He thought that they might have been gunshots, but then remembering that he didn't really know what gunshots sounded like, reasoning that it was probably just a car backfiring. This night's dream had been particularly mean. He'd been falling endlessly down through the void, but on this occasion he'd not been falling on his own. As he'd looked around him he'd seen Helen and Hector, Light and Tamara, Pepe Ortega, Antonia and Angel Guardiaro, Christina and Anna; there had been Michael Fry and Herschal, and even Father Paul from Ireland. They were all covered with thick glutinous globes of clotting blood and they were all dead, and yet even though they were dead, he'd still heard their screams. He shuddered and drank the scalding tea, wondering if in pursuit of his quest, he'd signed these peoples' death warrants.

Anna had stirred as her father had left the house and then had dreamed the most beautiful dream. She'd been back on the beach at La Bolonia and the beach had been totally deserted but for herself and Colin. Both of them were naked and Colin was touching her in that special place that Pedro had always wanted to get his fingers into. She writhed in juicy pleasure rising to climax and orgasm, and with the orgasm, woke to find her own fingers pressed deeply inside her vagina. With a feeling of self loathing she removed her fingers immediately and lay in her bed feeling bereft and uncomforted. As the town hall clock chimed five, she closed her eyes tightly, and imagining that her hand was Colin's hand, reintroduced her fingers to the wetness of her waiting sex. Beneath the light cotton sheets her legs opened wide as she pushed and probed ever more deeply – and it was all right as long as she imagined that it was Colin doing this to her, and not her doing it to herself.

She'd lost all concept of time – not that she'd had much concept of time in the first place. She'd not been happy at the hospital place but she hadn't known quite what to do until she'd heard her mother's voice in her head telling her to come home. That had seemed sensible so she'd walked for all of the night and all of the day and all of the next night as well. She was suspicious of roads and crossed them carefully when she had to, staying for the better part to the fields and bridal paths and the dark shade of the forests. When she got hungry she would eat a handful of berries or broad leaves from some of the plants and bushes. Some of them tasted bitter and unpleasant but as she didn't get ill or anything, she supposed that they were all right. Once, she thought it might have been in the afternoon, when she got *very* hungry, she found a small dead bird, and after pulling the feathers from it, ate it in her hands as she'd walked.

Always her mother's voice was whispering in her head. *This way, Lena! Just a little bit further,* or *That way dear, across the road and over the bridge and then back into the woods where nobody will see you...*

With the first lightening of the skies Lena Cortez arrived back at the edge of the village. She wondered if she should go back to their old house, but then her mother's voice said *no darling, I'm up here* so she'd headed up towards the cemetery near the castle, which was all rather strange because she remembered the stupid fat nurse in the hospital telling her that her mother was dead and was being put in the cemetery in Algy Neerus and it was fairly obvious to Lena's nine year old mind that you couldn't live in two cemeteries at the same time. Anybody knew that!

When she got to the cemetery it was almost full daylight and because she knew that the daytime was dangerous and because she did feel rather tired after her long walk, she climbed into one of the empty interment receptacles and fell fast asleep. She wasn't sure what she was supposed to do when she woke up, but was quietly confident that her mother would tell her.

At six a.m. the green Jaguar left Cordoba and began the last leg of its long journey towards Castillo. Dolorean was extremely pleased. He felt rested and refreshed and the female was in good condition, looking absolutely perfect... Well, perfect by human standards anyway...

At nine thirty Mage called Hector from the pay phone in the square and half an hour later, at ten, they met for breakfast at Jacinto's. Hector looked tired and drawn. There were big dark rings around his eyes and he'd nicked himself several times when shaving.

'Another disastrous night,' he said in response to Mage's query. 'And another death. This time it's Alvaro Alvarez. Rabies! Spain in the 21st century and we've still got outbreaks of rabies! Jaime's shot the boar that bit him and the rest of the herd is now under quarantine. Alvaro's wife is beside herself and his dim-witted sons don't know whether they're coming or going... Anyway, sorry to unload my problems on your shoulders but I've been up since three o'clock and I need to catch up on some sleep... I tell you, Colin, it puts me on edge. It makes me wonder what else can go wrong. Where is the next tragedy coming from?'

'What I would want to know is how a domestic pig contracts rabies in the first place,' Mage said uneasily. There was an odd link between boars and Djinn. They both had tusks, and in Helen's claivoyant vision, she'd said that the Djinn had squealed like pigs...

'That's the mystery that's worrying the health and hygiene people. Even as we speak they've got teams of people scouring the hillsides and the campo around Castillo trying to pick up some spore. Jaime's gone with them and they're obviously taking it all very seriously. They've got instructions to shoot to kill if they come across anything remotely suspicious. Anyway, to change the subject, how did you get on with your American friend last night?'

'I'm not sure yet that he's a friend, but he's certainly a very powerful ally and he's got a lot of knowledge and information that will help us with our problems here in the village. He's dealt with the same kind of problems back in The States, so I'm damn glad to have him here on our side. We talked for quite a while, and on the strength of that conversation there are a few things I need to tell you that I haven't told you before... Not because I've wanted to deceive you in any way, but only because I've not wanted to stretch you capacity to believe in what would seem to be unbelievable. All of the things that I've told you about Dolorean, about him not only being my enemy but being everyone's enemy... All the explanations I've given you for what is going on in Castillo... They're all true, but there's rather a lot more to it, I'm afraid. It goes deeper than you could possibly imagine. If I'm to be honest with you I don't know where to begin, and after the night you've had last night, I'm not even sure that this is the most appropriate time.'

'Hey, now that you have started you cannot leave me dangling!' Hector complained. 'I may be tired, but I promise you that I'm in a very receptive mood. After what's been happening here, after what I've seen, I'm quite prepared to believe anything you can tell me, no matter how fantastic it might sound.' Hector took a sip of the carajillo and looked at Mage levelly over the rim of the small white cup.

'Don't be so sure,' Mage met his gaze. 'There's fantastic and there's fantastic.'

They sat at a table next to the window. The street was grey in the flat morning light, and although the day was warm, an occasional spit of rain formed in the dampness of the atmosphere. In the sunlight Castillo sparkled like an Andalucian jewel, but on dull days it could be moody and depressingly claustrophobic.

They watched a heavily laden mule being tethered to a reja – it was the same mule that Helen's taxi had almost collided with two days previously, and Hector sighed worriedly. 'I hope they get this rabies thing sorted out soon,' he said, 'because if they don't it'll be just like it was back in 1974. There'll be a purge on anything that walks on four legs. I wasn't here then, of course, but I'm told that the carnage was quite awful. Anyway, Colin, what are these new revelations you wish to share with me?'

But Mage hadn't been listening. Coming to his feet, he leaned across the table, and stared out into the street, his eyes riveted on the dusty dark green Jaguar that was trying to edge its way round the hind quarters of the mule. Hector saw the his knuckles were white and that all the colour had drained from his face.

'Colin, whatever is wrong? You suddenly look quite awful!'

'They here,' Mage said tersely between tightly clenched teeth.

'Who's here?' Hector asked.

'Jadoc Dolorean and Alexandra.'

Hector became instantly alert. 'Where?'

'Out there in the street. In the green Jaguar.'

Hector followed Mage's eyeline, and he also came slowly to his feet. 'Yes,' he breathed. 'Yes, I see now. That is certainly Señor Dolorean, but...' The Jaguar brushed against the mule and accelerated away up the hill causing the animal to buck and whinny in fright and pain. '...But who is the woman who is with him? This Alexandra? Do you know her?'

'Yes Hector, I know her. She was my wife!'

'But,' Hector turned to Mage and saw that the Englishman was visibly shaking. 'But Colin, I don't understand. How can this be? When we talked before you told me that your wife was dead.'

'She is,' Mage replied, then he was pushing back the wooden chair with an angry scrape, and rushing from the bar, began running as fast as he could across the village towards Calle Sombra.

22.

Opening Salvoes

He ran quickly through the village, cutting through back alleys and taking the most direct route to Calle Sombra via Calles Roma, Llanette and Quieros. The car would have to go the long way around the complicated one way system and although he knew he couldn't get there before it, he wouldn't be far behind. Turning left at the end of Quieros he came to a heart pounding halt. Catching his breath he walked cautiously towards the end of Calle Sombra, paused, then stepped around the corner.

Fifty yards away the Jaguar was parked outside the house at the end of the street. Both the front doors were open, as was the front door of the house. Dolorean emerged from the house and walked over to the passenger side of the car. Slowly and carefully Alexandra climbed out of the vehicle and even at fifty yards Mage could see with a sickly sense of horror and confusion that she was heavily pregnant! Involuntarily he began walking towards them. He had no idea what he might say or what he intended to do. The important thing was that they should see him, that they should know he was there, that they should know that he hadn't given up and was still a force to be reckoned with.

They'd turned and were walking towards the open door. From twenty feet away his voice ricocheted along the narrow canyon of the cobbled street.

'*Alex!*'

They stopped and turned again. Alexandra stared at him expressionlessly but a slow cruel smile began to spread across Dolorean's face. He pursed his thin lips over jagged uneven teeth, and it was almost as though he was blowing Mage a kiss of sly greeting. Indeed, to Mage's eyes, a kiss *was* blown... He had no time to assess its meaning or to react to it, for something hit him and lifting him off his feet, hurled him back along the street all of the thirty feet he'd walked from the corner, and he ended up flat on his back staring at a swirling unfocused sky as a tornado of wind roared above his head.

He was hurting. Elbows, shoulder blades, coccyx, the back of his head, were all grazed and bruised by the impact of the incredible fall. But there was another hurting, and unwinding coil of hatred and fury that churned in his gut and forced him to his knees as the wind subsided, just in time to see Alexandra being ushered into the house. When the door closed it was with a resounding slam that echoed along the street and made his head wince. There was contempt and venom both in the sound and in the gesture.

He staggered slowly to his feet, feeling sick and dizzy and bewildered. What had happened here? What had the shapechanger done to Alex? She was like a fucking zombie, for Christ's sake! And what of the business with the wind? Dolorean had blown him a kiss and then something like a sledgehammer had hit him with such force that he'd been lifted and thrown half the length of Calle Sombra. It was like Glastonbury all over again, only worse! A spasm gripped his stomach, and bending double, he vomited his breakfast into the gutter, becoming aware of the fact that his nose was bleeding quite badly and that he was rendered partially deaf by an odd ringing in his ears. It was as if an energy had passed through him, taking his strength and befuddling all his senses.

He stared malevolently at the house and even more malevolently at the green Jaguar. There'd be no point in trying to get a line on Dolorean through the car, for Mage was very familiar with the vehicle. He'd had it registered in Alexandra's name when he'd bought it for her as an anniversary present two years before.

With a profound feeling of deep offence, he turned his back on the street and began the long walk back to Calle Granadillos. The opening salvoes in the battle of Castillo had just been fired and he'd been given a bloody nose.

Even as Dolorean had driven into the village he'd known that it was wrong... Sensing the changes, touching them, absorbing the atmospheres, he'd driven quickly to the house. He'd not been too surprised by the encounter with the magician. It was logical and predictable that he would be there to greet them, and had he had more time he would have dismissed him more permanently. As it was, he had given him something to think about and had bought himself a little time to settle the female in her new surroundings. Once he was sure that the incubator was secure he would deal with the manmate once and for all... And yet, as he moved through the empty house, settling the female in her quarters and unpacking their frugal belongings, he felt a profound sense of disquiet and unease. The magician had obviously violated the sanctity of these very rooms. He'd been in, nosing around, and had certainly done something of a ritual nature to announce his presence. Walking through the front door had been like passing through water and climbing the stairs had been like pushing through dense undergrowth. Thankfully, the female was so heavily tranced and pre-conditioned, that she was totally impervious to it all.

He spent an industrious two hours dealing with practical necessities and only then allowed himself the luxury of spreading his spore and essence. Standing next to the bed upon which the female slept, he closed his eyes and went into the abstract mental state that allowed him to assimilate the information that he needed. He was neither pleased nor amused in his assessment of the damage that had been done in his absence. For one thing, his circle of disciples and acolytes was shattered. While this was not a disaster, it was a serious set back. His social infrastructure was an important if not integral part of his plan, and he would now have to redefine his thinking. What people like Ignatious and Miriam Cortez would have done for him he would now have to do himself, and while this was not a major problem it was a most annoying nuisance. Certainly he might recruit and recreate a new circle, but that would take a little time and energy and it might be more advisable to proceed independently.

What concerned him more was the way in which the atmosphere within the village had changed. When he had last been here the ambience had been quite perfect for his mission... Mild and bland on a physical level but crackling with latent psychic energy produced by its varied inhabitants. But now there was another energy, dark and focused against him and he was in no doubt as to whom had brought this about. The manmate magician had been here for a number of Earthworld weeks and obviously he had done much to disperse and neutralise the powerful aura that the Djinn had worked so hard to create. He had seriously underestimated the powers of the manmate, not to mention the human's stubborn tenacity. With the psychic attacks he had launched at the time of the acquisition of the incubator he had religiously followed the instructions and rituals as given to him by the Clanfather, and to all intents and purposes based on the sum total of Djinnlore and knowledge gleaned from all previous incursions into the manworld, the attacks should have destroyed the manmate completely, reducing him either to death or to an imbecilic state. Clearly something had gone wrong. Neither of these things had happened, and if anything the magician was far stronger now than he had been when Dolorean had first encountered his energies the previous year.

He deeply wished that there was some way in which he communicate with his brethren but until such time as the opening was complete he knew that he must be denied this communication. He took much solace, however, in the knowledge that his brethren would be monitoring his progress and preparing for the ritual on their own side of the divide, and if there was anything that they could do to help him, especially in these late days, they would do it.

His greatest rage – and deepest worry – was reserved for the magician's desecration of the shrine in the garden. It indicated that the magician knew far more than he had any right to know and before he, Dolorean, could proceed further, the holy entrance to the labyrinth would have to be cleansed of the abominable obstruction that the manmate had placed in harm's way.

He opened his eyes, and making sure that the female was stable, moved down through the house and entering the garden, approached the well through the matted undergrowth. The high walls denied spying eyes, but to be safe, he threw a glamour around the area, and casting a passing glance at the slate grey skies, removed his clothes and stood naked in his human form at the lip of the aperture. Thrusting his arms behind him and bending his knees so that he was stooped to a crouch, he allowed the changing to flow through him. Within the ripples of displaced air the molecular metamorphosis happened fluidly and swiftly and like a billowing column of amber smoke the essence of the Djinn disappeared over the edge of the well and plunged downwards into the sightless darkness towards the silver pulsation of light that beckoned him like a beacon from fully forty metres beneath the surface of the earth.

Surrounding the circular stone with its disgustingly sigilled and bejewelled energies with his own energies and vaporous essence, he lifted it with will and telekinesis into the light and sent it hurtling into the air. It reached the height of its climb and then began its increasingly rapid descent towards the garden. Two metres above the earth the shapechanger's mind lashed out and the stone and crystal shattered into a million shards of dust. Even as the dust settled the amber smoke coalesced into the approximation of a human form, mauve lights flickered within and without it, and the nude form of Jadoc Dolorean reached for its clothes exhilarated by its expression of pure Djinn power which had been contained for so long – for too long – in the puny frame of the manshape.

***

Half an hour after Mage had rushed out of the bar Hector found Helen sitting writing a letter and drinking coffee on the terrace of The Miraflores.

'I need to talk to you,' he said abruptly. 'Something has happened. Colin's enemy, the man called Dolorean has arrived and Colin has gone running off somewhere... By the look on his face, I dare say it is towards some kind of confrontation.'

'Oh shit!' Helen swore uncharacteristically.

'There is something else.' Hector continued, very unsure of his ground, but determined to get to the bottom of what was troubling him. 'When Colin and I first became friends I clearly remember him telling me that his wife was dead and yet Dolorean has just arrived with a woman that Colin now says is his wife. Either Colin is married or he is not. Either his wife is dead or she isn't. And although I have great liking and respect for Colin, I must think of Anna... If Colin has lied to me, and to my daughter about this, then I...'

'He hasn't lied,' Helen said firmly, 'but I think there are a number of things that he hasn't told you, and from what I know of the situation, probably with very good reason. We were talking about this last night and agreed that you should be given all the facts. Colin said that he would handle it in his own way and in his own time. The secret we have to share is not something which is easily believable, and Colin knew he would have to pick his time and place.'

'I think he was about to tell me things this morning, but then Dolorean and the woman arrived and Colin ran out of the bar after them... And I wasn't sure what to do so I came here looking for you.' Hector's eyes narrowed. 'You said that there is a secret that you have to share. If you know what this secret is, then I think you had better tell me about it now.'

'Yes Hector, I think I better had. So sit yourself down and I'll do my best to explain.'

'What about Colin?'

'Don't worry about him for now. Where ever he is and whatever he's doing, he'll be all right... Or at least, I think he will be.' Helen looked across the table and wondered where to begin. 'Hector, I'm going to tell you a fairy story, but the thing about this particular fairy story is that it isn't a fairy story at all. It's all absolutely real and totally true.'

Helen talked solidly for over an hour, an hour in which Hector sat and listened intently with growing disbelief. When she had finished, Hector lit his pipe and looked down at the nicotine stains on the ends of his fingers. What he had just heard was totally preposterous and he felt faintly embarrassed about sitting here with this beautiful young woman who'd just told him this crazy cock and bull story expecting him to believe it.

'I don't expect you to believe it,' Helen said, accurately reading his mind, 'but it is true. This is what Colin would have told you himself this morning if he hadn't been interrupted.'

'And do you think the story would have been any more credible coming from his lips?' Hector asked, not entirely able to mask the trace of sarcasm in his voice.

'No, I don't,' Helen admitted. 'I know it's hard to accept, but Hector, it is the truth. I travelled all the way from Scotland to help a man I've never even met before on the strength of my own belief. John Light has travelled even further, all the way from America because he believes that Colin is right. Both John Light and I might seem a little strange to you... We're not the normal kind of tourist that you might get in a place like Castillo.. But neither of us is some easily conned weirdo. Neither of us is a gullable romantic in search of adventure or cheap kicks. We're both very serious people, and there are other serious people behind Colin in England, Ireland and even Israel. None of us is evangelical. Quite the reverse, in fact. You don't have to believe what I'm telling you Hector, but I am not lying to you.'

'Well, there's one way we can find out!' Hector said briskly.

'Oh yes, and would you mind telling me how?'

Hector stood up, squaring back his shoulders and sucking in his stomach. His eyes glittered and his moustache bristled with an anger that was hard to explain. 'Miss Ross, I might only be a simple village doctor to most people, but I've travelled around in my time and I've seen something of this world. I may not be a clever intellectual but I am not a fool. What I am is this village's only doctor. We have two new arrivals one of whom I have actually met and have had a drink with. I propose to walk around to the house in Calle Sombra and knock on the door, and I shall see for myself if anything is wrong. I am quite prepared to accept that Mr Dolorean is a very evil man who has within him the power of magic... Colin convinced me of this much... But to believe that he is not really a human being but some shapeshifting Goblin masquerading as a human being is absurd, and I will not believe this on the strength of anybody's word. This I must see with my own eyes.'

'Okay, I have to admit that if I was you I'd feel the same way. But hang on, I'll come with you and...'

'No thank you, Miss Ross, I am quite capable of going on my own and forming my own judgements and if you should happen to see Colin before I do, would you ask him please to make a point of talking to me first before he tries talking again to Anna.'

Hector turned abruptly and marched off the terrace, and again Helen said 'Oh shit!' before getting up and rushing after him.

Hamish Hamilton was puzzled. Eulalio and Jesus had dug down about a metre and a half before calling him down into the grave like confines of the excavation. 'What's the problem, hombres?' he asked cheerfully, clapping both the diggers on their respective backs.

'The problem is that!' Eulalio said, pointing the edge of his sharp shovel towards the freshly exposed stonework.

Hamish squatted down on his haunches and examined the odd phenomena that met his eyes. Against the wall and clearly covering the top of the arched entrance that the diggers had exposed there was a thin membrane of what appeared to be dark yellow plastic. The membrane disappeared beneath the soil and Hamish's first thought was that someone had already excavated the site since the last time he had done so himself and had covered the entrance with sort of semi permanent tarpaulin that could be removed to facilitate easier access.

'Just pull it off,' he said

'Won't move,' said Eulalio, who was a man of few words.

'You try, jefe,' Jesus added excitedly, 'because as Eulalio says, it won't budge for us!'

Hamish tried to get a grip on it, intending to either peel it or rip it away, but the surface was smooth and slightly oily to the touch. In the end he lost patience and with a dour 'Fuck it!' he grabbed hold of Eulalio's spade and took a hard swing at the dark amber substance. Surprised by the shock waves that reverberated up his arms he dropped the spade and took another more detailed look at the membrane. It had been scoured by the impact but even as Hamish watched the scarring seemed to disappear into oily smoothness before his eyes. This was weird. Tentatively he ran his hands across the surface of the obstruction and experienced the strangest of sensations. Yes, it was definitely oily but beneath the oily texture there was a resin like hardness from which there emanated a subtle tingle that was so slight that it barely registered at all. The membrane was semi opaque and beneath its amber plasticity he could quite easily see the formation of the brickwork that went into the arch and the dark wood and metal studs of the ancient door.

Taking a pick axe he tried prizing the point of the pick between the lip of the membrane and the stone wall. When this didn't work he chipped away some of the stone and tried to work the pick in that way, but even as he created a small cavity of potential purpose the amber eased into it like jelly settling into a mould. For God's sake, what was this stuff? What was it made of? Like all archaeologists, he had a rudimentary knowledge of geology but what he was dealing with here seemed to go against the rules and laws of both disciplines.

He sat back on his haunches, wondering what he might try next. At the end of the day there were only so many options. He stood and took a deliberate swing with the pick axe at the area just below the portal. Again there were the shock waves caused by the impact, but this time he had the satisfaction of seeing that the point of the pick had penetrated a couple of inches. He tried wiggling and prizing the tool to create some kind of hole, and although there was some movement in the pick point it was minimal. It came out easily enough when he jerked it free and again there was that crazy thing whereby the amber membrane seemed to reseal itself.

Neither nervous, nor apprehensive but incredibly frustrated and curious, he again ran his hands over the membrane, caressing the curious substance with his finger tips looking for a weakness, a fissure, or any kind of join. And yet there was nothing... Nothing at all that gave any purchase or any clue as to what this stuff actually was. Wiping his hands against the seat of his old cords he stood back in exasperation and defeat.

'What is it, jefe?' Jesus asked.

'Damned if I know. Never seen anything like it before. Anyone else been digging here since we were last at it?'

Both labourers shook their heads in the negative. 'Ay, well some bugger has, and that's for sure,' Hamish exclaimed angrily. 'Don't know what this stuff is exactly, but it'll be one of these new polymer sealers that they're using these days, although Lord knows how they've done what they've done.' Then, more to himself that to the others: 'I wonder if Mage knows about this?'

'What do we do, then?' Eulalio asked.

'No point in digging any deeper till we know what this stuff is.' Hamish said thoughtfully, still rubbing his hands to get the last residue of the oil off them. 'Throw a couple of boards and some canvas over the hole and mark it with poles and red tape. We'll call it a day and have another go tomorrow after I've found out how to get through this resinny stuff or whatever it is.' He saw the look on their faces and grinned broadly. 'Don't worry hombres, you'll be paid for a full day today and there'll be another full day's money in it for you tomorrow.'

Eulalio and Jesus packed up their tools and went sauntering off down into the village in search of lunch and Hamish went in search of Colin Mage. But first he wanted to find some soap and hot water. His hands were beginning to sting a little bit where they'd come into contact with whatever it was that was denying him access to the citadel.

Casting the green Jaguar an admiring glance, Hector marched up to the front door and without hesitation rapped hard with the brass knocker. He heard the sounds echoing through the house and wondered why it was taking so long for anyone to answer. Maybe they were in the garden... And he shuddered at the thought of that garden but made himself accept that whatever he'd experienced there was no more than an illusion. He banged on the door again and waited another minute. He was about to turn away when he heard the bolts being pushed over and then the door opened and Jadoc Dolorean was standing in the threshold.

Hector flashed his brightest and most blustery smile. 'Señor Dolorean!' he exclaimed. 'I'd heard that you were back in the village and I have called to pay my respects. You remember me, perhaps? I am Doctor Hector Sanchez and I had the pleasure of making your acquaintance last year. If you remember, we had a drink together once.'

'Ah yes, doctor, I remember you well. Your respects are graciously accepted.'

'I, um, understand that this year you are travelling with a lady companion?'

'News travels fast in Castillo,' Dolorean said – and it seemed as though there was some secret amusement in his voice. 'And indeed you are correct. I have returned to Castillo with my wife...'

'Your wife?'

'Yes, my wife... Who alas is not awfully well after what has been a long and tedious journey.' Dolorean's face broke into a sad smile and Hector noticed the oddity of the man's uneven and unusually sharp little teeth.

'Well, remembering that I am of course a doctor, if there is anything that I can do, please feel free to call on my services.'

'Thank you Doctor Sanchez. You are most kind. But I feel that after a little rest, Alexandra will be quite well again soon.'

Hector sensed that the door was about to be closed in his face and he desperately needed to prolong this conversation for a while yet. 'Er, how long have you been married?' he asked lamely.

'Not very long. Less than a year. It all happened very quickly... But such is the pathway of true love!'

'Quite so!' Hector laughed trying to force some humour into his voice. In truth he felt totally repelled by this man and the thought of anyone falling in love with that lopsided face with the receding hairline and those sharp little teeth was literally incredible to him. 'Er, if you'd like me to, I'd be quite happy to have a look at your wife right now?'

'Would you now, Doctor Sanchez?'

There was a curious note in Dolorean's tone that made Hector suddenly feel ill at ease, but he had no intention of backing away from this until something was proven one way or the other.

The shapechanger enjoyed the doctor's sudden discomfort and it wondered who had sent him knocking on the door so soon. The doctor's spore was all over the house so obviously he had been with the magician when the magician had forced entry. Ergo, this doctor was one of the manmate's followers and thus, an enemy of the Djinn. The shapechanger had been prepared to play with the doctor for a while, sending him back to report that there was nothing to report, but there were other options. Would it not be poetic justice to turn this man of poor earth medicine against his friends, to enrole him as the first of the Djinn's new circle of worshipful acolytes? Would it not give even more satisfaction to show the doctor around the garden, to glamour him with the magic of the well, and to eat him at leisure, limb by limb, morsel by morsel, until his hunger was satiated? Certainly the village might wonder what had happened to its doctor, and equally certainly, the village would never know.

'Why not step inside then, Doctor Sanchez? My wife is resting, but I'm sure she will be very pleased to see you.' Dolorean smiled crookedly and pushed the door back on its hinges... and suddenly Hector was very frightened. He didn't know why, but for all the world, he knew he did not want to step across that threshold! Whether it was an auto suggestive reaction based on all that he'd been told or a natural warning bell echoing up from his subconscious, it mattered not. He got the impression that Dolorean was mocking him in some way, daring him to step inside the house, almost taunting him. And then Hector's anger flared above his fear. He was about to step forwards when words rang out clearly inside his head.

Hector! No! Be careful! It's a trap!

Amazingly, the words were not his own, but Helen Ross's. At first he thought she must be calling to him from somewhere near at hand, but when the voice came again – *Hector, don't go inside! If you do, you'll never come out again!* – he realised that this was definitely not so. The words were in his head, not in his ears. Even so, he cast around and sure enough, spotted Helen Ross out of the corner of his eye. She was standing by the steps that ran up along the side of the convent and which linked Calle Sombra with Plaza de Santa Clara. As such, she was fully ten metres distant but Hector could still see her worried look of consternation and alarm. But how, he wondered... How on earth was she able to do this? To put her words directly into his head without the necessary formality of speech?

'Er, Señor Dolorean, forgive me, but I have just remembered that I am supposed to be somewhere else, so perhaps it would be better if I returned later when I have more time and after your wife has rested.'

'On no, please do come in now,' Dolorean said, casting his own glance at Helen, who was another of the manmate's friends judging by the empathy of the vibration she was transmitting towards the doctor.

'Thank you, no,' Hector said, taking a step backwards.

'As you wish,' Dolorean's mouth widened into a smile, a smile that carried on widening until the lower half of his face was split in two, virtually from ear to ear, and revealing double rows of black and amber teeth which were serrated like saw blades. Hector gasped in disbelief when Dolorean's eyes inexplicably changed from a weak hazel to a burningly malevolent orange, and he cried out with shock and total disgust when Dolorean's tongue, long and green and covered in a scaly diamond pattern, leapt out of the impossible cavity which now totally disfigured Dolorean's face and lashed out at him, slapping him viciously like the thong of a whip against the side of his cheek. There was more than a metre of distance between them. As Hector's whole face began to go numb, he staggered backwards, his legs coming up against the bonnet of the Jaguar. Dolorean, now Dolorean again and not the creature he'd been barely a second before, shut the door in his face with a crafty grin and a sibilant whisper: 'I'll see you again soon, Hector Sanchez!'

The strength went from Hector's legs and he half stumbled, half collapsed against the car. So concerned was he with the sound of his own long ululating moan of horror and his desperate attempts to wipe away the stinging slime that clung to his face where Dolorean's tongue had hit him, he didn't even hear the sound of Helen's footsteps as she dashed across the cobbles towards him. He was aware of someone trying to help him stand up... Dimly registered that it was Helen Ross, and then the blessed veil of unconsciousness descended upon him as his mind overloaded with the impossibility and the enormity of what had just happened.

Helen led Hector out of the street and sat him down in a quiet corner of the plaza. He'd been unconscious for only a few seconds, but even now was still numb with shock. His eyes were vacant and unfocused and he breathed deeply, almost hyperventilating, with an occasional sob catching at the back of his throat. Helen wiped his cheek with a tissue, noting the narrow red weal that ran across his face from the corner of his sideburn down the jawline. She thought she'd seen what had caused it, but couldn't be sure until Hector confirmed or denied it. She'd been fully thirty feet away and had seen everything clearly enough – she'd sensed the danger, heard nuances in Dolorean's voice, and above all, had felt the emanation of pure malice that had pulsed not only out of the man but also from out of the house behind him. There'd been a moment of panic when she'd thought that Hector might be rash enough to enter the shapechanger's domain and, in her head, her words of warning had taken form. Before she'd needed to shout them out Hector had stepped back and it had been then that she'd thought she'd seen Dolorean's face change – then that she'd thought she'd seen his tongue uncoil and strike out at Hector. It could have been a trick of the light or it could have been a product of her fertile imagination and although she knew that it had been neither of these things, she still needed to hear Hector's own words... And the words were not long in coming.

After a number of minutes Hector's eyes found focus and his breathing became more regular. His cheek still stung and he tentatively raised a hand to touch the side of his face where he'd been struck. He looked at Helen in trembling bewilderment.

'What happened?' he asked.

'You fainted,' she answered.

'Yes... I suppose I must have done...' He bowed his head and buried his face in his hands. 'My God, that was horrible!' he muttered through his fingers.

It was Helen's turn to ask: 'What happened? I mean before you passed out? I know what I think I saw, but I need to hear it from your own lips.'

'He hit me,' Hector said simply. 'He hit me with his tongue. His whole face changed and he hit me with his tongue!'

'I think,' Helen put her arm around the doctor's shuddering shoulders, 'that we'd better go and find Colin.'

Light and Tamara had spent the late morning exploring the village. They were emerging from the Bar España after having enjoyed an early lunch, and virtually cannoned into Helen and Hector. Without preamble Helen narrated the story of Hector's experience with the shapechanger and together the four of them walked briskly through the narrow streets towards Calle Granadillos. They spent several minutes knocking on the door and were about to turn away when the door opened and Mage bade them enter.

Helen thought that he looked awful and as she crossed the threshold she met John Light's knowing look. The atmosphere was alive with heavy energy and whatever Mage had been doing prior to their arrival it hadn't just been a little innocent candle burning!

He led them through to the kitchen. Helen wanted to know what was upstairs, for this was where the pulse of energy originated. Seating them as he did around the kitchen table, however, made any casual investigation impossible. Mage looked at them each in turn and managed a faint smile.

'Well, he's arrived,' he said flatly. 'But I expect you've already found that out for yourselves.'

'You could say that,' Helen responded, and went on to explain what had happened to Hector.

When she had finished, Hector looked at Mage sheepishly. 'Colin, I am sorry I disbelieved you... But the story Helen told me was so crazy that I couldn't believe it until I had found out for myself. And now, after I have found out for myself, if it is any consolation, I believe you completely.'

'How are you feeling?' Mage asked gently, examining the red mark that was now only beginning to subside.

'It is hard to put into words. Disgusted. Insulted. And I suppose, if I am to tell the truth, very confused and very very scared.' Hector's hand crept back towards his cheek. 'What happened back there in Calle Sombra was so alien. So fundamentally *wrong!*'

'I understand how you feel,' Mage said, unable to keep the bitterness from his voice. 'To me Dolorean has always been wrong ever since I first set eyes on the bastard. The thing is,' he addressed the others, 'now that he's here, how do we proceed? It's obvious that he's got a lot of abilities that none of us, perhaps with the exception of John, has ever encountered before. The business with the tongue is interesting enough, and although it might sound odd, I'm rather glad that it's happened. If nothing else it's given Helen some real evidence and it has persuaded Hector to believe in something he could never have believed in unless he'd experienced it first hand. I suspect, however, that Dolorean has a lot more nasty tricks up his sleeve. For one thing, he seems to command some kind of pneumatic energy...'

He went on to tell them of his own bruising experience in Calle Sombra that morning and, as he did so, Helen watched him carefully. He was relaxing slightly now and the frantic motion of auric energy that had surrounded him when they'd first arrived had noticeably subsided. Even so, she found herself wondering what the magician had been up to in the time between being bowled over by a pneuma of magic and this present gathering of minds. Whatever it had been, it had been fluid and vicious, churning up from the core of Colin Mage's soul and leaving his normally calm aura in shreds and tatters.

John Light shifted uncomfortably on the small straight backed chair. 'I've not seen this pneumatic thing before,' he said slowly, 'but I can tell you that they've got a lot more weapons in their armoury that are just as dangerously effective, if not more so. Their ability to change shape at will, to actually become discarnate while still maintaining some form of molecular presence, is probably their neatest trick. I don't pretend to know it all, but I do know from past experience that this is one little party piece we must be particularly on guard against. In the time it takes to pull out a gun these things can dematerialise in a puff of smoke... And yes, okay, I know I need to tell you about what happened that time in Demsville, but just bear with me a while longer, will you? I need to get my head round it myself, I need to know you guys better, and I need to choose my own time...'

'Okay John, no pressure. When you're good and ready,' Mage said lightly, but Helen could detect the undercurrent of impatience in his voice.

To bridge the gap, she addressed Light directly. 'John, from your experience, is there anything you can tell us about the Djinn that can help us at this stage? We know that he's here and we know what he's going to try and do, but we don't know how, where, exactly when, or even what with. We're working blind on this, and although we know so much, in real terms we know so little.'

Light got up from his chair and mooched restlessly around the kitchen. It was a small room, cluttered with the usual pots and pans and plates on shelves. In three recessed alcoves there were modest tables lamps with deep pink shades. Light absently turned them on, making the kitchen a warmer, more welcoming place. Outside the afternoon light was fading into a haze of gloomy drizzle.

'What you've all got to remember is that what happened to me happened a very long time ago and although in part I can remember what *did* happen, I never have known exactly *how* it happened. The other thing that is worth pointing out is that then and over the last dozen years, as far as I've been concerned I've been dealing with demons and a dimension of hell. The concept of these things being "Djinn" from a parallel universe is relatively new to me, and I've been working very hard recently to assimilate what I've learned from Colin with the information I've been carrying with me over the years. A third thing you've got to remember is that for the last twelve years I've been trying my damnedest to forget what I know – and I was doing pretty damn good until Colin here came and screwed me all up and called me out! Finally, there's something else you'd better be aware of, just so that there are no misunderstandings between us later on. Our friend Hector says he's scared, and in my opinion he's got every right to be. For myself, I'm absolutely fucking terrified, and that's no lie or exaggeration!'

He looked at Helen. 'I know what you're asking me, lady, but we've got to be very careful here. It might be logical to assume that this Dolorean guy and the Djinn are the same kind of motherfuckers that I encountered in Demsville, but that could be a very dangerous assumption and one of the first things I've got to do, hopefully with your help, is to push this guy Dolorean into a corner and see how he unwinds. Needless to say, that could be very dangerous in the extreme, but the sooner it's done the better. On their own these bastards are very tough cookies, but when they're together they're virtually Goddamn invincible. Right now, as I understand it, we've just got the one of them to deal with and I'm all for keeping it that way.'

'There might be two of them,' Mage said miserably. 'He's got Alexandra with him and from what I saw of her this morning, not to mention what happened the last time I saw her in Glastonbury – I just don't think she's human any more. The other thing is,' he looked at Hector appealingly, 'She's very pregnant, but Hector, this is impossible. When we were first married and we tried to have kids we were told it was impossible because Alexandra isn't just barren, she's got malformed fallopian tubes! Christ, we spent a small fortune with half a dozen specialists, and they all said exactly the same thing. No babies!'

Hector was suddenly looking very old in the rose pink shadows. 'Colin, what can I say? That I agree with you? That it would be impossible for a woman to become pregnant in the circumstances? Then yes, I shall say it... but I would also say that it is impossible for a man's face to change and that it is impossible for a man's tongue to uncoil a full metre out of his mouth, and yet those things happened as sure as I am sitting here at this table, so who is to say what is and what is not possible?'

A long sigh heaved its way out of John Light's chest. 'I think maybe I can provide some information on this... When I was on their side trying like hell to get back to my side, one of the demons, or let's call them Djinn if you like, offered me a deal. If I was prepared to work a ritual on their behalf they'd be happy to facilitate my safe return back to my own world and not necessarily to Demsville Louisiana... I was given a number of choices, and I actually emerged in Cancun down in Mexico, which is, if you'll pardon the cliché, another story.

'Anyway, what emerged from our conversation was the admission that the Djinn could not pass easily into our world, and certainly not en masse. We, however, could pass quite easily into their world and could get out again just as easily just as long as we knew where the exits were, which was downright fucking impossible because once you're on their side of the barrier you've got no points of reference! For the Djinn to come through in any numbers someone, and apparently not necessarily one of their own kind, has got to create a doorway from our side of things, and I was given a pretty clear idea of the ritual needed to create that doorway. Basically, I was asked to take a phial of Djinn sperm back with me, to impregnate it within any women of child-bearing age although preferably one with some degree of natural psychism or clairvoyance. I was to promise that I'd do everything in my power to protect the woman until she came to her time, and then when it was her time, I was to make sure that she gave birth to whatever she was carrying at the exact point where the two worlds joined up... One half of her in our world, the other half in theirs, so to speak. As soon as the kid was out, that was about the end of it, at least from my end of things. All I had to do was make sure that the woman stayed exactly where she was and they would do the rest.

'Cutting a long story short, I went along with it. I had no choice because if I hadn't gone along with it, well, they showed me how I was going to die, and it was not a very pretty sight. What amazes me is that they were so gullible! I'd have promised them the stars and the sun and the moon to get out of that place, so I just said yeah yeah yeah to everything they were telling me and as soon as I got back into the daylight, promptly forgot the lot. The container with the sperm went into a trash can outside the Cancun Hilton and I was home free and running.

'The point is that I've got a pretty good idea what's happening here with our pregnant lady. Dolorean has found a very psychic female, has impregnated her with Djinn sperm, either his own or something he's brought with him, and when she's at her full time he's going to make sure she drops whatever she's carrying right down the central bore of what Colin calls The Opening. I dare say there's going to be lots of words and rituals to drum up all kinds of crazy psychic energy, but in essence, the birthing of the baby is what it's all about... And let's not forget, it's Djinn sperm, so whatever the child will be, it sure as hell won't be human.' He looked pityingly at Mage. The Englishman looked sick and pale beneath his deep tan. 'Hey man, I'm sorry to be so blunt, but Helen here did ask, and sometimes there ain't no tactful way in which to put things.'

'It's okay. Don't worry...' Mage reached for a cigarette and Helen could see that his hand was trembling, though whether it was with emotion or suppressed rage, she wasn't sure. 'Michael Fry, The Druid, told me that I must regard Alexandra as being dead, and although it's difficult, that is how I do regard her. Glastonbury was my last chance and I guess that ever since then, it's become progressively easier. What John is telling us coincides with my own information from Israel and Ireland, but it still doesn't answer our fundamental question... How do we stop this thing? As I've told you, I'm fairly certain that the actual location of the veil is within or beneath the Moorish citadel and I've got someone digging us a way into it at this very moment... In fact, the door to the citadel should be excavated by now and it's something I would have checked on if events hadn't accelerated quite so fast. What we have to do is find the actual opening and do whatever we can to block it, but even then, that's only half our task. Dolorean and Alexandra, and whatever Alexandra is carrying inside her, have got to be stopped, and if that means killing them, then we have to find a way to kill them... But make no mistake, that actual deed is solely my responsibility. If there's going to be any fall out, either from the other side or from the authorities on our own side, mine is the elected head and this is not a subject that is open to discussion!'

He glared pointedly at his four companions. 'What we need to do right now is form a few plans and come up with some ideas. Hector,' he turned to the doctor, 'what you might like to do for us is to have a chat with Jaime Gomez and see if we can get a lead on Raul Castro. It might not be a bad idea if you also phone the retreat in Antiquera and the clinic in La Linea. If there's anything happening in either of those places with the two nuns and the Cortez family, I want to know about it as soon as possible... And Hector, needless to say, if you're with us on this, it means your lips are sealed. Not a word to anyone, and especially not a word to Anna.'

'I am with you,' Hector said simply.

'Good...' Mage looked at his watch, and then glanced uneasily out of the back kitchen window. It was barely five o'clock and yet the light was all but gone from the sky. Evening on this dark day had fallen unnaturally early. 'What I suggest that we do, not necessarily right now, and not necessarily involving Hector or Tamara, but certainly this evening, is sit in circle together... A formal ritual of alliance where we can meld our minds and conjoin our mental strengths. Out of that we might even get some insight as to what's going on in the enemy camp.'

'Count Tammy in,' Light said. 'By her own admission she's not particularly clairvoyant, but she's sure as hell one sensitive lady and she's got a lot of spiritual strength. We talked about this on the drive down and we talked about it some more this morning, and she's as much involved in this as I am. For what it's worth, I reckon we ought to have Hector sit with us as well. Any strength we can give him have got to make him feel better about being on our side, and besides, five in a circle is always more powerful than three or four.'

'Fair enough,' Mage agreed. 'Let's take a break for some food and for my part I need to do some more deep meditation, and let's say we all meet again here at seven o'clock.'

The meeting broke up and although Helen had no doubt that Mage fully intended to do some meditating, she also was fairly certain that he'd need some time to clear the upstairs room of whatever he'd been so deeply and darkly involved in before they'd arrived.

23.

The Binding

Jesus stood at the bar of the Venta El Vaquero just outside Castillo on the main road to the south. He was talking animatedly to the curvaceous blond lady who'd served him his drink, and because the lady seemed to be as interested in him as he was in her, he found himself hoping that Eulalio would be late, or better yet, that he wouldn't come at all. He was fairly certain that Eulalio *would* come, for had it not been Eulalio himself who'd told Jesus to meet him at the Venta for seven o'clock? Even so if Eulalio could just be a little bit late, that would be very helpful.

Eulalio was late, but only by five minutes. He accepted the fino Jesus bought for him without so much as a thank you, then with a nod of the head indicated that they should take a table away from the bar. There were plenty to chose from, for they were the Venta's only customers.

'How are you?' Eulalio asked abruptly, once they were seated.

'Why, I am very well, thank you,' Jesus answered. 'Is there any reason why I should not be?'

'Have you spent all the extranjero's money yet?' Eulalio wanted to know.

'No – but I dare say I shall have done by tomorrow. It is good that we have another day's work. It's better than digging storm drains for the ayuntamiento!'

'That is what I want to talk to you about,' Eulalio said uneasily. 'I was not happy up there today. I was not happy with what we were doing, and I was not happy with that stuff we found covering the entrance. We ourselves were the last people to dig on that site four years ago and we both know that nobody has been up there since, so how did that plastic stuff get there, and what exactly is it?'

'I do not know – but Señor Hamish said it was some new kind of sealer.'

'Yes he did, but I think the only reason he said that was because he didn't know what it was himself and that still doesn't answer the question of who put it there!'

'Well, maybe we'll find out when we go back tomorrow.'

Eulalio sipped at his sherry. 'I didn't like it up there today,' he said again, 'and I have decided that I am not going back there tomorrow. You can go on your own if you wish, but if you take my advice, you'll stay well clear!'

Jesus felt a ball of tension begin to build in his solar plexus. 'Is this one of your feelings?' he asked nervously, for Eulalio's *feelings* were famous throughout the campo. Once, or so the story went, he'd had one of his feelings when he'd been working down a mine in Albeciete. He'd simply downed tools and walked out, thirty seconds before the mine roof caved in, killing everyone else who'd been working at the coal face. Then there'd been the time when he'd had one of his feelings about going on a bus from Algerciras to Malaga and had actually got off the bus in San Pedro. His wife had been furious and his friends had laughed at him, but when, half an hour later the bus had gone off the road just outside Torremolinas, swept away by the floods of 1989, his wife's fury had abated and his friends, the ones that had laughed, had all been dead or badly injured and they laughed no more.

'This is one of my feelings,' Eulalio said very quietly. 'I'm telling you, Jesus, that there is something wrong up at that castle. I don't know what it is, and I don't even want to find out what it might be. All the time we were digging up there this morning, last night as well, but much more so this morning, it was as though there was an enormous evil spirit sitting on my shoulder and laughing in my ear, and I'm not going to do any more digging up there, not now or ever!'

'In that case, neither am I!' Jesus said vehemently. 'We will telephone Señor Hamish in the morning and tell him he must employ someone else, or better yet, he can dig his own grave.'

Hamish Hamilton's hands hurt. Despite the cream and the bandages that Hector Sanchez had wrapped around them at tea time when he'd visited the doctor's surgery, and despite the panadol tablets he was taking and had been taking every hour throughout the afternoon, the pain was intense. The moment they'd come into contact with soap and water at lunch time the stinging pain had started in earnest and it had got progressively worse during the course of the afternoon. Hamish wasn't stupid. He was able to put two and two together and recognise that the cause of his problem was the contact he'd had with the amber substance of the polymer sealer he'd encountered that morning at the excavation. When he'd told Hector as much the doctor had been very uneasy and on edge, almost to the point of being evasive. Come back in the morning, he'd said, and if there was no improvement, then perhaps a trip down to the clinic at La Linea... And no, he was sorry, but he couldn't easily account for the pustulating red rash that had appeared on Hamish's hands other than to say it was probably a very strong allergic reaction to something he'd touched.

And Hamish knew exactly what that was! He marched from Calle Santana up to the castle, getting wet in the drizzle and really not caring a damn. There were more important things to worry about than a little bit of rain... And yet, the closer to the castle he became, the less sure he was as to what exactly they might be. His mind focused on the pain, almost became one with the pain, and by the time he was standing at the excavation, folding back the canvas and kicking away one of the boards so that he could look down into the hole, the pain from his hands, moved by the motor neurones of his brain, coursed through the rest of his body, making his body feel, well, somehow *too small* to contain the waves of pain that flushed through it.

Standing above the excavation and staring down into the black void, Hamish could see nothing, but he was beginning to feel things... for one thing there was heat and it seemed as though his mind was on fire. No small temperature caused by some 'flu bug, but something bigger and all encompassing that fragmented his senses. There was also a feeling of strength – which may have been totally illogical, but it was there nevertheless, and with the feeling of strength, there was a rage of power that demanded that he use it. An anger found focus in the back of his mind and wrapped around the anger there were barbs of resentment, resentment against Colin Mage and Hector Sanchez who had sent him up to excavate... no, not to excavate, but to *desecrate* the citadel. As the rain slicked his hair against his forehead it seemed quite reasonable to think in terms of revenge. If his fucking hands were going to fall off – and in the back of his mind he knew that that was exactly what was going to happen – then Mage and Sanchez were primarily responsible and they should be made to pay.

Movement somewhere behind him made him whirl around... a twig snapped and a leaf sighed in the rain and although there was nothing to be seen, he knew there was somebody close. Never mind. Whoever they were or whatever they were, they were no threat. A small giggle escaped his lips as he realised that the most threatening thing in Castillo de la Frontera at that moment was none other than he himself! He turned and strode back down towards the village, still aware of the pain but now, in a perverse way, beginning to enjoy it. Although he knew it would probably kill him eventually, right at that moment it made him feel incredibly alive and destructively potent... and yes, potent was a very good word. The thought of what he was going to do caused him to become sexually erect and he found himself rubbing the front of his old cords with one of his bandaged hands. *Might as well enjoy it while I can*, he thought.

Jaime Gomez woke groggily from his siesta, a siesta which had inexplicably lasted for far too long. He was reaching for the packet of Ducados when he saw the face of The Virgin Mary hovering above the back of the bedside chair.

No, you do not need your cigarettes, Jaime! You need to know that you are needed. Look at your watch. Note the time. In six hours you must be on the corner where Calle Loba joins with Calle Principal. Take your gun and make sure that it is working, for you will need it.

The apparition vanished, leaving Jaime wondering if he'd really seen it at all, or whether he'd just dreamed it. Either way, the message was clear. He was to be armed and prepared on the corner of Calle Loba six hours from now. Six hours. That meant one a.m.

'Don't worry,' he said out loud to the empty room. 'I'll be there!'

Hector was late for the seven o'clock rendezvous at Granadillos, and with good reason. It had been an eventful couple of hours. Standing in the kitchen he excitedly told the group what he had learned.

'First of all, the sisters are still in Antequara. They are safe and according to the Mother Superior, they're not going anywhere! Raul Castro was there yesterday and the day before, trying to get in to see them. First he said he was their uncle and then that he was their godfather, and then that he was both their uncle and their godfather and that he had to talk to the girls on a matter of important family business. The Mother Superior wasn't having any of it and he was denied access. From what I can gather, the girls didn't want to see him anyway and became quite hysterical when they learned that he'd been there.

'Next, I phoned La Linea and here we have something very odd. Peter Cortez is still in a coma but his daughter Lena has been missing for the last three days. No one knows where she is or when exactly she disappeared. No one knows where she's gone and quite frankly no one seems to care much one way or the other. They've informed the police and I suppose, in all fairness, there isn't much else they can do...

'The third thing I have to tell you concerns Hamish Hamilton. He came to see me at the surgery this evening with a dreadful rash on his hands. The pain was quite intense and apparently it's been getting worse all day ever since he found something up at the citadel this morning. He says that someone has sealed the entrance beneath the surface of the soil. They have used some sort of resin or plastic. He tried breaking through it with a pick axe and when that didn't work he examined it with his hands and got himself covered in what he describes as being some sort of oily substance and it's obviously this, we both agree, that's causing him to have a massive allergic reaction... but that's not all of it, I'm afraid. Apart from having a very high temperature, he struck me as being very strange... certainly not the man I've known these last few years. It was almost as though he was in some sort of semi hypnotic trance or as if he'd been drinking heavily, although he swears that he hasn't had a drink all day. I have dressed his hands and have told him to go to bed. If he's no better in the morning he'll have to join my ever increasing list of referrals to the clinic!'

Mage bit his lip, casting sideways glances at Helen and John Light. 'Disturbing and interesting,' he said. 'Oily resin or plastic... this ring any bells with anybody?'

Helen shook her head but Light looked thoughtful. 'It might be nothing,' he said, 'but in 1991 there were a series of experiments carried out at UCLA dealing with ectoplasm and cryogenics. It went disastrously wrong, which is why very few people got to hear about any of it, and because the experiments were very unofficial UCLA was able to cover its butt. Basically, a paranormalist team pulled a medium into the laboratory. If I remember right she was a lady called Hilary Burton and she had quite a reputation for transfiguration work built on ectoplasm. The idea was that she'd go down into a trance, produce the ectoplasm and then the ectoplasm was to be sprayed with liquid hydrogen, giving the researchers all the time they needed to carry out a whole load of experiments on its molecular structure and DNA, this is if it had any kind of molecular structure or DNA.

'Well, the lady did her stuff quite admirably, but when they hit the plasm with the hydrogen they managed to hit her too. Froze her to death on the spot! But they *did* get the ectoplasm! It only lasted a few seconds after they'd chipped it out of the ice and one of the guys working on the team described it to me as grey globules of something half way between thick oil and soft plastic. Then the whole thing simply evaporated in front of their noses.'

'Ectoplasm,' Mage thought out loud, '...or at least, some form of ectoplasm. It's a very interesting theory and if we're all agreed we'll check it out first thing in the morning. No point in trailing up to the castle tonight in the dark, but if we can get a sample of this stuff and have a look at it in a laboratory, then it might answer a few questions.'

'I have all the basic equipment in my surgery,' Hector reminded him. 'I for one would like to see what it is that has done so much damage to Hamish's hands.'

'Thanks Hector, and point taken, but for now let's get on with this evening's business. If you'd all like to follow me upstairs?'

Mage led them up into the salon. The windows and shutters were closed and a substantial log fire burned brightly in the hearth. The round table had been drawn into the centre of the room, around which there were five assorted chairs. Upon the table, almost like place settings, there were five slim white candles. Apart from the fire the candles were the only source of light. The room was pleasantly warm and scented with mild but exotic incense.

He sat them at the table, Helen to his left, Light to his right. Tamara sat at Light's right, next to Hector who was positioned to the left of Helen. 'Let's meditate for a moment on what it is we're going to try and do here this evening,' he said. 'We five share a remarkable secret. One of the most closely guarded secrets of all time. There are probably less than fifty people in the whole world who know about the Djinn, and we five are certainly the only people in Castillo who know about them. With our knowledge there comes a responsibility to do something about the situation. It might sound awfully melodramatic if I say that we are the only people who can spoil the Djinn's plans, but that probably *is* the bottom line.

'Now, while there are many things we don't know about our adversary, one thing we *do* know is that he's a very psychic, very magical being. Although I am quite prepared to shoot the bastard in the back while he sleeps, I suspect that as John has already told us, it wouldn't work. Our Djinn has to be disposed of by magical means and, as far as I'm concerned, that fine! We *are* that magical means! I don't promise you that we can win this fight, but I do tell you that we've got to try and I do tell you that we can give our enemy one hell of a run for his money! If there is anybody alive on this planet who can stop the Djinn, then make no mistake, we are those people!

'What I want to do this evening is create a psychic bond between us, a spiritual binding, that will give each of us some insight into the other's mind... something that will give us a corporate magical identity. My strengths become John's, John's strengths become mine. Ours' become Helen's, Helen's become ours. Whatever weaknesses we have will be neutralised by our group strength and while I am not claiming that we will be able to create the power of telepathy between us, we'll certainly create an *empathy,* and this is very important because it means that we three,' he looked at Light and Helen, 'can offer a far greater measure of protection to Hector and Tamara, who don't have the training or the skills that we have. We are only as strong as our weakest link!'

'Also,' Mage smile faintly and Helen was well aware of the tension behind the smile. 'Later on this evening I intend to go over onto the offensive and if I can do that with your energies to back me up, my work is bound to be that much more effective.'

'What exactly are you planning?' Light asked curiously.

'I want to work a binding ritual and see if I can't keep our genie corked up in his bottle. I'm working on the hopeful assumption that his energy levels might be a little on the low side. He's just arrived in Castillo to find that Ignatious and his group no longer exist. Also he's had a run in with me and another with Hector. You know how magic works as well as I do. These things will have drained his energies rather than having added to them. It's no mean feat to conjure up wind with sufficient force to knock a man over, not to mention changing your face and sticking your tongue out for more than a yard! Maybe he thinks he's got us reeling. Maybe he won't be expecting an offensive strike quite so soon. Either way, I'll strike while the iron is hot and see if I can't do something to make sure that he doesn't stray too far from the house in Calle Sombra. If I can sow a few psychic mines at key places around the northern quarter of the village, it might slow him down and give him something to think about. Now that he's here, I don't want him disappearing on me again like he did back in England.'

'Is there anything we can do to help on a practical level?' Helen asked.

'Other than sharing your energy with me, no not really... leastwise, not at this early stage. If you both meditate between the hours of eleven and one, that's when I intend to work... crossing the divide of the day. In fact, I can see how it might be to our advantage if you and John keep a low psychic profile for a day or so. The Djinn knows about me, but there's no reason why he should know about you guys just yet.'

'Don't forget, he saw me in the street with Hector this morning.'

'No, I'm not forgetting that, but we don't know how much that's actually told him. We know that Dolorean is very powerful, even to the point of being superhuman, and we also know that he's incredibly dangerous... but he isn't God, he isn't all powerful, and we must be careful not to credit him with more abilities than he might actually have.'

'You still be very damn careful, my friend.' Light said sombrely. 'I hear where you're coming from, but until we have proof to the contrary, if I were you I'd proceed as though this guy *is* God and *is* all powerful... anyway, let's make a start, otherwise we'll be sitting here gassing all night. You want some physical contact?'

'Yes... let's join hands and form the circle.'

'Is there anything special you want me to do?' Hector asked with just a trace of uncertainty.

'Yes please, Hector,' Mage said promptly. 'Because this is in essence a religious ceremony, I'd simply like to relax and go with the flow of whatever comes down. Don't be worried or alarmed by anything that happens or by any feelings you might have and it will help if initially you can say a few prayers, asking for purity and wisdom... that kind of thing. And Tamara, the same goes for you, okay?'

'Okay... but I ain't too sure that my God is the same as Hector's God.'

'Doesn't matter,' Mage said simply. 'There is ultimately only the one God Energy, irrespective of the names and titles we bestow upon it – and if it isn't on our side, then I'll carry the Djinn to The Opening on my own back.'

Then Mage closed his eyes and began building the circle.

Helen had sat in more magic circles that she'd had hot Sunday dinners, but even so she was moved and impressed by Mage's handling of the ritual that took place in the upstairs room of the house in Granadillos that evening. Whatever might have happened in that same room earlier in the day, well, that had not involved her anyway, and whatever it was, it was past and done and none of her business. *This* ritual she was very much a part of and, both during it and after it, she felt very good about the whole thing.

Mage began by offering a simple prayer to The Great Spirit, asking for light, courage and guidance. He then made the statement of intent and purpose, indicating why the five of them were gathered in the circle and identifying each member of the circle by name, asking for the protection of the four prime guardian angels to be visited upon them. He identified their common cause and named their enemy and, Helen noticed, he included Alexandra in the naming! Finally, he invoked the Name of God in the seven ways known to man, asking for the gifts of trust, love, faith, strength and communication.

Throughout the ceremony Mage's voice was soft but never less than firm. There was none of the sycophantic supplication such as she'd heard from so many self styled wizards and warlocks in the past, and nor were there any of the melodramatic histrionics that frequently went with such circles and gatherings... Yet the power in Mage's words was never less than totally commanding and she increasingly became aware of the fact whoever or whatever this man was, he was a very old, very advanced spirit.

At one point she found herself drifting off, out of body, to survey the table and its five sitters from a point high in the corner of the room. It seemed to her clairvoyant mind that silver braids of energy coalesced around the table, linking each of the five sitters together... which was, of course, no more and no less than what Mage was working to create. She concentrated her attention on her own body and realised that she had fallen into a light trance; monitoring the rest of the table. It seemed that Light had also moved into a high state of alpha consciousness but was still very much bound within his own body aura and, what's more, she thought, very intentionally so. There was no way that Light was prepared to move out of body at this early stage. His demand for control was too great and although he may have been prepared to form an alliance with Colin Mage he was still very much testing the waters. She had little doubt that Light could move out of body at will – his psychic aura was really quite phenomenal – but that will, an iron bar of personal identity, was not prepared to relax just yet... which was fair enough. He was an extraordinary man who could not have survived over the years without that incredible force of willpower.

She focused her attention on Tamara, recognising that although Tamara's personality tended to be overshadowed by Light's larger than life character and presence, Tamara nonetheless had a mind of her own. That mind, it seemed to Helen, was finely tuned into Light's own psychic vibration and although she may have been very intuitive, any psychism she had was clearly borrowed from her partner's reservoir. And yet a powerful strength did emanate from Tamara's aura and when Helen examined it she found a multitude of facets. There was a stubborn streak as broad as the Grand Canyon and a towering pillar of pride, not based on bloody minded arrogance but upon a resonant chord of quiet dignity. Most of all, however, there was a shining prism of love, potent and powerful, and directed solely towards her man. It was a total love, uncontaminated by reserve or expectation of anything in return. Helen had always been suspicious, even to the point of being dismissive, of the concept of *Unconditional Love*, which she felt was a very glib cliché bandied about by New Age philosophers who had no idea of what they were talking about, but now she was seeing it in all its glory and was humbled by it. John Light was an extremely lucky man and she fervently hoped that he knew it.

Hector Sanchez surprised her. She found him in a deeply meditative state on the borders of trance. His psychic aura, while obviously not as strong as the three occultists sitting at the table, was actually a lot stronger that Tamara's and far stronger than she'd expected to find in someone uninitiated in mystic lore. He was surrounded by a pale blue effervescent light which she recognised as a healing energy. Up to a point this was logical, for after all, the man was a doctor and yet not all doctors were natural healers and it was glaringly apparent that even if Hector Sanchez had never set foot inside a medical school, he would *still* have had the power to heal! She pushed a little deeper into the man and found herself enveloped in the essence of his kindness and compassion... but she also made contact with his loneliness and felt the sharp edge of his fears. Channelling some of her own healing energy into the doctor's soul, she retreated, not wishing to intrude further.

She found herself rising again, through the ceiling and the eaves of the house and then through the rafters and the roof, until she was poised and hovering some fifty feet or so up in the air, surveying the scene beneath her with profound and distinct clarity. She was able to see through the roof of Mage's house, looking down upon the round table, recognising her own corporeal body to Mage's left, seeing also the subtle umbilical chord of silver light that spiralled upwards from the crown of her head, which was her guideline and lifeline and also the line of energy that made the astral projection possible. Broadening her vision she took in the vista of the village, seeing the different energies swirl and eddy through the streets. Streetlights dimmed amid the myriad patterns of soul light... and yet there were also areas of deep shadow that troubled and disturbed her. Elevating even further she came to recognise that for every shard and sparkle of light, there was a corresponding shadow of turbulence. Lightness and dark, good and evil... They were black and white words that did not do justice to the concept of what she was perceiving, but if she had deliberately sought an experience that illustrated the fine balance of conflicting energies within Castillo de la Frontera, try as she might, she could have done no better than this!

Something caught her attention towards the north and she allowed her out of body self to drift across the rooftops of the village until she was hovering above the town hall. A dark strand of energy flowed like a narrow stream from the top of the mountain down across the northern quadrant of Castillo, culminating near the convent adjacent to Calle Sombra. Within the dark eddies there were subtle discolorations of mauve and bile green, and in all her years of astral experience she had never seen anything like it before. It repelled and frightened her, but she was still excited by it, for if Colin Mage was seeking some evidence to link the Dolorean house with the citadel, then here was the proof! To be sure it was not the kind of evidence that would stand up in a court of law, but what did that matter? What they were involved in transcended any kind of secular evaluation or sense of justice.

Without effort she allowed herself to be drawn back towards Granadillos and descended through the roof to take up residence in her own body. Her eyes momentarily opened and she was aware of Mage watching her. He raised an eyebrow and she nodded in recognition of his awareness. He'd known that she'd been out of body, but he'd have to wait until the ritual was over before she'd be able to report what she'd seen flowing from the castle into the streets of the northern barrio. For the time being she was content to re-settle herself within the circle, feeling very safe and secure in the cradle of its power.

She closed her eyes again, aware of the protective energies channelling through her from the physical contact with Mage's hand... And then the process reversed itself as Mage began to draw the energies from the circle into himself. A breeze seemed to waft around the table, a breeze that became a gentle wind; the temperature in the room perceptibly dropped and she felt a hollowness rise in her solar plexus. She breathed the energy out of her mouth,and felt it being caught up in the vortex. The more she gave, the more the vortex demanded until she felt a breathless pain of tension beginning to build uncomfortably within her chest. She heard a gentle moan from her left and a gasping sigh from across the table – and knew that whatever she was experiencing, the others were experiencing it too. She wanted to open her eyes, but knew that she shouldn't... knew that she *couldn't* unless it was by a direct force of will.

Helen exercised that will and her eyes fluttered open half a millimetre, which was enough to see the five candles flames leaping to an impossible height and leaning towards Mage at the head of the table as though a mighty wind was blowing them in his direction. Also there was a clearly defined cloud of silver auric energy being drawn from the sitters at the table. It was held in stasis within the circle by the peripheral breeze, and it was from this reservoir that Mage drew it into himself through his crown chakra. *My God,* she thought. *He's taking too much! He's draining us dry!* She sent out a firm warning thought of restraint and immediately the pressure eased within her body. The wind began to subside and the atmosphere around the table relaxed.

Tamara's head fell backwards, her eyes rolling into her socket, while Hector slumped forwards with a shuddering moan. John Light opened his eyes and he spent several seconds trying to bring them into focus. When he'd regained full consciousness, he looked first at Helen and then at Mage. Helen's gaze also became riveted upon the magician who was sitting back easily in his place. His eyes were still shut but a smile played across the contours of his mouth.

It was one of the coldest smiles Helen Ross had ever seen.

Lena had spent most of the day sleeping in the cemetery but as the afternoon had worn on she'd become increasingly cold and hungry. When the light had begun to fade she'd scrambled out of her hiding place and had gone in search of food. She'd found a large bull frog but had not found it appetising enough to eat, so had let it go after ripping off one of its legs in absent minded frustration. Circumnavigating the cemetery and scrambling down the hillside, she'd come to Alvaro's pig farm. The place was deserted – there were not even any pigs! – but the back door to the house had been open and she'd let herself into the kitchen where she'd gorged herself on semi-stale bread and old churizo sausage before a sound at the front door had caused her to scuttle off out into the drizzle.

She needed to be somewhere. Somewhere safe, somewhere warm and, more importantly, somewhere that her mother wanted her to be. The trouble was Lena didn't know exactly where that place was, so she had to listen to her mother's voice which now seemed to be becoming increasingly garbled and indistinct. And yet her mother seemed to be telling her to go *up*... wherever *up* was. She'd been up to the cemetery, but obviously that wasn't where she was supposed to be, so where else was there an *up* place? The only answer seemed to be the ruins of the castle, so that was where she headed.

Once she got there her mother started talking to her about a stone... she had to find a stone, which was silly, because there were hundreds, no not hundreds but *thousands* of stones. Which stone was it that she was supposed to find? Her mother said that it was a special stone and that if Lena listened very carefully, she would lead her too it. So Lena did listen very carefully and her mother *did* lead her to it. It was there, rough hewn, glowing and buried beneath a cairn of other stones. But now, once she'd got it, what was she supposed to do with it?

Don't do anything with it, darling. Just find somewhere warm and safe to sleep and rest, and then everything will be wonderfully all right again.

But where to sleep and rest that was warm and safe? She was cold and wet, the only heat coming from the rock that she had to carry in both of her little hands because it was so heavy. A figure moved past her in the rain, heading towards the Moorish part of the ruins. Instinct said to follow him, so that was what she did. Maybe he would be able to show her somewhere safe and warm? And that was exactly what he did do!

After he'd gone, she crawled down into the burrow beneath the soil. And here, once the old bit of canvas tarpaulin had been pushed back into place, it was deliciously warm and safe. There was some plastic stuff to sit on and lean against, which moulded itself around her, almost like the waters of a soapy bath, although this water seemed more oily than soapy and, of course, there were no soap suds. With her mother's special stone set firmly in her lap, Lena Cortez fell into a deep and contented sleep, occasionally giggling as the plastic stuff wrapped itself more firmly around her body.

Annette Salt was tired by the time she arrived back in Castillo. The drive up from Gibraltar where she worked as a secretary for the Jiske Banking Company had not been too bad, but the queues at the border had been horrendous and it had been a long day. One little pearl of satisfaction made it worthwhile, however. The insurance company had paid up for the damage that lunatic Carlos had inflicted upon her car and when she actually worked it out, she was about fifteen pounds in pocket on the deal.

She parked outside her home in Calle Llanette, and grabbing her bag and briefcase, slammed the car door shut and locked it firmly. It was an old motor car, but it was going to have to do for another couple of years, by which time either she'd have got the promotion she was looking for – and that would mean boardrooms and company cars, or she'd be back in England. She was about to open her front door when she heard her name being called from the next house.

'Annette? Is that you?'

It was Hamish Hamilton's voice and when she looked, she realised that the front door of his house was ajar, emitting a faint light into the street. Although they'd lived next door to each other for a number of years and were good neighbours, they were by no means close friends. Even so she felt some sense of alarm when she heard the plaintive note of distress in Hamish's voice.

'Yes, just back from Gibraltar,' she called. 'Are you all right?'

'No... actually I'm not. Got myself into a wee pickle, as a matter of fact. Look, I'm sorry to be a nuisance, but you couldn't just pop in for a minute and help me out, could you?'

'Sure. Hang on half a sec...'

Annette slipped her keys into her pocket and entered the dim hallway of Hamish's home. Dumping her briefcase by the door she pushed on into the lounge to find the archaeologist sitting at his dining table, illuminated only by one single angle poise lamp. He sat, rather stiffly and unnaturally, hands tucked under the table, and there was a wild and worried look on his craggy face, a face that looked terribly pale and ill. She realised that he was soaking wet. His shirt clung to his chest and his hair was slicked across his forehead.

'Bloody hell Hamish,' she exclaimed. 'You look as though you need a hot bath and some dry clothes! What have you been up to?'

'Bit of an accident up at the castle,' he murmured with an odd note in his voice. 'Annette, come and sit down. I've got something to show you.'

Annette sat at the table, and as she did so, she heard the door close gently behind her. For a moment she thought someone else had come into the room, but when she cast a glance over her shoulder, there was nobody there. Must have been the wind, she thought, which was the only logical explanation despite the fact that it was a still night amid the drizzle.

'What's going on, Hamish? What's the problem?'

Hamish Hamilton sighed, half in sadness, half in childish delight and proud satisfaction. 'I want to know what you think of these,' he said, and drawing his hands from beneath the table placed them on the polished pine in front of her.

'Oh *God!*' Annette whispered in horror and revulsion at what she was seeing. The archaeologists hands – if you could call them hands – were twisted and discoloured. Hard scabacious growths covered his knuckles and finger joints, while the palms seemed to be covered in pulsating sores, which suppurated and wept even as she watched. His finger nails were extraordinarily long and hooked into dirty yellow claw-like talons. Overall, each hand seemed to be half as large again as it had any right to be and as Hamish flexed his fingers filaments of dead skin flaked away amid the distinct sounds of a crackling squelch.

'Oh Jesus! Hamish, you've got to get to a hospital....'

'Och, it's a wee bit late for hospitals,' he said mournfully.

'Well you can't just sit here like this. We've got to get you some help!'

'I know – that's why I called you in. I've been sitting here waiting for you.'

Annette, who at an earlier time in her life had had some training as a nurse, tried to be professional and businesslike. 'All right Hamish, but now that I'm here, what do you want me to do? If you don't want to go into hospital, at least let me go and telephone Doctor Sanchez...'

'No, I don't want you to 'phone Doctor Sanchez. He's already seen me and he couldn't do anything other than rub on a bit of cream and wrap me up in a few bandages that fell off within half a bloody hour... So no to doctors and hospitals, I'm afraid. But there certainly *is* something that you *can* do...'

A crafty, sly look crept across Hamish Hamilton's face as he looked at Annette expectantly across the table. Annette, still engrossed by the horror of what had happened to Hamish – what *had* happened, for God's sake? – failed to detect the nuance of something new and suggestive in his voice.

'Fine. How can I help?'

'You can start by getting undressed.'

'I beg your pardon?' The unexpectedness of Hamish's words slapped her across the face, focusing her senses, which were still recoiling from the state of Hamish's hands, into a sharper state of alertness.

'I said you can start by getting undressed,' Hamish repeated conversationally.

'Hamish this is not a time to be joking,' Annette said coldly, not at amused by what she took to be the Scotsman's humour, even if he was in abnormal state.

'Who's joking?' Hamish asked with a manic giggle and pushing his chair backwards from where it had been drawn tightly against the edge of the table, he stood up.

He was naked from his genitals down to his ankles and Annette gasped with surprise and revulsion at the size of his pulsatingly erect member that seemed to wave at her in the breeze from less than four feet away. She suddenly became aware of just how threateningly dangerous the situation was and knew she had to get out, and get out fast! Working on pure instinct for survival, she pushed her chair backwards and bolted for the door... actually had her hand on the handle and was trying to turn the knob, when one of those ghastly hands thrust its way through the curls of her hair and grabbed her by the neck. She felt the finger nails cutting into the flesh of her throat... Opened her mouth to scream, but for a scream there had to be air, and her air supply had suddenly been cut off. Thus, instead of the scream, all she managed was a muted gargle.

She could feel Hamish's hot breath and hear his giggles behind her. She tried writhing and stamping with the heels of her shoes, but for her every move he had a counter move. She felt her dress being rucked up above her waist and thrust forcefully backwards in an attempt to push her assailant off balance. She was rewarded by a stunning blow to the side of the head and the nails cut deeper into her skin... *Oh sweet God, not just the nails... His finger tips, his fucking fingers for Christ's sake, were inside her throat, wrapping themselves around her windpipe and that whistling gurgle she could hear, that was blood mixing with air as both blood and air escaped from her body. He wasn't just raping her. He was tearing her throat out. He was killing her!*

Distantly she heard the sound of ripping fabric as he tore her clothes from her, then she was being bent forwards with a massive pressure on the back of her neck. Her legs were kicked open and something mercilessly hard and cold forced itself up into her vagina pouring something that was scaldingly hot into her cervix.

As Hamish Hamilton's life seed spewed into her through her ravaged vagina, Annette Salt's life blood cascaded out of her through her equally ravaged throat.

Ever since the two black Americans had arrived in Castillo Christina had become increasingly agitated and distant. Angel had felt ousted and rejected, his insecurities wrapping themselves around his jealousies like strands of barbed wire. All that day there had been an unhappy knot of hollow tension in his stomach and when Christina had made it clear that she could not – or *would* not – spend that evening with him because she had to talk to her boss, his insecurity joined forces with his immaturity and he stamped out of Christina's bedroom in a childish tantrum. He needed to talk to El Moreno, for in truth El Moreno was the only person he could talk to about this, and certainly El Moreno was the only person who could do anything about it.

Angel banged on the door at Calle Granadillos and, receiving no answer, went back to the Miraflores to check the hotel bar and subsequently every other bar in the village. El Moreno was not to be found and Angel finally settled down to a moody and desultory dinner with his Grandmother, suspending his search until later.

Mage had sat silently in the darkened room. He'd heard Angel pounding on the door, had known who it was and had guessed what the boy had wanted, and yet had chosen to ignore the imperative summons. There were other, more important things afoot than Angel's growing pains!

At eleven o'clock he rose from his half lotus position from in front of the dying embers of the log fire and dressed himself in dark clothes. Before leaving the room, a room that had, over the previous hours, become more than just a room, he dipped his hands deeply into a bowl of pale blue liquid that he'd begun to prepare that afternoon and had completed only after the other four members of his circle had left to be about their own business earlier in the evening. The liquid was thick and syrupy and clung to his hands, lightly staining them, not only with its colour but also with its texture and vibration. With a muttered grunt of satisfaction, he walked out into the pressing dampness of the night.

It had stopped raining but the streets were still wet with a glistening sheen of moisture that clung not only to the paving stones and cobbles but also to the fabric of his clothes. The night air was thick with the smell of rain and the sharp acrid tang of wood smoke and, carried upon a warm blustery wind, there were the usual sounds of an Andalucian hill village battening down its hatches after an unseasonably dreary day. Shadows hovered in dark corners and gathered around the peripheries of dim and hazy light that spilled from the occasional street lamp and bar room window. Unaccountably, for that warm night wind was a definite entity, there were pockets of mist that drifted above the rooftops, clung to the eaves, gathered around the base of bushes and the boles of trees and blurred the architecture of sharp corners, diffusing the intermittent pools of light that illuminated his erratic pathway

Blending wraithlike into the shadow, he padded silently down the back alley that led past the Hotel Miraflores and, negotiating the lower part of Calle Consuelo, cut a sharp left that brought him up against the closed wooden doors of the church of Santa Maria. Here, he had decided, it would begin and thus – he closed his eyes and smiled cruelly – here it began. Releasing the mental brakes, he felt the power surge through him like a tidal wave.

He combined the resonant phonetic sounds of a repetitive mantra with the clear visualisation of Jadoc Dolorean and Alexandra being held captive in their lair... *May these streets be denied to them. May this street and this church be denied to them...* He marshalled his thoughts, thoughts that were fuelled by all the rage and frustration that he had contained and controlled within his being for so long, and focused them upon this one single objective. *Let this village be closed to them, let their hearts, if they have hearts, know pain and fear. Let them tremble at the sound of my name. May they know of my presence, let their opening be denied!* Feeling the power ferment to an explosive point within his solar plexus, he stretched both his arms out, about thirty degrees away from his body, and with his fingers rigidly spread and pointing down towards the ground, he began walking back up the hill along the side of the church and then beyond the church and into the streets of the village. Now he felt the power even more strongly as it pulsed through the deepest core of his spiritual being. He drew on it from his mind, channelled it through his chakras, held it within his solar plexus and then discharged it into the earth, through his hands, using his fingers like lightening conductors. There were sensations of pain and heat... Pain in his gut, pain in his arms, pain in his head... heat in his fingers and heat behind his eyes... both pain and heat in the centre of his soul as he discharged the binding power of magic out of him and into the ether of the astral and the sentience of the night.

Colin Mage was not the only man of magic to be abroad in the village of Castillo that night. Employing a naive and crafty magic of his own, Angel Guadiaro melded into the shadows and followed Mage at a respectful distance as he strode purposefully along the deserted streets. His long wait on the corner of Calle Granadillos had eventually paid dividends and, when Mage had finally emerged from the house, Angel had padded after him.

When El Moreno stood in from of Santa Maria, Angel held his breath on the corner of Calle Consuelo, occasionally peeping around the brickwork to make sure that Mage was still there. When Mage had started off up the hill, his arms held out from his body, again Angel followed after, always careful to keep at least one street and one corner between himself and his quarry. This was all very strange. What was El Moreno up to? What was he doing?

Soon things became even stranger, for as Mage navigated the latticework of small streets, moving ever closer towards the northern barrio of the village, occasionally touching a street lamp, once or twice stopping and placing his hands against the white walls of first one street corner and then another, it seemed to Angel's eyes that pale beams of blue firelight leapt from Mage's hands, arcing down and sizzling as they came into contact with the rain slick on the surface of the road. On those occasions when Mage passed through a pool of illumination thrown from a street lamp or distant window, the blue trails were invisible to the eye, and yet, when he walked through deep shadow and total darkness, they were plainly visible and to such an extent that Angel found himself following the light itself rather than the man who was the cause of it.

And Angel wondered as to what that cause might be. Was El Moreno holding a small torch in each hand? Torches covered with blue gel, perhaps, that caused the curiously coloured effect? This was the logical explanation, but when Angel looked carefully it was plain to see that El Moreno's hands were held open, fingers free and pointed downwards. He could not possibly be holding a torch! Therefore, what *was* the blue light? Angel did not know... Not in intellectual terms anyway, but deeply, intuitively, he knew that Mage was either making the light in some supernatural manner or was, if nothing else, at least the cause of it. And here was another curiosity... Once Mage had crested the brow of the hill and began to move down into the northern barrio, heading, it seemed to Angel, inexorably towards Santa Clara and Calle Sombra (and he shuddered at the memory of what had transpired in that street not such a long time ago) the blue firelight effect became increasingly stronger... Sharper, almost like twin lazer beams, blasting downwards out of his hands into the road and paving stones by his feet.

Helen had slept soundly for two hours. She woke at ten and showered, then took up a meditative position on the bed, clearing her conscious mind in preparation to beam out energy towards Colin Mage as he went through the rigorous and draining process of the binding ritual. Privately, she doubted that the ritual would do much good, but recognising Mage's need to try – his need to do something in retaliation against what had confronted him earlier in the day. From her own experience, she knew how effective binding rituals could be against fellow human beings – she'd woven a few of her own in her time and had frequently been involved in the breaking of them on behalf of other people who'd sometimes been caught in their snare – but that was against fellow human beings! She was quite prepared to give Alexandra Mage the benefit of the doubt at this point in time, but based on her own experience in Calle Sombra earlier that day, she was absolutely certain that Jadoc Dolorean was *not* a human being and, therefore, to what extent he might be bound by any ritual Mage might concoct was highly questionable.

Nonetheless, she was here to help and Mage had been reasonably specific in defining how she might be of assistance and she set to work, building her own mental magic circle in the confines of her room. Without even realising it was happening, she slipped into a light trance... and broke from it with such a sense of dark foreboding that she found herself sitting cross legged on the bed and shivering in a cold sweat of fear and apprehension. Something was going to go wrong. There was a tremendous sense of threat and danger and, despite what was expected of her, she knew she couldn't remain in the cosseted safety of the hotel while Mage faced the danger alone. Quickly, she climbed into some casual clothes and, leaving the Miraflores, slipped out into the dark streets.

Here, amid the blustery warmth of a wet night wind, the sense of danger became significantly more acute. It was difficult to know what to do, but it stood to reason that the greatest danger would come at the climax of Mage's ritual and it also stood to reason that Mage would bring the ritual to such a climax in close proximity to the Dolorean House at Calle Sombra. Getting her bearings, and recalling the geography of the village, she walked briskly and firmly up the main street and was actually entering the square outside Santa Clara long before Mage had even left Calle Granadillos.

She found a dark and dry corner beneath an orange tree at the entrance to the plaza. From here she could see the Dolorean house, the convent and the whole of the plaza without being seen herself. Thankful for the fleece lined warmth of her Barbour jacket, she settled down to wait and passed the time by building protective magic circles in her mind.

The square was uncannily silent and yet within the silence there was sentience. It came from no specific place but was in the very air, so strongly tangible that she felt that all she had to do was reach out and she would touch it. Her eyes kept darting back to the house in the far corner, but nothing stirred the ether around its walls and roof and no light shone forth from any of its windows. The reflective glow from a single street lamp in Calle Sombra illuminated the front of the building, but the steps that led up along the side of the convent and into the square were concealed within a void of impenetrable darkness. Another street lamp, somewhat closer, illuminated the narrow street the gave entry to the plaza from Calle Vasquez and she had the satisfaction of knowing that no one could leave or enter the square without her seeing them.

Midnight came and went and although she was becoming cold and tired, she maintained her silent surveillance. The tension in the night air lessened not one jot and the wind, still pregnant with rain, had become more truculent. An empty coke can clattered across the plaza, its metallic rattle making her jump and she jumped again as the wind lifted an old sheet of newspaper from a litter bin and sent it tumbling across the square in pursuit of the can. She realised how jittery she had become, especially during these last few minutes. If there had been something for her to focus on, that might have done something to help. As it was, she felt like an abstract character in an old black and white film noir movie... the plaza, the emptiness, the silence and the atmosphere, all acquired a surreal quality that made her feel out of step with time. She found that she was holding her breath and when, eventually, a human shadow did move around the corner from Calle Sombra, she nearly shouted out in surprise.

She could not see who it was at this distance, only that the figure was male, but slim and slight, and therefore definitely not Colin Mage. Her eyes locked on to him but it was virtually impossible to maintain visual contact. He was a blur of darkness in deep shadow and the only indication she had of his presence was the occasional movement of his head as he peeped around the corner from whence he'd come... And then he was moving, running diagonally across the plaza, and taking up a position almost opposite her, hunkering low behind a stone bench and occasionally glancing over to his left towards the other entrance to the square. Now she had a marginally better view of him and recognised him as the young boy, Angel Something, who'd been with Mage the first time she'd met him in The Miraflores. Hector had introduced them and if she remembered correctly he'd bought her a drink. Obviously he was associated with Mage in some way and there was also a link with John Light, for wasn't he dating the glamorous blond girl, Christina, who was one of Light's people? The question was, what was he doing here now and why was he acting so furtively?

Her attention became diverted and more intense as another figure slowly entered the plaza from Calle Vasquez. Even without the low brimmed hat and the man's stocky frame she would still have recognised Colin Mage by the emanation of raw psychic energy that exuded from him. He passed her, no more than twelve feet away, and was totally oblivious of her presence. In the one glimpse she had of his face, lit by the light of the distant street lamp, she saw that he was drawn and haggard... his eyes were sunken black holes and his skin was parchment white with a curious blue tinge. His every step seemed to be weighted with weariness and she realised that if he had descended so deeply within himself in pursuit of his magic to be oblivious of her presence, he must also be ignorant of Angel's presence on the far side of the square, and indeed, of any other threats that might be gathered against him.

She wanted to call out a warning, but then the discipline of her own training made her hold her peace. This man was a master magician and although she knew that many must scoff at the idea of magic being a real cosmic force controllable by man, especially now in the first years of the 21st century, she herself knew otherwise and credited Mage with all the respect she felt he was due. She had to assume that he knew what he was doing... that if there was danger – and there was always danger in the practice of high magic – then he himself must be aware of it.

She watched as Mage moved towards the middle of the small claustrophobic square and blinked as she became aware of the odd blue light that seemed to flicker around him. It was both translucent and opaque, hard to define clearly, but nonetheless most definitely there. Like some personal manifestation of Saint Elmo's fire, flames seemed to run down his arms then leap from his fingers to make contact with the rainy surface of the plaza. He turned on the spot, a slow and steady rotation of three hundred and sixty degrees, and the pale blue energy swathed across the square in expanding concentric circles of static electricity. She wasn't just sensing this, or imagining it in her psychic mind, but was actually seeing it with her own eyes. It may have been impossible, but even so this really *was* happening!

Mage stood like an enigmatic avatar and raised his hands towards the massively brooding structure of the convent. Two lines of blue fire arced from his fingers, crackling against the gnarled old wood of the ancient doors and coruscating around them like lightening in an electro-magnetic field. Then without warning he shifted his aim and the same lazer like lances of energy leapt from him towards the Dolorean house, rippling across the walls, kissing dark windows and running in latticed channels across the roof.

Helen had to rub her eyes. This was something out of the special effects box on the set of some science fiction move. Except that this was no movie! It was happening for real and, as if in confirmation of this fact, the blustering skuddy wind acquired fresh ferocity, hurling itself around the plaza in the cyclone of a small tornado. The empty coke can bounced off walls and the rest of the contents of the litter bin emptied in pursuit of the old newspaper that had previously given her such a start. She felt the wind buffeting against the side of her face, slicking her hair into her eyes, whipping the leaves off the tree and stripping the buds of orange blossom from the branches.

Above the roar of the gale she heard a long wailing cry of release rise in anguish and victory from the magician's lips – and then it was over. No wind, no chasing litter, no blue Saint Elmo's fire, just the silent square with the single hunched figure standing in the middle of it, hands hanging loosely by his side, head bowed. Then, as though he carried all the weight of the world upon his frail human shoulders, he turned and shuffled from the plaza.

Helen waited for the boy to follow after him from his concealed position behind the bench – wondered what he'd made of it all – then she herself forced some movement into her stiff limbs and quietly hurried after them both.
Mage was exhausted. After sealing the end of Calle Sombra with multiple layers of mental pentagrams carved into the ether with mantric prayers and sharply focused visualisation of the binding, he'd finally entered Plaza de Santa Clara and, summoning his last reserves of power, had flooded it with his spore. His head ached and his belly cramped in violent spasms as the power channelled out of him.

The blood curse that escaped his lips came from his soul, cut through the wind and ricocheted off the walls of the shuttered buildings.

Dazed and shocked by the savagery of what he had released from within him, he exited the square, totally unaware of the watching eyes that followed his movements. He'd launched his attack and all of his remaining mental energies were focused on maintaining a defensive shield against any counter strike Dolorean might unleash. He knew that he was both weakened and exposed and that it was important that he should return to his protective circle as soon as he could. With feet and legs that felt like lead he began the long trek back through the village, initially making for Calle Loba which would take him over the crest of the hill, bringing him down through Calles Alta and Misericordia to the sanctuary of Calle Granadillos and safe haven... or at least, the closest thing to safe haven he had any reasonable hope of finding in Castillo that night.

He was aware of other energies and entities moving around him, both physical and metaphysical, but could do nothing about them other than hope he would make it back to his circle of protection before they struck... if indeed they struck at all. He was not naive. He did not believe that his ritual would leave his enemies shaking in their shoes, but he did know that he had unleashed a terrible force that might yet give them some cause for thought. If not actually stopping them dead in their tracks, then at least binding them within the dimensions of their own space. With a little luck it might take them some time to recover, and even more time to test the strength of the binding magic that had been employed against them. Even so, from the depths of his exhaustion, Mage was on guard against any manifestation of incoming psychic counter attack... little thinking that when the attack did come, it would not be on a psychic, but indeed on a very physical level.

Calle Loba joined Calle Principal at an acute fifteen degree angle. There was a small triangle of municipal garden at the point of the joining which provided a meagre home for half a dozen stunted shrubs and a pair of dwarf palm bushes. There was also a municipal rubbish bin and a municipal bench.

Jaime discarded the idea of sitting on the bench. True, it might have been more comfortable than where he stood and it would have given him a commanding view of the junction, but it would also have put him on public view to all and sundry, and that was about the last thing he needed.

So instead he took up a position in the dark obscurity of the entrance to Emilio Estufado's stable, which was almost opposite the apex of the junction. It meant that he could observe most of Calles Loba and Principal, at least as far as the brow of the hill, and could observe the municipal garden itself and also keep an eye on the small alleyway, Caminette de los Serpientes, than ran steeply down into the darkness of the eastern barrio towards Calle Llanette. True, he had no vision of the northern stretch of Calle Principal that led up the turn off to Calle Vasquez and the area around Plaza de Santa Clara, but no one could pass in either direction along Castillo's main street without Jaime being able to identify them from the deep cover of his own vantage point.

He smoked a Ducados, carefully covering the glowing cigarette end in the cup of his hand. With his other hand he absently fiddled with the butt of the freshly oiled and loaded Beretta automatic pistol. Every few seconds, he checked the luminous dial of his watch, counting away the minutes. The Virgin Mary – he was no longer sure that it *was* The Virgin Mary, but the habit of thinking of Her in those terms had become established within his psyche – had told him to be where he was for one a.m. and he'd made sure he was ready and in position long before then. He had no idea what was expected of him, only that it was bound to be something important.

At one point he glanced at his watch just as the minute hand indicated half an hour past midnight and his head jerked upwards as a long animalistic howl echoed across the roof tops of the village from somewhere behind him, over in the northern barrio. His first thought was that a rabid dog was stalking the streets, baying in the madness of its rabid contraction, but if it *was* a dog, it was unlike any dog Jaime had ever heard before, mad, rabid, or otherwise! A blast of wind made him shiver, or more accurately, coincided with the shiver, for in truth the wind was warm and it was the long braying howl that made his blood run cold.

The silence of the night descended upon him again, but even the silence was unnerving. It was *too* silent, too still, too quiet, too empty. Even the Bar Vargas, over to his left and a little way up Calle Principal from the entrance to Caminette de los Serpientes, was shut and had been closing even as he'd arrived... which was all but unheard of. Vargas was one of the late night watering holes and seldom dropped its shutters much before three o'clock in the early hours.

No pedestrian walked the streets, no car slammed its door or hooted its horn, no peel of distant laughter broke the spell, and indeed to Jaime's way of thinking, it did in fact feel as if Castillo de la Frontera had fallen under some spell, a spell that persuaded its inhabitants to stay off the streets, to go to bed early, to distance themselves from the sense of expectancy that clung to the night wind. Something was coming on that wind... something dark and violent. He sensed it and waited for it with an inexplicable mixture of fear and glee. Perhaps the people of Castillo had also sensed it, but instead of going forward to meet it, they'd turned and fled from it, hiding behind their shuttered windows and locked doors, waiting, like The Children of Israel, for the Angel of Death to pass over their trembling heads.

Something caught his eye, over to the left, deep in the darkness of Los Serpientes. He strained to see what it might be – there had been the merest suggestion of some movement – but now, studying the alleyway carefully, there was nothing to be seen... Nothing to be seen, perhaps, but still he sensed the presence of someone, or something lurking...

He was concentrating so hard on the entrance to Los Serpientes, that the other figure, a figure walking very slowly with a wide brimmed hat pulled down low across his eyes, was fully two metres around the corner before Jaime saw him. Coming from the northern part of Calle Principal, he trudged diagonally across Jaime's line of vision, heading towards Calle Loba.

Now there was some definite movement in Caminette de los Serpientes and, almost without realising that he was doing it, Jaime found himself unbuttoning the studded flap of his holster. The action, when it came, came very quickly, and

Jaime's reaction was totally instinctive.

The figure in the hat had begun climbing the initial incline of Calle Loba's steep hill, when a second figure, screaming shrilly, broke from the cover of Los Serpientes, and charged after him. In both hands – hands that seemed to be much larger than they had any right to be – he held a wicked looking machete that he was waving wildly above his head, clearly intent on bringing it down upon his unsuspecting victim. In the fleeting glimpse Jaime got, he saw mania and murder in the aggressor's eyes.

Stepping out from his own concealment and bringing up the pistol, Jaime barked out a single imperative command.

'Halt!'

The figure in the hat, either alerted by Jaime's shout or by his assailant's scream, paused in his stride and began to turn. But it was too late and much too close. His assailant was almost upon him, the machete already swinging downwards in its announcement of imminent death.

Jaime didn't hesitate. His finger squeezed the trigger. Once, twice and three times. The sound of the gunshots rent the night asunder, and both figures fell to the cobbles in a melee of arms and legs. Jaime took a small amount of satisfaction in seeing the machete clatter away harmlessly against a nearby wall, but his heart was in his mouth as he approached the two prostrate figures, the taller of the two draped unlovingly across the other... for unless Jaime was very much mistaken, he'd managed to shoot them both.

24.

Aftershock

It was not often that Hector became really angry, but on this occasion he was furious. The object of his fury was his tear stained but defiant daughter, who stood facing him from the opposite end of their modest kitchen.

'I'm not going!' she cried, 'and that's all there is to it!'

Hector's hands bunched into fists by his side and he felt his blood pressure rising. 'That most certainly isn't all there is to it and believe me, my girl, you *are* going, whether you like it or not! I've tried asking you nicely, I've explained why I want you out of Castillo for a while, I've begged and pleaded with you, all to no avail... So now I'm *telling* you. You're leaving for Ronda on the one o'clock train. You're going to stay with Doctor Oliver and his wife for a few days and I'll come and get you when I think it's safe for you to come back to the village.'

'But *why?*' Anna sobbed plaintively.

'I've already told you why,' Hector said coldly, appalled and upset by his daughter's uncharacteristically childish behaviour. 'Last night a woman was raped and murdered in Calle Llanette and although the man who did it has been shot dead, it doesn't alter the fact that there is a dreadful atmosphere hanging over this place like a pall, and I want you out of it! Good God, Anna, I know you are young and inexperienced, but even you must have felt that there is something very bad going on in Castillo at the moment. One death after another, each more violent than the one before, rabid pigs, sick priests and now this morning, out of a clear blue sky, we have hail stones...'

The morning had dawned bright and sunny and as people had got down to the business of starting their day, not yet aware that two more of their number were dead, killed in the most dramatic of ways, the sudden hail storm had taken everyone by surprise. The day was fresh, the skies were clear and yet literally, out of the blue, at eight forty five the hail had cascaded over the village. Some of the hail stones had been the size of peas, while others had been the size of large marbles.

Car roofs were dented, windscreens shattered, canvas awnings were ripped and torn, as was the skin of bare arms and faces of those unlucky enough to be caught in the open. The deluge had continued for fully seven minutes then ended as abruptly and as mysteriously as it had started. As if he hadn't already been busy enough, Hector's morning surgery saw a run on iodine and plasters and, in the end, he'd simply gone down to the pharmacia in the high street and had worked in unison with the pharmacist and his assistants, dishing out the first aid. Thankfully, no one had been seriously hurt, but a lot of people were in a mild state of shock. Late May in Andalucia, and here there were hailstones, some as big as golf balls, so some people said, and falling out of a clear blue sky. Who'd have thought such a thing was possible!

As far as Hector had been concerned, that was the whole point. It wasn't possible.

Hector was tired. He'd been up half the night after having been summonsed by Jaime Gomez a little after one a.m. He'd met the police chief on the corner of Calle Loba and had listened in horror to what Gomez had to tell him. Together they'd prised the two bodies apart. Hamish Hamilton was very dead. One of Jaime's bullets had caught him in the small of the back, the other had taken him in his right shoulder while the third had entered through the back of his neck and had effectively blown half his head off. Mage, thankfully, was alive, but had been out cold. For the sake of secrecy – both men were aware of the need of some secrecy – and also expediency, they had carried Mage around to the police station and had laid him out in one of the cells. Hector had wanted to take him back to Santana or Granadillos, but Jaime had been insistent.

'I am quite prepared to accept that this extranjero is without blame or guilt for what has happened here,' he'd said, 'but this is still a very serious business and I must follow the correct procedures. If you tell me this man must go to a hospital, that is one thing, but if you are telling me he is simply unconscious and will recover in due course, then I must hold him at least until have questioned him.'

The other thing that hadn't helped very much was that Helen was obviously involved in this somehow. She'd been hovering, no, more a case of dancing in agitation over Mage as Hector had arrived and because her Spanish was minimal to non-existent, Hector had had to translate both what Jaime was saying, and what he was asking her. Basically, she'd seen nothing... Had heard the gun going off and had run around the corner to find Jaime standing over the two bodies with a smoking pistol in his hands. There had been a few moments of confusion bordering on hysteria, caused predominantly by the lack of communication, which to some extent had been resolved with Hector's ruffled arrival.

While Jaime had returned with two junior officers to Calle Loba, Hector had examined Mage more thoroughly, grilling Helen at the same time. Helen told him that she'd been following Mage as he'd walked the village, but made no mention of the blue fire she'd seen streaming out of his body. Hector had been aware that he was only getting part of a story, but for the time being, it had to be good enough. As far as he could ascertain, Mage was simply unconscious. There were no bones broken and the blood that covered him was not his own.

'Is there anything I can do?' Helen had asked.

'Yes. Find some warm water and clean him up while I go and sort out Jaime.'

Hector had gone down to the mortuary and had conducted a priliminary post mortem on Hamish.

'For God's sake, look at his hands!' Jaime had exclaimed at one point.

'Yes,' Hector had grunted noncommittally, 'I know all about his hands.'

It had been after four by the time he'd finished and had returned to Mage's cell. He'd still been unconscious and Helen had fallen asleep in her chair. He'd sent her back home and had left Mage in Jaime's care, returning to Calle Santana as the first cocks were beginning to crow. He'd collapsed, still fully clothed, on his bed, only to be woken again an hour later by the phone. It had been Jaime Gomez again, ringing from Hamish Hamilton's house in Calle Llanette.

'Please,' Hector had begged, 'can this not wait?'

'No, it can't. I need you here now... and Doctor, do you have a bottle of brandy anywhere?'

'Brandy? Yes, I suppose there'll be a bottle around somewhere.'

'Then bring it.'

Feeling like a zombie, brandy bottle in one hand and doctor's bag in the other, Hector had again ventured out into what he increasingly saw as the hostile environment of the village. Now there had been grey light in the sky, but it had done little to lift his spirits. He'd arrived in Calle Llanette to find Jaime and half of Castillo's police force gathered in the street milling around two police cars. Rotating blue lights flashed eerily, but what had been even more eerie had been the mood of silence that hung around the tableau. Jaime had stood on Hamish's door step, eyeing the doctor grimly. Without a word he'd reached for the bottle and had taken a long slug from the neck before passing it back.

'You too,' the policeman had said shortly.

'For God's sake Jaime, it's six o'clock in the morning!'

'Take a drink,' Jaime had commanded. 'You're going to need it, believe me.'

Too tired to argue, Hector had taken a long choking mouthful from the bottle of Magno and then, full of perplexity, had followed Jaime into the archaeologist's house.

Even as he crossed the threshold he smelt it... the strong sickly sweet tang of blood. Jaime had stood to one side letting the doctor see what he and his men had already witnessed. Annette Salt's naked body was propped against the wall. It was totally covered in blood – which was hardly surprising. She had been decapitated, with her head placed back on her torso back to front. Both her hands had been severed from her wrists and sat in their own pools of blood a few feet away from her blood drenched legs. Her arms, ending in ragged stumps, rested unnaturally across her lower abdomen. All that, horrific as it was, wasn't so bad as the fact that her eyes, although dead, were wide open and seemingly stared straight at Hector, in some mute and terrible appeal, even though she'd obviously passed the point of help many hours before.

Hector had known Annette Salt well. They'd been friends... not close friends, certainly not intimate friends, but friends nevertheless.

'Jaime, I can't handle this,' he'd gasped, then had turned away and vomited, stumbling from the charnel house to where there had been some semblance of fresh air. Jaime had followed him, tentatively resting a hand on the doctor's heaving shoulders as he'd brought up the contents of his stomach. Hector blindly grasped at the brandy bottle Jaime had offered him and had downed several long swallows before he'd been able to get his breath and focus on the policeman's face.

'Listen!' Hector had grabbed Jaime's sleeve. 'Listen, I've been a doctor for nearly thirty years! I've treated war wounds in Israel, the results of back street abortions in Barcelona and I've put people back together after they've suffered at the hands of some of the world's worst torturers – but I've never had to deal with anything like this before! Jaime, I *knew* her! She was a nice lady! I thought I knew Hamish too... How could he have done this? I tell you Jaime, I've seen more horrible deaths in this village over the last few months than I did when I was on the front line of a war zone... but this one...' he'd nodded towards Hamish's open door, '...this one is where I draw the line. I can't cope with this one at all.'

'You don't have too. The Guardia Civil are on the way from Algerciras, along with someone from the coroner's office...'

The two men sat down on the pavement with their backs to the wall. Jaime had taken off his peaked cap and had lit a cigarette, offering the packet to Hector in exchange for the bottle of Magno.

'You don't have to,' he'd said again. 'And I don't have to either... This,' he'd jerked his thumb towards the Hamilton house, 'isn't just an isolated incident. It's tied in with a lot of other things. I don't know what all those other things are exactly, and when the Guardia gets here, they will find me as ignorant and as confused as everyone else. I am just the village policeman. I know nothing. This case is too big for me to handle alone. And *you,* you are just the village doctor, you know nothing, and there is too much happening here for you to handle on *your* own, but,' he'd eyed Hector shrewdly, 'we *both* know there is something happening here which is dark and mysterious and very very rotten. This last night's business is only a little part of something much bigger. We both know this, although I get the feeling that maybe you know more than I do... But for both our sakes, when our friends arrive from the coast, we neither of us know anything. We will take some time to talk in private later if you have a mind to, but for now let us remember that I need more policemen on the ground in Castillo and you need some assistants to help you with your medical responsibilities. We both need some sleep... a man can't think clearly when he's dropping from tiredness.'

Hector had nodded, understanding exactly where Jaime was coming from. 'It makes you wonder just what's going to happen next,' he'd said absently.

'True. It does. And that is another thing that we both know... that there is something else waiting to happen. This, this *blasphemy*...' again he'd nodded in the general direction of Annette's corpse, '...isn't just the end result of a man's madness. There is something alive and eating at Castillo's heart. You and I, doctor, must find it and destroy it, whatever it is...'

'I don't see what a few hail stones have got to do with me being packed off to Ronda!' Anna snuffled petulently.

Hector, who had made the impulsive decision to get Anna out of the village just as the last hail stones had been bouncing all over the cobbles and had phoned his good friend Albert Oliver there and then from the pharmacist's office to arrange things, was intransigent. Had he been less tired and less stressed he may have handled things very differently, as it was...

'You are going to Ronda because I am your father and this is what I have asked of you. All of your life I have tried to be a good parent and I have given you all that it has ever been in my power to give. Never have I asked anything unreasonable of you in return. So now, I have asked you to go to Ronda for a little while because some terrible things are happening here which I can deal with more effectively if I don't have to worry about you all the time. Do you help me? Do you even listen to what I am saying? No, you do not. Instead you behave like a spoilt child and, if you are going to behave like a child, then I must treat you like a child and *tell* you that you are going to Ronda. Now, go and pack your things.'

'And what if I refuse?'

Hector looked at her bleakly. There were tears in his eyes and ice in his heart. 'Then it is over between us,' he said quietly. 'You can find somewhere else to live, or we will sell this house and I will give you half of the money and I shall find somewhere else to live. But as long as I am your father and you are living beneath my roof, you will obey me when there is something as important as this at stake.'

'You would not do this thing!' she said in a horrified voice.

'Yes Anna, I would. You leave me no choice.'

'All right,' Anna gulped... 'But I cannot leave without first saying good-bye to Colin.'

'Ahhh,' Hector sighed. 'This is what all this fuss is about, isn't it? Well, I wouldn't want to come between you and your precious Colin, but I'd have thought that right now he's got enough on his plate dealing with his wife, to worry too much about you.'

It was out before he'd realised that he'd said it, and it was only when Anna went rigid with shock that he understood how his words must have sounded to her ears. Indeed, even out of context and regardless of tone, he saw how the words themselves skewered into his daughter's heart. The pain in her eyes was quite awful to behold.

'His *wife?*' Anna echoed disbelievingly.

'Ex-wife, I think. If they're not actually divorced, they're certainly separated. The point is, she's here in the village now, with someone else, and that's one of the reasons that Colin himself is here...' Hearing his own words stumble out of his mouth, he realised that rather than helping, he was making things a lot worse and he retreated into lame silence.

'Colin never told me that he was married,' she said in an incredibly small voice that was so full of hurt and disappointment that Hector's heart bled for her.

'Maybe he had very good reasons... and maybe there are a lot of other things he hasn't told you... and maybe this is good enough reason for you to go to Ronda, just for a little while, until everything gets sorted out...'

'Yes Papa...' All the fight had gone out of her and she sounded totally distracted. 'Of course... I'll just go and throw a few things into a bag...'

Anna walked slowly across the room and Hector felt like cutting his throat. He'd been stupid and he'd been clumsy and he'd caused his daughter unnecessary pain... But then again, maybe the pain wasn't entirely unnecessary. Maybe it was just as well she knew some of the truth... Knew what she was getting into before she fell too deeply in love with someone she could never have. And then, with a sick twist of awareness, Hector recognised that it was probably already far too late for such thoughts and reservations.

After he'd put Anna on the train he drove to the police station. Jaime met him in his office and waived him into a chair. The policeman managed a rare smile.

'How did you get on with the Coroner's people?' he asked.

'Well enough. They asked all the wrong questions and I gave them all the right answers. The upshot of it is that they're sending me a trained nurse but she won't be here for another month and in the meantime I've got a hotline set up between my office and the medical examiner's office in Algerciras so that I can "keep them informed of any further developments in and around Castillo de la Frontera as and when they occur." What about you?'

Jaime laughed harshly. 'Just about the same. They pat me on the back, tell me what a wonderful job I'm doing, promise me more manpower when some manpower becomes available and, in the meantime, just carry on as normal. From their point of view, it's all cut and dried. There has been a terrible terrible murder but, thanks to the excellent work of Captain Gomez, the murderer has already been apprehended... and what's more, just in the nick of time to prevent another killing! There isn't going to be a firearms tribunal and from what that stupid fat asshole of a mayor has said, they might even end up giving me a medal, along with a promotion and a commendation! Either they are all crazy or I'm going crazy.'

'What about Señor Mage?' Hector asked.

Jaime's eyes narrowed. 'He's still down in the cells. Sleeping like a baby. Can't wake him up, but then to tell the truth, I've not tried all that hard. Not had the time. His friends have been in to see me and this man has got some very strange friends, I might tell you... The blond girl is okay, got a nice backside, but the other two, the American blacks... now they are odd. God knows what they're doing here in a place like Castillo. Anyway, I've told them that their friend is all right and that he is free to go after he has woken up and I have asked him some questions... Unfortunately I've had to admit that there's been a shooting because the blond girl, this Miss Ross, she was there at the time and knows more or less what happened anyway.'

Hector chewed the stem of his pipe and wondered whether he should tell Jaime some of the things behind Mage's presence in the village. He felt that he should, but really, he needed to talk to Colin about it first. He stood up.

'Let's go and see if we can rouse him,' he suggested.

'Good idea, although I don't know how much he can tell me.'

Enough to make you want to run away from this place just as fast as you can go... That's what he can tell you. As for what he will *tell you, ah well that's a very different matter!* Hector kept his thoughts to himself and as Jaime led him through the complicated sequence of corridors that led to the cellars than ran the length of the ayuntamiento and served as the town jail, he wondered at the odd quirk of serendipity that seemed to have thrown him into such a conspiratorial alliance with a man who up until now he had so actively disliked.

Mage slept serenely on the spartan cot. Helen had done a good job of bathing him and either she or John Light had brought him some fresh clothes to change into when he woke. The old garments which had been badly splattered by Hamish's blood were wrapped up in a plastic bag somewhere else in the building. Hector checked pulse and heart beat, both were strong, and although he could not say that Mage was not suffering from some concussion as a result of Hamish bringing him down on the cobbles, there was certainly no external indication of any such condition and in the end Hector had to assume that Mage was just in an extremely deep sleep. He tried calling his name and gentle pushing at his shoulder, but with no positive results. Finally he held a phial of smelling salts beneath Mage's nose which did begin to bring him back to a conscious state, albeit with a few coughs and splutters. Even then it took fully five minutes for him to wake properly and five more after that to realise that he was in a police cell with an increasingly impatient chief of police waiting to interrogate him.

A trip to the bathroom, a cup of awful coffee and two of Jaime's black cigarettes later, and Mage was reasonably compos mentis. Jaime asked his questions and Mage provided what answers he could. Yes, he knew Hamish Hamilton and, indeed, Mr Hamilton had been contracted by him to do some excavation work up at the castle... No, there was no feud or animosity between them; quite the reverse, in fact. They were on good terms – or so he'd thought. No, he didn't know anything about last night. He'd been out for a stroll around the village and was heading for home when the attack came. All he remembered was the sound of a gun going off, or it might have been a car back firing, then someone had cannoned into him and he'd fallen over, banging his head on the ground...

Jaime Gomez suspected that he was not getting the whole truth and Hector Sanchez *knew* that the policeman was only being told half a story. But Jaime wasn't finished yet.

'You say that Señor Hamilton was doing some excavation for you up at the castle?'

'Yes, that's right.'

'Did he have a permit?'

'Yes, I think so. At least, I know that he applied for the permit.'

'Where exactly was Señor Hamilton digging on your behalf?'

'He was excavating the entrance of the citadel for me. I wanted to get inside and have a look around. He told me it was the only way in.'

'And what is your interest in the citadel?' There was a very sharp edge to Jaime's voice. The memory of his own experience near the walls of the Moorish ruin were still excruciatingly fresh in his mind.'

'Historical and archaeological,' Mage answered blandly.

'Why did you not do the excavation yourself?'

'Mr Hamilton was a professional archaeologist. I'm just an amateur.'

'Why your particular interest in the citadel?'

'Curiosity. The Christian keep is wide open to the winds and holds no secrets. The citadel, on the other hand, is far better preserved and is closed to open view. I wanted to see what was inside.'

'Why?'

'I've already told you, Captain Gomez... I have an amateur interest in archaeology and I was curious.'

'I find it curious that you are curious,' Jaime said enigmatically. 'However, there is no reason for you to remain here now that you are awake and so you are free to go. There will, no doubt, be further inquiries with regard to the tragic events of last night and it is certain that you will be called by the authorities in Algerciras as a key witness. As such I must instruct you not to leave Castillo without first providing me with a forwarding address and, should you elect to leave Spain prior to the hearing in Algerciras, you may well be summoned to appear and at your own expense.'

'Thank you Captain Gomez. I understand perfectly, but you don't have to worry. I'm not going anywhere. I've only just arrived.'

'Phew!' Mage walked out into the street and squinted against the brilliant sunshine. 'That was hard work!'

'Gomez is no fool,' Hector warned. 'He may have no hard information, but he knows there is something happening in Castillo. He is suspicious of everything and everybody. He's certainly suspicious of you and I think that he is even suspicious of me. How do you feel, by the way?'

'Incredibly awful,' Mage admitted with a rueful smile, '...but if you steer me into this bar and buy me a couple of decent cups of coffee and a packet of cigarettes, I dare say I'll start feeling a bit better.'

'I dare say you won't,' Hector retorted. 'Not when you hear what I've got to tell you.'

Mage paused, mid stride in the street. 'Is it about Anna?'

'Why do you ask about Anna at a time like this?' Hector studied him quizzically.

Mage shrugged. 'I had a dream, that's all... that she was travelling on a train, somewhere away from here, somewhere to the north...'

Hector's mouth set in a grim line. 'Colin, I put Anna on the train for Ronda not two hours ago... I've sent her away for a while until this business in Castillo is dealt with one way or the other...' Mage sighed, seemingly with relief, but Hector held up a hand. 'But I'm afraid to say I have rather more to tell you than that. Inadvertently, or at least I think it was inadvertently, I have told her that your ex-wife is here in the village ...'

'Oh shit,' Mage muttered.

'...And putting it bluntly, this information did not go down too well with my daughter! You will now ask why I let the cat out of the bag and I will buy you your coffee and your cigarettes and tell you...'

Hector led Mage into the Bar España where they found a quiet corner and, armed with the required sustenance, proceeded to tell him of all that had happened, sparing him none of the gory details. Mage sat and listened in silence, chain smoking furiously, his hand tightening in such a fierce grip around the coffee cup that Hector fully expected it to explode at any given second. When he'd finished, Mage had looked at him wanly.

'You did the right thing, getting Anna out,' he said softly. 'If it's okay with you, I'll write her a letter – you can read it first if you like – and I'm just so sorry that she's been hurt. I am sorry too about Hamish and Annette Salt. If I could bring them back, believe me, I would. If I could change things, I wish I'd never asked Hamish to go anywhere near that bloody citadel! And the thing which makes all this so much worse, is that this is only the beginning. Things will get a lot worse yet before they get any better.'

'I don't see how things could be much worse than they already are,' Hector tried to smile, but failed miserably. He was beginning to feel dizzy and knew that if he didn't sleep soon, he would probably collapse on the spot.

'Oh believe me things could be much worse,' Mage said bitterly, so wrapped up in his own thoughts that he failed to detect Hector's exhaustion. 'We could all be dead.'

Hector found his bed a little before noon and slept solidly for three luxurious hours. His alarm clock woke him for three p.m. and by three thirty he was showered and shaved and ready when Mage's Land Rover pulled up outside the house. He climbed into the back of the truck finding a space between the two girls; John Light sat up front, next to Mage, his massive bulk taking up most of the two left hand passenger seats.

The old blue Land Rover roared up Santana, turned right on to Calle Principal, then hooked a sharp left around the acute fifteen degree bend that brought them into Calle Loba. Loba twisted into Misericordia and Mage brought the vehicle to a halt in the small car park beneath the castle. The quintet disembarked and carried on the rest of the way on foot. Mage had brought his carpet bag while Hector carried his usual black briefcase. Light swung a plastic carryall over one shoulder and his free hand swung a substantial axe which had been expertly honed to a razor sharp edge. Even to the most casual observer it would have been apparent that this group of people was not just out for an afternoon constitutional. They moved with a quiet sense of professional purpose, not needing to talk much for most of the discussion relevant to their mission had taken place earlier in the day. As it happened, while there was no casual observer, there was one very interested onlooker who carefully monitored the group's progress from his hiding place over by the keep.

'We're being watched,' Light said tersely as they moved towards the abandoned excavation.

'Yes, I feel it too...' Helen glanced nervously around her. 'I think there's someone over there, in the rocks by the keep. I can't see them, but damn it, I know there's somebody there!'

'Don't worry about it,' Mage said. 'I suspect I know who it is and they pose us no threat.' Kicking the planks and tarpaulin to one side he looked down into the hole that Jesus and Eulalio had dug two days before. 'Now then, people, what do we make of this?'

The sun was low in the sky, but there was more than enough light to see down into the excavation. The plastic resin was clearly visible beneath a dusting of soil. Incongruously, a child's white sneaker rested in the bottom of the pit.

'Let's get on with it,' Light said.

'Yes,' Mage agreed. 'Let's!'

The three men rested their respective bags on the ground. Hector produced three pairs of surgical gloves which they snapped over their hands and wrists. Mage brought out the magic mirror box and wedged it between two stout stones on the lip of the excavation. He also took out the crystal wand and tucked it firmly into his belt. John Light handed him a thick pair of rubberised gardening gloves from the carryall and pulled on a pair himself. Their eyes met and Mage grinned feebly.

'You don't have to do this, you know,' he said.

'Oh yes I do,' Light countered.

'Okay - ' Mage addressed the group. 'Let's just be very careful about this. We need a sample of the plastic resin and although we don't know exactly what it is, we do know how dangerous it can be... We know what it did to Hamish, so don't anybody get too close and, whatever else you do, don't even think about touching the bloody stuff. We'll try getting a sample of it on the mirror box, then from the mirror box it goes into Hector's sterilised container and hopefully that should hold it in stasis for a while.' He glanced at Helen. 'You're okay with your bit?'

Helen nodded. 'I monitor the psychic emanations and give you as much warning as I can if I feel anything nasty building in the ether...'

'And I keep watch and make sure we're not disturbed on a physical level,' Tamara added, making it clearly understood that she too was part of this operation, even though her role may have been a relatively minor one, at least in her own eyes.

'Fine.' Mage looked at Light. 'Let's do it!' Then he jumped over the edge and dropped into the bottom of the hole.

Light eased himself down into the confined space with a greater degree of circumspection. Jesus and Eulalio had dug their trench about six feet deep, eight feet long and six feet wide. There was not a lot of room in which to manoeuvre but working in unison they approached the partially revealed archway and began brushing the detritus of earth away from the membrane of resin, using a pair of stiff bristled hand brushes that Light had brought with him. It took them the better part of ten minutes to clean up the surface and fully reveal the layer of plastic substance that seemed to have moulded itself to the stonework and the top of the door. Just as Hamish Hamilton had discovered, the membrane was transparent but had a curious amber opacity.

'Whoever's done this has done a damn good job of it,' Light remarked. 'Let me try with the axe...'

Light took a swing at the resin where the top of the door joined with the stonework of the wall and met with the same lack of success as Hamish had done. The axe bounced back in Light's hands without making so much as a mark on the alien surface. With a grunt and a curse, he swung again, with precisely the same result.

He looked at Mage. 'Got any ideas, man?'

'Nope, but I get the feeling that whatever this stuff is, it isn't man made... if you catch my meaning.'

'Too damn right I do... Okay, well let's try something else...'

Again duplicating the dead archaeologist's earlier attempts, Light tried prising the blade of the axe between the resin and the stonework but could neither find purchase nor leverage. With another grunt of frustration, he stepped back, looking at Mage with perplexity.

'That ain't working either,' he said, stating the obvious.

'The question is,' Mage mused out loud, 'how far down does it go? From what Hamilton told me, these doors are about seven feet high. So far, only the top of the doors has been uncovered. What if this plastic stuff needs air as a catalyst? I mean, what's happening a yard under our feet?'

'The soil is soft enough, so let's dig down a little way and find out,' Light suggested. 'Back up and give me some space. There's a pretty mean shovel in the carryall. You get that while I do some loosening.'

Using the axe as a pick, Light laid about it while Mage scooped up the results. They created a bore hole some two feet square up against the door, but found no difference. The resin still clung evenly to the dark wood as though it had been heat sealed in place.

'Fucking shit!' Light exploded in disgust.

'Yes, I know how you feel!' Mage agreed. He glanced upwards and realised that the light was beginning to fade. Not enough to worry, but enough to remind him that their time in this place was finite. He had no desire to be here after dark and would have preferred to have begun this operation in the morning of the day, but neither he nor Hector had been in any fit state and he was certainly not going to ask anyone else to do what he should have done himself in the first place.

'Time to change tactics, John.'

Light raised an eyebrow in question and in answer to the question, Mage extricated the crystal wand from his belt. 'Okay John, ease back and give me a little space.'

Light moved to rest his bulk against the wall of earthworks, tripping slightly as something snagged against his heel. He stooped and picked up the white sneaker, gave it a cursory glance, then tossed it to the ground again. Even as the small shoe left his hand he found himself wondering how the hell it had got down there in the first place.

Mage stroked the sharp quartz crystal with his forefinger and thumb; his psychic energies were much depleted from the previous night, so at best it was a token gesture of ritual. The wand had been an intrinsic part of his magical armoury for many years and thus was already impregnated with his spore, perfectly in tune with his personal vibration. It was almost a part of him and when, as now, he held it in his hand, it became a natural extension of his etheric being. He'd made it with his own hands, albeit under his Grandmother's careful guidance, when he was only eighteen years old – *the crystal is just a lovely piece of quartz and the wood is just a branch of ash, but it's what you put into the wand and channel through it that counts... how you use it and what you use it for.*

Consequently, the loss of the wand was, to Mage, a serious blow.

Initially, as he pressed the point of the crystal against the surface of the resin, nothing happened but then, imperceptibly, the tip of the quartz slid a couple of millimetres into the plastic substance and Mage became aware of the faintest vibratory thrum. It travelled up the handle of the wand, but he also felt it beneath his feet, emitting from deep within the earth.

'Hey, you feel something kind of humming or buzzing?' Light asked.

Mage nodded but said nothing, maintaining his mental concentration on the point of the crystal. Helen Ross's strained and distant call of *'Careful!'* seemed to come from a long way away as a new sensation assailed his senses. There was a crackling tension in the ozone and a tangy smell, that was familiar and reminded him of rotting seaweed. He'd experienced that smell before on the top of Glastonbury Tor and Helen's warning was obsolete, for he was already totally on his guard. Without warning the smooth plastic resin suddenly fractured into a thousand hairline cracks. A weird mauve light began to dance behind the membrane and Light's indrawn gasp of alarm was lost beneath the sound of Mage's own shout of surprise as the wand was torn from his grasp and dragged in one all powerful sucking movement into the resin. For a brief second the crystal flared in a miasma of coloured lights then the ash handle burst into flame even as it disappeared from sight, following the crystal into the amber plastic. The thrumming vibration beneath Mage's feet became a definite and pulsating tremor, and then Helen Ross was shouting:

'Out! Out! Out! Out!'

Neither Mage nor Light needed second bidding. They exchanged one frightened glance and then were scrambling furiously out of the pit as the floor gave way and the walls collapsed. A second more and they would have been buried alive. As they looked down through the choking cloud of acrid dust an alien and chilling phenomena met their eyes. For up against what was visible of the top of the door, stretching a full metre out and away from the wall, a glutinous amber liquid gurgled and congealed within the sods of soil and earth. The tremors subsided, making the gurgling squelching sound significantly more audible, then even that diminished into silence. Mage stared at what remained of the excavation, for now, instead of there being a deep pit, there was but a shallow indentation of distressed soil.

'What the fuck was that stuff?' Light finally exploded.

'I don't know,' Mage answered softly, 'but whatever it is it's determined to stop us from getting into the citadel.' He made eye contact with Light. 'Did you see what happened to the wand?'

'Yeah, I saw. Reminds me of Demsville. Now you see it, now you don't.'

Mage rubbed his right hand with his left, still feeling the tingle that had been caused by the wand being pulled so violently and unexpectedly from him. He stooped and retrieved the mirror box, sadly noting that both main reflective surfaces were cracked and broken. Mirror box smashed, wand lost, the citadel door more firmly sealed than it had ever been... Not exactly the most successful operation he'd ever undertaken. He managed a feeble grin for Hector and Tamara, neither of whom had had any idea that anything was amiss until Mage and Light had come scrambling out of the hole as though the devil himself was after them, and then turned his attention towards Helen, who was standing a little to one side, still visibly shaken. He walked over to where she stood and lightly rested his hand upon her shoulder.

'Thank you for the warning,' he said quietly. 'Without it, we'd have had it! What did you pick up?'

'Hard to put into words,' she said, groping for self expression. 'Everything was okay until I saw you touch the plastic with the crystal. As soon as you did that I got the most terrifying impression of something dark and powerful rushing up from the bowels of the earth. It was sentient and angry, and it was angry at you... Almost as though it knew who you were and what you were doing. It all happened so quickly and I didn't realise I was yelling until the words were out of my mouth... What happened down there? I couldn't see it all.'

'Like you say, it happened fast. I put the crystal against the resin, the resin cracked, then the whole wand was simply sucked out of my hand and disappeared in front of my eyes. There was a smell and a vibration and you were shouting at us to get out and you know the rest...

'Okay...' he raised his voice and dusted his hat against his thigh, 'unless anyone else has got a better idea, I suggest we go back to the hotel. Let's find a quiet corner and have a drink and a chat.'

'Amen to a drink!' Light said vehemently.

'Right, I need about three minutes on my own first. I just want to check on something... see you at the Land Rover.'

As the main party moved gratefully away from the citadel, Mage strode over towards the keep. He had no difficulty in locating the small cairn of stones where he'd buried Ignatious's lode stone, but was not particularly surprised to see the cairn of stones toppled over and the lodestone gone from where he'd placed it. Somehow, although he did not know how, he knew that the stone had been recaptured by the enemy. In itself, that wasn't the end of the world, but what was worrying was the idea of someone still abroad, working on Dolorean's behalf. His thoughts immediately went to Raul Castro and he would have been bemused the know that stealer of the stone was not the hunter but a nine year old girl! All that concerned him at that moment, however, was the fact that the lodestone was gone. Strike another victory in favour of the opposition. It seemed that his binding ritual of the previous night had been anything but effective.

He glanced up and caught a furtive movement fifty metres further up the hill. Pretending not to notice and giving no indication that he'd seen Angel, he lit a cigarette, gave the village a cursory look as it began to nestle within the shadows of the evening, then strode off in pursuit of his companions.

They sat around a table in a quiet corner of the sheltered court yard. One of Henry's girls served them a light supper of fish and yellow peppers, deep fried and stuffed with mushrooms and garlic. Hector ordered wine from Rioja and even Mage downed a liberal glass full, savouring the oaky taste on his palate and appreciating the warmth of the alcohol as it reached his stomach. Their conversation was conducted in low undertones for there were other diners in the Miraflores that evening and all were aware of how easily voices could carry on the night air. Fortunately there was some gentle back ground music and there was little chance of them being overheard as they discussed in some repetitive detail the events that had occurred up at the citadel.

'I'll bet you anything you like, we could go up there now and try excavating that bloody entrance, and we're going to find that instead of just a thin sheet of that resin, there's a whole block of the stuff covering the door. It'll remain dormant until we try to get into it, but the moment we do try, it'll become unstable and we'll have a repeat performance of this evening's show, only a damn sight worse! We can't fight it or counteract it until we know what it is, and even after all that's happened I'm still in the dark.' Mage looked around the table for help.

'We could always bring in the people from Algerciras,' Hector suggested. 'They have all the equipment, and they *did* say I should inform them of anything unusual and, if they *did* get involved, it might be one less thing for us to worry about. What's more, it might alert them to the fact that there is more happening here in Castillo than meets the eye. I know what you have said, but I'm beginning to think that the more people who know about what we're up against here, the safer it might be.'

'Hector has a point,' Light observed, 'but how are we going to feel if, say, half a dozen lab boys start messing around up there and the same thing happens to them that happened to the archaeologist guy? That way our problem is not only multiplied, it's compounded.'

'I'd love to be able to walk away from this,' Mage said tiredly, 'but as you all know, I can't. I feel terrible about Hamish and, the way I see it, the problem is our responsibility. The idea of dumping the resin into the hands of the authorities is greatly appealing, but I feel fairly sure that if we did do that, then as John says, we'd have a lot to answer for, both on a karmic level as well as a physical one. I simply know that somehow I've got to get inside the citadel. I think I could probably get to it through the well in Dolorean's back garden, but I consider that a very dangerous option, even more so now that he's actually here. The way I see it, I've got to go in through the roof and although that may be illegal and I may get nabbed, it does offer one advantage. I can work my way down through the building by degrees and get out fast the moment anything goes wrong.'

'That might be an easier option now than we first thought,' Hector mused. '... As you know, I've had some dealings with Jaime Gomez and if, to some extent, he could be brought into this, if nothing else it would expedite matters if we need to break the law. Don't misunderstand me. I am not saying that I like the man or even that I vouch for him, but I've acquired some new respect for him lately and, apart from anything else, he's in tune with what's happening in the village, even if he doesn't know what's causing it.'

'It's an idea,' Mage said doubtfully. 'Tell you what, Hector. Let me sleep on that one and we'll look at it again tomorrow. I'm just so bitterly disappointed that we couldn't even get you just a tiny sample of that resin!'

'I think I know what it is,' Helen said quietly from her end of the table, eliciting immediate and unreserved attention from the rest of the group, 'but only on a deep subliminal level that I don't know how to express in words.'

'For God's sake, sweetheart, do at least please try!' Light ejaculated in exasperation.

'Okay, but you've got to remember that this is just a feeling, not a theory or anything as tangible as that... I think it's what you thought it was. Some form of ectoplasm. Not the sort of ectoplasm we associate with spiritualists and seances in our own world, but maybe some kind of Djinnlike equivalent. That feeling I had up at the citadel of something dark and evil rushing up to the surface... Well, I think that the "something" was the resin itself. I didn't feel that the resin was particularly sentient, but that it was being directed by something that most certainly was. Now, I've been told that the Djinn are very magical and psychic entities who have travelled a different evolutionary pathway to ourselves and, bearing in mind that they're shapechangers, well, what if they've not only learned to change shape and project thought... what if they can project some form of changed ecological state? What if the resin is a product of their own psychism or even their imagination? They want to make sure an entrance is sealed, then send out the mental picture of an impervious sticky substance and, hey presto, you've got your resin. Battering it with an axe isn't going to shift it, nor is pounding it with half a dozen JCB's, because it's in a constant form of creation from what is fundamentally another dimension. Now the moment Colin touched it with the crystal wand, there *was* a reaction... there would have to have been a reaction! Unlike a JCB or a sledgehammer, Colin's wand is essentially a magical tool and, when it made contact with the resin, all of the energies would have been transmitted directly to the source. The source immediately perceives a threat and there is a massive protective reaction, which is what nearly cost you your necks...'

'Which *would* have cost us our necks if it hadn't been for you!' Mage was adamant in his praise. 'Helen, you undervalue your own strength of perception. That's a good solid tangible theory! It sounds right and it rings true and, even if it didn't, it's still the only one we've got! John, what do you think?'

'As a *theory?* Yeah, sure, it works well enough and, as you say, it's the only one we got... But I wouldn't want to have to act on that theory or stake my life on it till we've got some more proof, one way or the other. So, what I want to know is can we figure out any way of putting Helen's theory to the test?'

'Yes, we could do with getting our head around that one. Anyone got any ideas?'

No one had, and the table fell into silence as the waitress presented them with an enormous fresh fruit pavlova. There wasn't much further conversation until the pavlova had disappeared.

'I'll tell you one thing that *does* worry me,' Light said, dabbing his lips with a knapkin, 'and that is that we have no intelligence about what's going on in the enemy camp. While we're chasing around like blue assed flies, what exactly is the guy Dolorean doing? We know what we know about him but how much exactly does he know about us? Let's face it, we're all sitting here assuming that he's sitting in his part of the pueblo when, for all we know, he could be half way back to England. None of us has actually seen him for more than thirty six hours and I figure that one of our priorities must be in getting a line into this guy. What's he doing, where and when is he doing it, what's he thinking, what does he know?

'Now, as I see it, we've got two ways of handling this and maybe we need to employ them both. The first way is easy. We sit in circle for at least an hour every day with the express purpose of tapping into Señor Dolorean's thoughts... Sure it might not work, but I've done a lot of work in this area over the years and I'd be damned surprised if we didn't pull in some results sooner or later. He may be strong in his own way, but with the three of us pulling together, no offence at all to Tammy or Hector, we're not psychic weaklings. We've got some tough medicine of our own to dish out if we need to!

'The second way is something far more practical. We need to mount a watch on this house of his. We need to know when he's in it and when he's not, and we need to know where he is when he isn't in it. This presents us with an obvious problem – we're undermanned! I can't see how the five of us can manage it on our own, so we need to bring in some more people. They don't have to know all the details... in fact, come to think of it, they don't have to know any of the details, do they? Now, I've got one soldier in this village. No one knows who she is, she's got no obvious link with me and, more importantly, she's a total stranger to Dolorean. I've been wondering what to do with her as a matter of fact, and it seems crazy not to use her.'

'You're talking about Christina,' Mage said thoughtfully, his mind revolving around what Light had been saying. 'And if we use Christina in this way, then maybe we can use Angel as well...'

'Angel was following you last night,' Helen said. 'I'd have mentioned it before, but what with everything else, this is the first chance I've had.'

Mage chuckled. 'Was he now? Well, that comes as no great surprise. For what it's worth, he was with us up at the castle this evening... our secret watcher. He's a bright lad. Very psychic and, of course, he thinks he's in love with Christina...'

'He needs to be damn careful then,' Light growled, lighting a cigar. 'That girl goes through men like I go through Havanas!'

'So what do we tell them?' Helen asked.

'Angel already knows something about Dolorean,' Mage admitted, 'while, as I understand it, Christina knows nothing. So, we could tell them part of the truth. That Dolorean is a dangerous criminal or even, as Angel already believes, that he's a very powerful black magician who's come to Castillo for a very evil purpose. We can tell them that we need them to watch the house in Sombra and that they can either do it in shifts or they can do it together, which is something that I'm sure Angel would prefer.

'We've got a bit of a problem wqith mobile phones in this place insofar as they don't work very well if they work at all. Something to do with atmospherics and the mountains blocking the signals. We're going need some reliable communications system so obviously, we're going to have to find a couple of walkie talkies or CBs, one for them and one for us, and we're going to have to establish a base from which they can carry out their surveillance, but that's something that shouldn't pose too much of a problem. What we can't do, however, is coerce or con them into anything. We've got to stress how incredibly dangerous this is and let them know what risks they might be running. If they want to volunteer, that's fine, but we can't just order them into our service.'

'Don't have a problem with that,' Light said easily. 'How do you want to handle it?'

'Let's see if you and I can get Christina and Angel together, if not tonight, first thing in the morning, but before we do,' Mage grinned, 'maybe we'd better have a few words first so that we can get our story straight.' He leaned back and lit a cigarette. 'Anyone got any other thoughts?'

'Yes,' Helen said emphatically. 'We've all got to be very much on our guard. We've all got to watch each others backs. We don't know what powers may be launched against us, so wherever we are, whatever we're doing, especially when we're settling down to sleep, keep whatever protective circles you've got wrapped closely wrapped around you. It's important that we all know where we are at any given time, so if someone's going to be buying walkie talkies then maybe they should buy a few. One for each of us. Hector,' she turned and looked directly at the doctor, 'I'm particularly concerned about you. Colin and John and I know enough to be able to protect ourselves. Tammy is under John's protection, but you are very much out there on your own. I'm also very aware of the fact that your home is much nearer to Calle Sombra than is Colin's place in Granadillos or the Miraflores, so I think it might be better if you moved into the hotel for a while. That way, we're all in much closer proximity.'

'I'm very sorry but I really can't do that,' Hector smiled apologetically. 'Whatever else I am, I'm also the village doctor. If people are sick or there is some emergency, then my house in Santana is where they know they will find me. I do appreciate your concern, and I do appreciate the grave importance of what we are all involved with, but I cannot, no matter what the cause, ignore my other responsibilities.'

'In that case one of us, either Colin or myself, must move in with you.' She looked directly at Mage. 'Colin?'

An uncommon spark of merry mischief flashed across Mage's face, which either Helen didn't see or was not aware of. 'I agree with you completely,' he said soberly. 'But I've spent over a month building my circle in Granadillos. It won't transfer, at least not easily, and so it's going to have to be you, love – providing, of course, Hector doesn't mind.'

Hector looked acutely embarrassed but even so, he beamed at Helen. 'You will be most welcome,' he said. 'And, naturally, now that Anna is in Ronda, I'm sure she will not mind you taking over her bedroom for a while.'

In fact, Hector knew that Anna would be furious if she ever found out, but what her eyes didn't see her heart wouldn't grieve over. The idea of having Helen Ross beneath his roof, no matter what the circumstances, filled him with a tingling sense of excitement from head to toe.

Mage, aware of Hector's embarrassment, was also aware of Helen's embarrassment, but in Helen's case, he was also aware of her deep sense of satisfaction. She had, he thought, manipulated the situation quite perfectly.

Later, in the privacy of their room, Tamara made Light lie back on the bed and brought him to a long and lingering orgasm that released not only the sexual tension, but most of all the other tension that had been building up since they'd arrived in Spain. She did so with love and dedication, still unable to come to terms with the fact that now, instead of just being Tamara, she was Mrs John Light. Their wedding had been a simple civic affair in New Orleans and had taken place the day before their departure for Spain. In some ways it made no difference, and yet in others, it made all the difference in the world. If she'd had to spell out in specific terms what exactly those other ways were, she couldn't have done so and therefore made no attempt to, but the one overpowering fact that she *could* get her head round was that the man she had suddenly become married to was not the man she had lived with and served these past fourteen years. Some things, she realised, were better not examined too closely anyway.

'How are you feeling?' she asked, stretching out on the bed next to him and drawing a long red finger nail tantalisingly along the inside of his thigh.

He didn't answer immediately and the bed creaked as he rolled over onto his side to look at her. 'Good,' he said presently. 'Weird - but good!' He reached for a half smoked Havana. 'I'm feeling good about what we've just done and I feel very good about what we did in New Orleans.'

'Tell me about weird,' she prompted.

'Weird - well, weird is out of my depth. LA and The Church seems a long way away and a long time ago, and I've been wondering if I'll ever go back – if I *can* ever go back.. My life has been a series of chapters and being here makes me feel like a new chapter is beginning and I'm not even sure that I *want* to go back!'

He lit the cigar, took one puff and stubbed it out again. The stale smoke tasted foul and contaminated the sweet after scent of sex and the exotic musk of Tamara's perfume. 'Being here in Castillo is strange,' he mused. 'There are no flashing lights, no TV cameras, no hoards of people clamouring for my time and attention...'

'No one but me to tell you what a great guy you are,' Tamara slipped in.

'Yeah, there is that,' Light laughed, 'but believe it or not, I don't miss that at all. Instead, it's a bit like the very early days back in Demsville. I'm part of a tight little group with survival on its mind, where it's who I am that counts, not what I represent or pretend to be. There's something inside that says that what I'm trying to do here is more important than all that crap back in The States. Sure, I'm trying to help Brother Mage, and I sure as hell don't mind playing second fiddle to him for the time being, but what's more important is the fact that I'm fighting my own demons and laying my own ghosts that should have been laid years ago.'

'Tell me what do you make of him?' Tamara asked curiously.

'Mage? He's very dangerous.' Light said bluntly. 'Reminds me of the way Vern plays chess. Vern can know that he's lost the game, but he'll never topple his king and capitulate. Takes it far too personally and wages a war of attrition, taking as many of my pieces as he can until he's left with his king in a corner, all boxed in with no place to go and not a piece of his own left to protect it with. Vern won't quit until it's all over and Mage is just like that, which isn't just dangerous, it's also stupid, because like Vern, he can never look forward to the next game.

'Colin Mage will stop his enemy on this mountain, and if he can't, he'll get himself killed trying, and Tammy, I ain't got no doubts about that at all! He's got *jihad* wrapped around his aura like a fucking funeral shroud. I ain't saying he's got a death wish, but he's quite happy to die for this cause, and that's the big difference between us. He might be, but for your sake as well as my own, I'm not! Even if these Djinni demons break through here, I sure as hell don't automatically accept that it's the end of the world. Earth is a big old planet, Tammy, and people like me and Mage ain't the only magical heavyweights living on it. There'll be more than one battle, you can rest assured on that, and if we don't win here, we'll win somewhere else. Where there's life there's hope, that's what Aunt Epiphany used to say, and humanity ain't gonna role over on its back with its legs up in the air at the first sight of a few scaly lizards. They might win in the end, but we'll give 'em one hell of a run for their money, not just here in Spain, but all over the world.'

'Are you saying that when the going gets tough, the tough get going?'

'Not exactly, Kiddo, no. Let's say that I intend to help Brother Colin all that I can, because if we can stop this opening gambit then we've won this particular game... But the moment the enemy's bishops and knights come charging into our ranks, gobbling pawns up like plankton and toppling our castles, then *this* king and queen are out of here and we'll live to fight again on another board.'

'Well,' Tamara said frankly and with a sigh of relief, 'all I can say is thank you Lordie for that! This is a pretty little place, but I don't relish the idea of dying here.'

Light was suddenly mindful of a grassy bank filled with the same scent of sex where another conversation that had taken place only yesterday and a thousand years before and had revolved around the fear and thought of death. 'One thing I can promise you,' he said firmly, 'and I promise you this on my own life. You ain't gonna die, not here or anywhere else, not for at least another sixty years! Believe me?'

'Sure,' she said. 'I believe you.'

And then Light held her fiercely and possessively, making a silent promise to himself and his gods. Had Tamara heard it she may have been pleased at the passion of Light's emotions, but she would not have been particularly reassured by the implications of the pledge.

25.

States Of Grace

The following few days were very busy ones. On the Thursday, Light and Tamara had gone to Gibraltar returning with no less than seven CB radio hand sets while Mage had tackled Pepe Ortega about an empty house that belonged to him in Calle Rincon. The building was semi derelict, but had one important thing going for it. The view from the upstairs bedroom looked down the whole length of Calle Sombra and anyone watching from that vantage point could monitor the front of the Dolorean house with ease.

Ortega had been quite amenable to the idea of letting it to Mage on a short term basis, but when the subject of money had been discussed, the old man had shaken his head adamantly. 'No Señor, you will pay me nothing. I am not blind. I can see why this casita may be of use to you and the calm in my belly and the fear in my heart remove the need for payment. Come back tomorrow and at least one room will be clean and tidy for you.'

On the Thursday afternoon Helen had checked out of the hotel and discretely moved her things to Hector's house in Calle Santana, and on Thursday evening Light and Mage had had a long conversation with Christina and Angel. By Friday lunch time the two observers were in place and, true to his word, Pepe Ortega had swept out the upstairs bedroom, providing some basic furniture, including a substantial mattress, which Christina and Angel promptly put to good use. Forty eight hours without sex had done neither of them any harm.

On the Friday evening they'd experimented with the CBs and had designated some appropriate call signs based upon the zodiac; Christina and Angel became respectively Leo One and Leo Two, Helen and Hector became Capricorn One and Capricorn Two, Light and Tamara were Taurus One and Taurus Two which left Mage with the singular designation of Scorpio.

On Saturday both Mage and Helen were interviewed by two senior police detectives from Algerciras, and by that Saturday Jaime Gomez had become a cause célèbre in the village. The story had become significantly embellished and twisted. It was understood that Jaime had first found the woman's dead body and had then, by brilliant police work, deducted who her murderer must be. He'd gone in pursuit of the perpetrator and had shot him dead as he was in the act of trying to commit another murder. Thus, although no one could put their hand on their heart and say that they actually liked their Chief of Police, Jaime nonetheless became a local hero. Everyone said what a good policeman he was and what a good job he was doing and wasn't it fortunate that they should have someone as good as Captain Gomez as their Chief of Police in such troubled times as these! A few months before and Jaime would have basked in the fame and glory, but as it was, knowing what he knew, it bounced off him like so much water off a duck's back.

On the Sunday Hector drove to Ronda, taking with him a letter from Mage to Anna. Although Mage had given it to him in an unsealed envelope, he did not read it... but he did monitor his daughter's reactions as she read it. Either Anna had become very good at hiding her emotions or the letter elicited no emotional reaction. She simply folded the piece of writing paper, tucking it away in her purse, and began to tell him of the work she had been doing with Doctor Oliver. To Hector's eyes, she looked tired and listless; she did not ask when she might return to Castillo and Hector avoided making any mention of the subject. He also refrained from mentioning that Helen Ross had, for the past three nights, been sleeping in her bed.

Anna spent most of Monday reading and re-reading the letter Mage had sent her, wondering what she should do about it. Finally, deciding that when you didn't know what to do it was better if you did nothing, she put the letter away in the bottom of her suitcase and decided to try and forget about it. At least, for the time being.

Also on the Monday, during the afternoon, Mage, Helen and Light inspected the excavation up at the citadel. Someone had removed the planks and tarpaulin and for all the world it was as if no excavation had ever taken place. Digging half a meter beneath the top soil they came upon the unyeilding layer of resin which now stretched in a crescent moon all around the subterranean entrance to the ruin. None of them had picked up any particularly strong psychic vibration other than the unambiguous impression that the doors to the citadel were now irrevocably sealed.

On the Tuesday, one week since Dolorean and Alexandra had arrived in Castillo and Mage had performed his binding ritual, the quintet sat around what had become their usual table in the Miraflores courtyard restaurant and assessed the progress that they'd made.

'All things being equal, I think we have achieved quite a lot over these past few days,' Mage said. 'On the debit side we have made no psychic contact with the Djinn and we have no idea what he's doing, but to our credit, we've built a really strong psychic circle and we've all become very much in tune with each other. We've got Christina and Angel in place in Calle Rincon mounting a twenty four hour surveillance operation, and nothing can move in or out of Calle Sombra without them knowing about it.'

'What about the back entrance?' Hector asked tentatively. 'We got out over the wall, so couldn't they?'

'Yes they could,' Mage readily agreed, 'but the question is why should they when they've got a perfectly good front door? The other thing to remember is that Alexandra is heavily pregnant and if what John told us is right, they're not going to want to risk anything going wrong at this late stage. Getting over that wall was no piece of cake for us and we were scared shitless! I can't see a pregnant woman doing it and again, going by what John has told us and my own instincts, I shouldn't think that Dolorean would be much inclined to leave her on her own if she is so integral to the opening ritual. Frankly, what worries me more is that bloody well!'

'That will worry me till my dying day!' Hector said forcefully.

'I think that your binding ritual has probably worked,' Helen offered tentatively. 'At least up to a point. We seem to have found a breathing space, a state of grace in which to get our act together, which I agree with you, Colin, we've done quite a good job of doing. I think we all thought that things were going to start hitting the fan last week, but unless I'm very wrong, it seems as though everything has quietened down quite a lot over the last couple of days.'

'Helen is right,' Hector confirmed. 'We've gone six whole days without a death or an accident or anything odd occurring. It's almost as though things are getting back to normal at long last.'

'Yeah, well my instincts tell me that this is the lull before the storm,' Light commented, but was hard pressed to develop his theme. 'Don't exactly know why I feel this way, but I guess I do feel it pretty strongly.' He changed tack. 'There are a couple of things which do concern me which we need to talk about. First of all, I cannot believe that after all the time we've sat in circle together we haven't picked up one trace of these peoples' psychic presence. We must be doing something wrong here and maybe need to change our tactics... And the other thing that worries me slightly is the way in which we're all conveniently forgetting that the Djinn are shapechangers. It might be difficult for a pregnant woman to scramble over a high wall, but it'd be a different story if the Djinn chose not to be a pregnant woman but something that could slide over that wall without any great effort at all. Even if we assume that the woman can't change shape because she's pregnant or because she's not a fully fledged Djinn as yet,' Light was aware of the pain in Mage's eyes but carried on regardlessly, 'that still leaves Dolorean himself. We mustn't evaluate his powers by human standards. He could have been wandering around this village for the last week watching our every move, but if he don't look like the guy we know as Dolorean, how are we gonna know any better?'

'That is one very scary and sobering thought,' Mage admitted.

'Good,' Light responded. 'If we're gonna survive in this game we need to be very scared and very sober! Sure, I think we've achieved a helluva lot in a very short time, but for crying out loud, let's not get too complacent or give ourselves too many pats on the back. This war ain't over yet and if you want my opinion, it ain't even started yet. Not properly, anyway. We'll know when it has when the Djinn goes over onto the offensive. That's when the shit's really gonna start hitting the fan.'

'I don't know how important this might be,' Tamara spoke softly. She was the least voluble member of the group but when she did have something to say, she usually had a valid point. '...And ladies and gentlemen, forgive me if this sounds uncharitable, but I guess it's gotto be said. We're relying on Christina and Angel to feed us information from their stake-out, but how much can we rely on them? They're so wrapped up in themselves that I sometimes get the impression that thermo nuclear war could break out without them noticing the bangs or the mushroom clouds.'

'I think they're pretty sound.' Mage looked at Light for confirmation.

'Yeah, I guess so,' Light said, 'but Tammy has a point and it wouldn't be a bad idea to make sure they're on the ball rather than just balling.'

'At least,' Mage grinned wryly, 'it's good to know that the great love affair is still on. This time last week, and I wouldn't have given it a snowball's chance in hell.'

This was an opinion most ardently shared by Angel... An Angel who, despite the severity of the warnings he'd received, was none-the-less delighted by the sudden turn of events that had brought him into such close and legitimate proximity with Christina.

The day after he'd watched Mage and his friends up at the citadel, he'd quietly taken himself out of the village and had gone to Colmenar on the train. He'd rented a room in a cheap pension, spending the evening and most of the following day getting his thoughts and feelings not only about El Moreno but also about Christina into some semblance of order.

Colmenar was a curiosity. Nominally it functioned as the railway stop for the much larger village of Gaucin, but the fact that Gaucin itself was some fifteen kilometres away on the other side of the mountain didn't seem to phase anyone in the slightest. To get to Colmenar by road was an arduous hour's journey from Castillo along narrow switch backs that dipped and dived through dense woodland and jagged mountain peaks, and yet by rail it took barely twenty minutes. The pueblo itself was a ragged collection of adobe houses strung along the railway line; to the south there were rolling acres of tilled and furrowed fields, while to the north and north west forests of tall pine climbed majestically into the mountains.

There were three cafes, one of which was associated with the pension. It was here that he had asked for the room, and the gaunt woman who'd given him the key, taking his money in advance, had shown him to his quarters. It had been a small rectangular box, washed in blue paint, with a single cot and a wash stand. There was no running water and if he needed the lavatory, it was out in the yard. The bar stayed open until midnight and the pension rates did not include breakfast.

He'd nodded his understanding and had been grateful when she'd withdrawn. Being neither thirsty nor hungry, he'd stretched out on the cot, hands behind his head, and had studied the cobwebs that hung around the naked light bulb in the middle of the ceiling. Which problem to deal with first, he'd wondered? Christina or El Moreno? Maybe he couldn't deal with them separately at all, for in his own mind both situations were inextricably intertwined.

He had gone to El Moreno for help. *Give me one night with Christina,* he had begged. *Just one night!* Well, he'd had more than his one night, that was for sure. There had been five nights, five mornings and four afternoons, and he'd learned more about sex in one week than he had done in all the previous years of his young life gone before. He'd not known much to start with, but Christina had been a good teacher and had introduced him to areas of knowledge and pleasure that he had not even known existed, let alone experienced. But herein lay the problem. If she had this knowledge she must have acquired it somewhere and with someone else. How many somewhere's were there? How many someone else's? These thoughts skewered into his belly causing real physical pain, but where had they come from? They had not been there when he'd first met Christina and they had not been there the first two or three times they had made love... They'd insidiously crept up on him over the last few days and were playing havoc with his emotions and screwing up his mind.

He'd reached out, and pulling on the long piece of cord that controlled the light, plunged the room into semi darkness. Night came early in the mountains and the light had long since fled the day, but even so reflections streamed in through the uncurtained window casting strange blue shapes across the ceilings and the walls. Outside in the street, Colmenar was beginning to hum as Colmenatos came out for the evening, strolling along the railway line, hanging around the tabacalera kiosks and filling up the cafes. There had been the sounds of rock and roll music, revving motor cycles, clinking glasses, the roaring gurgle of a coffee machine, laughter from carefree folk who knew nothing of the heartache felt by the woebegone youth who languished in the isolation of the pension's bleak back room. Instinctively, his hand had gone to the talisman that hung around his neck and he'd found himself praying, not knowing whether he was praying to Colin Mage, Jesus Christ, or The Lord God Almighty. *Let it be all right,* he prayed. *Let me have Christina for ever and make this pain in my heart go away!*

The room had remained silent. There had been no sign or indication that his prayer had been heard, and yet he would have been enormously reassured had he been a fly on the wall of the Miraflores court yard, for at that very moment he was the subject of a certain conversation that was destined to bring him closer to Christina in ways that he'd never thought possible.

Later, he'd gone out into the street and had eaten a frugal supper, drinking wine rather than his usual bacardi. He'd received more than one passing glance of interest from more than one pretty girl and, ironically, had been oblivious to the small stir that he was causing among the available female population of Colmenar. He'd not have been interested in them anyway. Dark dewy eyes and coquettish giggles could not compete with the blond vision of brazen sexuality that filled his heart and mind. At one point a group of young men had come and sat at the next table. They'd paid him no heed, but he'd been aware of their presence, their crude language and rough jokes. He'd realised with a sense of shock that to all intents and purposes, he was the same as they were, a village boy of no breeding, caught in a loop of time that offered tradition and frustration from the past and a continuation of the same for the future... Unless he could break the loop. He'd recognised in that one fleeting moment of dawning awareness that he *had* to break the loop! Christina was a successful model, a cosmopolitan American with a tradition of success and sophistication. When she looked at him, what did she see? What *could* she see, other than the ignorant Spanish peasant boy with a big penis and a besotted heart? This, he'd vowed solemnly, was something that would have to change. She could never become a part of his world other than as a dalliance or a passing fancy, so he would have to become a part of hers! He'd had no idea as to how he might bring about this transformation – but El Moreno was sure to know.

This had brought him neatly to the other matter that needed some thought and assessment. He'd watched El Moreno walk through the streets of his village with blue fire dripping from his fingers. He'd seen him enter the Plaza de Santa Clara and raise up a tornado as he exploded with blue fire, blue fire that had swept over everything in his sight. How was it possible for a man to do this? Angel had read his books and understood how a magic spell might have worked to get him inside Christina's knickers. He also understood how it might be possible for El Moreno to have a power inside him that healed sick people and made them well again, now matter how ill they might have been... But to control the wind? To summon up tornados? To be able to create blue fire that went wherever he'd pointed his fingers? No, this had to be something different. No man had that amount of power. Therefore, because Angel knew what he'd seen and there'd been nothing wrong with his eyes, there was only one conclusion that he could come to. It was beautiful in its simplicity but awe inspiring in its implication. Señor Mage, El Moreno was not just a man. He was *more* than a man! Perhaps he was an angel or a god, maybe he was a devil or a superhuman spirit in human form, but as far as Angel Guardiaro was concerned, he was definitely more than just a man... And whoever or whatever El Moreno was, he was Angel's friend. Had he not already proved this by taking away the herpes, by putting money in his pocket, by giving him the talisman that had brought him to Christina?

Angel had slept surprisingly well that night. He'd breakfasted early the following morning and then had spent several hours wandering through the forests that encroached upon Colmenar from the other side of the railway line. The air had been crystal clear spiced with the scent of pine and fresh earth and it had not been difficult for him to formulate his plans. He'd taken a strange delight in talking out loud, for there were only the trees to hear him and he knew that they would keep his secrets.

'First of all, with Christina, I shall apologise for being childish and then I shall become strong and very sensible. I will learn to speak better English and I shall spend less time making love and playing my guitar and make more time for studying and learning. I shall remember that she is more important to me than I am to her, and I shall remember that it is to my advantage if she does not know this... What do you think of that, trees? A good idea, yes?

'Always I keep in mind that one day she will become tired of me and will go back to America. Always I keep in mind that she has had many many lovers...' He'd bitten his lip and had kicked his feet through the thick springy grass as he'd come to grips with that one. '...But always I remember that there are miracles, for El Moreno has shown me miracles, and maybe I have a chance of getting a big miracle, of being Christina's last lover even though I am not her first! In the meantime I shall enjoy fucking her and try to become the best fuck she's ever had, and that way maybe she'll never want to go back to America or, if she does, she won't go there without me. Yes! Yes! Yes!' his triumphant shout was muffled by the verdant branches. 'My brains need some development, I'll admit to it, but there's nothing wrong with my balls. Maybe they will yet become my salvation.'

He'd worked through the first line of trees and had emerged on a craggy buttress of bare rock that gave a panoramic view of the surrounding country. A train, toy-like in the distance, had been straining up the steep incline from Castillo and an eagle had swooped low over his head, glaring at him with a black predatory eye and condemning him for his trespass. He'd sat on the rock, then had stretched out on his back, watching the eagle as it glided upon the currents of air, occasionally soaring as it found an unexpected thermal.

'Now what do I do about El Moreno?' he'd wondered. 'More to the point, what *can* I do about El Moreno, other than to be his friend and to be of service if he needs me. Maybe I should go and talk to him. Maybe I should tell him what I have seen. Maybe he will explain things to me and maybe he won't, but even if he doesn't, at least he will know that his secret is safe with me and that in all things I am his ally.'

He'd thought about this for a good deal longer before his belly started singing lunch time songs and he'd made his way down into Colmenar for a beer and a sandwich. He'd caught the afternoon train back to Castillo and El Moreno himself had come knocking on his door that evening asking if he'd join him for a drink and a chat at the Miraflores.

Angel had been pleased to accept and was even more pleased to discover the reason behind the invitation. He'd sat with Christina listening in rapt attention as El Moreno and El Negro outlined their proposition, and had needed no time to think about his answer for Christina had answered for them both.

'Right on!' she'd exclaimed. 'So *this* is what it's all about! Reverend, Colin, don't you worry about a thing. Angel and me are the guys for the job. When do we start?'

'We'd like to try and get you in place some time tomorrow,' El Moreno had said.

Later that evening Angel and Christina had walked through Castillo on an independent reconnaissance mission. Angel had haltingly apologised for storming out on her and Christina had been dismissive.

'Don't worry about it,' she said lightly. 'I know what you guys are like.'

Angel hadn't known exactly what she'd meant, and maybe it was just as well. Either way, Christina hadn't given him too much time to dwell upon it. As they'd turned the corner from Rincon into Quiros, Christina had pulled him into the concealment of a dimly lit and little used passageway and her arms had gone persuasively around his neck.

'I missed you,' she'd breathed into his ear.

And so now it begins, he'd thought.

They'd made love in the passageway, and again later in her hotel room. On the following day, once they were ensconced in the room overlooking Calle Sombra, they'd made love on the mattress that Pepe Ortega had provided.

'Are we not supposed to be keeping watch on the street?' Angel had said worriedly.

'Sure we are,' Christina had grinned slyly, 'but that only takes one pair of eyes at a time, so *I'll* watch the street and you can watch me.'

She'd kneeled on the mattress facing the window, bending forwards until her chin touched the sheet, her bottom thrust provocatively upwards. She'd eased her skirt up around her waist and Angel had needed no further encouragement. He'd pulled her flimsy briefs to one side and had entered her with ease. *Do not come quickly*, he'd told himself. *You make this last and last and last...* Then struck by the incongruity of the situation he'd burst out laughing.

'We must always do it like this and then we can both watch the street at the same time!'

'Only...if...you've...got...your...eyes...open!' Christina had gasped and panted through the waves of her orgasm.

'My eyes are open wide,' Angel had said in Spanish, and Christina wouldn't have known what he meant even if she'd heard him say it.

For Angel it was a beautiful week. They made love frequently and spontaneously and even when they were not making love, they were either thinking about it or talking about it. Occasionally one would leave the stake-out, but never for long, always returning with something delicious... Hot churros in the morning, cold beers in the afternoon, chocolate at night, which on one occasion they didn't bother eating but smeared over Christina's body that Angel might take carnal delight in licking it all off afterwards. The weather was warm and for most of the time they wore the minimal of clothes, sometimes spending hours on end totally naked. Christina's sexual appetite was as insatiable as Angel's sexual confidence was unassailable. Their biggest and only problem, was sleep. For their surveillance to be effective, one of them had to be awake at all times, thus they fell into a pattern of "watches" – Angel would remain awake during the early hours and sleep solidly during the siesta, while Christina would sleep the better part of the night, maintaining a state of alertness during the long afternoons. On one particular night Christina fell asleep with Angel's penis still deeply embedded within her, and on the following afternoon he awoke from his siesta to find her riding gently upon his erect member with her eyes wide open and staring coolly out of the window. At all times Angel insisted that they speak in English and, by the end of their first week his command of the language had come on leaps and bounds. For a whole week nothing happened, and then on the Friday morning, the pattern broke.

'Leo One to Taurus One, do you read me? Over.'

Light was sitting on the terrace at the Miraflores, enjoying a late breakfast with Tamara and Mage. He immediately put down his coffee cup and lifted the CB handset to his lips.

'Taurus One reading you loud and clear. Over.'

'We've got some action here,' Christina said excitedly. 'Two people have just come out of the front door. One skinny little guy with a pregnant lady. They're ignoring the car and are walking down the street towards us...'

'Okay Leo One, just you keep your heads down and make Goddam sure you ain't seen. You got that? Over.'

'Loud and clear and understood.'

Mage was already on his feet. 'Looks like our state of grace is suddenly over,' he said grimly. 'I'll cut up through the back alleys and stake out the main street, so why don't you and Tammy take the other direction and check out the square. It's market day, so the whole place will be heathing and seething, but if you hang around Jacinto's bar, they'll not get past you without you knowing about it. They shouldn't be too difficult to spot.'

'Okay, get going man. We'll buzz Helen and Hector and let 'em know something's coming down. Keep your channel open.'

While Mage rushed up Consuelo, Light and Tamara moved with rather less urgently down towards the Plaza de Constitucion. As Mage had said, it was market day and the square was covered in stalls, some selling flowers, others fruits and vegetables, while still more had racks and rows of clothes, everything from denim jeans to the formal black and grey pin stripe of Spanish country tradition. One stall displayed two dozen different varieties of olive, while upon another there were alarm clocks and inexpensive watches amid cheap and trashy transistor radios. Nestled next to the white walls of the Bar El Paseo there were cages of livestock, chickens and cockerels, wood pigeons and rabbits. Many of the stalls had candy stripes awnings and the whole vista was one of vibrant colour and movement. The Friday markets were popular. Not only did they present one with the opportunity to buy things a little more cheaply, they gave one the chance to see and be seen. Market days were excuses for wearing new skirts or new hats, for meeting people whom one wouldn't see from one week to the next, for exchanging gossip and catching up on a thousand and one minor scandals. Perhaps this particular Friday market was exceptionally busy. The weather was good, the long winter and erratic spring had passed to make way for early summer. Perhaps now, some of Castillo's past problems and tragedies could be forgotten about.

Light and Tamara took up position in the window of Jacinto's bar. They did not have to wait long before their "targets" came into view. A pregnant woman with a skinny angular man... no, they were not difficult to recognise. As they moved past the window, Light moved to follow them.

'Tam, you stay here. Watch out for Colin and the cavalry. If our targets move back up the hill, you'll see 'em from here. Don't try following 'em yourself, just give me a squawk on the box, okay?'

With that he moved out into the crowd, following Dolorean and Alexandra at a discreet distance. Normally he would have stuck out like a sore thumb, but there was a contingent of at least half a dozen Moroccan Africans touting their wares within the market place. He couldn't exactly lose himself among their number, for they were far too few, but at least they created a situation whereby he was not the only black man in the square, and thus they afforded him some degree of cover.

Dolorean and Alexandra cut an erratic path from stall to stall. People moved out of their way with smiles and murmurs of approval, for a pregnant woman in Southern Andalucia carries with her an aura of mystique that commands respect not found anywhere else in the civilised world. Dolorean smiled effusively, nodding here and there with a few murmured words *muchos gracias* and *buenas dias* while Alexandra's smile, Light noted, was firmly and inflexibly frozen to her face. Yes, she nodded her head in imitation of her companion's gestures, but the face itself was devoid of all animation.

Light realised that he was looking for something odd, and therefore it was inevitable that he should find it. What he found even more odd was that the other people milling around in the market saw nothing wrong or remiss about the strange couple that wandered in their midst.

After some ten or fifteen minutes of browsing, they went and sat at a table outside the Bar El Paseo. A generous green and white awning protected them from the brilliance of the sunshine and the black American was able to watch them from the corner of the olive stall without having to squint against the light. While it was not the most perfect place from which to see without being seen, he'd picked up a few tips of the surveillance trade over the years and was able to put such skills as he had to good use. He bought three different kinds of olive and struck up an amicable conversation with the stall holder, keeping Dolorean in constant view out of the corner of his eye.

Note: he's drinking - looks like water - but she ain't. He's doing the talking, even if it's only to the waiter, but she ain't saying a word. He looks okay... At least he looks like a human being... But there's something really weird about her... Like she's some kind of life sized doll and he's pulling the strings. Okay, wise ass, what do you do now?

The last thing that John Light had been looking for was any kind of direct contact or confrontation, but he was an impulsive man and if it felt right and the signs were good, he believed in following his instincts. Two people at the next table got up to go just as the camarero was emerging from the entrance to the bar. Light fixed his own evangelist's smile firmly in place and danced up the steps to the table that had suddenly been vacated.

'Hey, bring me a long cold beer would you?' he called to the waiter, and then turned the full force of his smile towards Alexandra Mage. 'Phew, sure is a hot day lady. Guess you're gonna feel it more than me in your condition and I sure do bet you're glad of the shade. By the way,' he let the Louisiana charm ooze out of every pore as he stuck out his hand. 'Mah name is John Light. The Reverend John Light, an' ah sure am glad to make your acquaintance!'

What happened next was extremely educational.

It had been a difficult ten days for the Shapechanger. On the Tuesday of the binding ritual the female had become critically unstable and he'd had to fight all night to preserve the Newlife that struggled within her. His attention had been so wrapped up in this quest that he was not even aware of the fact that there had *been* a binding ritual. It had only become obvious when he'd tried to leave the house the following afternoon. He'd not reached the end of Calle Sombra before the nausea had hit him accompanied by dazzling blue light motes that danced before his eyes, denying him vision and confusing his sense of balance.

He had retreated the few yards back to the house and waited until the evening before he'd tried again. This time he'd gone out through the garden, clambering over the high wall, and dropping into the narrow alleyway. Both the garden and the alley had been clear, but the moment he'd tried to make an exit from either end of the narrow cobbled passage, it had been like pushing through thick cloying waves of life draining magma. Again the shards of iridescent blue light, hovering like a thousand miniature stars against the retinas of his eyes, forced him back over the wall into the sanctuary of the garden.

He'd changed shape, sacrificing the constraints of his human form in favour of the unmetabolical entity of mist – had glided over the wall and had edged tentatively towards the end of the passage to be met with an icy blast of freezing wind which was very nearly his undoing. Retreating in a sense of rising panic, he'd reverted to his human shape, realising just how close he had come to being destroyed, for although gifted with the ability to change shape, the mass and volume of shape had always to remain constant and had that psychic wind dissipated any of the mass of his mistform, he would have been hard pressed to compensate for its loss in the other forms available to him.

In the early hours of Thursday morning he tried for a third time to break free of the binding and on this occasion did meet with some limited success, being able to break the bonds that bound him within the house. But to do it, he'd had to play a dangerous game, metamorphosing into the state of pure Djinn in the warrior form. He was well aware of his vulnerability, for if he was seen he must kill, and in killing would inevitably draw unwanted attention upon himself. It was also in those early Thursday hours that he realised the extent of the binding; it wasn't just Sombra and Santa Clara that had been charged with binding energy, but indeed the whole village. Castillo was latticed with magical lay lines of restriction. To cut through them in his warrior form would take many hours in which the chances of exposure and discovery would become increasingly inevitable.

Thus, during the daylight hours of Thursday he entered his own meditative state of grace in search of a solution to his problem. It was now apparent that there had been a most serious miscalculation. The forces arraigned against him were far more powerful than he would have believed possible. He could no longer write the manmate magician off as a minor nuisance – indeed, he was emerging as a formidable adversary. Undoubtedly he was getting help from somewhere and the help had to be effective magical help, not just the good will and support of the local peasantry.

The Djinn found itself experiencing a crisis in energy management. Much of it's mental powers were constantly dedicated to maintenance of the incubator's stability and, after the earlier crisis, it could not afford to let its guard drop for a minute... At the same time, changing form and maintaining any form that was not its own natural state, was also a significant drain on its reserves. Certainly, in its warrior form it could sever the binding, but that would mean withdrawing some of the energy needed to stabilise the female and he doubted the Newlife's ability to survive in those circumstances. All of his training and preparation had instilled within him the importance of protecting the Newlife at all costs, and so another method of release would have to be found.

In the last hours of darkness before the dawn of Friday, the Shapechanger took a calculated risk and, assuming the mistform, descended through the well into the labyrinth of tunnels and natural caverns that riddled the earth beneath Castillo. Here, in these dark and airless spaces, the manmate's magic was ineffectual and following its innate homing instincts the Shapechanger flowed rapidly through the subterranean fissures until finally it came to a perpendicular shaft. Moving up the shaft and recognising that there might be some subsequent difficulty when it came to moving the female to this place, the Shapechanger emerged at the well head within the dungeons of the Moorish citadel, immediately aware of familiar spore. No Djinn had ventured here in the flesh, but the place was redolent with Djinn magic and for the first time in many hours he experienced a sense of safety and relief. He had not been forsaken by his brethren. They may not have been able to communicate with him or he with them other than in spirit, but here in this sacred place, the most holy ground in two worlds, he felt that spirit most strongly. The magic of the Worldshapers crossed between the dimensions of the Great Divide and he was mindful of the enormous effort and energy that it had taken, not only to get him here but to sustain during his time within this world.

Being here on this earthly side of the divide, he had clear imagery of all the preparations that would be taking place on the other side of the opening that very moment in his own world.

The Worldshapers and the Shamans would be in deep mystical trance, constantly monitoring the energies filtering through from the Earthworld, countering any malignancy or intrusion by their own powers of High Magic. Behind them the Clanfathers would be marshalling the regiments of warriors in preparation for the transition and initial assault. It did not matter that the opening could only channel a single Djinn at a time – the transition took no more than a second and once the opening was open it could never be closed!

Deliberately changing to his naked Djinn form, the Shapechanger stood at the edge of the well, inhaling the pungent aroma of its own kind. Directing a prayer down towards the stagnant waters many feet below and beyond these waters directly into the monitoring minds of the Shamans and Worldshapers it had no way of knowing whether the prayer would be heard – but the same is true of all creeds and cultures and it took simple strength and comfort from being able to articulate the invocation in its own tongue, thus strengthening the mental images he was projecting. One prayer shouted was worth three prayers whispered, providing the supplicant's heart was true and his motives pure.

To human ears the sounds emitting from the shapechanger would have been a series of staccato barks and long squeels, to the Djinn, however, it was sheer poetry.

"Supreme Clanfather, sire of our race, hear the words of your most dedicated warrior. In this dark hour. I am alone and our enemies are gathered round me. Fill my blood with the heat of my forefathers' courage! Fill my eyes with spume from The Sea Of Visions! Strengthen my arms that they may bear the weight of The Marak Mountains! Uncoil The Serpent Of War within my soul! Take away my fear and fill my ears with wisdom. Take away my fear and sharpen fine my tusks for battle. Take away my fear and fill my being with your presence and approval that I may not fail you in my chosen duty. I am born within The Brethren and I am The Seed of Djinn!"

After some further minutes of contemplation he started back on his journey, deliberately doing so in his human form. It was not that he sought to make things any more difficult for himself than he needed to, but when the time came to move the female he knew he could not do so in the mistform. Therefore this was necessary practice. It made the journey three times longer and he fretted for the welfare of the incubator, but arriving back at Calle Sombra, he found everything as he had left it and was able to relax in preparation for the magical rituals that had now become imperative for his continuing survival.

The Shapechanger spent several critical hours with the female. It served him well to keep her in a comatose state, but he was well aware that long before the birthing he would have to re-animate her. This in itself would make inroads upon his energy levels and there would be even greater cost in the maintenance of her human form, and yet it had to be done for did not the ritual demand that "a female of The World Of Man shall deliver Newlife born of the seed of Djinn through the very veil of The Great Divide"? Thus, when he led her to the place of the birthing she must arrive at the opening as an Earth born female. At least in appearance. It mattered not that she had been altered both physiologically and psychologically beyond the realms of human understanding – that Djinn blood now pulsed through her human veins and that many of her internal organs had been restructured to enable the Newlife to live and feed within her. Once the Newlife left the incubator within her belly she would become redundant. He could release his hold. The body would degenerate rapidly, and as for the mind, that had already departed many months before

He wondered about the much vaunted human spirit. Had that also gone, chasing after the mind to the sanctuary of the human death state, or did it linger, unable to depart until the life spark – that life spark that he alone had created and was responsible for – was allowed to fail when he no longer had use for her body? He had frequently looked for the evidence of that spirit, but had never found it. The occasional crises which had de-stabilised her were not caused by a rebellious spirit but by human tissues striving to reject the Djinnform that clamoured for life of its own within her.

Uplifted by his foray to the citadel and reassured by the condition of the female, he allowed his mind to spiral down into deep trance. He would be instantly alerted if anything untoward occurred, either on a physical or psychic level, but short of any such emergency, he was now able to explore the essence of his inner spiritual being and in so doing knew he would find the solutions to the problems which beset him.

He longed to be able to communicate with his Brethren. There was so much he had to tell them, so much that he had learned! In some ways the information he carried was almost as important as the opening itself and even if the ritual should fail, it was imperative that his Clanfather should know what he himself had come to know. In any future attempt made to penetrate the veil it was essential that not one but two shapechangers should cross the divide, one to incubate the female and the other to be responsible for offensive and defensive measures as well as all the practical matters such as concealment and transport. He knew that this was impossible, but a way would have to be found. The sum total of these many responsibilities was too much for one warrior to bear alone.

He realised, quite clinically, that for the first time throughout this whole operation he was actually considering the possibility of failure. He did not like this, but appraised it realistically. The intelligence gathered by years of research and study was painfully not infallible. There should not have been any opposition from the manmate. There should have been no disruption of his carefully chosen circle of disciples. He should not now be having to work against what was obviously a most powerful binding, bound in place by a human mind bequeathed with energies that would have made a Worldshaper sit up and take notice!

But he would not fail. He had come too far. If a mind had woven the braids of the binding then it had been a human mind. Now another mind, *his* mind, a Djinn mind, would unravel those braids, one by one, knot by knot, street by street, until the binding was undone. It may take some hours, it may even take days, but working from the state of deep trance where there was no threat of discovery or intrusion, he methodically went about the business of destroying the manmate's magic. By the nature of his race the Djinn was not an emotional creature. True, duels were frequently fought for the sake of honour or to settle disputes, but the notion of blood feuds for the sake of personal revenge, while not totally absent from Djinn lore, were none-the-less relatively rare. Even so, as the Shapechanger went about the business of wrecking the manmate's binding, he vowed to himself that it was a precursor to the destruction of the man himself. One way or another the magician would die. He would eat the manmate's beating heart and make sure the manmate lived just long enough to watch him do it!

Four days later the binding was undone and now it was time to initiate another process. He began the arduous business of reforming the female from the glutinous mass that had become her natural state in these latter days of incubation to something that would be acceptable and normal to other human eyes. He deeply wished that these adherences to the ritual could be passed over. But the Shamans had been adamant. They needed to be carried out to the letter: *"And at the beginning of the time before the Newlife is come full term, the female shall be shown to her own people that they might praise and approve her. And in this doing Man's blessing shall fall upon the Djinnseed. Thus when the Djinn shall come again to the World of Man it shall be by invitation born of the blessing."*

He knew that this was to be a test of his powers of perception and control, but he was rested and strengthened and looked forwards to the challenge. He also knew that instead of friends that should have been there to offer him a measure of protection, there were instead enemies...The manmate, the witch, the bumbling doctor and whoever else the manmate had been able to recruit. But now it was time to take the fight to them, to unnerve them, to worry them, to make them aware of the puny inefficiency of their magics when compared to the higher magic of the Djinn. It was also time to effect that part of the ritual that brought praise and approval.

It came in reassuring waves of abundance. Old men nodded knowingly. Young boys winked and pointed. Teenage girls giggled in admiration. Mothers with their own children smiled approvingly... *Muy Bien, Señor y Señora. Muy Bien, muy Bien!* More mature matrons positively beamed. *Felicitaciones!* one called. *Ah, bien echo, bien echo* whispered another, tentatively patting the female's swollen stomach. *Cuantas semanas ma? Cinco? Oh mucho suerte Señora, mucho suerte.* Old grandmothers, long since barren themselves, patted their own shapeless bellies and cackled in delight. *She's big* said one. *Twins!* chortled a second. *Triplets!* exclaimed a third. *Welcome to our village* one stall holder called cheerfully. *I'm here every Friday and I've got the best fruit in town!* Hands, sometimes just finger tips, belonging to both the young and the old, lightly brushed against the female as she passed them by, almost as if by making this most elusive of contacts, they might be invested with some of the fertility magic blooming and blossoming within her. *One for me!* murmured a skinny woman with sagging breasts. *May my crops grow tall* a short man muttered.

He'd sensed the manmate's presence, of course, but more so on the high street rather than here in the swirling bustle of the market. Inevitably they were being watched, but he didn't worry about it too much. It was to be expected. In any case, that was what they were here for... in part. Perhaps now it might be advantageous to do some watching and for this purpose, he led the female by the arm and sat her at the cafe table outside the Bar El Paseo. He ordered mineral water and settled down to watch the crowds.

From his vantage point at the corner of the square Mage watched, aghast, as Light moved from the olive stall to sit next to Alexandra and Dolorean. His horror increased as Light leaned across the division between the tables and engaged Alexandra in conversation. He bowed his head to kiss her fingers, then he was stretching over in front of her to shake Dolorean's hand.

'What's the crazy bastard playing at?' he cursed, taking a tentative step forwards.

Tamara's restraining hand fell lightly upon his arm. 'Take it easy Colin. The Man knows what he's doing.'

'For Christ's sake, I hope so,' Mage retorted from between clenched teeth. 'He's leaving himself wide open.'

'No,' Tamara said wisely, 'he ain't doin' that, believe me. Let's just wait a while an' see how this comes down.'

Light sat chatting for fully five minutes before getting up from his table. Again he shook Dolorean's hand and again he lifted Alexandra's fingers to his lips before turning and walking away from them, sauntering through the busy market in the general direction of the Miraflores. A few seconds later Dolorean and Alexandra got up to leave, heading in the opposite direction and moving towards the taxi rank and the start of Calle Principal.

'Tammy, you go left. Find John and tell him to meet me back at the hotel. I'll be there in a few minutes... or however long it takes.'

'Okay. What are you going to do?'

'I'll know that when I've done it!'

Keeping half an eye on Alexandra, Mage walked briskly around the perimeter of the square, arriving at the taxi rank a few paces behind Dolorean. While Dolorean and Alexandra carried on slowly up the hill towards the ayuntamiento, Mage cut right into Calle Roma and pounded up the street as fast as he could go, cutting left again through a side alley where Roma forked into Santana and Llanette, to emerge panting and out of breath a good hundred yards ahead of the advancing couple. Regaining his breath and composure, he held his ground until they drew level. *If Light can do it, then so can I,* he thought.

Ignoring Dolorean he locked eyes with Alexandra. He was blocking their pathway and the road was busy with market traffic. They had no choice other than to stop.

'Good morning, Alex!' he said firmly.

'Good morning,' she answered politely in a voice that was a travesty of what once had been her own. She did not avoid his penetrating gaze – he saw that she saw him, was studying him, but he failed to find one single spark of recognition in her eyes. Instead there was a vacant stare of distracted indifference that seemed to say who are you? What do you want? Why are you standing in my way?

'Alexandra! It's me! Colin! For God's sake, Alex, talk to me!'

'I'm most terribly sorry,' Alexandra said in that same polite voice, eyes never blinking, smile never shifting, 'but I don't know who you are and I don't know anybody called Colin.'

Shaking with barely suppressed rage, Mage turned on Jadoc Dolorean – Dolorean who was smiling at him triumphantly, not bothering to conceal his elation. This had been the female's hardest test and she'd passed with flying colours.

'You bastard!' Mage spat, his voice dripping with loathing and contempt.

Dolorean laughed, and it seemed that there was genuine humour in his voice. 'Leave,' he said good naturedly. 'Leave while you can. She's mine now. You have lost.'

'I'm not going anywhere, Shapechanger!' Mage snarled in his face, taking a certain pleasure in seeing Dolorean's eyes flicker in reaction. 'Oh yes, Mr Jadoc Dolorean, I know all about Shapechangers, all about The Djinn, all about your opening! I know all about *you!* I know who you are, I know *what* you are, I know where you've come from and I know why you're here. I also know why Alexandra is so important to you and I know that before long you expect to see cohorts of your brethren charging through this village, but believe me, you fucking son of a lizard, that isn't going to happen!'

'I promise you it is!' Dolorean hissed through compressed lips.

'Over my dead body!'

'Then I assure you it *will* be over your dead body!' Dolorean's eyes began to flicker with amber light, the irises becoming fluid in indeterminate movement.

'Great!' Mage laughed tauntingly taking one step backwards. 'Take a look around you, Pigface. You've got an audience! I'm sure they'd love to see you strut your stuff. C'mon Dolorean, show them something to remember you by! Give 'em a tusk, show 'em a snout, flash them a talon! Maybe you could blow 'em a kiss?'

The Shapechanger cast an eye around him and sure enough this public altercation had attracted an audience of at least a dozen shoppers on their way down the hill towards the market. They stood in bemused and amused little groups watching this crude display of extranjero temperament, wondering how this unexpected cabaret might end. Who would hit who first... And what of the poor pregnant woman who stood watching these ill-mannered proceedings with such an angelic and patient smile upon her tired face? It was, of course, totally disgraceful... but at the same time, quite wonderfully entertaining!

Dolorean's eyes returned to their normal state and Mage pushed a quivering finger under his nose. 'You've been trying to kill me for months,' he sneered. 'You've done a damn fine job on Alexandra, and don't worry, you'll have plenty more chances with me, because wherever you turn, you'll find me waiting for you. Wherever you go, I'll be there first. Whenever you dream, leave a part of yourself on guard because I'll be listening in, whenever you sleep, keep your door bolted because I'll be just outside! I know *what* your opening is, I know *where* it's supposed to take place, I know *when* and I know *why*! But like I say, you'll have to kill me first before it happens and whenever you feel like trying, just remember I'll be waiting for you and I'll be ready for you. You've got to kill me, Dolorean, because if you don't, it'll be me that serves your head on a Djinn war shield at your Clanfather's supper and, if I have my way, it'll be long before mid-summer's eve!'

Mage turned on his heel and strode down the hill towards the market place, not once glancing behind him, and not caring about what the consequences of the confrontation might yet be. Certainly, he'd shown his hand... Had alerted the Shapechanger to the extent of his information. That might have been a stupid move to have made, no matter how good he felt about it in that moment, but also it might yet work for him if the extent of his knowledge was enough to rattle or provoke the Shapechanger into doing something over-reactive or impulsive of his own.

'It was ill-advised, Colin,' Light said moodily a little while later, in a quiet corner of the Miraflores terrace.

'What was ill-advised? Me tackling them in the street, or you going over and talking to them in the market?'

'Colin, when I went and sat down at that table outside the bar, I knew *exactly* what I was doing. Can you say the same for your actions?'

Mage lit a cigarette. It was a reflexive and defensive action, which gave him a few seconds in which to think. 'No,' he said shortly. 'I was playing it by ear. Going where the energy took me. I probably wouldn't have done it if I hadn't seen you pull your stunt in the market place... Hey, look John, I'm not passing the buck or making excuses. I'm just trying to explain how it happened.'

'Okay. Don't know how much good you've done, or how much harm either. At least it might hurry things along a bit. If our Wicked Genie thinks he's under some threat it might make him make a mistake, but man, you're sure gonna have to be very much more on your guard from now on.'

'Well, if I'm his number one target, at least it'll take some of the heat off you.'

'Colin, there wasn't and isn't any heat on me.'

'What happened in the market place,' Mage asked, needing to know, but also needing to redirect the way this conversation was going.

'That was *very* interesting,' Light laughed. 'Strike one high score for evangelists and niggers!' He was smiling, but it was a hard humourless smile. 'I thought I'd get some "hands on" experience. I'm the only one of us, apart from Tammy, who hasn't met this guy so I figured it was about time that I did. I kept my mind full of nice bright pictures of prayer meetings and TV cameras so if either of 'em did get inside my head, that's all they were going to see. The Reverend John Light in all his glory! Everything else I kept well hidden and compartmentalised. They weren't going to catch me off guard like you did in LA.

'...And anyhow, I just went over and said hello...'

Alexandra had looked deliberately at Dolorean before allowing Light to take her hand. 'I'm Alex Dolorean,' she had said politely, 'and this is my husband Jack. We're very pleased to meet you.'

The words had sounded stilted and hollow to Light's ears and her hand had felt cold and clammy. As he'd raised her fingers to his lips he'd detected an odd smell. Subtle and certainly not heavy, it had been elusively familiar but not particularly attractive. He'd tried the gentlest of psychic probes, but had found nothing. There had been no etheric emanation at all whatsoever, which was extremely disturbing for every living thing carried its own vibration and an expectant mother in the latter stages of her pregnancy had her own – or *should* have had her own – highly amplified charge of protective energy. Furthermore, while not every expectant mother enjoyed a state of gently blooming spirituality, it was common among many. And yet, this energy, this spiritual aura that should have made eyes shine with inner knowledge and skin glow with burgeoning fecundity, had been highly noticeable by its absence in the woman seated next to him.

He'd turned his extrovert attention towards the man. 'Delighted to meet you sir,' he'd drawled, pumping Dolorean's hand enthusiastically and welcoming him into the inner visions of TV parties, press conferences, gospel songs and rousing hallelujahs. Dolorean's hand had been dry and warm and it had also been uncommonly hard, the hardness a contradictory reflection of the man himself who was slim to the point of being frail, a weak, wimpish figure, rendered almost comical by the receding line of spiked and tufty hair. There had been nothing comical about the man's eyes, however. They'd been dark and beady, coldly glittering like that of a raven or some other bird of prey.

'Reverend Light,' Dolorean's voice had been high in timber and silkily smooth. 'May I ask what brings you to this part of Spain? Forgive me for being curious but Castillo is a little off the usual tourist trail.'

'Lookin' all over this beautiful country,' Light had ad-libbed expansively. 'Partly it's a sabbatical. Ah tell you sir, the pressures back in The States have been quite phenomenal this last year or so! Ah guess it's also what you might call a kind of reconnaissance mission. Ah been thinkin' about openin' a chapter of mah church here in Europe, an' where better than right here in Southern Andalucia! The weather is just fine and ah sense that the soil might be rich with potential converts.'

'I do hope you will not be seeking to convert either myself or my wife to your faith,' Dolorean had said in an amused tone. 'I assure you that neither of us would be at all interested, I'm afraid.'

'Lord no!' Light had exclaimed. 'As ah say, this is just a look around trip, but ah saw you guys sittin' here an' figured that as you didn't look Spanish, you might be American or English, so ah just kinda moseyed over to say hi...' He'd switched his attention back to Alexandra. '...And to offer mah good wishes an' congratulations! Tell me, Ma'am, when is the happy even due?'

There had been a short but significant pause before Alexandra had answered. 'Another few weeks yet, Reverend.'

'An' you gonna be here for the duration?'

'Of course,' Dolorean had answered. 'We have a house here. We live here. But why do you ask?' A sharp edge had crept into his voice.

'Just naturally inquisitive, ah guess,' Light had allowed a sly smile to creep across his face. 'These are always tense an' worrisome days for parents, so if you find you've got some spare time between now an' the baby comin' Ah do happen to have with me some wonderful religious tracts that make for some very interesting reading, oh yes siree, even though ah do say so mahself, some *very* interesting reading. Ah would be more than happy to give you...'

Dolorean had laughed. 'I'm sorry Reverend, but you're wasting your time.'

Light had rolled his eyes. 'Bringin' the Word of The Lord to the ears of man is never a waste of time,' he'd said devoutly, noticing that his deep South Louisiana accent was slipping slightly into East Texas. 'But ah surely have no desire to impose mahself upon your company, so shall bid you good day – an' it's been a real pleasure talking with you folks.'

He'd shaken Dolorean's hand again, still hot and curiously hard, and again had lifted Alexandra's fingers to his lips – and again there'd been that peculiar scent of something muskily unpleasant – and finally he'd walked away, considerably wiser than he'd been before.

'Well,' Mage asked in agitation, 'what do you make of it all?'

'I've been thinking about it and, yeah, I guess you could say I've come to a couple of conclusions. First of all, he didn't rumble me... never got through my defence net. But I figure that one of the main reasons for that was because he was expending an awful lot of energy on Alexandra. Man, I know you're not going to like this, but she simply wasn't there! The lights were on, running off Dolorean's batteries, but there was no one at home. Frankly, she was just like a zombie, and I don't mean that allegorically, but literally.' He threw Mage a sideways glance. 'You know anything about zombies, Colin?'

'Not really,' Mage admitted uneasily. 'My interests and research have taken me in other directions.'

'Yeah, well I guess that's understandable. For what it's worth, because it's closer to my own back ground and culture, I know quite a lot and believe me, man, zombies are for real. Forget the bullshit you see on the movies. There ain't no resurrection of the dead or anything like that, but on some of the Caribbean islands, not just Haiti but throughout the archipelago and also in the deep South, places like Louisiana and the Delta, and increasingly in Florida, the cult of voodoo is alive an' kickin' and getting stronger every year. Zombies have always been a part of the scene.

'It's all a question of mind control. The high priests and master magicians – they're called Barons, by the way – need to control their followers and fear is as good a way as any. So they make a zombie out of someone which not only strikes fear in the hearts of the faithful, but also creates a tangible manifestation of their power. The way they do it is to find some unsuspecting dupe, hypnotise them into a deep, and I do mean a really deep hypnotic trance that takes them down into a state of catatonia and the Baron takes total control of their mind. He says sit and the zombie sits, he says walk talk and shit and the zombie walks talks and shits. He even says kill and the zombie will kill. The longer he's under the deeper he goes and the deeper he goes the more power the Baron has over him. The more power the Baron has over him the more difficult it is – hey, what am I saying? It isn't *difficult*, it's down right fuckin' impossible for the poor bastard to break free from the Baron's hold.'

'What happens,' Mage asked carefully, 'if the Baron deliberately relinquishes his hold over the zombie?'

'It's not a good scenario,' Light retorted flatly. 'In some cases the zombie will remember what's happened and go totally ape shit... Freak out like the proverbial mad hatter which usually leads to suicide or complete mental collapse, sometimes even to execution if the Baron feels threatened in anyway. But more often than not, the brain cells have become irreparably damaged or he's become so psychologically dependent on the controlling mind that he just sits there like a vegetable for a week or so and dies of natural causes like starvation or dehydration. After the Baron's had him, he can no longer think for himself and all the instincts have gone. Man, he doesn't even know that he's hungry or thirsty let alone what his name might once have been or what time of day it might be.'

'And you think that Alexandra is playing zombie to Dolorean's Baron?'

'I'm pretty sure of it Colin, yeah. She didn't say anything or do anything without clearing it with Dolorean first. I'd ask her something and there was a time lapse of half a second or so before she answered or responded. Her smile never wavered, her voice never altered in pitch and I swear to you there wasn't a single sparkle of life in her eyes. If he's had her for, what, nine months? Ten months? Then she is really gone down very deep – and Colin, whatever happens, no matter what we might be able to try and do, I just don't think she's ever coming back from where she's at. I tell you, man, that the lady I was talking to might have had a body, but the mind inside her mind was Dolorean's and wherever souls go to when they depart this world, well I guess that where her soul is right now, and I get the distinct feeling that it's probably been there for quite a while.'

'You're probably right,' Mage responded in a tight and neutral tone.

'Figure I am Colin, but I also think that there is more to this than the voodoo bit.' He told Mage in greater depth and detail about the lack of aura and absence of etheric or spiritual presence, and also about the odd smell that he had detected when bringing Alexandra's hand up to his face. 'Damnedest thing. It's so familiar, but I just can't get it to click in my brain, maybe because it's so totally out of context.'

'It wouldn't have been anything like what we got a whiff of the other day up at the excavation, would it? You know, that kind of old seaweedy smell?'

Light shook his head. 'No, negative, nothing like that. More like, well look, I know this sounds crazy, but more like moth balls!'

They were sitting at a small table set back in a shaded alcove and surrounded by tall plants. They had the terrace to themselves, as most of the people who might have been there on a sunny Friday morning in May were still caught up in the social whirl of the market. Mage looked at Light shrewdly and stubbed out his cigarette.

'John, will you let me come inside for a moment and see if I can fish it out of your subconscious?'

Light looked uneasy, but still he nodded. 'Sure. If you think you can do it.'

'Oh certainly I can do it all right.' Mage murmured confidently, 'but not without asking you first.'

'Okay, go ahead then. Want me to do anything?'

'Just shut your eyes and remember holding Alexandra's hand.'

So Light closed his eyes and Mage slipped in and out of his mind. It was over in less than three seconds. It might have taken longer had he not had Elsie Maud to guide him.

'Violets,' he said.

'Violets?' Light echoed. 'No, not really. I don't...'

'Violets,' Mage insisted '...old violets, and the moth balls you spoke of. Disinfectant and dirt and decay. That fusty old smell you get sometimes from very elderly people who don't always look after themselves properly... This ringing any bells with you, John?'

'Damn right!' Light exclaimed exultantly. 'It's the smell of old age!'

'And this was the smell you picked up from Alexandra?'

'Yeah...' Light's exultancy faded and he became introspective, '...but it's totally illogical.'

'Not really,' Mage said tersely. 'Our olfactory psychic senses are some of the strongest that we have, but like many of the clairvoyant impressions we receive, we have to break the psychic code to get to the true meaning of what we're seeing or hearing, or in this case smelling. What you picked up was the smell of corruption and death.'

'I'll go along with that, but whose death exactly?'

'Alexandra's, of course,' Mage's voice was bleak. 'I think you're right when you say her mind has gone so far away that it can never come back. Michael Fry obviously knew more than he was saying all those months ago when he told me to regard Alexandra as being dead... although I didn't appreciate it at the time. I think Alexandra's been dead for quite a long time now. There was still something, just something of her still fighting for life that last time I tried to get close to her on top of Glastonbury Tor, but whatever that was, it's long gone I'm afraid. So, when I kill her, I'll be killing a corpse.'

Light was silent as he digested Mage's words. 'If it's got to be done, it's got to be done,' he said very softly. 'And I guess I know why you've got to do it. Her mind and her will have gone, that's for sure, but we can't be so certain about her soul. If there's just the remotest chance that her soul is still trapped in her body, man, it's got to be released.'

'I know. I've always known, and when the time comes, I'll release it and take the consequences.'

'You do what you've got to do, but let me worry about the consequences. I'm pretty good at that kind of shit, and who knows, maybe that's one of the karmic reasons for me being here. In the meantime, what next?'

Mage smiled thinly. 'Carry on playing our waiting game, I suppose, but after this morning, we'd better prepare ourselves for some form of incoming psychic attack. Now that he knows the extent of my knowledge I can't see Dolorean sitting up in Calle Sombra just twiddling his thumbs, can you?'

'No,' Light grinned ruefully, 'I guess I can't. You got any idea what he might throw at us?'

'None at all, but one thing's for sure, it won't be very nice.'

26.

Reinforcements

Leon stared beyond the bowed head of his unhappy companion, gazing out of the restaurant window at the twinkling late night lights of Hayarkon Street. Tel Aviv was a busy city at the best of times, but on a Friday it positively throbbed with youth and vitality. The restaurant was full and raucous with its late evening clientele and Leon was troubled, not only by the atmosphere within the bistro, but also by the tense and moody atmosphere that hung above their table like a shroud. It had, Leon realised, been a mistake to come out. If they'd stayed at the apartment they could at least have had their argument in peace. And then he remembered that the only reason he'd suggested that they should dine out had been as a tactic to avoid the full-scale fight that had been festering all afternoon ever since he'd arrived from Jerusalem.

Dov had been pleased to see him, but less pleased to learn that the stay was to be such a short one. He'd been horrified to hear that Leon intended to leave for Madrid on Sunday morning! He'd made the inevitable protests, had delivered all the logical arguments, but Leon had been tactfully intransigent and what should have been a joyful reunion soon became an area of resentment and conflict. In the end, Leon's patience had worn thin. He'd reminded Dov of his position with Mossad and had pointed out that an order was an order and if his superiors had to sends him to Spain for a few weeks, then he was in no position to refuse.

While this was essentially the truth, he thought it best that Dov should not know why he was going to Spain or indeed that it had been he himself who had petitioned Gideon Lemski to let him go.

At first Lemski had been reluctant, but Leon had been persuasive and in the end the DG had capitulated, but not without first issuing some warning words of admonition.

'Let us go over this once more just so that I have it clear in my own mind about what you're telling me,' Lemski had said from behind his spartan desk in the cheerless Mossad office. 'You get the old man back to his bolt hole in the Negev and he tells you about this bunch of international terrorists based in Spain who have developed this mind control drug that they intend to use against the State of Israel. You tell him you don't believe him, so he takes a sample of the stuff to prove his point. This leads to him going completely off his head and he explodes a home made bomb made from thirty two kilos of semtex. Now you want to go and find this character called Colin Mage who has been working with Herschal, to pass on some information about the drug which will be essential in helping this Mr Mage destroy the terrorists. You're effectively asking me to grant you field agent status for this one operation and facilitate your transport to Spain with full diplomatic immunity and, if I say no, you intend to apply for sick leave and go off half-cocked under your own steam. Is that about it?'

'Yes,' Leon had said sheepishly. 'That's it.'

'It's a total crock of shit,' Lemski had said conversationally. 'You know it, I know it, and now you know that I know it. One, if there was any such terrorist organisation in Spain, there was no reason why Herschal shouldn't tell us this in Ashquelon. Two, given that there was such an organisation, our people in Spain would have known about it long since and would be far better placed to handle it effectively than you could – which is something that you yourself must be fully aware of. Three, the only reason that an IDF helicopter was dispatched on a search and rescue mission was that the seismic shock of that explosion knocked the seismograph at Dimona right off the Richter scale and the heat that came from the blast was picked up by infra red cameras, not only at Dimona, but also by passing satellite. Whatever the hell blew up back there was a fuck sight more than thirty two lousy kilos of semtex! I was out there myself three days ago and for your information there's a crater fifty meters wide and more than a hundred metres deep... Almost the kind of thing you'd expect from a subterranean nuclear detonation. There isn't any trace of radiation so we know it wasn't a nuke, but nor was it simply semtex.'

'Herschal said it was semtex,' Leon said truthfully.

'Leon, my lad, you've been lying through your teeth. This is a cock and bull story you've concocted to cover something up... but I'm going to let you run with it all the same, on the assumption that you do know what you're doing and you'll bring me in on it when you feel you're in a position to do so. If it wasn't for Herschal's involvement in all of this, you'd be out of this organisation on your ear so fast you wouldn't have time to say thanks for the memory, but as it is... There's a reservation in your name on the El Al flight to Madrid eight o'clock Sunday morning. You've got full DI and you'll be met at the airport by our people and taken on to the embassy. The embassy have been told that you're on a covert operation controlled directly from this office but that it's low risk and low key. Officially you are on sick leave. Unofficially you're on your own. You are free to contact me direct, but I trust that when you do so you'll be prepared to tell me the truth.'

Leon had stood up, flushing with gratitude and embarrassment beneath the paleness of his skin. 'Thank you Gideon,' he'd said – had been tempted to say more and then had thought better of it. He'd turned to go but just before he'd got to the door, Lemski had called him back.

'Tell me one thing,' he'd asked softly.

'If I can.'

'Is there any reason for me to worry out the state of Israel's security on or around the 21st of June?'

'Yes,' Leon had said equally quietly. 'There is every good reason. I'll contact you from Spain if the threat is averted, but if you don't hear from me before the 21st, put everything you've got on red alert. And if you don't hear from me before the 21st, well I guess you won't be hearing from me at all...'

'What will we be looking for?'

'I – ' Leon's tongue had become tied with the mental vision of Herschal's decapitation, ' – you'll know it when you see it,' he'd finally stammered.

Dov looked up from the dregs of his coffee cup. His finely boned face, more Greek than Jewish, was a mask of forlorn tragedy. Six years younger than Leon, he looked even younger with his tightly cropped white blond hair and clear blue eyes.

'I wish you didn't have to go,' he said simply.

Leon's heart went out to him, but this was a public place and he kept his emotions in check. 'I wish I didn't have to go,' he said 'but I do. Come on, let's pay the check and get out of here.'

They walked across Namir Square, dodging youngsters on roller skates and skateboards and, cutting down by the marina, strolled along the promenade. On their left were the concrete mountains of the Plaza, Diplomat and Ramada hotels while to their right the Mediterranean lapped against the shale and shingle sand of the deserted beach. A warm blustery wind blew in from the sea, carrying with it the occasional spit of rain or plume of spray. From somewhere in the near distance, perhaps from a cafe or somebody's portable ghetto blaster, Jennifer Rush's powerful voice belted out evocative lyrics as she bared the emotions of her soul to The Power Of Love. Here, where it was dark and there were no prying eyes, they found a quiet wall and Leon allowed his arm to fall across his lover's shoulders.

'Listen Dov, I do have to go. I shouldn't be away for more than a few weeks and after that, well, I don't know. Maybe I've had enough of Mossad. Maybe it's time to look for some other kind of lifestyle where we can have more time to ourselves instead of just a handful of stolen moments. You've been so patient with me over this last year... just hang on in there for a little while longer, will you?'

'Of course I will,' Dov's voice was muffled. 'But sometimes – sometimes I get frightened. I'm frightened now! You seem to have changed so much in the last few weeks.'

'It's been a very rough time,' Leon said noncommittally. *Oh yes, a very rough time! I've seen the face of Satan so close I could smell the bile of his breath. I've had a preview of Armageddon! I've watched an old man have his head bitten off and I can still hear his scream and smell his blood as it spewed all over me. And oh yes, I've been blown up. But don't worry Dov, this is the kind of thing that a*

Mossad agent is trained for and I'll soon get over it all – maybe in about fifty to a hundred years, should I live so long!

'I'll miss you Leon – and I'll be here for you when you get back.'

'I'll miss you too – and as for you being here when I get back, I'm counting on it...'

As an El Al Boeing 747 carried Leon westwards towards Spain, Gideon Lemski met with Arial Sharon in a small private office at The Knesset.

'Has he gone?' Sharon asked without preamble.

Lemski glanced at his watch. 'The flight left on time two hours ago. He'll be landing in Madrid at noon.'

'And what about this tale of terrorists and mind control drugs?'

'In my opinion it's a fabrication. Total rubbish... and I told him as much at our Friday briefing. He didn't deny it.'

'So what's the real story?'

Lemski tugged at his lower lip thoughtfully. 'Arial, I really don't know. When Megiddo One made contact I thought that he'd become senile and was having delusions, but then I started getting a bad feeling. You can't just dismiss The Elijah File out of hand, can you? So I allowed Shapiro to take him back to the Negev. There was a transponder hidden in their vehicle that not even Shapiro himself knew about, so the chopper knew exactly where to go when the shit hit the fan. You've seen Dimona's report from the site of the explosion and I'm sure that you'll be aware of the anomalies: the dimensions of the crater and the blast effect within the oasis don't add up. To all intents there must have been two explosions, one following on immediately after the first. The initial detonation near the surface triggered something significantly more powerful at least sixty or seventy metres underground.

'Shapiro was in shock for several days and you've also seen the psychologist's report. The boy was scared to death about something that he certainly wasn't telling us about and no amount of pushing and probing was going to get it out of him. By the time I was able to interview him he'd got his story all worked out and he's stuck to it throughout. The only thing is that he now knows that I know it's false.'

'What about this man in Spain? This Colin Mage, who is supposed to be working against these fictitious terrorists?'

Lemski grinned. 'We haven't been idle on this one. First of all he's not on any of our computer files, he's not known to the CIA and he's as clean as a whistle with the British SIS. When we pushed the Brits the only thing they were able to come up with was the fact that he's an academic with a handful of books to his name. But mark this! The books all deal with various aspects of the paranormal and the occult and he is regarded as being an expert in his field. Now, given what we know about Meggido One and the contents of The Elijah File, I find this to be a curious little quirk of coincidence. There is a link here somewhere, although I'm damned if I can find it.'

'So you're using Shapiro as a sprat to catch a mackerel, aren't you?'

Lemski nodded. 'Yes, if indeed there is a mackerel out there to be caught. A better analogy is to say that I'm throwing him like a stone into the pond and shall be watching very carefully to see what happens to the ripples. He was very badly shaken by whatever happened in the Negev and in his present state he's absolutely no use to me here. I'd have insisted that he took some sick leave but as he was quite determined to go to Spain one way or the other, I thought he might as well go in a controlled situation, and at least this way we'll be able to keep an eye on him.'

'So he's going to this place – what's it called, Castillo? – as an independent field agent?'

'Good Lord no!' Lemski grinned again. 'Certainly he thinks he is, but he'll have a P3 unit on his tail every inch of the way from Madrid. They'll keep him out of trouble, and if there is any trouble, we'll know exactly what that trouble is without having to rely on young Shapiro's reports.'

'Isn't a P3 team a little excessive?' Sharon asked.

'Perhaps, but I'd rather have them there just in case.'

'Won't Shapiro get wise to them?'

'Arial,' Lemski said matter of factly, 'he's not a field agent. Out of the office and away from his precious modems and computers, he doesn't know his arse from his elbow!'

Leon was met at Madrid International Airport by a short compact man with sharp green eyes and short brown hair. He introduced himself as Asher and described himself as a junior military attaché. Leon smiled and shook hands and thought *military attaché like hell! He's Mossad through and through. One of the guys at the sharp end! Mossad's cutting edge overseas!*

Asher drove them through the heavy traffic which crawled fumily along the crowded auto route and it took them the better part of two hours to reach the embassy.

'We've been asked to provide you with everything you need,' Asher said conversationally.

'Thanks. Right now I need a shower and a bed for couple of hours.'

'No problem. We anticipated that.'

'I also need a car, preferably one without diplomatic plates, and a half decent map of Southern Spain. And,' Leon paused, 'I want a Little Ruben.'

Asher raised an eyebrow. 'Okay,' he said cautiously. 'That's something you'll have to sign for, of course, and, look, forgive me for saying this, you will be damn careful how you use it, won't you? We're on pretty good terms with the Spaniards these days and neither the ambassador nor our people back home would be very pleased if anything came along to spoil things.'

'I'll be careful,' Leon said neutrally.

'It'll take a couple of hours to arrange. Are you staying in Madrid overnight?'

'No. I only had a couple of hours sleep last night so I'll rest up this afternoon and leave this evening when the traffic dies down a bit.'

Asher laughed. 'Sorry, but in this town the traffic never dies down! If you can think of leaving mid-evening, say eightish or nineish, at least the traffic's coming into Madrid, so it should be a little easier for you. You have any preference car-wise?'

'Nothing flashy, but something comfortable.'

'Leave it with me.'

Leon left Madrid a little before nine, feeling relatively refreshed after a decent sleep and a light meal. Asher had provided him with a four year old Mercedes diesel in dark grey. Although it was hardly what Leon would have called fast, it was certainly extremely comfortable. The Little Ruben was stashed away innocuously in the boot with the rest of his things and with passport, papers, and no shortage of euros, he felt reasonably confident about his mission. His first step was to get to Castillo. He'd studied the map and it was a straight run south from Madrid, with optional routes opening up for him at a town called Bailen. Here he could either carry on south to Granada before turning west for Malaga and Cadiz, or he could make for Cordoba and then drop down on Castillo via Antiquera and Ronda. Asher had recommended the Granada route but to Leon's eye, the Cordoba route looked quite a lot shorter.

'We'll see how I feel at Bailen,' he muttered to himself as, with some relief, he found himself leaving the outskirts of Madrid and heading south along the N4 at a steady one hundred and twenty kph.

Driving doggedly through the long night and taking several breaks to rest his tired eyes, he did not reach Bailen until nine the following morning. He stopped for a leisurely breakfast at a roadside venta, aware of the balmier atmosphere and warmer temperature. Studying his map again he still couldn't make up his mind which way to go and ended up by tossing a coin, heads for Granada tails for Cordoba. Cordoba won, and by ten o'clock he was on the road again. Despite the fact that he was not making particularly good time, he estimated that he would be in Castillo well before evening. What he would do then, he wasn't sure... He had no pre-formed plans, but decided that would be best if he kept a low profile. He had no idea what to expect and had not thought further than his quest to find Colin Mage. He'd tell him about Herschal and what had happened in the Negev and, depending upon Mage's reaction, would take his lead from that.

During the night drive his mind had mulled over the bizarre and horrific sequence of events that had placed him upon this course of action. He'd found himself trying to remember all that Herschal had told him and although the exact words were elusive he felt that he'd got the gist of it. The vision of Herschal's demise was an ever haunting spectre and he took some comfort from the Little Ruben nestling in the boot. Southwest of Cordoba after he'd turned off the E5 in favour of the N331 he pulled off the road north of Montilla and rescued the squat black case from the back of the car. To all intents and purposes it was a photographer's camera case made from black aluminium with the usual hand grip and carrying strap. Although it was not particularly heavy Leon slung the strap across his shoulder and walked a good quarter mile from the roadside before sitting the flat box on the table top of a convenient rock and using the keys Asher had given him, unlocked the lid.

Instead of the usual selection of cameras and lenses nestling in the rubber foam there was an Uzi mk III machine pistol and six clips of ammunition. In a separate section to the right of the case there were three hand grenades and a small mine. The grenades were of the high explosive anti-personnel variety, standard Israeli army issue, while the mine was something of a curiosity. On one side of the disk there was a suction pad clearly indicating that it could be used as a limpet mine, while on the other there was a sharp spike which also acted as a detonator, indicating it could be equally well used as a land mine. The bomb could be set to explode upon impact, but there was also a timing device that could delay detonation for anything up to twenty four hours. The whole package, the camera case and it's contents, was known as Little Ruben. Leon didn't know how the name had come about, but it had certainly been in use since the early 1960's.

Taking the Uzi from the case he tried it in his hand for balance taking mock aim at distant trees and boulders. The Mossad issue of the Uzi took a clip of thirty six 9mm rounds and was effective up to about fifty yards. It could be used on single shot mode, or on fully automatic which would empty the clip in under two seconds. Leon was mindful of the black ooze that had belched from the creature in the cavern as Herschal's Remington had discharged its load – *Let's see how the fucker deals with thirty six rounds of 9mm nickel between its eyes!* Leon thought viciously, and lining up on a small sapling some twenty yards distant, he squeezed the trigger.

'What's he doing?' asked the man called Yuri who lounged behind the wheel of the pale blue Volkswagen camper van, idly rolling a cigarette.

The woman who sat behind him didn't bother looking up from her magazine but she did pick up the miniature walkie talkie and press the send button. 'Situation?' she asked, speaking boredly into the mouthpiece.'

'He's conducting a weapons check,' came the crackling reply above the hiss of static.

'Weapons check,' she said in the same bored tone to man behind the wheel.

'Yeah, I heard,' he retorted. And then, 'Shit, I hope this isn't going to be another wild goose chase!'

'Who cares if it is – as long as we stay alive and get paid.' She turned the page of her magazine avidly absorbing the vibrant images that leapt out at her from the colour plates. It was the latest edition of Art International and this month's special feature was on the masterworks of Titian.

'I care!' Yuri said testily. 'All I've done for the last six sodding months is drive this bloody van across Northern Spain, Bilbao across the border to Biarritz, Biarritz back to Bilbao... I'm bored frigging stiff.'

'Well now we're driving to Southern Spain,' she said sarcastically, 'and I'm sure that'll make a very nice change for us all.' Basically she did not want to talk. She wanted to breathe art and feel the kiss of Titian's genius in her soul.

'Aren't you just the teeniest bit interested in just seeing the weeniest bit of action?' he asked with equal sarcasm, mimicking her tone.

Tanja Hein closed her eyes and fought to control her temper. At forty six years old she may have lost the first bloom of her youthful beauty but she was still strikingly attractive with short spikey red hair and a lithe responsive body. Apart from one nine month period back in 1984, she'd seen active service initially with the IDF and then Mossad for twenty two consecutive years and in those years she'd seen enough action to last her a lifetime.

'No,' she said. 'I'm not.'

There was a crunch of gravel and the passenger door swung open. Micky Vordeman swung himself into the right hand seat, passing the powerful Zeiss binoculars to Tanja. He grinned broadly. 'Heaven help us if we have to rely on Mr Shapiro to save us from the bad guys. I hope he's got other talents, because believe me, shooting isn't one of them.'

'He's a non-combatant,' Tanja said mildly.

'He may have been but not any more,' Micky retorted. 'He's here directly from The Man Himself in Jerusalem, he's got full DI and is playing around with a Little Ruben when he probably hasn't had his hands on a gun since he was in his basic training. There's something here that isn't quite kosher.'

'Look,' she said, 'I don't know any more than you do. Our orders are explicitly vague, just as they always are, so let's just do our job as best we can. We follow our Mr Shapiro, ride shotgun for him, haul his balls out of any hot spots and in the meantime stay completely covert... Yuri!'

Yuri turned on the engine but did not pull off the grass verge until the radio signal from the transponder concealed beneath Leon's Mercedes began beeping to indicate that he was on the move again. When the small green light on Tanja's monitor indicated that the Mercedes was two kilometres ahead, just as it had been all the way from the suburbs of Madrid, the P3 unit relaxed and settled down to the last part of their journey.

Leon's first sight of Castillo came at seven thirty that evening. His car cornered the last bend on the road down through the mountains from Ronda, and there it was, on the far side of the valley, stretching across the spine of the distant ridge, the battlements and keep of the ancient castle in inky black silhouette against the crimson panorama of a blood red sunset. Street lamps twinkled in welcome anticipation of his impending arrival, but Leon shivered in his seat. To his eyes the village seemed to be bathed in blood, as did the surrounding fields and vineyards. A trick of the light, to be sure, but somewhere over there in that huddle of houses hunched beneath the castle, there dwelt the brother of the thing that had bitten off Herschal's head with one swallowing snap of its jaw. There was no use denying it. Now that he was here he was frightened and the bloody sunset seemed to be an omen of evil things to come.

He drove slowly into the village and cruised the narrow streets absorbing the atmosphere and geography. The sun had gone and night had fallen quickly, bringing with it a more welcoming ambience. Children played on street corners, people stood talking in shop doorways, lights from several cafes and bars spilled across the cobbles. Not knowing what he was looking for but knowing that he needed somewhere to stay that could offer him a bed and a hot bath, it was inevitable that he should find his way to the Miraflores. It was the only hotel in town and he was encouraged by its appearance.. Henry Holloway was delighted to receive him and helped him carry the cases from the Mercedes. By quirk of serendipity Leon was given the very room that Helen Ross had vacated the week before.

He contemplated exploring the village on foot but dismissed the idea almost immediately. He was not long out of a hospital bed and his body, still bruised in a number of places, ached for sleep. He took the hot bath that his tensed muscles craved for and was asleep almost as soon as his head hit the pillow. The drive from Madrid had taken much longer than he'd anticipated and his quest to find Colin Mage could reasonably be put on hold until the following day.

He woke late on Tuesday morning and went in search of breakfast. Henry served him on the terrace and, like most people, Leon was enchanted by the place. Flowers of deep and varied colours nestled within a hundred shades of green, their intoxicating scent born on the clear fresh air. The sky was vibrantly blue without a cloud in sight and the plants and foliage were alive with scores of broad winged butterflies of a dozen different hues. As he stood, leaning against the adobe wall, taking in the panoramic view of the village while finishing his third cup of superb Spanish coffee, his feelings of foreboding caused by the previous evening's sunset evaporated completely. Yes, there was still the hollow tingle of fear that had been ever present since the moment he'd regained consciousness in the IDF's military hospital in Jerusalem, but that was something he'd learned how to live with.

He heard the scrape of chairs behind him and casually turned to see who else had come to breakfast in this idyllic spot. He nearly dropped his coffee cup, for there, not four metres distant, Yasser Arafat was sitting with Saddam Hussein! Arafat was lighting a cigarette from a soft blue and white packet, while Hussein was filling a pipe!

Leon's knees were trembling, and he sat down. Of course, it *wasn't* the PLO leader and the President of Iraq – after all one was dead and the other was in prison but the resemblances were striking. The two men were talking in low but animated tones and they ignored him completely until Henry brought them their cups of coffee. Then they looked up and noticed him staring in their direction. Yasser Arafat nodded in a surly manner while Saddam Hussein shot him a friendly half smile and called out a polite *Buenas Dias.* They went back to their conversation in even more muted tones and Leon deliberately averted his eyes. His Spanish was passable, although not good by scholarly standards. He'd taken languages at university and while he spoke English, German and Arabic like a native, Spanish and French had always been his weak areas. He strove to pick up an odd word but the two men were taking care not to be overheard.

After fifteen minutes Yasser Arafat got up and left, leaving Saddam Hussein puffing thoughtfully on his pipe. Another few minutes elapsed before he was joined by an exceptionally attractive woman in her early thirties. Saddam put down his pipe and reached up to kiss her cheek.

'How did you get on?' she asked in clear English.

'Well enough,' Saddam answered, also in English. 'He's suspicious, of course. Wants to know what's going on, and it was difficult to know how much to tell him. We must either tell him everything and risk his disbelief or we must come up with a credible water tight story that answers all his questions. We're going to have to talk to Colin about this – I can't act on my own – and in any case Jaime wants to talk to Colin anyway. In the meantime I think it's safe to say we have a potential ally and if we do decide to go in through the roof, Jaime will cover for us – providing he knows, or thinks he knows what it's all about. He's very very curious and, of course, I can hardly blame him.'

Leon, whose ears had pricked up when he'd heard the name "Colin" – after all, how many people with that name were there likely to be in a place like this? – got up from his table and coughing politely to signal his approach, took a few steps towards Saddam and his girl friend.

'Excuse me,' he began tentatively, 'I couldn't help but hear that you were speaking English and as my Spanish is quite deplorable, I wondered if you could help me?'

As the couple looked up he watched the colour drain from the woman's face. 'My God,' she exclaimed. 'I know you!'

'I beg your pardon?' Leon floundered, for this was obviously a case of mistaken identity. He'd never seen this girl until a few moments before and he'd have remembered her if he had, for now on closer inspection he saw that she was quite lovely. Despite his homo sexuality, indeed, perhaps even because of it, he had a finely tuned appreciation for beauty.

'I know you,' the girl said again. 'I've seen you before and I know where I've seen you!'

'Actually,' Leon felt acutely embarrassed, 'I'm fairly sure you must be wrong. I only arrived last night and I'm trying to locate someone. He's an Englishman, a friend of a friend, and when I heard you mention someone called Colin, I wondered, as this is such a small place, if your Colin could possibly be the Colin I'm looking for?'

The girl's face broke into a broad smile. 'Mage,' she said.

Leon nodded. 'Yes, his name is Colin Mage.'

'I knew that I knew you,' she said. And then: 'Have you got a funny kind of gun with you? One that's all handle and no barrel?'

Leon's jaw dropped. It was an odd but accurate way of describing an Uzi, but how in the name of God could she possibly have known about it? There was something very peculiar happening here and his Mossad training stepped in to help him.

'I really do need to speak with Mr Mage,' he said urbanely, totally ignoring the subject of the gun.

'Then you'll have to wait a while,' Saddam Hussein said, entering the conversation for the first time with an odd pinch in his voice. 'He's not here.'

'Well can you tell me where he is?' Leon asked. 'My business with him really is very urgent.'

'Right now?' Saddam glanced at his watch. 'Right now he's just getting on a train for Ronda and he won't be back until tonight.'

'Maybe not even until tomorrow morning,' the girl said innocently.

At first Saddam scowled, then his face broke into a small grin. 'He should be so lucky,' he chuckled reluctantly.

He'd been told that it was one of the most wonderfully scenic railway routes in the whole of Europe, but as the train from Castillo struggled up the steep mountain passes with rock and forest crowding in from both sides, Mage's thoughts were not on the spectacular views, but on the Djinn. The expected counter attack had not developed! The circle had sat on guard throughout Saturday night and most of Sunday, but there hadn't been so much as a presentient twitch. On Monday he'd spent several hours with Angel and Christina watching the house in Calle Sombra through powerful binoculars. No one had entered or exited from the building, the shutters had remained closed and when, on one occasion, out of exasperation he'd walked along Sombra to stand defiantly outside the front door, there had been that uncannily familiar feeling of emptyness... and yet Dolorean and Alexandra had to be inside. There was no where else for them to be! But if they *were* in the house, what were they doing and why this profound sensation of enigmatic absence?

On the Monday evening Anna had telephoned from Ronda, and that had given him something else to think about. In the letter he'd sent with Hector ten days before, he'd told her that he would make a point of being in the Miraflores every day at six o'clock if she wanted to talk to him. If he was to be totally honest with himself, he'd been disappointed that she'd taken so long to make the call, but perversely, now that she had, he found himself looking forwards to their meeting with no small degree of trepidation. He had already hurt her once, and at all costs, must not do so again. The only way he could avoid doing so was by telling her everything, which, of course, he could not do. How could she believe him? How could anyone believe without having had first hand experience? Inevitably, then, he would have to lie. He found this notion abhorrent, and thus determined to keep his dishonesty to the minimum, building, perhaps, on the tale that had been told to Christina and Angel. Even so, he was still uncomfortable with the option. Above all, he suspected, Anna was going to want to know about Alexandra and he would have to be both sensitive and careful in how he handled her questions.

On time to the minute the train pulled into Ronda and Mage spent a pleasant hour exploring the centre of the old Roman town. His appointment with Anna was not until one o'clock so there was plenty of time to play the tourist. Being out of Castillo made a welcome change and he realised that the last time he'd been out of the village for any length of time had been on the occasion of the day out to the beach at La Bolonia. It seemed like a long time ago, but the memory of Anna's firm breasts pushing into his hands and the taste of her salty kisses were vividly clear in his mind. He wondered how this day's reunion mind end. Would there be more kisses or would it end in bitter tears?

Ronda was built on the edge of a sheer cliff, dissected by a deep ravine. Mage stood on the bridge looking down into the vast gorge, turbulent with the tumbling waters of the river five hundred feet below. It was a very long drop. No "cry for help" if you did a swallow dive over the parapet; jump from this bridge and you were deadly serious about dying! He remembered that during the civil war, prisoners had been executed by being heaved over the very balustrade against which he now so casually leaned. Across more than half a century there was still a trace echo of their terrified screams. The ether was still disturbed by their panic filled struggles to avoid what by any standards was a most horrendous death.

Shaking his head in an attempt to dispel the mood of negativity, he turned from the bridge and retraced his steps back towards the bull ring, one of Spain's oldest cathedrals dedicated to the blood and carnage of man's cruelty to animals... And paused. There was something familiar about this place. He knew he'd never been here before, but the shape of the square, the statue on the central reservation, the row of shops over on his left, sheltering from the hot sun beneath the shade of a porticoed arcade... All whispered seductively in his ears, persuading him to open his eyes and see that which he needed to see. Following the powerful pulse of intuition, Mage cut across the square. He was only half way across when he saw the shop with its faded sign – *The Armouria of Juan Cordoba Al Andaluz*.

He leapt out of the way of an oncoming tourist bus and landed up outside the shop, staring excitedly through the accumulated layers of grime that covered the window. There were fishing rods, sheath knives, air rifles and shot guns but the object of his inspection remained elusive until he walked into the shop itself and there he saw it, hanging on the wall above the counter. The shop had changed little from the way it had been when he'd seen it in his dream, and the crossbow was exactly as he remembered it, with its polished olive wood stock and curious firing mechanism, incorporating the double gunnals for the two bolts, one perched upon the top of the other. Just by looking at it, he could see that the weapon was as clean and as well oiled as it had been on the day that it had been made. The one who had commissioned its construction had never returned to collect it, and the one who had made it had never sold it.

As the rippling sensations of *déjà vu* coursed through him, he was beset with a feeling of giddiness and nausea – and sat down on a convenient three legged stool watching the old man who served behind the counter measure out a phial of black powder for the equally grizzled old customer who demanded it, promising to bring it back if it didn't ignite properly in the chamber of whatever antiquated blunderbuss of a weapon that required its explosive qualities. The shopkeeper was the same man that he had seen in his dream, which was as impossible as the dream itself was impossible.

None the less, he had had the dream! In it, he had been the patron, the commissioner, and the man he had been talking to was now stood, talking to someone else less than ten feet away. Despite all his research and training, Mage did not know how precognition really worked. At best there were vague theories based upon a variety of suppositions unique to the supposer and subtly different in each and every case – but here was the living proof that precognition was an energy within the cosmic world! He'd had the dream in which he had visited this shop, had talked to the old man behind the counter, had even threatened the man's life if he so much as spoke to anyone with regard to the commissioning of the crossbow! And now here he was, in the flesh and reality of his own time space continuum.

As Old Grizzly departed with his black powder Mage got up and approached the counter. He stared openly at the armourer, and the armourer looked back with interest and curiosity, but with no sense of recognition. In the end Mage broke the gaze and nodded to the weapon on the wall above the old man's head.

'I wish to purchase the cross bow, Señor.'

The shop keeper raised an ancient eyebrow while thin lips pulled into a smile across tobacco stained teeth. 'I am sorry Señor. That is impossible. The weapon is not for sale.'

'Everything is for sale,' Mage responded ' – at the right price. Name your price and I shall pay it.'

The shop keeper's smile broadened. 'You do not understand, Señor. The weapon, the cross bow, she is not just a weapon, she is an *heirloom!* My Grandfather made her in 1887 for Duke Cristobal de Cordoba and she has been in our family since that day. If she were to be for sale, it would be as an antique and the price would be phenomenal.'

'Tell me what phenomenal price that might be?' Mage asked easily, his confidence rising.

The old man shrugged. 'It would have to be something in the region of four thousand euros,' he said off handedly.

'That's not a bad profit on something that was commissioned for only four hundred presetas,' he mused out loud, taking some satisfaction in watching the old man's jaw drop half an inch. 'Tell me, if you were to sell me the crossbow, would you be selling it on behalf of the descendants of Cristobal de Cordoba, or on your own account?'

'On my own account, of course! As I have told you Señor, the bow has been in my family for more than one hundred years!'

'In which case, Señor, you would be a thief! For while undoubtedly the crossbow has been in your family for all the years you claim, it has never belonged to you. Duke Cristobal de Cordoba paid for the weapon in advance. I must tell you that it is the rightful property of his heirs and descendants and what ever else you might be, Señor, you are most certainly not one of those!'

The old shopkeeper was no longer smiling. Indeed, his lips were pursed in a tight thin line and he bristled with hostility. 'The weapon has full provenance,' he snapped. 'Every transaction that has taken place in this armouria has been recorded in our ledgers since my Grandfather came to Ronda from Cordoba in 1884. If you know so much about this weapon,' with a note of triumphant glee, he hauled a huge black book onto the top of the counter, 'perhaps you can tell me how much the Duke is supposed to have paid?''

'I've already told you,' Mage said mildly. 'It was the sum of four hundred pesetas – which, incidentally, included six specially made bolts in a flat wooden case. I expect the bolts to be included in today's transaction at the price we have yet to agree on. Assuredly I will pay you a lot more that the four hundred pesetas that has already been paid, but certainly nothing like four four thousand euros.'

'I've told you,' the armourer cried shrilly. 'The crossbow is not for sale. Now get out of here before I call the police!'

'The bow *is* for sale,' Mage persisted doggedly, 'for if it is not, it is I who shall go to the police and ask them to examine your ledger for the year 1887, and while I am there denouncing you I shall mention how it is that you sell black powder without demanding signatures from your customers or entering the transaction on the necessary government forms. After I have done that, I shall drink in every bar and tavern in Ronda and speak freely of the way in which you and your family have cheated the heirs of Cristobal de Cordoba by claiming ownership of something that does not, and never has belonged to you since the day it was made.'

The old man had turned pale and Mage felt like a total bastard. He was determined to have the bow at any cost, however, and now sweetened the pill that he was forcing the old man to swallow. Taking out his wallet, he extracted his Amex Gold Card and laid it casually on the counter in full view of the armourer's eyes.

'Providing you're not going to talk in thousands, you may name your price,' he said easily.

'Two thousand five hundred euros! ' the shop keeper exclaimed.

'Don't insult me. Remembering that the weapon has been paid for once and that four hundred pesetas was a small fortune a hundred years ago, I'll offer you eight hundred!'

'It is you who insult me!' the armourer challenged.

'Then let us be realistic.'

'Two thousand euros, then!'

'One thousand.'

'But this is a hand made antique!'

Mage nodded. 'That's true. One thousand, and that's it,' he said firmly, and although the haggling went on for several more minutes, the transaction was completed at one thousand euros. At no small cost, in Sterling a little over six hundred pounds, he had acquired a valuable antique at very fair price, but it had been a lot of money to pay for a weapon – and it was very much as a weapon that Mage wanted the crossbow. Hunches, instincts and intuitions were part of his stock in trade; he was fighting a war wherein dreams could be likened to arms and ammunition. He'd been given this weapon in a dream and now, as he hurried across Ronda to meet Anna, he held the same weapon in his arms and knew that when the time came he would use it.

In some ways it was easier than Mage had imagined it might be, but in other ways, especially during the first hour of their reunion, it was worse. Anna was cool and frosty to a point verging on impoliteness and it took some time for her even to begin to thaw. Mage rode with it and didn't push it. He supposed that from her point of view she was entitled to exact a degree of revenge and, furthermore, she didn't look at all well. She'd lost weight and much of the colour had gone from her cheeks. Indeed, her skin looked pale and almost transluscent beneath the dark green canopy of the cafe where they sat, at the junction of the main road and The Plaza del Torros. The streets were snarled with fume belching traffic and the plaza was crawling with early summer tourists; it would not have been his natural choice for a lunch time tete-a-tete, but even the short walk from the Clinica Olivera, which was situated a few hundred yards away opposite the Reina Victoria Hotel, had tired her and he'd grabbed the first free table that he'd seen in the first restaurant they'd come to. She sipped iced tea while he drank coffee. They waited for a pasta dish that neither of them actually wanted, for they were both tense and neither was in the least bit hungry. Their waiter had been insistent, however. Between noon and three p.m. only lunches were served and so Mage had ordered for the privilege of being able to sit somewhere in the shade where they could talk. Their conversation was stilted.

'How have you been?' he asked tentatively.

Her mouth twitched. It might have been a smile but he thought otherwise. Her fingers played nervously with an angry spot on the side of her chin. 'Why should I lie to you?' she said, clearly implying that she considered him guilty of having lied to her. 'I have not been good. I have not been well. I have not been happy! Oliver and Laura have been extremely kind – they have done their best to keep me occupied and entertained, but they have not been able to prevent me from catching a cold and they have not been able to take away the pain that I have felt in my head – and in my heart.' She looked at him directly. There were tears in her dark eyes, but her voice was firm. 'Colin, why did you not tell me that you had a wife?'

He chose his words carefully and spoke with great restraint. 'I did not tell you that I had a wife because for the last year and a half of my life I have not had a wife.' He reached for cigarettes. 'To be sure, I am still technically married, although I do have papers that prove that I am legally separated. When I left England a divorce was pending. For all I know it might already have gone through, although if it has, I've not heard about it.'

'But my father says that your wife is here. In Castillo – and this is the reason why you yourself have come to Spain!'

'These things are true,' Mage admitted, fiddling with the Zippo before finally lighting the cigarette. He had no desire to be patronising but knew he would have to keep the story simple. 'Eighteen months ago, my wife and I met a man. The man wanted my wife and he took her from me. We'd been married for a number of years and we'd been very happy, so perhaps you can imagine how I felt when she chose to go with him.'

He drew on the cigarette, blowing a cloud of blue smoke up towards the green canvas roof. 'Under normal circumstances, this would have been bad enough. Painful to be sure, but tolerable and survivable. Marriages break down all the time for a whole host of different reasons. Two people can work their hearts out to make a relationship work, but there are never any guarantees. In my situation, however, the circumstances were far from normal. This man I'm telling you about is in some ways, but only in some ways, a lot like me – not only stole my wife's body, he also stole her mind and her free will. I can't prove it, of course, but I don't think she would ever have gone with him had he not been able to do those things first.'

He watched her surreptitiously, trying to gauge her reaction. She saw that he was waiting for her to make some response. 'Is it possible for a man to have this kind of power?' she asked.

'Oh yes,' Mage answered. 'It's rare, but in some people it's there all right.'

'And you also have this power? You said that this man, the one who stole your wife, was like you in some ways...'

'You *know* I have this power,' he answered gently. 'It's the power that can take away your headaches, that can cure Pepe Ortega's ulcer, that can make Antonia Guardiaro forget about her arthritis for a while and that can dispel her Grandson's herpes. You saw some other examples of this power on the night we went to San Pablo. With this other man it is different. He has more power than I have, but he uses it to hurt people, not to help them. The best way I can describe him to you is to tell you that he is a very bad *bruho*... a black witch who takes pleasure in inflicting pain for his own dark purpose. He doesn't like people like you and me, people like your father and all the other friends you've ever known. He's using his power, his magic if you like, to try and make this world a better place for people like himself, and if he does that, it's going to be a terrible world for the likes of us... So terrible, in fact, that we wouldn't fit into it at all!

'Anyway, he has come to Castillo to perform some magic that can only be performed in Castillo. The village is a very special place and it's possible to do things in Castillo that can't be done anywhere else. Please don't ask me to explain this, just accept it as a fact for the time being. He's brought my ex-wife with him, because he can't do what he wants to do without her. Alexandra is, or should I say was, very psychic in her own right, which is why he latched onto us – onto her – in the first place. What they're planning to do is quite awful! I don't think Alexandra is aware of what's happening or even of what has happened. Either way, I'm here to stop them if I can.'

'And what about your wife?' Ann asked solemnly. 'Do you still love her?'

The question threw him, even though he had been expecting it. 'I don't know,' he answered honestly. 'We had a good marriage and we were very close as a couple until Dolorean split us appart, and yet this last year has been the longest year in my life – and the most painful. My time with Alexandra seems like it was all a very long time ago. I remember the good times and I remember how my wife was... I'm deeply sorry that the marriage is over and I'm angry and troubled about the way in which it ended.' He paused, and then; 'I've found it very hard to let go of the memories, especially when I remember *how* everything ended. In any case, you can't live with a person for a number of years and not have some residual feelings for them when you're still only eighteen months down the road... But I saw her in Castillo on Friday morning – and I'll tell you this! My wife is dead. The person I loved and was married to died a long time ago, killed by the man who now calls himself her husband.'

'Do you want her back?'

'The question doesn't arise. It's too late for that.'

'But if you could have her back? Would you?'

He knew well enough what Anna wanted, but even so, did not answer immediately. Instead he allowed his mind to wander back over the events of the past year, remembering in particular the words of Michael Fry and, more recently, those of John Light.

'No,' he said. 'The answer is no. I wouldn't – because I couldn't. Too much has happened. There's been too much pain and suffering and regardless of what has caused the pain it's been enough to act as a catharsis. You get to a point where you can't go back, even if you want to. It's the point where the good, no matter how good it was, becomes spoiled and contaminated by the bad.'

A score of connected thoughts crowded his mind and one in particular took precedence. Even if Alexandra knocked on his bedroom door that very night, he would not let her in. No matter how attractive she might look or how reasonable she might sound, his fear would keep her at bay. She was no longer the woman he had married. Indeed, she was no longer a woman at all! The dream vision of the ravening crone danced behind his eyes and he was totally repelled by it. He grieved for what he had lost, but the words of his friends combined with his own experience had found root in his own consciousness, and what he had said to Anna was correct; Alexandra was dead! She had died the previous year, the last gram of human breath extracted from her being upon the top of Glastonbury Tor. That she still walked and talked, bloated with an impossible alien pregnancy, was a mind bending conundrum.

He found himself gazing into space, eyes lingering on the traffic, registering a party of Germans who climbed into a pair of horse drawn landaus, and across the square he watched two Spanish children as they romped on the grass with brightly coloured balloons tied to their wrists. Here in this healthy mountain town there was a sense of every day normality. It was a place devoid of Djinn, magicians and dark magic, where peoples' fears were ordinary every day fears – the fear of poverty, of illness, of death. Any other fears were the fears that he himself had brought with him and were his alone to carry; they hung heavily in his heart, clouding the natural beauty of the sparkling sunshine, muting the happy laughter of carefree children.

His fugue of thought was broken by the waiter who unceremoniously clattered two plates of grey macaroni in front of them. Mage muttered a cursory *muchas gracias* but the food looked totally unappetising. He pushed the plate to one side and drained the remnants of his coffee.

'I'm sorry,' Anna said.

'You don't have to eat it.'

'I'm not going to eat it, but that's not why I'm saying I'm sorry.' She looked utterly dejected and could not meet his eyes. 'For the last ten days I have been feeling very sorry for myself and, it is true, I have known much pain, but my pain is nothing in comparison with that which you have suffered. I now feel very small. Very childish.'

'We cannot measure pain,' he said, reaching over and lightly covering her hand with his own. 'It is unique to the individual and you have as much right to your pain as I have to mine. I'm just so sorry that I have been the cause of yours.'

'I have caused myself the pain by being so immature and so *stupid!*'

'No. You have every right to be upset.'

'I should never have left Castillo,' she exclaimed vehemently..

'I'm glad that you did,' he said, and watched her flinch at his words. 'Anna, your father was right to send you away for a while. Some terrible things have been happening in Castillo and, if I'm right, there are some worse things to come. It's better that you're out of it.'

'But I want to be with you,' she said openly. 'I want to help you... My father is helping you, isn't he?'

'Very much indeed,' Mage confirmed. 'And if you want to help me and your father, the very best thing that you can do for us is to remain here. That way we know you are safe and we can get on with what we're doing without worrying about you. Hector cares about you more than words can say and, knowing what he knows, he has done what any father would do in the circumstances.'

'And do *you* care?' her voice was little more than a whisper.

'Yes Anna, I care. You know that I care.'

'I love you,' she said simply.

He felt his heart lurch as the hollowness within his solar plexus spread to all parts of his body. 'I know you do,' he answered softly. 'But I'm not yet free to say those same words to you. Not until I've sorted out this business with Dolorean and Alexandra. If, after that, you still feel the same way... then at least I'll be free to come to you whole, rather than in shreds and tatters.'

'I promise you, I shall still feel the same way!'

Will you? Even though I may be in a worse state then than I'm in now? Will you, even after Jaime Gomez has arrested me on a double murder charge? Will you, if I manage to get your father killed?

'Then it gives us both something to hope for – to look forward to.'

'Do you...' she struggled to find the right words. 'Do you know how long...?'

He was mindful of the date on the calendar. 'A few weeks, and it'll be over one way or the other.'

'I have waited for twenty two years,' she said, trying to suppress the rising tide of excitement within her. 'I can manage another few weeks!'

'What do you want to do now?' he asked, eyeing the untouched grey mess on their plates and seeking to divert their conversation on to safer ground.
Some of the colour instantly returned to her cheeks and she averted her eyes. 'I think you would be shocked if I told you.'

'Believe me, Anna, I don't shock easily.'

'Very well, then. I want to be alone with you somewhere. Somewhere quiet and private, away from the noise and the prying eyes, where you can hold me and kiss me and make me feel good again.'

He looked at her obliquely. 'That could be very dangerous,' he warned, trying to keep his voice on an even keel.

'I know,' she said. 'But I'll risk it if you will.'

They checked into the Reina Victoria and were shown to a cool spacious room with pale green curtains and blinds. There was a large modern bed and while there was a fair sprinkling of other furniture, their attention remained riveted upon the bed.

Shit, I'm not ready for this!

He rested the crossbow, wrapped in its hessian covering, against one of the chairs. Anna sat on the edge of the bed, looking down at her hands, which were clasped on her lap.

Were they clasped or were they clenched?

'You must tell me what you want me to do,' she said tremulously.

Do? he thought. *Sweet Goddess Venus on a Friday, you'd better help me, and do it quickly. I haven't got a clue how to handle this!*

'Anna,' he said tenderly. 'You don't have to do anything.'

'I know I don't have to.' She looked up and met his eyes. '...But I want to. And that's different.'

He found that he was biting his lip. 'Okay,' he said. 'Okay...'

He walked across towards the window, kicking off his boots as he went. He closed the shutters, denying the bright sun its intrusive present and dimming the room to softer shadows. From the window he went to the bed and stretched out on top of the cool counterpane. Anna half turned to watch him and took his hand as he reached for her.

'Come here,' he said.

'Do you want me to...?'

'Just come here.'

She swung her feet up from the floor and lay next to him. His left arm went around the back of her neck while his right curved around her waist. He drew her face close to his own, kissing her lightly on the lips.'

'I...'

'Hush,' he whispered. 'Don't talk. Kiss me, relax, sleep and dream. You don't have to do anything. You have nothing to prove that isn't already proven by your being here.'

She snuggled up against him, returned his gentle kisses, felt his hands stroking her hair and her back and began to shake off the cords of tension that had been her constant companions for so many long days. Even the pain behind her eyes began to ease as a new pain, deep and pleasurable, began to rise low in her belly. She found herself waiting in anticipation for a more intimate caress, a caress which, when it came, caused her to squirm with desire for more daring adventure. His hand cupped her breast, so lightly, so hesitantly, that she could hardly feel it. She *wanted* to feel it, and covering his hand with her own, pressed it more firmly against her body. She heard him utter a low groan and she smiled in silent satisfaction. At least she was doing this bit right!

How she might have reacted had Mage taken full advantage of the situation was something she was not destined to discover – at least, not then. True, their kisses became longer and more passionate and, true, she had welcomed his hands as they had found their way between buttons that had mysteriously come undone, his fingers stroking the bare flesh of her stomach, sometimes moving up to scratch tantalisingly at the hardness of her nipples as they thrust against the flimsy lace of her bra, sometimes drifting downwards to glide against the flesh of her thighs. True, it had seemed the most natural thing in the world to open her legs as his hand had curved upwards along the inside of her thigh, and when he had touched her in that most private and sacred of female places, causing her to gasp in surprise and delight as her juices flowed in response, it had seemed totally natural for her to open her legs even wider, thrusting her pelvis upwards to meet the insistent but exquisitely gentle pressure from his fingers until they were moving in a rhythm of union that had but one purpose and one inevitable destination.

The orgasm came as he took her breast in his mouth, running her nipple against his teeth, pressing his fingers more firmly into the wetness between her legs. It exploded within her like a rolling wave of thunder, making her cry out in shock and amazement. Nothing had prepared her for this experience, its majesty and its magnitude, its all encompassing, soul tilting pleasure. This was not how her friends in the village had described it... They'd said it was nothing, or that if it was something, it was something messy and distasteful... That it certainly was not a pleasant experience, at least not for the girl it wasn't! They said that boys were only out for what they could get... and yet what had Colin got out of this? He had been the bringer of the greatest pleasure she'd ever known. What had he, the giver, taken in return? Although their clothes were rumpled, they were still fully dressed; surely, if her friends were right, they should now both be naked? If her friends were right, Colin should have taken her, plucking the cherry of her virginity in response to the brazen unambiguity of her words. If Colin Mage had been Pedro of San Pablo then there was no doubt in her mind what the outcome of the afternoon would have been!

'Thank God,' she murmured.

'For what?' he asked, smiling down at her.

'I thank God that you are you. Even in tatters and shreds, I thank God for you.'

He lowered his head to kiss her breast. It was still exposed and she had made no attempt to cover it. 'It's not all one way,' he murmured, feasting his eyes as much as his lips.

'It certainly won't be the next time we do this,' she laughed quietly, not unlike the cat who's caught the canary, Mage thought, and then has fallen into the vat of cream.

'The next time?' he asked innocently.

'Oh Señor Mage,' she looked at him with feigned sadness, 'you really don't know what you have done, do you?'

They slept through the siesta and then with the balmy descent of evening, went in search of food. Now they were ravenous and wolfed down two enormous plates of gambas with freshly baked bread and a litre of wine. They talked and laughed like old lovers, and it was easy for him to forget the impending nemesis that loomed sixty kilometres away in Castillo de la Frontera. After they had eaten, they walked through quiet lamp lit gardens that were alive with courting couples, either strolling hand in hand as they were themselves, or sitting in fond embraces in dark grassy corners, sometimes kissing openly upon wrought iron benches, or laughing in youthful gatherings around metal tables by one or the other of the two open air chiringuito bars.

They came to a point where they could walk no further. There was an elderly eucalyptus tree, an old Victorian street lamp, and a row of railings. Beyond the railings the sheer cliff face dropped two thousand feet from the plateau to the valley below. In the distance rows of mountain tops rolled across the horizon, hazy blue against the ink blue of the night sky. Stars winked in harmony with pinpricks of light that were dotted all over the valley, a farmhouse here, a hacienda here, a tiny pueblito in the foot hills, all of forty kilometres distant. They stood watching for many minutes before Anna turned to him hesitantly.

'Will you think I am a bad girl if I tell you that I enjoyed what we did this afternoon?'

'No. I think you would be a bad girl if you told me you did not enjoy what we did this afternoon.'

She was silent again, and then: 'When will you return to Castillo?'

He grinned to himself, thinking briefly about Hector. 'There's a train, the last one, I think, in...' he glanced at his watch, '...just over half an hour. I could catch it, but it would be a rush. I'd far rather spend the rest of this evening with you, providing you're not too tired, and I'll catch a morning train tomorrow.'

'This is good,' she said. 'We must call in at the clinic. I must tell Laura that I shall be out late, otherwise she will worry.'

'Fine. You want to go now?'

'No. Now, I want you to kiss me some more.'

Mage laughed and swung her in his arms until they were leaning up against the protective shadows of the tree and many more timeless moments were lost as their lips explored each others mouths.

'You must teach me how to kiss properly,' she whispered at one point.

'You need no teaching from me,' he replied.

'You must tell me what you like,' she insisted.

'I like you.'

She made him wait on the corner in a small bodega. 'I will only be a few moments,' she explained. 'If I take you inside, there will be introductions and explanations and it will be an hour before we escape. You will not be offended if I ask you to wait for me here? I shall be in and out in five minutes.'

The five minutes was nearer twenty, but Mage didn't mind. He was happy to stand at the bar sipping a diet coke and watching the world go by. Towards the back of the bodega, hemmed in by giants wine vats and barrels, a jovial crowd of students clustered around an old man who sang unaccompanied flamenco songs in a raucus nasal whine; he sang of ancient Andalucia and forgotten Spanish pride. Lost in his own turbulent poetry, he was oblivious to his audience, singing neither for them nor for his supper, but for his own spiritual salvation. A couple of the young men were deliberately winding him up, but others listened in thoughtful contemplation, hushing their less serious friends into half embarrassed silence.

Out in the strteet throngs of meandering people wandered up and down the Via Sindicato. Macho boys called out provocatively to big breasted girls who either giggled in response or turned their heads away in aloof superiority. Children danced around the feet of their parents, a taxi deposited a group of serious businessmen on the corner, and again Mage was struck by the normality of his surroundings, feeling it even more profoundly when he measured it against the abormality of this day. At two o'clock he had been battling with Anna, resigned to returning to Castillo on the four o'clock train, but by four o'clock he been sprawled out upon a hotel bed with her, gently stroking her to what had probably been her first proper orgasm.

His mind ran back over some of the things he had said to her, and in a gentle way, without dramatic impact, he came to realise that despite all of the darkness and distress he had experienced, there *were* one or two plus points.

Had Dolorean not come into his life he would have been living and working in York, doing much the same thing that he'd been doing for the past dozen years. Yes, there would have been another couple of books to his name, and yes, he would have continued to help the unending stream of clinets and pateints that found their way to his door. With Alexandra by his side he would have have begun to inevitable descent into complacent and academic midle age. His finances were sound, his marriage was secure, and he could look forward to encroaching years of predictable comfort. In all honesty he would have welcomed this. This was what he'd worked for, what he'd expected...

And yet what would he have achieved in The Grand Design? Certainly not the status of Spiritual Warrior! Spiritually aware academic, perhaps, but that was a far cry from his present position.

Dolorean *had* come into his life and Alexandra had gone with him. Yes, there *had* been great pain, but out of that pain there had come great knowledge of profounbd secrets. As a result of that pain he had been elevated and promoted within the ranks of the cosmic heirachy. Now he was no longer the complacent academic, but a warrior with a mission, the outcome of which would either change the world in which he lived, or prevent it from being changed. Along the pathway of the warrior he had been exposed to energies and powers that he never knew existed in the modern world; he'd made friends with spiritual giants like Michael Fry, Paul O'Connor and Herschel of The Negev – people he would never have come close to but for the tragedy that had so successfully wrecked his old life. He was now allied with the darkly angelic powers of John Light, had been a catalyst in Light's life, bringing him forward to face the demons of his own history and nudging him into recognising and formalising a love match of great worth and value. Indirectly, as a result of Mager's pain and his reaction to that pain, he had brought great happiness ti Tamara, for would Light's awareness of Tamara have changed to the extent that it had, had Mage not made him aware of his own vulnerability and responsibility?

Nor did it stop there. If he had never come to Spain, Helen Ross would not have come to Spain, and thus, would never have met Hector Sanchez. He wasn't sure when exactly Helen and Hector had become lovers, but it had certainly been somewhere towards the end of Helen's first week beneath the roof of the doctor's house in Calle Santana. Neirther of them, he knew, had either been looking for or expecting to find a relationships at this stage in their respective lives, but they had found it none the less – and judging by their attitude towards one another, it was no light weight thing.

Thinking of Hector brought him full circle back to Anna.

Like Hector and Helen, nor had he been looking for a relationship. Indeed, it had been the last thing that he'd wanted or expected, and yet, like it or not, he'd found one. There was no ambiguity in Anna's attitude. She had dealt with the problem of being with a man who was not only twice her age but who was still technically married to someone else. Her emotions had triumphed over catholic restriction and sobriety. Mage knew that he could not think in terms of an affair when it was abundantly clear that Anna was thinking in terms of a committed relationship... Which was fair enough, but he foresaw a thousand potential problems that he knew she could not possible foresee herself..

A disturbing thought enveigled its way into his conciousness, one that he didn't like and didn't want to have to deal with. *What would have happened if I'd met Anna while I was still happily married to Alexandra?* He assumed that the answer was nothing – nothing would have happened. On his part his relationship with Alexandra had been sacrosanct, and yet he knew, deeply down in his belly and his loins, that it was a very dangerous assumption to make. He did not want to think that Anna might have had the power and charisma to detract him from his marital committments; it was an ugly, intolerable thought, and he was gratefulo put it to rest, secure in the knowledge that he would never be in a position to find the answer to the hypothetical question. As it stood, here and now, there was no contest. Alexandra represented pain, death and decay, and danger in the first degree, while Anna represented life and hope and the freshness and challenge of all that was new. Alexandra was the past while Anna was the future. Oh true, she was also very dangerous, especially with that Damoclean sword of a brain tumour hanging like a cloud above her head. It wouldn't do, would it, he mused, to allow himself to fall in love with Anna Sanchez, only to stand at her grave two years down the road, weeping and wearing white lillies of bereavement! *She isn't going to die,* he told himself firmly. *Whatever else happens, she isn't going to die!*

He watched as she walked out of the narrow door and crossed the street towards him. She had changed out of the while summer dress with all its buttons and now wore a very short cocktail number in deep rose pink that swished evocateivly around her legs, legs that ended in high heeled while sandals. Pendant earings made from coral dangled from her ears, and in her hand she carried a small canvas bag.

'What's in the bag?' he asked, walking forwards to meet her.

'A few things for the morning,' she answered.

'The morning?' he echoed.

'The morning,' she confirmed.

Once again they stood in the bedroom. Neither of them made any effort to turn on the lights, but the room was flooded with the soft yellow reflection from the street lamps. It was all the illumination they needed. She leaned with her back to the bedroom door, receiving Mage's kiss and kissing hard in return. He made no move to touch her until she took his hands and brought them up from her waist to cover her breasts.

'My God, I hope you know what you're doing,' he breathed between kisses.

'Yes, my Colin, I know exactly what I am doing. You might not yet be my man, but from this night, I am your woman.'

He said nothing. There was nothing he could say. Moving his hand, he lowered his head to her breast, feeling her nipple pressing against the fine silk of the pink dress, hard and thrusting, longing to be set free from its concealment and captivity. Acting on instinct, Anna unfastened the two small bows at her shoulders, then reaching down for the hem, she eased the dress up over her hips, then over her head, and allowed it to fall where it would, not knowing or caring where that might be as Mage's tongue described a low and descending arc across her rib cage and her stomach. He fell to his knees before her, his head moving ever lower until his tongue was pushing and licking at the white lace of her lingerie. His hands curved down along her sides, picking up the inconsequential material of her briefs and easing them down, first over her hips and then along her legs.

She gasped in disbelief as the tip of his tongue probed through the tight curls of her pubic hair, the gasp becomming a small strangled cry as he pushed her legs more widely open, running the top of his tongue along the outer lips of her vagina before pressing against her clitoris...

And then he was lifting her, and carrying her to the bed... Laying her down and spreading her legs wider than she'd thought they would ever spread. Her first orgasm came as he covered her sex with his mouth, his tongue darting in and out of her, licking her to heights of pleasure that defied description. Then he was towering above her, removing his own clothes, and her second orgasm came as she felt his rigid member, first brushing against her, and then, so very gently, easing into her, filling her up with a fullness that touched every fibre of her being. There was one small tear of pain but the pain was lost in the explosion of a hundred other sensations. It was only when he began to move rythmically in and out of her, sometimes kissing her fiercely on the mouth, sometimes rubbing his face against her breasts, that she began to become aware of the fact that all which had gone before was a precursor for something different, something so much greater, something so incredibly *awesome*, that was beginning to build up inside her. It grew and grew with the increasing urgency of his thrusts, but it was only when he hooked his arms around her legs, bringing her knees up so that they almost touched the pillow beneath her head, that it finally exploded like the flooding eruption of a long dormant volcano. Her sweat streaked body twisted and turned and writhed within the agony and the extacy. To hang on to any sense of reality, she clung fiercely to him, digging her fingers deeply into the flesh of his back... But now, oh God, there was something else.... He was trembling and shuddering, harder within her than before... And then she felt it. A hot stream of lava shooting up inside her, and she heard it too in the long wolflike cry that emitted from his lips as he flung his tawny head back, eyes closed in the power and the passion of his own release, bellowing like a wounded bull at the shadows on the ceiling.

Later, she didn't know what time it might have been but they had both slept and had awoken simultaniously, she took him in her arms, holding his head maternally against her heart, stroking his hair and kissing the palm of his hand which she held firmly in her hand. She spoke to him, not knowing whether he heard or not.

'Tomorrow, you will go back to Castillo and you will fight your battle. I shall stay here, but shall come with you in my mind. When you fight your fight, you will not fight it alone. You have the colour of my love, red, like the colour of my blood, to wear like your lady's colours. I am your lady and if you are to be my man, you must win, Colin. You must win, for my sake as well as your own. You *will* win! I love you... I love you... I love you...'

Mage heard. Said nothing. Wept silently.

27.

Advances

This time, as he travelled on the train, he did notice the magnificent scenery. His senses were alive and he noticed everything. High wheeling eagles that hovered arrogantly above the mountain passes, herds of goats that roamed semi wild through dense olive groves, shards of silver water that cascaded down steep hillsides in sparkling streams. The soup stain on the ticket collector's tie, the wedge of cheese that was about to tumble from the sandwich being eaten by the old peasant woman who sat surrounded by her bags on the opposite side of the aisle. In particular he noticed Anna's canvas overnight bag that sat on the seat opposite him. In it was the dark pink dress she'd worn the previous evening and the sheet from the hotel bed with its powerfully symbolic bloodstain.

They'd looked at the bloodied sheet with a mixture of delight and horror.

'We cannot leave it like that,' she had said.

'No,' he'd agreed. 'So we'll take it with us.'

'I'm glad you have seen it... You know?'

'I know, and you know that I did not need to see it!'

He'd watched her dress, marvelling at her lack of shyness as she'd climbed into a pair of jeans and a denim blouse. 'You're very beautiful,' he'd said.

'I'm very skinny,' she'd riposted. 'But it is my own fault for not eating. Now that I know we are together, I shall probably eat like a pig and when you see me again I shall be enormously fat.'

'Fat or skinny, you'd still be beautiful.' He'd folded the sheet up and for want of somewhere to put it, had placed it in her bag. The pink dress had been where it had fallen the night before, crumpled in a little heap by the bedroom door. He'd picked it up, immediately aware of the scent of her perfume that still clung to the silk. Thoughtfully, he'd placed it in the bag with the sheet.

'You are taking my dress with you?' she'd laughed.

'I'd like to.'

She shaken her head sorrowfully. 'Somehow I do not think it will fit you!'

He'd grinned. 'I dare say it won't, but I'll hang it up somewhere in the house and every time I see it I shall remember how I came to get it.'

'You will think of me sometimes?' she'd asked seriously.

'More than sometimes.'

'I will be thinking of you all the time.'

They'd been by the door, ready to leave. He had kissed her gently. 'I know you will,' he'd said, '...and that will give me great strength.'

'Can you come back to Ronda soon... I mean, before everything is all over in Castillo?'

'I'll try. I want to. If I don't, it will only be because I honestly can't.'

'Colin...' she'd glanced at the desecrated bed in a meaningful way. 'I want you to know that I have no regrets.'

'Good,' he'd said. 'Neither have I.'

Certainly none that he was going to tell her about, anyway.

He'd walked her back to the clinic and they had stolen a last moment together.

'You're not going to get into trouble, are you?' he'd asked.

'Probably,' she'd giggled, 'but what are they going to do? Send me back to Castillo? Despite all that you have said and all that my father has said, I really would not protest too much if they did that!' Her tone had changed. 'My darling Colin, do promise me that you will take great care.'

'I promise.'

'And even if it is in shreds and tatters, promise me you will come back to me when you can.'

'That I also promise,' he'd held her tight, kissing her, praying to God that she would be strong and would not cry and then, hessian sacked crossbow in one hand, the overnight bag in the other, he'd marched away, doing battle with his own moist eyes and the wicked lump of emotion that had risen in his throat.

Even now he could still smell her perfume. Her spore covered the essence of his being and he could even taste the honey and champagne taste of her sex. The magician within him argued that he had lost two valuable weapons, his chastity and his detachment. But the man within him rejoiced, for had he not also acquired two new weapons that might yet prove to be even more valuable? Was he not returning from Ronda, not only with that magical and mysterious crossbow, but also with a woman's love?

It would be an exaggeration to say that Mage arrived back to a reception committee, but even as he'd driven through the village from the railway station, he'd sensed a subtle hardening in Castillo's atmosphere. The sky had been a bright unforgiving blue and the heat of the morning had been unusually harsh. There had been a note from Light, pushed under the door at Granadillos, with instructions to meet him at the Miraflores a.s.a.p. and after showering and changing his clothes he'd walked into the hotel bar to find everyone waiting for him. He could see by their faces that the news was not good.

Hector was glowering but, Mage assumed, there was inevitably a personal angle to Hector's mood. He'd have to do something about it in due course, but now was obviously not the right time. Helen looked agitated while Light was his usual inscrutable self. Only Tamara appeared relatively calm.

There was another man present in the group. Thin hair, thick horn rimmed glasses and a weak chin. He was wearing an expensive lightweight grey suit and seemed noticeably more tense than the others. Mage didn't know him and he wondered what he was doing here. His presence obviously had something to do with Light's note and this impromptu gathering. He focused on Light and raised a quizzical eyebrow.

'There's some good news and bad news – and more bad news,' the black American drawled. 'Which do you want first?'

'You choose,' Mage said, swinging himself up onto one of the high bar stools.

'Well, let's start with the bad news. Dolorean's car has gone missing. Don't ask me how or why, but when Christina checked this morning the car was gone. Neither she nor the boy have got any idea when it went.'

'Oh shit!' Mage exclaimed. 'What happened? Were they both asleep at the same time?'

'Probably, but go easy man. They've been on that stake-out for nearly two weeks with nothing much to do other than screw each other into a coma. It's inevitable that by now they've got lax and lazy. It would happen to anyone, even experienced pros, which, of course, they're not. They're both pissed off with themselves, so there's no point in giving 'em a harder time than they're already having. The other thing to remember is that this doesn't mean our bird has flown. For all we know the car could have been lifted by some local bad boy. Maybe Dolorean doesn't even know it's gone yet.'

'One way or another, we have to find out,' Mage said emphatically. 'Christ knows how, but we have to get into the house and see if they are still there and, if they are, then I don't give a shit about the car. But if they've gone, we have to find that car and fast... Hector, will Jaime Gomez help us on this one?'

'I think he will, yes... but you are going to have to talk to him first. He is curious about you, and has put two and two together. He knows that you are a part of the problem he is having with Castillo but, of course, he can't work out the mechanics and angles of it. I must also tell you that he is not too kindly disposed towards you. The way he sees it, he saved your life the other week, and you haven't even bothered to say thank you.'

Mage scratched at his beard sheepishly. 'Shit,' he said for the third time in as many minutes, 'he's got a point, hasn't he? Okay, my first point of call from here is the police station. Let's see what I can salvage.'

'Do you want me to come with you?'

'Yes please Hector, I do...' He turned back to Light. 'What's the good news, John?'

Light waved a hand in Leon's direction. 'This is Leon Shapiro. You haven't met him, but he's a friend of a friend of yours in Israel. He says he's come here to find you, that he's got valuable information for you and that he's here to help. He ain't telling us anything else, but Helen and I both agree. The guy's a spook. He's got "government" stamped all the way through his aura. The complication is that he isn't here on his own. He's got at least two, possibly even three people on his tail. Helen and I both spotted them in the square last night. We thought, first of all, that we were under observation, but when we sorted it out and played a few games, it turns out that Leon here is the object of their interest. He swears blind that he doesn't know anything about all of this and we believe him... but it doesn't altar the fact that he's come here to find you and someone has seen fit to put a very professional surveillance team on his tail, whether he knows about it or not.'

'Mr Mage,' Leon pushed through between Light and Tamara, 'it's very important that I talk to you alone!'

'We can do that if you like, but there's very little point. Anything you tell me will be immediately passed on to my friends here. We could save a lot of time if you're prepared to trust us as a group.'

Leon glanced around nervously. The bar was empty, but he still felt exposed and not a little intimidated by these people. His preconception of this meeting was that it would be an intense and private head to head conversation with a man who stood alone against their common enemy, and yet in reality Mage did not stand alone and he, Leon, was being asked to unburden his soul, almost, as it were, in public. It was a far cry from the romantic notion that he'd had of riding to Mage's rescue like the Seventh Cavalry in pursuit of marauding Indians. There may have been marauding Indians, but it seemed that Mage already had plenty of reinforcements. Deflated by this scenario, Leon shrugged.

'I've come from Herschal,' he said simply.

Mage smiled broadly and warmly. 'I guessed as much!' he exclaimed, reaching forwards to shake Leon's hand. With the physical contact a shiver ran up his arm and constricted his heart. The smile froze on his face as the psychic emanations pulsed into his mind from the other man's memory cells. 'Herschal's dead?' he asked softly in shocked disbelief.

'I'm afraid so.'

'When did this happen – and how?'

'As for when, about two and a half weeks ago. I say "about" because I'm still a little hazy about time...'

'I didn't pick up a thing!' Mage interrupted, the disbelief worming its way ever more deeply into his psyche.

'...And as for how,' Leon continued, 'a Djinn bit his head off.'

During the tenure of his stay at the hotel Light had built up an enviable rapport with Henry Holloway. They shared a love of good wine and a quirky interest in bizarre cocktails. After the second week of their acquaintance Henry had given Light free run of the bar on an honour system, and thus Light felt at ease as he strode behind the counter and dispensed a round of strong drinks while the others pulled up chairs around a table in the furthest corner of the bar. Leon told his story directly and in detail. He did not need to embellish anything, for even the barest bones of his tale made fascinating and grim listening. For the better part Mage sat in silence, but Light asked a number of sharp and pertinent questions, frequently making Leon go over various parts of his story twice and three times. He was particularly interested in Herschal's offensive actions against the Djinn..

'Let me get this right in my mind,' he said slowly. 'Out of the vortex of turbulent air, you see this shape. It''s big and humanoid, but fat and squat with it. It's got a face half way between a man and a pig. It's got tusks and rows of serrated teeth, and the whole of its body is covered by what you describe as scaly armour, including the thing's arms and legs. It hasn't got fingers as such, but claws, that are like an animal's, only these claws are much longer and sharper, right?'

'It's an accurate description, yes.'

'Did you notice anything peculiar about its navel?' Helen asked. 'Something that might have looked like a coiled whip?'

'No, I can't remember anything like that.'

'Never mind that,' Light said. 'This thing takes form above the surface of the water. It's clearly very aggressive. You shout at Herschal to shoot and the old man pumps a couple of rounds into it's chest. You said, if I heard you right, that you actually saw the rounds hit their target? Tell me about that again. Everything you can remember.'

Leon closed his eyes in concentration. 'It all happened very very fast. Hershal fired three times. The first two shots hit the Djinn in the chest. There wasn't a spurt of blood or anything like that, but black stuff started oozing out of the two holes. There was about a second, no more than that, then he fired a third shot. I didn't see what happened to that one because by then the Djinn was already well into a state of change.'

'Okay, tell me all you can remember about that!'

'This is where it gets difficult...'

'Do the best you can. Take your time. I can't tell you how important this is.'

'All right...The thing just changed, in less than a second. One minute it was this scaly thing, gnashing its tusks or whatever they were, and then the next it was a swirling mass of grey and brown smoke curving up and clinging to the roof of the cavern. It came across the ceiling towards us like a bat out of hell, then it simply dropped on top of Herschal. I heard the gun go off again and just for a second, after I heard the old man scream, I saw the thing's face in the smoke. It had Herschal's head it its mouth and it was looking straight at me. That's when I lost it, I'm afraid. That's when I ran.'

Leon opened his eyes. They were full of humiliation and apology.

'Don't get worked up about it, man,' Light said frankly. 'If it'd been me in your shoes, I'd have been out of there long before you made your exit!'

Mage entered the interrogation for the first time. 'Do you know,' he asked quietly, 'if Herschal did anything to summon the Djinn?'

'No, I don't know that. As far as I was concerned we were just going to spend the night down in the cave by the water's edge and wait and see what happened. I know that everything seemed to be all right and then I fell asleep. When I woke up there was all this swirling mist and these weird flickering lights and within a few minutes after that all hell was breaking loose.' He looked at Mage in mute appeal. 'The thing which is so difficult for me is that I didn't believe him... Not a word of what he told me. If I *had* believed him, he'd still be alive today.'

Mage leaned across the table and rested his hand on Leon's wrist. 'Don't blame yourself too much. Even with all the facts and terms of reference, things that you didn't have, it would still be an unbelievable story. Let's change the subject for a moment, can we. If John and Helen say that you're under surveillance, then I think it's fairly safe to assume that this is the case. Have you any idea who these people might be?'

Leon nodded his head miserably. 'I don't know for certain, but I could hazard a guess. Gideon Lemski let me go far too easily. I thought he was giving me a free rein, although I knew he didn't believe my story about international terrorists. What I suspect he's done is put the Spanish P3 unit on my case, which if nothing else just goes to show he's more impressed and worried about Herschal and The Elijah File than he was prepared to admit.'

'What's a P3 unit?' Mage asked blankly.

'Mossad hit squad,' Light said grimly.

Leon shot him a curious look. 'You seem to be very well informed.'

'I am,' Light grinned humourlessly.

'It's not really a "hit squad",' Leon said defensively to Mage. '...But we do have resident teams in just about every country in the world and if Mossad needs any really dirty work done quickly and quietly, then they're the people who usually do it. It's true that a P3 team will carry out an assassination if called for, but frankly the occurrences are few and far between. They're the strong arm of Mossad's overseas operations, but more like the British SAS than, say, the CIA.'

'Lord,' Mage muttered, 'how do we go about keeping them out of our hair?'

'I'll phone Gideon Lemski and tell him to call them off.'

'No don't do that,' Light said quickly. 'Look, as far as they're concerned, their purpose for being here is to keep tabs on you, right? They don't know anything about the Djinn, Herschal or the Elijah File. They figure that if there's any kind of threat it's going to come from terrorists or some other such crap. As long as they see you're okay, they not actually going to *do* anything and, therefore, they're no real threat to us and, who knows, there might be some circumstances wherein they might actually be useful. I assume they'll be armed?'

'They'll have quite an arsenal on hand somewhere,' Leon confirmed.

'Good. So, if we need some fire power, we've got three pros hanging in the wings who've got it and know how to use it. That kind of makes me feel a little happier rather than worried. I say we ignore 'em until we need 'em and let's keep our fingers crossed that we never do! Let's face it, we're a little light on firepower ourselves. At least old Herschal had a shot gun and, incidentally, I'm gratified to learn that he managed to do some damage with it. When I had my run in with the Djinn, all I had was a hand gun. Sure, it was a Colt Python .357 magnum, but like I told you guys once before, I actually watched the bullets bounce off that armour plate stuff that they pull around them when they're in the warrior mode.'

'Just a minute,' Leon asked urgently. 'Are you telling me that you've actually been in combat with one of the things that killed Herschal?'

'Yep, that's what I'm telling you and for the sake of the record I've got to report that I came off a damn sight worse than he did. And I'll tell you something else which you might like to chew on. From what Colin has told me, it seems that quite a few people know about the Djinn, but as far as I know there are only two people alive on this planet who have actually seen one. They're both sitting in this bar right now, because I'm talking about you and me!'

Leon looked at Mage. 'But haven't you... I mean, I thought...?'

Mage shook his head. 'No, sorry Leon. I've seen him in his human form and in the process of partial transformation, but not as the full blown warrior.'

'I see,' said Leon, somewhat vaguely and not really seeing at all. And then – 'Herschal led me to believe that there was a Djinn here, in this village. Is this true?'

Mage and Light exchanged dark looks. 'There certainly was up until last night,' Mage said eventually, 'but whether or not he's still here this morning is a debatable point, and this is a question we have to find an answer to sooner rather than later.'

Mage walked briskly up the hill with Hector by his side.

'How is Anna?' Hector asked.

It was a loaded question and Mage knew it. 'She's fine,' he said lightly. 'Happier for having seen me and prepared to stay in Ronda for the time being.'

'And you're not going to tell me anything else?'

'No, I'm not. How is Helen?'

'That's different.'

'I'm sure it is,' Mage demurred, content at having made his point.

Jaime Gomez received them in his office and Mage went straight on to the attack, squeezing the policeman's hand warmly and pressing his index finger firmly against the pulse point at Jaime's wrist.

Jaime hadn't been sure what he'd been expecting from the meeting, but it certainly wasn't this. The extranjero was polite, almost to the point of being deferential. His apologies and thanks were nothing if not sincere and he behaved not so much like the foreigner that he was, but more like an Hidalgo or an Alcalde. Jaime found himself warming to the man, admitting to himself that he could have been wrong in his initial judgement of this Señor Mage, for he was most unlike any of the other extranjeros that had crossed his path over the years.

Mage made a passing remark, humorous and about nothing of any great consequence. Jaime laughed in response and Hector blinked in surprise. To hear Jaime Gomez laugh in anything approaching genuine humour was a rare occurrence indeed. Surprise turned to wry admiration as Jaime waved his hand expansively and asked: 'How may I help you Señor Mage?'

How could Jaime help Mage? Mage had been semi-officially summoned to help Jaime, so how had their roles become so reversed? How had Colin managed to twist things round so completely? Hector listened and watched, only gradually becoming aware of the fact that he was seeing magic in the making. He saw that Colin was drawing the policeman in, covering him with a glamour of bonhomie that had them chatting with the familiarity of old friends within less than fifteen minutes. Jaime sent for coffee and even went so far as to produce a bottle of Magno to go with it when it came. Colin helped himself to the policeman's black Ducados cigarettes, and Jaime chain smoked Mage's Marlboros. Hector, sitting in the corner by the window, felt ignored and forgotten as the policeman settled more comfortably into the web that the magician was weaving. Hector was in no doubt that Jaime had no idea of what was happening.

For Mage's part it was hard work, though not as hard as he'd expected it might be. Jaime Gomez had changed a lot since their first encounter in the Miraflores all those weeks before and, as he drew the policeman's vibration ever more closely in tune with his own, he became increasingly impressed with what he found in the other man's subconscious.

When, that day in the hotel bar, he had brushed against Jaime's psyche, he had found it darkly repulsive and so full of turbulent negativity that he had chosen to retreat quickly rather than be contaminated by the dirt that clung to the policeman's soul. Now, by force of necessity, he looked more deeply into the man and found that some form of cleansing had taken place. Certainly there were still many layers of psychosis that were ugly in their ardour and their anger, but at least, now that he was taking the trouble to look, he could begin to understand why Jaime's spirit was so pitted and scarred. The fury, the resentment, the contempt for his fellow men born of the injustices perpetrated by them were all still there, borne of Jaime's belief that he had been borne for greatness and yet had only attained mediocrity, held back by the flukes of fate that made his physical appearance as appealing as his politics. Isolation and rejection had pushed him into the safe sex of glossy magazines and hard films; the commercial sex bought in the sweaty whorehouses of Madrid and the bordellos of Marbella and Barcelona were real substitutes for the union found in loving emotional relationships. Indeed, for Jaime Gomez, relationships such as these were abstractions, unreal in the reality of his own experience.

And yet beneath this cyclone of anti-social bitterness, Mage found something pure and worthwhile. A spark of human brightness cast a flickering light into the dark morass of the policeman's bitter dispair. Finding the spark, Mage blew on it, kindling it to a small but steady flame.

'Doctor Sanchez tells me that you have become deeply concerned by the many tragic events which have taken place in Castillo,' Mage said evenly. 'That you see that there is a pattern to these events...'

'Yes, but I do not understand this pattern.'

Mage nodded thoughtfully. 'It is a hard pattern to understand, Jaime.' Incredibly, they were now on first name terms. 'But I understand it, and I am here today to offer you my help and also to ask for your help in return.'

'We will help each other!' Jaime exclaimed vehemently, 'and together we shall put an end to the curse that has descended upon this village.'

'It is curious that you think of what is happening here as a curse, for in a way, that is exactly what it is...'

Mage presented Jaime with the same story, albeit with a few embellishments, that had been offered to Christina and Angel. Jaime listened intently but with mounting confusion and inner conflict. On the one hand, he found the idea of magic, black witches, bruhos and curses a difficult pill to swallow – but on the other hand he was very mindful of his own terrifying experience up by the citadel. That had been like a magical force, hadn't it? And what power, other than something horribly weird and mystical, could do to a pig what he had seen done to a pig? Furthermore, it was obvious, glaringly, magnificently obvious that this extranjero was a good *good* man who had come to Castillo to help the village with its many horrific complaints and yet, if it were not for him, Jaime Gomez, being in the right place at the right time, this extranjero would be dead, his head cloven in two by a mad man's meat cleaver. And how had he come to be in the right place at the right time? Because the Blue Lady had *told* him to be there, and what was The Blue Lady, if not a manifestation of the spirit and the power of the magic that the extranjero was trying to explain to him at this very minute? A month before and Jaime would have thrown this Englishman out of his office without a second thought. Now, he sat thoughtfully, trying to make sense of what he'd been told.

'If this man Dolorean is such a bad man, why has he not been arrested in England?'

'Because he has not broken any criminal law, either in England or in Spain. The laws that he has broken are not brokered by governments or secular authorities... But he is still a criminal, and is known to be a criminal by different people in different places. This is why there are unofficial policeman already here in the village who have come to try and neutralise the threat he poses.'

Jaime looked up with quickened interest. 'Who are these "unofficial policemen"?' he asked.

'There is myself, for one, from England. Helen Ross, from Scotland, is another. The black couple from America, Señor and Señora Light, are here to represent the American interest in Dolorean's destruction. Another gentleman, a Mr Leon Shapiro, arrived from Israel yesterday and, of course, there is Doctor Sanchez, sitting quietly there in the corner. None of us belongs to any official police force, apart, that is, for Mr Shapiro, but we are all aware of the threat that Dolorean poses and we are all here to police and arrest his activities. Apart from Hector, we have come from many different places across the world at no small financial expense, to put an end to the dark happenings that have caused so many problems in this place.

'And yet, even with all our combined knowledge and resources, we are powerless without your help and co-operation. Dolorean's car has disappeared. We need to find it, but what is more important, is that we need to know whether Dolorean has disappeared with it or whether he is still lurking in his lair in Calle Sombra. Certainly, we could break in, but then we would be breaking the laws of Spain. Far better that I come to you at this time, for you are The Chief of Police, and if a house must be entered to ascertain the whereabouts of a criminal, far better you do it than us. There is something else... I must find a way of entering the citadel. For reasons that we will show you, it is impossible to excavate down to the door, so I seek to force access through the roof, which is something else I cannot do without your co-operation.'

'Why is the citadel so important?' Jaime asked uneasily.

'I'm not sure, and even if I was, I'm not sure that I could explain it. As men, we all take our strength from something, whether it is belief in the workings of law and order or, in Doctor Sanchez's case, a belief in the power of healing. Some men take their strength from a belief in God, others take it from a belief of their own rightness. Some take it from the possession of money and material things, others take it from the power of love, while others still find it in concepts such as freedom and equality, or, on the dark side, through domination and cruelty. Dolorean takes his strength from something that is within, or beneath the citadel!' Mage leaned across the table and lowering his voice so that Jaime had to strain to hear the whispered words, he laid the palms of his hands across the policeman's wrists. 'Jaime, the thing that nearly killed you up there must itself be killed! You have a powerful pair of friends in Doctor Sanchez and myself, and there are other people also waiting to offer you the gift of friendship if you're prepared to accept it. You also have a very powerful spiritual ally, and if you find it hard to accept what I am telling you, then find some faith in the words of your Blue Madonna!'

Jaime reeled in shock. The extranjero knew! Not only about the suffocating darkness up at the citadel but also about his visions and visitations! But how? How? How?

'How?' he finally managed to croak.

'By the power that you doubt. The power that is real and is within us all. Brightly within you and me and Doctor Sanchez and our other friends, but darkly, so terribly darkly within our enemy. Now, Captain Gomez, tell me that you're on our side and that you're going to help us!'

Jaime looked for words. Failed to find them, but nodded numbly.

Accompanied by a young patrolman, they spent five minutes banging on the front door. When there was no response, they climbed the wall at the back of the house and negotiated the garden, now curiously devoid of atmosphere or psychic phenomena. After rattling shutters and doors, Jaime effectively snapped the lock on the French windows and the quartet tentatively entered the building.

'Be very careful,' Mage warned as they made their way across the kitchen towards the hallway that led to the front door. Jaime needed no warning. The holster flap was unbuttoned and his right hand constantly rested on the butt of his loaded gun. Even so, after only a very few minutes, it was clear to all that the house was empty. There was a deserted musty feel to the rooms, along with a lingering smell of dirt, reminiscent of stale and contaminated chemicals. There was no sign of habitation in any of the down stairs rooms, but in one of the upper bedrooms they did find evidence of occupation. Two single beds had been slept in, three suitcases stood open revealing a jumble of ordinary everyday clothes. Upon a vanity table there were the basic ingredients of a woman's cornucopia of cosmetics.

'Christ,' said the young patrolman. 'It stinks like shit in here!'

Indeed the smell of decay and excreta was particularly strong and Patrolman Sancho Ferro was not the only member of the quartet to wrinkle his nose.

They moved back out onto the landing and Mage lit a cigarette, feeling both frustrated and dejected. 'They've gone,' he said flatly, 'and by the feel of it, they've been gone for quite a while.'

'This is all very strange,' Jaime commented. 'According to what you say, Dolorean and his female, who is lately pregnant, have been living here for the better part of two weeks, but there is no evidence of such occupation. There is no food in the cupboards, the refrigerator is turned on but is also empty. There is no sign of the cooker having been used, although there is a full bombona of gas. There are bottles of water, but no tea or coffee or alcohol. Everything is covered in dust and, if they have been living here, they've contained their residence to this one bedroom, which is in itself unlikely. What have they been doing here all this time? What have they been eating and drinking? What kind of person can live on bottled water for the better part of a fortnight?'

Hector and Mage exchanged looks. *A person who isn't a person at all!* Hector thought with a deep thrill, that was half fear and half relief. Wouldn't it be just too wonderful if they'd gone for good. If they'd taken stock of the opposition arraigned against them and had fled in their car to some other place, taking their malignancy with them!

'Let's have a look at the passage that leads to the church,' Mage suggested.

Underground, in the cellar, the atmosphere was as bland and as indifferent as it was in the upper rooms. With deliberate effort, Jaime and Ferro forced the lock and they explored the dimly lit passage that led beneath Calle Sombra and emerged in the vestry of Santa Clara. Jaime felt that he was in receipt of secrets, embodied by the discovery of this tunnel.

'Is there any link between Dolorean and the fact that Father Ignatious is so seriously ill?' he asked. 'It seems more than coincidental that this tunnel runs from Dolorean's house to Ignatious's church.'

'We think that there is a very strong link,' Mage told him. 'Anyway, there's nothing here. Let's go back and check out the garden.'

'The garden?' Jaime echoed. 'What is there of interest in the garden?'

'The well,' Hector said morosely.

Mage grinned, but said nothing, and led the party back out into the open air. At the well, he knelt by the rim and peered down into the bottomless pit. Here there was some trace of psychic disturbance, although nothing on the scale of what he and Hector had experienced on their last visit. He wondered what effect his "bomb" had had, and wondered more pointedly what might happen were he to try lowering himself down the narrow bore hole. Even as he thought the thought, a vague but vivid picture flowed into his mind of malefic glee. *Dolorean would love it if I tried. He's discarded the defences to sucker me into making a silly move. I go down there, thinking everything has quietened down, but I sure as hell don't come up again!*

'Okay, our birds have flown. We don't know whether they're coming back here or not, but I suspect that the answer is that they won't be. They've gone to ground somewhere else... God knows where, but it won't be too far away from Castillo, that's for sure. What we have to do now is find the car.'

'Give me what details you can,' Jaime said, 'and I'll get my people onto it straight away.'

They found the Jaguar towards the end of the afternoon. It was parked down by the river, half a mile upstream of the iron bridge which spanned the Hozgarganta. No real effort had been made to conceal the vehicle, but it had been left behind a thick scree of ferns and oleanders, the dark green paintwork blending its soft lines in with the back drop of the foliage

For the purpose of the search they had split into small groups; Jaime and his men in two Seat police cars, Light and Tamara in their hire car, Hector and Helen in Hector's old green Renault Four, Leon with Mage in the Land Rover. They'd tuned their walkie talkies into the local police band and thus had been able to stay in radio contact with each other throughout the day. Given that Mage had the only four wheel drive, he'd drawn the short straw of checking the more inaccessible outlying districts. Leon had carried the black camera case over his shoulder, sitting with it firmly on his lap as the Land Rover had bounced along the pitted cart tracks around the outskirts of the village.

Mage had eyed the case obliquely on a number of occasions. Helen had reminded him of the vision she'd had at The Oaks, and also of how Leon had avoided making any comment when she'd asked him about the gun. In the end, his curiosity had got the better of him.

'What's in the case, Leon?' he'd asked at one point when they'd been cruising down a winding back lane that ran parallel with the main road to San Pablo.

Leon had grinned openly. 'I was wondering when you'd ask!'

'So I'm asking now.'

'A sub machine gun, six clips of ammo, three grenades and a limpet mine.'

'You being serious?'

'Dead right I'm being serious...' Leon had twisted in his seat, 'and I'm also seriously curious as to how your friend Helen knew I had a gun with me that was "all handle and no barrel".'

'She saw you with it in a dream that she had, about a month ago.'

'That's crazy,' Leon had responded, not totally sure what was crazier – someone he'd never met seeing him in a dream, or careering around the Spanish campo in search of an alien being from another dimension in time and space.

'Not really. Not if you're someone like Helen Ross.'

As they'd criss-crossed the lattice work of cart tracks, Mage had told him of his own time in the Negev and, indeed, the whole story behind his meeting with Herschal. He'd quietly grieved at the loss of the old shaman and had made Leon tell his own story yet again. Leon had obliged, albeit tersely, with words filled with emotion.

'That's why I've got this with me,' he'd concluded, slapping his hand against the aluminium case. 'If ever I'm in the unfortunate position of coming face to face with one of those creatures again I'm not even going to think twice. I'm going to annihilate the thing!'

If you can, Mage had thought grimly, not at all sure that bullets were the answer to the problem. His mind had come to rest on the crossbow and the unusual sextet of hollowed bolts. Regardless of their original purpose, he had a few ideas of what could be done to them to make them potent against the Djinn. Bullets did not equate with magic, but maybe, if the bolts could be doctored in some way... if he could fill the hollow projectiles with the right ammunition, the right *ingredients*...

They'd checked in with the rest of the team every half hour or so, despondent that the others were having no more luck than they were. Mage had felt sure that Dolorean had not strayed far from Castillo, although logically he could have been anywhere on the Iberian peninsular by now if he'd so chosen. Jaime had radioed an APB appeal through the Guardia Civil, but so far nothing had come to light. Instinctively Mage had not been surprised. He'd been quite sure that the shapechanger was still within spitting distance of the citadel.

By four o'clock both men had been gagging for a drink. They'd stopped briefly to quench their thirst at the Venta El Vaquero, and then had crossed the main road, trailing back towards Castillo across the open country by the side of the river, south of the village. Mage had missed a turn and their route had taken them along the river bank to the west of the village, bringing them to the firmer surface of the tarmac road by the iron bridge. He'd been in the process of swinging the Land Rover to the right when Leon had suddenly demanded that he stop.

'What's up?' Mage had asked.

Leon had scrambled out of the cab and, crossing to the edge of the road, had studied the dirt track that carried on northwards between the river and the rising massive of rock and stone that was Castillo's mountain.

'Come and look at this,' he'd called.

Mage had jumped out of the Land Rover, joining Leon at the point where the dirt track left the road. Leon had pointed wordlessly towards the dusty earth. 'If I remember my Jaguars, they *do* have rather wide tyres, don't they?'

Mage had looked and, sure enough, faintly etched into the hard packed ground there were the unmistakable tracks of a wide tyred vehicle. 'Could be from a Nissan Patrol,' Mage had mused softly.

'Uh huh,' Leon had shaken his head in the negative. 'Look at the occasional scuff marks between the tracks. That's been done by a sump or a low slung exhaust. A Nissan or any of the other big four wheel drives have got more than enough ground clearance to get over this terrain without their undercarriages getting in the way.'

'You're right,' Mage had looked at Leon with new found respect. He'd raised a quizzical eyebrow. 'So, do we call in the cavalry now, or wait till we find the Jag?'

'Let's find the car... and that way, if we *don't* find it, we haven't got egg splattered all over our faces.'

'Okay, do we walk or do we drive?'

'Let's walk. No disrespect, but that's not the most comfortable vehicle I've ever travelled in.'

'True.' Mage had cast an affectionate glance over his shoulder. 'But I wouldn't swap it for all the Nissans in Japan.'

They had followed the tracks, realising that there was only one set of tyre marks. What ever had driven down that way had not driven back and, from what Mage had remembered of the topography, there was nowhere for anything other than a four wheel drive to go. The track clung to the river bank for half a mile or so, then disintegrated into a goat path that wove its way northwards through canyons of smooth stone and boulders the size of small houses. If you were brave, you could force a passage across country towards the east, skirting around the northern barrio of Castillo, but it was extremely rough terrain, difficult even for a Land Rover and impossible for an ordinary car.

They had come to the end of the track, had eyed the boulders speculatively, and then had turned their attention towards the surrounding bushes. The afternoon was perfectly still but imperfectly silent. A sharp glint of reflected light caught Mage's eye.

'There it is,' he said, his voice sounding strangely loud. 'Over there, behind the oleanders.'

They brushed through the thick sea of ferns until the Jaguar was only a few yards distant. It looked forlornly out of place and, incongruously, the passenger door had been left open on its hinge. Leon took another cautious step forward but Mage restrained him.

'No, careful Leon. There's something not quite right here. Let's take this very slowly.'

He used the walkie talkie to call off the search, giving their location and issuing specific instructions. Then, knowing that it would be at least fifteen minutes before any one arrived, he and Leon circumnavigated the car looking for any signs of flight.

'Over here,' Leon called after only a few seconds and Mage joined him where a swathe of trampled ferns led away from the car towards the goat path. Still mindful of the eerie stillness, they followed the spore. There was a stretch of grass between the ferns and the rocks that revealed no secrets, but at the beginning of the goat path there were tell tale scuff marks in the sand.

'That's where they've gone,' Leon said, stating the obvious, 'but what's up there that would make them leave the car like this?'

Mage's eyes clouded as he remembered the first time he'd stood up at the castle gazing along the cut of this river and its deep ravine. *Caves* he had thought. *There would have to be caves.*

'There'll be a cave,' he said quietly, casting a glance over his shoulder at the massive buttress of rock that supported the keep and the citadel and, on the far side of the mountain, the village of Castillo. From the river to the castle it was little more than a quarter mile as flew the crow, but it would have taken several hours of careful climbing to negotiate the distance, and only then if one was an experienced climber. How long, he thought, might it take to stroll along an easy subterranean tunnel? Twenty minutes? Half an hour?

He put himself in Dolorean's shoes and tried to look at things from the shapechanger's point of view. There had to be a problem with practical logistics, surely? Given that for whatever reason he had needed to move Alexandra from Calle Sombra into the citadel, how could he do it easily and without bringing unwanted attention upon himself. He could hardly drop a heavily pregnant woman down that narrow garden well, and even if he could wave a magic wand and remove the resin which sealed the entrance to the citadel, there was still a ton of earth pressed up hard against the door. How much easier, how much more *convenient* if there was a cave that gave access to and easy passage through the base of the mountain.

Of course, there was no guarantee that the citadel *was* the place of the opening, but it *felt* right and everything pointed in that direction. Helen's clairvoyant visions coincided with Hamish Hamilton's descriptions, and the protective barrier of resin had to be significant of something, hadn't it? The fact that the Djinn was prominent in Arab mythology and that the citadel had emerged from Arab culture could not be forgotten and Mage's own instincts made it difficult for him to look elsewhere. Indeed, he couldn't look elsewhere until the citadel had first given up its secrets. If he was wrong about the citadel, the wrongness had first to be proved.

He studied the goat path as it disappeared among the rocks. Somewhere ahead, and probably not very far, there would be a cave... a cave which gave access to the labyrinth within the mountain. He knew with total certainty that this was enemy territory and, when he invaded it, as he knew he must, he knew he would find the tunnel which had so frequently terrorised his dreams.

The sound of labouring engines made him break from his reverie. He turned to observe the oncoming vehicles, Jaime's police car in the lead followed by Hector's old green Renault, dangerously low on its springs, for now as well as Hector and Helen it also carried Light and Tamara, and both Light and Hector were big heavy men. A flash of light momentarily caught his eye from the far side of the river bank, but he was preoccupied and ignored it. As the two cars came to a halt disgorging the occupants, Mage went forward to meet them.

Sancho loved cars. In particular he loved a certain breed of car. At home, where he still lived with his mother and father and three sisters, his bedroom wall was covered with photographs of Lambourginis and Ferraris with occasional Porches, BMWs and, of course, the English Jaguar. He had special regard for the Jaguar. Its understated style and quiet opulence made it particularly appealing. He'd never actually seen a Lambourgini or a Ferrari, and until now he'd never seen a Jaguar.

Despite the foreigner's admonition to leave the car well alone, while his Jefe and the extranjeros gathered around the goat path in ardent debate, he was drawn towards the dark green XJ12 in a semi-mesmeric daze, like iron filings to a magnet. He ran his hand along the gently curving roof, feeling the metal tingle beneath his fingers, almost sighing like his sister sometimes sighed when she let Juan Carlos Robero kiss her tits. He'd heard her do it, he'd even watched them do it when they thought they were alone in the house...

From the car's tantalisingly open door came the delicious smell of rich soft leather. He rested his hand upon the door to peer inside...

...And the door slammed shut with shocking force, shattering four fingers in an instant and trapping his hand against the bulkhead. Sancho Ferril's piercing scream violated the stillness of the afternoon and brought the others racing from the goat path.

Either unhearing or unheedful of Mage's warning shout, Jaime Gomez dashed towards the car and grabbed the door by the handle, his one thought being to release his officer's hand. The door flew open with the same ferocity with which it had slammed shut, catching Jaime full in the chest and sending him sprawling. Then it slammed shut yet again, shattering Sancho's shins and pinioning him half sprawled across the front seats, his mangled legs dangling limply over the sills. For a millisecond there was a seething mass of rippling black smoke within the vehicle, and then in the blink of an eye it had gone and all the tension and pressure departed from the door. It eased open gently, untrapping its victim.

The return to stillness after the incredible violence of the kinetic energy left them all dazed for a second, then Hector moved quickly towards the bloodied Sancho and the spell was broken. Light and Mage also moved forwards to help.

'What the fuck happened?' Light asked as together they eased the patrolman out of the car and laid him down upon a bed of fern leaves.

'The bloody car was booby trapped,' Mage snarled angrily. 'Christ Almighty, I knew there was something wrong about it! I *told* every one to stay clear!'

Jaime picked himself up slowly. He was bruised and dishevelled, but not seriously damaged. Blood trickled from his nose but he wiped it away as an irritation rather than an injury. He took one look at Sancho Ferril and swore bitterly.

'How is he?' he asked Hector.

'He's sick, but he'll live. Needless to say, he needs the clinic in La Linea and we've got to get him there quickly. I can't say for sure, but I think that both his legs are broken and, frankly, his hand is a total mess.'

Mage and Helen exchanged knowing looks. The same thought was in both their minds. Mage shook his head imperceptibly and Helen nodded in understanding. There was nothing that they could do here that the clinic could not do more effectively. Sancho Ferril had passed out and was therefore oblivious to the pain that caused his unconsciousness. With some luck he wouldn't wake up until he was swathed with bandages in a hospital ward. Time then to apply some healing if it was needed. Right now, apart from anything else, both knew that they had to conserve their energies.

With some rapid deliberation, they got Sancho loaded into the police car, then with Hector driving and Jaime sitting on the back seat, nursing his patrolman's head upon his lap and intermittently wiping his own bloody nose, the car drew away along the bank of the river, heading back towards the iron bridge and the road to the coast. Mage looked down at the big flash light that he'd retrieved from the back of the patrol car, then looked up at his four remaining companions.

'"And then there were five!"' he said neutrally.

Only Helen understood the full significance of his remark. 'What do we do now?' she asked, seeking to recreate their sense of direction and purpose.

'We've still got plenty of daylight, so before it goes, let's find that cave.'

'You seem pretty sure that there *is* a cave,' Light said dubiously.

'Oh yes John, I'm certain all right. The more important question is what are we going to do when we find it.'

'What's going on?' Tanja Hein's voice sounded tinny in Micky Vordeman's ear, but they were using the hand set radio's at maximum range and the mountains played havoc with reception.

'Been some sort of accident,' Vordeman reported back. 'Didn't see what happened, but the two cops and the doctor are heading back your way in the police car, so keep your heads down. The other five, our boy included, are heading further up the river on foot.'

'Can you follow them?'

'Sure. No problem. They've only got one path to follow and they'll be in clear view all of the time. I've got plenty of cover over here and the going is much easier on my side of the water.'

'Can you cross the river quickly if you have to?'

'Sure. It's not deep.'

'Have you got *any* idea where they're heading?'

'Uh huh,' Vordeman responded negatively, swinging his binoculars up stream. 'The only thing I can see are a couple of caves, about three of four hundred meters upstream.'

'Okay. Talk to me when they get to the caves.'

'Will do boss lady, out.'

'Out.'

It did not take them long to arrive at the caves Micky Vordeman had seen. There was a dirty shingle strip between the water's edge and the sheer face of the cliff, and the two caves stood almost side by side, the shingle stretching into the darkness of their apertures. Jaime had said that there might be caves. Hector had said that he thought there was a cave. Mage had *known* that there would be a cave, and now there were two to choose from.

The goat path carried on northwards but up the steepest of inclines. An agile man might have been able to follow it, but not a pregnant woman.

They approached the caves with caution, all of them mindful of the booby trapped car. Leon had felt that he was the only one who had not grasped the significance of the incident with the car and he knew that he was certainly ignorant of the mechanics. Knowing that she was dealing with someone who had no terms of reference had made it difficult, but none-the-less Helen had tried to explain it to him as best she could.

'You might find it hard to accept the notion of magic and magic spells,' she'd said as they'd worked their way around the bend in the river, '...so think instead of energy and think in terms of a magician being someone who can *control* that energy, bending it and using it for his own purposes. What our friend Dolorean has done is to leave a bolt of controlled and pre-programmed energy either in or around the car, destined to be triggered the moment anyone came too close. In this case he's worked on the door, probably because it was the easiest thing to do, and maybe because he was short of time. If he'd really put his mind to it he could have rigged the car to start by itself, and maybe ram us all into the rocks or the river... Colin twigged it, but the policeman walked into the trap before he'd had time to do anything about it.'

'What you're telling me isn't humanly possible,' Leon had protested.

'Maybe it is and maybe it isn't. I don't intend to argue the point with you because I'm by no means sure of my facts. Suffice to say that it *is* possible in theory and if you happen to be a Djinn, it's possible in practice. He's proved it by doing it.'

Reminded of another cave in another place, Leon now looked with equal trepidation at the two caves that faced him. 'Which one?' he asked hoarsely.

'The one on the left,' Mage answered immediately.

'Yeah, I guess you're right,' Light drawled in easy agreement.

'How can you know?' Leon exclaimed.

'"Evil treads the left hand path",' Helen quoted softly.

'Yes, but it's more than that,' Mage added.

'Tell me about it, man,' Light said, squatting on his haunches and reaching for a cigar.

'Look at the two caves. One is a narrow cut and the other is a round open mouth. In a dream that I've had fairly regularly over the last year, I'm in a round tunnel. It's not conclusive, but to my mind a round cave equates with a round tunnel, but apart from that, have a look at that bit of bracken to the left of the cave mouth. See anything?'

'Shit, yes. I didn't notice that before!'

'What are we looking at?' Leon asked peering through his thick glasses.

'There's a strip of cloth caught in the thorns. Part of a woman's dress, and unless I'm much mistaken, it looks very much like the dress Alexandra was wearing last Friday. John?'

'Yeah, looks about right.' He rose to his feet. 'You thinking what I'm thinking?'

'Oh I'm way ahead of you! Helen?'

'It stinks,' she said simply.

'Will someone please tell me what's going on!' Leon snapped in impatient exasperation.

'It's a trap, man,' Tamara said emphatically. 'Our guy knew that sooner or later we'd find the car, so he hexes it, full well knowin' that it ain't gonna stop us. He makes sure his foot prints lead us along the goat path, and he makes sure we know which cave is the right cave by pointing the way by this scrap of stuff. He *wants* us to follow him inside, an' you can bet your asses that if we do, he's got some more surprises in store for us that are gonna make that crap back at the car look like chicken shit.'

Mage had to laugh, albeit ruefully. 'Tamara, I couldn't have put it better myself!' Then, more soberly, 'but the question is, what do we do about it? Walk into it or walk away from it? Either way, he wins. Either way we lose.'

Leon rested the black aluminium case on the pebbles and, kneeling before it, unlocked the hinge clips. He looked up coldly. 'I can't believe what I'm hearing from you people,' he said, the contempt in his voice hiding the fear. 'We establish that this is where the Djinn has gone and now you're holding back wondering whether or not you should follow him. Okay, so it might be a trap, but so what? If we're expecting it, we can counter it!' He brought the Uzi out of the case and rammed a clip of ammunition into the handle. 'As you can see, we're not entirely defenceless!'

'Oh oh, looks like we've got a situation developing,' Vordeman spoke into the walkie talkie.

'What's happening?' Tanja's broken tones scrambled back through the hiss of static.

'They're at the caves. Having a row by the look of it. Shapiro's introducing them to Little Ruben and clipping up the Uzi.'

'--- et any closer?'

'Yeah, I'll try...'

'We have a number of problems,' Mage said placatingly. 'The first is that among the five of us we have one gun and one torch. The second is that we have absolutely no idea of what we've going to find inside that cave and Tamara is right, it'll be booby trapped just like the car. Whatever we do find in the cave, well, there's no guarantee that a gun, even a gun like the one you've got, will do any good. Even if we exercise extreme caution, whatever is in there could get us long before we even get the chance to see what the hell it is. The force we're up against is a magical force and we have to fight fire with fire. Now we *do* have some magical power, but it has to be loaded and sighted, just like your machine gun. When we go into that cave it needs to be as spiritual warriors not gung ho commandos.'

'We're being watched,' Helen interrupted.

'I'm not surprised,' Tamara wrapped her arms around her chest. 'This place gives me the creeps.'

'No,' Helen shook her head in minor irritation. 'This is on a physical level.'

'Any idea from where?' Light asked casually, '- and don't anyone look round.'

'The far side of the river – I think.'

'Could be Leon's shadows,' Mage suggested.

'We're all very worried about shadows,' Leon said sarcastically, standing up and swinging the case over one shoulder, leaving both hands free to cradle the Uzi. 'I'm more concerned with the shadows in front of me, not those that might or might not be there. If you want to go and work up some mumbo jumbo that's fine with me, just give me the Goddam torch and I'll go in on my own!'

'Didn't you learn anything in the Negev?' Mage asked caustically.

Leon faced up to him. 'Yes,' he said. 'Yes I did. I learned that a creature such as the one that's scaring you all shitless actually exists and I've travelled a lot of miles to find its brother... which according to you has done a disappearing act into that cave over there. Something else I learned is that you don't run away from something like this and I'm going into the cave to find it, and when I've found it, I'm going to blow the bastard's brains away. What you have to do is decide whether you're going to come with me or whether you're going to try and stop me, which I wouldn't advise because,' the barrel of the Uzi came up an inch or two, 'I have this and you don't!'

Light put himself between Leon and the cave. He spoke to Leon but his eyes were fiercely quartering the foliage on the far side of the river. 'So shoot me,' he said easily, ''cos I ain't moving till we've got something sensible sorted out here!'

Leon glowered belligerently at the black giant, but realised that he was boxed it. The American was being serious and he knew that he *would* have to shoot him to move him.

Mage came to his rescue. 'Okay,' he said. 'Let's find a compromise here. You've got the gun and I've got the torch. If you're prepared to give me five minutes to get my act together, we'll do a preliminary, and I do mean a preliminary examination of the cave. Ten minutes in and ten minutes out, no matter what we find, okay?'

'Colin, my man, this is very dangerous!'

'Yes John, I know it is, but Leon does have a point. We might as well go carefully and get some idea of what we're up against, then at least we'll know what steps we have to take to neutralise it. We can come back in the morning cleansed and prepared, and I do have something back at the house which might be useful to have with us if we're going into combat.'

'You've got another reason too, haven't you?' Helen asked astutely.

Mage nodded. 'Yes. I don't know how you feel, but since this morning I've sensed that we're suddenly working on a much tighter time scale. We've all assumed that we've got plenty of time. June 21st is a long way off as yet, but what if we're wrong about this date? Sure, it's the "longest day" in our calendar, but how do we know that Dolorean is working to our time table? How do we know that, even if he was, he hasn't changed his mind and brought everything forwards. From his point of view, things can't have gone as he'd expected. His carefully prepared little group was gone even before he got here, and when he did get here and found that not only did he not have a clear field but that there were powerful opponents on that field determined to bring him down. If you were him, what would you do?'

No shadow passed over the sun, but as one the group shivered.

'Okay,' Light said, stepping to one side. 'Ten minutes up and ten minutes down. Twenty minutes in all. Keep the CB link open if you can and let Tammy have a running commentary. Me an' Helen will med down and try to channel whatever we can your way. At the first sign of a barrier, the first smell of a trap and you're out of there fast, you got me?'

Leon, no longer sure that he was so pleased to have got his own way, nodded his agreement.

'If Colin says run, you run like fuck,' Light insisted pointedly.

'Sure, just like I did in the Negev.'

'Just like you did in the Negev,' Mage confirmed. 'For Herschal you now read Colin Mage, all right?'

'All right,' Leon agreed testily, and it would be all right just as long as they didn't come face to face with the Djinn, for if they did, Mage or no Mage, he intended to be true to his own promise to himself and would use the Uzi to blow the creature's head off.

A few minutes later Leon and Mage entered the cave.

'Shapiro and the Englishman have just gone into one of the caves,' Vordeman spoke into the walkie talkie. He waited for a reply but all he got for his trouble was an offensive burst of static.

They've entered through the cave! Half a mile away Dolorean, who was no longer Dolorean and would never be Dolorean again (Praise The Winds of Zoof!) opened amber elliptical eyes and smiled gleefully in the gloom. Now, at last and not before time, there would be the working of the *Zkernowii*, that highest form of Djinn magic used exclusively to bring the chaos of revenge raining down upon an enemy's shoulders. Now, having reverted to his true form, the Djinn carved a sigil in the dry air with its first digit claw. Mauve light emanated from the serrated creases around its scaly navel and down in the river cave, the first of many such potential traps was sprung.

As Jadoc Dolorean, the Djinn had known after the confrontation with Mage on the day of *The Showing* that The Opening was now seriously compromised. There was no choice. Somehow the timing *had* to be brought forwards. The manmate's power had been effervescent, and so too had been that of the black interloper. When the so called reverend had chatted at their table he had not seen beneath the disguise, but he had picked up the thoughtforms from the manmate and had realised then just how precarious his position had become. His enemies were groping their way forwards. Sooner or later they would get too close and he knew he could not deal with them all simultaneously and maintain the stability of the incubator at the same time. Thus the female would have to be moved to The Sacred Place as soon as possible. A message must be dispatched to his brethren (he had no idea how) and The Birthing must be induced.

Seething with a desire for revenge, the shapechanger had escorted the female back to the house. Indeed, he had fully intended to conjure up a counter offensive, but the female herself had made that impossible by going into a fit of rejectional spasms that had lasted on and off for the rest of the day and most of that night. She had stabilised by the morning but was in too precarious a state to be left for any length of time. Towards noon she had again started showing some signs of agitation and he'd taken the dangerous but logical step of allowing her to lapse into her natural state. Without the veneer of human form she'd become a gelatinous ovoid with vaguely appendaged limbs. The vital organs and circulatory system were more easily monitored this way, as was the incubator itself, a pulsing mauve mass, egg shaped and opaque. The form of The Newlife had been clearly visible behind the opacity of the membrane and at one point the Djinn had felt a mixture of delight and pride as The Newlife's snout had pressed against the wall of the incubator, its curled tail clearly twitching with sentient life. Now he had been able to exercise control over the incubator and reassure its occupant – but may the brethren help him, he'd thought, if he had to move the female quickly.

In the late hours of Saturday night he had assumed the mist form and again had descended down the well, weaving wraithlike through the channels and cuts until he came to The Sacred Place. Here he had prayed ardently for some help and guidance. None had been forthcoming, so he had looked objectively at his problems, seeking to find their solution on his own. First, The Opening could not take place without his brethren's help. The date of The Opening had been planned eighty moons before to the most perfect minute of the most perfect hour. It might be difficult, but not impossible, to alter the arrangements on his own side of the divide, providing he could let his people know. Their preparations could be re-calibrated, but only if they *knew!* Working out of synchronisation with the shamans would achieve nothing, other than bringing about the unnecessary destruction of the incubator and the premature death of The Newlife.

So, the prime problem had been in discovering a way to convey a message across the divide. Certainly, he could have constructed a magic circle and, with the power of its amplification, projected telepathic messages – but without any guarantee that they would be received by the worldchangers waiting on the other side. No, that might have to be done as a last resort, but surely a more fool proof way could be found? He fretted at the Djinn's inability to cross between worlds freely and, in his fretting, had found his answer. It was so glaringly obvious that he'd marvelled at the fact that he'd not thought of it before and marvelled more that no one else had thought of it either.

A Djinn could not cross between worlds but a human could! This was well known and well documented. Thus, all he had to do was find a human to dispatch on his behalf, carrying the messages he needed to send. The human did not have to go willingly, but could be sent through The Opening in a mind fugue. His brethren would mind meld with the human and the vital information would be removed with the rest of the contents of the human's mind and memory. True, he had first to find a human subject and, while that might not be easy, it certainly should not be hard.

Elated, no, not just elated but positively triumphant, he had allowed his essence to swirl around the chamber, disturbing layers of dust and sending a shower of pebbles cascading over the edge of the well. There'd been a long pause before the sound of disturbed water had echoed up from the bowels of the earth. He'd come up against a spiralling flight of stone stairs that led up to the higher levels of the citadel and, without a thought, had ascended. Arriving at ground level, his senses had become immediately alert to a foreign presence and with a single twist of thought he'd changed his molecular structure, assuming the carapaced form of the warrior. Standing like a statue, he'd projected his senses in pursuit of the faint, but still clearly detectable presence. The walls of this chamber were still covered in thick layers of *ghambon*, the protective psychic manifestation projected by the shamans to guarantee the sanctity and the security of the citadel. Such was the powerful emanation of Djinn that the minute vibrancy of human intrusion had been almost undetectable, although still maddeningly there.

He'd homed in on the vibration like a beacon and had found the cause of it, suspended and cocooned in the *ghambon* by the door. A human child, female, minus one shoe, eyes closed, held in stasis by the magic of the substance. He had trembled in humility and self condemnation. All this time he had believed that his prayers had gone unheard and yet here was the proof that his prayers *had* been heard, perhaps even before he had made them. Here, here within the confines of his own citadel, was the means of communication he so desperately needed and it had seemed to him that perhaps his brethren were more aware of events on this side of the divide than he had given them credit for. He'd cursed himself for not thinking of the human messenger many days before, for surely, and here was the evidence, his brethren most certainly had.

He'd reached up to release the child, using the navel coil to melt the resin around her encapsulated form. Still covered in the sticky membrane, he'd taken her back down to the lower level, laying her to rest at the edge of the well. His mind had worked furiously as he'd thought about the necessary ritual. She would have to be purified before she could be dispatched, and before the dispatching he would have to build a circle of projection. This would take time but providing he was not distracted it could be done within a day. Allow for the other preparations that would be required and The Opening could be achieved two or three days after that. He had become exultant and had paced the dungeon chamber with mounting excitement. Much, of course, could go wrong and yet clearly this was the best course of action. Were he to wait for the longest day, that day might never dawn. His brethren must have known this themselves, otherwise they would not have placed the thoughts in his mind and would not have given him the means by which he could act on them.

For the rest of that night and the following day he had drifted back and forth between Calle Sombra and the citadel, and at sundown on the Sunday he had built his circle around the dungeon well. Using every age old invocation in correct and proper sequence, he had focused his channel of power and looking down the well had been gratified to see the rippling mauve lights that indicated that the bridge between worlds was not only viable but in place..

Then had come the sensitive and difficult task of cleansing the girl child. Using the umbilical coil he'd removed the residue of the membrane and after removing her clothes, had used his saliva to purify her emaciated flesh. At no time had she become conscious, although she did stir and moan when his mind had entered her own mind, implanting the right words and picture patterns that would convey the urgency of his requests and instructions to his waiting brethren. Inevitably he had taken something of the girl's life patterns into his own consciousness, marvelling at how those who served were able to do so even after death, for was this child not the child of one of his own disciples? He'd acquired a picture of the mother bleeding to death in the blood bath of her own arrogance and stupidity, and superimposed upon this vision had been the vision of the manmate lurking powerfully in the back ground. Again he'd cursed himself for not having dispatched the manmate directly when he'd had the chance. Thoughts of the manmate had made him work faster, for while he was not afraid of the magician, the magician's powers could no longer be described as puny. Furthermore, he had acquired powerful allies. How much different things might have been had he had the common sense to kill the manmate a year ago. There had, after all, been plenty of opportunities.

At the mid-night hour he had dropped the girl into the well. Long before she hit the water, Lena Cortez had flicked out of sight and out of time as she was consumed by the mauve lights and transported into a different dimension.

The shapechanger had sat until dawn meditating and waiting for some acknowledgement of receipt, either by thoughtform or physical manifestation. None had been forthcoming but he'd put the time to good use, preparing himself for the more exhausting process of performing the opening ritual.

The daylight hours of Monday had been spent preparing the incubator and in building the strength of his own psychic and mental reserves. Also, he had had to deal with the problem that Colin Mage had so eruditely defined. The female could not be transported to The Sacred Place via the well in the garden, for while it was true that the female sub species of Djinn were far superior than their male counterparts in the art of shapechanging, they could not assume the discarnate mistform while in a state of pregnancy. Furthermore, while his female was no longer human, she was not yet full blown Djinn and nor would she be so until she had discharged her duties to The Newlife... and even then, only if she survived The Birthing. Easier access would have to be found and *had been found* in the late hours of Monday.

The mountain beneath the citadel was honeycombed with tunnels. Most of them were natural, while a few of them were partially man made. Upon priliminary inspection none of them provided the access he needed and it had only been after he had mounted a much more thorough search that he had found what he'd been looking for.

The dungeon beneath the citadel was a large square place, in the centre of which was the circular well. Apart from the worn flight of stone steps set into the wall there was no other entrance or exit. However, unlike the well in the back garden of Calle Sombra, this water bore was much wider and steps had been cut into the wall, leading down to the water level. Half way down this spiral was the narrow cleft in the stonework which gave access to the labyrinth. Instead of following his usual route he had explored in detail and had found a series of interlinking caverns and passages that had led him consistently downwards until he'd come to a long tunnel, worn smooth by winter torrents, that had brought him to a cave mouth beyond the bend of the river.

It would be a hard climb, but he'd estimated that the female could manage it without too much difficulty even though it might take her two or three hours. He'd travelled the route in his mistform, then had travelled it again, carnately and clothed in armour scale, constantly becoming more enthusiastic with each completion of the journey. Not only was this the logical way to bring the female into the citadel, it was also eminently defensible! His jaws had clicked in anticipatory pleasure as he'd contemplated the obstructions he could and would place along the way. The manmate could lead an army of magicians into the mountain, but they would not travel far before the dark retribution of the *Zkernowii* would descend upon their heads.

More than satisfied with his progress he had returned to the incubator, preparing it for its last journey. The female had been carefully brought back to a semblance of human form, and in the first light of Tuesday morning, he had transferred her to the car, driving at a sedate speed, as far as the car would take them to the riverside cave. He had left the car with a *Zkernowii* vaporised around the door mechanism, and as the female had begun to negotiate the labyrinth in gradual stages, he'd had ample opportunity to close the pathway behind them with a variety of tricks and traps that would be viciously effective should they be sprung. His hands had caressed a sleeping bat, his fingers had trailed through a spider's web, his breath had fallen upon smooth stone, his feet had stamped with unnecessary force against the various surfaces of the ground – and throughout all, his incantations had echoed eerily through the lofty caverns.

The journey had taken longer than he'd anticipated, but by noon he had effected the transfer of the female to her ultimate resting place and, with both of them enfolded in the armour of his protective circle, he had allowed himself the luxury of resting. He had gone for more than ninety hours without sleep and sleep had become an imperative necessity. Thus he had slept throughout the afternoon of Tuesday, his eyes only opening when he had been alerted by the mental warning bell that told him that the first of his defences was in the process of being breached.

'*Zkernowii!*' he breathed in predatory satisfaction. '*Zkernowii!*'

28.

Zkernowii

They entered the cave, Mage playing the light downwards and ahead of them, Leon holding the machine pistol, cocked and ready in the crook of his arm. Twenty yards into the cave, the shingle became shale and as the cave narrowed, inclining steadily upwards at an angle of ten or twelve degrees, the shale gave way to solid bedrock. In the winter months and especially during the rainy seasons, this cave would be inaccessible, the cave mouth under water, the cavern filled with a raging torrent as it channelled the spill off from the mountain. Even now it was damp and dank and smelled badly of old mud and rotting vegetation and, beneath that smell, something darker that might, providing Mage's imagination wasn't playing tricks on him, have been faintly reminiscent of seaweed. He was not happy about this expedition. It was ill-planned and ill-prepared for, but both Leon's fear and determination had acted as goads upon his subconscious, reminding him of his own fear and his own determination to conquer it.

Fifty yards in, the cave narrowed to such an extent that their shoulders touched, and then swung sharply to the right. They had to lower their heads to duck beneath a low proscenium of stone and found themselves in a long straight passage, that disappeared beyond the range of the probing beam of the powerful torch. It wasn't the tunnel of Mage's nightmares, but it was bad enough. They advanced cautiously and as they went, the pathway became significantly steeper. Now that they were cut off from the incidental illumination that had spilled into the cavern from the mouth of the cave, it became pitch black and freezing cold. Noting the sudden drop in temperature, Mage paused, resting his free hand upon Leon's right shoulder.

'What's up?' Leon asked.

'Do you feel the change in temperature?'

'Sure. It's damn cold in here, but then, all caves are cold, aren't they?'

Yes, some of them are, but not like this Mage thought. 'Just be on your guard and very careful,' he said non-committally, realising that Leon was completely the wrong person to have as a companion on an adventure such as this. Despite the Mossad man's experiences in the Negev, it still seemed that Leon had not grasped the enormity and implications, either of what they were up against or what they were trying to achieve. As such he was a dangerous ally and Mage found himself fervently wishing that it was either John Light or Helen Ross who walked by his side. Although he channelled all the energy he possessed into his psychic awareness, his psychic senses seemed dulled and unable to cope in the stygian darkness and he would have preferred Helen's clairvoyance for company rather than Leon's gun.

As they negotiated the steep incline Mage made a firm decision. Once they had seen where and what it led to, they would turn back and retrace their steps. He glanced at his watch and frowned. They were only four minutes into their mission and already it seemed like four hours.

After another hundred yards or so, the tunnel widened and flattened out. Beneath their feet there was now a light covering of sand, while the roof of the tunnel lifted into a vault of church-like proportions. Above their heads something of indeterminate shape moved sibilently with a hiss and a creak. Mage, heart pounding, swung the torch upwards in time to catch the peripheral edge of movement, the hint of a dark shape displacing air.

'What is it?' Leon asked in alarm, the fear in his voice clearly audible..

'Don't know,' Mage retorted tensely, 'but whatever it was, it was big. Either way, it's gone now – and Leon, I think we should be going too...' His voice echoed upwards and outwards and although he had only spoken in a whisper it was profoundly amplified and played back to him by the subterranean acoustics.

'You're scared!' Leon challenged.

'Look, let's just forget this macho shit, shall we. Yes, I am bloody well scared half to death and if you're not, then you damn well should be!'

'Yes, well okay... do we know how much further this passage goes?'

Mage sighted the torch along the tunnel. It seemed to be never ending but the craggy outcrops of rock created shadows at all quarters and the shadows were deceptive. 'No,' he said shortly, 'but I do know that to do this job properly we need a lot more people and a lot more light, and I dare say we could use a lot more fire power.'

'We've got the Uzi,' Leon reminded him.

'True, but while I don't know anything much about guns, I've seen a helluva lot of movies where someone shoots a gun underground and before you know it you've got a full scale cave in on your hands. I mean, do *you* know what might happen if you shot that damn thing down here?'

'No I don't. You want to turn back then?'

'Hey, I didn't want to come in here in the first place! But yes... I'm as twitchy as a cat in a fire and all my psychic defences are screaming at me to get out of here as fast as I can. Apart from anything else, I don't like the idea of something big, black and nasty hanging above my head and this coldness is really getting to me. I can hardly feel my hands or feet and although I'd expect it to be chilly down here, this degree of coldness is unnatural.'

'All right. You've convinced me.'

'Thank God for that,' Mage sighed in relief. 'We've been gone long enough as it is.' He glanced at his watch. 'We're eight minutes in which gives us twelve minutes to get back to the others before they start panicking. And at least it's down hill all the way.'

They'd turned and were heading back the way they'd come, when Leon paused. 'What's that?' he asked

'What's what?'

'Shine the torch on the ground in front of our feet.'

Mage obliged and Leon pointed downwards. 'That!' he said, making reference to the straight and narrow line that had been gorged into the rock.

'I haven't a clue,' Mage said, kneeling to examine the mark. 'I didn't notice it before on our way up, and whatever it is, it must be man made.' He played the torch along the mark which stretched backwards into the dark between their two sets of footprints. 'Nature doesn't like straight lines.'

He was about to say more but a long ear piercing shriek from somewhere behind them cut him dead. He came to his feet, pivoting and swinging the beam of the torch all around him. There was nothing to be seen, but there was a new atmosphere in this enclosed space, which was one of impending threat and danger.

For a second the torch light fell of Leon's face and Mage took no delight in seeing that it was creased in a rictus of terror.

Mage grabbed him by the elbow. 'Start walking,' he said. 'Don't rush. Don't panic, and don't look behind you.'

'What *is* it?'

'I don't know and I don't want to hang around to find out. Five minutes hard walking and we're out of here, so let's just *go!*'

They started off at a brisk pace, Mage's vision straining in projection to see the low proscenium that would herald their escape and exit. The vision became tantalisingly elusive and Mage found himself counting off the seconds with each stride of his feet. The massing threat of malignant presence was constantly hovering just behind them and he had to employ all of his mental training to stop himself from breaking into a run. He tried familiar occult techniques, such as the visualisation and projection of the pentagram, to keep his fear at bay, but as the tunnel showed no signs of ending, he was aware of a rising tide of panic. There was something wrong here. This tunnel was just too fucking long!

'Oh *shit!*' The words escaped his lips in an angry exhalation of air. 'Do you see what I see?'

Their pace slowed slightly. 'Yes I see what you mean,' Leon answered, registering the fact that ahead of them the tunnel forged into two paths. On their upwards journey they had obviously failed to notice this tributary joining. The question now was which was the tributary and which the main line. 'Do we go left or go right?'

Mage hesitated and hovered, feeling incapable of making a decision. Both tunnels were enigmatic black holes, both tilted downwards, both could have been the way out, and yet neither might be the way out! His watch told him that nine minutes had elapsed since they'd begun their return journey and, if they'd been on the right path, they should have been back in the sunshine several minutes since. Turning back the way they'd come, he flashed the torch in that direction. At first there was nothing to see and then he became aware of a deeper shadow of darkness that seemed to be moving very slowly towards them, clinging to the roof of the tunnel. It was distant and indefinable but drawing closer with every heartbeat and with every heartbeat the temperature seemed to drop another degree. As if to confirm his bodily senses a sheen of frost had begun to form upon the rocks and there was a sensation of iciness beneath his feet. These things had not been apparent when they'd entered the tunnel, *for they had not been there when they'd entered the tunnel*!

By the minute hand of his watch that had been less than twenty minutes ago, but Mage was no longer convinced of the sanctity of time. The watch may have said minutes but his body clock was talking to him in terms of hours and he was more inclined to believe what his own body was telling him.

'Left or right?' Leon said again, but this time, his voice was oddly muffled and distant.

Mage turned and saw immediately that something weird had happened and was happening even as he watched. Leon seemed further away than he had been a second earlier. He shone the torch full in his face but there seemed to be a barrier between them that both reflected and absorbed the light. Reaching towards the Israeli it was like plunging his hand into a bucket of icy water. So cold was it that it actually seemed to burn and the pain was quite intolerable.

It seemed that Leon was three or four feet away and covered in a film of grey light that had nothing to do with the beam of the torch. Somewhere from the bowels of the mountain there came a dull rumble. It registered on Mage's consciousness but he paid it no heed as he tried to walk forward to where he perceived Leon to be. He came up hard against an invisible barrier that repelled him with what felt like an electric shock. Indeed, around him there were small blue sparks of static electricity and his nostrils flared at the unmistakable smell of seaweedy ozone.

'Leon!' Mage bellowed at the top of his voice – and now there was no echo. Quite the reverse in fact, it was like yelling into a muffled ball of cotton wool.

'Mage! Where the fuck are you? Where's the fucking light?' Leon Shapiro was seemingly less than six feet away and yet his voice sounded as though it came from six hundred yards away. Mage watched him turning on the spot. There were small flashes of light and tinny popping sounds – *Christ almighty he's shooting at something* Mage thought – and then Leon completely faded from his sight.

The dull rumble was becoming a sonorous roar and Mage lost his nerve. He ran as fast as his legs would carry him into the right hand tunnel, praying that it was the right one, and kept on running until the roaring noise behind him filled his whole world.

The rock that tripped him and sent him flying face down to the ground probably saved his life. Had he been upright when the wall of turgid water hit him, it could easily have broken every bone in his body with the force of the impact. As it was, the water lifted him and bore him like a tumbling twig. He gasped for breath as he was pummelled against the unforgiving walls of the tunnel, but there was no air to be had. The water filled the tunnel completely and began to fill his lungs, bringing him to the very gateway of death. And then the mountain gave him up and spat him out.

Twenty eight minutes after Mage and Leon had disappeared into the cave John Light had looked at his watch. 'They're taking too long,' he'd said.

Forty minutes after Mage and Leon had departed, the tension and concern hung over the waiting trio like a cloud. 'We should never have let them go in!' Helen had exclaimed.

After an hour had elapsed they were arguing bitterly as to what they ought to do. Helen was all for going into the cave after them, even though she knew that it would be a wrong move. Light vetoed the suggestion and Tamara refused point blank to go anywhere near the cave.

As they'd arrived at the compromise solution of Helen remaining at the cave mouth while Light and Tamara returned to the village in search of torches, ropes and whatever arms the village might give up, all three of them had become aware of the vibratory rumble beneath their feet. Light had been the first to react.

'Pull back,' he'd snapped, and they had managed to retreat a few yards up the goat track before a tumultuous wall of water exploded from the narrow mouth of the left hand cave, carrying Mage like so much flotsam and jetsam and depositing him bruised and bleeding and barely conscious amid the reeds and lilies at the river's edge while the tidal wave of filthy black water cascaded over him to spend its force in the greater body of the Hozgarganta.

Helen was off like a sprinter, Light jogging at a more sedate pace. *Retrieved one and lost one* he thought ominously.

Micky Vordeman found some higher ground where the RT reception was considerably clearer.

'We've got a crisis on our hands,' he snapped into the mouthpiece.

'What's going down?' Tanja Hein's voice crackled back.

'Shapiro and the Englishman went into one of the caves a couple of hours ago. Ten minutes ago the Englishman emerges on the bow wave of a tidal wave, but he doesn't come out of the same cave he went into. The two women and the black guy are helping him back along the goat track to where they left the car. There seems to be some urgency.'

'What about Shapiro?'

'Sorry boss, of him there ain't no sign. What do you want me to do?'

There was a moment's silence, and then 'Can you get over to the cave?'

'Sure, no problem.'

'Carry out a preliminary. Yuri's on his way. Wait till he gets there, then skirmish.'

'Got you. What about you?'

'I'm going to pick up the Brit and his friends, then I'm going to stick to them like glue. I don't like the way this is coming down.'

'No...' Vordeman looked at the caves through his binoculars. The sun was now low in the sky and everything leapt out in harsh relief. 'Neither do I. Tell Yuri to hurry it up and tell him to bring a couple of torches. There's not a lot of daylight left. What do you want us to do with Shapiro if we find him?'

'Haul his ass out of there, then bring him to me. Fuck Jerusalem, I want to know what's coming down. The little shit will tell us one way or the other.'

'Dangerous ground lady, but you're calling the shots.'

It was six thirty before Yuri joined Mickey Vordeman at the entrance to the caves. He carried two heavy rucksacks and, dropping one of them at Vordeman's feet, eyed the caves speculatively.

'Which one?' he asked abruptly.

'Good question,' said Vordeman, checking the contents of the bag and extricating the extra clips of ammunition for the Uzi that he'd had strapped to his belt for most of the afternoon. 'Shapiro and the Brit went into the cave on the left at four thirty two, and at six twenty one the Brit came out of the cave on the right, surfing on a ton of water, and alone. There was panic in the ranks and they all left here about twenty minutes ago. Surprised you didn't see them.'

'I did!' Yuri passed Vordeman one of the torches he had brought. 'They passed me in the Renault.'

'Did they see you?'

Yuri looked scornful. 'No, of course not, but I saw them.' He threw the rucksack over his shoulder. 'The Englishman looked in a pretty sorry state. You got any idea what happened in there?'

'No.'

'So we're going in blind?'

'Looks like it, but there shouldn't be too much of a problem. All we've got to do is find Shapiro and haul his ass out of there.'

'And what if we don't find him?'

Vordeman grinned. 'Should we worry? We tell the boss lady that we looked and we can't do any more than that.'

'No, I don't like this,' Yuri spat on the ground and looked at his colleague shrewdly. 'Shapiro went in there with his weapon cocked and ready. So *he* must have been expecting to find something.'

'Yeah, maybe, or maybe he was just trying to impress his friends?'

Yuri grunted. 'Perhaps, but if you don't mind, let's handle this one like it's a maximum threat situation, okay?'

'Okay... So, do you take the left cave while I take the right, or do you want to do it the other way round?'

Yuri looked thoughtfully pensive. 'Let's take the cave on the left, but let's take it together.'

'Oh sure!' Vordeman scoffed, 'and while we're going up the left hole Shapiro could be coming out of the right hole and we'd miss him completely!'

'You're right, but look, just humour me on this one will you, Micky? Let's check out the cave on the left together, and then let's check out the other one. When we've done that, we'll figure out our next move.'

Vordeman gave his partner a curious look. They were not friends and indeed their personalities had frequently clashed over the previous months of being on operations together. On two occasions, once in Barcelona and once in Bilbao, they'd nearly come to blows and probably would have done had Tanja Hein not intervened with her iron hand. And yet, each had a begrudging professional respect for the other and there had been a few times, especially during the Basque operation, when Mickey Vordeman's balls would have been in a sling had Yuri not acted as quickly and promptly as he had done. But despite this, for six months, Vordeman had been "Vordeman" or "hit man" with occasional hailings as "shit face" and "motherfucker." Yuri had never called him Mickey. Not until now. Vordeman was tempted to try and score from his partner's sudden change of attitude, but something made him change his mind. Maybe it was the way in which Yuri was looking at him, openly and candidly, waiting for a straight answer to what had been at best a veiled question.

'Okay,' Vordeman said. 'We'll do it your way.'

They entered the narrow cave on their right, shining their lights upwards into the tight crevice of the roof and along the damp walls of the smooth sides. At its furthest recess the cave degenerated and became an oval tunnel, about the size of a small storm drain. Vordeman stooped and shone the torch into the circular black channel. There was nothing to see but darkness.

'This is obviously where the Englishman came out,' he observed, 'but unless we want to go in on our bellies I think we'd better check next door.'

Yuri made no protest and together they reconnoitred the larger of the two caves. Here they encountered the proscenium arch and discovered the tunnel beyond it.

'This looks more like it!' Vordeman offered, trying to inject some enthusiasm into the mission.

'If you say so,' Yuri agreed, only marginally happier than he had been a minute before. He would never have described himself as being claustrophobic but he could not shift the curious mood of negativity and apprehension that had descended over him; something deep and primal inside his subconscious told him to get out of this place now while he still could, and as for Mr Leon Fucking Shapiro, the namby pamby boss's boy wonder from Jerusalem, well he could stew in his own juice!

They moved cautiously along the tunnel, skirmishing in well practised harmony. Their two torch beams were never static, criss-crossing each other in constant motion while their ears strained for any distant sound that might alert them to Leon's whereabouts.

'It's damn cold in here,' Vordeman said at one point.

'But at least it's dry, which is more than can be said for the other cave. What I want to know is what the hell Shapiro and the Brit were doing in here in the first place?'

'Maybe they were looking for buried treasure!' Vordeman grinned in the gloom.

'Yeah, maybe, but it's got to be dangerous treasure if you go looking for it with an Uzi under your arm. You said Shapiro had the Little Ruben with him?'

'You've got a point,' Vordeman acknowledged soberly.

They emerged into the church-like cavern where Mage and Leon had called a halt to their own incursion and also like Mage, both Mossad agents noted the sudden drop in temperature. It did not deter them, however, and they pressed on until the roof lowered again. Another hundred meters along a narrow passage and they emerged in a circular cavern that had three other tunnels leading off from it. Yuri's heart sank, for now logic dictated that they would *have* to separate, and if there was one single thing that he knew for certain concerning the cock-up of an operation, it was that he did not want to be alone in this place.

'Well?' he asked pointedly.

'Let's throw some light on the subject.' Vordeman dropped the rucksack to the ground, noting with satisfaction that they now had dry sand beneath their feet. Rummaging in the back he produced a candle flare and, sticking it firmly in the earth near the mouth of the tunnel that they had just emerged from, he pulled the self ignite cord and the flare burst into harsh incandescent radiance. With this quality of illumination the cavern looked reassuringly smaller than they had first thought. 'This thing will burn merrily for about ten minutes. 'You take the left hand tunnel, I'll take the one on the right. Synchronise watches, and I'll meet you back here in six minutes. Then we'll check out the middle tunnel together. Okay?'

'Sure,' Yuri said, summoning a veneer of confidence that he did not really feel. 'Six minutes, right?'

'That'll give us enough time to assess the lie of the land. Let's move out.'

Yuri watched Vordeman march cheerfully into the right hand tunnel before he himself turned and entered the one on the left. He wondered to what extent Mickey Vordeman was putting on an act, or if he genuinely was unaware of the sense of danger that seemed to cling to every particle of air within this dark and repellent place. If it was an act it was a damn good one. He examined his own feelings. Was he not over reacting to his own imagination? After all, wasn't this place enough to spook anybody? *Of course it damn well is!* he thought emphatically, admitting to himself that he was spooked out. But he was wise enough not to berate himself too much for feeling this way. There had been too many times over too many years when being spooked had saved his life and he had come to trust his sixth sense more implicitly that he would have cared to admit to someone like Mickey Vordeman, and even to himself, for that matter.

Gritting his teeth and exercising great caution, he entered the tunnel and although he could quite easily have walked upright, chose instead to move forwards at a crouch. He glanced behind him on more than one occasion, reassured by the bright light emitted by the burning flare. It enabled him to measure his distance and provided him with a solid term of reference.

For a hundred meters or so the pathway was straight and level, then suddenly it dipped steeply downwards at an angle of forty five degrees. Had he been walking normally he might easily have missed this sudden decline with dire and catastrophic consequences. As it was, he was able to drop to his knees and examine the way ahead with care and circumspection. The bore of the tunnel seemed unnaturally smooth, and as he smoothed his free hand across the ground surface, the stone beneath the fine sand seemed to be polished to a slippy gloss. *Could have broken my stupid neck!* he thought, quietly pleased that the sixth sense which had advocated extreme caution had again saved him from something unpleasant.

It was that same sixth sense that, without warning, made his hackles rise and his blood freeze. Without knowing how he knew, he knew that he was no longer alone. That there was someone or something behind him, and whoever or whatever it was, it wasn't Mickey Vordeman! To his credit, although he was assailed by the most unreasonable fear, he did not panic. Gently releasing the safety catch on the Uzi, he turned slowly and carefully brought the short stubby barrel of the gun into line with the beam of the torch, his finger taking up the first pressure on the trigger. He saw nothing. There was nothing to see. And that was the problem. A hundred meters away there should have been the bright light of the flare, but instead there was jet black inky darkness, a darkness so profound that not even the beam of the torch could penetrate it.

And then, half through his eyes and half through other senses that up until then he did not know he had, he saw that the darkness was moving and rushing towards him at phenomenal velocity. Even as his finger was squeezing the trigger, something soft and solid hit him, poured over him like a tornado of hot wind, and propelled him backwards over the edge of the incline. He fell like a parachutist without a parachute, and above the furious detonations that came from the Uzi as he discharged a whole clip of 9mm ammunition, he heard his own inarticulate scream of terror echoing around him as he fell unchecked into the black abyss.

Mickey Vordeman had negotiated the tunnel of his choice and had emerged into a foul smelling high ceilinged cavern that was littered with uneven boulders. This was, as far as he could see, the end of this particular road. The only way out of the cavern was the way he'd come in, unless he wanted to try climbing up to the apex of the roof to see if there was a an exit route up there... which was something that Vordeman did not want to do, for although he was extremely fit, it had been a long afternoon sprawled out on his rock beneath the constant beating of the Spanish sun, and in words of one syllable, he was tired. Walking through caves was one thing, scaling unkind and unforgiving walls with a torch in one hand and an Uzi in the other, well, he was prepared to pass on that degree of conscientiousness, and without a qualm. Wherever Leon Shapiro was beneath this mountain, it certainly wasn't here.

He turned to go and stifled a long yawn. The yawn almost choked in his throat as he heard a noise above his head. Immediately the torch beam probed upwards as he played it high against the irregular roof. There was nothing to see, but again the sound impinged upon his ears, a leathery scuffling creak. Then, out of the darkness, something pale and globular dropped and splashed in front of his feet with a sickening squelch, stinking of something like diarrhoea or stale vomit.

He gagged at the stench, taking two involuntary steps backwards and focusing the torch on the splatter that coagulated in a mucussy pool before him. Whatever it was, there was more of it, covering the surface of the boulders and splashed up against the walls like shit stains from a flock of gulls, and it was this, he now realised, that was the cause of the awful smell.

He shone the torch upwards again but still nothing moved... Not until there came the distant staccato burst of sub machine gun fire and then something *did* pass across his line of vision. Something broad and dark like a privateer's black sail, first creaking open and then folding back inwards upon itself. Whatever it was, it was big, and now he became aware of other things... That rather than the cold he had become accustomed to, it was hot in here... That there was another smell, dirty and feral, almost a furry smell, that lingered tantalisingly beneath the more obvious syrup of excreta... and most horrific of all, that there *was* something, something powerful and alien, in this cave with him!

Vordeman was crucified with indecision. On the one hand the sound of firing made it imperative that he find Yuri and lend whatever support was needed. Yuri had had the wobbles about this investigation, but even so, he would not fire his weapon by accident and if he was firing, he was firing at something that deserved to be fired upon. On the other hand, he was rooted to the spot by the presence of whatever creature shared this cave space with him and although it would be wrong to say that he was quaking with fear, a deep sense of trepidation and unease filled his spirit. He eyed the exit tunnel, only a few meters away, and came to a decision.

With a stride and a leap, he dashed for the exit and almost got there before a sudden rushing of displaced air made him turn.

Had he not turned he would not have seen what killed him, which in the circumstances might have been significantly more merciful. As it was, the torch beam fell on the hideous countenance of the bat that swooped towards him. Its mouth was pulled open in the rictus of an angry scream, blind pink and red eyes seemed to focus on his own and then there was a searing wrench of the most excruciatingly pain as talons embedded themselves in his belly and chest. Both torch and gun were dropped as leathery wings wrapped themselves around him, crushing arms and shoulders, and pulling him into the airlessness of the creature's fur.

His dying thought, as he was hauled upwards into the dark vaults of the cavern, was that this was no ordinary bat. Bats were tiny creatures, inoffensive and benign to man. But this bat was big, certainly as big as he was, and with a wingspan measured in metres. What's more, it was angry, and it was killing him.

In the dungeon chamber the shapechanger smiled. The *Zkernowii* was working wonderfully, joyfully well. Four had entered the labyrinth and three had been destroyed or neutralised. A fourth had escaped, but had certainly not escaped undamaged.

Had the shapechanger been able to function totally as the Warrior Djinn, it would have been able to identify the spore of its victims. Much of its energy, however, was still focused on the incubator and its abilities were finite. It did not know who had been caught in the traps, but was content to rest in the knowledge that the manmate's army of interlopers was now sustaining collateral damage. The scales were being re-balanced and the sensation of revenge was deliciously sweet.

That said, the shapechanger would have been marginally less pleased had it known of the existence of the P3 unit, and that two of its three victims were still alive. It would have been furious had it had an inkling that the one escapee was none other than the manmate magician himself.

They got Mage back to Calle Granadillos in record time and within a very few minutes Hector, only just returned with Jaime Gomez from La Linea, had arrived to administer stitches, plasters and bandages. Mage had a nasty gash across his forehead and a badly cut lower lip. Two ribs had been cracked and a number of muscles had been badly strained. He was also covered by a host of minor lesions and major, external bruises. He was conscious and put up an argument when Hector produced not one but three hypodermic syringes. Hector was not to be deterred and, with Helen and Light backing him up, took a certain satisfaction in giving Mage the injections.

'One for tetanus,' he explained, 'one as a relaxant and the third, a precaution against typhus. You swallowed a lot of dirty water.'

'I'll live,' Mage croaked weakly.

'Only if you sleep for a while and rest for a few days.'

'We don't *have* a few days,' Mage rasped, and looking at Helen for support, tried to prop himself up on one arm. 'For heaven's sake, Leon is still trapped down there somewhere!'

'I know,' she answered soberly. 'We'll do what we can to find him and get him out, but Hector's right. You can't do anything in your present state. You've got to rest.'

'And,' Light cut in pointedly, 'if it hadn't been for Shapiro's obsession, you wouldn't be in this state now. It was his decision Colin, and if there's a price to be paid, it's his to pay, not ours! Anyway, for crying out loud, what happened in there, man?'

Forcing the words through the sorest of sore throats, Mage briefly narrated the events that had led to his separation from the Israeli, emphasising his belief that a power of magic had been focused against them. No-one disagreed with him, but everyone had an opinion with regard to what should be done next. An argument raged above his sick bed, and it was one that he became increasingly disassociated from as Hector's second injection began to take effect.

Before he finally slipped into the sleep of healing he whispered a few firm instructions into Helen Ross's ear and then gave himself up to the welcome waves of unconsciousness.

Ever since she had been in Castillo, Helen Ross had made a point of telephoning Michael Fry every three or four days to give him a detailed update of all that was happening. She had done this with Mage's full knowledge and, apart from her own personal involvement with Hector Sanchez, had been totally candid in her reports. She phoned him now to give him a detailed briefing and also to ask his advice and opinion.

The Druid was adamant. 'I don't care if Mage is half dead on his feet and I don't care what your doctor says, Mage is right when he says things are speeding up. We feel it here at The Oaks, and we have our corroboration from Glastonbury and Cael. You must follow through on Mage's instructions. I know it sounds callous, but don't worry about the Israeli. Your prime priority must be to get into the citadel and stop the Djinn, and if that is what Colin is trying to do, you're duty bound to help him every way you can.'

'I don't need a lecture, Michael,' Helen said gently. 'I'm quite prepared to follow Colin's instructions. In fact, they're already in hand. Light is performing a healing ritual even as I speak and Doctor Sanchez is arranging with the Chief of Police for us to go in through the roof of the citadel early tomorrow morning.'

'Be careful,' Michael Fry said quickly. 'And don't you be tempted to go in with the raiding party!'

'I might have to.'

'No, no don't! After your clairvoyancy at The Oaks you'll be a sitting duck for anything that comes your way on the astral plane. You've got their scent, but I'll bet an oak tree for an acorn that the Djinn has also got yours!'

'I still might have to,' Helen said evenly and then, to change the subject, 'Providing he can get out of bed, we'll be performing a ritual at dawn. Colin was very anxious that you should know that he intends to be in the Christian keep. That you should visualise him there if you're in a position to perform your own ritual concomitant with our own.'

'Tell him that there'll be rituals performed all over Britain,' Fry said formally, assuming the mantle of The Merlin. 'Stonehenge, Avebury, Glastonbury, Anglesea, Caernarfon, The Oaks, Edinburgh, Culloden – even Cael in Ireland – we'll all be projecting our protective energies towards you in Castillo!'

'Thank you. I'll tell the others that. They'll be reassured and I'll phone you tomorrow evening if I'm in a position to do so.'

'Make sure that you are.'

Helen replaced the receiver on the cradle arm and pushed her way out of the phone box in the village square. It was a hot balmy evening, and it was a with a weird feeling of detachment that she surveyed the sight of children playing in The Plaza de Constitucion while their parents sat drinking wine and wafting Andalucian fans around the cluttered tables that crowded out onto the street from Jacinto's bar. Everything seemed so normal. Everyone seemed so unconcerned. Would they be sitting there so complacently if they knew that this might be their last free night on earth? That it might be their last night, period! She doubted it, and while part of her wanted to hurry from table to table, telling parents to flee with their children while they still could, the other part of her knew that it would be to no avail. Fights, sick priests, deaths and suicides, along with a handful of bad births, well, that might be one thing, but were she to tell them of an alien species that had designs of territorial conquest and that at that very minute they were preparing a ritual, a *magical* ritual that would give them free access not only to this little paradise of Andalucia but also to the rest of the world, she'd be carted off in a straight jacket before she could say the first line of The Maiden's Prayer!

Leon had fired blindly at the wave of darkness that had suddenly overcome him. In a single heartbeat Mage and the precious light had vanished, plunging him into a black world devoid of parameters. Even with the cacophony of the nine millimetre detonations ringing in his ears he had screamed Mage's name over and over again, cursing him to his grave for having deserted him. It was only after he had collapsed to the ground – at least there was still something beneath his feet – and had had time to reflect on the sudden horrific turn of events, that he came to realise that Mage would not, *could* not have disappeared so abruptly through any natural cause. Something equally dreadful had befallen the Englishman and it was a moot point as to who had the greater advantage. Leon had the Uzi, but Mage had the light.

He had been aware of the sound of rushing water, but it had been a distant sound, and irrelevant to his predicament, which was quite terrifying! He was lost beneath a mountain with no idea where he was or how he could get out, without even a pin prick of light to give him any sense of direction. Tentatively he'd brought his hand up to his eyes. The darkness had remained constant, and for the first time in his life he had wished that he'd been a smoker, for then at least he might have had a lighter or a box of matches in his pocket.

With his heartbeat thundering in his ears he had fought for some calm and composure and had taken stock of what he *did* have. There was the Uzi, of course, and the rest of the Little Ruben's arsenal. He had the clothes that clung to his body in a sheen of sweat and although he had panicked and, indeed, was still extremely frightened, he had his reason and rationale. He had to find his way back to the river bank and fought now to remember a few salient facts. On their way into the mountain, they had travelled up a noticeable gradient. Therefore, despite the confusion of the split tunnel and Mage's unaccountable disappearance, if he could define which way was *down,* then he might be in with a chance.

He had also been subtly aware of the fact that the sense of threat and pursuit that had filled himself and Mage alike with such a profound sense of urgency was now absent. Furthermore, it was no longer bitterly cold. Quite the reverse, in fact. It had become oppressively warm and airless. He had no idea why there should have been such sudden variance in the temperature, but given the choice he was glad of the warmth. At least he would not freeze to death, although – and he'd shivered at the thought – death was a very real possibility. Anything, *absolutely fucking anything* could be in this tunnel with him and he wouldn't know about it until it was far too late. Deprived of both vision and sound his imagination had gone into overtime, threatening even greater paralysis. In an effort to overcome it, he had forced himself into action.

First he'd pulled the aluminium case in front of him and, going purely by touch, had sprung the catches. Groping through the contents, he'd extricated the spare ammunition clips and had stuffed them into the belt of his trousers. The grenades had gone into his jacket pockets and he'd tucked the limpet mine inside his shirt. It had been far from comfortable, but now at least he could ditch the cumbersome case, and with the Uzi slung around his shoulder he'd had both hands free to feel along the surface of the ground in search of any sense of inclination. He'd found none, but after only a very short time his fingers had made contact with a very slight groove scarred into the rock. He'd been immediately mindful of the mark that he'd drawn Mage's attention to and had felt sure that this was the same mark. Filled with a disproportionate sense of achievement, he'd started crawling forwards. Here at least had been some term of reference. All he had to do was follow the line and if he found himself travelling upwards, he'd simply turn and retrace his steps. He'd been so totally confidant that the groove in the ground would lead him somewhere that he'd conveniently forgotten to consider what might have been responsible for putting it there in the first place. Had he known, he would not have felt quite so pleased with himself.

Edging forwards on all fours he'd soon lost track of time and time came to be measured in increasing waves of pain as his body had stiffened with the unaccustomed posture. His hands had soon become grazed with minor cuts as they'd brushed against sharp pebbles, but it was his knee caps which suffered the most. Eventually, to take the pressure off his knees, he'd slithered along on his belly and, while this had made the going marginally more comfortable, it had also made it considerably slower. After a while, he'd had to rest and stretching out on his back, again had brought his hand to his face. Although he'd had ample time to get used to the dark there'd still been nothing to see. The ticking of his wristwatch had brought a measure of reassurance, but he regretted the fact that his father's old timepiece did not have a luminous dial. There had been a further three rest breaks before he had come to realise that as far as he could tell he was neither travelling uphill nor down and that he had no idea of how much distance he might have covered. The almost imperceptible groove had still been there beneath his sore fingers, but it had been obvious, even to Leon, that it wasn't leading him anywhere.

Not for the first time in his adult life, he'd felt like crying. Apart from anything else he'd been desperately thirsty and the thirst had acted as a barb in the flank of his increasing desperation to be free of this Godforsaken place. One thought had led to another and he'd found himself praying to a God that had been too long ignored and too long forgotten. He'd never been sure whether he had forgotten God or if God had forgotten him. At the time, the time of his transitional youth, it had seemed as though God had been the guilty party!

His parents had both been religious more by cant than conviction, and from his own macrocosmic point of view, God had been an abstract idea rather than a living energy. Therefore there'd been no conviction, only desperation, when he'd been cornered into praying as a last resort. His prayers, like the prayers of all adolescents doing battle with wakening emotions and sexual urges, especially complicated and confused in Leon's case, were prayed with his knees to the ground and his back to the wall. They had, in Leon's critical evaluation, all gone unheard and relatively early in life he'd formed the conclusion that if you wanted a prayer answered, you had to answer it yourself. God had had enough chances to prove his existence, and in every case had failed miserably.

Leon had prayed for the love of Leah Goldman, but the lovely Leah Goldman, had, with a disdainful shake of her thick black curly hair, gone with Alexis Dronstein. He had prayed for the heterosexual genes within his being to become the dominant genes, but they had failed miserably in the face of the homosexual onslaught. Later he had prayed that he might at least remain aloof to the sexual urges that had so frequently placed him in potentially embarrassing and hazardous situations... But God had not heard those prayers either, and it had only been after Leon had severed his tenuous links with the Godhead that he'd been able to find any semblance of self acceptance.

His mind had freewheeled, remembering the day he had joined Mossad fresh from the IDF basic training programme. He'd remembered the day that his father had died, and he'd remembered feeling even then how much he regretted that he and his father had not been closer. There's had been a working relationship rather than the normal father and son relationship that he had so desperately longed for.

He'd remembered his Bar Mitzvah in Jaffa all those years ago and tried to remember Herschal being there. The memory had been obstinately elusive, but at least he'd remembered some of the prayers. Leon's God had been dead to him since late in his teens, but now in acute distress, there had been a reincarnation of faith and the prayers came thick and fast. There had been several, loosely wrapped around the theme of *Oh God, I'm in the shit so get me out of it as fast as you can and if you do I promise I'll pray in the synagogue every day for the rest of my life...*

The detonation of small arms fire had been all the more shocking by its unexpectedness. It came from somewhere directly ahead and now, when Leon peered into the gloom, there was just the faintest opaque glow of dim light. With an exhalation of relief and mindless of what he might be getting himself into, he scrambled to his feet and made haste towards the source of the illumination. *Thank you God, thank you, thank you, thank you!*

Heedless of the many obstructions and hardly feeling the frequent collisions with sharp protrusions of rock, he half jogged half stumbled until he came to the light, and when he found it, he was confounded by it.

He arrived in a small circular chamber with what felt to be an extremely insecure base beneath his feet. There were small stones and layers of fine sand which created a sense of impermanence. He felt that this flooring might give way at any given moment, and what was beneath was anybody's guess. From where he stood, a torch beam shone obliquely downwards from a point some two meters above his head. It illuminated a gossamer mist of cobwebby stuff that clung to the walls of the vertical shaft and in matted folds across it. The torch was caught in the latticework of this weird and curious fabric – it was something half way between an enormous spider's web and folds of transparent cotton wool – and clearly visible above the light there was the shadowy silhouette of a human form, caught and spread-eagled in the net.

'Are you all right?' Leon called inanely, his voice emerging as a croak.

'Of course I'm not fucking well all right,' came the muffled reply from above him. And then – 'Who the fuck are you?'

'Leon Shapiro.'

'Oh *shit!*'

'What's the matter?' Leon asked, taken aback by the vehemence of the suspended figure's exclamation.

'What's the matter? I'll tell you what the matter is! If it wasn't for you, I wouldn't be strung up here like this!'

'Well who the hell are you?' Leon asked indignantly, not understanding why he should be blamed for the other man's predicament.

'Yuri Bogdanovitch, Mossad P3. We saw you come into the caves with the Brit. The Brit came out but you didn't, so we came in looking for you. My wing man must be around here somewhere – unless he's met with an accident too. I thought you might be him.'

'You say Mage got out of the mountain?' Leon asked excitedly.

'Yeah...'

'When? I Mean, how long ago are we talking about? I've lost track of time...'

'Curious that, isn't it?' Yuri mused conversationally. 'You and Mage went into the cave just after four o'clock, he came out alone at twenty past six. Vordeman and I entered the cave at twenty minutes to seven, but I don't know if that was two hours ago or two days ago. I can't get my hand free to look at my watch... So you tell me, what's the time?'

By angling his wrist Leon could now see the face of his watch in the diffused light of the torch beam. 'It's eight fifteen,' he said cautiously. 'At least, that's what it says, but...'

'Yeah, I know. Eight fifteen, but when? Eight fifteen this evening or eight fifteen tomorrow morning?'

'I don't know... I'd have said that I'd been stuck down here for an awful lot longer than four hours... Anyway, what happened to you?'

'Ah, I was looking down this hole when something hit me like an express train and bowled me over the edge. Thought that was it, but I did a couple of somersaults and ended up in this crap. All very interesting...'

'I'll see if I can climb up the side of the shaft and help get you unravelled.'

'No!' Yuri said quickly. 'No, don't do that! Where are you – I mean, in relation to me?'

'About four or five metres beneath you, but look, there are some fairly good hand holds and I should...'

'No,' Yuri cut in. 'Don't come anywhere near this mesh stuff! I tell you, man, it's got a life of its own. The more you move the more it wraps itself around you. I'm trussed up like a fucking cocoon and I'm not going anywhere without a three man team with winches and harnesses. I can't see below me, but I get the impression that I'm suspended in mid air?'

'Yes, you are... but what are we going to do then?'

'Hey, Shapiro, I thought you were the guy with all of the answers! I'm just one of the foot soldiers following orders, although that doesn't mean I don't have a few questions!'

'On the subject of orders, what were they and where did they come from?'

'Word came direct from Jerusalem to keep you under close surveillance, to ride shotgun for you without letting you know we were around, and to haul your ass out of the fire if it looked as though you were getting burned.'

'And were you told why?'

'Nope!'

'Fucking hell!' It was Leon's turn to swear.

'You going to tell me?'

'Mr Bogdanovitch, I wouldn't know where to start and you wouldn't believe me even if I did. Suffice to say that we're in a lot more trouble than you could conceivably imagine.'

'No, Mr Shapiro, no... I can quite easily imagine that we're in a *lot* of trouble. The question is, how do we get out of it? The only thing I can think of is that you find some way out of here and get back as fast as you can with all the help you can muster. I'm not forgetting that something *pushed* me down this fucking hole, and don't ask me how I know, but I just get the strongest feeling that it's got me exactly where it wants me and it'll be back to finish me off sooner or later.'

'But I don't know how to get out!' Leon exclaimed in acute frustration. 'I'm more lost than you are and I don't have a light. Maybe if I could reach your torch....'

'Is it caught up in the stuff?'

'Yes.'

'Then forget it, unless you've got a nice big stick. You haven't got a big stick, have you?'

'No.'

'Then like I say man, forget it. Push your arm into this stuff and you won't get it out again!' Yuri chuckled with deliberate melodrama. 'You have been warned!'

'Are you hurt?' Leon asked miserably, in a feeble attempt to change the subject.

'I don't think so... but the truth is I don't know. I can feel my head ticking and my heart beating, but not much else. Like I say, I'm totally trussed up in this fucking cocoon and I can't move a muscle hardly. My back or my neck might be broken for all I know... I can't feel a thing. Almost as though I've been anaesthetised in some way. But at least there isn't any pain.'

Leon sat down in the entrance to the chamber and looked forlornly up at his suspended companion. He was becoming increasingly aware of his own pain and exhaustion, exacerbated by the different pains of hunger and thirst. The heat in this part of the mountain was quite profound, and the airlessness of the atmosphere made him breathe in short rasping breaths. Upon the air there was a sharp acrid tang, acidic to the tongue and unsettling on the stomach. It reminded him of dirty hospitals and fouled sheets. But at least, here there was some semblance of light and, far more importantly, another human being. True, Yuri Bogdanovitch was in an unenviable and inextricable position, but his presence meant that whatever else, Leon was not alone, and right then, that meant more than words could say.

He found himself becoming drowsy, and indeed was beginning to nod off when Yuri's words brought him back to the depressing and frightening reality of the moment.

'Are you still there?'

'Yes... sorry. I was just thinking...'

'Do you still have your Uzi with you?' There was an edge to Yuri's voice that had not been there before.

'Yes. Why?'

'Unless I'm wrong, you're going to need it!'

'Why? What's wrong? What's happening?' Leon was instantly alert now, standing and straining his eyes upwards.

'I think it might be feeding time,' Yuri said dreamily.

'Bogdanovitch, what the hell are you talking about?'

'Hey, Leon, you ever killed a man?'

'No. I'm not a field agent!'

'Well I hope you've got balls enough to do it, because in a little while from now, I might be asking you for one big favour!' A note of hysteria had crept into Yuri Bogdanovitch's voice.

'What is happening up there?' Leon demanded.

'Can't you see?'

'No, I can't see a damn thing. Well, sure, I see the torch and I see you, but...'

'You can't see what's above me?'

'No.'

'Just as well, Leon Shapiro. Just as well. But I'll tell you what *I* can see, shall I? I can see the motherfucker that pushed me down this hole. It's about four metres above me, coming down the shaft quite slowly... We're talking about something that might once have been a spider, but that would have been before it got sprayed with some very bad chemical shit out of Fort Detrick or Dimona. Ooh, this baby is big! Only got six legs, but each one of 'em is about a metre long... and this little lady's got teeth like a shark. And she's grinding 'em together in such a way to tell me that she's very *very* hungry, and not only am I the hors-d'oeuvre, I'm also the main course! You see it yet?'

'No,' Leon wailed. 'I can't see anything!'

'Cock your hammer, Leon, and when you shoot, shoot straight.'

'I can't just shoot you!' Leon exclaimed in acute distress.

'You fucking shoot me when I fucking tell you to!' Yuri Bogdanovitch screamed at him. 'I'd rather be shot by a fellow Israeli than be eaten by this bastard! You can't see the frigging thing, but, oh shit shit shit, I can! It's got eyes and big scaly things clinging to it and it fucking well stinks like an Auschwitze oven... and it's pissing and dribbling all over me...'

Leon heard a muffled slithering and scraping, then a globular ball of mucussy stuff dropped through the cobwebs and exploded with a venomous stench against an oval boulder. The whole framework of the latticework of cobwebs began to dance and shimmer before his eyes, dislodging the torch slightly and altering the angle of the beam. And now, with the light out of his eyes he did see something dark and shapeless descending upon the web. It filled the shaft, not only with the bulk of its size but also with its all pervading sense of menace.

'Now... Now... *Now!*' Yuri half screamed and half sobbed. 'If you're any fucking kind of fucking Jew, for fuck's sake, do it now!'

With the memory of Herschal's death indelibly scored across his mind, Leon raised the Uzi and squeezed the trigger. Yuri's body danced in mid air as the nine millimetre parabellums tore into him. If he emitted a death scream Leon never heard it above the ear shattering cacophony of the gun. But in the silence that came after there was a sibilant hiss as the thing that had been about to devour the P3 agent lowered itself into the web, pushing the Israeli's still twitching corpse to one side, making straight for Leon, who stood in shock at the bottom of the pit. Seeing his predicament he swiftly inserted a fresh clip of ammunition, and raising the stubby barrel once again, took careful aim at the centre of the descending abomination and again squeezed the trigger, discharging half of the thirty six round clip in one long burst into the underbelly of the alien entity.

The thing quivered, spewing out streams of lava like liquid that cut a swathe through the web, then folding its legs, it dropped like a stone. Leon leapt back to the side of the wall as the hunched and deformed bundle crashed at his feet with an incredibly squelching thud, then the floor of the cave gave way and the beast disappeared from sight through a gaping black hole. Leon tried to jump towards the sanctuary of the tunnel he had followed from the lower levels, but he was milliseconds too late. The floor disintegrated beneath his feet and he too found himself falling in hot pursuit of the creature he had just killed... At least, he *hoped* that he'd killed it – not that it mattered now, of course, now that he too was going to die.

He inhaled the breath that he needed to scream his last farewell to the world, then hit ice cold water that immediately carried him away in the spume and spray of its careering torrent. He felt his leg snap beneath him as he hit something less pliable than bone and flesh, then something else, even less pliable, struck him across his head and he was saved from the waves of pain by the embalming blackness of unconsciousness.

The shapechanger had heard the intermittent bursts of small arms fire, and for a while had focused in on them with some interest. The interlopers were fighting back, which was to be expected, although guns and bullets would have little or no effect against the *Zkernowii*. At one point, however, he did feel a small charge of energy pass from him which suggested that one of his defence mechanisms had been destroyed. Not that it mattered. There were plenty more waiting to be employed when the need arose. He strained his ears and nostrils and forced his other senses into the focus of an investigative sweep. There had been the gun shots, but all was still and silent now but for the steady regular inhalations of the incubator. He was sure that there would be further incursions, but they would be dealt with in the same way as had been the first. The magic of the *Zkernowii* was all powerful and would bring death to all those who sought to deter him or bring him harm.

It was the pain in Leon's lower left leg that finally persuaded him to open his eyes. Yet even with his eyes open he was no better off. He was confined to the totality of darkness once again and had to use his other perceptions to take stock of his new but equally terrible predicament. First of all, he was half in and half out of water, shoulders and torso resting upon solid rock while his hips and legs trailed down a gentle incline, small waves lapping over his sodden trousers. With a groan and supreme effort of self will, he eased himself more firmly onto the shallow ledge, coming into contact with hard wall. In the process he inadvertently bandaged his left leg against the lip of the stone, causing waves of pain that plunged him into a flirtatious alliance with unconsciousness again.

When he came round for the second time he was sitting with his back to the wall, his legs splayed out in front of him, the Uzi nestling firmly in his lap. He wondered if the damn thing would still work after its dousing, and vaguely remembered from some half read office circular that all Mossad Uzi's were now being waterproofed at the factory before dispatch. He hoped that the waterproofing was effective, absolutely certain that he would be using the gun again before he got out of this mess... Always assuming he *could* get out of this mess. But even if he couldn't, the gun would have to be fired at least one more time...

He thought with horror of what he had had to do to Yuri Bogdanovitch... and absently wondered what had happened to the other thing that had claimed half a precious clip of ammunition. One thing was certain. What he could do for Yuri Bogdanovitch he would certainly do for himself if he had to!

He tried moving his legs. The right one was no problem, but the left leg was useless, apart from the pain. Oh no, the pain wasn't useless at all, for that was the only thing in this coffin like environment that told him he was still alive. *I am alive,* he told himself, over and over again, realising that his problem was how to remain that way.

Tentatively he ran his hands along his left shin and found the break in the bone midway between the knee cap and the ankle. It seemed to be a clean break, but having little or no medical knowledge, there was no way he could be sure. He *did* know that walking on the thing was out of the question, and that unless it was seen to soon and the bone re set, he might end up being lame for life – however long that life might be.

'Help!' he called out more in frustration than desperation. His voice was little more than a hoarse whisper that brought his attention back to the burning sensation in his chest and throat. Once, many years ago, he'd been caught up in a cloud of tear gas used to dispel a Palestinian demonstration at the Damascus Gate and had been ill for days after with laryngitis and the most colossal chest infection. It felt now as if he was having a relapse of mammoth proportions.

Despite the water that lapped at his feet – what was it? An underground lake, a stream, a river? And if the latter, where was the rushing torrent that had brought him up upon this hostile shore? – the air was warm and dry, and from somewhere there was the imperceptible suggestion of just the faintest breeze. Working by touch alone he extricated the spare clips of ammunition and laid them on the rock next to him, taking stock as he did so. He'd used half a clip to test and site the weapon, and had used the other half of that clip in his blind panic when he'd been separated from Mage. There was a half used clip in the gun right now and another four in reserve... That meant over one hundred and fifty rounds, providing, of course, *they* still worked after their submersing. And then there was the other hardware. The grenades and the limpet mine. He laid them out to his right, and with the nine millimetre clips to his left, settled down to wait.

It might be a long wait and he wasn't even sure what he was waiting for. He had no voice to shout with, only one leg to carry him and his eyes were blinded by the darkness. But he did have his ears! And the moment he heard anything that might be identified as a search and rescue, he'd yell if he could yell, or fire the bloody gun, or get someone's attention somehow. One thing that gave him a small glimmer of hope was the wall behind his back, for rather than being raw stone, it had been constructed from rough hewn bricks. Man made bricks. Therefore, wherever he was, he had to be somewhere close to the world of men.

29.

The Keep

Mage dreamed a dream that was more than a dream and while he did so, Helen and Light sat at his bedside pouring their healing energies into him. Sometimes they acted together, linking hands across the bed, their free fingers making physical contact with Mage's temples, other times they worked independently, but at no time through the evening and the middle hours of the night was Mage ever alone.

At around eleven o'clock his temperature rocketed to over 103 degrees Fahrenheit and he became delirious but within half an hour it had subsided to more acceptable levels and by midnight he was cool and calm.

Helen had filled the bedroom with various herbs and wild flowers and she had also lit nine white candles; this novena burned slowly and steadily and filled the room with a warm and glowing ambience. Occasionally a waft of soft night air would breeze in from the open window, causing the candles to flicker and making shadows dance across the white walls beneath the oak beamed ceiling.

Hector sat in a corner chair, sometimes dozing but for the better part very alert to the miracle which unfolded intermittently before his eyes. In the space of a few short hours the bruises on Mage's battered body bloomed to their full and violent hue, and then of their own volition began to subside. The split lower lip became a golf ball of yellow puss – then John Light had touched it with great tenderness, gently using the back of his hand, and the huge blister had burst. Helen had wiped it clean with a moist tissue covered with the sticky balm of an aloe vera plant, and within an hour Mage's mouth, which would always be scarred, had none the less returned to the semblance of its normal shape.

At midnight, as if in unspoken communion, Light and Helen had stood, one on either side of the bed, and with their heads bowed, they had laid their hands upon Mage's chest. Was it Hector's imagination or had he actually heard the fractured ribs cracking as they had knitted together? He was not sure and could not tell, but that was what it had *sounded* like! He was in no doubt, however, that there was a great charge of power being unleashed here in this room and that he was witness to something that was impossible by any medical or scientific standard. Mage should have been in a hospital bed with several days of rest and recuperation ahead of him, and yet with the intercession of these two people, one of whom he had come to love, a healing process that should have taken days was being concentrated into hours.

'He should go to the clinic,' he had said after his initial examination. 'He has concussion, there are many bruises and there might even be some internal bleeding.'

Helen had looked at him almost serenely, then had stood on tiptoe to brush her lips against his unshaven cheek. 'There isn't time, Hector. Trust us. We know what we're doing and what we've got to do. This is one of the reasons why we are here. You've done your bit, so just sit back and rest for a while, get some sleep if you can and let me and John have him.'

By one in the morning Mage had fallen into a deep and natural sleep and Helen and Light had visibly relaxed. Tamara had prepared herb tea and sandwiches, and the four of them had gathered in the salon around the modest log fire that Tamara had lit more for comfort than for warmth. The door to the bedroom was wide open and the candles still burned. From where she sat she could watch Mage with ease.

Light was trying to explain to Hector, in the most basic lay terms, how the concept of spiritual healing worked, when Helen reached over and lightly touched his arm. 'Excuse me, John,' she said quietly, 'but look into the bedroom and tell me if you see what I see?'

Light did as he was told and as a long sigh escaped his lips, he gripped Helen's hand firmly. 'Oh yes lady, I most surely do!'

'Hector, Tammy... Can you see what we're seeing?'

'I see – well, *something,* but I don't know what I'm seeing,' Hector muttered, coming to his feet and taking a cautious half step forwards.

'It's the spirits, man,' Tamara said in awe. 'You guys started the healing an' now the spirits are doin' their work!'

Helen was suddenly aware of the tears that were streaming down her cheeks. In her simple statement, Tamara had hit the nail on the head. There could be no other explanation for the dancing motes of light that hovered above Mage's face and body, sometimes ascending towards the gnarled old black beams, then dropping like fireflies, sometimes quivering above a certain bruise or lesion, sometimes moving in slow deliberation up and down the form of the unconscious man. She tried to count the incandescent pin pricks of light, but couldn't. They were too numerous and moved too quickly.

'The candles...?'

'No Hector.' She stood at the doctor's side, wrapping her arm around his waist and tucking her thumb into his trouser belt, 'Tammy's right. If ever you needed evidence for the existence of spirit, you're getting it now. If you have found it hard to believe some of the words you have heard, simply believe now what your own eyes are telling you!'

And while the spirits danced, and the watchers watched, Colin Mage dreamed on.

He was in the keep, sitting in the centre of the dry circle of grey sand. Light streamed in through the open portals, and yes, while it was sunlight, it was a different kind of sunlight to any he had ever known. There was a kaleidoscopic ethereality that defied and denied the hard forms of perspective and focus, but he clearly understood that he was not alone in the keep. Around him there were figures wearing robes of different pastel hues. Some of them he knew, others he did not. Many of them he knew to be dead.

His Grandmother, Elsie Maud, wearing silver grey and looking far younger than he could ever remember, was the first to step forwards. He knelt and taking her outstretched hands, kissed her fingers.

Up yer gets, Colly my lad. This is the time you was born for!

'But Nan,' he said. 'Why? For good God's sake, why did it have to be me?' He had felt the pressure of her spindly fingers as she had gripped his hands.

Ask it the other way round, Colly. Why not you?

Father Paul O'Connor of Cael rested an emerald arm upon his shoulder. *We are all with you, Colin. You will not be allowed to fail.* As the elderly priest spoke there was the sound of monks singing Gregorian Chant somewhere in the distant background.

'Why are you here?' Mage asked. 'Are you dead?'

Several weeks ago. I knew I could pass over as soon as you arrived in Castillo. That's all I was hanging on for. My only task was to make sure you got here...

Mine also said Herschal of The Negev, wearing Judaic red. *Now you must face the beast, the creature of all our fears, and slay him without mercy. You will not fight alone. We are all here to lend weight to your arm.*

'Do you know what's happened to Leon?' Mage asked.

He fights his own battles and awaits his own destiny. Concerning your own fate, your plan is a good one. Enter the citadel after the sunrise. Your foe will be expecting you to attack from below, not above...

I am Rajad said a small dark skinned boy, dressed in pure white. *I come in the dreams of my aunt to tell you that all the other gateways are firmly closed. You need have no worry about your flanks. The battle will be won or lost on this mountain alone...*

'Your aunt?' Mage asked, perplexed by the unfamiliarity of the boy.

My aunt is Kiku.

'Ah yes, I remember writing to her. How is she?'

Saddened by the thought of my impending death, for should you fail here she will sacrifice me to Shiva to ensure that the opening on my continent remains sealed... I am very young sir, and have no wish to die, so I pray for your success..

The figures moved silently round him, diffusing and diffused within the light. And now another stepped forwards, dressed in purple with iron grey hair. *I am Marcus Sutonious of the Spanish Legion. I fought with the Djinn on this mountain top nearly two thousand years ago and, although I lost, I do have intelligence that* might help you. His body armour is impregnable, but if you strike at his eyes, you may blind him. Know that your enemy has no heart, but that he does have two brains, one in his head and one in his belly. To destroy the one you must destroy the other.*

The light was becoming brighter and the walls within the keep were becoming more indistinct. *I am Carlos, Hidalgo of Castille* said another masculine voice, but when Mage tried to place the source could not do so for now the figures were turning and fading from vision. *My friends and I did battle against the magic of the Djinn in 1249. His magic is powerful, but I come to tell you that it is flawed by the blindness born of arrogance...*

...And then there was a crackling coruscating lightening flash of pure brilliance and he was alone in the keep, levitating upwards towards pin pricks of different light which he gradually identified as candle flames as he slipped quietly into consciousness.

'Hi,' Helen said encouragingly. 'How are you feeling?'

'Good,' he said in a low voice. 'A bit disjointed, but good. What time is it?'

'Three a.m. Now, drink this.' She brought a cup to his lips filled with a dark sweet liquid that smelled of mint and honey.

'What is it?'

'Just drink it. It'll help you wake up and make you feel better.'

He took a tentative sip, tasted the mint and honey and a deeper darker herbal bitterness that neither the mint nor the honey could entirely conceal. He coughed once. 'Your own potent little witch brew?' he asked tiredly.

'Something like that.'

He took another mouthful, amazed at the speed with which the concoction was working. He must ask her for the recipe sometime. 'The others?' he asked.

'We're all here.'

'Good. There's a lot of work to do.'

'Yes, but just take it easy for a wee while. You've had quite an ordeal and you're still very weak.'

'I'm going to be fine,' he responded, knowing something that she didn't. He pushed himself up on to one elbow. 'Any sign of Leon?'

Helen's face clouded. 'No, I'm afraid not.'

'Okay. Let me get out of this bed.'

'I'll get Hector.'

'Don't worry, I can manage.'

'I'll get him anyway.'

She beat a hasty retreat and when Hector entered the bedroom it was to find Mage standing naked by the side of the bed, his body a weal of blue and yellow bruises. He eyed the bruises with professional interest. They appeared to be several days old.

'You heal quickly, my friend,' he said pointedly.

'I had a lot of help,' Mage responded with a pale half smile.

'I'm not unaware of it. Helen and John have sat with you throughout the night. I don't know about John, but I know that Helen needs some sleep before whatever the morning might bring.'

'They can both rest for a while now.'

'And what about you?'

'I have some things to do.'

'Good God Colin, you can hardly stand!'

'I'll be all right Hector, I promise you.' Tentatively and not without effort, Mage climbed into fresh clothes. 'How's our friend Jaime Gomez?'

'Jaime's nursing a broken nose and he's looking for a fight. He'll be at the citadel at first light with ladders and ropes He should be able to make a big enough hole, although I've no idea how long it might take him.'

'Make sure you're with him,' Mage said. 'Tell him I don't care how long it takes, but silence is more important than speed. At the first sight of trouble, if you come across anything like the membrane of resin, pull back quickly and forget it. I'll find some other way in.' He zipped up his trousers, and with a small groan, bent to pull on his shoes.

'Colin, you're not well.'

'I'll be better before I get worse,' Mage said enigmatically. Then he managed a small laugh. 'Seriously, Hector, there's not much pain. I'm just as stiff as a board.'

They went through into the other room. Light and Tamara were sprawled out on the sofa while Helen had her legs folded beneath her within the depths of the overstuffed arm chair. 'John, Helen, Tamara – I'd like to say thank you...'

'Hey man,' Light came to his feet. 'Forget it. Just as long as you're in one piece!'

'I'm okay. My greatest concern at the moment is for you. You've been up all night and now you've got to get some rest. It starts getting light at six o'clock and the sun comes up around seven. By then I need to be in the keep with you and Helen riding shot gun for me outside. It'll be a crucial piece of ritual for me and I can't afford to be distracted or disturbed. Jaime Gomez will force an entry for me at the citadel, and Hector will let you know as soon as he's done it. When you know, I'll know, so I should be going in around eight o'clock unless Gomez comes unstuck, in which case I'll go down through the well at Calle Sombra.'

'Not alone!' Helen said sharply.

'Obviously I'll be going alone,' Mage argued gently. 'No point in exposing more of us to risk than we have to, and if I can't succeed on my own, we'll need you to organise a second line of defence. Apart from anything else, I'll benefit more from having you focus your mental energies on the mission rather than your physical presence.'

'It makes some sense, sure,' Light looked solemn, 'but in the spirit of the thing, it sucks!'

'Colin you are not going by yourself!' Helen was quite emphatic. 'You might be working within your own parameters of destiny, but I have my own agenda and I'm coming with you.'

Mage felt a slow burn of anger begin to ignite within him. 'Helen, if Michael

Fry...'

'This has got nothing to do with The Druid,' she snapped more aggressively than she'd intended. 'Think about this logically for a moment. If you go in there with a light you're going to be a sitting duck for anything that's waiting for you, but if you go in without a light you're going to be as blind as a bat! If I come in with you though, that'll be different. My clairvoyancy will work like radar. I'll be your eyes and your ears. I'll direct you to the Djinn and alert you to any countermeasures he might throw in your way! Ever since The Oaks, I've had the shapechanger's spore. I've got a score to settle, and I know that sooner or later I'm going to have to face the Djinn in the flesh, rather than in the sanctuary of clairvoyant vision. Given that, I suppose I'm being selfish. I want you by my side when it happens. But you must remember that I have *seen* us, you and I, together beneath the citadel, and if we're going to beat this nasty son of a bitch, we're going to do it together. In any case,' her eyes flashed and she found that she was tapping her foot as her knuckles balled into fists, 'while you may be all that you are, you have absolutely no authority to tell me what I can and can't do. I'm a free agent, and I'm here on my own account.'

Hector Sanchez looked horrified at the idea of Helen accompanying Mage, but Mage himself was reminded of this woman's authority. She was not just Michael Fry's ambassador, but also High Priestess of The Clans, and she had as much right as anyone present to make her own decisions. Mage simply didn't have the energy to fight. He'd told Hector that he was fine, but in reality it felt as though his head was detached from the rest of his body. There was half a second's time lag between the brain initiating an instruction and the body carrying it out. He knew that he would be all right later, once he had sat in ritual with himself and had balanced his own energies and chakras, but for now he demurred to Helen's adamancy and sat down at the head of his altar table, noting that despite the fact that there had been other people milling around this room for several hours, nothing had been disturbed. He would fight with Helen later when he had regained more of his strength or maybe he would simply let Hector do it for him. By the look on the doctor's face, if Helen Ross was going into the citadel, it would be over Hector's dead body! In any case, for the time being, there were other things to discuss.

'I need some time to work and meditate,' he told them, 'and I have a weapon to prepare. You've all been up for half the night, and it's going to be a helluva day tomorrow, so you all must get some sleep, even if it's only a couple of hours. Let's think about a six o'clock breakfast, and we'll comb out some of the fine details of our battle plan then.'

By and large Mage's suggestion was met with enthusiasm, but Light shook his head.

'Not me. I'm on my second wind and it'll be twenty four hours before I'm able to sleep. Right now I need to be occupied and busy.'

'Fine,' Mage said. 'Hang around. I may yet need another pair of hands.'

Tamara tucked herself into the folds of the generous sofa while Helen and Hector retired to the spare downstairs bedroom. There was an obvious element of tension between them and Mage knew that Hector would do his best to dissuade

Helen from her chosen course of action. Somehow, he didn't think that the doctor would be very successful with his protestations and it might only be when Helen looked into the black hole of the unknown from the roof of the citadel that there may be some chance of persuading her to change her mind.

After some initial searching for the right ingredients and arranging the lighting to their liking, the two men sat at Mage's table and meditated for twenty minutes before Mage chanted the mantra that opened his circle. He lit a single red candle as a token gesture, then leaning down to one side, hauled the crossbow onto the table and stripped away its hessian covering. Light's eyes lit up with interest, but at this stage, while Mage went through the process of cleansing and blessing, he said nothing. When this was done, at least in the first part, he allowed himself the luxury of a low whistle.

'That is a beast,' he murmured appreciatively. 'Where did you find it?'

Mage told him of the circumstances behind its purchase and then produced the six hollow pointed bolts. 'These...' he said. 'I don't know... I just have a feeling about them. You've said yourself that bullets don't seem to have much impact on the Djinn, and from what Leon told us, even Herschal's twelve bore loaded with solid shot couldn't prevent the damn thing that killed him from changing its shape and form. So if lead can't kill it and silver won't stop it, what will? What do we fill these bolts with that might be effective? I can forge points from shards of crystal and superglue or maybe the crystal itself might be enough, but if I've got a hollow shaft every instinct screams at me that something must go into it. Dreams, such as the one that I had about finding the bow, are there for a purpose. The Lords Of Light have put a powerful weapon in my hands, but what they haven't made clear is how exactly I'm supposed to use it.'

Light picked up one of the bolts and rolling it between his fingers and thumb, he looked at it thoughtfully. 'Bullets don't work,' he confirmed. 'At least, not against the armour, they don't. Shoot one of the bastards in the eye, or get a round between the scales and that might be a different story. I don't know what the results of that kind of shooting might be. The trouble is, when these bastards are in combat mode they move very very fast and that's something you need to remember. You don't really have time to take proper aim. Leastwise, I didn't. But...' he put the bolt down on the table and stroked the sharp feathering of the goose feather flight '...you remember how Leon described the shoot-out in the Negev? I quizzed him about it quite thoroughly and he clearly said that he saw Herschal's rounds drawing blood, or what might be described as blood, before the Djinn changed shape and came at them from the roof. Now, I know that a round of solid shot from a Remmy is a helluva sight bigger and heavier than a slug from a 357, but the 357's muzzle velocity is fantastically greater, and I reckon that old Herschal might have known something that we don't. You remember that he joked with Leon about silver bullets? Okay, so Leon didn't definitely say that Herschal's ammo was made from silver, but what if it was? It certainly gives us a working direction.'

Mage smiled thinly. 'Yes, all right, but John, it's nearly four o'clock in the morning and we're in an Andalucian hill village in the middle of nowhere. We don't have the equipment to start melting down silver, even if we had any silver to melt.'

'True,' Light sounded smug. 'But I can think of two places where we'll find what we want without even moving out of this house!'

'You have my undivided attention!'

'Behind you on the wall and in Hector's medical bag.'

Mage swung around and studied the plain white wall on the far side of the room. There was little to see other than the fastening hook for the curtain and a thermometer. He made the connection immediately, for obviously there would be at least one thermometer in Hector's bag, and thermometers contained mercury – or quicksilver. It may have been a different chemical compound than that which might have forged Herschal's silver bullets, but it was close enough and, indeed, in spirit was in total harmony with the concept. Furthermore, to Mage's way of thinking, there would be far greater magical symbolism in using mercury than solid metal..

'What you're suggesting,' he said slowly, 'is that we fill the bolts with quicksilver and then seal them with the crystal?'

'It's my best idea.' Light had been stroking the but of the cross bow. 'This thing is going to pack one God almighty punch and combined with the follow through weight of the bolt, the impact should be tremendous. I don't know what damage the crystal might do, but these quarrels are made from solid steel and if they can puncture the Djinn's hide, it'll be like injecting the quicksilver directly into the bloodstream. Even if the crystal and the steel fail, the quicksilver might just give us an edge.'

'John, it feels right. Let's do it.'

This was easier said than done and they had to work very carefully, breaking the seals of the wall thermometer and decanting the small amount of mercury into a thurible before pouring it with the aid of a makeshift funnel into the hollow tip of the first bolt. While Light held the bolt upright, Mage tipped it with a smudge of superglue. Taking no chances, Light still held on to it while Mage took a pure piece of crystal quartz from his bag, and using a lapidary hammer, smashed it into several fine shards. Choosing one of the wickedest slivers, he dabbed more superglue at its base and held it in place at the tip of the bolt until the glue set.

'One down, five to go,' Light said in satisfaction.

'Won't be time.' Mage observed. 'And I don't think there'll be enough mercury either. Let's be content to do one more and, as it is, we'll have to rouse Hector. I don't want to go rummaging in his bag without asking him first. If I get the chance to shoot off a couple of the bolts, I'll consider myself lucky.' He grinned wryly. 'Do you want to go down and knock on their door, or shall I?'

'They're probably not asleep anyway.'

'I suppose,' Mage mused, 'this would be a good time to see how good Helen is at receiving telepathic impulses?'

'Yeah, and to see how good we are at sending 'em. You want to try it?'

'Might as well. If we *can* forge a link, it might serve us well later on.'

Then two men bowed their heads and closed their eyes. They concentrated on Helen's name, sending out a firm but gentle summons. They were gratified and rewarded when, a few moments later, they heard the bedroom door open and close, and Helen emerged at the head of the stairs. She looked tousled, but alert, folded in the generous proportions of Hector's shirt.

'I got the feeling...' she began.
'You sure did!' Light was on his feat, beaming like a Cheshire cat.
'Were you trying to make contact?'
'We were and we did!' Light exclaimed.
'Sorry to bother you,' Mage said, also standing. 'But it seemed to be an important experiment and in any case we need to wake Hector. If he has a spare thermometer in his bag, we could use it for what we're working on.'
'Hang on...'

Helen disappeared and then, a couple of minutes later, reappeared with the required object. There were sounds of activity from the bedroom below and Tamara stirred herself from her slumbers on the sofa. Mage and Light put the second bolt together with an audience and when they had done, they surveyed their handiwork with satisfaction. The two bolts gleamed with their own dark malice and when Mage held them, one in each hand, he was powerfully aware of their vibration. *This one,* he thought, tightening his grip on the bolt in his right hand, *this one is for Dolorean, and this one,* he rubbed his thumb along the shaft that he held in his left hand... *This one's for Alex!*

It was now well past five o'clock. They sat at the kitchen table, still in the dark of night, and ate a frugal breakfast. There was no sign of the dawn when they left the house a few minutes before five thirty, but from their elevated position up at the castle, they were all aware of a lightening in the eastern sky. At five fifty five Mage climbed the ragged wall and dropped into the keep. Light, Tamara and Helen settled down to wait and meditate and Hector went in search of Jaime Gomez.

Angel woke before the dawn... not that he had been properly asleep anyway. The argument that he had had with Christina the previous evening had not been resolved and he had spent most of the night tossing and turning, trying to find a way in which he could reverse the sudden downwards trend that seemed destined to dash his hopes of a long term relationship upon the rocks of inevitability.

During the long lazy days when they had been concerned with keeping the house in Calle Sombra under observation, everything had been perfect. They had watched the house and had made love with uninhibited passion. She had taught him things that had made his young mind boggle, and he had learned not to ask where she herself had learned these pleasure enhancing techniques. He'd been so caught up in the excitement of the *now* that he had paid little heed to what might be around the corner of the after, and then suddenly that time was upon him and he didn't know how to handle it. Dolorean's car had gone and Dolorean had gone with it, and although he and Christina had been left with a watching brief, the point and purpose seemed to have gone from their presence in Pepe Ortega's *casita.* Christina had become restless and moody, and the previous evening two things had happened to send thrills of fear racing through his heart. For the first time she had declined to have sex with him, and while that was bad enough, she'd also been talking about going back to The States, and that had been even worse.

'But Christina, what about me?' he had asked tentatively and in some distress.

She had looked at him sadly. 'Oh, you'll survive. Men always do. And in any case, nothing lasts for ever.'

'I want us to last for ever!'

'Yeah, I guess you do, but you've got a lot to learn. Anyway, I'm going for a walk.'

'I'll come with you.'

'No thanks, I want to be on my own. Besides, someone's got to watch the house.'

'I don't care about the house. I want to be with you!'

'And I want some space!'

She had gone, and had been gone for more than an hour. When she'd returned she'd been even more uncommunicative, and had curled up on her half of the mattress, face to the wall.

'I want to talk!' Angel had pleaded.

'And I want to sleep.'

Whether she had really gone to sleep or whether she'd just been feigning it to avoid confrontation, he didn't know. Sleep was certainly difficult for him. How could he sleep with that hollow ball of tension screwing up his insides?

Thus, he climbed into his clothes and went out into the street. Christina didn't stir, and he thought about her with angry resentment. How could *she* sleep while *he* was suffering so much anguish? He leaned with his back to the cool white stone and contemplated the answer. There was only one answer, as obvious as it was painful. She simply didn't care!

Angel, who knew nothing of homesickness or pre-menstrual tension, allowed the anger to ferment within him and, in a moment of impulse, pushed himself away from the wall and began to walk the familiar streets of the village that had been the only home he'd ever known. He remembered his vows, made to the skies above Colmenar, and accepted that Castillo would remain his only home. There would be no high life in America for him. Christina would go, leaving him here, and that would be that. Inevitably she would forget all about him and how long would that take? A week? A fortnight? A month? while he was doomed to spend the rest of his life dreaming about the love that he had lost. He remembered his pact with Colin Mage. El Moreno had promised him one night in Christina's bed, and when he worked it out he'd had almost a month of sheer unadulterated carnal delight. How much better might it have been if he had had nothing, for then there would be nothing to miss. Angel knew his village, and he knew that none of the village girls that might one day replace Christina in his affections and thoughts would ever please him the way in which Christina had. Ask Immaculada Conception or Paquita Alonso to sit on his face and suck his cock until he came, and they would fly to their parents or the nearest priest screaming high treason and unholy perversion at the tops of their shrill little voices. Compared to Christina, they were shit... But then, in mounting frustration, he realised that Christina probably saw him in exactly the same light when she compared him to the other men she had known back in America.

He drew back his foot to kick at a can, but then paused. He was marching down the main street, heading towards the Ayuntamiento. Unusually for that time of night the building was ablaze with light. A police car was drawn up outside the entrance and there seemed to be a determined hive of activity going on, conducted with gusto by none other than Jaime Gomez.

Angel slunk into the shadows – he still hated the police chief's guts – and moved closer until he could hear what was going on. The two deputies, known colloquially as Diego Uno and Diego Dos were loading things into the back of the car while Jaime stood in the entrance, puffing irritably at a cigarette. Angel saw that half of Jaime's face was covered in a white dressing that stretched across his nose and was taped with elastoplast to his cheeks. *Good,* he thought, knowing nothing of the circumstances behind Jaime's injury, *the bastard's had an accident!*

'Be sure you get it all in and don't forget anything.' Jaime snapped, grinding the but of his smoke beneath his boot.

'Yes *Jefe.*'

'You've loaded the ropes and the torches?'

'Yes *Jefe*'

'The shot guns and the shells?'

'Yes *Jefe.*'

'What about the hammers and chisels and the masonry drill?'

'Yes *Jefe,* it's all loaded.'

'Then where the hell is Tobias with the long ladders and the winch?'

'*Jefe,* you told him to be here at six o'clock and it is only a quarter to the hour.'

'Just as long as he isn't late,' Jaime said ominously. 'I want to be up at the castle before the dawn.'

The castle? Angel retreated into one of the back lanes. What were they going to be doing up at the castle that required hammers and chisels and torches and ropes, not to mention shotguns and Toby Cristobal's winch and long ladders? Instinctively he knew that it had something to do with El Moreno and, if it had to do with El Moreno, then, as far as he was concerned, it had something to do with himself. So, there was something happening up at the castle, was there? Well, the only way to find out what that might be was to go and look.

Tanja Hein knew that she was two men down. This fact had impinged itself upon her consciousness long before midnight and she'd had too many years of combat and covert experience to doubt her own assessment of the situation. Whether two men down meant two men dead was a different matter, but without intelligence to the contrary, it seemed prudent to assume the worse and act accordingly. Her problem was in defining the right action. She could certainly use the radio and call in reinforcements, but that would be premature. Better to find out what had happened to her two operatives first, then at least she would know what she was dealing with, what to report and what reinforcements to ask for.

After Yuri had left to make his rendezvous with Vordeman, she had followed the green Renault back into the village and had established the injured Englishman had been taken into the white house in Calle Granadillos. The girl had left, but had returned within fifteen minutes, and also during that time, the Spanish doctor had arrived, flustered and on foot. She had taken up station at the top junction of the street, parking discreetly off the road on a small square of waste land. No one could come or go without her seeing them, and she'd sat there for two full hours observing the sum total of nothing. She'd tried to contact Yuri and Vordeman every five or ten minutes, but had got nothing but a hiss of static for her trouble.

This had placed her in an awkward dilemma. Should she remain on station and watch the house, or should she go in search of her two absent team members? To do the latter, she would have to compromise on the former. But after two hours of inactivity the desire to do *something* overcame her and she'd driven back down to the river, walking the last few hundred metres to the caves with a flashlight in one hand, Uzi under her jacket, and the walkie talkie in her hand. Even at the entrance to the caves all she'd got from the RT was a bland band of white noise. She'd contemplated going into the caves but had thought better of it. To her sure knowledge four men had gone into those dark caverns and only one had come out and he'd come out in a worse state than he'd gone in. It had been obvious to her that the Englishman had the answers that she needed and so she had returned to Castillo, taking up her original position at the top of Granadillos, and wondering how she might get to the man that she desperately needed to interview.

She didn't know who he was or what he was, but her intuition combined with her common sense told her that he was integral to this operation... An operation that had suddenly gone very sour. At midnight she'd climbed into the back of the Volkswagen and had radioed Madrid. Madrid had patched her through to Jerusalem and she'd made a cautious and coded report. *Shapiro missing twelve hours, P1 and P2 missing ten hours in search. No contact. Information please British National Colin Mage.*

She was told to hold, and then thirty minutes later she received what she considered to be a totally ambiguous reply. *Mage friendly. Close and assist. Disregard casualties.*

Disregard casualties? What did that mean? It was against the ethos of all IDF philosophy, so how was she supposed to interpret it? Forget about Shapiro and Vordeman and Bogdanovitch and concentrate on helping the Brit, or was she being ordered to help this unknown Mr Mage and to disregard any casualties that might be incurred in the process?

At one a.m. she got out of the Volkswagen and prowled the perimeters of the house. The ground floor of the building was dark and silent but there were lights and the soft murmur of voices coming from the upstairs rooms, which told her that at least the occupants were still in residence and hadn't done a bunk while she'd been prowling down by the river. Back in the Volkswagen she settled down for a long night. She'd tackle this Colin Mage in the morning, by which time she might have heard something further from Jerusalem, or better yet from Yuri or Vordeman. She checked her armoury and then, as a token gesture, had tried to raise a response from the RT. Nothing was forthcoming, so wrapping her coat around her, she settled down to doze, knowing that she'd be alert in an instant the moment anything or anybody stirred down at the house.

She became awake and on guard at thirty minutes past five. The front door of the house was opening and figures spilled out into the street. She recognised the huge bulk of the black American and the only marginally smaller dimensions of the Spanish doctor. Between them, the Englishman seemed dwarfed. There were also the two women. As one the quintet started up the hill towards her, then cut off to their left, climbing higher and out of sight through the narrow maze of shadowy streets that led up towards the castle. Taking care not to make any noise, Tanja slipped out of the VW and followed at a safe distance. She smiled to herself in the darkness, for if this hadn't been such a serious business, the melodrama might have been amusing. Armed with the Uzi, three spare clips of ammunition, two grenades, a 357 Desert Eagle automatic pistol, with two spare clips for the hand gun, she felt like a walking arsenal. *Mossad to the rescue,* she thought. *Israel into action...* But her smile hardened. Three of her countrymen were missing, possibly dead, and she was being directed by her control into a course of blind action, which was something else that was out of sympathy with Israeli military philosophy.

Disregarding the weight, which in all fairness was evenly distributed about her incredibly fit body, she followed the mysterious quintet to the ramparts of the castle. Here she let them get well ahead of her before she made her own ascent of the steep path that led through the Moorish arch and into the arena of ruins. Staying low by the Eastern wall, she picked her way carefully forwards, monitoring the progress of the group on her right, which were following the more direct route to towards the circular tapering tower of the keep. From somewhere in the distance and behind her there came the sound of revving engines and a crunch of gears. Headlights cut a swathe through the night and she hurried forwards to find some deep cover midway between the rampart wall and the tower. Confident that she had not been seen, she settled down between two ancient balustrades and awaited developments. They were not long in coming, for a few moments later two vehicles lurched in convoy through the narrow arch, their headlights sweeping over the vista of ruins before turning right and, instead of heading towards the keep as she might have expected, headed instead towards the squat citadel over on the Northern perimeter of the castle ground. A male figure – was it the doctor or the American? – detached itself from the shadows surrounding the base of the keep and strode purposefully towards the mechanised unit. The figure carried a bag, so it might have been the doctor, but both the Englishman and the American had also carried bags, so there was no way of being sure.

She realised that despite all the hardware she'd brought, she'd forgotten to bring the one item that at this time might have been more useful than the rest of the stuff put together. She'd left the VW in such haste that she'd not thought to bring the binoculars. *Silly bitch* she thought, and then shivered with the familiar feeling of being watched. *So who's watching the watcher?* she wondered, and narrowing her eyes, quartered every centimetre of her surroundings. There was some activity over at the citadel and a few shadowy movements ahead of her up at the keep, but other than that it was as silent and as still as a graveyard. She knew that she was tired and was working on her reserves, and put her feelings down to her overstretched nerves and the sombreness of her surroundings. It was a natural conclusion to arrive at – but still the wrong one as she was to find out to her cost within a very short while.

Imperceptibly the stars disappeared as the dark of the night gave way to the paler pastel shades of the pre-dawn morning. Over at the citadel, Jaime and Hector, aided by Tobias Cristobal, propped their ladder against the wall and began loosening the tiles from the roof. Within the confines of the keep Mage drifted down into deep psychic trance, drawing together the fabric of two worlds within the dimensions of the astral planes. At three points around the keep, one within sight of the other, Light, Tamara and Helen sat facing outwards, eyes closed but minds wide open, relying on their senses rather than their vision to alert them to any intrusion. Their guardianship was focused against any psychic or paranormal intrusion, and thus they failed to anticipate anything that might come against them on a purely physical level. From his spread-eagled position upon an elevated flat rock to the north east of the keep, Angel observed all and wondered just what the hell was going on. When Tanja Hein decided it was time to make a move, Angel Guadiaro moved with her.

He had drawn the motif of the pentagram in the sand and had placed white candles at each of the star points. Generous with his proportions, he'd given himself plenty of space to sit in the centre of the star, the cross bow over his knees, loaded with the two magical bolts. Around him in a semi circle were his amulets and talismans – the athame dagger, the flask of most precious oil, a representative selection of prime crystals, pure quartz, smoky quartz, citrine, rose and amethyst. Missing was the wand, lost and gone for ever, and he mourned its passing.

Even before he began the recitation of ancient words that would not only open the circle, but would also open him to any vibration of a spiritual or paranormal nature, he was profoundly aware of the power and the positive energy within this place. He'd stood in this space before and he had felt protected, but now the energies were so much stronger. Slowly, and with great precision, he tuned himself into them, not knowing precisely what was causing them, but being well aware of the law of opposites. If the energies here were so much brighter it was perhaps because the energies at the citadel had become so much darker. He spared more than a passing thought for Hector and Jaime and hoped that they would be all right – knew that they *would* be all right, providing he could get his act together quickly. Once he was out of his body he could give them some protection from the astral.

Regulating his breathing, the trance took him relatively quickly, this in itself a powerful indication of how much he had changed in the last few hours – or more accurately, how much he had *been* changed by the concentrated energies of Helen Ross and John Light. He felt their presence strongly and knew that they were in position, just a few yards away. Just a few yards, but increasingly in another world as his head fell forwards in semi consciousness. His own mumbled words – *Yod heh vauv heh, adoni, eh heh yeh, ahgehlah, ve geburah, veh gedulah, le olahim ohm* – became increasingly distant as the cone of bright light crackled above his head. Initially the light was imaginary, a projection of his own psychic mind, but then the light became real and his spirit moved out of self with a small sighing wrench and became part of the light.

Out of body, yes, but definitely not out of control. Using the focus of his mindpower, he unravelled the knots of memory, turning back the hands of time to the very beginning of his life, remembering in a series of flash visions all that had been the sum total of his life, right up to the time when he first met Alexandra. Here he deliberately slowed the process and went through every event, in sequence, that had brought him to this time and place. It was a painful process, but a necessary one, that reminded him of his purpose and honed the point of his quest. He remembered every detail of his battle with the Djinn from the day they had first clapped eyes on each other beneath the palm trees of Marbella, and recalled every scrap of intelligence he had gleaned of the creature since. He remembered the handful of people who had helped him, the two good friends in York, Michael Fry at The Oaks, Blanc Villiers in Paris, Paul O'Connor in Ireland, Herschal in Israel, Light and Helen... And added to this list were the names of Hector and Anna Sanchez, Pepe Ortega, Angel and Antonia Guadiaro... Even the policeman, Jaime Gomez. Without these people, he realised, he could not have done what he had thus far done, and could not do what he was attempting to do. He thought also of Leon Shapiro, and if he wasn't already dead, hoped that he might be in time to save him.

Then the trance deepened as he deliberately projected himself into the nightmare that had plagued his dreams for so many months. He was in the circular tunnel heading towards the circular portal, but now instead of being propelled and dragged against his will, he marched with purpose and deliberation. When the portal swung open upon its single hinge he stepped through it without hesitation into the stygian blackness, but instead of falling, felt himself being catapulted upwards towards a canopy of unrecognisable stars. And then he was among the stars, pacing and hunting, cross bow at the ready, strings cocked and tensioned, crystal quarrel points glinting in the star light.

A figure fell in step with him and he recognised it as being a projection of himself, but it was more than just a projection, for in the keep he was wearing rough denim, but here upon the astral, this other self wore silver and green and red. He melded his mind with the figure and in so doing became one with his higher spiritual persona, the ambassadorial avatar that bridged the gap between the worlds of life and death. From the fusion of this union there was a heightened perception, not just of cosmic identity but also of protection and safety.

Now he found himself hurtling upwards and forwards through a kaleidoscope of coalescing stars towards a broader brighter glow that seemed to fill the horizon. The stars faded when he came to this light place, supported effortlessly in the firmament by the interlocking seals of the pentagram that stretched across the heavens for as far as the eye could see. Within the central sanctuary of the sigil stood a group of familiar figures; here were the souls that had filled his sleeping dream – his Grandmother, Paul O'Connor, Herschal, the Roman Marcus Sutonious, the hidalgo Carlos of Castille. The boy Rajad was missing but there were others present who's names he did not know, yet whose faces were elusively familiar, either from half forgotten dreams or a dozen other lives long gone before.

This was the borderland between psychic imagination and spiritual reality. He had gone searching for this place and having found it, did not question its objective existence. It was real to him, and just because he had been brought here by the power of his own dream, this did not mean that it was not equally real to the other spiritual beings also present at this astral gathering. Who could define spiritual reality anyway? Suffice to say this was the destination he had striven to reach. Through the discipline of his mind and the training of his craft he had been successful. Projected by the force of his own will and aided by his powers of creative visualisation, he had come to make clearer and more verbose contact with these spiritual identities, who having beckoned him once from the dreamstate, stood waiting now within the safety of the pentagram. As he drew nearer the circle parted and they welcomed him to their midst.

Time warped and became an abstraction within the abstract. Later, he would remember his journey to the celestial pentagram, and he would remember the overpowering feelings of love and kinship that he had received from his spiritual allies... But as for what exactly was said and done, this intelligence remained vague and elusive, filtering through little by little, degree by degree in the time that came afterwards. One clear memory that he was to hold, however, was the overwhelming feeling of remorse and regret that he experienced when it became apparent that his time within the astral circle was over. As again he became discarnate, discarding the confines of his other, higher self, he descended into the identifiable configuration of the circular keep, a keep that was now filled with diagonal bars of sunlight as the sun rose in the east, pushing and pulsing the morning rays through every portal and each tiny crack in the Christian stonework.

From the top of the tower he looked down and observed his bowed form in the middle of his own rough sign of magic. The candles burned unwaveringly and there were the reassuringly familiar smells of candle wax, dry sand and goat dung, the more distant but no less familiar tangs of jasmine and wild garlic wound up with wood smoke and the pungent scents of pine and eucalyptus that together constituted all the hallmarks of an early summer dawn in Southern Andalucia. Then the candles *did* flicker, in turn and in sequence around the circle, and above the circle the striations of sunbeams danced out of sequence with the direction of the light. The keep became redolent with a different scent, one that evoked visions of lush English meadows, brooks that burbled and babbled with British heritage through fields of freshly cut grass. There was the unmistakable perfume of lavender carried on the wind that brought north country rain to bleak moors that were dotted with phallic standing stones and thick enigmatic carpets of purple heather. Atlantic waves cascaded in salty spume against unyeilding Celtic coastlines while acorns clung to giant oaks defying both nature and gravity to take them before English summer had kissed the heavily laden bows within the sacred oaken groves. There was the whiff of warm straw, the aroma of old leather and saddle soap, but above all there was the all pervading earthy trace of an English oak forest in full and fecund season. Mage retreated within the magic circle and made ready to greet the inquiring mind of Michael Fry.

With hooded eyes John Light watched the dawn break above the Castillato valley. The sun rose in a fiery orb above the distant Sierra Morenos, covering the village below him with a mantle of liquid gold and solvent coalescing shades of rose pink. And yet, although he was aware of this magical transformation from night to day, he only half saw it. His mind had found a different resting place within the deeper levels of his consciousness and he was clinically aware of the waves of psychic turbulence which emanated from within the keep. Indeed, he had tuned his own psychic mind into the vibration, was at one with it, an essential part of it. Had there been a manifestation of incoming psychic attack, either from the shapechanger or any other paranormal source, he would have been alert to it immediately – as it was, he was not aware of the physical threat until the barrel of Tanja Hein's .357 Desert Eagle stroked icily across his cheek and came to rest just beneath his left eye. He recognised it for what it was, but it still took several seconds to bring himself back to the reality of the moment and to understand what the owner of the gun was saying to him.

'I'm not playing games,' Tanja spat with low intensity. 'Tell me where he is or I'll shoot you where you sit.'

'Tell you where who is?' Light asked, fighting hard to find some clarity within his muddled state and at the same time sending out a mental distress signal to Helen and Tamara. There was some doubt as to whether either of the girls would pick him up. If Helen was as deep in her protective meditation as he himself had been, she would be oblivious to earthly distractions. While he was very close to Tamara on a mental level and while she was knowledgeable in her own right, they neither of them had the rapport of telepathy to such an extent that he could summon her at will.

'The Englishman,' Tanja said, edging to one side so that he could see who was interrogating him. The gun barrel moved and came to rest a few inches away from the end of his nose. It wasn't the worse gun he'd ever been threatened with, but it was bad enough. He gathered the weight of his sentience and projected it over the gun barrel to make contact with the woman's steely green eyes that stared at him coldly and unblinkingly.

'Mossad?' he drawled conversationally, rapidly regaining his composure.

Tanja was visibly taken aback by Light's question and he pressed home his advantage. 'Ah yes, lady, we had you spotted from the moment you rolled into the village square. Leon hadn't got a clue that he was being tailed, but we blew your cover in all of five minutes.'

Tanja's eyes narrowed to angry slits. 'What are you? CIA?'

'CIA?' Light echoed, allowing a laugh to roll up from his belly in the hope that it might attract some allied attention. 'For Chrissakes lady, no way! Is that what they told you? That the CIA is involved with this?' He pulled an important name out of the memory of his conversation with Leon. 'It's obvious that you weren't briefed by Gideon Lemski, or if you were, he's spun you a line of crap!'

The gun barrel lowered half an inch. 'Gideon Lemski's is not a name that's widely known,' Tanja purred menacingly. 'So how is it so familiar to you?'

Light shrugged – and Tanja's trigger finger stiffened. 'From Leon, of course.'

'And talking of Leon,' the gun edged upwards again. 'Maybe you can tell me where *he* is right now?'

'Lady, I would if I could, but the truth of the matter is that I just don't know.'

'You must have some idea!'

'Only to say that he's somewhere under this mountain. More than that, your guess is as good as mine.'

'I see. We'll go back to my first question then. Where's the Englishman?'

'Busy looking for Leon,' Light smiled his friendliest smile, but Tanja was not impressed.

'My friend, I am rapidly loosing my patience. I am very tired, I'm very frustrated and I am very pissed off. I've followed you up here so I know the Englishman's with you somewhere. I also know that the last time anyone saw Leon it was in the Englishman's company. They went into the caves together down by the river. Your pal came out, but Leon didn't. Now you give me some straight answers or I'm likely to get very mean and nasty.'

Light could see that she was being serious. 'Colin Mage is in the tower behind me,' he said soberly. 'And seriously, he is looking for Leon, so I'd leave him be if I were you.'

Tanja stepped backwards. 'On your feet, please, and let's go.'

Light stood up. 'Go where?'

'Into the tower. I want to talk to your friend Mr Mage, and I want to talk to him now!'

'Sorry lady, but no. Like I said, the man is busy and what he's doing is too important. I'm not going to disturb him, and neither are you. You'll just have to wait 'till he's done doing what he's doing. You can talk to him then.'

'Bull shit mister, I am going to talk to him right now!'

'Over my dead body, lady.'

'Then it'll be over your dead body!'

Light folded his arms and looked Tanja calmly in the eye. 'Let's cut the melodrama. If you're going to shoot me, get on with it... Personally, I don't think you've got the balls.'

'No?' Tanja Hein smiled thinly. 'Then on your own head be it.'

Later, when they compared their relative experiences, both Mage and Michael Fry's impressions of their astral meeting in the keep were totally corroborative. The Druid was able to describe the circular tower in some detail, even down to Mage's clothing and posture, while Mage was quite correct in his perception of the Druid, robed in white and dark sage green, standing before the underground altar beneath the roots of the sacred oaken grove. No actual words passed between them, but each was electrifyingly aware of the other's presence and they communicated by thought alone.

 Hail Spain!
Welcome England!
You are prepared?
Almost!
I am with you and bring you the strength of oak trees!
And the blessings of The Merlin?
And the blessings of The Merlin! You have come far and have done well!
There is yet much to do.
The Priestess has been useful?
The Priestess is invaluable but insists on combat.
This is ill-advised but she is her own soul. When will you engage the enemy?
This morning.
We feel his presence here and fear he is forewarned of your coming.
There are friends here who have pledged their help.
We project all the power of our protection from this sacred place. We have been in preparation since before the Priestess left us.
I am reassured.
What remains?
The ritual of battle and the battle itself.
Thirteen bards shall sing for your success.
I succeed or fail before this sunset.
I see you have a weapon!
It came to me in dreams!
You have tried it out?
No. There has been so little time.
Take this as a token of your effectiveness. If the shapechanger has changed his schedule it is because you have forced his hand. You will kill with the weapon of your dreams?
Yes.
You will kill both?
Yes.
Test your aim and shoot the dawn. When you know your eye is true, purify yourself for war. Always we are with you and shall be with you when you fight, and whatever the outcome, always ever afterwards. In the service of your destiny you serve the world of Man....

 From a position still outside of self, Mage watched as he removed the crystal tipped bolts from their grooves on top of the cross bow, replacing them with a single hollow pointed quarrel from the wooden quiver. With great effort he tensioned one of the strings, then bringing the bow to his shoulder, he aimed the weapon at one of the high portals to the east. The rough portal was an ovoid block of brilliant light as the almost parallel sun streamed through it, creating a thick wedge of light motes with sharply defined borders. Without hesitation he released the trigger mechanism and with a loud thwack and continuing whine, the quarrel leapt towards the light and disappeared into it, arcing effortlessly, ever upwards, towards the burning star...

Something white and silver and tinged with gold hurtled obliquely above Tanja Hein's head. It seemed to have come from the keep and was racing towards the sun like a miniature guided missile.

'What the hell's that?' she exclaimed in sudden wonderment.

Light acted instinctively. In the split second while she was distracted, his arms shot forwards like a black cobras. One massive hand grabbed her diminutive wrist, while the other closed around the gun and wrenched it from her grip. The movement was so swift and fluid that she didn't realise quite what had happened until she herself was looking down the barrel of her own gun.

'You bastard!' she exclaimed, more in surprise than fear.

'No, I promise you my Ma and Pa were married all legal and true before I came along – leastwise, that's always what my aunt Epiphany told me anyway. Sorry if I hurt your wrist, but I just don't like people waving guns under my nose.'

The Desert Eagle was pointed directly at her heart. She knew that long before she could get to the Uzi or any of the other hardware deposited around her body, this black giant could splatter her vital organs all over these rocks for yards around. The Eagle was a gas loader and the .357's were wad cutters designed to drop a man in his tracks at a hundred yards.

She looked at him glitteringly. 'Now what are you going to do?' she asked, unable to keep the bitterness out of her voice. This mission had been a bummer ever since they'd left Madrid.

'Do? Guess I'll give you you're gun back if you promise to be a good girl and just hang patient for a while.'

To her amazement Light let the pistol pivot forwards on its trigger guard and he, handed the gun towards her, butt first. 'Believe it or not, sweet heart, we're all on the same side. So just you tuck this thing away and sit your skinny white ass on the nearest rock. I shouldn't think you're gonna have to wait too long...' He cast an eye to the east where the sun was now sitting on the rim of the mountains. His watch said seven thirty. '...I guess another half hour at the most.'

Tanja sat down, not at all sure how to deal with these curious turns of events. 'Just what the hell is coming down here?' she asked evenly.

'All in good time, lady. Just be patient...'

He sat down on the rock opposite her and at first she thought he was looking at her, but upon closer inspection realised that he was looking over her head towards the rising sun. She watched the sun reflecting in his eyes turning them from dark brown to burning red, causing him to take on the persona of some black demi-god, and despite the warmth of the new day shivered as his features took on a mask of malevolence. She thought of the gun – it was still in her hand. She could become provocative again, but felt that the initiative had passed from her. She was now in this man's hands, and she found herself wondering to what extent he had ever been in hers. If you weren't scared of a .357 Desert Eagle pushing its barrel up your nose, just what the fuck were you scared of?

Her attention was diverted by the sound of... Well, it was something half way between singing and chanting. It came from within the keep, so weirdly alien and evocative that she shivered again. This time there were goose bumps on her goose bumps and the hairs on the back of her neck began to tingle of their own accord.

'And just what the shit is *that?*' she glared aggressively at Light.

'That's the man you want to talk to, lady, and if you listen a while, you'll understand just why he's too busy to talk to you right now. Leastwise, a part of you might.' Then he closed his eyes and dipped his hands into the sand, tossing it in repetitive explosions of dust and grains into the air and letting the light breeze take it where it would. When he spoke again it was in the form of a recurring doggerel and his voice assumed the accent of the deep black south. *'"Dis hexing be vexing, de wicked deceived, de voodoo she workin' to bring man his need."'*

The more this went on the more unnerved Tanja Hein became. She found herself wishing she was back in Jerusalem, eating falafel and drinking tea in Emdee's Cafe... Or failing that, a stiff drink in any of the village bars would do just as well. And yet she felt bound and rooted to this spot, and was content to sit here waiting for things to happen as they would. Part of it was fear. She didn't want to move for fear of finding that she couldn't.

Mage, now wearing the mantle of most high magician, descended ever deeper into the spiral of the ritual. He absorbed the earth energies into his being and also those other energies from the astral and the realms of pure spirit. Using ancient words in even more ancient thoughtforms of address, he announced his presence and his purpose and intentions, asking help of those who might grant it, lashing out in condemnation against those who chose to decline. Mindpower fused with phonetics and acoustics and his song of war caused the keep to reverberate with the resonance and the power of his spiritual essence. The keep, its own properties enhanced and released by Mage's investiture, acted as an amplifier and hurled the magician's battle cry out into the cosmos.

John Light heard it, and ignoring Tanja Hein's curious gaze, went with it within the rhythms of his own body. For a while he was Jonty Golightly again being taught by his elders what to do when you felt the magic working through you.

Tamara heard it and curled up within herself, hugging her arms around her chest, and wishing she was anywhere but here. Her memories flew back to the first fourteen years of her life, memories that she'd spent the latter twelve years of her life trying to forget.

Helen heard it loudly and clearly with a skirl of angry pipes as she raced with Rob Roy Macgregor across the sodden turf of a Scottish moor towards the implacable red line of smoking muskets and fixed bayonets. Her own pagan ululations picked out the counterpoints and harmonies of Mage's song, and as she sang with him she wept silently for the dead and for those who were about to die.

In their own way, both Hector and Jaime heard it as they worked swiftly and silently on the citadel roof. They laboured to free a stubborn pantile and when the thing suddenly and soundlessly came free in their hands, both felt the surging rush of new strength and energy that not only rippled through their bodies, but also coursed through their minds. They exchanged a knowing look, each aware that the other had felt the same blast of raw power working through them and for them.

Anna Sanchez felt it in Ronda. She woke from dreams that had been filled with images of the man she loved. Her head was free from pain and her eyes, although moist, saw more clearly than they done for days. She had fallen asleep the night before half way through trying to write Mage a letter... Now, still not yet fully awake, she reached for the pad and pen by her bedside and wrote *"sleep softly sweet butterfly, for in the morning you will be gone, leaving me, your lover, behind"*. She did not know what she meant by these words, but they seemed appropriate to both her emotions of joy and her deep feelings of inexplicable fear.

Michael Fry heard it and felt it at The Oaks, as did Master Santorini and the thirteen guardian bards who sat in private enclave around the sacred altar beneath the trees. They had been in training and preparation for this event for almost forty days, and as one they lifted their spirits out of self in readiness for the forthcoming psychic battle to be fought above the mountains of Andalucia. If they lost they would have to fight again above the Oaken Groves in preservation of their own existence and heritage.

It was heard by many, although not all, on the island of Cael. Those that did hear were already in their defensive trances at the mouth of the cave on the shingle beach, while those who did not still knew well enough what was at stake and what was expected of them. Thus, while their masters strove to serve on a temporal level, the acolytes prepared their own supportive service of secular Catholicism.

It was heard by Pepe Ortega, who woke early in his bed, and felt an all consuming need to dress quickly and hurry across the village to Antonia Guadiaro's house. It was felt also by Antonia, who was awake and ready to meet him at the door. They had spoken of strange things for many days, this early summer, and when Pepe arrived, he arrived excited and out of breath.

'Something will happen today,' he told her. 'I feel it!'

'It has already begun,' she said. 'I have felt it all night.'

It was heard by a dying priest in the Seville seminary hospital. As the first strange notes of the song brushed against the sides of his mind, Ignatious's heart palpitated for the very last time and he died without opening his eyes or uttering a word. In the La Linea clinic Peter Cortez slipped ever more deeply into his brain damaging coma, and in Antiquera, two noviciate nuns began bleeding profusely despite the fact that neither was expecting a period at that time. On the road to Ubrique Raoul Castro fell asleep at the wheel of his Nissan Patrol... He had been driving around the campo for most of the night, but if anyone had asked him, he'd have sworn he was wide awake. No one did ask him, and by the time any one came along to pose the question, Castro was in no position to give them a coherent answer. He was in no position to give them any answer at all.

It was heard within the mountain of Castillo, not only by the Djinn, but also by the incubator and the Newlife within the incubator. An energy that he had never felt before pressed against the shapechangers temples, making him bellow in surprise at the ferocity of the onslaught. He screened himself from the pain, but this took several minutes of strict mental discipline and by then the female was contorted by writhings as The Newlife struggled to be free from the last fine membranes of constraint. *Not yet! Not yet!* the shapechanger prayed as he worked frantically to retrieve the situation. And although he did retrieve the situation, he only did so in part for it was obvious that the birthing process had begun. Thus no longer could he incorporate the birthing with his magic. It was too late for that, and he had no choice other than to weave the ritual of the The Opening around the advent of the birthing. This was all wrong! This was not as it should be! Not as it had been planned, not as he had so frequently visualised it!

Pulling the protective power shield of the *Zkernowii* around him, he dragged the incubator to the edge of the well. Extending the shield until it covered not only himself but the female and the contents of her belly, he squatted beside the quivering mass of distended flesh and began the preliminary stanzas of the opening ritual. The pain in his head was still present, but he was successful in holding it at bay until the power of his own magic began to wash over him, removing the discomfort completely as he became more deeply involved in what he was doing. At a certain point he uttered three guttural words and his body changed form, and became that of the warrior. Even as the polished scales of body armour took shape and clicked into place, the scales emitted a pale silver phosphorescence of light that coalesced within the confines of the shield and cast a wan and shadowy light around the stygian darkness of the chamber.

He worked with well rehearsed smoothness, allowing himself to get caught up in the majesty and the sheer art of what he strove to create. The calm born of discipline and dedication descended upon him, and as his power gathered momentum, then so both the incubating female and the Newlife also found calm in his omnipotent presence. Even so, in a quietly recessed private corner of his mind, there burned a rage of fury and resentment, focused fairly and squarely against the manmate magician who had contaminated the splendour and the beauty of this most magical happening. When The Opening was done, when his brethren rent the veil and forced the breach, he would be free of his responsibilities towards his mission. Then, if the manmate was still alive, he would find him and destroy him utterly, taking long and lingering pleasure in the process.

Hector dashed across the open ground, came first upon Tamara who stood to greet him with tired eyes. They collected Helen – she was like a coiled spring, he thought – and together they moved round to Light's position.

'We're in!' Hector called triumphantly, then the trio froze as they became aware of the fact that Light was not alone. Sat next to him was a harassed looking woman with a very large gun in one hand and another strapped to her belt beneath the folds of her lightweight jacket.

Light came to his feet and Tanja followed suit. 'This is Mossad,' he said tiredly as he became aware of the fact that he was again on the earth plane. 'She wants to talk to Colin.'

Tanja surveyed the three new arrivals. They all looked dishevelled and both the girls seemed slightly spaced out. The Spanish doctor was covered in dust and grime and although he was obviously highly excited about something, the smile was frozen to his face as he stared at her suspiciously. These people – and there was still one missing – were Leon Shapiro's associates and she felt it was time to lay a few cards on the table.

Slipping the Desert Eagle back into its holster under her left arm she stood with her thumbs tucked into her belt, coat pulled back, so that they could all see the Uzi.

'My name is Tanja Hein,' she said, 'and yes, I work for the Israeli government. My instructions are to offer close but covert support to one of our people in this area, namely Leon Shapiro, but he seems to have gone missing and so too have the two agents that I dispatched to find him yesterday afternoon. You people, to the best of my knowledge, were the last to see Shapiro alive and I'd like to know who you are, what you're doing, and what you know about my missing people. I particularly want to talk to your Mr Mage. I radioed a report in last night and the word that came back was that I should regard him as friendly and offer assistance. The message didn't say anything about the rest of you...' She looked half apologetically at Light, realising that she had probably been guilty of over reaction in her challenge. '...This gentleman has indicated that we're on the same side, but what side is that? Who are we fighting and where are the bad guys?'

Mage's quartet remained uncomfortably silent for here again, both as a group and as individuals, they faced a familiar problem; how to explain the inexplicable and how to explain it to someone with no terms of reference? In the end it was Light who took the initiative.

'Miss Hein, I'm sorry lady, but we just don't have the time for complicated explanations. Please be patient and ride with us for a little while. We lost Leon yesterday afternoon and have no idea where he is or whether he's alive or dead, but I promise you, we've been doing all that we can to help him and we'll be launching a search and rescue mission within the hour. With regard to your two missing agents, what happened to them? How did they get lost?'

'They went into the same caves down by the river and just like Shapiro, they haven't come out.'

Light sighed. 'Well, we'll all hope that they're gonna turn up okay, but I guess it's only fair to tell you that the chances are a bit slim.'

'Why?' Tanja demanded. 'What's in those caves that's so Goddamn dangerous?'

Light paused, then diverted his attention towards the others. 'Hector, you want to go and tell Jaime that we're almost on our way? And Helen, why don't you go and check on Colin?'

'Of course,' Hector nodded and strode off around the base of the keep, closely followed by Helen who proceeded to clamber up the rubble until she came to the crack in the stonework which gave access to the interior. Casting a glance behind her, she marvelled at the beauty of the new day, and in the perfect stillness of the morning, was able to hear quite clearly what Light was saying to the Israeli.

'I guess I'd better introduce myself. I'm John Light from California and this is my wife Tammy. Before I can even begin to answer your questions, let me ask you one of my own. Tell me, Miss Hein, do you believe in magic?'

'That depends,' Tanja answered guardedly, 'on what you mean by magic?'

'Put it this way, I don't mean stage magic. I mean the magic of fable and legend, if you like, fairy tale magic, the magic of witches and magicians...'

Tanja snorted in derision. 'Of course I damn well don't!'

And Helen's lip curled downwards in contempt, not just for this woman, but for all those like her across the world who so quickly condemned and ridiculed that which they had no knowledge of, who dismissed ten thousand years of tradition with a careless wave of modern sophistry, and who conveniently ignored all the evidence of their own eyes and senses!

She turned away angrily, and eased into the entrance. She drew breath to call Mage's name, but then that breath stilled in her breast as the magical splendour of the vision before her unfolded in front of her eyes. Beneath her, ten feet down, she saw the unmistakable lines of the pentagrams, highlighted by the candles that burned at the star points. Within the central reservation the crossbow sat upon the earth behind the single red candle, but of Colin Mage, there was no sign... Until she looked upwards. Diagonal shards of sunlight lanced across the keep causing a wild confusion of lines and patterns... And it was here within this matrix, some ten feet *above* her and twenty feet *above* the ground, that she found the form of Colin Mage, cross legged, straight backed, head bowed, hovering unsupported within the sunbeams and shadows. Even as she watched, he descended gently through the kaleidoscope, sometimes a dark smudge as he passed through shadow, at other times brilliantly lit as he passed through bars of sunbeams, until without a sound he passed through her direct line of vision and finally came to rest within the pentagram. The light which surrounded him was not just from the sun but came from some other sublime source, sparkling and coruscating around his head and shoulders like a waterfall wherein each drop of water had sentient and spiritual life of its own. Again she opened her mouth to speak, but succeeded only in exhaling her pent up breath in a long emotional sigh. A sigh of extacy and triumph.

30.

The Opening

The shapechanger stood tall and proud in his full armour. His arms were outstretched in parody of some unholy crucifixion while his head was thrown back in exultation as he petitioned the spirits of his ancestors to aid him in his quest for control and conquest. The silvery scales that covered his body glowed and pulsed with their own inner light, and combined with the presence of the *Zkernowii* shield he had drawn down upon him, he felt omnipotent within his self created capsule of power. He was inviolate and invincible.

Before him, and between where he stood and the lip of the well, the female lay stretched upon the earth, her elbows and fists beating a steady tattoo against the clay as she panted and gasped in rhythm with the contractions and contortions coming from the huge ovoid of palpitating membrane that rose symmetrically from her breast bone and curved critically down towards her pubis. The membrane of the incubator glistened gelatinously and was constantly rippling and changing shape as the Newlife within gradually took up its requisite position for the physical act of birthing.

An eerie glow began to illuminate the central area of the chamber. In part it came from the shapechanger himself, the silver of the scales diffusing with the pale amber emanation being emitted by the incubator, but there was another source, subtle and indistinct, that seemed to come from within the well itself. Nominally this was a pale green, but striated with refractions of mauve, it defied precise description. The shapechanger was aware of it, indeed was responsible for having created it, and now submerged his senses within it, strengthening it with form and body and revelling within the experience, for this curious light was the very fabric of the substance within which he would create the opening.

With a series of staccato grunts he extended his arms towards the female. The green mauve light eddied around her and she began to tremble as tiny entrails of mist made themselves present, creeping and curling surreptitiously from her ears, mouth and nostrils and from the tangled mat of hair between her legs. He elevated his arms upwards, no more than an inclination of his desire, and she rose from the floor. Initially no more than an inch or two, then with strengthening momentum, one foot and then two, until she hovered fully three feet above the ground. He nodded his head and swept his right arm forwards, and the female glided imperceptibly towards the centre of the well, the manoeuvre ending when she was suspended directly above the orifice. The light folded around her, seemingly holding her in suspension and casting weird shadows of silhouette against the distant roof. Uttering another staccato growl, the shapechanger brought his hands together and then parted them. As they parted the female's legs opened impossibly wide. There were two muffled but clearly audible crunches as her hips dislocated. He stepped forwards to within a foot of the well and to within five feet of the female's disfigured and distended vagina, and extending his clawed talons towards it in supplication, he began to chant the invocation of the summoning.

Throughout the long night, a night in which time had no meaning, Leon slipped in and out of consciousness. His dreams and waking visions – and it was frequently impossible to know which was which – alternated between being with Dov in Hayarkon Street and being in that other place where he'd had to kill Yuri Bogdanovitch. Sometimes the dreams merged and it was Dov who was caught in the web, and Dov whom he had executed with half a clip from the Uzi. In another dream sequence he found himself in bed with Yuri.

I'm sorry I had to shoot you, he said.

Hey, think nothing of it, Bogdanovitch answered. *You did me a great favour, and besides, you were only following orders...*

Intermittently, Herschal's face danced before his eyes exclaiming "I told you so! I told you so!" in childish glee. Leon told the torsoless head to piss off, which sometimes it did and sometimes it didn't.

Deprived of light and any awareness of time, Leon's mind focused on the one tangible thing that told him he was still alive: the pain was excruciating, skewering through his head and body like fiery lances. His throat was closed by glands that had swollen up like small footballs and a tight band of constricting heat wrapped itself around his chest, holding his heart and lungs in a vice of unrelenting pressure. But it was his leg which caused the greatest problem. Throbbing in perpetual torment and pulsing with feverish heat that caused the leg to swell and his whole body temperature to rise, he knew that not only was it badly broken, but also badly infected. On the rare occasions that he tried to move it, even just a centimetre, the explosions of pain were so severe, so all encompassing, that his mind retreated from the agony and he passed out.

After one such lapse into unconsciousness he came round aware that something was different. It took him a few moments – *seconds? hours?* – to register the fact that he was hearing something, a muted consonant chatter of sound coming from somewhere far above him. It was unrecognisable as language but contained enough similarity to speech to make him strain to define what he was hearing. If it *was* someone talking, then they were talking to themselves in the strangest of tongues! He tried calling out, but while earlier he had at least managed a croak, now there was nothing. His throat had closed totally. He considered firing the Uzi and then thought better of it. Partly he was worried about ricochets and to some extent Mage's warning still held true, but it was more an intuitive thing. If that distant sound of chatter had been in Hebrew, or Spanish, English, French or German, if it had been even faintly recognisable as human speech, he'd have risked it. As it was, it defied recognition, and even though he cradled the Uzi in his arms, caution stayed his hand. He was temporarily content to sit and listen, ears straining for any nuance of change. And there was change, subtle, imperceptible, though not in Leon's sense of sound, but in his sense of vision.

It was difficult for him to define what he was seeing or when indeed he started to see it, but there was a gradual lightening within the darkness, almost as though the dimmest and most opaque of spotlights was glimmering downwards from some great height high above him. It created an indeterminate pillar of dark grey within the total blackness of his surroundings.

He watched it grow in strength over some considerable period of unmeasured time, until the dark grey became lighter in tone and hue, acquiring a silver greeny sheen that eddied on the water in front of him... And now he could see the water, black and oily calm, and wondered what deep currents ran beneath the surface of this subterranean pool, currents so strong that they had pulled him from the torrent, washing him up upon this eerie shelf?

Leon was fascinated by the light but also deeply frightened by it. It was unearthly and unnatural and unnervingly familiar. As the light grew ever stronger so did Leon's fears and suspicions and he found himself trying to push himself further backwards against the unyeilding stone, even though he was already as far back as he could get, away from the waters of the pool. Leon's worst fears were confirmed when the surface of the pool, one tight circular area in the centre of the otherwise still water, began to simmer with tiny bubbles that emitted wisps and tendrils of mist, mist that hovered over the water before being drawn inexorably upwards into the pillar of light, a light that had taken on a curious life of its own with gyrating striations of green and mauve. He'd seen this phenomena before, in Herschal's cave, deep beneath the surface of the Negev. In Herschal's cave the light had ended at the curved dome of the roof, but here it carried on straight up through the circular bore, a shaft within a shaft, and at least, there was now enough light for him to determine his surroundings.

The flat ledge that was his refuge was about a metre in depth apart from the one section where he sat, which indented a further metre creating a narrow V shaped defile. He was cut off on both sides by the black water that lapped against the rough walls. It could have been centimetres deep, or kilometres. On the far side of the cavern, some ten metres distant, there was another small landing and, incredibly, unless his eyes were deceiving him, set in the wall and leading upwards, was a steep and irregular set of steps! His heart leapt with hope as he perceived a way to freedom and escape and then, just as swiftly, it came crashing down again like a sand castle before the incoming tide. Assuming he could get from one side of the pool to the other, something he certainly could not do without leaving his precious armoury behind, he knew he would never be able to negotiate those steep and daunting steps. Furthermore, even if he was not lame, there was no way he could cross the pool without coming into the illumination of that unwholesome light. Remembering the rocks he had tossed in Herschal's tomb and the way they had flashed out of existence before they came anywhere near the water was a sobering reason to stay put, exactly where he was...

And there was another more pressing reason. The waters in the middle of the pool were now boiling and broiling madly and the pillar of light had become a significantly more clearly defined column, filled with bursts of static electricity that threw the cavern into harsh black and white relief. There was a powerful smell of sulphur and ozone, and although he wasn't sure what exactly it might be, he knew that something, and something quite awful, was about to happen.

From his concealment Angel watched as Mage emerged from the keep. He was fully thirty metres away but even at this distance, he could see that El Moreno was intangibly different; perhaps it was a trick of the light caused by the rapidly rising sun, but it seemed to Angel's eyes that the man was covered in a corona of gold and silver haloes that shifted shape and form even as he strode down from the rubble strewn entrance to the tower towards the waiting trio. La Señorita Helen walked with him, and she too seemed to be covered by the same shimmering mantle. If the other three extranjeros were aware of this phenomena they gave no sign, and the quintet stood talking for a brief moment before making off towards the citadel. Once away from the shadows of the keep the curious light began to fade, but Angel was unperturbed. He knew what he had seen! Keeping his head down, he edged backwards to beyond the sanctuary of the ramparts and then ran around the boundary of the ruins, keeping low and out of sight until he was beneath the northern wall. Beneath him was Alvaro's farm and what was left of his prize herd of pigs. After the rabies scare, the Algercirans had culled ninety percent of them and now no more than three or four healthy young specimens remained, snuffling through the bushes in search of truffles or dead relatives. For all Angel knew, they may even have been in search of both. He didn't really care. His main preoccupation was what was happening over on the far side of the wall, and stretching himself out on the narrow external balustrade of the battlements, he was able to hear most of the conversation and, albeit with restricted vision, see some of what was going on. Angel wondered why he didn't just get up and go over and say hello. Certainly Gomez was there, but beneath the umbrella of Mage's patronage, the policeman could do him no harm... No, it had nothing to do with Gomez, but something told him that, at least for the time being, it would be better to remain unseen.

Mage looked up towards the roof of the citadel. Against a sky that was rapidly losing its blueness in favour of pale levanter cloud that scudded in from the north, Jaime Gomez and Tobias Cristobal stood out in sharp silhouette, sitting, as they were, on the edge of the roof some thirty feet up in the air. Their perch looked precarious but he had to presume that they were safe enough. Both men smoked nonchalantly, waiting, he supposed, for him to make the next move.

A long aluminium ladder had been propped against the wall, raking away from the roof at about fifteen degrees. Mage studied the ground between the wall and the base of the ladder and wondered about the resin that might – or might not – be sentient beneath the surface. Nothing was visible, and there was no time now to effect any kind of experimental exploration.

A small but powerful winch, weighted down by heavy stones, paid out a long rope along the length of the ladder, culminating at a fly wheel which had been securely wedged on the top of the wall. Mage saw immediately how it would work. He'd secure himself to the rope, then Gomez and Cristobal would lower him down through the roof, the winch acting as a break. If he had to come out the same way, the winch would come into its own and haul him up. A hundred things could go wrong and there were a dozen imponderables, but in principle the plan was simple enough.

He felt afraid and suppressed a shiver as the fear threatened to get the better of him – and then made contact with the calmness and resolve that had been gifted to him within the confines of the keep. Whatever happened this morning would be the culmination of a year and a half's search and preparation, a year's pain and sacrifice during which there had been many times when he'd doubted his own sanity. It may have been corny and melodramatic, but in the privacy of his own thoughts he recognised that this time was the culmination and fulfilment of his destiny. All that had gone before had led him to this moment, and all of whatever happened afterwards was an essential part of it also.

He turned to his friends. 'John, unless you're afraid of heights, I'd like you on the roof. Tamara and Hector stay on the ground and be prepared to be flexible as circumstances dictate. Miss Hein, I'd like you to stay with Hector and Tammy... just keep an eye on things and take your lead from my people. If anything goes wrong, you'll know about it and in that event, don't be afraid to use whatever fire power you've got available. Anyone or anything that comes out of this citadel that you don't recognise is to be regarded as hostile, and if you'll pardon the cliché, shoot first and ask questions afterwards. Helen...'

'I'm coming in with you,' Helen Ross said flatly.

'I'm not sure that it's such a good idea,' Mage responded reasonably.

'I forbid it!' Hector exclaimed hotly.

Helen closed her eyes briefly and sighed in exasperation. First she turned to the doctor. 'Hector, you're a sweet and darling man, but even though I love you to death, I'm my own person. I do what I want to do, when and how I want to do it. You either accept me on those terms or not at all. You're the bonus in my life, but make no mistake, I didn't come to Castillo to fall in love with you, but to go into this citadel with Colin and do whatever I've got to do when I come face to face with whatever is inside.' She turned then to Mage. 'I want no arguments from you Colin. You know what I'm doing and why I'm doing it. I've already given you my reasons and you know full well that they're valid. Now, rather than talking about it, let's get this show on the road, shall we?' From her bag she produced her priestess's athame, a long dagger sharpened to a razor edge on both sides. Slipping the knife into her boot, she smiled at Mage candidly. 'I'm ready when you are.'

Mage made eye contact, not just with Helen, but individually with each of the others standing around at the bottom of the ladder. Tanja Hein was an unknown entity, but he was crystal clear in his own mind that he could not have come thus far without the help and co-operation of these people who had laid so much on the line for him, and who had given up so much of their own lives in pursuit of his own bizarre and by no means totally proven beliefs. He smiled quietly, the smile conveying not only his thanks and appreciation, but also his love and trust.

'Okay,' he nodded slowly, swinging the cross bow into a comfortable position across his back and resting one foot on the first rung of the ladder. 'Let's do it!' Then he turned his back on them and began to ascend the ladder.

Helen waited till he was half way, then began to follow. Given the few seconds grace, Light turned to Tanja Hein. 'Lady, as you're so loaded with firepower, you got something you want to lend me? That big automatic pistol, for example?' Tanja didn't want to let it go, but there was something in the black American's eyes that made the request sound like an order, a very compelling order that could not be ignored. She passed over the Desert Eagle.

'I take it you know how to use it?' she asked begrudgingly.

'You take it right, lady. You take it right.' Then he too began the ascent, the ladder bowing and bending noticeably beneath his not inconsiderable weight.

Once on top of the citadel Mage realised that there was a lot more room than he'd first thought there might be. Between the crenellations and the gently curving cupola of the domed roof there was a good metre of walkway that gave a firm base for the operation. Jaime Gomez and Tobias Cristobal had forced free half a dozen of the gently bevelled tiles, creating a vaguely circular entry point where the cupola met the flat roof. There was nothing to be seen other than darkness and shadow, which to Mage's eye made it even more menacing. Jaime had been efficient, however, and among the paraphernalia that lay littered and strewn across the parapet, there were three heavy duty police torches, which could, if necessary, be clipped to a belt or chest harness. Indeed, there were even a couple of harness rigs laid out on the stonework and Mage nodded in recognition of the policeman's thoroughness.

'You've done extremely well, Jaime Gomez – and I thank you very much for your efforts.'

Jaime's eyes glittered as he met Mage's steady gaze. 'You intend to enter the citadel, and The Saints know why, but I have helped you all I can – yet still I do not know what you search for – what is inside this old tomb that is of so much importance.'

'But you *do* know that it is important, that it is dark and that it is evil. Don't ask me how I know, but I *do* know that you have felt its presence and its power...'

'This is true, oh yes indeed this is very true, but still I do not know the cause!'

'And perhaps it's just as well that you don't, but take it from me, that whatever is resident beneath this roof is your enemy – and the enemy of the visions of your own mind...'

Mage let it hang, allowing his words to make contact with Jaime's subconscious. There was no mention of the Blue Madonna but the wraithlike presence was in both their minds, drawing them together in strange and unspoken alliance. The rapport between them was broken as Helen, soon followed by Light, clambered over the battlements.

Together they inspected the opening and the harnesses, and after some discussion, the harnesses were rejected as being too restrictive and cumbersome. Tobias Cristobal came ingeniously to the rescue by rigging two stirrups to the end of the rope. In this way, Mage and Helen had firm foot supports, could hang on to the rope with one hand, leaving the other hand free to hold whatever needed to be held and, if necessary, to fend off obstacles. After further deliberation they decided to take the torches. They were secured in something approaching a shoulder holster, and could be worn, lens pointing forwards, from the side of the rib cage. The extra weight was negligible, and although they were carrying marginally a little more bulk, the pros significantly outweighed the cons.

Jaime and Tobias took up the slack of the rope while John Light sat himself down, back to the parapet, a few feet to one side. From this position he could view the proceedings with his line of vision unimpaired. Tanja Hein's Desert Eagle could be in his hand within a split second, but to all intents and purposes he appeared to close his eyes in preparation for a morning nap. Jaime and Tobias glanced his way curiously but both Mage and Helen knew exactly what he was doing. While they would be making the descent into the citadel in the flesh, Light would be making it with them in mental projection of his astral spirit.

'Will the winch take our combined weights?' Mage asked.

Cristobal nodded. 'Of course, Señor, and more besides. I use it during the week for unloading bags of cement from the backs of lorries.'

'Good, then I'll go first, and Helen, you come down behind me.'

He squatted down by the opening and slipping his foot into the stirrup, eased his legs over the edge. Helen took up position behind him, and as Jaime and Cristobal first took up the strain then started paying out the line, first Mage and then Helen were lowered through the roof of the citadel.

Haloed by the shaft of light that flooded downwards from the aperture in the cupola, they were none-the-less surrounded by darkness, a darkness that seemed to be filled by darker shapes that penetrated reason and caused the imagination to run wild. It was only when Mage clumsily flicked on the torch and the beam from the light illuminated the latticework of beams, some of them as thick as small trees, that his heart stopped pounding. Although not exactly unnerved by the experience, it sharpened the edge of his fear and made him aware of just how scared he really was. Well may he have been fulfilling the role of the spiritual warrior, but he was also a man, and the man within him was badly frightened..

Twenty feet down from the cupola he came into contact with a firm flat surface. Steeping out of the stirrup, he held the rope taught, easing it down until Helen also alighted from the line to stand by his side. The air was stale and thick with dust and the light from the opening in the roof seemed to be very dim and distant.

'Where are we?' she whispered, her voice barely audible.

'Working from my memory of what Hamish told me, we're on the top floor. What would have been the sleeping quarters. There's another floor beneath us, two thirds of which is technically underground if you measure the citadel by it's present day external dimension, and then beneath that the cellars and dungeons where Hamish said we'd find the old well. Let's go careful and find a way down, but for heaven's sake, watch out for the resin and let's go as quietly as we can.'

'I don't like this atmosphere... and I'm not just referring to all the dust!'

'I know exactly what you mean and, no, I don't like it much either!'

Intermingled with the powerful odour of dust and dirt and rotting wood there was something tangibly corporeal that was reminiscent of decomposing flesh. Mage found himself flashing the torch from side to side, probing with the beam of light to discover what, if anything, had chosen to die in any one of the four corners. The room was empty of anything that might have caused the subtle stink, but it was still there, emanating from below along with a vibratory thrum that impinged not only on the psychic senses but also upon the physical senses. The torch beam – and he was now most heartily glad that he'd decided that they should bring the torches – fell upon a darker area of shadow in the wedge of the most distant corner.

'Over there,' he murmured.

'Yes, I've got it,' Helen touched his arm, half in a gesture of reassurance, half in support. 'That's where all this crappy stuff is coming up from – I think.'

'I think you're right.'

They moved silently and cautiously towards the orifice.

'There'll be some sort of staircase,' Helen said from behind him.

From the top of the hole in the floor Mage flashed the torch briefly downwards and sure enough, there was a staircase of sorts, formed by short stocky beams, about a metre long, set deeply into the stonework. The stairs *looked* secure enough, although there would obviously be no way of telling for sure until they tested them with their weight. Each step would have to be tested independently upon their descent, for although they looked more than adequately sturdy, for all Mage knew they could be rotten with dry rot. Apart from a cursory inspection by one of Hamish Hamilton's students, these steps had been unused for the better part of four hundred years.

There was another element that unnerved Mage and made him extremely cautious. Flashing the torch once again he sought confirmation of his first impressions. The torch beam reflected from the shiny glistening substance that covered the stonework of the wall, and from behind him he heard Helen draw breath.

'The resin?'

'Looks like it,' he confirmed. And then, 'It's going to be very difficult getting down those steps without hanging on to the wall for some sort of support and I don't know about you, but I sure as hell don't feel like getting any closer to that stuff than I have to. Let's get the rope. If we lower it down from this side we can get down to the next level and if we make a point of keeping the steps between ourselves and the wall we should be able to avoid contact.'

'What happens if we get to the bottom and find that it's all over the floor?'

'We'll cross that bridge when we come to it. In the meantime, let's get the rope and keep our fingers crossed.'

They brought the line over to the stair head and Mage talked quietly into the walkie talkie, telling Jaime that they were descending to the next level and to pay out more line. 'Do it very slowly,' he instructed, 'and if I press the panic button, get me up fast.' Then he turned to Helen. 'Let me go down on my own first. If everything's okay, shin down afterwards, but if it's not it'll be easier if only one of us has got to beat a hasty retreat.'

'Okay,' Helen agreed. 'There is some danger down there, but I don't think it's critical. Our problem is, well, deeper... further down. Even so, be on your guard.'

'Don't try telling Grandpa to suck eggs,' he responded in mock jocularity, trying to lighten the tension between them. Then, foot in the stirrup, he eased himself over the edge and dropped into the waiting void of darkness an inch at a time.

The smell of death and decay was much stronger and now there was a pungent tang of something else that reminded him of bad eggs and sulphur... And there was also that unmistakable whiff of rotting seaweed. The temperature seemed to rise radically and the concept of fresh air became a distant memory from a previous life. One sweep of the torch told him the grim truth. Each of the four walls was covered in the shiny mucussy membrane with what appeared to be a significant shapeless concentration of the stuff over by the remains of the main entrance doors. Something glinted briefly in the torch light, but then was lost and gone. When he swept the light back he was another few inches lower in the descent which altered the angle sufficiently to cause the glinting sparkle to remain elusive. Twisting the torch so that the light shone downwards he was gratified to see that the resin did not cover all of the floor surface. Certainly, there were a few patches of the stuff where it had spilled and dribbled from the walls but most of the central area was clear. Having said that, his foot, when it came to rest upon smooth flag stone of the floor was barely eighteen inches from the nearest patch of resin. He eyed it dubiously and studiously, watching for any indication of movement or sentience. When he was as sure as he could be that it was dormant, he tugged lightly on the rope indicating that Helen should make her descent.

As Helen shinned silently down the rope he became increasingly aware of a flickering glow of light that emanated from the far corner. It was diffused and multi coloured but gave off enough illumination for him to discern that it came from a similar opening in the floor to the one that they'd just descended from. The hues of light changed from mauve to green and then blue to orange, and with these lights there was an audible mutter of sound, distant and muted.

'That's where it is,' Helen said, her own voice sounding curiously muffled and distant although her mouth was only inches from his ear. 'That's where we've got to go.'

Mage nodded, but said nothing. Instead, he slipped the cross bow from his back, and placing his foot in the brace, drew back both of the strings until they cocked on the knock. From the quiver of quarrels he withdrew the pair of crystal tipped bolts and loaded them both, securing them firmly in their gunnels, one above the other.

He could see Helen's face faintly illuminated in the unholy glow from the distant corner. It wore a quizzical expression.

'If we find Dolorean down there, I'm not even going to think about it. I'm going to shoot the fucker.' His voice was flat and devoid of emotion.

'And if Alexandra is down there with him?'

'Of course she's down there with him. That's why I prepared two bolts.'

Taking care to stay as far away as possible from the dark stains of resin, they crossed the floor, coming ever closer to where the floor fell away, and ever closer to the weird lights and the incomprehensible sounds that floated up from the room below. Both took some reassurance in recognising that the lights that they were seeing were no more than reflections, but both also became increasingly aware of the overpowering smell of seaweed and sulphurous ozone.

Coming to the opening they did not need their torches to see that this descent would be much easier. The stairs down were of solid stone and of the resin there was no sign. And yet here the atmosphere seemed to be so much thicker with a scarcity of oxygen. They had to breathe deeply to capture what little air there was, and with the air came the taste of something sickly and corrupt that made the bile rise in their throats and their stomachs heave.

Mage stole a quick glance at his companion. Her eyes were three quarters closed, pulled into slits of concentration and she looked as ill as he felt.

'They're down there,' she hissed. 'I can feel them. They're doing it and they're pretty damn close to the climax.'

'Then let's go and see exactly what it is that they *are* doing and see if we can put a stop to it.' Mage ducked his head and bending low with the bow held out at the ready before him, he started down the stone stair case. He had not gone more than five steps down before Helen heard a low animalistic moan escape his lips. Cautiously creeping down the steps after him, she too came to behold the sight that caused the magician so much obvious distress.

What met her eyes was the most surreal vision of hell, and even though she'd been mentally prepared for something fairly horrendous, nothing could have prepared her for the total *wrongness*, the complete *alienness* of the picture which unfolded beneath her.

While the parameters of the chamber were shrouded by unnaturally dark and impenetrable shadow the middle of the dungeon was filled with swirling and coalescing shards of light that reached up from within the well in a column that touched the ceiling then spilled back down to the floor to sweep around the lip of the well like a tornado moving in slow and controlled motion.

Two figures, exactly as she had seen them in her clairvoyant vision, were bathed in the unholy vortex, and against her will, her eyes were drawn towards them in horror and disgust.

The larger figure was standing facing away from them in three quarter profile, scaly legs and scaly arms that ended in a matrix of webbing and sharpened claws, thrown open wide as the light wove its presence round its gross form, bouncing off and reflected from the scales... Scales which in one breath seemed to be silver, then in another a pale yellowy green. A reptilian lizard like tail, fat and ridged and just failing to reach the floor, switched back and forth with a sense of malevolent purpose; the ridges which began at the narrow tip carried on up the centre of the creature's back, then split in two between powerful shoulder blades to form the rim of two bony epaulets which carapaced the shoulders, sitting around the muscular neck like an armoured collar.

The neck supported the Djinn's head, a head that seemed disproportionately large even for the squat barrel-like body beneath it. Nominally it could have been described as piggish, but that told only a small part of the story. A pig's face, yes, perhaps, but one that was covered with scales and small bony protrusions, that had a low Neanderthal brow with protuberant horns forcing upwards and outwards above deep-set gimlety eyes. And yes, there was a snout like a pig's snout, but beneath the snout there was a maw of a mouth with rows of wickedly glittering teeth, and two razor sharp tusks, fully a foot long, that jutted out like sabres, almost as an extension of the creature's jaw bone.

Because of the angle she was hard pressed to see the front of the Djinn's torso, but she could see quite enough to realise that she was looking at the archetype of all Man's perceptions of evil since the beginning of recorded time. Here was the church's satanic devil, the demon of Man's darkest nightmares, the dark destroyer God summoned in the tribal chants of Africa, the avenging angel personified in paintings upon the walls of Indian temples and crafted into the contorted writhing of Balinese death masks. Here was the energy behind every fearful myth from every continent of the world, hinted at by secret writings, and confused but present in occult art from the Haitian juju wand to the gargoyle clinging to the buttress of the Christian cathedral.

To see it as an abstract energy was one thing and to see it in the form of a specific clairvoyant vision was another, but to see it in the flesh, alive and real, active and aggressive, barely twenty feet away, ah this was another thing entirely! She pressed herself to the stonework, wanting flight and retreat, but mesmerised by the proceedings she was witness to. She fought for control, reminding herself of why she was here, and centred her attention on the other, if anything, more magical and more disgusting figure whose presence, or should she say *presences* filled the room.

Logically it had to be Alexandra, but she could only think of Mage's ex-wife as *it* rather than *her*.

Exactly as she had visualised that terrible day at The Oaks, *it* hung in a state of levitational suspension above the circular orifice of the well. It too had scales, clinging to and peeling from its grey slime covered torso. Its arms, thin spindly sticks, hung weightless beneath it. Its legs were opened at impossible right angles from its body. Its hair lank and matted, fell in tangled tresses, while its face, still recognisable as something that might once have been female, was constricted into a mask of something that only hinted at and mimicked human force. It was white and ancient, ravaged by time, ravaged by death – the face of a corpse dug up after a year of lying in its grave. While the figure itself was quite enough to give Helen nightmares for the rest of her life, what was happening to the figure was even worse.

Its belly was a huge pulsating membranous mound and even as Helen watched she could see something writhing and whipping within it. She was about to say something but there was a sudden squeal followed by a mulching squelchy sound – liquid, half blood, half a viscous white slime belched and splattered out of Alexandra's vagina, and then she saw it, something like a giant tadpole but with thickly matted black hair and viscous red eyes, something with appendages that might be described as arms that ended in a trident of small black talons, was clawing its way out of the opening, screeching shrilly as it emerged inch by bloody inch.

She heard Mage gag... Actually saw the vomit as it ejected from his mouth and cascaded over his clothes and the stone of the steps.

'For God's sake, Colin,' she prayed out loud in a feeble whimper, not sure whether he heard her or not. 'For God's sake, do something!'

Mage, in fact, did not hear the prayer, but he acted anyway. He'd seen enough to push him towards the final sanctuary of madness, but this was the moment he'd trained and prepared himself for. This was the moment he'd worked so hard to attain. Maybe he was here by destiny and karma, but he was also here by the sheer force and persistence of his own will, and he was here by right. He was as frightened and as disgusted as Helen, but this would not stop him doing what he knew he had to do... And he knew he'd better do it soon before the final dregs of oxygen were pressed from this place and they were overcome by the poisonous fumes that he imagined were clinging to the ether like cells of some dark and malignant cancer.

Clearly revealed in the cone of light, and less than twenty feet distant, the Djinn presented him with an easy unmissable target. Bringing the cross bow to his shoulder he aimed at the creature's head, and with his own small prayer of vindication, released the trigger mechanism.

The crystal tipped bolt flew from the bow with a velocity that almost matched a bullet leaving the barrel of a gun and with a flat direct trajectory that took it directly towards its intended target.

At first he'd thought he'd scored a hit, but Helen's in drawn gasp of shock and surprise made him suspicious of his own initial reaction. At first he couldn't see what had happened, but then Helen pulled him down to her level and he fully beheld the bizarre impossibility of the situation.

The bolt was held in stasis, suspended in mid air, some five feet short of it's intended victim's back... Almost as though it had hit an invisible wall where the dark of the peripheral shadows came into contact with the wildly unstable lights. The crystal quartz at the end of the quarrel was glowing incandescently, throwing off minuscule showers of sparks.

Not knowing what to do for the best, but knowing he had to do something, he brought the bow to his eye again and was about to shoot his second bolt, when

Helen's arm restrained him.

'No,' she hissed. 'Not now... wait. There's some kind of force feel around that scaly bastard. Just wait and let's see what happens. I think...'

Mage never did find out when Helen thought for at that moment there was a final shriek of victory the thing that had been trying to escape from the confines of Alexandra's body tore itself free, hovering in obeisance before the Djinn who had sired it and summoned it forth. A roar of staccato sounds emanated from the Djinn's throat and its taloned hands crashed together in symbolic command. With another screel, the fury eel with red eyes and the long chord of tail that even now was still being ejected from its mother's birth canal, suddenly dropped from sight, falling from between Alexandra's legs into the waiting opening of the well.

Leon watched the light show with growing awe and wonderment. It broiled in a perfectly cylindrical column, its base upon the troubled waters of the pool, its zenith somewhere far above him and out of sight. From his restricted position he strained to look upwards to see where it went and in so doing became aware of a dense black speck falling towards him. Falling was the wrong word. Spiralling was more apt, for the shape came down the column of light in a circular descent, like a child coming down a transparent helter skelter, controlling its velocity by using its feet as brakes. He tried to see what was making this purposeful and menacing journey but its shape was blurred and it was never in one place long enough for him to make an accurate assessment. Only when it entered the confines of the cavern did he realise how small it was, and yet despite its size, it was enough to terrify him. He had one clear impression of the malevolent entity, something that looked like a slimy giant tadpole with red eyes, matted fur, two short forearms ending in a triclaw of hooks that reminded him insanely of some miniature Tyrannosaurus Rex. For one brief second the thing looked directly at him. Thinking that he was about to be attacked, he raised the Uzi to his shoulder, and then barely a metre above the surface of the boiling water, the malicious little monster quivered once and with a flick of its vicious whippy tail, disappeared from sight. One nanosecond it was there, and in the next it had gone.

Leon did not relax. While it was true that he was terrified and totally unnerved, he had not lost all reason. Something else was bound to happen soon and he had learned enough from Herschal and Colin Mage to hazard a fairly good guess as to what that might be. On impulse, he disengaged the half used clip of ammunition from the gun, and loaded a fresh full clip from his arsenal. He didn't know exactly how many rounds he had discharged at Uri Bogdanovitch or at the thing that had been coming to get him, but if it had been about half a clip, far better to have thirty six rounds at the ready and not just eighteen.

He became aware of a subtle but distinct vibration... And while it was a sensory thing in the atmosphere around him, he also felt it in the ground beneath his buttocks. As if in confirmation, the lights within the column began to change, become less psychedelically wild and more stable, while at the same time significantly brighter. A pale sickly green was the predominant hue but with motes of mauve that appeared from nowhere and rose upwards as if carried upon some unseen and unfelt breeze. The effect was hypnotic and becoming drawn into it he was totally unprepared for what happened next.

At the base of the column, just about where the tadpole from hell had disappeared, the green light rippled, took on another dimension of depth, and a figure – this time a very *large* figure began to take shape. Squat, silver scaled, covered by transparent oily mucus, it was the brother of the creature than had done for Herschal... The mirror image of the countenance Leon had seen etched upon stone walls and a certain copper plate. Unbeknown to Leon, it was also much in the likeness of the brother who had opened the door for it, and who now stood, tranced and transfixed, forty meters above him at the head of the well.

Its eyes were closed and its arms, ending in those webbed mandibles with their horrific barbs, were crossed across its breast, the razor sharp black claws resting upon the carapaced epaulets of its shoulders. Very slowly, although with gradually gaining momentum, the thing lifted and levitated upwards within the column of green, the mauve light motes keeping pace with the ascent, occasionally brushing and caressing against it as though in worship and adoration of the beast's hideous countenance.

The Djinn was fully two meters into its ascent and was moving towards the roof of the cavern before Leon broke free of his fugue. With a strangled inarticulate gasp, he brought the Uzi to his shoulder, sighted upwards and the ascending horror, and squeezed the trigger.

Nothing happened.

He squeezed the trigger again, and still nothing happened.

Fucking bastard gun he screamed silently inside his own head. *Work, damn you, work!*

By the time he realised that he had neither released the safety catch nor cocked the bolt the Djinn was eddying out of sight, opaque in the cloying green light above his line of vision. But even as, in his fury of despair, he primed the weapon, another figure, identical to the first, was materialising in the rippling ether. While the first Djinn had been profile to him, this second faced him directly, barely three meters distant. Leon waited until it was fully formed, sighting carefully along the stubby barrel and aiming directly between the creature's closed eyes. As it began to levitate in pursuit of its companion – *please nice gun, please please please work this time* – Leon again pulled back on the Uzi's trigger.

In the space of less than two seconds and above the cacophonous continuous roar of the discharging weapon, thirty six nickel jacketed 9mm rounds flew across the short divide, and without a single misfire or shot that went wide of its mark, ploughed into the Djinn's unprotected face, centred in a perfect grouping in and around the eye sockets and the bridge of the creature's snout.

Its head flew back like a trap door hinged to a steel spring as jets of black steaming liquid cascaded upwards and all around it. There was one short shrill screech, and then even that was cut off as Leon, having rapidly ejected one clip in favour of another, fired again. Four shorter bursts, one aimed at his original target, one aimed at the throat, another at the chest, and the fourth at the curious umbilical coiling wrapped around the area of the navel.

Let's see you change shape now, you frigging bastard! Leon railed in hysterical elation, ramming a third clip home into the Uzi's breach.

There was, however, no indication of the metamorphosis that he had witnessed in the Negev. Instead, the dead or dying alien being, ever more enveloped in the cascades and splatterings of what Leon took to be its blood, folded inwards upon itself and gradually dematerialised from sight, leaving only the rippling waves of green light in its wake.

Mossad strikes back! Leon giggled inanely, leaning forwards slightly in anticipation of the next materialisation and the next round of the conflict.

He knew, of course, that he could not ultimately win and that therefore he was going to die. But he would not die without taking a few of these bastards with him, and he would not die in vain. No one else might know of his death, but at least, he reasoned, his death would not be without purpose. Although not a soldier it would be a soldier's death, and he took some solace in that. His father would be proud, so too would Gideon Lemski. Dov, dear sweet Dov, well Dov would be distraught, of course, although not so distraught as he might be if one of these Djinn things came wandering through his precious Tel Aviv hospital and started eating up his patients! He hoped that he might be doing something worthwhile to help the Englishman, if he was still alive, and if all the prophets and new age gurus were right, he'd find out soon enough on way or the other. Leon giggled to himself again, inanity edging towards insanity as his fractured mind began to disintegrate. *What a mess I'm in,* he thought. *I've pissed and shit myself and I must look awful!. What's even worse is that I used up almost half my ammunition.*

He scrabbled around, allowing his hands to glide appreciatively over the egg shaped curves of the grenades. More for reassurance than any practical purpose he sat the limpet mine on his lap. There was plenty of light now... Quite enough to see what you had to do to arm the detonator. You simply flicked this little red switch here, and then it was purely a matter of setting the timer. Leon pondered over that. He could set it for thirty seconds, or five minutes, or even an hour, but then, he knew he wasn't going anywhere in a hurry, so instead he set it to detonate immediately upon contact. All he had to do now was press down on the flat red plastic pad and *boom!* Leon didn't know how much explosive the mine contained, or even what type of explosive it was, but he knew it was enough to blow a main battle tank to bits, or, if you put it in the right place under the water line, sink a small ship. Yes, Leon felt very reassured by the mine as he hugged it to his chest. If things looked as though they were going to get really shitty, all he had to do was press on the detonator pad, and he'd be well out of it. With all that much explosive there surely couldn't be any pain, could there? It'd be all over in a flash – he chuckled comfortably to himself, yes there'd be a flash and a *bang,* - and then he'd be wherever he was going. Despite his strict religious upbringing, he wasn't quite sure where that might be, but wherever it was, it had to be a fuck sight better than where he was right now!

The attack, when it came, took Leon totally by surprise. He been sitting there, somewhat dreamily, waiting for the light to start rippling and for another Djinn to start forming at the base of the column. Instead there was a single rending sound and the damn thing was there, sentient, awake, amber elliptical eyes wide open as it lunged across the water towards him. His fear and shock broke through the spasmic grip of the laryngitis and a scream escaped his lips as he raised the Uzi, but even as he began to squeeze the trigger a whip like tentacle shot out from the Djinn's navel and slashed the weapon from his hands with such force that Leon's wrist and three of his fingers were instananeously broken.

Leon didn't even feel the pain. Reflexively he grabbed at the mine with both his bad hand and the good, but then the Djinn was upon him. The umbilical whip wrapped itself around his legs tightening like a garrotte – and then he did feel pain as his injury shrieked in protest against the cruel and unrelenting pressure that was brought to bare upon it...

... And yet he had good cause to be thankful for the broken leg. The pain was chasing him into unconsciousness even as the Djinn's talons sunk themselves into his shoulders, breaking bone and cartilage and desiccating flesh and muscle. He was hauled into a vertical position as his attacker drew him closer to the slobbering gash of a fetid mouth; Leon felt himself being lifted into space as the Djinn dragged him backwards towards the centre of the green column, and once within the light, either because he was running out of air as his life ebbed away or because there was no air, he starting choking within the alien atmosphere. The Djinn's tusk was nuzzling at his throat as its amber eyes bore into him with baleful contempt. Leon smiled once, then dropped his arms and leaned forwards to embrace his foe.

The explosion tore a hole in the heart of Castillo's mountain. Compressed within the confines of the small cavern the heat and kinetic energies of the blast found their own pathways to release and freedom. The waters of the pool were immediately evaporated and the external layers of stone walls melted. The blast forced itself downwards, shattering the basalt beneath the pool and opening up a fiery chasm that channelled earth quaking energy through the deeper labyrinth of caves and tunnels. It punched outwards through three hundred and sixty degrees, shredding rock and causing fissures until it found exit through the side of the mountain, causing small avalanches to cascade down towards the river in the west and the village in the east. For the better part, however, the main force of the detonation was channelled upwards through the bore of the well which acted like a giant run barrel, shooting the furious forces up towards the citadel...

Mage and Helen had watched in impotent fascination as the light from the well had taken on its more verdant hue. Independently of each other they had both felt the raw energy of the Djinn's telekinetic power as it had motioned with its arm, causing the haggard and deflated wreck that had once been Alexandra to drift away from her levitational position above the well. She'd keeled to one side like a listing ship, still hovering a few feet above the ground but further away in the more distant shadows of the dungeon.

The reason for this manoeuvre had become horrifically apparent as the second Djinn had emerged within the centre of the well shaft and with one gracefully fluid movement stepped out of the ether on to the firm and real foundation of Spanish soil. The two invaders from the other world had bowed in deep greeting to each other, emitting staccato barks of welcome in their own inimitable tongue.

Then things had started happening very quickly indeed. From somewhere beneath them, Mage presumed from the bottom of the well, there had come the sharp and unmistakable roaring chatter of small arms fire. It had been muted by the distance and the weird acoustics, but none the less the imperious and aggressive bursts of gunfire had been music to Mage's ears.

'Leon! He's still alive!' Helen's excited voice had been exultant with delight and Mage had grabbed her arm, euphoric with this sudden turn of events that might yet, he'd hoped, redress the impossible imbalance of power.

The Djinn were also aware of this unexpected threat, and in becoming alert to one, became alert to another. Without warning the beast that had once been known as Dolorean whirled to face the two intruders, letting out a squeal of rage and recognition. In the space of a heartbeat the umbilical whip had uncoiled from its navel and was lashing towards them, but then, either because the Djinn's concentration had lapsed or because the crystal tipped bolt had finally worried its way through the invisible shield that was no longer acting as a deterrent, the bolt leapt forwards in resumption of its deadly journey, arcing towards its target like a fiery cannon shell. Instinctively alert to this new threat, Dolorean stepped nimbly to one side. The bolt hurtled past, missing his snout by an inch, and carrying on to imbed itself firmly and deeply into the throat of the second Djinn who had been moving position to see what had been causing its brother so much distress and fury.

Even above the diminishing sounds of the subterranean gunfire, the creature's bellow of anguish and agony had been deafeningly loud. It's hands had grasped at its throat as streams of black liquid squirted and spurted in violent jets, splashing across the walls and floor of the dungeon, splashing too over its compatriot, who, Mage and Helen now forgotten, was advancing to assist. By the time he'd got there, the wounded Djinn was on its knees, its grotesque form shimmering in and out of focus as it tried to attain the shapechanging power of metamorphosis. Either by force of Mage's magic, or the effect of the small amount of quicksilver injected into the alien's system, perhaps even by the penetrative power of the crystal alone, the Dolorean Djinn had been too late. Even as he'd reached down to extract the bolt, buried up to its flight feathers in the mess of fractured scale and black slime, the kneeling invader's silver scales had turned to a static and lifeless mauve, its torso toppling over to one side and out of reach.

With an ululating howl that sounded as though it might have originated from the bowels of hell, Dolorean had turned and with salivating tusks and air curving claws, had launched himself at the two figures hunched upon the stone staircase. Mage, cross bow sights to his eye, was already taking up the pressure on the trigger and had been about to discharge the second bolt into his adversary's rapidly advancing face, when the world suddenly exploded with the detonation caused by Leon Shapiro's last embrace.

The floor of the dungeon blew up and a stab of red and white fire stabbed upwards from within the well, smashing a huge hole through the rood above it, and indeed causing the roof to collapse in a shower of burning timbers and slabs of stone. In the split second before they were covered by rolling clouds of thick acrid smoke, Mage saw one such piece of stone, the size of a small coffee table, smash down upon the Djinn's shoulder and deflect the oncoming assault.

Choking on the hot debris and blinded by the brilliant flash that still burned behind the retinas of his eyes, Mage groped his way back up the steps. It was not so much a case of him helping Helen, but of Helen helping him. He steadfastly refused to let go of the cross bow; common sense said leave it – it was cumbersome and had served its purpose, but instinct and intuition said no. Marshalling his rapidly dwindling reserves, he hauled himself up on to what was left of the flag stoned floor. A gaping hole had been rent in it at the centre, and pieces of masonry and flagging still crumbled and gave way, falling into the abyss below. What made things even more dangerous was the fact that some heavy debris, including some of the beams, was falling from the floor above, for not only had the explosion torn a hole in the roof of the dungeon, it had gone on to blast a path straight up to the top of the citadel. Indeed, through the swirling clouds of dust and smoke, a shard of light stabbed downwards from above and although his mind was cluttered and confused by the shock of the detonation, Mage spared a muddled thought for the people who had been waiting for them on the roof. He hoped they had survived the blast, but at that moment his and Helen's survival was paramount on his list of priorities.

Even though their ears were ringing, both of them virtually deafened, they were both aware of an insecure rending and creaking as the damaged foundations of the citadel began to give way. Without warning a crack appeared in the wall next to them and the floor lurched a little to the right. Mage knew that they had to get out of there and get out fast before the whole structure came tumbling down on them. The question was how? Their escape route was closed and there was no other visible means.

Then, in answer to his unspoken prayer, there was the unmistakable sound of splintering wood as the great door of the citadel, no longer supported by the pressure of the surrounding stone, collapsed and came crashing down, half of it disappearing into the dungeon, the other half piling up on itself in a jumble of broken beams and panels. A wide wedge of light came flooding into the chamber to reveal the true extent of the damage that had been caused, but at the same time, showing them their way out. There was no sign of the resin which had caused them so many earlier fears, but even if it had been present, Mage would have risked it in favour of being buried alive.

Mouthing the words *come on*, he took Helen's hand and led her carefully around the perimeter until they came to what appeared to be the more stable pile of rubble that had come avalanching in after the doors had fallen. They were both covered with several layers of filth and grime, their hands and faces black with soot. Their clothes and also some of their hair was singed, but when he caught Helen's eye, he saw the look of elation spread across her dirty face as they clambered up the forty five degree slope towards light fresh air and freedom. His own elation soared to dizzy heights as he put his hand on a sharply pointed object, and instinctively pulling it away, realised that the offending protrusion was nothing less than the sharp crystal tip of his wand – the wand that had been lost in such distressing and alarming circumstances on the day they had investigated the excavation, trying to make some sense of Hamish Hamilton's demise. Now the wand had found its way back to him in the most remarkable of circumstances and he tore it from its resting place with all the vigour and enthusiasm of being reunited with a long lost friend.

They were almost at the lip of the mound, within a foot of being able to strole out of their prison into the daylight, and with Mage a little ahead, when Helen's shrill and terrified scream of panic stopped him dead in his tracks. He turned to see the cause of Helen's terror and his bowels loosened. The Djinn was standing on the rim of the blown out floor glaring at them with bane and malice, and even as Mage looked, the umbilical whip lashed out to the extent of its extraordinary length, flying up the land spill and wrapping itself tightly around both of Helen's legs. With a high pitched squeal of triumph it began to reel her in like a fish on a line while at the same time advancing steadily towards its captive.

For Helen this was the realisation of her worst nightmare. The creature was fifteen feet below her and advancing all the time, and now in the dim light of day she saw its true countenance clearly for the first time. It was the ugliest, most horrific sight she'd seen in her life, an exact replica of the visualisation she'd had at The Oaks, but made so much worse by the clear knowledge that this was not just a vision. It was covered in the same streaks of soot that covered both herself and Mage, but apart from what appeared to be a shard of broken carapace on the Djinn's shoulder, it was otherwise undamaged. A rigid phallus protruded from between its legs, emitting small ejaculations of something she didn't even want to contemplate the nature of, and its mouth hung open to reveal the rows of shark like teeth that were snapping and masticating with mounting anticipation. The twin points of its tusks glinted wickedly and wetly, and unless she was much mistaken, they two ejaculated small mists of spray from their tips. Darkness and panic began to overcome her as the pain in her legs increased beyond endurance, and without realising that she was doing it, she started to scream, and not just a single shriek of surprise, but one long wail of terror that even to Mage's deafened ears, went on and on without end.

Mage was badly compromised. With one hand he clung to the less than permanent earth face, made more difficult by his purchase on the wand. With his other hand he hung on to Helen's wrist. To get to the cross bow, half slung across his shoulder, he would first have to release his grip on Helen, and even if he did that he had no means of being certain that he'd be in time to shoot at the Djinn before the Djinn put paid to Helen. But Helen had a free hand, hadn't she? And did she not also have her athame tucked somewhere in one of her boots?

'Helen!' he roared at her, not sure whether she heard or not. 'For God's sake, where's your knife, girl? Helen, use your knife!'

Helen made no response, although her screams diminished. But by then it was too late anyway and as the Djinn started climbing the mound behind them, the cord of the umbilical whip becoming tauter and tighter as the distance between them closed, Mage felt her wrist slip through his fingers.

On the roof of the citadel John Light had become instantly alert a few seconds *before* they had heard the distant stammer of small arms fire. Jaime Gomez and Tobias Cristobal had been peering into the opening in the cupola, flashing their torches in an attempt to discover what was going on, and had it not been for Light's forceful and intuitive intervention, both men would have been killed by the blast that tore the cupola from its anchor points and sent it spinning like a wounded flying saucer over the edge of the battlements.

'*Back!*' Light had yelled imperiously. '*Quickly! Back against the wall!*'

Not knowing exactly what the problem was but sensing the urgency of the command, the two Spaniards had pulled back and were standing in agitation next to Light when they'd felt the citadel quiver beneath their feet. Jaime had opened his mouth to say something, but then the cupola had been shattered and lifted into the air on a long finger of flame, that belched outwards as well as upwards, singeing their hair and sucking the breath from their bodies. A tile, the size of a paving stone, hit Jaime full in the chest, propelling him backwards. He'd have gone over the edge to a certain death had Light not caught him, deflecting his backwards trajectory so that he came up against one of the higher crenellations. Even then, the police chief was out cold, and, Light suspected, quite seriously damaged. With Toby's help, he eased the piece of masonry to one side and started unbuttoning the police man's tunic. Blood tricked from his already damaged nose, and more alarmingly from the side of his mouth. He was about to call for Hector's help, but a squelching thump from beneath his feet, from somewhere just *within* the ruined citadel, stayed his call and distracted him.

Old Tobias had heard it too and he looked at Light with fearful expectancy, waiting for some guidance and direction.

The aluminium ladder had been blown away from the side of the wall and when Light risked a fast glance downwards he saw Hector and the two women struggling to walk it upright again. Hector saw him, waved and shouted.

'Is everything all right up there? What in God's name happened?'

'Jaime's injured,' Light shouted down in response. Don't know how bad, but it doesn't look too good. There's been an explosion of some sort down on one of the lower levels. We copped the top of the blast. Half the Goddamn roof has gone, but I guess we're okay for a while.'

'I'll come up and help you with Jaime!'

'No, hang on Doc. Wait 'till I let you know that it's okay.'

Again Light heard what could only be described as a squelch, and this time it was followed by a creak of snapping wood. He turned his attention to the gaping hole that had appeared in the sunken centre of the roof. There was little to see amid the rolling clouds of dust and grey smoke, but it was obvious that the whole roof was in danger of imminent collapse. A large spar of timber had thrust itself up from the room below, and was now resting on the lip of the hole, putting it under great weight and pressure. Under any other circumstances he would have waited for Hector and the ladder, leaving the roof to its own fate. He was, however, all too well aware that somewhere beneath his feet Mage and Helen might be looking for a way out – at least, they would if they were still alive – and he didn't want to walk away, couldn't walk away, until he was absolutely sure that they were not coming out. There was still plenty of rope wrapped around the drum winch, and certainly enough for him to lower himself down into whatever lay below if he had to... He didn't want to, and was honest enough with himself to admit it openly, but if he *had* to...

'Let's see if we can move that wooden spar,' he suggested to Tobias. 'It'll take some pressure off the roof, and if my friends are coming out this way, it'll give them more space?'

'What about Jaime?' Tobias asked.

'Doctor's on his way.'

'Okay!' Tobias suddenly grinned. 'But you better let me move the beam, Señor. No offence, but with your weight, I think the roof she come tumbling down.'

'All right old man, but just you be very careful.'

'Pah, you tell me to be careful after I have just been blown up! You a little late with your warning Señor, but *si,* I shall be careful.'

The spindly carpenter edged delicately towards the rim of the ruptured roof, testing each tile with his foot before he put any weight on it. When he was satisfied that it was going to hold his sparse frame, he wrapped his old but muscular arms around the stem of the offending beam and was in the process of taking the strain when something long and silver grey flashed out of the darkness just beneath his feet, whipping across his throat. Without so much as a cry – just a long rasping gurgle – the carpenter fell backwards with blood spuming like a fountain from his throat that had been cut deeply open almost from ear to ear. As his frame toppled to collapse almost where he stood, Light moaned in distress and fear as the old man's killer emerged from beneath and behind the beam.

In the past, and in a tale he had never yet told to another living soul, John Light had faced the Djinn, but what was emerging out of the smoke was unlike anything he'd ever encountered in either of the two worlds. It was long and grey and humanoid, but really that was where any human resemblance ended. Although the figure was not scaled as such, small lozenges of fishy substance clung to its skin amid tufts of matted substance that might once have been hair or fur. It was obviously female by virtue of its sagging teats and absence of any visible genitalia, and Light had no doubt with regard to the apparition's identity. He was looking at Alexandra, or what was left of her. In all truth, there was little resemblance to the being he had seen and talked to in the market place only a few days before. Her nose had gone, leaving two small nasal cavities beneath her reptilian eyes and above an impossibly wide mouth from which a long forked tongue danced and darted between yellow teeth, that seemed to Light's eyes, to be pointed like long brightly coloured needles. Her feet had become both webbed and clawed, and there were claws too at the end of each of her long tentacular arms that were, to all intents and purposes, now minus their elbow joints. It had been one such set of claws that had killed and almost decapitated old Toby.

He did not consciously know how she'd ended up on the roof, but *subconsciously,* well, somewhere below there had been an explosion, and if she'd been anywhere near the blast, it was quite conceivable that she could have been blown upwards to the roof of the citadel. It would have killed anything human, but whatever this female thing was, it was certainly no longer human! Either way, it was all a bit academic. She was here, heading towards the prostrate form of the still living Jaime Gomez, that tongue darting and green vapour spuming from her open mouth.

Light danced a few steps to his left to give him a clearer line of sight through the opacity of the smoke and with both hands on the butt, he brought up the pistol. His target was eighteen feet away and at this range confident of scoring a hit. *Fuck that cops and robbers bullshit about yelling freeze! Fuck the frigging bitch, full stop!*

He squeezed the trigger and although the heavy automatic bucked in his hand the kick-back was surprisingly light, aided as it was by the dampening effect of the gas recoil. The noise of the gun going off was, however, quite shocking, and it dulled his senses, but not to the extent that he couldn't see the bullet hit the target. The .357 round took Alexandra in the side of her scraggy neck – he saw it go in and he watched it come out the other side, almost in the process of cinematographic slow motion. It neither dropped her nor stopped her, but it did cause her to divert her attention from Jaime as she became aware of Light for the first time. With a long sighing, spume blowing hiss, she turned from her original victim and started advancing across the roof towards the more threatening adversary.

Oh fuck, here I go again pumping three fifty sevens into something that shouldn't exist! Light held his ground and oblivious to the horrendous soul wrenching pain of the noise, squeezed the trigger four more times in succession. All four rounds slammed into Alexandra's torso, passed through the alien inhuman body, and either expended themselves a mile away in open countryside or smashed into the battlements. But with the impact of each of the heavy calibre rounds Alexandra was pushed backwards, until, when the last bullet found its mark the parapet wall came up against the back of her legs and she soundlessly toppled backwards, disappearing from sight.

Light had time to catch his breath but once before the world exploded yet again, this time with the multiple detonations of a machine gun being discharged. He rushed to the edge of the roof, expecting to see Tanja Hein finishing Alexandra off with the Uzi. Instead he was presented with a view of total carnage. Alexandra must have dropped virtually on top of the Israeli agent, and far from being dead, she was in the furious business of beheading and disembowelling her victim. Tanja's Uzi was being discharged into the earth as her finger spasmodically jerked in its death throes against the trigger.

Hector and Tamara were less than ten feet away, backing away in shock and revulsion.

'*MOVE!*' Light roared at them with all the air in his lungs. Run for it. Get out! Run like hell!

With a single apprehensive look at the gobbling feast going on before his eyes

– Alexandra had her head well into Tanja's stomach – Hector grabbed Tamara's arm and together they fled around the far side of the citadel until they were out of Light's sight. Light looked down at the unholy feast and shuddered, at the same time thankful that the ladder was still laying flat on the ground where it had been dropped. He wondered if Alexandra had the strength to lift the ladder herself... Wondered whether she needed too! She'd survived five rounds of three fifty seven at close range and a thirty foot drop. Maybe the bitch could fly as well! He cast an eye at the hole in the roof and wondered what else, apart from Mage and Helen, might make its exit via that route. It was a sobering thought, and one that he knew he was going to have to get used to. Until someone put the ladder back in placer, he was trapped up here – *all dressed up and got no place to go* – he sung to himself as he squatted down next to Jaime and carefully purloined the unconscious policeman's nine millimetre Beretta. Ten rounds in the Beretta, maybe three left in the Desert Eagle, but what the fuck good were bullets? With a snort of disgust, he rifled Jaime's pockets until he found the crumpled packet of Ducados, and lighting a cigarette, settled down to wait and worry.

Mage's words cut through Helen's panic and she grabbed for the knife that was more than just a knife... It was her priestess's athame, used in her work and religion since she'd been initiated by her parent's when she'd been sixteen years old. Although highly decorous, it was wickedly pointed, the blade almost a foot long, razor sharp on both of its curving edges. The Djinn was almost upon her – she could smell the creature's fetid breath and almost count the minute scales beneath its amber elliptical eyes, eyes that bore ever more deeply into her as its hideous head drew closer – but she was in a poor position to launch an attack, *unless....*

Tearing free of Mage's weakened grip up her wrist she wrapped both hands around the hilt of the dagger. Even as the Djinn's talons were closing upon her, she launched herself forwards and upwards, plunging the athame into the creature's right eye.

The noise of it's hypersonic scream cut through to the core of her soul threatening to destroy her already damaged eardrums. But as the Djinn flailed backwards, the travesty of hands reaching to grasp at the offending weapon, the whip like cord released itself from around her legs, and then Mage had her by the shoulders and was dragging her into the open air and sunlight, although it was the weirdest sunlight she'd ever seen.

The sun was there, true enough, but it was hanging like an amber orb, dulled and distorted behind a concealing cloud of yellow opaque mist that seemed to stretch as far as her eye could see from horizon to horizon. Within the mist there were striated layers of blacker cloud, perhaps the smoke from the explosion, creating a tiger's eye effect, which, for a few seconds, until she got her bearings, made her feel as though she had entered a dreamscape world rather than the reality of her own time and place.

There was the sound of running footsteps, and half turning as she clambered unsteadily to her feet, she saw Hector and Tamara racing round the side of the citadel. They were heading off at a tangent until Mage bellowed *"Over Here!"* at the top of his voice. Only then did they divert from their path of flight, and come rushing over. Hector swept Helen up in his arms. Neither could speak but both were crying, and it fell to Tamara to brief Mage on the sequence of events that had taken place on the other side of the citadel.

'John's still up there,' she finished breathlessly, 'up on the roof with the other two. They're trapped until we can get them down. We gotta do something man! You hear me, we gotta do something...'

Mage's eyes had narrowed. He was looking over her shoulder.

'What we do is move backwards, very slowly and steadily.'

Tamara was about to protest, but then caught the note in the Englishman's voice. Instinctively she looked behind her and would have burst into tears had the emotions not locked themselves in her throat with a paroxysm of fear. For while the bloody monster that had not only killed but had half eaten Tanja Hein was walking towards them around the left hand side of the citadel, something twice as big, twice as ugly, twice as awful was clambering out of the hole at the bottom of the wall. It had scales and horns and tusks... There was even a horny tusk sticking out of its eye, or so Tamara thought until she recognised that it wasn't any such thing, but the hilt of a knife. Black liquid dribbled down its face to splash down upon its scaled and war scarred chest.

"Oh shit!" Tamara moaned, her legs beginning to buckle.

Mage grabbed her under the arm. "Helen, Hector!' he called authoritatively. 'We still have problems... Move back towards the keep.'

As the quartet retreated, never taking their eyes from the two alien entities, Mage slowly brought the bow to his shoulder. The trouble was, of course, that he had two targets, but there was only one bolt.

'Get behind me,' he snapped at his companions. 'Try and get to the keep. Helen, there's energy in there for us. Tap into it and use it if you can... and even if you can't, it's still the safest place I can think of.'

'We can't just leave you,' she protested from behind him.

'Yes you can if you have to... but don't worry, I won't be far behind you.'

The Djinn were a good forty yards away. They had come together at the base of the citadel and there they had stopped while the female had withdrawn the athame from her creator's eye, casting it with power and disdain over the edge of the castle wall. Now they separated, and with the female hanging a few feet behind, began to advance with malice and deliberation towards their retreating quarry.

He was wounded and he knew the wound was serious, possibly even fatal. In his own sphere or in the care of his shaman, the wound could be healed, but that world was closed to him. That world would always be closed to him now. The opening was closed, the magic betrayed or flawed. No brethren would be making the metamorphosis through this veil....The veil was in tatters, torn and shredded, not only by the physical destruction wrought by the explosion but also by the destruction of the delicate and complex link of magical and psychic energies that had been forged between his temple in this dimension and the hallowed efrit halls of his homeworld.

He was in pain and yet failed to care whether or not the pain might cost him his life. His life was forfeit anyway. He had failed in his mission – despite every plan, every preparation, every effort and sustained struggle – he had still failed! His homeworld closed to him he was now trapped in this dimension, and although he knew that with some further manoeuvring and shape changing he might exist for a while in human disguise, the will to do so was absent. But where there was a will, a will so strong and all consumingly powerful, was to exact revenge and retribution against the force which had denied him his destiny. The manmate magician and his cohorts would pay dearly for their success. They had eluded him so far, but only because he had been preoccupied with other responsibilities. Those responsibilities removed, he was now free to pursue his personal jihad of death and destruction.

True, the manmate had a powerful weapon, and one that had slain his newly come brother, and true, these human entities were prepared to fight when all previous intelligence had indicated that they could have no defence against the Djinn, but this did nothing to defer him from his quest.

He was oddly grateful to the female when she pulled the *zhoofuk* – the painmaker – from his eye, but there his sentiment ended. She had fulfilled her role and his responsibilities towards her were also ended. She would rise or fall, not on the strength of her own desire to live or die, but on his own for it was his mind and energy that gave her life – and thus, of course, she would die. She had no real knowledge or training, no shapechanging defences, no life spark she could truly call her own to enable her to survive in this hostile human environment. Even so, he was glad of her presence. She had proved her ability to fight and she may yet be useful as a weapon.

Even with his impaired vision he was easily able to target his adversary. He was standing some little way distant... Not running now, but waiting and prepared for combat. Through the waves of pain and fury the Djinn found an icicle of respect for his foe, a foe that he had consistently underestimated, and a foe who now refused to flee, but stood his ground waiting for the final battle.

The Djinn threw back his wounded head and howled the blood chilling opening stanza of The Battle Hymn Of The Brethren - *You have won! You have succeeded! You have destroyed my temple and have pulled down the veil which prevents the holy opening for the Great Transition. For these transgressions your life is mine!* – Venom spurted from the needle jets at the tips of his tusks and the umbilical whip quivered in pre-strike tension. He gathered all his energies in preparation for the last lightening leap which would have him at the manmate's throat even before the manmate knew that he was under attack, when something caught his psychic attention. He angled his head slightly to see a figure, obviously not Djinn and therefore human, racing past him in an attempt to reach the manmate the illusion of safety offered by the enemy lines. Acting purely on instinct the Djinn lashed out with the whip, caught the figure around its leg, toppling him to the ground. Even as the whip tautened and hauled him in, he was upon his prey, talons hooking into the soft flesh of rump and curving around scalp and face, lifting his quarry with outstretched arms high above his head. He could snap its back, break its neck, bite out its gut, or throw the writhing screaming figure over the edge of the castle wall where it would fall to the rocks below. It did not mater as long as it died painfully and as long as the manmate saw it die. Even now the manmate was walking forwards and the Djinn roared in anticipatory pleasure. It would simply tear its human prey in half, casting one part to the east and the other to the west and while the manmate was distracted, it would attack in the centre.

From the moment the explosion blew a hole in the side of the mountain not ten metres beneath where Angel was perched upon his precarious ledge, his position there became increasingly precarious and untenable. A cascade of vile smelling liquid, thicker than water but not as stodgy as mud, had gushed out in a torrent to splash down upon the rocks and stunted foliage of Alvaro's pig field. Angel's slab of stone had dropped fifteen degrees to the right, threatening to slide him off into the melee below – and he'd have gone too had he not grabbed at one of the battlement stanchions, hanging on for dear life as the mountain seemed to collapse around his ears.

It had been the sound of gunfire, deafeningly close, that had made him dip into his reserves, finding the strength, although God knew from where, to haul himself over the edge of the wall, but by then it was all over. The firing had stopped, and there was nothing to be seen – except for a winch and a ladder and – he'd stumbled over to the red bundle at the base of the wall, wondering what it was, not recognising its identity until he was almost upon it. And when he *did* realise that he was staring down at a headless torso that had had half of its belly torn away along with half a leg and both of its arms, he promptly threw up and panicked. There were no thoughts in his head, no feelings in his heart, just a blind instinct that said go, run, fly, move – put as much space as you can between yourself and this horrible gut wrenching *thing* that offended every fibre of his sensitive young soul.

Thus, not knowing what had happened, and certainly not knowing what was taking place only a few meters away and out of sight on the far side of the citadel, Angel ran and ran like the wind – straight into the arms of the waiting Djinn.

Mage watched in horror as Angel was downed then hauled off his feet to be held aloft above the shapechanger's head. Without thinking about what he was doing he began moving forwards to close the range, but by some instinct or other psychic impression – he caught the whiff of oak trees and thought of Michael Fry – the Djinn's intentions were obvious, and he knew that he simply didn't have the time. He watched the red blood trickle down the Djinn's arms as it escaped from Angel's damaged body, and he knew by the boy's screams that he was still alive, but for as how long depended upon a split second decision. Mage stopped in his advance, he had closed the distance by fifteen yards but his target was still twenty five yards away which seemed just too far distant to his way of thinking, but he knew he was out of time and out of options. He steadied the bow, stock pulled tightly into his shoulder, and aiming at the centre of the Djinn's chest, squeezed the trigger.

This time he was unable to follow the trajectory of the bolt. He did not see it going and nor did the Djinn even see it coming. Neither of them knew that a hit had been scored until the crystal tipped bolt squelched with tremendous velocity into the soft part of the membrane surrounding the base of the umbilical whip in the region of the creature's belly.

Mage knew that his bolt had found its target when the Djinn suddenly staggered backwards, dropping Angel without ceremony at its feet, and howling upwards at the yellow sky as black liquid oozed from its navel, covering its lower body and legs.

The Djinn knew that all was lost as it felt the fire well up in the very seat and pit of it's psychic soul. The manmate's magic had struck it deep within its armoury and prime heart, for here behind the umbilical were the dwelling places for the complex matrix patterns of neurones that not only gave the Djinn its ability to change shape, but gave it too, all of its psychic and magical energies... The very essence of its being that gave it individual identity and made it what it was. It was not the pain that told the Djinn that its existence was ending, but the lack of pain. It had *been* in pain since the day of its birth, and a pain which had been horribly intensified during its time in the manworld, but now that pain was receding as the sun, the sun that it had sought to capture for the sake of its kind, became ever stronger in the alien sky, sucking his spirit from within the scaled shell, and spitting it out again, born on the winds of *Zoof* to be transported back from whence it came.

Mage walked forwards with steady deliberation. From somewhere behind him he heard the sound of running feet and someone was calling his name, but there was a roaring in his ears and his head felt as if it was disengaged from the rest of his body. Within the cone of roaring there seemed to be a distant thunder of applause that came not from the earthplane but from some other astral dimension. For a brief second he was aware of other figures walking with him, one of whom was a smiling Michael Fry, then as suddenly as the vision had come, it departed, leaving him standing to one side of the injured and unconscious Angel de Guadiaro, looking down at the corpse of the Djinn. There was no doubt in his mind that the shapechanger was dead. The energy had gone from it, and even now, even as he watched, its silver scales were turning a dark rusty brown, stained in many places by the dark patches of flash burn and the streaks of black blood.

There was nothing that he could do for Angel, and any case, he instinctively knew that within seconds Hector would be at the boy's side. Even so he wondered at the synchronicity of the boy's arrival on the battle field. True, the magician had slain the Djinn, but would it have been quite so easy had not the Djinn's attention been distracted at the crucial moment? Without Angel's intervention, could the Djinn have been defeated at all? No one would ever know, but in that part of his brain that still reasoned on a human level, he marvelled at the complexity of life's jigsaw. From his first day in Castillo Angel had played an integral and essential part in Mage's quest, and although the boy was obviously badly damaged by his encounter, it seemed so fatalistically right that he should be there playing such an important role at the end. He hoped that Angel's life would be spared this encounter with destiny, but then an alien sound attracted his attention and he was harshly reminded that this business was not quite over yet. One last onerous task remained.

Alexandra... It was not Alexandra, of course, but he could not help but think of the female entity in these familiar terms, stood a few feet to one side. Her arms, awfully inhuman, excessively long and without elbow joints, hung limply by her side, as she stood swaying mournfully, a keening whimper emitting from her mouth as saliva dribbled through the rows of blood stained needle points of teeth. Her eyes were open but vacant, and they did not flicker as he approached.

He didn't know – and didn't care – whether or not she still posed a threat. He stood before her, making himself look at her, studying the amber elliptical eyes, and trying to make contact, any kind of contact, with what ever spirit might still rest within the shell.

There was nothing. Just the overpowering stench of decay and corruption. It was like looking at a corpse that had been disinterred and re-animated after a year in the grave.

And yet, once, in another form, this alien creature had been his wife. He knew not what might have happened to her spirit, and while this troubled him greatly, he *did* know what had happened to her body. It had not died, but had been twisted and changed, contaminated by alien spore. Somewhere within its disgustingly changed form there might just be a residual spark, not of the mind, but of the spirit that had once made this creature human, and he sought to make contact with it, perhaps in search of permission or just to say farewell. But there was nothing, no sign, no hint, no indication, not a single clue to suggest that anything of the human spark remained within.

He dropped the bow, letting it clatter to the ground, and never taking his eyes from the amber slits that gazed at him sightlessly from the slack and unanimated face, he withdrew the wand from his belt. With both hands wrapped around the handle he drew it back above his head, and then, after only the briefest pauses of hesitation, plunged it downwards with all of his force and might, driving the crystal point deep into Alexandra's breast.

There was little resistance, just the sound and sensation of tearing fabric. She did not scream, there were no writhings of death agony, there was no attempt at self defence or counter attack. A small gasp, the blinking of an eye, and then she crumpled, twisting to one side as she fell forwards, face down top the ground. Mage stood motionless and without emotion, staring dispassionately at the crystal tip of the wand which now protruded from her back. Some of Tanja Hein's blood still clung to Alexandra's form, but the turgid stuff that covered the tip of the wand was black and glutinous. It was not human blood, but the blood of the shapechanger, the blood of the Djinn.

Mage searched for a tear, but too many tears had already been shed, and his eyes were dry. He looked up at the curious sky, the sun no longer visible behind the curious mist that was descending over Castillo and the Castillato valley, and in his mind, laid the spirit of his dead wife to rest.

While Helen and Tamara went to rescue Light and Jaime Gomez, and while Hector carried Angel some way distant to tend to the boy's wounds, Mage dragged Alexandra over towards the Djinn, depositing her in a heap next to him.

Tobias Cristobal's pick-up truck still had the keys in the dashboard, and he drove the vehicle over to the two corpses, bringing it to a halt almost directly above them. With the engine still running he lifted the bonnet, and disconnecting the fuel line, sprayed petrol over the two dead beings until they were both saturated. Then he stood back, and while the petrol stilled spewed force, covering not only the Djinn and its mate, but also running in puddles around the tyres and forming various small reservoirs within the engine bay, he retrieved the very crumbled pack of Marlboro cigarettes from his pocket. Selecting the only cigarette that was not broken, he put it in the corner of his mouth and took out the old brass zippo. The lighter, as always, worked first time.

He drew the smoke deeply into his lungs, then, with an almost casual under arm swing, he tossed the lighter towards Toby's truck...

There would be no evidence of the other world and Man would continue to live in ignorance of its presence, content to get on with the business of life and the battle of living without being distracted by something so dark and fearful that what joy could be had out of life would be contaminated by that knowledge. Besides, there would always be people like Herschal, like Paul O'Connor, like Helen Ross and Michael Fry, and, God bless him, John Light, to fight Man's battle for him against the secret enemy allied against Man since the beginning of the world. Leave the corpse of the Djinn and there might be alarm, more likely there would be derision... There would certainly be questions, arguments, recriminations which Mage wanted no part of. As far as he was concerned the business was over. He'd done what he'd come to do, what he'd been sent to do, and that was the end of it. If the Djinn attempted to force passage in some other place at some future time, that would be someone else's battle, not his. He'd fought his fight in Castillo, and now if nothing else, this opening was closed, access to the age old enemy denied...

The zippo arced through the morning air, landing with precision just beneath the front wheels of the pick up. For two seconds nothing happened, then the truck and the two figures it partially covered went up with a whoompf of heat and flame, followed a few seconds after that by a louder more destructive detonation as the main fuel tank ruptured and exploded. A fire ball topped by a mushroom of black billowing smoke lifted into the air, but Mage's eyes were on the two figures, and he smoked his cigarette calmly, watching as they began to crumble, falling in upon themselves, as they were devoured by the ferocity of the flames.

Epilogue:

Closing Rituals

He stood silently and alone on the terrace of the Miraflores Hotel watching the last vestiges of light disappear from what had been another stupifyingly hot Spanish day. The sky, marginally lighter in the west, settled like dark blue velvet over the Castillato valley; the glow from village street lamps and the open doors and windows of the tightly huddled white houses doing nothing to diminish the brightness of the vast panorama of stars that stretched majestically from horizon to horizon.

On the balmy and heavily scented night air drifted the usual sounds of children playing and the chatter of a score of different inarticulate conversations – and from behind him came the enchanting peel of Anna's laughter and the more stentorian rumble of her father's chuckle. He stole a glance through the palm fronds at the table he had just left... It was a celebratory table underpinned by subtle moods of sadness and uncertainty. On the following day John Light and Tamara would be leaving Castillo, and although this party had come together to celebrate their victory over the Djinn and Angel Guadiaro's release from hospital, it was also a farewell dinner for the two Americans.

Almost three weeks had elapsed since the battle which had brought about the closing of The Opening and the destruction of the Djinn...Three intensely full and busy weeks wherein for a very short while Castillo had had it's moment of fame upon the world stage.

A cell of international terrorists had been discovered by the local police chief, who almost single handedly, and at great risk to himself, had not only destroyed the terrorists, but had also blown up their not inconsiderable cache of arms. For two days Jaime's photograph had adorned most of the Spanish newspapers. There had been letters of commendation, a visit to Madrid, a medal and an offer of promotion... Which, rather curiously, Jaime had declined, telling his superiors that he was now very settled in Castillo, and if he had a choice, Castillo was where he would prefer to remain.

Mage had written a thoughtful and carefully worded letter to Gideon Lemski, care of the Israeli military attaché in Madrid, and in the ensuing wave of publicity and investigations, no mention was ever made of Leon Shapiro or the Mossad P3 team. Tanja Hein's body was quietly buried almost where she had fallen; Mage had dug the grave himself, and as there was a marked absence of Rabbis in Southern Andalucia, Father Francisco had come up to the still smouldering ruins of the citadel to say some appropriate religious words... A far cry from the recitation of Kadish, but in the circumstances, certainly better than nothing.

Jaime Gomez sat at the table between Hector and John Light, relaxed and at ease and wearing light casual clothes. He was still one of the ugliest men Mage had ever come across, but now the tension and darkness, which had made him so much more unattractive at their first meeting, was acutely noticeable by its absence.

Sitting opposite, and between Christina and Anna, Angel looked positively rakish with the black leather eye patch stretched across his face; the patch hid the fact that his left eye was missing, but could do little to hide the scar that ran from his temple down across his cheek to his jawbone. In the fullness of time there would be some more plastic surgery and the insertion of an artificial eye, but for the time being he was content to be walking, content to be part of the great secret, even more content with the knowledge that Christina had elected to remain in Castillo for at least a few more weeks before following John and Tamara back across the Atlantic. He was reassured by the promise of a long holiday in the United States after the next and necessary round of operations.

Mage's eye fell caringly upon Helen. She openly held Hector's hand and worked hard to create the party mood, and yet Mage knew full well the depth and extent of her divided loyalties. One part of her desperately wanted to remain in Castillo and to accept Hector's tentative and half terrified offer of marriage, but the other part pulled her back to her native Scottish glens and to the responsibilities of the life she'd worked so hard to create for herself within the worlds of Wicca and Druidism. It had been left that she would seriously consider Hector's offer, but would make no final decision until she'd spent a lot more time in Castillo and until Hector had spent some time in Scotland.

Some days previously Hector Sanchez had taken him to one side, and beneath the bullish bluster Mage had accurately identified both the doctor's fear of losing that which he held so precious and his determination not to lose...

'Colin, I tell you, if she does not come back to Castillo, then I shall go and camp on her doorstep in Scotland! Wherever she is, this is where I shall also be!'

'And what about Anna?' Mage had quietly asked.

'Ah yes, I was forgetting about Anna!' The doctor's face had fallen, then he'd looked at Mage shiftily. 'But then, I could ask you the same question, couldn't I?'

Mage had nodded thoughtfully. They had been sitting in the small cantina bar near the garage where they'd enjoyed their first drink so many weeks before. The place was still littered with discarded cigarette packets and wood shavings and the windows had been even more grimy with the rime of summer dust. He'd failed to notice these things, however, as he'd mulled over the significance of the other man's question.

'Anna thinks she is in love with me,' he had begun slowly.

'No,' Hector had jumped in quickly. 'She doesn't *think,* she knows! And in any case, I do not believe that my daughter would go to bed with a man that she did *not* love!'

Mage had raised a questioning eyebrow and Hector had nodded confirmation. 'Oh yes, Colin, it was the first thing she told me when she returned from Ronda. I did not ask, I did not pry. She told me of her own volition. She is my daughter and I am her father, and despite our recent disagreement, we are best friends. Anna wanted me to know, as her friend, of the wonderful thing that had happened to her. The point is, however, not how Anna feels about you but how you feel about her, and what, if anything, you intend to do about it.'

'I'll be staying in Castillo,' Mage had answered neutrally, stubbing out one cigarette and immediately lighting another. '...Partly because there's nothing left for me in England any more and partly because there's no where else for me to go. It seems right that I should stay here. I've fought a battle here, and to my own amazement, it seems that I've won... But perhaps because of all that has happened, I'm tied to this place now, just as Herschal was tied to his place in the Negev. And partly, I'll be staying here because of Anna. Make no mistake, Hector, I do not dismiss her feelings lightly, but even if she had no feelings for me, I'd still be staying here on her account. I made a promise, to you, to her, and more importantly to myself, that should we survive the Djinn, I'd do my utmost to make Anna well again... Well, we have survived the Djinn, and so now I'm going to concentrate on your daughter...' He'd paused, choosing his words with great care. 'I do not know how successful I might be, but you, more than many others, know that I am not without power and talent and I intend to use all of these energies on Anna's behalf. If I fail in this new quest, it won't be through want of trying!

'As far as the emotional side of things is concerned, that can develop at its own speed. I'm not in any rush and I'm under no illusions. Anna is very young, and one way or the other, her feelings are going to change. They'll become more intense or more diluted, and I'll deal with them which ever way I have to when the need arises.'

A broad grin had suddenly stretched across his face. 'But Hector, there's one thing you can be sure of! With a new nurse and an associate doctor scheduled to arrive any day now from Algerciras and with me around to look after Anna, you'll have plenty of time to go and sit on Helen Ross's doorstep for as long as it takes. I wish you luck, and with a little patience and determination, it might not take you as long as you think!'

'But there's still one thing that's puzzling me...' Helen's voice drifted across the courtyard. Mage watched as she turned to John Light. 'John, in my clairvoyant trance I clearly saw you covered in blood and very badly damaged from a wound in your chest. Everything else that I saw in that trance has happened more or less... Leon with his funny gun, Colin with the crossbow, the Djinn's magical ceremony, Alexandra giving birth, even being attacked and caught by the Djinn – but you're my one failure, so to speak...'

'No, not really,' Light said uncomfortably and enigmatically. Then with a wry self conscious smile around the table he unfastened his shirt to reveal the long white scar that stretched down diagonally across his rib cage, almost from shoulder to waist. It was an old wound, but still livid and puckered, suggesting that it had had little or no medical attention at the time of its infliction. 'You saw it right, but from twelve years ago. This was what I got from my first bust up with the Djinn.'

'And you never have told us that story, have you?' Helen mused out loud.

'Nope, and I guess I'm never going to now, now that I don't have to!'

Anna quietly left the table and went to join Mage on the terrace. He slipped his arm around her narrow waist, reassured by the way in which she came quite naturally into his arms – reassured also by the fact that since she'd returned from Ronda she'd begun to gain some weight, and although she still frequently suffered from bad headaches and blurring vision, the attacks were no longer quite so violent or prolonged as once they had been... And this even before he had begun a formal pattern of healing therapy.

She brought her arms together around his neck, and pressing her body against his chest as he kissed her, tingled with the familiar anticipatory excitement. They had made love three times in the past ten days and, incredibly, each occasion had brought more pleasure and excitement than the last. Anna had not yet learned to ask outright for what she wanted, but she most dearly hoped that later this evening Mage would say the right words that would bring her naked and eager to his bed in Calle Granadillos. If he *didn't* say anything then perhaps, just perhaps, she might suggest they take a walk somewhere dark and quiet before he took her home. She was still unsure about many aspects of their relationship, still insecure with regard to his feelings for her, but neither insecure nor uncertain about her own feelings for him.

Like Angel, she had been told the full story of the Djinn. She did not fully understand it – it was difficult and very confusing to understand, but from what both Colin and her father had said to her, she did at least grasp something of the enormity of what had been happening while she'd been waiting impatiently in Ronda. More importantly, she intuitively understood that although Colin's ex-wife was no longer a threat to her own place in Colin's heart, he was still going to need some time to adjust to the new situation. Her father had told her that if she wanted her man, she would have to be patient, and while she did not have patience in abundance, she would find what was needed from somewhere, and it might not be too difficult as long as she had Colin by her side and as long as she knew that he cared.

But there were times, such as this moment, when she was scared by his dreamy eyed distance... Times, when although she held his body close to her own, his mind was a million miles elsewhere. These were the times when she needed most reassurance.

Applying some of the lessons she was only recently learning, she kissed him deeply, and seeking his hand, brought it up to cup her breast. 'You are happy, my love?' she breathed in his ear. 'Tell me, my love, that you are happy now...'

He felt the hardness of her nipple beneath his hand, tasted the sweetness of her kiss, was filled with the heady scent of her perfume, and heard the urgency behind her whispered words.

'Yes,' he said, feeling her gently and brushing his lips against her hair. 'I'm happy now.'

...I'm happy to be alive, to be here holding you, to feel your love washing over me in great waves of protection. I'm happy that the danger has past and that after so many long, long months of darkness I can see some light again. I'm happy to think that I might, after all, have a future, even though I don't know what that future holds for me. I'm happy that Angel is alive. I'm happy that Hector and Helen have found something worth fighting for. I'm happy that we survived even though we did not all survive intact and some of us did not survive at all...

He thought, inevitably, of the casualties... Of Herschal, of Leon and the two members of the P3 team, whose bodies had never been recovered, perhaps because there were no bodies left to recover... Of Old Tobias Cristobal and Tanja Hein whose bodies were buried, one publicly the other privately, on the top of Castillo's mountain. Without guilt, but none the less with great sadness, he thought of Miriam Cortez, of her still missing daughter and her still comatose husband... He thought of Ignatious, now in his grave in Seville, of Diego Matan who had inadvertently given his life for such an unworthy cause. Of Immaculada Morro, who despite his warning, had not got out of Castillo in time... He remembered Hamish Hamilton, and here there was a dark stab of conscience. If he'd done his own dirty digging rather than leaving it to the archaeologist, then maybe Hamilton and the poor woman he'd so brutally murdered might still be alive!

He thought of all the people, both good and bad, whose lives had been changed by the impending presence of the Djinn, and not for the first time, he thought of the Djinn themselves, trapped within the confines of their own dimension, restless with resentment and aggression, seeking to vent their fury by rending the veil between worlds. Could no approach be made from this side? Could no pact of peaceful co-existence be entered into? Perhaps, perhaps, but it would be a long time coming, and not in his lifetime, and not until there were more souls like John Light, Michael Fry and Herschal of The Negev alive on the planet... And in any case, perhaps Man was not yet ready to share the planet which he so thoroughly dominated by his presence and culture with any alien presence, be it from the stars or from within the confines of Earth's own etheric dimensions.

He thought of Jadoc Dolorean, both as the man and the monster, and for many reasons, not all of them wholesome, he rejoiced at that creature's passing. Inevitably, he thought too of Alexandra, and here his mind splintered. In some ways she had been dead for a eighteen months, and in others ways, only for a few weeks. But either way, his wife was dead, dead to him, dead to the world and dead to the Djinn. These were early days yet, but at least now his own healing process could begin.

He held Anna ever more tightly, deeply aware of the fact that she not only represented life, but also the challenge and point of his own future. It was not the future he had seen for himself a few short months before, but what did that matter now? He *would* heal this woman, and in giving her life, would find life for himself in the bargain.

'Yes,' he said again, this time more forcefully, 'I am happy now...'

Not as happy as I have been, and not as happy as one day I know I shall be... But happier than I ever thought I could be, happier than I have any right to be. So be patient with me, my beautiful Spanish Anna. Give me some time, just a little more time, and in the end it will all work out for the best, not just for you, but for both of us!

Rajad looked down on the familiar terrain of his home village from the distant hill. He was pleased to be back, secure in the knowledge that he would soon be reunited with his mother and father and his brothers and sisters. It had been an interesting journey, this long ride to and from the high mountains, but one that he had not always enjoyed. There had been times when his Aunt Kiku had been somehow strangely threatening, and there had been many nights when they had lodged in the cave of the shrine when his sleep had been assailed by dark and menacing dreams. Then, just in the space of a day, all had changed. Aunt Kiku had become brighter and more merry and had told him to pack his things in preparation for the long trek home. He had been happy to oblige, for, to tell the truth, the dark cave, with its less than beautiful shrine to Kali, had frequently made him afraid.

Michael Fry strolled through the gardens of The Oaks with Leonardo Santorini by his side. They made an odd couple, the young aesthetic Merlin in his expensive silk suite and the craggy old man with his jutting chin and shock of silver hair, dressed, as he was, in the simple homespun tunic of the bard. It was a warm afternoon in the height of full summer and the garden was alive with butterflies and the droning hum of honey bees. The mid-summer solstice had come and gone; there had been no leadership challenge from within the High Council of Thirteen and, indeed, partially though the voluble and unexpected support from Martyn of Glastonbury, his tenure of the movement was more secure than ever before.

As they approached the grove of oak trees they were passed by a young bard pushing a wheelbarrow full of cut grass. His hair was as fair as the summer corn and his eyes shone a brilliant green as he bowed in favour of his two superiors. Michael Fry dazzled him with a warm and friendly smile that broke through all formality of rank.

'Good afternoon Matthew, I see you have quite enough to keep you busy!'

The young Druid called Matthew laughed. 'Yes, Lord Merlin, quite enough thank you!'

He carried on pushing the barrow in the direction of the compost heap, and Fry watched his progress, a thoughtful smile of appreciation playing at the corners of his mouth.

'They did very well, didn't they?' he mused out loud, making reference to the fact that it had been Matthew and twelve young bards like him who had sat in almost permanent ritual for forty consecutive days and nights while Mage had prepared for and had fought and won the battle in Castillo.

'Yes they did,' Santorini agreed without hesitation, 'and so did we. So did you!'

'One wonders if the outcome might have been any different had we not sat in our circles, creating the energy that we created and directing it to Mage's assistance...'

'I doubt we'll ever know, but even if it didn't help Mage a single jot, it certainly has had other benefits closer to home. None of our own people can have failed to detect the emanation of energy we created. It has proven the need and usefulness of magical practice within the movement, and if you were looking for evidence of loyalty among the rank and file, the fact that eight men and five women put their lives and sanity on the line for more than a month is more than enough!'

Fry changed the subject slightly. 'I accept that it can't happen all at once, but I want both Colin Mage and Helen Ross fully integrated within the Order of Bards. I want them both on The High Council Of Thirteen within a year!'

Santorini looked at his Merlin obliquely. 'All things are possible, but what you're suggesting will be difficult. You'll find some resistance from within our own ranks, of that I have no doubt – but I suspect you'll meet with even greater resistance from the two people themselves. They may not wish to be integrated.'

Fry smiled sweetly at his old friend and mentor. 'We'll see,' he said enigmatically. 'We'll see.'

Gideon Lemski sat alone in his spartan office. Two files, one fat and one thin, sat on his desk, along with a meticulously written letter. The larger of the two files was The Elijah File, while the slimmer volume which carried the code name of SHAPIRO/NEGEV was little more than a precis written in his own hand, detailing the events which had led to Leon Shapiro's journey to Spain and the subsequent loss, not only of Shapiro, but also of the highly trained P3 team.

He read again the letter from Spain... The letter from this man called Colin Mage, a man he had never met, but a man who knew what had really happened on that Spanish mountain. The letter contained details of a combat with international terrorists and, as such, echoed and corroborated the tale that Leon Shapiro had told him here in this very office. Gideon Lemski had not believed Shapiro then and nor did he believe Mage's version of events now – and yet, what Mage *had* done, was to give him a nice neat and tidy end to The Elijah File. With Mage's letter, along with the official report from the Spanish police, there were no loose ends, no dangling strings...

But it was too tidy, too glib, and if he chose to read between the lines, this Colin Mage character knew it, and knew that he, Gideon Lemski, would know it too. Maybe his choice and nuance of words had *meant* Lemski to know!

"*...thus with the actions and events narrated above, I am pleased to inform you* *that the threat to Israel and other sympathetic nations has now been neutralised. It is with profound sadness and deep regret that I tell you of the loss of Leon Shapiro, Tanja Hein, Michael Vordeman and Yuri Bogdanovitch, but I hope that you and the families of the deceased can find some solace in the knowledge that they died fighting for the cause of freedom against a vicious and merciless enemy. That which Leon and Herschal might and might not have told you, along with this report, should at least enable you to understand, in part, what has happened here. It keeps the record straight, and you may now, if you so choose, use this as your final entry in The Elijah File..."*

It was bullshit! Pure, unadulterated bullshit... But it would keep the politicians happy, and it would, he had to admit, make a fitting final entry to the bulky file that sat before him on his desk. Slipping the letter into the back of the SHAPIRO/NEGEV file, he, in turn, placed that file in back of The Elijah File. Taking an expensive fountain pen, he wrote across the bottom of back page *"This file is now closed"* dated it, and signed with an expansive and angry flourish.

"This file is now closed."

The words stared up at him mischievously from the page. Was it really over? Was it really closed? He hoped that it was, but couldn't be quite so sure. As Mossad's Director General, he was privy to certain information that Colin Mage and the Spanish Police had no knowledge of, and he was mindful of another report that he'd been reading only earlier that day.

After the massive and uncharacteristic explosion that had torn a hole in the middle of the Negev desert, killing Herschal and injuring Leon, he had acted purely on intuition and had set up a small observation post close to the rim of the crater. They had been given a watching brief, and had been frustrated when he'd been unable to tell them what they were watching for. Their reports had initially centred around the formation of a pool of natural water at the base of the crater, for here was a new oasis in the making, and anything that brought green life to Israel's arid backlands was something to be celebrated, almost with a sense of wonderment, especially when it seemed that the hand of God was at work rather than the hand of Man. But this latest report, the one he had received this morning... now where was it...

He rummaged in the right hand draw, found the fax sheet, and studied it thoughtfully, trying to make sense of what the message was trying to tell him. It was nothing really... just that a corporal, one Ari Ben Yehuda, had been on patrol the previous night and had noticed some flickering mauve and green lights hovering just above the surface of the water...

ooOoo

ALSO AVAILABLE FROM HUMDRUMMING...

The Imagineer
By Gregory Ashe

ISBN 1-905532-00-8 - Snowscape Edition
ISBN 1-905532-01-6 - Fire Eye Edition

"If it were that easy, we'd all be heroes"

This is not it. The world you know - normal, safe, boring - is just a stepping stone to other worlds, other places. Places of magic, monsters and limitless imagination.

Like most eleven year olds, Charlie Whittaker always hoped this was true. Now he knows it is.
Because somebody's kidnapped his Uncle and he's forced to give chase.

Leaving normality far behind...

He will make friends on the way: the enigmatic Lashram, the absurd Squintillion, the noble Algernon. He will see sights that will make the wildest dreams of his life seem bland.

But will he survive long enough to enjoy them? There are horrors out there, ravenous cannibals, lethal assassins and, of course The High Lord Jethryk – a man who wears shadows torn from his victims and could snuff out all life in the universe using no more than his smooth fingertips. There is, in fact, only one power Jethryk doesn't possess, a power he intends to steal from Charlie's uncle.

By whatever means necessary.

It's all about story you see, and the power of imagination, one false word and creation as we know it will cease to exist...

The Imagineer is a beautifully illustrated novel that hearkens back to the child in all of us, a modern fairytale that will excite older children and adults alike. There are other worlds to explore: sometimes wonderful, sometimes terrifying, always spectacular.

All you have to do is believe...

More Than This
By Guy Adams

ISBN 1-905532-05-9

"There was something in the water"

Kiss me quick and squeeze me slow, there's something amiss in the crumbling seaside resort of Gravestown: Children are vanishing and nobody can understand how.

Gregory Ashe watches them go, sees them hanging from their tatty 'wanted' pictures and the wilting bouquets of flowers left by well wishers. Like most thirteen year olds he feels it's nothing to do with him, he's far too busy with his face in a book and a head full of dreams.

Then, amongst the seaweed and shingle, a solitary foot is washed up and the violence begins.

Gravestown is infected. People are beginning to lose their minds, changing, becoming other. Blood is spilt, over and over and over...

Through it all the waves roll and, in the dark building on the cliff tops, the lunatics howl by the light of their moon.

Slowly the safe walls of reality are crumbling and it seems nobody can stop it.

Nobody that is except The Magician, a man who takes young Gregory under his wing and shows him how hollow those dreams of his really are, a man with more than just spare decks of cards hidden up his sleeve.

Gregory's never been in so much danger...

A dark fantasy laced with humour and terror. More Than This *is a fast paced journey from innocence to maturity, fear to hope, heaven to hell. Exciting, horrifying and filled with the sort of imagination, escapism and, above all, magic you remember from books you read as a child - magic you thought lost.*

DEADBEAT
BY GUY ADAMS

ISBN 1-905532-02-4

"I think you're missing something, what did you notice about the woman in the coffin? ...She was breathing. Not a common habit amongst the dead."

It's the middle of the night and, in a dark suburban churchyard, a group of men are loading a coffin into the back of a transit van.

But why would you be taking a full coffin away from a graveyard and, more importantly, why is the occupant still breathing?

The matter obviously needs thorough investigation by the best, most capable authorities.

Which is a pity as the only two witnesses are a pair of drunken ex-theatricals with reasons of their own to avoid the police.

Tom Harris (nightclub owner) and Max Jackson (habitual barfly) are on the case.

God help us...

Deadbeat *is the first in a series of adventures set in the secret underbelly of contemporary London, a place where the dead walk, magic can be bought on street corners and anything is possible.*

Frankly, it's just like every other Pulp Crime/Horror/Zombie/Comedy/Thriller you've ever read.